Captain Jack's Woman

STEPHANIE LAURENS

A Gentleman's Honor

AVON BOOKS
An Imprint of HarperCollins*Publishers*

FIRST EDITION

ISBN-13: 978-0-06-112161-6
ISBN-10: 0-06-112161-4

06 07 08 09 RRD 10 9 8 7 6 5 4 3 2 1

Captain Jack's Woman

Prologue

April 1811
The Old Barn near Brancaster
Norfolk, England

Three horsemen pulled out of the trees before the Old
Barn. Harness jingled, faint on the night breeze, as
they turned their horses' heads to the west. Clouds shifted,
drifted; moonlight shone through, bathing the scene.

The Old Barn stood silent, watchful, guarding its secrets.
Earlier, within its walls, the Hunstanton Gang had gathered
to elect a new leader. Afterward, the smugglers had left,
slipping into the night, mere shadows in the dark. They
would return, nights from now, meeting under the light of
a storm lantern to hear of the next cargo their new leader
had arranged.

"Captain Jack!" As he swung his horse onto the road,
George Smeaton frowned at the man beside him. "Do we
really need to resurrect him?"

"Who else?" Mounted on his tall grey, Jonathon Hendon, better known as Jack, gestured expansively. "That
was, after all, my *nom de guerre.*"

"Years ago. When you were dangerous to know. I've
lived the last years in the comfortable belief that Captain
Jack had died."

"No." Jack grinned. "He's merely been in temporary
retirement." Captain Jack had been active in more devil-
may-care days, when, between army engagements in the

1

Peninsula, the Admirality had recruited Jack to captain one of his own ships, harassing French shipping up and down the Channel. "You have to admit Captain Jack's perfect for this job—a fitting leader for the Hunstanton Gang."

George's snort was eloquent. "Poor blighters—they've no idea what they've let themselves in for."

Jack chuckled. "Stop carping—our mission's proceeding better than I'd hoped, and all in only a few weeks of coming home. Whitehall will be impressed. We've been accepted by the smugglers—I'm now their leader. We're in a perfect position to ensure no information gets to the French by this route." His brows rose; his expression turned considering. "Who knows?" he mused. "We might even be able to use the traffic for our own ends."

George raised his eyes heavenward. "Captain Jack's only been with us half an hour, and already you're getting ideas. Just what wild scheme are you hatching?"

"Not hatching." Jack threw him a glance. "It's called seizing opportunity. It occurs to me that while our principal aim is to ensure no spies go out through the Norfolk surf, and perhaps follow any arrivals back to their traitorous source, we might now have the opportunity to do a little information passing of our own—to Boney's confusion, needless to say."

George stared. "I thought that once we'd investigated any recent human cargoes, you'd shut the Hunstanton Gang down."

"Perhaps." Jack's gaze grew distant. "And perhaps not." He blinked and straightened. "I'll see what Whitehall thinks. We'll need Anthony, too."

"Oh, my God!" George shook his head. "Just how long do you imagine the Gang will swallow your tale that we're landless mercenaries, dishonorably discharged no less, particularly once you take full command? You've been a major for years, landed gentry all your life. It shows!"

Jack shrugged dismissively. "They won't think too hard. They've been looking for months for someone to replace Jed Brannagan. They won't rock the boat—at least, not soon. We'll have time enough for our needs." He twisted, glancing back at the third rider, a length behind to his left.

Like himself and George, a native of these parts, Matthew, his longtime batman, now general servant, had merged easily into the smuggling band. "We'll continue to use the old fishing cottage as our private rendezvous—it's secluded, and we can guard against being followed."

Matthew nodded. "Aye. Easy enough to check our trail."

Jack settled in his saddle. "Given the smugglers are all from outlying farms or fishing villages, there's no reason they should stumble on our real identities."

Checking his horse, Jack turned left, into the narrow mouth of a winding track. George followed; Matthew brought up the rear. As they climbed a rise, Jack glanced back. "All things considered, I can't see why you're worrying. Captain Jack's command of the Hunstanton Gang should be plain sailing."

"Plain sailing with Captain Jack?" George snorted. "When pigs fly."

Chapter 1

May 1811
West Norfolk

Kit Cranmer sat with her nose to the carriage window, feasting on the landmarks of memory. The spire atop the Customs House at King's Lynn and the old fortress of Castle Rising had fallen behind them. Ahead lay the turning to Wolferton; Cranmer was close at last. Streamers of twilight red and gold colored the sky in welcome; the sense of coming home grew stronger with every mile. With a triumphant sigh, Kit sat back against the squabs and gave thanks yet again for her freedom. She'd remained "cabin'd, cribb'd and confin'd" in London for far too long.

Ten minutes later, the entrance to the park loomed ahead in the gathering dusk, the Cranmer arms blazoned on each gatepost. The gates were open wide; the coach trundled through. Kit straightened and shook old Elmina awake, then sat back, suddenly tense.

Gravel scrunched beneath the wheels; the carriage rocked to a halt. The door was pulled open.

Her grandfather stood before her, his proud head erect, his leonine mane thrown into relief by the flares flanking the large doors. For one suspended moment, they stared at each other, love, hope, and remembered pain reflected over and over between them.

"Kit?"

And the years rolled back. With a choked "Gran'pa!"

Kit launched herself into Spencer Cranmer's arms.

"Kit. Oh, *Kit*!" Lord Cranmer of Cranmer Hall, his beloved granddaughter locked against his chest, could find no other words. For six years he'd waited for her to come back; he could barely believe she was real.

Elmina and the housekeeper, Mrs. Fogg, fussed and prodded the emotion-locked pair inside, leaving them on the *chaise* in the drawing room, before the blazing fire.

Eventually, Spencer straightened and mopped his eyes with a large handkerchief. "Kit, darling girl—I'm *so* glad to see you."

Kit looked up, tears unashamedly suspended on her long brown lashes. She hadn't yet recovered her voice, so she smiled her response.

Spencer returned the smile. "I know it's selfish of me to wish you here—your aunts pointed that out years ago, when you decided to go to London. I'd given up hope you'd ever return. I was sure you'd marry some fashionable sprig and forget all about Cranmer and your old grandfather."

Kit's smile faded. Frowning slightly, she wriggled to sit straighter. "What do you mean, Gran'pa? I never wanted to go to London—my aunts told me I had to. They told me you wanted me to contract a fine alliance—that as the only girl in the family, it was my duty to be a credit to the Cranmer name and further my uncles' standing." The last was said with contempt.

Spencer's pale gaze sharpened. His bushy white brows met in a thunderous frown. "*What?*"

Kit winced. "Don't bellow." She'd forgotten his temper. According to Dr. Thrushborne, his health depended on his not losing it too often.

Rising, she went to the fireplace and tugged the bellpull. "Let me think." Her gaze on the flames, she frowned, long-ago events replaying in her mind. "When Gran'ma died, you locked yourself up, and I didn't see you again. Aunt Isobel and Aunt Margery came and talked to you. Then they came and told me I had to go with them—that my uncles were to be my guardians and they'd groom me and present me and so on." She looked directly at Spencer. "That was all I knew."

The angry sparkle in the old eyes holding hers so intently was all the proof Kit needed of her aunts' duplicity.

"Those conniving bitches! Those witches dressed up in silks and furs. Those hell-born harpies! The pair of them are nothing but—"

Spencer's animadversions were interrupted by a knock on the door, followed by Jenkins, the butler.

Kit caught Jenkins's eye. "Your master's cordial, please Jenkins."

Jenkins bowed. "At once, miss."

As the door closed, Kit turned to Spencer. "Why didn't you write?"

The pale old eyes met hers unflinchingly. "I didn't think you'd want to hear from an old man. They told me you wanted to go. That you were bored, buried here in the country, living with old people."

Kit's violet eyes clouded. Her aunts were truly the bitches he called them. Until now, she'd never appreciated just how low they'd stooped to gain control of her so they could manipulate her to suit their husbands' ambitious ends. "Oh, Gran'pa." Sinking onto the *chaise*, her elegant gown sushing softly, she hugged Spencer for all she was worth. "You were all I had left, and I thought you didn't want me." Kit buried her face in his cravat and felt Spencer's cheek against her curls. After a moment, his hand rose to pat her shoulder. She tightened her arms fiercely, then drew back, eyes flaming with a light Spencer remembered all too well. She rose and fell to pacing, skirts swishing, her vigorous strides well beyond society's dictates. "Ooooh! How I wish my aunts were here now."

"Not half as much as I," Spencer growled. "Those *mesdames* will get a lambasting from me when next they dare show their faces."

Jenkins noiselessly entered; coming forward, he offered his master a small glass of dark liquid. With barely a glance, Spencer took it; absentmindedly, he quaffed the dose, then waved Jenkins away.

Kit paused, slender and elegant, before the mantelpiece.

Spencer's loving gaze roamed her fair skin, creamy rather than white, unmarred by any blemish despite her predilection for outdoor pursuits. The burnished curls were the same shade he remembered, the same shade he'd once possessed. The long tresses, confined in plaits at sixteen, had given way to cropped curls, large and lustrous. The fashion suited her, highlighting the delicate features of her small heart-shaped face.

From age six, Kit had lived at Cranmer, after her parents, Spencer's son Christopher and his French emigrée wife, had died in a carriage accident. Spencer's gaze dwelled on the long lines of Kit's figure, outlined by her green traveling dress. She carried herself gracefully even now as she resumed her angry pacing. He stirred. "God, Kit. Do you realize we've lost six years?"

Kit's smile was dazzling, resurrecting memories of the tomboy, the hoyden, the devil in her blood. "I'm back now, Gran'pa, and I mean to stay."

Spencer leaned back, well pleased with her declaration. He waved at her. "Well, miss—let me see how you've turned out."

With a chuckle, Kit curtsied. "Not too deep, for after all, you are *just* a baron." The twinkle in her eye suggested he was the prince of her heart. Spencer snorted. Kit rose and dutifully pirouetted, arms gracefully extended as if she were dancing.

Spencer slapped his knee. "Not bad, even if I say so myself."

Kit laughed and returned to the *chaise*. "You're prejudiced, Gran'pa. Now, tell me what's happened here."

To her relief, Spencer obliged. While he rattled on about fields and tenants, Kit listened with half an ear. Inside, she was still reeling. Six years of purgatory she'd spent in London, for no reason at all. The months of misery she'd endured, during which she'd had to come to grips with the loss of not only a beloved grandmother, but effectively of her grandfather as well, were burned into her soul. Why, oh *why* had she never swallowed her pride and written to Spencer, pleaded with him to allow her to come home? She'd almost done it on countless occasions but, deeply wounded by his apparent rejection of her, she'd always allowed her stubborn pride to intervene. Inherently truthful, she'd never dreamed her aunts had been so deceitful. Never again would she trust those who professed to have her welfare at heart. Henceforth, she silently vowed, she'd run her own life.

Gazing at her grandfather's white mane, Kit nodded as he told her of their neighbors. The six years had wrought their inevitable changes in him, yet Spencer was still an impressive figure. Even now, with his shoulders slightly stooped, his height and strength made a definite impact. His patrician features, his hooked nose and piercing pale violet eyes shaded by overhanging brows, commanded attention; from his rambling discourse, she gathered he was still deeply involved with county matters, as influential as ever.

Inwardly, Kit sighed. She loved Spencer as she did no other on earth. And he loved her. Yet even he was demonstrably fallible, no real protection against the wolves of this world. No. If she was to come to grief, she'd rather it was self-inflicted. From now on, she'd make her own decisions, her own mistakes.

Later that night, finally alone in the bedroom that had been hers for as long as she could remember, Kit stood at the open window and gazed at the pale circle of the moon, suspended in night's blackness over the deep. She'd never felt so alone. She'd never felt so free.

Kit was astonished at how easily she slipped back into her Cranmer routine. Rising early, she rode her mare, Delia, then breakfasted with Spencer before turning to whatever task she'd set herself for the day. The afternoon saw her riding again, before evening brought her back to her grandfather's side. Over dinner, she'd listen to his account of his day, giving her opinions when asked, shrewdly interpolating comments when she wasn't. Between them, the six years of separation were as though they'd never been.

From that, Kit took her direction. It was useless to wail and gnash her teeth over her aunts' perfidy. She was free of them—free to forget them. Her grandfather was in good health and, she'd learned, would remain her legal guardian until she was twenty-five; there was no chance of her aunts interfering again. She would waste no more time on the past. Her life was hers—she would live it to the full.

Her daily tasks varied from helping Mrs. Fogg about the house, in the stillroom or the kitchen, to visiting her grandfather's tenants, who were all delighted to welcome her home.

Home.

Her heart soared as she rode the far-flung acres, the sky wide and clear above her, the wind tugging at her curls. Delia, a purebred black Arab, had been a gift from Spencer on Kit's eighteenth birthday. Since he'd taught her to ride and had always taken enormous pride in her horsemanship, she hadn't placed any undue emphasis on the gift. Now, she saw it as a call from a lonely and aching heart, a call she had not, in her innocence, recognized. It only made her love Delia more. Together, they thundered over the sands, Delia's hooves glistening with wave foam. The sharp cries of gulls came keening on the currents high above; the boom of the surf rumbled in the salt-laden air.

Word of her return spread quickly. She dutifully sustained visits from the rector's wife and from Lady Dersingham, the wife of a neighboring landowner. Kit's *ton*nish grace impressed both ladies. Her manner was assured, her deportment perfection. In the faraway capital she might hold herself insultingly aloof, but at Cranmer, she was Spencer's granddaughter.

Chapter 2

On the afternoon of her third day of freedom, Kit donned her green-velvet riding habit and asked for a sidesaddle to be put on Delia. When with Spencer or alone, she'd taken to riding astride, scandalously dressed in breeches and coat. The clothes had been made for her years before; Elmina had let down the hems and remade the breeches to fit. The coat was an old one of her cousin Geoffrey's, recut to her slighter frame but still loose enough to disguise her figure should the need arise. Now that her hair was cropped, leaving the flame-colored curls rioting about her head, she hardly needed the protection of the old tricorne that completed her highly irregular outfit. When garbed in her male attire, a hat shading her features, her sex was moot.

Today she was bound for Gresham Manor. Her closest friend, whom she hadn't seen in years, lived quietly there with her parents. Amy had never had to go to London. She'd contracted a suitable alliance with a local gentleman of acceptable birth and reasonable fortune; that much, Kit knew from her letters. Amy's gentleman was with Wellington's forces in the Peninsula; their wedding would take place once he returned.

Kit rode up the long drive of Gresham Manor and directly around to the stables.

"Miss Cranmer!" The groom came running to take her horse's bridle. "Didn't recognize you for a minute there, miss. Back from London town, are ye?"

"That's right, Jeffries." Kit smiled and slid from Delia's back. "Is Miss Amy in?"

"*Kit?* It *is* you!"

Turning, Kit barely had time to verify that the figure descending on her was indeed Amy, golden hair in fashionable ringlets, peaches-and-cream complexion still perfect, before she was enveloped in a warm embrace.

"I saw you ride past the library windows and wondered if Mr. Woodley's sermons had sent me to sleep, and I was dreaming."

Kit laughed. "Goose! I've been back only a few days and couldn't wait to see you and hear all your news. Is your fiancé back yet?"

"Yes! It's the most wonderful thing!" Amy gripped Kit's fingers, her eyes shining. "First him—now you. Clearly the gods have decided to be especially kind."

Amy drew back, holding Kit at arm's length to study her elegant attire, the short velvet coat, clasped with gold frogs, and the gracefully sweeping velvet skirts. Amy's brown gaze returned to Kit bobbed curls, and she grimaced. "Drat! You make me feel positively dowdy. I don't know whether I'll introduce you to George after all."

Kit laughed and drew Amy's arm through hers. "Fear not. I've no designs on your fiancé—very likely he'll be either terrified or disapproving of my wild ways." They started for the house.

"George," Amy declared, "is utterly sensible. I'm sure you'll approve of each other. But I'm dying of curiosity. *Why* are you back? And why didn't you write and warn me?"

Kit smiled. "It's a long story. Perhaps I should meet your mother first, then maybe we can find a nice quiet nook?"

Amy nodded; arm in arm, they entered the house. Lady Gresham, a motherly woman who ruled her household with a firm but benevolent hand, had always had a soft spot for Kit. She insisted the girls take tea with her but, beyond extracting the information that Kit was still unbetrothed, made no effort to learn more of her recent past.

Eventually released, Amy and Kit took refuge in Amy's

bedchamber. Settled in the billows of the bed, Kit smiled. She and Amy had been closer than sisters since the age of six; six years' separation, bridged by letters, hadn't dinted their easy familiarity.

At Amy's prompting, Kit recounted the tale of her aunts' machinations and how they'd contrived to hold her for six long years. "If it hadn't been for my cousins, I'm sure their persuasions to marry would have been a great deal more drastic. Once, they locked me in my room for two days, until Geoffrey appeared on the doorstep and insisted on seeing me." Kit grimaced. "After that, they were reduced to nagging. But when they wheeled in the earl of Roberts, I decided enough was enough. The man was old enough to be my father!" Kit frowned. "And he was altogether . . . not nice," she ended lamely. "After that, my aunts finally conceded defeat and declared me unmarriageable. So I was allowed to come home—I knew Gran'pa would at least give me houseroom."

Amy sent her a stern look. "He was heartbroken when you left. I did tell you."

Kit's eyes clouded, violet hazed with grey. "I know, but my aunts were very clever." A short silence fell; Kit broke it with a sigh. "So now I'm finished with London *and* with men. I can live very happily without either."

Amy frowned. "Is it wise to go that far? After all, who knows what delicious gentleman might be lurking around the next bend in your road?"

"Just as long as he stays *out* of my road, I'll be satisfied."

"Oh, *Kit*. Not all men are old dodderers or fops. Some are quite personable. Like George."

With a "Humph," Kit turned on her stomach and propped her chin in her hands. "Enough of my affairs. Tell me about this George of yours."

George, it transpired, was the only son of the Smeatons of Smeaton Hall, located some way beyond Gresham Manor. He was twelve years Kit's senior; she could not recall meeting either him or his parents before.

"It's reassuring knowing I'll not be too far away," Amy concluded. "We must have you and your grandfather over for dinner and introduce you to George and his parents.''

Noting the happiness shining in Amy's face, Kit agreed with what enthusiasm she could. It was obvious to the meanest intelligence that Amy was head over heels in love with George, and that soon Kit would lose her best friend to matrimony. Amy chattered on; eventually, a frown tugging at her brows, Kit broke into her narrative. ''Amy, *why* do you want to marry?''

''Why?'' The question stopped Amy in her tracks. Then, realizing Kit meant the question literally, she marshaled her thoughts. ''Because I love George and want to be with him for the rest of my life.'' She looked hopefully at Kit, willing her to understand.

Kit stared back, violet eyes intent. ''You want to marry him because you love him?'' When Amy nodded, she asked: ''What's love feel like?''

Brow furrowed, Amy considered. ''Well,'' she began, ''you know all about the . . . the act, don't you?''

''Of *course* I know about that.'' They were both country bred—such matters were inescapable facts of country life. ''But what's that got to do with love?''

''*Well*,'' Amy continued, ''when you love a man you want to . . . do that with him.''

Kit frowned. ''Do you really want to do that with your George?''

Blushing furiously, Amy nodded.

Kit's brows rose, then she shrugged. ''It seems such a peculiar undertaking—so undignified, if you know what I mean.''

Amy choked.

''But how do you know you want to do that with George?'' Kit focused on Amy's face. ''You haven't, have you?''

''Of course I haven't!'' Amy stiffened.

''How then?''

Drawing a deep breath, Amy fixed Kit with a long-suffering look. ''You can tell because of what you feel when a man kisses you.''

Kit frowned.

''You've been kissed by a gentleman, haven't you? I

mean, not one of your relatives. What about your London gentlemen—didn't they?''

It was Kit's turn to blush. "Some of them," she admitted.

"Well? What did it feel like?"

Kit grimaced. "One was like kissing a dead fish, and the others were sort of hot wriggling things. They tried to put their tongues in my mouth." She shuddered expressively. "It was awful!"

Amy bit her lips, then drew an unsteady breath. "Yes, all right. That's probably just as well—that means you don't want to go to bed with any of them."

"Oh." Kit's face cleared. "What should it feel like if I do want to . . ." She gestured. "You know."

"Sleep with a man?"

Kit glared. "Yes, damn it! What does it feel like to want a man to make love to you?" She turned onto her back and, dropping her head into the pillows, stared upward. "Take pity on me, Amy, and tell. If you don't, I'll probably die ignorant."

Amy chuckled. "Oh no, you won't. You're just in the doldrums, what with your aunts' machinations and all. You'll come about and meet your man."

"But I might not, so just tell me. Please?"

Amy smiled and settled beside Kit. "All right. But you must remember I haven't had much experience of this either."

"You've had more than me, and it's only fair to share."

"And you've got to promise you won't be shocked."

Kit came up on one elbow and looked into Amy's face. "You said you didn't . . ."

Amy blushed. "I—we haven't. It's just that there are . . . well, preliminaries, that might be a bit more than you expect."

Kit frowned, then dropped back onto the bed. "Try me."

"Well—when he kisses you, you should like it for a start. If you're revolted, then he's not the man for you."

"All right. He's kissed me, and I like it. What then?"

"You should want him to go on kissing you, and you should like it when he puts his tongue in your mouth."

Kit bent a skeptical look on her friend.

Amy frowned. "It's true. And you should feel all hot and flushed—like having a fever only nicer. Your knees tend to go weak, but that doesn't matter because he'll be holding you. And for some reason, you can't hear very well when you're kissing—I don't know why. It's just as well to remember that."

"Sounds like a disease," Kit muttered.

Amy ignored her. "Sometimes it's a bit hard to breathe, but somehow you manage."

"Wonderful—suffocation as well."

"He might kiss your eyes and cheeks and ears, too, and then move on to your neck. That's always nice."

A distinct purr was slowly infusing itself into Amy's soft voice; Kit blinked.

"And then," Amy went on, "depending on how things are going, he might touch your breasts, just gently, sort of squeezing and stroking. It always feels as if my laces are too tight by that stage."

Kit stared, openmouthed, but Amy was well launched on her subject.

"Soon, my nubbins go all hard and crinkly, which is a rather odd feeling. And then comes the hot flushes."

"Hot flushes?"

"Mmm. They start in your breasts and move down."

"Down? Down where?"

"To between your legs. And then—and this is the important bit." Amy wagged a finger. "If you feel all hot and wet down there, then he's the man for you. But you'll know that anyway because all you'll be thinking about by then is how nice it would feel if only he'd come into you."

Aghast, Kit stared. "It sounds positively dreadful."

"Oh, *Kit*." Amy threw her a commiserating glance. "It's not awful at all."

"I'll take your word for it. Thank you for warning me."

Kit lay silent, staring at the ceiling. Her one brush with love hadn't been anything like that. From Amy's description, it was clear that she, Kit, had never been touched by love. Feeling as if she'd succeeded in understanding some particularly difficult point that had eluded her for years, Kit shook her head. "I can't see myself getting hot and wet for any man. But then, I'm obviously not destined for love at all."

"You can't say that."

Kit lifted a haughty brow, but Amy was not to be gainsaid.

"You can't just *decide* you're not susceptible. With the right man, you won't be able to help yourself. It's just because you're . . . innocent of love that you say so."

Kit's eyes widened. "Innocent? Did I tell you I lost my innocence one fine summer evening on my Uncle Frederick's terrace?"

Amy gaped.

Kit shook her head. "Not physically. But I found out what most men think of love that night. I grant your George may be different—there are exceptions to every rule. But I've learned that it's women who fall in love and men who take advantage of our weakness. I've no intention of succumbing."

"What happened on your uncle's terrace?"

Kit grimaced. "I was eighteen. Can you remember what eighteen felt like? I suppose I'd started to get over leaving Cranmer. My uncles and aunts had already been urging me to marry. Then, miraculously, I found myself in love. Or so I thought." Kit paused, eyes fixed on the ceiling, then she drew a deep breath. "He was beautiful—a captain of guards, tall and handsome. Lord George Belville, the second son of a duke. He said he loved me. I was so happy, Amy. I don't think I can explain what it felt like, to have someone who really cared about me again. I was . . . oh— as you are now. Over the moon with joy. My aunts gave a ball, and Belville said he'd use the opportunity to ask my uncle for my hand. They disappeared into the library midway through the evening. I was so excited, I couldn't bear not knowing what was being said. So I slipped out on the small terrace and listened outside the library windows. What I heard—" Her voice broke. She drew another breath and forged on. "All I heard was them laughing at me."

Amy's hand found hers amid the bedcovers; Kit barely noticed. "It was all deliberate. They'd presented me with four suitors up till then, all much older men, none particularly attractive. My aunts had decided I was too much of a romantic—tainted with the wildness of my father's and mother's blood was the way they put it—to accept such eminently suitable alliances. So they'd searched out Belville. He was as ambitious as they were. He was destined for some position in military affairs, something high, organized through his connections. Through our marriage, he'd get the backing of my uncles in furthering his career. They'd get his support in furthering theirs. I was the token to cement their alliance. It was all made perfectly clear while I listened. Belville spoke of how easy it had been to ensnare me.''

Kit stretched her arms out, forcing her long fingers to straighten from the claws they'd curled into. She uttered a hollow laugh. ''They were so sure of themselves. When I refused Belville the next day, they couldn't believe it.''

Abruptly, she sat up, swinging about to face Amy. ''After that, I always listened to my so-called suitors' meetings with my guardians. Most instructive. So, you see, Amy dear, while I may envy you your experience, I know how rare it is. I don't expect love as you know it to find me. It's had six years to do so and failed. I'll soon be well and truly on the shelf.''

Kit saw sympathy in Amy's brown eyes and, smiling ruefully, shook her head. ''There's no earthly point feeling sorry for me, for I don't feel the least sorry for myself. What man do you know would allow me the freedom I presently enjoy—to go about as I please, to be myself?''

''But you don't do anything scandalous.''

''I see no point in inviting the attentions of the gabblemongers, and I would never bring scandal to my grandfather's name. But I recognize no restrictions beyond those. A husband would expect his wife to behave in accord with certain strictures, to be at home when he was, not riding the sands. He'd expect me to follow his dictates, have my world revolve about him, when I'd be wanting to do something quite different.''

Amy frowned. ''I can understand your disillusionment, but we vowed we'd marry for love, remember?''

Kit smiled. "We'd marry for love—or not at all."

Amy flushed, but, before she could speak, Kit went on, her tone one of acceptance: "*You're* marrying for love; *I'm* not marrying at all."

"*Kit!*"

Kit laughed. "Don't fuss so, my dearest goose. I'm enjoying myself hugely. I promise you—I don't *need* love."

Amy held her tongue but, to her mind, love was the very thing Kit did need to make her whole.

Chapter 3

Kit spent the following two days paying visits to various tenants' wives, hearing about their families, their troubles, renewing the women's direct contact with Cranmer Hall, which had lapsed since her grandmother's death. Yet between the chatter-filled visits, she brooded, surprised at herself yet unable to shake free.

Discussing love with Amy had been a mistake. Ever since, she'd been restless. Until then, Cranmer had seemed the perfect haven. Now, something was missing. She didn't appreciate the feeling.

Luckily, the next day was too busy for brooding, filled instead with preparations for the dinner Spencer had organized to reintroduce her formally to their neighbors. Kit managed to squeeze in a ride in the afternoon but returned in good time to change.

The guests arrived punctually at eight. Waiting to greet them at the drawing room door, Kit stood beside Spencer, impressive in a silk coat and white knee breeches, his white mane wreathing his proud head. His expression was one of paternal pride, for which Kit knew she was directly responsible.

She'd chosen her gown carefully, rejecting fine muslins and low-cut satins in favor of a delicate creation in aquamarine silk. The free-flowing material did justice to her slender length; the neckline was scooped and scalloped as befitted her age but remained high enough for propriety. The color heightened the glow of her burnished curls and drew attention to the creaminess of her skin.

Her eyes sparkled as she curtsied to the Lord Lieutenant, Lord Marchmont, and his wife, drawing an appreciative look from his lordship.

"Kathryn, my dear, it's a pleasure to see you back in the fold."

Kit smiled easily. "Indeed, my lord, it's a pleasure to be back and meeting old friends."

Lord Marchmont laughed and tapped her cheek. "Very prettily said, my dear."

He and his wife moved into the room to make way for the next guests. Kit knew them all. She couldn't help comparing the real joy she felt in such a simple affair with the boredom she'd found in the elaborate entertainments of the *ton*.

The Greshams were the last to arrive. After exchanging compliments with Sir Harvey and Lady Gresham, Kit linked her arm in Amy's. "Where's your George?" At her suggestion, the Greshams' invitation had included Amy's betrothed. "I'm dying to meet this paragon whose kisses get you hot and wet."

"Sssh! For heaven's sake, Kit, keep your voice down." Amy's eyes were fixed on her mother's back. Perceiving no sign that her ladyship had heard, she switched her gaze to Kit's teasing face. And sighed. "George had to cry off. It seems he's still on duty—assigned to some special mission." Amy grimaced. "He does steal time to drop by now and then, but it's hardly what I'd hoped—I haven't seen much of him in the last few weeks."

"Oh," was all Kit could find to say.

"But," added Amy, drawing herself up, "it will only be for another few months. And at least he's safe in England, not facing the French guns." Smiling, she squeezed Kit's arm. "Incidentally, he said he was most desirous of making your acquaintance."

Kit looked her disbelief. "Did he really say that or are you just being loyal?"

Amy laughed. "You're right. What with his apologies for not being able to accompany us, I'm afraid we never got around to discussing you."

Kit nodded sagely. "I see. Too feverish for sense."

Amy grinned but refused confirmation. Together, they strolled among the guests, chatting easily. The conversation in the drawing room revolved around farming and the local markets, but once they were all seated about the long dining table, the talk shifted to other spheres.

"Hendon's not here, I see." Lord Marchmont sent a glance around the table, as if the recently returned Lord Hendon might have slipped in unnoticed. "Thought he would be."

"We sent a card, but his lordship had a prior engagement." Spencer nodded to Jenkins; the first course was promptly served, footmen ferrying dishes from the kitchen.

Pondering a dish of crab in oyster sauce, Kit realized it was rather odd of Lord Hendon to have a prior engagement. With whom, when all the surrounding families were here?

"Pity," Spencer continued. "Haven't met the fellow yet."

"I have," replied Lord Marchmont, helping himself to the turbot.

"Oh?" said Spencer. All paused to hear his lordship's response.

Lord Marchmont nodded. "Seems a solid sort. Jake's boy, after all."

Jake Hendon had been the previous lord of Castle Hendon. Kit's memory supplied a hazy figure, broad, powerful, and extremely tall with a pair of twinkling grey eyes. He'd taken her for a ride on his stallion when she'd been eight years old. She couldn't recall having met his son.

"What's this I hear about Hendon's appointment as High Commissioner?" Sir Harvey glanced at his lordship. "Another attempt to stamp out the traffic?"

"So it appears." Lord Marchmont looked up. "But he's Jake's boy—he'll know how to pace his success."

All the men nodded, comfortable with that assessment. Smuggling was in the Norfolk blood; control was one thing, suppression unthinkable. Where else would they get their brandy?

Lady Gresham looked pointedly at Lady Marchmont. "Amelia, have you met this paragon?"

Lady Marchmont nodded. "Indeed. A most pleasant gentleman."

"Good. What's he like?"

Amy and Kit exchanged glances, then rapidly looked down at their plates. While the men ignored the very feminine question, the ladies fastened their attention on Lady Marchmont.

"He's tall, just like his father. And he's got the same odd hair—you remember, Martha. I believe he's been in both the army and the navy, but that might not be right. It doesn't sound normal, does it?"

Lady Gresham frowned. "Amelia, stop beating about the bush. *How much* like his father is he?"

Lady Marchmont chuckled. "Oh, that!" She waved dismissively. "He's as handsome as sin, but then, all the Hendons are."

"Too true," agreed Mrs. Cartwright. "And they can charm the birds from the trees."

"That, too." Her ladyship nodded. "A silver-tongued devil, he is."

Lady Dersingham sighed. "So pleasant, to know there's a personable gentleman about one has yet to meet. Heightens the anticipation."

There were nods of agreement all around.

"He's not married, is he?" asked Lady Lechfield.

Lady Marchmont shook her head. "Oh, no. You may be sure I asked. He's only recently returned from active service abroad. He still carries a wound—a limp in his left leg. He said he expected to be very much caught up in executing his commission as well as taking up Jake's reins."

"Hmm." Lady Gresham's gaze rested on Kit, seated at the end of the table. "Thinks he'll be too busy to find a wife, does he?"

Lady Dersingham's gaze had followed her ladyship's. "Perhaps we could help?" she mused.

Kit, busy conveying her compliments to their chef via Jenkins, did not catch their assessing glances. She turned back to see the ladies Gresham and Dersingham exchanging satisfied nods with Lady Marchmont.

As the ladies' attention returned to their plates, Kit

caught a quizzical glance from Amy. Briefly Kit grimaced, then looked down, eyes gleaming cynically. A silver-tongued devil as handsome as sin sounded far too much like one of her London suitors. Just because the man was tall, wellborn, and not positively ugly, he was immediately considered a desirable *parti*! Stifling an unladylike snort, Kit attacked her portion of crab.

Chapter 4

Shortly after eleven, the coaches rumbled down the drive, well lit by a full moon. Beside Spencer on the steps, Kit waved them away, then impulsively hugged her grandfather.

"Thank you, Gran'pa. That was a lovely evening."

Spencer beamed. "A rare pleasure, my dear." Arm in arm, they entered the hall. "Perhaps in a few months we might consider a dance, eh?"

Kit smiled. "Perhaps. Who knows—we might even entice this mysterious Lord Hendon with the promise of music."

Spencer laughed. "Not if he's Jake's lad. Never could stand any fussing and primping, not Jake."

"Ah, but this one's a new generation—who knows what he'll be like."

Spencer shook his head. "As you get older, my dear, one thing becomes clear. People don't really change, generation to generation. The same strengths, the same weaknesses."

Kit laughed and kissed his cheek. "Good night, Gran'pa."

Spencer patted her hand and left her.

But once in her room, Kit couldn't settle down. She let Elmina help her from her gown, then dismissed her; enveloped in a wrapper, she prowled the room. The single candle wavered and she snuffed it. Moonlight streamed in, shedding more than enough light. Thinking of Spencer's dance, Kit bowed and swayed through the steps of a cotillion. At its end, she sank onto the window seat and stared out over the fields. In the distance, she could hear the swoosh of the waves, two miles away.

The odd emptiness remained, that peculiar feeling of lack that had settled deep inside her. In an effort to ignore it, she fixed her senses on the ebb and surge of the tide, letting the sounds lull her and lead her toward slumber. She'd almost succumbed when she saw the light.

A flash of brilliance, it flared in the dark. Then, just as she'd convinced herself she'd imagined it, it came again. There was a ship offshore, signaling to—to whom? On the thought, the muted reflection of an answering flash from beneath the cliffs gleamed on the dark water.

Kit searched the blackness, separating the darker mass of the cliffs from the background of the Wash. Smugglers were running a cargo on the beach directly west of Cranmer Hall.

Within minutes, she'd pulled on her breeches and bound her breasts in the cloths she used for support when riding. She pulled a linen shirt over her head and shrugged on her coat without stopping to tie the shirt laces. Stockings and boots followed. She jammed on her hat, remembering to wrap a woollen scarf about her throat to hide the white of her linen. She headed for the door but paused at the last. On impulse, she turned back and crossed to where, above a dresser against the wall, a rapier with an Italianate guard lay in brackets, crossed over its belted scabbard. It was the work of a minute to free both. Seconds later, Kit slipped out of the house and headed for the stables.

Delia whinnied in welcome, then stood quietly as Kit threw a saddle onto the black back, expertly cinching the girth before leading the mare, not into the yard where the clop of iron-shod hooves would rouse the stablelads, but into the small paddock behind the stables. Swinging into the saddle, she leaned forward, murmuring encouragement to the mare, then set her directly at the fence. Delia cleared it easily.

The black hooves effortlessly ate the miles. Fifteen

minutes later, Kit reined in under cover of the last trees before the cliff's edge.

Fitful clouds had found the moon. Her senses straining into the sudden darkness, Kit heard the soft splash of oars, followed by an unmistakable "scrunch." A boat had beached. In the same instant, a jingle from her left drew her eyes. The moon sailed free, and Kit saw what the smugglers on the beach beneath the cliffs couldn't see. The Revenue.

A small troop was picking its way across the grassy headland. For a full minute, Kit watched. The soldiers were armed.

What crazy impulse prompted her she never knew. Perhaps a vision of fishermen's children playing under nets on the beach? She'd seen such a sight just that afternoon, while riding past a fishing hamlet. Whatever, she pulled her scarf high, covering nose and chin, and yanked her hat down. Drawing Delia around, she set the mare on a silent course parallel to the shore. There was no pathway where the Revenue were headed. Kit knew every inch of this stretch of coast, the section she most frequently visited on her rides. She left the Revenue behind but didn't turn Delia to the shore until she was out of their sight. The clouds were unreliable; she couldn't afford to be seen.

Once on the beach, she turned the mare's head for the smugglers, a dark blotch on the shore. Praying they'd realize a single rider was no threat, she galloped directly toward them. The dull drubbing of Delia's hooves was swallowed by the crash of the surf; she was nearly upon them before they realized. Kit had a momentary vision of stunned faces, then she saw moonlight flash on a pistol's mounts. Struggling to turn Delia, she all but snarled in fright: "Don't be a fool! The Revenue are on the cliff. They're some way from a path, but they're there. Get out!"

Wheeling Delia, Kit glanced back. The smugglers stood frozen in a knot about their boat. "Go!" she urged. "*Move*—or they'll nail your hides to the Custom House in Lynn."

Afterward, she realized it was her use of the shortened name for the town, a habit with locals, that prompted them to turn to her. The largest took a tentative step toward her, warily eyeing Delia and her iron-tipped hooves. "We've a cargo here that's got nowhere to go. All our blunt's sunk in't. If we don't get it out, our families'll starve."

Kit recognized him. She'd seen him that afternoon at the hamlet, busily mending nets. Fleetingly, she closed her eyes. Trust her to stumble onto the most helpless crew of smugglers on the English coast.

She opened her eyes, and the men were still there, mutely begging for help. "Where are your ponies?" she asked.

"Didn't think we'd need 'em, not for this lot."

"But . . ." Kit had always thought smugglers had ponies. "What were you going to do with it then?"

"We normally put stuff like this in a cave up beside the knoll yonder." The big man nodded southward.

Kit knew the cave. She and her cousins had played in it often. But the Revenue troop was between the smugglers and the cave. Moving the goods in the boat was impossible; with the moon out they'd be seen.

On the other hand, a boat could be a perfect distraction.

"Two of you. Take the boat out to sea. You've got nets in it, haven't you?" To her relief, they nodded. "Get the cargo out. Put it close to the cliffs." She glanced at the cliffs, then up at the moon—a large cloud swept up and engulfed it. Thanking her guardian angel, Kit nodded. "Now! Move!"

They worked fast. Soon, the boat was empty. "You two!" Kit called to the pair elected to remain with the boat. The surf was pounding in; she had to yell to be heard. "You're out fishing, understand? You pulled in here for a break, nothing more. You don't know anything about anything except fish. Take the boat out and act as if you really are fishing. Go!"

A minute later, the oars dipped and the small boat struggled out through the surf. Kit wheeled Delia and made for the cliff.

The large man was waiting for her there. "What now?"

"The Snettisham quarries." Kit kept her voice low. "And no talking. They must be close above us. Head north and keep in the lee of the cliff. They'll be expecting you to go south.''

"But our homes are south.''

In the blackness, Kit couldn't tell who'd said that. "Which would you rather—being late home or ending in the cells beneath the Custom House?''

There was no further argument. Huffing and puffing, they followed her. Once they were clear of where she'd seen the Revenue, Kit found a path to the cliff top. "I'm going to find out where they are. There's no sense in walking into an ambush with your arms full.''

Without waiting for their opinion, she set Delia upward. She followed the cliff edge back toward the soldiers, keeping under cover. She was in a stand of oak waiting for the next spate of moonlight to study the area ahead when she heard them coming. They were grumbling, loud and long, having belatedly realized they were nowhere near a path downward. The moonlight strengthened, and she could see them gathering in a knot in the middle of the grassy expanse directly in front of her.

A shout came from the cliff's edge. "There's a path here, Sergeant! What are we to do? The boat's gone, and there's nought to be seen on the sands.''

A burly man nudged his horse to the cliff and looked down. He swore. "Never mind that now. We saw that boat. Half of you—down onto the sand and go south. The rest keep to the cliffs. We're bound to come up with them, one way or t'other.''

"But south's Sergeant Osborne's region, Sergeant.''

The burly man cuffed the speaker. "I know that, fool boy! But Osborne's out to Sheringham way, so's it's up to us to police this 'ere stretch. On you go, and let's see what we can find.''

To Kit's delight, she saw them split, then both groups head south. Satisfied, she returned to the small band trudging doggedly northward, still on the sands.

"You're safe. They've gone south.''

The men downed their burdens and sat on the sands. "Thanks be we only had one boatload.'' The speaker glanced toward Kit and explained: "Normally we have a lot more."

The large man, who seemed to be their spokesman, looked up at her. "This quarry you spoke of, lad. Where be it?"

Kit stared. It had never occurred to her that they wouldn't know Snettisham quarries. She and her cousins had spent hours playing there. It was a perfect hiding place for anything. But what if she took them there?

Delia pranced sideways; Kit gentled her. "I'll give you directions. You won't want me to know exactly where you've stowed your goods." Using the mare's nervousness as an excuse, Kit backed her up. At least one man had a pistol.

"Hang about, lad." The large man stepped forward. Delia took exception and danced back. He stopped. "You've got nothing to fear from us, matey. You saved us back there, no mistake. Smugglers' honor says we offer you a cut of the booty."

Kit blinked. Smugglers' honor? She laughed lightly and drew Delia around. "Consider it a free service. I don't want any booty." She set her heels to the sleek black sides and Delia surged forward.

"Wait!" The panicky note in the man's voice made Kit rein in and turn. He stumbled through the sand toward her, stopping when he was close enough to talk. For a moment, he stared at her, then looked to his companions. In the dim light, Kit saw their emphatic nods. The spokesman turned back to her.

"It's like this, lad. We don' have a leader. We got into the business thinking we could manage well enough, but you saw how 'tis." His head jerked southward. "You thought fast, back there. I don' suppose you'd like to take us on? We got good contacts an' all. But we're not good on the organization, like."

Disbelief and consternation warred in Kit's brain. Take them on? "You mean . . . you want me to act as your leader?"

"For a slice o' the profits, o'course."

Delia shifted. Kit glanced up and saw the others hoist

their burdens and draw nearer. She didn't need to fear a pistol while they were so laden. "I'm sure you'll manage well enough on your own. The Revenue just got lucky."

But the big man was shaking his head. "Lad, just look at us. None of us knows where these quarries of yours be. We don' even know what's the best road home. Like as not, as soon as we're back on the cliffs, we'll run slap bang into the Revenue. And then it'll all be for nought."

The moon sailed free and Kit saw their faces, turned up to her in childlike trust. She sighed. What had she got herself into now? "What do you run?"

They perked up at this sign of interest. "Show 'im, Joe." The big man waved the smallest one forward. The man shuffled over the sand, one wary eye on Delia. He smiled up at Kit as he drew near—an all but toothless grin—then stopped beside the mare and peeled back the oilskin enclosing the packet he bore, a rectangle about three feet long and flatish. Grubby hands brushed back layers of coarse cloth.

Moonlight glimmered on what was revealed. Kit's eyes grew round. Lace! They were smuggling Brussels lace. No wonder the packages were so small. One boatload, carried to London and sold through the trade, would surely feed these men and their families for months. Kit rapidly revised her assessment of their business acumen. Organizationally hopeless they might be, but they knew their cargoes.

"We sometimes get brandy, too, depending." The big man had drawn closer.

Kit's eyes narrowed. "Nothing else?" She'd heard there were things other than goods brought ashore in the boats.

Her tone was sharp, but the man's face was open when he answered: "We ain't done no other cargoes—this's been enough t'present."

She could sense their entreaty. Her Norfolk blood stirred. A leader of smugglers? One part of her laughed at the idea. A small part. Most of her unconventional soul was intrigued. Her father had led a band for a short time—for a lark, he'd said. Why couldn't she? Kit crossed her hands over her pommel and considered the possibilities. "If I became your leader, you'd have to agree to doing only the cargoes I think are right.''

They glanced at each other, then the big man looked up. ''What cut?''

''No cut.'' They murmured at that; behind her muffler, Kit smiled. ''I don't need your goods or the money they'll bring. If I agree to take you on, it'll be for the sheer hell of it. Nothing more.''

A quick conference ensued, then the spokesman approached. ''If we agree, will you show us these quarries?''

''If we agree, I'll take over right now. If not, say so, and I'll be off.'' Delia pranced.

The man sent a glance around his companions, then turned back to her. ''Deal. What moniker do ye go by?''

''Kit.''

''Right then, young Kit. Lead on.''

It took them an hour to reach the quarries and find a suitable deserted tunnel to use as a base. By then, Kit had learned a great deal more of the small band. They contracted for cargoes through the inns in King's Lynn. Whatever they brought ashore, they hid in the cave for a few nights before transferring it by pack pony to the ruined abbey at Creake.

''S'been a clearinghouse for years, hereabouts. We show the goods to the old crone who lives in the cottage close by, and she's always got our cut ready an' waiting.''

''The old woman has the money?''

''Oh, aye. She be a witch, so the money's safe with her.''

''How very convenient.'' Someone, somewhere, had put considerable effort into organizing the Norfolk smugglers. An unwelcome thought surfaced. ''Are there any other gangs operating about here?''

The large man went by the unenviable name of Noah. ''Not on the west here, no. But there's a gang east of Hunstanton. Big gang, that is. We've never come across 'em, though.''

And I hope you never will, Kit thought. These poor souls were a remarkably simple lot, not given to unnecessary violence, fisherman driven to smuggling in order to feed their families. But somewhere out there lurked real smugglers, the sort who committed the atrocities proclaimed in the handbills. She'd no desire whatever to meet them. Keeping clear of this Hunstanton Gang seemed a good idea.

Once the lace was stored, she gave orders, crisply and clearly, about how they were to pass the cargo on. She also insisted they operate from the quarries henceforth. "The Revenue men will be suspicious of that stretch of beach, and the cave's too close. From now on, we'll work from here." Kit threw out a hand to indicate their surroundings. They were standing before the dark mouth of the abandoned tunnel in which they'd stashed their goods. "We'll be safer here. There are places aplenty to hide, and even in broad daylight it's not easy to follow people through here." She paused, then paced before them, frowning in concentration. "If you have to go out in your boats to bring in the cargo, then the boats should just land the goods and go directly back to your village. If the rest of you bring ponies, then we can load the goods and transfer them here. When it's safe, they can go on to Creake."

They agreed readily. "This be a dandy place for hiding, right enough."

As they stood to leave, Noah noticed the rapier at Kit's side. "That's a right pretty toy. Know how to use it?"

A heartbeat later, he was blinking at the soft shimmer of moonlight on steel, the rapier point at his throat. Swallowing convulsively, his gaze traveled the length of the wicked blade, until, over the top of the ornate guard, he met Kit's narrowed eyes. She smiled tightly. "Yes."

"Oh." The big man remained perfectly still.

Kit relaxed and expertly turned the blade and slid it back into the scabbard. "A little conceit of mine."

She turned and walked to where Delia waited, ears pricked. Behind her, she sensed the exchanged glances and hid a smug smile. She swung up to the saddle, then looked back at her little band.

"You know the road home?"

They nodded. "And we'll keep a watch for the Revenue, like you said."

"Good. We'll meet here Thursday after moonrise." Kit wheeled and set her heels to Delia's sides. "And then we'll see what comes next."

Chapter 5

"Damn!"** George flung his cards down on the rough deal table and glared at Jack. "Nothing's changed in well-nigh twenty years! You still win."

Jack's white teeth showed in a laughing smile. "Console yourself it's not the title to your paternal acres that lie under my hand." He lifted his palm, revealing a pile of wood-chips.

Pushing back his chair, George snorted disgustedly. "As if I'd risk anything of worth against such a dyed-in-the-wool gamester."

Jack collected the cards and reshaped the pack, then, elbows on the table, shuffled them back and forth, left hand to right.

Outside, the east wind howled, whipping leaves and twigs against the shutters. Inside, the lamplight played on Jack's bent head, exposing the hidden streaks of gold, bright against the duller brown. Aside from the table, the single-room cottage was sparsely furnished, the principal items being a large bed against the opposite wall and an equally large wardrobe beside it. Yet no farmworker would have dreamed of setting foot in the place. The bed was old but of polished oak, as was the wardrobe. The sheets were of linen and the goosefeather quilt simply too luxurious to permit the fiction of this being a humble dwelling. True, the deal table was just that, but smoothed and cleaned and in remarkably good condition. The four chairs scattered about the room were of assorted styles but none bore any relation to the crude seating normally found in fishermen's abodes.

Jack slapped the pack on the table and, pushing his chair back, stretched his arms above his head.

Hoofbeats, muffled by the wildness outside, sounded like a ghostly echo. Dragging his gaze from the flames flickering in the stone hearth, George turned to listen, then sent an expectant look Jack's way.

Jack's brows rose fleetingly before his gaze swung to the door. Seconds later, it burst open to reveal a large figure wrapped in heavy frieze, a hat pulled low over his eyes. The figure whirled, slamming the heavy door against the tempest outside.

The tension in Jack's long frame eased. He leaned forward, arms on the table. "Welcome back. What did you learn?"

Matthew's lined face emerged as the hat hit the table. He shrugged off his coat and set it on a peg beside the door. "Like you thought, there's another gang."

"They're active?" George drew his chair closer.

At Jack's nod, Matthew pulled another chair to the table. "They're in business, all right. Ran a cargo of brandy last night, somewhere between Hunstanton and Heacham, cool as you please. I heard talk they did that consignment of lace we refused—the run that clashed with that load of spirits we took out Brancaster way."

Jack swore. "Damn! I'd hoped that night was all a piece of Tonkin's delusions." He turned to George. "When I went into Hunstanton yesterday, Tonkin was full of this gang he'd surprised running some cargo south of Snettisham. Preening that he'd found another gang operating on Osborne's turf that Osborne hadn't known about. I spoke to some of Tonkin's men later. It sounded like they'd seen a fishing boat pull in for a break and Tonkin invented the rest." Jack grimaced. "Now, it seems otherwise."

"Does it matter? If they're a small operation . . ." George broke off at Jack's emphatic nod.

"It matters. We need this coast tied up. If there's another gang operating, no matter how small, who's to tell what cargoes they'll run?"

The wind whistled down the narrow chimney and played with the flames licking the logs in the hearth. Abruptly, Jack pushed away from the table. "We'll have to find out who this lot is." He looked at Matthew. "Did you get any hints from your contacts?"

Matthew shook his head. "Not a whiff of a scent."

George frowned. "What about Osborne? Why not just get him to clamp down along that stretch?"

"Because I've sent him to clamp down on the beaches between Blakeney and Cromer." Exasperation colored Jack's tone. "There's a small outfit operating around there, but for most of that coast, the silts are so unpredictable no master in his right mind will bring his ship in close. The few reasonable landings are easy to patrol. But I sent Osborne to ensure the job was done. Aside from anything else, it seemed preferable to make certain he wouldn't get wind of our activities and seek to curtail them. Tonkin, bless his hopeless heart, is so bumblingly inept we stand in no danger from him. Unfortunately, neither does this other gang."

"So," George mused, "Tonkin's now effectively responsible for the coast from Lynn to Blakeney?"

Jack nodded.

"Whoever this other lot are," said Matthew, "seems like they know the area well. There's no whispers of pack trains or any such, but they must be moving the goods, same as us."

"Who knows?" Jack said. "They might actually be better set up than us. We're only novices, after all."

George turned a jaundiced eye on Jack. "I don't believe any man in his right mind would call Captain Jack a novice—not at this sort of devilry."

A broad grin dispelled Jack's seriousness. "You flatter me, my friend. Now, how are we to meet this mystery gang?"

"Must we meet them?"

"How else, oh knowledgeable one, are we to dissuade them from their illegal pursuits?"

"Dissuade them?"

Jack's face hardened. "That—or do Tonkin's job for him."

George looked glum. "I knew I wasn't going to like this mission."

Jack's chair grated on the floor as he rose. "They're smugglers, for Christ's sake."

George sighed, dropping his eyes from Jack's stern grey gaze. "So are we, Jack. So are we."

But Jack had stopped listening. Turning to Matthew, he asked, "What cargoes do they usually take?"

Chapter 6

Aweek later, from the cliff top screened by a belt of trees, Kit watched her band beach their boats at much the same spot as on the night she'd first rescued them. This time, there was no Revenue troop about; she'd reconnoitered the cliffs in both directions.

Still she was nervous, twitchy. Since she'd taken over, her band had run five cargoes, all successfully. Her band. At first, the responsibility had scared her. Now, each time they came off safely, she felt a thrill of achievement. But tonight was a special cargo. An agent, Nolan, had met them in Lynn last night. For the first time, she'd joined Noah for the negotiations. Just as well. She'd intervened and driven their price up—because Nolan was in a fix. He had a schooner with twenty bales of lace and no one to bring it in. They were his last resort. She'd already heard of the Revenue raids about Sheringham and, for some reason, the Hunstanton Gang had refused the run. Why, she didn't know—which was the root cause of her nervousness.

Everything, however, was going smoothly. The night was dark, the sky deepest purple. Beneath her, Delia peacefully cropped, undisturbed by an owl hooting in the trees behind them.

Watching the orderly way the men swiftly unloaded the boats, Kit smiled. They were not unintelligent, just unimaginative. Once she showed them a better way of doing things, they caught on quickly.

Suddenly, Delia's head came up, ears pricked, muscles

tensing. Kit strained her senses to catch what had disturbed the mare. Nothing. Then, far to the left, another owl hooted. Delia sidled. Kit stared at the great black head. *Not an owl?* She didn't wait for confirmation. Pulling Delia around, she set the mare onto the path down to the sands.

In the trees on the cliff top, two riders met a third.

"Spotted them," Matthew murmured, as Jack and George came up, walking their horses over the thinly grassed ground. He pointed to where ten ponies were being loaded with the consignment of lace they'd refused. As they looked, a mounted figure all in black broke from the shadow of the cliff and raced across the sands. "Cripes," muttered Matthew. "What's that?"

"A lookout we've alerted," came George's laconic answer.

"But where did a smuggler get a horse like that?" Jack watched as horse and rider flew toward the boats, a single entity in effortless motion. "This gang has signed up a little unexpected talent."

George nodded. "Do we go down now that they know we're here?"

Jack grimaced. "Let's wait. They might think we're the Revenue."

It appeared he was right. The rider reached the group on the sands. Immediately, their pace increased. Within minutes, the boats pulled out to sea. The rider backed from the ponies as the men tugged straps and girths tight. The black horse danced; the rider scanned the cliffs. He did not look directly their way.

Squinting, George whispered: "The horse—is it all black?"

Jack nodded. "Looks like it." He took up his reins. "They're heading in. Let's follow. I've a desire to see where they're stashing their goods."

Kit couldn't get rid of the feeling of being watched. Like Delia, her nerves were at full stretch. She hadn't explained to Noah why she came bolting out of the dark, urging him on. She'd just issued a warning: "There's someone out there. I didn't wait to find out who. Let's get going."

Five minutes later, she and Delia gained the cliff top. She waited until Noah, walking beside the lead pony, crested the cliff, then leaned down to say: "Go east by Cranmer woods, then cut back to the quarries. I'll scout around to make sure we're not followed."

She wheeled Delia and made off into the surrounding trees. For the next hour, she tracked her own men, sweeping in arcs across their trail. Time and again, Delia skittered. And every time, Kit felt the hair on her nape lift.

In the end, she realized it was she, the rider, the unknowns were tracking. Abruptly, Kit drew rein. Her followers were mounted, else they wouldn't have kept up thus far. They weren't trying to catch them but were following them to their hideout. But they were on Cranmer land and none knew that better than she. Her men would soon be turning north toward the quarries. She, with her unwelcome escort, would continue east.

Kit patted Delia's glossy black neck. "We'll have a run soon, my lady. But first let's do a little deceiving."

They were nearing the village of Great Bircham when Jack realized they'd lost the pack train. He reined in on a crest overlooking a moonlit valley. Somewhere ahead, the rider still ranged. "Damn! He's moving too fast to be following ponies. We've been had."

George stopped beside him. "Maybe the ponies were faster through the woods. The rider went slow there."

Jack shook his head emphatically. Then, as if to confirm his deduction in the most mocking way, the rider appeared, crossing the fields below at full gallop, a streak of black against the silvered green.

"Christ!" breathed George. "Will you look at that."

"I'd rather not look at that," Jack replied. After three seconds of silence, in which the rider gathered the fluid black into a soaring leap over a pair of hedges, he continued grudgingly: "Well, whoever he is, he can ride."

"What now?" asked Matthew.

"We go home and try to figure out another way of contacting this accursed gang." With that dampening answer,

Jack shook his reins and set his grey stallion, Champion, down the ridge.

Kit raced with the wind, the scenery a blur about her. She took her usual route to Gresham Manor, circling it, then pulling up on a hill overlooking the house to let Delia rest.

What would Amy say if she went down and threw gravel at her window? Kit grinned. Amy had a streak of conservatism that was quite wide, despite her predeliction for becoming hot and wet for her George.

Sighing, Kit folded her hands across her pommel, staring at the dreaming countryside. She hadn't thought of Amy's disturbing revelations for weeks, not since she'd taken up smuggling. Had excitement filled in that odd gap in her innermost self? After a moment's consideration, she admitted it had not. Rather, the demands of smuggling had left no time for dwelling on ill-defined regrets. Which was just as well. Shaking the cramps from her shoulders, Kit picked up the reins. It was time for the quarries.

The trio of riders cantered north in no great hurry. Jack drew rein as they topped a hill and turned to George, who pulled up beside him. Champion's head came around, but not to look at George, or George's gelding. The grey stallion shifted, craning his long neck to stare past George. The movement caught Jack's attention; he followed the horse's gaze.

"Hold very still," he commanded, his voice a bare murmur. Carefully, he turned in the saddle and looked back. The flash of black that had caught Champion's attention appeared in the fields behind them, this time heading west. Then horse and rider crossed the road, still flying. Jack watched until they disappeared into the trees bordering the next field.

Only then did he relax his rein and let Champion turn. The horse came about and stared in the direction the unknown rider had taken.

A grin of diabolical delight spread over Jack's features. "So that's it."

"What?" asked George. "Was that the rider again? Why aren't we giving chase?"

"We are." Jack set Champion back down the road, waiting until George and Matthew caught up before shifting to a canter. "But we mustn't get too close and warn him. I've been wondering what gave us away. I'd wager that black is a mare. Not having been introduced to Champion here, like any other well-bred female, she gets skittish whenever he gets close."

"Can Champion lead us to them?"

"I've no idea." Jack patted the silky grey neck. "But we can't risk getting too close until the rider dismounts."

Kit reached the quarries as the last pony was unloaded. Noah and the others greeted her with relief.

"Thought as how somethin' might have come upon you, lad."

Feeling thoroughly alive, her blood stirred by her long gallop, Kit swung her leg over Delia's neck and slid to the ground. "I'm sure we were followed, but I didn't catch sight of anyone. I went a very long way around, just in case." She looped Delia's reins to a wooden strut at the edge of the clearing, well away from the men, who had an almost superstitious fear of the black horse. "What's the stuff like?" She headed for the tunnel entrance.

Noah waved to a packet opened on a rock. "First-class stuff, it looks."

Kit bent over the lace, resting both palms on the rock to protect against the impulse to draw off her gloves and finger the delicate tracery, a far too feminine gesture. "This is better than that other stuff you ran. What's the price?"

The other men sat in the cave entrance, chewing baccy and talking quietly, while she and Noah reviewed their plans.

What warned her, she never knew. The hairs on her nape lifted. The next instant, she whirled, her rapier singing from its sheath, sweeping in an arc before the three men silently approaching.

What happened next made her blink. The foremost man—tall, well built, and hatless was her first impression—

took one step back and her rapier clashed against solid steel. Kit's eyes grew round. She swallowed a knot of cold fear at the sight of her elegant blade countered by a longer, infinitely more wicked-looking sword. The two men following the first drew back, leaving a wide area to the fighters.

Heavens! She was involved in a sword fight!

Resolutely, Kit quelled the impulse to drop her rapier and flee. Drawing a deep breath, she forced her mind to function. If this man was a smuggler, he'd have no knowledge of the finer points of swordsmanship. She, on the other hand, had been trained by an Italian master, a close friend of Spencer's. She hadn't practiced for years but, as her opponent drifted left, she instinctively drifted right, the blades hissing softly.

He made the first move, a tentative prod Kit easily pushed aside. She followed immediately with a classic counter, and was dismayed to meet the prescribed defense, perfectly executed. Two more similar exchanges sent her heart to her boots. The man could fight and fight well. The strength she sensed behind the long sword was frightening.

In growing panic, she glanced at her opponent's face. The moon shone over her shoulder, leaving her own face in shadow. Even in the weak light, she saw the frown on the handsome face watching her. A second later, the effect of that face hit her. Kit blinked and dragged her mind and her gaze back to her blade, poised against that other. But her disobedient eyes flicked upward again, drawn by that face. She sucked in a painful breath. *God, he is beautiful.* Sculpted features, aquiline planes below high cheekbones, lips long and firm above a stubbornly square chin. His hair was fairish, streaked silver in the moonlight. Despite her every effort, Kit's senses refused to bend to her will, irresponsibly continuing their dangerous detachment, roaming over the outline of the large body facing hers.

An odd sensation bloomed in Kit's midsection, a warm weakness that sapped what little strength she had. She wondered whether it was fear of impending death. At the thought, from deep inside, she heard a laugh, a warm, rich, seductive laugh. *What are you waiting for? You've been fantasizing about meeting a man who could do to you what*

George does to Amy—here he is. All you have to do is put down your rapier and step forward.

Kit's guard wavered—she came to herself with a sickening start. In that instant, her opponent launched an attack. Her blade had nowhere near enough strength to counter the sword effectively. By dint of sheer luck and fancy footwork, she survived the first rush, her heart pounding horribly, a metallic taste in her mouth. She knew she'd never survive the second.

So much for my dream come true, she sneered at her inner self. The man's about to skewer me, no thanks to you.

But the clash she feared never came. Her opponent took a decisive step back, just one, but it was enough to get him out of her reach. His sword was slowly lowered until it pointed at the ground.

Glancing up at that distracting face, Kit saw his frown deepen.

Jack's mind was reeling, overloaded by conflicting and confusing information. Champion had led them unerringly in the wake of the black mare. As soon as they saw the jumble of jagged rocks on the horizon, they'd recognized their destination. Respect for the smaller gang grew—the quarries were a perfect hideaway, made to order. They'd left their horses at the edge of the quarries, to ensure that Champion's presence did not give them away.

They'd come into the clearing openly but quietly. He'd immediately seen the slim figure in black poring over something on the opposite side. His feet had taken him in that direction. That was when his problems started.

Even before the lad whirled to face him, sword in hand, he'd been conscious of a quickening of his pulse, an increase in his heartbeat, a tightening of expectation which had nothing to do with the dangers of the night. Being presented with a rapier, wrong end first, only compounded the confusion. His reaction had been instinctive. It was not common practice for men to wear swords, but neither he nor George had yet adjusted to walking abroad without theirs on their hips. His hand had grasped his hilt the instant he'd heard the hiss of steel leaving a scabbard.

The poor light put him at a disadvantage from the first.

The young lad was an outline, nothing more. Straining into the gloom, he'd moved cautiously, testing his opponent, despite the likelihood he could walk over the lad without difficulty. His opening move had been tentative. The lad's response had been another revelation—who'd have expected Italian ripostes from a smuggler? But the following moves left him wondering what was wrong with the lad. The arm wielding the rapier had no strength in it.

He'd peered hard at the boy then, and the impulse to shake his head grew. Something was damnably wrong somewhere. Despite not being able to see the lad's eyes, he could feel the boy's gaze and knew he was staring. At him. It was the effect of that stare that totally threw him. Never before had his body reacted so definitely, certainly never in response to a stare from a male.

The lad's point had wavered, and he'd pressed forward, without any real aim, more a matter of keeping up pretenses while he decided what to do. The lack of response made his mind up for him. He didn't know enough about the gang, and about this strange boy, to make forcing a submission wise. The lad was no fool; he'd know a fight between them could have only one end; they both knew that now. He stepped back and lowered his sword.

The boy's head came up.

A moment passed, pregnant with expectation. Then the rapier lowered. Inwardly, Jack sighed with relief.

"Who are you?" Fear had tightened Kit's throat; her voice came out gravelly and, if anything, even deeper than usual. Her eyes remained fixed on the man before her. His head turned slightly, as if to catch some half-heard sound, yet she'd spoken clearly. His unnerving frown didn't waver.

Jack heard the question but couldn't quite believe what he'd heard. His senses registered not the fear, but the underlying quality in the husky voice. He'd heard voices like that before; they didn't belong to striplings. Yet what his senses kept telling him, his rational mind knew to be impossible. It had to be some peculiar effect of the moonlight. "I'm Captain Jack, leader of the Hunstanton Gang. We want to talk, nothing more."

The lad stood perfectly still, shrouded in shadow, his face invisible. "We're listening."

Moving slowly, deliberately, Jack sheathed his sword. The tension eased, but he noted that the stripling kept his rapier in his hand. His lips quirked. The lad had his wits about him—if their situations had been reversed, he'd have done the same.

Kit felt much safer when the long sword settled back into its scabbard and felt no compulsion whatever to sheathe hers. The man was more than dangerous, particularly when his features eased, as they'd just done. The slight smile, if it was even that, drew her eyes to his lips. What would they feel like against hers? Would they make her feel . . . Kit dragged her errant thoughts from the brink of certain confusion. Then another thought struck, out of the blue. What would she feel if he smiled?

But he was talking. Kit struggled to concentrate on his words, rather than letting her mind slide aimlessly into the rich, velvety-deep tones.

"We'd like you to consider a merger." Jack waited for some response; none came. His cohorts shifted, but the lad made no sign. "Equal footing, equal share in the proceeds." Still nothing. "With our gangs working together, we'd tie up the coast from Lynn to Wells and farther. We could set our conditions, so we get a decent share of the profits, given the risks we take."

That idea caused a stir. Jack was pleased with the result, given that only half his mind was concentrating on his arguments. The better half was centered on the lad. Now, with his mates looking pointedly to him, the boy shifted slightly. "What exactly's in this for us?"

It was a sensible question, but Jack could have sworn the lad paid scant attention to his answer.

While ostensibly listening to Captain Jack extol the obvious virtues of operating as part of a larger whole, Kit wondered what on earth she was to do. The merger would be in the best interests of her small band. Captain Jack had already demonstrated an uncommon degree of ability. And good sense. And he didn't seem overly bloodthirsty. Noah and company would be as safe as they could be under his guidance. But for herself, every sense was screaming the fact that remaining anywhere near Captain Jack was tantamount to lunacy. He'd eat her for breakfast, or worse. Even in bad light, she wasn't sure of her ability to fool him—he seemed suspicious already.

He'd come to the end of his straightforward explanation and was waiting for her reply. "What's in a merger for you?" she asked.

Jack's feelings for the stripling became even more confused as grudging respect and exasperation were added to the list. He hadn't entered the clearing with any real plan; the idea of a merger had leapt ready-formed to his mind, more in response to a need to accommodate the lad than anything else. His explanation of the benefits to them had been easy enough, but what possible benefits were there to him? Other than the truth?

Jack looked directly at the slim figure, still wreathed in shadows before him. "While you're operating independently, the agents can use you as competition to force us to accept whatever price they offer. Without competition, we'd be better off." He stopped there, leaving the other way of reducing competition unvoiced. He was sure the lad would get the message.

Kit did, but she was not convinced she understood the full ramifications of a merger, nor that she ever would, not while Captain Jack stood before her. "I'll need time to consider your offer."

Jack smiled at the formal phrasing. He nodded. "Naturally. Shall we say twenty-four hours?"

His smile was every bit as unnerving as his frown. In fact, Kit decided, she preferred his frown. She only just managed to stop her bewildered nod. "Three days," she countered. "I'll need three days." Kit glanced around at the faces of her men. "If the rest of you want to join them now . . ."

Noah shook his head. "No, lad. You rescued us, you took us on. Decision's yours, I'm thinking." A murmur of agreement came from the rest of the group.

Jack's look of surprise was fleeting, wiped from his face by the lad's next words.

Kit spoke to Noah. "I'll be in touch." Inside, she was feeling most peculiar. Decidedly fluttery and weak at the knees. She had to get out of this, and soon, before she did something too feminine to overlook. Steeling herself, she faced Captain Jack and inclined her head regally. "I'll meet you here, seventy-two hours from now, and give you our answer."

With that, Kit walked off toward Delia, praying their unexpected and unnerving guests would accept their dismissal.

Her unconscious arrogance left Jack reeling again. He recovered his equilibrium in time to see the slim figure swing up to the saddle of the black. The horse was pure Arab, not a doubt about it, and a mare as he'd supposed. Jack's eyes narrowed. Surely there'd been too much swing in the lad's swagger? When on a horse, it was difficult to judge, yet the boy's legs seemed uncommonly long for his height and more tapered than they ought to be.

With no more than a nod for his men, the lad headed the mare out of the clearing. Jack stared at the black-garbed figure until it merged into the night, leaving him with a headache and, infinitely worse, no proof of the conviction of his senses.

Chapter 7

By the time they reached the cottage that night, Jack didn't know what he thought of Young Kit. They'd learned the lad's name from the smugglers, but it was clear the men knew little else of their leader. They were sensible, solid fishermen, forced into the trade. It seemed unlikely such men, many fathers themselves, rigidly conservative as only the ignorant could be, would give loyalty and unquestioning obedience to Young Kit if he was other than he pretended to be.

Leaving Matthew to see to the horses, Jack strode into the cottage. George followed. Halting by the table, Jack unbuckled his sword belt and scabbard. Turning, he went to the wardrobe, opened it, and thrust the scabbard to the very back, then shut the door firmly. "That's the end of that little conceit." Flinging himself into a chair, Jack rested both elbows on the table and ran his hands over his face. "God! I might have killed the whelp."

"Or he might have killed you." George slumped into another chair. "He seemed to know what he was about."

Jack waved dismissively. "He's been taught well enough, but he'd no strength to him."

George chuckled. "We can't all be six-foot-two and strong enough to run up cathedral belltowers with a wench under each arm."

Jack snorted at the reminder of one of his more outrageous exploits.

When he remained silent, George ventured, "What made

you think of a merger? I thought we were just there to spy out the opposition.''

"The opposition proved devilishly well organized. If it hadn't been for Champion, we wouldn't have found them. There didn't seem much point in walking away again. And I've no taste for killing wet-behind-the-ear whelps.''

A short silence descended. Jack's gaze remained fixed in space. "Who do you think he is?''

"Young Kit?'' George blinked sleepily. "One of our neighbors' sons, I should think. Where else the horse?''

Jack nodded. "Correct me if I'm wrong, but I don't know of any such whelp hereabouts. Morgan's sons are too old—they'd be nearer thirty, surely? And Henry Fair-clough's boys are too young. Kit must be about sixteen.''

George frowned. "I can't recall anyone that fits, either. But perhaps he's a nephew come to spend time on the family acres? Who knows?'' He shrugged. "Could be any-one.''

"*Can't* be just anyone. Young Kit knows this district like the back of his hand. Think of the chase he led us, the way he rode across those fields. He *knew* every fence, every tree. And according to Noah, Kit was the one who knew about the quarries.''

George yawned. "Well, we knew about the quarries, too. We just hadn't thought of using them.''

Jack looked disgusted. "Lack of sleep has addled your wits. That's precisely what I mean. We know the area be-cause we grew up here. Kit's grown up here, too. Which means he should be easy enough to track down.''

"And then what?'' mumbled George, around another yawn.

"And then,'' Jack replied, getting to his feet and hauling George to his, "we'll have to decide what to do with the whelp. Because if he is someone's son, the chances are he'll recognize me, if not both of us.'' Propelling George to the door, he added: "And we can't trust Young Kit with that information.''

What with seeing the somnolent George on his way be-fore riding home with Matthew and stabling Champion, it was close to dawn before Jack finally lay between cool sheets and stared at the shadow patterns on his ceiling.

Neither George nor Matthew had found anything especially odd about Young Kit. Questioned on the way home, Matthew's estimation had mirrored George's. Kit was the son of a neighboring landowner, sire unknown. There was, of course, the possibility that Kit was an illegitimate sprig of some local lordly tree. The horse might have been a gift, in light of the boy's equestrian abilities, or alternatively, might be "borrowed" from his sire's stables. Whatever, the horse provided the best clue to Young Kit's identity.

Jack sighed deeply and closed his eyes. Kit's identity was only one of his problems and certainly the easier to solve. His odd reaction to the boy was a worry. Why had it happened? It had been decades since any sight had affected him so dramatically. But, for whatever incomprehensible reason, the slim, black-garbed figure of Young Kit had acted as a powerful aphrodisiac, sending his body into a state of immediate readiness. He'd been as horny as Champion on the trail of the black mare!

With a snort, Jack turned and burrowed his stubbled cheek into the pillow. He tried to blot the entire business from his mind. When that didn't work, he searched for some explanation, however insubstantial, for the episode. If he could find a reason, hopefully that would be the end of it. There was a strong possibility that it might prove necessary to include Young Kit in the Gang. The idea of having the young whelp continuously about, wreaking havoc with his manly reactions, was simply too hideous to contemplate.

Could it have been some similarity to one of his long-discarded mistresses, popping up to waylay him when he least expected it? Perhaps it was simply the effect of unusual abstinence?

Maybe it was just wishful thinking on his part? Jack grinned. He couldn't deny that a nice, wild woman, the sort who might lead a smuggling gang, would make a welcome addition to his current lifestyle. Elsewise, the only sport to be had in the vicinity consisted of virtuous maids, whom he avoided on principle, and dowagers old enough to be his mother. Ever fertile, his brain developed his fantasy. The tension in his shoulders slowly eased.

Insidiously, sleep crawled from his feet to his calves to his knees to his hips, ever upward to claim him. Just before he succumbed, Jack hit on his cure. He'd unmask Young Kit—that was it. The sensation would disappear once Kit was revealed as the male he had to be. George was sure of it, Matthew was sure of it. Most importantly, the smugglers who followed Kit were sure of it, and surely they must know?

The problem was, *he* was far from sure of it.

Kit spent the following day in a distracted daze. Even the simplest task was beyond her; her attention constantly drifted, lured in fascinated horror to contemplation of her dreadful dilemma.

After incorrectly mixing a potion for the parlor maid's sore throat, twice, she gave up in disgust and headed for the gazebo at the end of the rose garden. The morning had cleared to a fine afternoon; she hoped the brisk breeze would blow away her mental cobwebs.

The little gazebo, with its view of the rose beds, was a favorite retreat. With a weary sigh, Kit sank onto the wooden bench. She was caught, trapped, squarely between the devil and the deep blue sea. On the one hand, prudence urged that she accept Captain Jack's proposal for her crew and decline it for herself, slipping cautiously into the mists, letting Young Kit disappear. Unfortunately, neither her men nor Captain Jack would be satisfied with that. She knew them—knew them far better than they knew her. She didn't, in truth, know Captain Jack, and if she was intent on following prudence's dictates, she never would.

Coward! sneered her other self.

"Did you see him?" Kit asked, annoyed when her heartbeat accelerated at the memory.

Oh, yes! came the thoroughly smitten answer.

Kit snorted. "Even in moonlight he looked like he could give the London rakes lessons."

Indubitably. And just think what lessons he could give you.

Kit blushed. "I'm *not* interested."

Like hell you're not. You, my girl, turned a delicate shade of green when Amy was describing her experiences. Now fate hands you a gilded first-ever opportunity to do a little experiencing of your own and what do you do? Run away before that gorgeous specimen gets a chance to raise your temperature. What's happened to your wild Cranmer blood?

Kit grimaced. "I've still got you to remind me I haven't lost it."

Putting a lid on her wilder self, Kit brooded on her folly in getting involved with smugglers. That didn't last long. She'd enjoyed the past weeks too much to dissemble, even to herself. The excitement, the thrills, the highs and lows of tension and relief had become a staple in her diet, an addictive ingredient she was loath to forego. How else would she fill in her time?

The alternative to disappearing grew increasingly attractive.

Resolutely, she shook her head. "I can't risk it. He's suspicious already. Men can't be trusted—and men like Captain Jack are even less trustworthy than the rest."

Who said anything about trust? If he realizes Young Kit's not all he seems, well and good. You might even learn what you're dying to know—what price a little experience against the years of lonely spinsterhood ahead? You know you'll never marry, so what good is your closely guarded virtue? And who's to know? You can always disappear, once your men have settled in with his.

"And what happens if I get caught, if things don't go as planned?" Kit waited, but her wild self remained prudently silent. She sighed, then frowned as she saw a maid looking this way and that amongst the rosebushes. With a rustle of starched petticoats, Kit rose. "Dorcas? What's amiss?"

"Oh! There you be, miss. Jenkins said as you might be out 'ere."

"Yes. Here I am." Kit stepped down from her retreat. "Am I wanted?"

"Oh, yes, if you please, miss. The Lord Lieutenant and his lady be here. In the drawing room."

Hiding a grimace, Kit headed indoors. She found Lady Marchmont ensconced on the *chaise*, listening with barely concealed boredom to the conversation between her husband and Spencer. At the sight of Kit, she perked up. "Kathryn, my dear!" Her ladyship surged up in a froth of soft lace.

After exchanging the usual pleasantries, Kit sat on the *chaise*. Lady Marchmont barely paused to draw breath. "We've just come from Castle Hendon, my dear. *Such* an impressive place but sadly in need of a woman's touch these days. I do believe Jake hadn't had the curtains shaken since Mary died." Lady Marchmont patted Kit's hand. "But I don't suppose you remember the last Lady Hendon. She died when the new Lord Hendon was just a boy. Jake raised him." Her ladyship paused; Kit waited politely.

"I thought I should pass the word on directly." Lord Marchmont's voice, lowered conspiratorially, came to Kit's ears. She glanced to where Spencer and the Lord Lieutenant sat on chairs drawn together, the two grey heads close.

"Mind you, such being the case, it's a wonder he's not positively wild. Heaven knows, Jake was the devil himself in disguise, or so many of us thought." Lady Marchmont made this startling revelation, a dreamy smile on her lips.

Kit nodded, her eyes on her ladyship's face, her attention elsewhere.

"Hendon's made it clear he's not particularly interested in the commercial traffic, as he put it. He's here after bigger game. Seems there's word about that this area's a target for those running cargo of a different sort." Lord Marchmont paused meaningfully.

Spencer snorted. Kit caught the sharpness in his comment, "What's that supposed to mean?"

"But I dare say one shouldn't judge a book by its binding." Lady Marchmont raised her brows. "Perhaps, in this case, he really is a sheep in wolf's clothing."

Kit smiled, but she hadn't heard a word. She was far too concerned with learning what sort of cargo interested the new High Commissioner.

"Human cargo," Lord Marchmont pronounced with heavy relish.

"Mind you, I'm not sure but what it's better the other way around." Lady Marchmont brightened.

"Seems they've blocked the routes out of Sussex and Kent, but they didn't catch all the spies." Lord Marchmont leaned closer to Spencer. "They think those left will try this coast next."

"But just fancy, my dear. He keeps city hours down here. Doesn't rise until noon." An unladylike humph escaped Lady Marchmont. "He'll have to change, of course. Needs someone to help him adjust. Must be hard to pick up country ways after so many years."

A frown nagged at Kit's brows. As Lady Marchmont's bemused stare penetrated her daze, she wiped her expression clean and nodded seriously. "I dare say you're right, ma'am."

Her ladyship blinked. Kit realized she'd slipped somewhere and tried to focus on her ladyship's words, rather than her lord's.

Lady Marchmont's face cleared. "Oh—are you imagining he's a fop? Not a bit of it!" She waved one plump hand, and Kit's mind slid away.

"Hendon suggested I quietly let the message get about. Just to the right people, y'know." Lord Marchmont set down his teacup.

"His dress is very precise—the military influence, I dare say. But you'd know more about that than I, being so newly returned from the capital." Lady Marchmont chewed one fat finger. "Elegant," she pronounced. "You'd have to call him elegant."

Kit's eyes glazed. Her head was spinning.

"Did he now?" Spencer eyed Lord Marchmont shrewdly.

Lady Marchmont leaned forward and whispered: "Lucy Cartwright's got her eye on him for her eldest, Jane. But nothing'll come of that."

"Seemed to think he might need a bit of support if it came to a dustup," Lord Marchmont said. "The Revenue are stretched thin these days."

"He doesn't strike me as being the sort of man who'd appreciate having a young girl to wife. He's a serious man, thirty-five if he's a day. A more mature woman would be much more useful to him. Being the Lady of Castle Hendon is a full-time occupation, not the place for a giddy girl.''

Spencer's barking laugh echoed through the room. ''That's certainly true. Have you heard of the raids out Sheringham way?''

Her grandfather and his guest settled to review the latest exercises of the Revenue Office. Kit took the opportunity to catch up with her ladyship.

''Of course, there's the limp, though it's not seriously incapacitating. And he's at least got the Hendon looks to compensate.''

Kit attempted to infuse some degree of mild interest into her features.

Lady Marchmont looked positively thrilled. ''Well, Kathryn dear, we really must see what we can organize, don't you think?''

The predatory gleam in her ladyship's eyes set alarm bells ringing; Kit's interest fled. *Good God—she's trying to marry me off to Lord Hendon!*

To Kit's immense relief, Jenkins chose that precise instant to enter with the tea tray. If not for the timely interruption, she'd never have stilled the heated denial that had risen, involuntarily, to her lips.

Conversation became general over the teacups. With the ease born of considerable practice in company far more demanding than the present, Kit contributed her share.

Suddenly, Spencer slapped his thigh. ''Forgot!'' He looked at Kit. ''There's a letter for you, m'dear. On the table there.'' His nod indicated a small table by the window.

''For me?'' Kit rose and went to fetch it.

Spencer nodded. ''It's from Julian. I got one, too.''

''Julian?'' Kit returned to the *chaise*, examining the packet addressed in her youngest cousin's unmistakable scrawl.

''Go on, read it. Lord and Lady Marchmont'll excuse you, I'm sure.''

Lord Marchmont nodded benignly, his wife much more avidly. Kit broke the Cranmer seal and quickly scanned the lines, crossed and recrossed, with two blots for good measure. "He's done it," she breathed, as Julian's meaning became clear. "He's enlisted!"

Her face alight, Kit looked at Spencer and saw her happiness for Julian mirrored in his eyes. Spencer nodded. "Aye. About time he went his own road. It'll be the making of him, I don't doubt."

Blinking, Kit nodded. Julian had wanted to join the army forever but, as the youngest of the Cranmer brood, he'd been protected and cosseted and steadfastly refused permission to break free. He'd reached his majority a fortnight ago and had signed up immediately. A passage toward the end of his letter sent a stab of sheer, painful pride through her.

You broke free, Kit. You made up your mind and went your own way. I decided to do the same. Wish me luck?

Her grandfather and Lord Marchmont were discussing the latest news from Europe; Lady Marchmont was eating a queen cake. With a happy sigh, Kit refolded the letter and laid it aside.

Jenkins returned, and the Marchmonts rose to take their leave, Lady Marchmont evolving plans for a ball to introduce the new Lord Hendon to his neighbors. "We haven't given a ball in years. We'll make it a large one—something special. A masquerade, perhaps? I'll want your advice, my dear, so think about it." With a wag of her chubby finger, Lady Marchmont sat back in her carriage.

On the steps, Kit smiled and waved. Beside her, Spencer clapped the Lord Lieutenant on the shoulder. "About that other matter. Tell Hendon he can count on support from Cranmer if he needs it. The Cranmers have always stood shoulder to shoulder with the Hendons through the years— we'll continue to do so. Particularly now we've one of our own at risk. Can't let any spies endanger young Julian." Spencer smiled. "Just as long as Hendon remembers he's Norfolk born and bred, that is. I've no mind to give up my brandy."

The twinkle in Spencer's eye was pronounced. An answering gleam lit Lord Marchmont's gaze. "No, b'God.

Very true. But he keeps a fine cellar, just like Jake, so I doubt we'll need to explain that to him.''

With a nod to Kit, Lord Marchmont climbed in beside his wife. The door shut, the coachman clicked the reins; the heavy coach lurched off.

Kit watched it disappear, then dropped a kiss on Spencer's weathered cheek and hugged him hard before descending the steps. With a last wave to Spencer, she headed for the gardens for a last stroll before dinner.

The shrubbery welcomed her with cool green walls, leading to a secluded grove with a fountain in the middle. Kit sat on the stone surround of the pool, trailing her fingers in the water. Her pleasure at Julian's news gradually faded, giving way to consideration of Lady Marchmont's fixation.

It was inevitable that the local ladies would busy themselves over finding her a husband; they'd known her from birth and, naturally, not one approved of her present state. With the appearance of Lord Hendon, an apparently eligible bachelor, on the scene, they had the ingredients of exactly the sort of plot they collectively delighted in hatching.

Grimacing, Kit shook the water from her fingers. They could hatch and plot to their hearts' content—she was past the age of innocent gullibility. Doubtless, despite his eligibility, Lord Hendon would prove to be another earl of Roberts. No—he couldn't be that old, not if Jake had been his father. Fortyish, a dessicated old stick but not quite old enough to be her father.

With a sigh, Kit stood and shook out her skirts. Unfortunately for Lady Marchmont, she hadn't escaped London—and her aunts' coils—to fall victim to the schemes of the local *grandes dames*.

The sun dipped beneath the horizon. Kit turned back toward the house. As she passed through the hedged walks, she shivered. Were spies run through the Norfolk surf? On that subject, her opinions matched Spencer's. The trade was tolerable, as long as it was just trade. But spying was treason. Did the Hunstanton Gang run ''human cargo''?

Kit frowned; her temples throbbed. The day had gone and she was no nearer to solving her dilemma. Worse, she now had potential treason to avoid.

Or avert.

Chapter 8

A quiet dinner with Spencer did not advance Kit's thoughts on Captain Jack's offer. She retired early, intending to spend a few clear hours pondering the pros and cons. But once in her bedroom, the fidgets caught her. In desperation, she threw on her masculine clothes and slipped down the back stairs.

She'd become adept at bridling and saddling Delia in the dark. Soon, she was galloping over fields intermittently lit by a setting moon, half-hidden by low, scudding clouds. On horseback, with the breeze whistling about her ears, she relaxed. Now, she could think.

Try as she might, she couldn't see a way off the carousel. If Young Kit simply disappeared, then riding alone dressed as a youth, by day or by night, became dangerous in the extreme. Young Kit would have to die in truth. Of course, Miss Kathryn Cranmer could still ride sedately about the countryside. Miss Kathryn Cranmer snorted derisively. She'd be dammed if she'd give up her freedom so tamely. That left the option of joining Captain Jack.

Perhaps she could retire? Individual members often withdrew from the gangs. As long as the fraternity knew who their ex-brothers were, no one minded. "I'll need to develop an identity," Kit mused. "There must be some place on Cranmer I could call home—some family with whom the smugglers have no contact." An old mother hysterical over the wildness of her youngest son, the last of three left to her . . . Grimly, Kit nodded. She would need to concoct a convincing reason for Young Kit's early retirement.

Which brought her to the last, nagging worry, a hovering ghost in the shadows of her mind. Were the Hunstanton Gang aiding and abetting spies?

If they are running spies, shouldn't you find out? If you join them for a few runs and see nothing, well and good. But if they do make arrangements to run "human cargo," you can inform Lord Hendon.

Kit humphed. Lord Hendon—wonderful! She supposed she'd have to meet the man sometime.

She turned Delia northeast, toward Scolt Head, a dense blur on the dark water. The sound of the surf grew louder as she approached the beaches east of Brancaster. She'd ridden north from Cranmer, passing in the lee of Castle Hendon, an imposing edifice built of local Carr stone on a hill sufficiently high to give it sweeping views in all directions.

Delia snuffed at the sea breeze. Kit allowed her to lengthen her stride.

Surely it was her duty to join the Hunstanton Gang and discover their involvement, if any, with spying? Particularly now that Julian had joined the army.

The ground ahead disappeared into blackness. At the edge of the cliff, Kit reined in and looked down. It was dim and dark on the sands. The surf boomed; the crash of waves and the slurping suck of the tide filled her ears.

A muffled shout reached her, followed by a second.

The moon escaped the clouds and Kit understood. The Hunstanton Gang was running a cargo on Brancaster beach.

Blanketing arms recaptured the moon, but she'd seen enough to be sure. The figure of Captain Jack had been clearly visible at the head of one boat. The two men who'd been with him the other night were there, too.

Kit drew Delia back from the cliff edge into the protection of a stand of stunted trees. The gang was nearly through unloading the boat; soon, they'd be heading . . . where? In an instant, Kit's mind was made up. She turned Delia, scouting for a better vantage point, one from which she could see without being seen. She eventually took refuge on a small tussocky hill in the scraggy remnants of an old coppice. Once safely concealed, she settled to wait, straining eyes trained on the cliff's edge.

Minutes later, they came up, single file, and passed directly beneath her little hill. She waited for Captain Jack and his two cohorts, bringing up the rear, to clear her, then counted to twenty slowly before taking to the narrow path in their wake. She followed them in a wide arc around the little town of Brancaster. In the fields west of the town, the cavalcade went to ground in an old barn. Kit watched from a distance, too wary to get closer. Soon, the men started leaving, some on foot, some riding, guiding ponies on leading reins.

At the last, three horsemen drew away from the barn. The moon smiled; Kit caught the gleam of Captain Jack's hair. The trio divided, one heading east. Captain Jack and the third man went west. Kit followed them.

She kept Delia on the verge, the drum of hooves of her quarries' horses making it easy to follow them. Luckily, they weren't riding fast, else she'd have had difficulty keeping up without taking to the telltale road herself.

They traveled the road for no more than a mile before turning south along a narrow track. Kit paused at the turn. The sound of heavy hooves at a walk reassured her. She pressed on, careful to hold Delia back.

Jack and Matthew set their mounts up the steep curve that took the track over the lip of the meadowland. At the highest point, just before the track curved into the trees edging the first Hendon field, Jack glanced down onto the stretch of track below. It was a habit instituted long since to ensure none of the Hunstanton Gang followed them to their lair.

The track was a pool of even, uninteresting shadow. Jack was turning away when a slight movement, caught from the corner of one eye, brought every faculty alert. He froze, gaze used to the night trained on the track below. A shadow darker than the rest detached itself from the cover of the trees and crept along the verge.

Matthew, warned by the sudden silence, had reined in

too, and stared downward. He leaned closer to whisper in Jack's ear. "Young Kit?"

Jack nodded. A slow, positively devilish smile twisted his long lips. "Go on to the cottage," he whispered. "I'm going to invite our young friend for a drink."

Matthew nodded, urging his horse to a walk, heading south along the narrow track.

Jack nudged Champion off the path and into the deeper shadows by a coppice. Young Kit's excess of curiosity was perfectly timed; he hadn't been looking forward to another night like the last, tossing and turning while grappling with his ridiculous obsession with the stripling. What better way to cure his senses of their idiotic misconception than to invite the lad in for a brandy? Once revealed in full light for the youth he was, Young Kit would doubtless get out from under his skin.

Approaching the upward sweep of the trail, Kit heard the steady clop of hooves above cease. She reined in, listening intently, then cautiously edged forward. When she saw where the track led, she stopped and held her breath. Then the hoofbeats restarted, heading onward. With a sigh of relief, she counted to twenty again before sending Delia up the track.

She crested the rise to find the track, innocent and empty, leading on across the meadowland. Ahead, a coppice bordered the trail, darker shadows pooling on the track like giant ink puddles. She paused, listening, but the hoofbeats continued on, the riders invisible through the trees ahead.

All was well. Kit put her heels to Delia's sleek sides. The mare sidled. Kit frowned and urged the mare forward. Delia balked.

The sensation of being watched enveloped Kit. Her stomach tightened; her eyes flared wide. She glanced to the left. Fields opened out, one adjoining the next, a clear escape. Without further thought, she set Delia at the hedge. As eager as she to get away, the mare cleared the hedge and went straight to a gallop.

In the trees bordering the track, Jack swore volubly. Be damned if he'd let the lad lose him again! He set his heels to Champion's sides; the grey surged in pursuit.

Champion answered the call with alacrity, only too ready to give chase. Jack held him back, content to keep the bobbing black bottom of Young Kit in clear view, waiting until the Arab started to tire before allowing the grey stallion's strength to show.

The thud of hooves behind her told Kit her observer had come into the open. She glanced behind and her worst fears were confirmed. Damn the man! She hadn't seen anything worthwhile, and he must know he couldn't catch her.

By the time the end of the fields hove in sight, Kit had revised her opinion of Captain Jack's equestrian judgment. The grey he had under him seemed tireless and Delia, already ridden far that night, was wilting. In desperation, Kit swung Delia's head for the shore. Riding through sand would hopefully slow the heavier grey more than the mare.

She hadn't counted on the descent. Delia checked at the cliff's edge and took the steep path in a nervous prance. The grey, ridden aggressively, came over the top in a leap and half slithered through the soft soil to land on the flat in a flurry of sand, mere seconds behind her.

Kit clapped her heels to Delia's sleek flanks; the mare shot forward, half-panicked by the advent of the stallion so close.

To Kit's dismay, the tide was in and just turning, leaving only a narrow strip of dry sand skirting the base of the cliffs. She couldn't risk getting too close to the rocks and boulders strewn at the cliff foot. There was nowhere else to ride but on the hard sand, dampened and compacted by the retreating waves. And on such solid ground, the grey gained steadily.

Crouched low over Delia's neck, the black mane whipping her cheeks, Kit prayed for a miracle. But the sound of the grey's heavy hooves drew inexorably nearer. She started considering her excuses. What reason could she give for having followed him that would account for her bolting?

There was no viable answer to that one. Kit wished she'd had the nerve to stand her ground rather than fly when confronted with her nemesis. She glanced forward, contemplating hauling on the reins and capitulating, when, wonder of wonders, a spit of land loomed ahead. A tongue of the cliff, it cleaved the sands, running out into the surf, its sides decaying into the sea. If she could gain the rough-grassed dunes, she'd have a chance. Even tired as she was, climbing, Delia would be much faster than the heavy grey. As if to light her way, the moon sailed free of its cloudy veils and beamed down.

A length behind, Jack saw the spit. It was time to wind up the chase. The lad rode better than any trooper he'd ever seen. Once in the dunes, he'd be impossible to catch. Jack dropped his reins. Champion, sensing victory, lengthened his stride, obedient to the direction that sent him inland of the black mare, cutting off any sudden change of tack.

Kit was breathless. The wind dragged at her lungs. The dunes and safety were heartbeats away when, warned by some sixth sense, she glanced to her left. And saw a huge grey head almost level with her knee.

She only had time to gasp before two hundred odd pounds of highly trained male muscle knocked her from the saddle.

The instant he connected with Young Kit, Jack realized his error. He tried to twist in midair to cushion her fall but was only partially successful. Both he and his captive landed flat on their backs on the damp sand.

The breath was knocked out of him but he recovered immediately, sitting up and swinging around to lean over his prize, one leg automatically trapping hers to still her struggles. Only she didn't struggle.

Jack frowned and waited for the eyes, just visible beneath the brim of her old tricorne, to open. They remained shut. The body stretched beside and half under his was preternaturally still.

Cursing, Jack pulled at the tricorne. It took two tugs to free it. The wealth of glossy curls framing the smooth, wide brow sent his imagination, already sensitized by her nearness, into overload.

Slowly, almost as if she might dissolve beneath his touch, Jack lifted a finger to the smooth skin covering one high cheekbone, tracing the upward curve. The satin texture sent a thrill from the tip of his finger to regions far distant. When she gave no sign of returning consciousness, he slid his fingers into the mass of silky hair, ignoring the burgeoning sensations skittering through him, to feel the back of her skull. A lump the size of a duck egg was growing through the curls. In the sand beneath her head, he located the rock responsible, thankfully buried deep enough to make it unlikely it had caused any irreparable hurt.

Retrieving his hands, Jack eased back to stare at his captive.

Young Kit was out cold.

Grimacing, he eyed the heavy muffler wound over her nose and chin, concealing most of her face. The conversion of Young Kit into female form was certain to wreak havoc with his plans, but he may as well leave consideration of such matters until later. Right now, he doubted he could raise a cogent thought, much less make a wise decision. Which was simply proof of how much of a problem she was destined to become.

He should get that muffler off—she'd recover faster if she could breathe unrestricted. Yet he felt reluctant to bare any more of her face—or any other part of her for that matter. What he'd already seen—the perfect expanse of forehead, gracefully arched brows over large eyes set on a slight slant and delicately framed by a feathering of brown, the rioting curls, glossy even in moonlight—all attested to the certainty that the rest of Young Kit would prove equally fatal to his equanimity.

Jack swore under his breath. Why the hell did he have to get a case of the hots just now? And for a smugglers' moll, no less!

Metaphorically, and in every other way he knew, he girded his loins and reached for the muffler. She'd wound it tight, and it was some moments and a good few curses later before he drew the woollen folds from her face.

Just why she wore a muffler was instantly apparent. Grimly, Jack considered the sculpted features, rendered in flawless cream skin, the straight little nose, the pert, pointed chin and the full sensuous lips, pale now but just begging to be kissed to blush red. Young Kit's face was an essential statement of all that was feminine.

Intrigued, Jack let his gaze slide over the figure lying inert beside him. The padding in one shoulder of her coat was pressed to his arm, explaining that point. He stared at her chest, slowly rising and falling. The fullness of her shirt made it difficult to judge, but experience suggested her anatomy was unlikely to be quite so uneventful. Jack decided he wasn't up to investigating how she accomplished that feat of suppressing nature and turned instead to an expert inspection of her legs, still entwined with his. They were, in his experienced opinion, remarkably remarkable, unusually long and slender but firm with well-toned muscle.

Jack's lips curved appreciatively. She obviously rode a lot. How did she perform when the roles were reversed? He allowed his imagination, rampant by now, a whole three minutes to run riot, before reluctantly calling his mind to order. With a sigh, he gazed once more at Young Kit's pale face. Female skulls were weaker than male. She might take a few hours to come to.

Jack looked along the sands to where Champion stood in the lee of the dunes, reins dangling. Beside him stood the black mare, uncertain and skittish. Disengaging his legs from Kit's, Jack stood, brushing sand from his clothes. He whistled, and Champion ambled over. The mare hesitated, then followed.

Catching Champion's reins, Jack murmured soothing nothings to the great beast while watching the mare. The Arab approached slowly, then veered to come up on Kit's other side. The black head went down. The mare softly huffed into the bright curls. Kit didn't stir.

"What a precious beauty you are," Jack breathed, edging closer. The black head came up; one large black eye looked straight at him. Slowly, Jack reached for the mare's bridle. To his relief, she accepted his touch. He lengthened the reins, then looped the ends through a ring on his own saddle. Then he stood back to see how Champion would take to the arrangement. The big stallion did not normally tolerate other horses too close, yet a single minute served to convince Jack he didn't need to worry about the Arab.

Champion clearly possessed equine manners when he chose to employ them, and he was all out to make a good impression on the mare.

Grinning, Jack turned to consider the female he had in charge. He bent and lifted Kit from the sands, then sat her in his saddle and held her draped over the pommel while he mounted behind her. Swinging her once more into his arms, he settled in the saddle, balancing Kit across his thighs, her head cradled against his chest.

Jack turned Champion toward the dunes, touched his heels to the grey's flanks, and set course for the cottage.

Chapter 9

By the time he reached the cottage, Jack's jaw was clenched with the effort of ignoring the thoroughly female body in his arms. With every stride, Champion's gait pressed the warm swell of Kit's bound breasts against Jack's chest, alternating with the even more unnerving rub of her firm bottom against his thigh. The ride was torture— a fact he was sure Kit, whoever she was, would delight in, if he was ever fool enough to tell her. He suspected she'd wake with a headache. On the sands, he'd felt a touch guilty about that. Now, he considered it only her due—he was sure he'd have a splitting head by dawn. And no chance of sleep, either.

Champion's hooves thudded on the packed earth before the cottage. The door opened, and Matthew came out. "What happened?"

Jack drew rein some paces from the door. "The lad didn't take kindly to my invitation. In fact, he didn't even wait to hear it. I had to exert my powers of persuasion."

"So I see." Matthew advanced, clearly intent on taking Jack's burden from him.

Jack brought his leg over the pommel and slid to the ground, Kit's inanimate form clasped to his chest. He brushed past Matthew and headed for the door. "Stable Champion and the mare. I doubt she'll give you much trouble." Jack paused in the doorway and looked back. "Then you may as well go home. He's apt to be out for a while." He smiled. "I think Young Kit would probably feel more

67

comfortable if he thought no one but me had seen him *in extremis*."

Wise in the ways of lads and young soldiers, Matthew nodded. "Aye. You'll be right enough there, no doubt. I'll be off then." So saying, he caught Champion's reins and headed for the small stable beside the cottage.

Jack entered the cottage and kicked the door shut, leaning back on the rough panels to juggle the latch with his elbow. Then he straightened and looked down at his burden. Thank God he'd put Kit's hat back on. The wide brim had shaded her face enough for him to get her past Matthew. Quite why he was keeping her little secret from his unquestionably loyal henchman he wasn't entirely certain. Perhaps because he hadn't yet had time to consider just what Kit's secret meant and how he was going to deal with it, and, from long experience, he knew Matthew would unhesitatingly avail himself of the license accorded longtime servitors to disapprove, vociferously, should his master elect to follow some less than straightforward course.

But before he could think of anything, he had to get rid of the distracting body in his arms.

Jack strode to the bed and dropped Kit onto the coverlet as if she was a lump of hot iron. In truth, she'd set him alight, and he couldn't see any prospect of dousing the flames. Making love to unconscious women had never appealed to him. He stared down at the slender and still silent form. The muffler had shaken loose and lay about her throat. Her hat had fallen off, exposing her curls and telltale face to the lamplight.

Abruptly, Jack took a step back.

Now that she was out of his arms, he could think clearly. And it didn't take much thought to conclude that making love to Kit at any time was likely to prove dangerous, if not specifically to himself, then certainly to his mission. He'd already dropped the appellation "Young"—having carried her for half an hour, he knew she wasn't that young. Certainly not too young.

With a growl of frustration, Jack swung around and crossed to the sideboard. He poured himself a generous brandy, wryly wondering if Kit actually drank the stuff.

What would she have done if he'd invited her back to share a bottle?

Jack grinned; the grin faded when he glanced toward the bed. What the hell was he to do with her?

He prowled the room, intermittently shooting glances at the figure on the bed. The brandy didn't help. He drained the glass and set it aside. Kit hadn't stirred. With a long sigh, Jack approached the bed and stood beside it, staring down at her.

She was too pale. Tentatively, he touched her cheek. It was reassuringly warm. Leaning over her, he pulled off her leather gauntlets and chafed the small hands, fine-boned and delicate. It didn't help. Jack grimaced. Her breathing was shallow, her chest constricted by the tight bands she wore to conceal her breasts. He'd felt them when he'd carried her.

His arms felt leaden; his feet wouldn't move. His body definitely didn't like what his brain was telling it. But there was no help for it. And the sooner he got it over with, the better.

Jack forced his limbs to function. He turned Kit over, making sure she didn't suffocate in the soft folds of the coverlet. He bundled her out of her coat, then pulled her shirttails free of her breeches, trying to ignore the most unmasculine curve of her buttocks. Pushing the back of the shirt up to her shoulders, he located the flat knot securing the linen bands, craftily tucked under one arm. The knot was well and truly tight. Jack swore as he tugged and fumbled, fingers brushing skin that felt like cool silk and burned like a brand. By the time the knot finally gave, he'd exhausted his repertoire of curses, something he'd hitherto believed impossible.

He sat on the edge of the bed, garnering strength for the next move, willing his mind not to see the beauty revealed to his senses, the slim back, delicate shoulder blades sheathed in ivory silk. With slow deliberation, he loosened the bindings and shifted them until they gave. Quickly, he pulled the shirt back down, wisely refraining from tucking it in and, rising, turned Kit onto her back once more.

Almost immediately, her breathing deepened. Within a

minute, her color improved, but still she didn't stir. Resigned to more waiting, Jack drifted to the table and pulled out a chair. Leaning back, he gazed broodingly at his unconscious visitor. He reached for the brandy bottle.

Consciousness trickled into Kit's mind in dribs and drabs, a flash of memory, a tingle in her fingertips. Then her eyelids fluttered, and she was awake. And confused. She kept her eyes shut and tried to think. The memory of the wild chase on the beach, and Captain Jack riding her down—it must have been his body that had hit her—crystallized in her brain. That was all she could recall. Warily, she let her senses search out her surroundings, stiffening with apprehension at the incoming information. She was lying on a bed.

From under her lashes, Kit surveyed what she could see of the room—rough walls and an old oak wardrobe. Beyond confirming the fact she was in someone's bedroom, in someone's bed, they told her little.

But you can guess who that someone is, can't you? And now you're in his bed.

Don't be silly, Kit lectured her wilder self. *I'm still dressed, aren't I?* On the thought, the looseness of her bands registered. Kit sat up with a gasp.

The bands immediately slipped lower, freeing her breasts. Her head swam. With a weak, "Oh," Kit fell back on her elbows, closing her eyes against the pain in the back of her head. When she opened them, she saw Captain Jack watching her from across the room. He was lounging in a chair on the other side of a table, a look of aggravation on his handsome face.

For the life of him, Jack couldn't tear his gaze from the proof of Kit's womanhood, thrust provocatively against the fine cotton of her shirt. The front was pulled taut by her reclining position, revealing the rich swells beneath tipped by the tight buds of her nipples. When she just lay there and stared at him, Jack felt his temper stir. Hell and the devil! Was she doing it on purpose?

Kit raised a hand to her head, stifling a groan. "What happened?"

The shirt eased, and Jack could breathe again. "You hit your head on a rock buried in the sand."

Kit sat up and gingerly felt her skull. She'd forgotten how velvety deep his voice was. Her fingers found a sizable lump on the back of her head. She winced and shot a frowning glance at her nemesis. "You could have killed me with that foolish stunt."

The accusation brought Jack upright, the legs of his chair crashing onto the floor. "Foolish stunt?" he echoed in disbelief. "What the hell do you call a woman masquerading as a boy and leading a gang of smugglers? Sensible?" Real anger at the risks she'd courted rose up. "What the hell do you think would have happened after your first slip? Do you swim well with rocks tied to your feet?"

Kit winced. "Don't bellow." She dropped her head into her hands. She didn't feel all that well. Coping with Captain Jack at any time would have proved problematical, but right now, feeling as woozy as she did, this was shaping up to be a disastrous encounter. And he was already annoyed, though what he had to be annoyed about she couldn't imagine. She was the one with the lump on her head. "Where are we?"

"Where we won't be interrupted. I want some answers to one or two questions—understandable in the circumstances, don't you think? We can start with the obvious—what's your name?"

"Kit." Kit grinned into her hands. Let him make what he liked of that.

"Catherine, Christine, or what?"

Kit frowned. "You don't need to know."

"True. Where do you live?"

Kit reserved her answer to that one. Her head ached. A quick reconnoiter yielded the information that they were in a small cottage, alone. The fact that the door led directly outside was reassuring.

Frowning, Jack stared at the glossy curls crowning Kit's bent head. In the lamplight, they glowed a rich coppery red. In sunlight, he suspected they'd be redder and brighter still. The color tugged at his memory, an elusive recognition that refused to materialize. When she pulled her knees up, the better to support her hands which in turn were supporting her head, Jack grimaced. He supposed he should give her some brandy, but he didn't really want to get closer. The table was a protective barricade and he was loath to leave its shelter. At least he was wearing his "poor country squire" togs; the loosely fitting breeches gave him some protection. In his military togs, or, heaven forbid, his town rig, she'd know immediately just how much she was affecting him. It was bad enough that he knew.

Her head was still down. With an exasperated sigh, Jack reached for the bottle. Rising, he fetched a clean glass and half filled it with the best French brandy to be found in England. Glass in hand, he approached the bed.

She'd glanced up at the sound of his chair on the boards. Now, she raised her head, to look first at the glass, then into his face.

Memory returned with a thump. Jack stopped and blinked. Then he looked again and suspicion was confirmed. "Kit," he repeated. "Kit Cranmer?" He allowed one brow to rise in mocking question. Her eyes staring up at him, liquid amethyst, were all the answer he needed.

Kit swallowed, barely aware of his words. Heavens—it was worse than she'd thought! He was perfectly gorgeous—mind-numbingly, toe-curlingly gorgeous—with his wild mane of hair, wind-tousled brown streaked with gold. His brow was wide, his nose patrician and autocratic, his chin decidedly square. But it was his eyes that held her; set deep under slanted brows, they gleamed silver-grey in the lamplight. And his lips—long and rather thin, firm and mobile. How would they feel . . .

Kit clamped off the thought. Parched, she reached for the proffered glass. Her fingers brushed his. Ignoring the peculiar thrill that twisted through her, and suppressing the panic that swam in its wake, Kit sipped the brandy, very aware of the man beside her. He'd stopped by the side of the bed, towering over her. Entranced by his face, she'd spared no more than a glance for the rest of him. How did he measure up? She leaned back on her elbows the better to bring him into view.

Her shirt drew taut.

Beside the bed, Jack stiffened. Kit shifted to stare up at him. She saw his jaw clench, saw the planes of his face harden. Then she noticed his gaze was not on her face. She followed its direction, and saw what was holding him transfixed. Smoothly, she sat up, taking another sip of brandy, telling herself it was just the same as when London rakes had sized her up. There was no need to blush or act like a missish schoolgirl. Another sip of brandy steadied her. She hadn't answered his question. Perhaps it would be wise to do so. Trying to hide her paternity was hopeless; the Cranmer coloring was known the length and breadth of Norfolk.

"Now you know who I am, who are you?" she said.

Jack shook his head to clear his befogged senses. Christ! It'd been too long. His mission was in grave danger. With some vague idea of safety, he walked to where a chair stood against the wall and, swinging it about, sat astride, resting his arms on its back, facing her. He ignored her question; at least she hadn't recognized him.

"I doubt that you're Spencer's." He watched her closely but could detect no reaction. Not the current Lord Cranmer's child, then. "He had three sons, but if memory serves, the elder two don't have the family coloring. Only the youngest had that. Christopher Cranmer, the wildest of the bunch." Jack's memory lurched again. His lips twisted wryly. "Also known as Kit Cranmer, as I recall." A lifting of the corners of Kit's lips suggested he'd hit the target. "So you're Christopher Cranmer's daughter."

Kit allowed her brows to rise. Then she shrugged and nodded. Who was he, to have such detailed recollections of her family? At the very least, he was a local, yet she'd never seen him before yesterday. From under her lashes, she glanced at the broad shoulders and wide biceps, bulging as he leaned forward on his forearms. There was no padding in the simple jacket—those bulges were all perfectly real. Powerful thighs stretched his plain breeches. Seated as he was, she couldn't see much beyond that, but anyone who rode as he did had to be strong. The lamplight didn't illuminate his face, but she supposed him in his thirties. There was no chance she would have forgotten such a specimen.

"Who was your mother?"

The question, uttered in an amiable but commanding tone, jerked Kit's mind back from whence it had wandered. For a full minute, she stared uncomprehendingly. Then the implication of Jack's question struck her. Her eyes kindled; she drew breath to wither him. Belatedly, her wilder self tumbled out of its daze and scrambled to clamp the lid on her temper.

Hang on a minute—stop, cease, desist, stow it, you fool! You need an identity, remember? He's just handed you one. So what if he thinks you're illegitimate? Better that than the truth—which he wouldn't believe anyway.

Kit's eyes glazed. She blushed and looked down.

The odd expressions that passed over Kit's face in rapid succession left Jack bewildered. But the blush he understood immediately. "Sorry," he said. "An unnecessarily prying question."

Kit looked up, amazed. He was apologizing?

"Where do you live?" Jack remembered her mare. The stubborn pride of the present Lord Cranmer was as well-known as his family's coloring. Jack hazarded a guess. "With your grandfather?"

Slowly, Kit nodded. Her mind was racing. If she was her father's illegimate daughter, nothing would be more likely. Her father had been Spencer's favorite. Her grandfather would naturally assume responsiblity for any bastards his son had left behind. But she had to tread warily—Captain Jack knew far too much about the local families to allow her to invent freely. Luckily, he obviously didn't know Spencer's legitimate granddaughter had returned from London.

"I live at the Hall." One of her cousin Geoffrey's maxims on lying replayed in her head. *Stick to the truth as far as possible.* "I grew up there, but when my grandmother died they sent me away." If Jack was a local, he'd wonder why he'd never seen her about.

"Away?" Jack look interested.

Kit took another sip of brandy, grateful for the warmth unfurling in her belly. It seemed to be easing her head. "I was sent to London to live with the curate from Holme when he moved to Chiswick.'' Kit grabbed at the memory of the young curate—the image fitted perfectly. ''I didn't really like the capital. When the curate was promoted, I came back.'' Kit prayed Jack didn't know the curate from Holme personally; she'd no idea if he'd been promoted or not.

Neither did Jack. Kit's tale made sense, even accounting for her cultured speech and sophisticated gestures. If she'd been brought up at Cranmer under her grandmother's eye, then spent time in London, even with a boring curate, she'd be every bit as confident and at ease with him as she was proving to be. No simple country miss, this one. Her story was believable. Her attitude suggested she knew as much. Jack's eyes narrowed. ''So you live at the Hall and Spencer openly acknowledges you?''

Now that, my fine gentleman, is a trick question. Kit waved airily. ''Oh, I've always lived quietly. I was trained to look after the house, so that's what I do.'' She smiled at her inquisitor, knowing she'd passed the test. Not even Spencer would raise a bastard granddaughter on a par with the trueborn.

Grimly, Jack acknowledged that smile. She was certainly quick, but he could do without her smiles. They infused her face with a radiance painters had wasted lifetimes trying to capture. Whoever her mother had been, she must have been uncommonly beautiful to give rise to a daughter to rival Aphrodite.

''So by day, Spencer's housekeeper; by night, Young Kit, leader of a smuggling gang. How long have you been in the trade?''

''Only a few weeks.'' Kit wished he'd stop scowling at her. He'd smiled at her once at the quarries. She'd a mind to witness the phenomenon in the stronger lamplight, but Jack didn't seem at all likely to oblige. She smiled at him. He scowled back.

''How the devil have you survived? You cover your face, there's padding in your coat—but what happens if one of the men touches you?''

''They don't—they haven't.'' Kit hoped her blush didn't

show. "They just think I'm a well-born stripling, not built on their scale."

Jack snorted, his gaze never leaving her face. Then his eyes narrowed. "Where did you learn to swagger—and all the rest of it? It's not that easy to pass as a male. You've not trod the boards, have you?"

Kit met his gaze—and chose her words with care. She could hardly lay claim to her cousins, much less their influence. "I've had opportunity aplenty to study men and how they move." She smiled condescendingly. "I'm more than passing familiar with the male of the species."

Jack's brows rose; after a moment, he asked: "How long did you intend playing the smuggler?"

Kit shrugged. "Who knows? And now that you've found me out, we'll never learn, will we?" Her smile turned brittle. Young Kit's short career was at an end—the excitement and thrills were no longer to be hers.

Jack's brows rose higher. "You plan to retire?"

Kit stared at him. "Aren't you . . ." She blinked. "Do you mean you won't give me away?"

Jack's scowl returned. "Not won't—can't." He'd never thought of himself as conservative—Jonathon was his conservative side and at the moment he was definitely Jack— but the thought of Kit trooping about in breeches before a horde of seamen, laying herself open to discovery and God only knew what consequences, awoke in him feelings of sheer protectiveness. Outwardly, he frowned. Inwardly, he seethed and swore. He'd known she'd be trouble; now, he knew what sort.

He stifled a groan. Kit was looking at him, uncertainty plainly writ in her fine features. He drew a deep breath. "Until your men are safely accepted as part of the Hunstanton Gang, Young Kit will have to continue a smuggler."

Kit heard but was barely listening. She knew she wasn't an antidote; if she'd wanted it, she could have had men at her feet the entire time she'd been in London. Yet Captain Jack, whoever he was, wasn't responding to her in the customary way. He was still scowling. Deliberately, she lay back on her elbows and surveyed him boldly. "Why?"

The sudden stiffness that suffused his large frame was unnerving to say the least. Deliciously unnerving. Kit moved her shoulders slightly, settling her elbows more firmly, and felt her shirt shift over her nipples. She looked up to see how Jack was taking the display, ready to smile condescendingly at his confusion. Instead, she froze, transfixed by an overwhelming sense of danger.

His eyes were silver, not grey, clear and sparkling, like polished steel. And they weren't looking at her face. As she watched, a muscle flickered along his jaw. Suddenly, Kit understood. He wasn't responding because he didn't wish to, not because she wasn't affecting him. Only his control stood between her and what he would do—would like to do. Abruptly, Kit rolled to the side, on one hip, ostensibly to take a sip of brandy.

Shaken, Jack drew a deep breath, grimly wondering if the silly minx knew how close she'd come to being rolled in the bed she was lolling so provocatively upon. Another second, and he'd have given in to the urge to stand up, set the chair aside, and fall on her like the sex-starved hellion he was.

Luckily, she'd drawn back. Later, he fully intended to pursue a more intimate relationship with her, but at the moment, business came first. What had she asked? He remembered. "I want to make one gang out of two. If I expose you, your men will be a laughingstock, which won't help me in my aims. If you suddenly disappear, your men will think I've done away with you—scared you off at the very least. They'll probably decide not to join us so there will still be two gangs operating along this coast."

Kit frowned and looked down into the amber fluid swirling in her glass. He was suggesting she remain a boy—her true sex known only to him and herself—for an indefinite time. She wasn't sure she could keep up the pretense for a day. It was all very well to prance about in breeches when everyone watching thought you were male; she suspected it would be quite a different matter when one watcher, this particular watcher, knew the truth. Besides, she didn't really want to play the boy with Jack. Determinedly, Kit shook her head. "If I explain it to them—"

"They'll think I've scared you off."

Kit glared and sat up. "Not if I tell them—"

"Regardless of what you tell them."

The finality in his deep tones was not encouraging. But his scheme was the epitome of madness. "You said yourself it was a foolish thing to do. What if they, and the rest of your gang, discover the truth?"

"They won't. Not while I'm there to make sure of it."

His conviction sounded unshakable. How illogical, Kit thought, to be arguing for an outcome she didn't really desire. Yet the more she considered his scheme, the more dangerous it seemed. Luckily, she had herself well in hand. He was offering just the sort of excitement that appealed to her wilder self. She narrowed her eyes and chose her words carefully. "How do I know *you* won't give me away?"

Jack's eyes glittered. She was getting very close to the bone. What did she think he was—an overreactive schoolboy? Coolly, deliberately, he let his gaze wander, lingering on her breasts—not visible anymore, but he knew they were there—before drifting downward for a leisurely perusal of her long legs.

Kit blushed. And pounced the instant before he did. "Like that!" It hadn't been what she'd meant, but it would prove her point.

Jack blinked, then flushed with annoyance. He scowled ferociously. "I won't! What would I have to gain from giving you away?" His eyes narrowed as he studied her. "I can assure you I'll behave exactly as if you were the lad they all think you are." He didn't consider it wise to tell her what it was more likely the men would think if they realized he was overly interested in Young Kit. "I can't, of course, answer for your reactions."

Kit's temper ignited. Of all the insufferable, conceited louts she'd ever faced, Jack took the cake. Presumably he knew he was gorgeous. Doubtless scores of women had told him so. Hell would freeze before she heard those words from her! Kit tilted her nose in the air. "What reactions?"

Jack hooted with laughter. Abruptly, he stood and flung the chair aside. All thought of his mission, of sense and safety, fled at her challenge. No reactions to him? He advanced on the bed.

Kit's eyes felt as if they'd pop from her head. Horrified, she tried to shuffle back in the bed but her elbows tangled in the covers and she sprawled full-length instead. Then he was towering over her, his shadow engulfing her. Hands on hips, he looked down at her from the foot of the bed. He held out one hand. "Come here."

He was mad. She had no intention of going anywhere near him. He was smiling now, devilishly. She decided she preferred his scowl—it was infinitely less threatening. She tried a scowl of her own.

Jack's smile gained intensity; his eyes grew brighter. He had every intention of putting the vixen in her place once and for all. She was giving him more trouble than a troop of drunken cavalry. First she played the tease, curling on the bed so much like a cat he was quite sure that if he'd stroked her she'd have purred. Now, because he'd forced her into a blush, she was playing the threatened virgin.

But he wasn't so far gone in lunacy as to get on the bed with her. When she continued to scowl, her amethyst eyes spitting purple chips, he made a grab for her hand.

Unfortunately, Kit chose the same moment to sit up, the better to deliver a verbal broadside. She saw his movement; he saw hers. Both tried to compensate. Jack's fingers curled about her hand as he tried to straighten to avoid a collision of heads. Kit half rose, then fell back, wrenching her hand in an effort to free it. The result was the reverse of both their intentions. Jack's leg hit the bed end and he stumbled, then was pulled off-balance by the unexpected violence of Kit's tug. He landed on the bed beside her.

Kit smothered a shriek and tried to roll off the bed. A large hand grabbed her hip and rolled her back. A curse she didn't comprehend fell on her ears. Memories of tussles with her cousins awoke in her brain. Instead of fighting the pull, she turned with it.

It was purely reflex action that saved Jack's manly parts from Kit's rising knee. Giving up any attempt at gentlemanly behavior, he grabbed both her hands and swung over her, straddling her hips, pinning her beneath him.

To his amazement, she continued to struggle, her hips writhing between his thighs.

"Be still, you witless wanton, or I won't answer for the consequences!"

That stopped her. Wide eyes stared up at him. The front of her shirt rose and fell rapidly. Jack couldn't see through it, but the memory of what lay beneath it acted powerfully on his brain. The temptation to let go of her hands and cup the sweet mounds grew stronger by the second. His palms tingled in anticipation.

Jack forced his gaze upward. He met her eyes and saw the panic there. Panic? Jack closed his eyes against the plea in the violet depths and drew a deep breath. What the hell was going on? Now, she even looked like a threatened virgin. As sanity slowly seeped back into his brain, the rigidity of the slim form between his thighs registered.

Could she be a virgin? Jack's worldly brain rejected that idea out of hand. A woman of her background, of her age, with her attributes—one who declared herself "more than passing familiar" with men—could not be a virgin. Besides, she'd made moves enough that smacked of experience. No. The truth was, she didn't, for whatever reason, want him. Because he wanted her? Some women were like that. Jack prided himself on his knowledge of the female sex. He'd spent fifteen and more years in an extensive study of the fascinating creatures. In between fighting a few wars. If she really had taken an aversion to him, he could use it to his advantage in the short term. And when the need for Young Kit had passed, he could look forward to spending countless interesting hours changing her mind.

Jack opened his eyes and studied Kit's face. She was scowling again. He smiled crookedly. He was aching with need, but she wasn't about to welcome him aboard. Not yet.

He changed his hold on her hands, so that his thumbs rested in her palms. Slowly, deliberately, he moved his thumbs in a circular motion, caressing her sensitive skin. He watched as her eyes grew larger, rounder.

Kit was speechless. Worse, she was close to mindless. Neither her own experiences nor Amy's had prepared her for the effect Jack was having on her. Despite the fact that he hadn't even kissed her, she couldn't think straight. His touch on her palms was driving little shivers down every nerve, focusing her mind on her hands, as if to distract her from the heat seeping insidiously through every vein, radiating from the junction of her thighs. There was a complementary heat above, where he straddled her. Dimly, she sensed a growing urge to lift her hips and press heat to heat. She resisted it, struggling to break free of his spell. "Let me go, Jack." Her words were soft, feminine, not the decisive demand she intended at all.

Jack grinned, inordinately pleased to hear his name on her lips. "I'll let you go if you promise to do as I ask."

Kit frowned. Was he threatening her? It was an effort to put her thoughts into words. Particularly when he looked as if he'd like to eat her. Slowly. "What do you mean?" She asked.

"Be Young Kit for two months. After that, we'll arrange your retirement." *And you can start your next assignment— as my mistress.* Jack smiled into her beautiful eyes. He was sure they'd turn deepest violet when she climaxed. He was looking forward to conducting that experiment.

Kit couldn't steady her breathing. She shook her head. "It'll never work."

"It'll work. We'll make it work."

The idea was tempting, very tempting. Kit struggled to get a grip on the situation. "What if I won't?"

Jack's brows rose but he was smiling—that devilish smile again. Then he sighed dramatically and stopped stroking her palms. Kit relaxed, relief surging through her. Only to be overridden by panic when he raised her hand to his lips and kissed one fingertip. Her lips formed an O of sheer shock.

Watching her, Jack nearly laughed. No reaction to him? If she was any more responsive she'd be climbing the walls. "If you won't join me in a business venture, we'll just have to consider what other type of . . . partnership we can enjoy."

Kit stared at him in undisguised horror.

Jack turned her hand over to press a kiss to her palm.

He felt her entire body tense. "The first thing we'll have to investigate is whether this aversion of yours is any more than skin deep." Involuntarily, his gaze dropped to her shirt and his mind shifted to a contemplation of the delights it concealed. Just a single thickness of material was all that protected her breasts from his hungry gaze. And his ardent attentions. Almost, he wished she'd hold firm to her resolve not to be Young Kit. At least long enough to make a little persuasion necessary.

Kit's mind was sluggish. Aversion? Her aversion? Here she was, in a flat panic lest he realize just how very attracted she was, and he thought she held him in aversion? She almost laughed hysterically. If she hadn't been so frightened by her response to him, she would have. Having him so close drained her willpower; every little attention he bestowed only made matters worse. Another few moves and he'd have her egging him on. The idea of what would happen if he kissed her brought her to a rapid decision. "All right."

Jack hauled his gaze back to her face and his mind back to her words. "All right?"

Kit heard the disappointment in his voice. He'd have carried out his threat with enthusiasm. "Yes, all right, damn you!" She pushed hard at his hands. "If the others agree, I'll be Young Kit, but only for a month. Until my men settle in with your gang."

Jack's sigh was heartfelt. Reluctantly, he released her. Before moving off her, he smiled winningly, directly into the large eyes lit by violet sparks. "Sure you won't change your mind?"

The look he got set him chuckling. He rolled to her side and lay back on the pillows, content for the moment. Her capitulation wasn't exactly complimentary, but he'd a month to work on that.

Beside him, Kit lay still, struck by the revelation that, although he was still close, now that he wasn't touching her, her mind was functioning again. Recalling her uncertainties about the Hunstanton Gang's cargoes, she remembered what had led her to such questions. "I take it you've heard about Lord Hendon, the new High Commissioner, and his interest in the trade?''

Jack managed to suppress the start her words gave him. What had she heard? He settled his hands behind his head and spoke to the ceiling. ''It's well known the Revenue are working out an excess of zeal about Sheringham.''

Kit frowned. ''That's not what I meant. I heard that Lord Hendon has been appointed specifically to take a greater interest in the traffic.''

From under his lashes, Jack watched her profile. ''Who told you that?''

''I overheard someone tell my grandfather about it.''

''Who?''

''The Lord Lieutenant.''

Jack pursed his lips. It wasn't exactly the message Lord Marchmont had been sent to deliver, but it was close enough. He was sure the Lord Lieutenant would have communicated his message accurately but if Kit had been flapping her ears at a distance, she might not have caught the whole of it. He couldn't imagine the two peers openly discussing such business in front of Spencer's housekeeper. ''If that's the case, we'll have to keep a close eye on his lordship's activities.''

Kit snorted derisively and sat up. ''If he ever actually stirs himself to anything that can be so described. I'm beginning to think he's gone to ground in that castle of his and just issues orders to the Revenue from his daybed.''

Jack looked at her in amazement. ''What makes you think that?''

''He's never seen about, that's why. He's been here for a few months, yet most people haven't sighted him. I know because Spencer gave a dinner party. Lord Hendon was invited but had a prior engagement.''

The disgust in her voice made Jack blink. ''What's wrong with that?''

Kit's lip curled. ''A prior engagement with whom— when all the surrounding families were at Cranmer that night?''

Jack looked much struck, a fact Kit missed. She found the glass of brandy, now empty, amid the covers and, with the trailing ends of her muffler, ineffectually dabbed at the small stain where the dregs had spilt in their tumble. Suddenly, she giggled.

"What's funny?"

"I was just wondering if I should pity the poor man, when he finally condescends to make a public appearance. The ladies of the neighborhood are all so *anxious* to meet him. Mrs. Cartwright has designs on him as a husband for her Jane, and Lady Marchmont—" Kit broke off, horrified by what she'd nearly said.

"Who's Lady Marchmont got in mind for the poor devil?" The laughter bubbling beneath the smooth surface of Jack's voice was encouraging.

"Someone else," Kit replied repressively. "And I don't envy the chit one bit."

"Oh?" Jack turned a fascinated eye on her. "Why's that?"

Kit was enjoying the unexpected sensation of sitting beside Jack, feeling oddly at ease and totally unthreatened, despite the panic of only minutes ago. For some inexplicable reason, she was quite sure he intended her no harm. His conviction that he could make her welcome his advances was frightening purely because she knew it was the truth. But when he wasn't engaging in that sort of play, she felt completely at one with him, perfectly ready to share her opinion of the new High Commissioner. She pulled an expressive face. "From all I've heard, Hendon sounds a dry old stick, positively fusty." She studied the glass in her hand. "He must be fifty and he limps. Lady Marchmont said he was 'Hendonish' but I've no idea what that means—probably stuffy."

Jack's brows had risen to considerable heights. He could have informed Kit precisely what "Hendonish" meant— she'd just been treated to a sample, albeit restricted—but he didn't. He was too taken up with grappling with a sense of outrage. "You've met the man, I take it."

"No." Kit shook her head. "Hardly anyone has, so he can hardly take exception to our visions of him if they're unfairly unflattering, can he?"

And that, thought Jack, was a deucedly difficult argument to counter.

A sudden shriek of wind brought their situation forcibly to Kit's mind. Heavens! Here she sat in Captain Jack's bed, with him beside her, chatting the night away. She must have rocks in her head! She wriggled toward the edge of the bed. "I must go."

Long fingers encircled her wrist. Jack didn't exert any great pressure, yet Kit didn't fool herself into thinking she could break free. "I take it we're agreed, then. Your men and mine to join from now on."

Kit frowned. "If the others agree. I'll have to ask them. I'll meet you at the quarries as we planned and tell you what we've decided."

She glanced at Jack. His face was blank, his expression unreadable. But she sensed he didn't like her conditions. Unconsciously, she tilted her chin.

Jack pondered her defiant expression and considered the advisability of pulling her to him and kissing her into agreement. Her lips were temptation incarnate, soft and full and devastatingly feminine. Particularly in their present half pout. Abruptly, he dragged his mind from its preoccupation. What she'd suggested was fair enough, but he didn't trust her in the quarries. He'd a shrewd suspicion she knew them better than he did. "I'll agree to wait two nights for your answer on the condition that you, personally, bring it to me here—not at the quarries."

Kit forced herself not to look down at the hand trapping hers or at the long body stretched at ease on the covers. She needed no demonstration to understand her vulnerability. She looked into Jack's eyes and read cool determination in their depths. Did it really matter if she came here again?

How deliciously dangerous, her wilder self purred.

"Very well." The hand about her wrist was withdrawn. Kit stood. Then immediately sank back on the bed, blushing furiously. Her bands were still undone. She couldn't ride back to Cranmer with them about her waist; and she didn't fancy the idea of stopping along the way to get undressed and do them up.

It took Jack a moment to work out the reason for her

blush. Then he laughed, a low chuckle that set Kit's nerves skittering. He sat up. "Turn around and let me do them up for you." When Kit sent him a scandalized look, he grinned wickedly. "I undid them, after all."

At his teasing tone, Kit blushed again and reluctantly turned about, wriggling to work the bands into position. What else could she do? He'd already seen her naked back—and her seminaked front, too. She felt his weight shift on the bed, then he rolled up the back of her shirt.

"Hold them where you want them tied."

Kit slipped her hands beneath her shirt to settle the bands over her breasts. "Tighter," she said, as she felt him cinch the ends only just tight enough to stay up.

An unintelligible mutter came from behind her, but he tightened the knot.

"More."

"Christ, woman! There ought to be a law against what you're doing."

Kit took a moment to work that out, then giggled. "There won't be any permanent damage."

The knot was tied, just tight enough, and her shirt pulled down. Kit stood and tucked the shirt into her waistband, then shrugged on her coat before winding the muffler tight about her nose and chin.

Lounging on the bed, Jack watched the transformation critically. Even knowing she was a woman, he had to admit her disguise was good. "Your mare's in the stable out back, keeping company with my stallion. Don't get too close to him; he bites."

Kit nodded. She found her tricorne in the corner by the bed and crammed it over her curls. "You didn't say where we are."

"About two miles north of Castle Hendon."

Beneath her muffler, Kit's lips twisted wryly. Jack seemed a man very much after her own heart. "You do like to live dangerously, don't you?"

Jack smiled brilliantly. "It keeps boredom at bay."

With a regal inclination of her head, Kit sauntered to the door.

Jack grinned. With her husky voice and the mannish airs

she assumed with such ease, he was confident they'd manage her charade for the requisite month.

At the door, Kit paused. "Until the night after tomorrow, then."

Jack nodded, his expression leaching into impassivity. "Don't try to disappear, will you? Your men might do something rash. And I know where to find you."

For the first time that night, Kit confronted the side of Captain Jack that had, presumably, made him the leader of the Hunstanton Gang. She decided she wasn't going to give him the joy of knowing how unnerving she found it. With a flourish, she swept him a bow before unlatching the door and pausing on the threshold to say, "I'll be here."

Then she left.

In the cottage, Jack dropped back onto the pillows and fell to a contemplation of the first woman to have ever left his bed untried. A temporary aberration but a novel one. He was deep in dreams when the quick clop of hooves told him Kit was on her way. With a sigh, he closed his eyes, wishing that Young Kit's month of service was already past.

Chapter 10

Next morning, Lord Hendon, the new High Commissioner for North Norfolk, visited his Revenue Office in King's Lynn, accompanied by his longtime friend and fellow ex-officer, George Smeaton.

His long limbs elegantly disposed in the best chair the Office possessed, his shoulder-length hair confined by a black riband at his nape, Jack knew he looked every inch the well-to-do gentleman lately retired from active service. His left leg was extended, kept straight by the discreet splint he wore under his close-fitting breeches. He'd carried such an injury for months after the hell of Corunna; the splint jogged his memory into a limp, increasing the overt difference between Lord Hendon and one Captain Jack.

One long-fingered hand languidly turned a page in the Office's logbook, the sapphire in his signet ring catching the light, splintering it through prisms of blue. His ears were filled with the drone of Sergeant Tonkin's explanations for his continuing lack of success in apprehending the smuggling gang operating between Lynn and Hunstanton. George sat by the window, a silent witness to Tonkin's performance.

"A devilish wise lot, they are, m'lord. Led by one of the more experienced men, I'd say."

Jack suppressed a smile at the thought of what Kit would say to that. He made a mental note to tell her when she returned to the cottage. Listening with apparent interest to Tonkin's summation, he was very aware that just the thought of that problematical female had been enough to instantly transform his body from listless lassitude to a state of semiarousal. Deliberately, he focused on Tonkin's words.

A burly, barrel-chested individual, Tonkin's coarse, blunt features were balanced by cauliflower ears. Since Tonkin's reputation was murky, bordering on the vicious, Jack had sent the efficient Osborne out of the area of their operations, leaving Tonkin to bear any odium as a result of the continuing high level of traffic. "If we could just lay hands on one of this 'ere lot, m'lord, I'd wring the truth from 'im." Tonkin's beady eyes gleamed. "And then we'd string a few up on our gibbets—that'd teach 'em not to play games with the Revenue."

"Indeed, Sergeant. We all agree this gang's got to be stopped." Jack leaned forward; his gaze transfixed Tonkin. "I suggest, as Osborne is engaged around Sheringham, you concentrate on the stretch of coast from Hunstanton to Lynn. I believe you said this particular gang operates only in that area?"

"Yes sir. We ain't never got a whiff of 'em elsewheres." Trapped beneath Jack's penetrating stare, Tonkin shifted uneasily. "But if you'll pardon the question, m'lord, if I'm to send my men down this way, who's to watch the Brancaster beaches? I swear there's a big gang operating thereabouts."

Jack's face expressed supercilious condescension. "One thing at a time, Tonkin. Lay the gang operating between Hunstanton and Lynn by the heels, then you may go haring off after your 'big gang.' "

His insultingly cynical tones struck Tonkin like a slap. He came to attention and saluted. "Yes, m'lord. Is there anything else, m'lord?"

With Tonkin dismissed, Jack and George quitted the Custom House. Crossing the sunny cobbled square, George adjusted his stride to Jack's limp.

Artistically wielding his cane, Jack struggled to ignore the stirrings of guilt. He hadn't told George about Kit. Like Matthew, George would disapprove, insisting Kit be retired forthwith, somehow or other. Basically, Jack agreed with the sentiment—he just didn't see what the "somehow or other" could be, and he was too experienced an officer to put the safety of a single woman before his mission.

The other matter troubling his conscience was a sinking feeling he should have behaved better with Kit, that he shouldn't have stooped to sexual coercion. Henceforth, he'd ensure that his attitude toward her remained professional. At least until she retired from the gang. After that, she'd no longer be tangled in his mission, and he could deal with her as personally as she'd allow.

Fantasizing about dealing with her personally had kept him awake for much of last night.

"Lord Hendon, ain't it?"

The barked greeting, coming from no more than a yard away, startled Jack from his reverie. He glanced up; a large man of advanced years was planted plumb in front of him. As his gaze took in the corona of curling white hair and the sharp eyes, washed out but still detectably violet-hued, Jack realized he was facing Spencer, Lord Cranmer, Kit's grandfather.

Jack smiled and held out his hand. "Lord Cranmer?"

His hand was enveloped in a huge palm and crushed.

"Aye." Spencer was pleased to have been recognized. "I knew your father well, m'boy. Marchmont spoke to me t'other day. If you need any help, you need only ask."

Smoothly, Jack thanked him and introduced George, adding: "We were in the army together."

Spencer wrung George's hand. "Engaged to Amy Gresham, ain't you? Think we missed your company, some nights back."

"Er—yes." George rolled an anguished eye at Jack.

Jack came to the rescue with consummate charm. "We were sorry to miss your dinner, but friends from London dropped by with news of our regiment."

Spencer chuckled. "It's not me you should be making your excuses to. It's the ladies get their noses out of joint when eligible men don't join the crowd." His eyes twinkled. "A word of warning, seeing you're Jake's boy. You'd do well to weather the storm before it works itself into a frenzy. Fighting shy of the *beldames* won't scare them off—they'll just try harder. Best to let them have their try at you. Once they're convinced you're past praying for, they'll start off on someone else.''

"Great heavens! It sounds like a hunt." Jack looked taken aback.

"It is a hunt, you may be sure." Spencer grinned. "You're in Norfolk now, not London. Here they play the game in earnest.''

"I'll bear your warning in mind, m'lord." Jack grinned back, a rogue unrepentant.

Spencer chuckled. "You do that, m'boy. Wouldn't want to see you leg-shackled to some drab female who's the dearest cousin of one of their ladyships, would we?" With that dire prediction, Spencer went on his way, chuckling to himself.

"The devil!" Jack heaved a sigh. "I've a nasty suspicion he's right." The memory of Kit's words, uttered while she'd been sitting on his bed last night, echoed in his brain. "Fighting shy of society seemed a wise idea, but it looks like we'll have to attend a few balls and dinners.''

"*We'll*?" George turned, eyes wide. "Might I remind you I've had the good sense to get betrothed and so am no longer at risk? I don't have to attend any such affairs.''

Jack's eyes narrowed. "You'd leave me to face the guns alone?''

"Dammit, Jack! You survived Corunna. Surely you can fight this engagement unsupported?''

"Ah, but we haven't sighted the enemy yet, have we?" When George looked puzzled, Jack explained: "Lady Whatsit's drab cousin. Just think how you'll feel if I get caught in parson's mousetrap, all because I didn't have you to watch my back.''

George pulled back to eye the elegant figure of Lord Hendon, at thirty-five, a man of vast and, in George's opinion, unparalleled experience of the fairer sex, consistent victor in the amphitheaters of *ton*nish ballrooms and bedrooms, a bona fide, fully certified rake of the first order. "Jack, in my humble opinion, the ladies of the district haven't a hope in hell.''

*   *   *

There was no moon to light the clearing before the cottage door. Kit stopped Delia under the tree opposite and studied the scene. A chink of lamplight showed beneath one shutter. It was midnight. All was still. Kit slackened her reins and headed Delia toward the stable.

In the shadow of the stable entrance, she dismounted, drawing the reins over Delia's head. The mare tossed her head sharply.

"Here. Let me."

Kit jumped back, a curse on her lips. A large hand closed about hers, deftly removing the reins. Jack was no more than a dense shadow at her shoulder. Unnerved, her wits frazzled by his touch, Kit waited in silence while he stabled Delia in the dark.

Were there others about? She peered into the gloom.

"There's no one else here." Jack returned to her side. "Come inside."

Kit had to hurry to keep up with Jack's long strides. He reached the door and entered before her, heading straight for the table to take the chair on the far side. Irritated by such cavalier treatment, Kit bit her tongue. She closed the door carefully, then turned to survey him, pausing to take stock before sauntering across the floor to the chair facing his.

He was scowling again, but she wasn't about to try for one of his smiles tonight. Pulling off her hat, she unwound her muffler, then sat.

"What's your decision?" Jack asked the question as soon as her bottom made contact with the chair seat. He'd been steeling himself for this meeting for more than twenty-four hours; it was galling to find the time had been wasted. The instant she'd appeared on his horizon, the only thing he could think of was getting her back onto his bed. And what he'd do next. He wanted this meeting concluded, and her safely on her way, with all possible haste.

From her expression, he knew his frown didn't meet with her approval. Right now, she didn't meet with his. She was the cause of all his present afflictions. Aside from the physical ramifications of her presence, he was having to cope with untold guilt over his deliberate support of her hoax.

He hadn't told Matthew or George. And now he was uncomfortably aware of Spencer, previously a shadowy figure he'd had no difficulty ignoring, transformed by their meeting into a flesh-and-blood man, presumably with real affection for his wayward granddaughter, even if she was illegitimate. Impossible to tell him, of course. What could he say? "A word in your ear, old man—your bastard granddaughter is masquerading as a smuggler"?

Dragging his gaze from Kit's lamplight-sheened curls, Jack stared into her violet eyes, alike yet quite different from Spencer's.

Kit's response to Jack's abrupt question had been to pull off her riding gloves, with infinite slowness, before glancing up to meet his gaze. "My men have agreed." She'd met her little band earlier that evening. "We'll join you as of now, provided you let us know what the cargoes are beforehand." It was her condition; the fishermen had been only too glad to accept Jack's offer.

Impassivity overtook Jack's scowl. Why the hell did she want to know that? His mind ranged over the possibilities but could find none that fit. "No." He kept the answer short and waited for her reaction.

"No?" she echoed. Then she shrugged. "All right. But I thought you wanted us to join you." She started to draw her gloves back on.

Jack abandoned impassivity. "What you ask is impossible. How can I run a gang if I have to check with you before I accept a cargo? There can be only one leader, and in case you've forgotten, I'm it."

Kit leaned one elbow on the table and cupped her chin in that hand, keeping her eyes on his face. It was a very strong face, with its powerful brow line and high cheekbones. "You should be able to understand that I feel responsible for my little band. How can I tell if you're doing right by them if I don't know what cargoes you're accepting or declining?"

Jack's exasperation grew. She'd hit on the one argument he couldn't, in all honesty, counter. If she'd been a man, he'd have applauded such a reason—it was the right attitude for a leader, of however small a troop. But Kit wasn't a man, a fact he was in no danger of forgetting.

Artfully, Kit continued. "I can see it might prove difficult to keep an agent waiting for confirmation. But if I was with you when you arranged the cargoes, there'd be no time lost."

Jack shook his head. "No. It's too dangerous. It's one thing to fool semicivilized fishermen; our contacts are not of that ilk. They're too likely to penetrate your disguise—God only knows what they'll make of it."

Kit received the assessment coolly, drawing her gloves through her fingers. "But you deal mostly with Nolan, don't you?"

Jack nodded. Nolan was his primary source of cargoes although there were three other agents in the area.

"I've already met Nolan without mishap, so I doubt there's any real danger there. He'll accept me as Young Kit. Seeing me with you will confirm we've joined forces, so he won't go trying to contact my men behind your back. That's what you wanted, wasn't it—a monopoly on this coast?"

Jack made no comment. There wasn't any he could make; she was dead on target with her reasoning, damn her.

Kit smiled. "So. Where and when do you make contact?"

Jack's expression turned grim. He'd been maneuvered into a corner and he didn't like it one bit. Their meeting place had been expressly chosen to be as unilluminated as possible, to ensure Nolan and his brethren had little chance of recognizing him, or George or Matthew. He was most at risk—he'd learned long ago that effectively disguising the streaks in his hair was impossible—so they'd found a venue where the light was always bad and keeping their hats on raised no eyebrows. But taking Kit to a hedge tavern frequented by local cutthroats and thieves was inconceivable.

"It's out of the question." Jack sat up and leaned both elbows on the table, the better to impress Kit with the madness of her suggestion.

"Why?" Kit fixed him with a determined stare.

"Because it would be the height of lunacy to take a woman, however well disguised, into a den of thieves." Jack's growl was barely restrained.

"Quite," Kit affirmed. "So no one will imagine Young Kit to be anything other than a lad."

"Christ!" Jack ran long fingers through his hair. "I wouldn't give a *sou* for Young Kit's safety in that place—male or female."

For a minute, Kit stared at him, incomprehension stamped on her fine features. Then she blushed delicately. Determined not to lower her head, she let her gaze slide to a consideration of the brandy bottle. "But you'll be there. There's no reason why any of them should . . ."

"Proposition you?" Jack kept his voice hard and matter-of-fact. If there was any possibility of scaring her off, he'd take it. "Allow me to inform you, my dear, that even I don't frequent such places alone. George and Matthew always accompany me."

Kit perked up. "So much the better. If there's four of us, and the three of you are large, then the danger will be minimal." She cocked an eyebrow at Jack, waiting for his next argument.

Her attitude, of patiently awaiting his next quibble in the calm certainty that she'd top it, brought a wry and entirely spontaneous grin to Jack's lips. Damn it—she was so cock-sure she could pull the thing off, he'd half a mind to let her try. She wouldn't find the Blackbird at all to her liking; maybe, after her first trip there, she'd be content to let him manage their contacts on his own.

His thoughts reached Kit. She smiled, only to be treated immediately to a scowl.

Hell and the devil! He was going mad. Jack fought the impulse to groan and bury his head in his hands. The effort of ignoring his besotted senses, and the pressure in his loins, was sapping his will. If only she was angry or frightened or flustered, he could cope. Instead, she was calm and in control, perfectly prepared to sit smiling at him, trading logic until he capitulated. He could render her witless easily enough, but only by unleashing something he was no longer sure he could reharness.

"All right." His jaw set uncompromisingly. "You can come with us next Wednesday night provided you do exactly as I say. Only I know your little secret. I suggest we keep it that way."

Content with having gained her immediate goal, Kit nodded. She was perfectly prepared to do as Jack said, as long as she could learn, firsthand, of the cargoes on offer. If there was any "human cargo," she'd have time to sound the alarm without risking her little troop, and, if possible, without endangering Captain Jack or his men, either.

Pleased, she reached for her hat. "Where do we meet?"

Engaged in an inventory of all the dangers attendant on taking Kit to the Blackbird, Jack shot her a decidedly malevolent glare. "Here. At eleven."

Kit grinned, then hid her face with her muffler. Her mood was buoyant; she wished she dared tease him from his grouchy attitude, but her instinct for self-preservation hadn't completely deserted her.

Jack slouched in his chair. This wasn't how this meeting was supposed to have gone, but at least she was leaving. He watched her assume her disguise and decided against going to the stable to help her with her horse. She could saddle her own damned mare if she was so keen on playing the lad. He acknowledged her flippant bow with something close to a snarl, which didn't affect her in the least. She seemed impervious to his bad temper—thrilled, no doubt, to have got her way. The door shut behind her, and he was alone.

Jack stretched but didn't relax until the sound of the mare's hooves died. He wasn't looking forward to Wednesday—the potential horrors were mind-numbing. To cap it all, he'd have to watch over her without letting on it was a *her* he was watching. Freed of Kit's inhibiting presence, Jack groaned.

Chapter 11

Kit's initiation into the dim world of the Blackbird Tavern was every bit as harrowing as Jack had anticipated. Sidelong, he studied the top of her hat, all he could see of her head as she sat at the rough trestle beside him, her nose buried in a tankard of ale. He hoped she wasn't drinking the stuff; it was home brewed and potent. He had no idea if she was wise to the danger. The fact that he wasn't sure of her past experience only further complicated his role as her protector. And Young Kit certainly needed a protector, even if the blasted woman didn't know it.

She'd seemed oblivious of the stir her appearance at his elbow had caused. Garbed in severe black, her slim form drew considering glances. Luckily, the Blackbird's patrons were not given to overt gestures. He and George had made straight for their usual table, taking Kit with them. He'd wedged her between the wall and his own solid bulk. The curiosity of the motley crew who'd taken shelter within the Blackbird's dingy walls on this drizzily June night washed over them, Young Kit its focus.

"Where the hell's Nolan?" George growled. Sitting opposite Kit, he nervously eyed the section of the room within his orbit.

Jack grimaced. "He'll be here soon enough." He'd warned both George and Matthew of Kit's heritage but continued to keep her sex a secret. Her coloring was so obvious it was impossible not to comment; to them, she was Christopher Cranmer's bastard son who lived at the Hall under Spencer's wing. Over "the stripling's" wish to join them in negotiations over cargoes, George's tendency to watch over youngsters had been of unexpected help.

He'd agreed Kit should accompany them. "If the place serves to put the lad off smuggling, so much the better," he'd said. "At least in our company he'll see a bit more of life in greater safety than might otherwise be afforded him."

It was a view that had not occurred to Jack—he wasn't sure he agreed with it. Certainly, George had not foreseen the interest Young Kit would provoke. Like him, both George and Matthew were edgy, nerves at full stretch. The only one of their company apparently unaffected by the tension in the room was its cause.

His gaze slid to her once more. She'd lifted her head from the tankard, but her gaze remained on the mug, cradled in both hands. To any observer, she gave every appearance of unconcerned innocence, idly toying with her drink, completely ignorant of the charged atmosphere. Then he noticed how tightly her gloved fingers were curled about the handle of the tankard.

Jack smiled into his beer. Not so ignorant. With any luck, she'd be scared witless.

Kit was certainly not unaware of the cloying interest of the other men in the room. The reason for it she found distasteful in the extreme, but she could hardly claim she hadn't been forewarned. For all she knew, Jack was relying on her disgust to make her balk at similar excursions in the future. But as long as the men in the room stared and did nothing, she couldn't see any real reason for fear. She'd been stared at aplenty, and far more overtly, during her Seasons in London. And Jack was only an inch or so away, on the crude bench beside her, an overwhelmingly large body that radiated warmth and security, reassuring with its aura of commanding strength governed by steely reflexes.

A stir by the door heralded an arrival. Jack looked over Matthew's shoulders. "It's Nolan."

The agent went to the bar and ordered a tankard, then, after scanning the room, made his way without haste to their table. He drew up a rough stool and perched at Jack's left, his eyes going to Kit. She'd raised her head at his approach and returned his stare unblinkingly.

Nolan's eyes narrowed. "You two in league?" He asked the question of Jack.

"A merger. To our mutual benefit."

Jack smiled, and Kit was very glad he didn't smile at her like that. The thought brought a shiver, which she sternly repressed.

"What does that mean?" Nolan didn't sound pleased.

"What it means, my friend, is that if you want to run a cargo into North Norfolk, you deal with me and me alone." Jack's deep voice was steady and completely devoid of emotion. In the hush, it held a menacing quality.

Nolan stared, then switched his gaze to Kit. "This true?"

"Yes." Kit kept it at that.

Nolan snorted and turned to Jack. "Well, leastways that means I won't have to deal with young upstarts who skim a man's profit to the bone." He turned to receive his tankard from a well-endowed serving wench, and so missed the inquiring glance Jack threw at Kit. She ignored it, letting her gaze slide from his, only to fall victim to the serving wench's fervent stare. Abruptly, she transferred her attention to her tankard and kept it there.

Once Jack and Nolan were well launched on their dealings, Kit looked up. The serving girl had retreated to the bar but her gaze was still fixed, in a drooling fashion, on her. Under her breath, Kit swore.

"Twenty kegs of the best brandy and ten more of port, if you can handle it." Nolan paused to swill from his tankard. Kit wondered how he could; the stuff tasted vile.

"We can handle it. The usual conditions?"

"Aye." Nolan eyed Jack warily, as if unable to believe he wasn't going to push the Gang's cut higher. "When do you want it?"

Jack considered, then said: "Tomorrow. The moon'll be new—not too much light but enough to see by. The delivery conditions the same?"

Nolan nodded. "Cash on delivery. The ship's the *Mollie*

Ann. She'll stand off Brancaster Head after dark tomorrow.''

"Right." Pushing his tankard aside, Jack stood. "It's time we left."

Nolan merely nodded and retreated into his beer.

Hurriedly standing, Kit found herself bundled in front of Jack. Matthew led the way and George brought up the rear. Their exit was so rapid that none of the other customers had time to blink. Outside, she, Jack, and George waited in the road while Matthew fetched their horses. Even in the gloom, Kit sensed the meaningful look Jack and George exchanged over her head. Then they were mounted and off, across the fields to the cottage.

There, they all sat around the table. Jack poured brandy, raising a brow in Kit's direction. She shook her head. The few sips of ale she'd taken had been more than enough. Jack delivered his plans in crisp tones that left Kit wondering what he'd been before. A soldier, certainly, but his attitude of authority suggested he hadn't been a trooper. The idea made her grin.

"How many boats can your men muster?"

Jack's question shook her into life. "Manned by two?" she asked. When he nodded, she replied: "Four. Do you want them all?"

"Four would double our number," put in George.

"And double the speed we could bring the barrels in." Jack looked at Kit. "We'll have all four. Get them to pull inshore just west of the Head—there's a little bay they'll likely know, perfect for the purpose." Turning to Matthew and George, he discussed the deposition of the rest of the men. Kit listened with half an ear, glancing up only briefly when George left.

Matthew followed. "G'night, lad."

Kit returned the words with a nod and a smile, hidden by her muffler. As soon as the door shut behind him, she tugged the folds free. "Phew! I hope the nights don't get too warm."

Replacing the brandy bottle on the sideboard, Jack turned to stare at her. In a month, long before the balmy nights of August, she wouldn't have need of her muffler. In a month, she wouldn't be masquerading as a smuggler. In a month, she'd be masquerading as his mistress. The thought brought a frown to his face. He'd still be masquerading, too, for he couldn't tell her who he was until his mission was complete. With an inward sigh, Jack focused on the present. "I take it you were edified by the company at the Blackbird?"

Kit lounged in her chair. "The company I could do without," she admitted. "But everything passed off smoothly. Next time, they'll recognize me, and I'll be less of an attraction."

Jack's exasperated look spoke volumes. "Next time," he repeated, drawing a chair to the other side of the table and straddling it. "I assume you're aware that the only reason you came off safely was because George and Matthew and I were there, rather too large to overlook?"

Kit opened her eyes wide. "I hadn't anticipated going there alone."

"Christ, *no!*" Jack ran his fingers through his hair, the golden strands catching and reflecting the lamplight. "This idea of yours is madness. I should never have agreed to it. But let me educate you on one point at least. If you'd made the slightest slip back there, unwittingly led one of the men to believe . . ." Jack struggled to find the right words for his purpose. One glance at Kit's open face, her eyes clearly visible now that she'd removed her hat and muffler, made it clear she wasn't entirely *au fait* with the way things were in dens of iniquity. "Led them to believe it'd be worthwhile to make a push for you," he continued, determined to bring her to a sense of her danger, "then we'd have had a riot on our hands. What would you have done then?"

Kit frowned. "Hid behind a table," she eventually conceded. "I'm no good with my fists."

The answer overturned Jack's deliberate seriousness. The idea of her delicate hands bunched into fists was silly enough; the notion of them doing any damage was laughable. His lips twisted in a reluctant grin.

Kit smiled sweetly. Immediately, all traces of mirth fled Jack's face, replaced by the scowl she was starting to believe was habitual. Dammit—he could smile, she knew he could. Charmingly.

Go on! Make him smile.

Shut up, Kit told her inner devil. *I can't afford a tussle with him—if he touches me, I can't think and then where will I be?*

Flat on your back, with any luck, came the unrepentant answer.

All I want is a smile, Kit told herself, repressing the inclination to scowl back. "You worry too much," she said. "Things will work out; it's only for a month."

Jack watched as she wound her muffler loosely into place and jammed her hat over her curls. He knew he should put his foot down and end her little charade, or at least restrict it to those areas he believed inevitable. He knew it, but couldn't work out how to do it. He argued and she returned a glib answer, then smiled, scattering his wits completely, leaving only an urgent longing in their place. He'd never worked with a woman before; socially, they were a push-over but professionally—he obviously didn't have the knack.

The scrape of her chair as she stood brought Jack's gaze back to Kit's face. "Until tomorrow, then." She smiled and felt a distinct pang of irritation when Jack glared back. Deliberately, she sauntered to the door, allowing her hips full license in their sway. She paused at the last to raise a hand in salute; his scowl was now definitely black. Her teeth gleamed. "Good night, Jack."

As she closed the door behind her, Kit wondered if the low growl she heard was from the distant surf or a some-what closer source.

The run was her first taste of Jack's planning in action. All went smoothly. She was the main lookout, stationed on the cliff above and to the east of the bay into which they ran the goods. In answer to her protest that surely any danger would come from the west, Jack had pulled rank and all but ordered her to the headland. She had a fine view of the beach. Her men were there. They dropped the cargo, then, together with the others in boats, pulled out into the Roads and headed straight home. The land-bound smugglers transferred the barrels to pack ponies, and the cavalcade headed inland. This time, Jack chose to hide the cargo in the ruins of an old church.

Overgrown with ivy, the ruins were all but impossible to discover unless you knew they were there. The old crypt, dark and dry, provided a perfect spot for their cache.

"Who owns this land?" Kit turned to Jack, sitting on his stallion beside her. They'd pulled back into the trees to keep watch over the gang as they worked, unloading the barrels and carting them down the steps to the crypt.

"It used to belong to the Smeatons."

Jack's tone suggested it no longer did. "And now?" Kit asked.

She knew the answer before he said, "Lord Hendon."

"Do you have a fetish of sorts, to constantly operate under the new High Commissioner's very nostrils?" Delia sidled to avoid the grey's head. Kit swore, and reined the mare in. "I wish you'd make your horse behave."

Jack obediently leaned forward and pulled Champion's ears. "Hear that, old fellow?" he whispered *sotto voce*. "Your advances are falling short of the mark. But don't worry. Females are contrary creatures at the best of times. Believe me—I know."

Kit ignored the invitation to take exception to his statement, quite sure there'd be a trap concealed amongst his words. In their few exchanges since the previous night, she'd detected a definite edge to Jack's remarks; she assumed it sprang from a corresponding sharpening of his temper. "You were about to tell me why you use Lord Hendon's lands."

Jack's lips twisted in a smile Kit couldn't see. He hadn't been about to do any such thing but hers was a persistent curiosity, one he should perhaps allay. She was also a persistent distraction, a persistent itch he couldn't yet scratch. But soon, he vowed, soon he'd attend to her as she deserved. The vision of her bottom, swaying in deliberate provocation as she'd walked to the door of the cottage, wasn't a sight he was likely to forget. "Sometimes, the safest place to hide is as close to your pursuer as possible."

Kit thought about that. "So he overlooks you while searching farther afield?"

Jack nodded. The men came out of the crypt; the last barrels had been stowed. Jack urged Champion forward.

Within minutes, the gang was scattering, ponies led off, other men disappearing on foot. Soon, the only souls left were Kit, Jack, Matthew, and George. They waited a few minutes, to make sure all the men were safely away. Then George nodded to Jack. "I'll see you tomorrow."

George rode into the trees. At Jack's signal, Matthew drew away, to wait for him just beyond the clearing.

Kit looked up; it was time for her to depart. She smiled, not knowing how weary she looked. "My men and I'll come up for the meeting on Monday. That's right, isn't it?"

Jack nodded, wishing he could escort her home. He hadn't thought of her riding alone through the dark before; he'd never watched her leave the cottage. To let her head into the night, tired and solitary, seemed an act of outright callousness. He considered insisting on escorting her, but rejected the idea. She'd refuse and argue, and he'd probably lose. And he didn't wish to remind her of his very real interest in her just at present. Ignoring her while she believed he was uninterested was hard enough. Ignoring her once she knew he was hooked would be impossible if her actions of last night were any guide. Like any other woman, she'd be incapable of leaving him alone, teasing him for attentions he was too wise to bestow—at least, not yet.

Half-asleep and dreaming, Kit found she was staring at the pale oval of Jack's face. She shook herself awake. "I'll be going then. Good night."

Jack bit his tongue. Rigid, he watched her leave the clearing, heading south on a ride of close to six miles through the dark.

Stifling a curse, he turned Champion to the east and found Matthew. Wordlessly, they set off, Champion leading Matthew's black over fields and meadows, somnolent under dark skies. They'd covered nearly a mile when Jack abruptly drew rein, startling Matthew who'd been asleep in his saddle.

"Dammit! You go on ahead. I'll be in later." Jack wheeled Champion and set his heels to the grey's sleek sides, leaving a bemused Matthew in his wake. When he reached the ruined church, Jack turned the grey's head south and loosened the reins. He was sure Champion would follow his Arab mare no matter which way Kit had gone.

Chapter 12

A fter that first run, Kit had been sure she'd face no real problem in being Young Kit for the requisite month. Unfortunately, affairs did not run so smoothly. Her pride was her problem: it rose to the fore on two different counts, both stemming directly from Jack's irritating behavior.

In the third week of their association, she sought solitude in the gazebo to thrash out how to counteract Jack's stubborn refusal to deal reasonably with her. She was always the lookout—that she could understand—but for all his apparent experience, Jack persisted in placing her to the east of the run area, away from Hunstanton. Yet if the Revenue were to mount a sortie, surely they'd be coming *from* Hunstanton?

Plonking herself down on the gazebo's wooden seat, Kit stared at the roses. Any attempt to question Jack's peculiar orders met with a highly discouraging scowl, topped by a growl if she pushed him. A snarl would no doubt be next, but she'd never had the nerve to test him. She had the distinct impression she was being bundled aside, out of harm's way. Kit narrowed her eyes. It was almost as if Jack knew there'd be no interference from the Revenue but sent her in the opposite direction just in case.

Damn it! It had been at *his* insistence she'd continued her charade; being given token tasks was not what she'd expected. Enough! She'd have it out with him this evening. There was to be another run, on the promontory between

Holme and Brancaster. Since they'd joined forces, the traffic had been constant—two runs a week, always on different beaches, mostly for Nolan, once for another agent. Spirits and lace had been the staple fare, high-quality merchandise that brought good returns to the smugglers.

With a rustle of skirts, Kit stood. Descending from the gazebo, she wended her way between the rose beds, indifferent to the perfect blooms nodding on every side. Lack of meaningful participation in the gang's affairs was one of her points of contention. Her personal interaction with Jack, or rather, lack of personal interaction with Jack, was the other.

His behavior during her first visit to the cottage she'd understood. What had her confused was all that had, or hadn't, come since. He'd blown hot for her initially, but ever since that night he'd appeared uninterested, as if he'd found her unattractive on second glance. For one who'd had the rakes of London at her feet, Jack's failure to succumb was galling.

Kit dropped the petals she'd pulled from a fading white rose and headed for the house. All the other personable males who'd hovered on her horizon had done so without her exerting any effort to attract their notice. Jack's notice, short-lived though it had been, had stirred her interest in a way none of the others had. She wanted more. But Jack, damn his silver eyes, seemed distinctly disinclined to supply it. He now acted as if she was a lad in truth—as if he couldn't be bothered responding to her as a woman.

Climbing the steps to the terrace, Kit realized her teeth were clenched. Forcibly relaxing her jaw, she made a vow. Before she quit the Hunstanton Gang, she'd have Captain Jack at her feet. A rash resolution, perhaps, but the thought sent a thrill of delicious daring through her.

Her lips quirked upward. This was what she craved—what she needed. A challenge. If Jack insisted on removing all chance of other thrills, surely it was only right he provide her with suitable compensation?

Entering the morning room, Kit sank onto the *chaise* and considered the possibilities. She'd need to be on guard to ensure Jack didn't take things farther than mere dalliance.

His behavior on that first night in his cottage had been ample proof that he could and would take matters far farther than she would countenance. He was not of common stock. No fisherman had such an air—of command, of authority, and, frequently, of sheer arrogance. His diction, his knowledge of swordplay, his stallion—all bore witness that his origins were considerably higher than the village. And, of course, he was gorgeous beyond belief. Nevertheless, a liaison, however brief, between Lord Cranmer's granddaughter and Captain Jack, leader of the Hunstanton Gang, did not fall within the bounds of the possible.

But he thinks you're illegitimate, remember?

"But I'm not illegitimate, am I?" Kit pointed out to her wilder self. "I couldn't possibly forget what I owe the family name."

Why? The family was ready enough to sacrifice you for their own ends.

"Only my uncles and aunts—not Spencer or my cousins."

Sure it's not just an old-fashioned dose of maidenly nerves? How will you learn if Amy's right if you don't give it a try? And if you're ever going to take the plunge—he's the one. Why not admit you go weak at the knees at the thought of all that lovely male muscle and those silver devil's eyes?

"Oh, shut up!" Kit reached for her embroidery. Prying her needle free, she poked it through the design. Drawing the thread through, she set her lips. She was bored. Excitement was what she needed. Tonight, she'd make sure she got some.

The roar of the surf as it pounded the sand filled Kit's ears. She stood in the lee of the cliff, holding Delia's reins, watching the Hunstanton Gang gather. The men huddled in small groups, their gruff voices barely audible above the surf. None approached her. They all viewed Young Kit as a delicate youth, a young nob, best left to Captain Jack to deal with.

Kit looked up and saw Jack approaching, mounted on his grey stallion and flanked by George and Matthew. Her confidence in Jack's ability to organize and command was complete. She'd heard tales, some decidedly grisly, of the Hunstanton Gang's activities before Jack had taken over. In the past three weeks, she'd seen no evidence of such excesses. Jack didn't even exert himself to impress his will—the men obeyed him instinctively, as if recognizing a born leader.

Kit peered out at the waves, black tipped with pearl in the weak moonlight. She could see no sign of the boats.

Jack drew rein some yards away and the men gathered about to receive their orders. Then they were off down the beach to wait, huddled on the sand like rocks just above the waterline. Dismounting, Jack set Matthew and George to watch for the signal from the ship that would tell them the boats were on their way in, then trudged through the sand toward Kit.

He stopped in front of her. "Up there should give you a good view."

To Kit's surprise, he indicated the cliff above the western end of the beach. Then she remembered they were out on the headland—if the Revenue came from anywhere it would have to be from the east; beyond the western point was sea. Her time had come. "No!" She had to shout over the din of the waves.

It took Jack a moment to realize what she was saying. He scowled. "What do you mean, 'No'?"

"I mean there's no sense in my keeping a lookout from that position. I may as well stay on the beach and watch the boats come in."

Jack stared at her. The idea of her scurrying around among the boats, being shoved aside by the first fisherman into whose path she stumbled, was one he refused to contemplate. A shout told him the signal had come. Soon, the boats would be beaching. He eyed the slight figure before him and shook his head. "I haven't time to argue about it now. I've got to see to the boats."

"Fine. I'll come, too." Kit looped Delia's reins about a straggling bush clinging to the cliff and turned to follow Jack.

"Get up to that cliff top immediately!"

The blast almost lifted her from her feet. Kit stepped back, eyes widening in alarm. Jack towered over her, one arm lifted, one finger jabbing at the western cliff. Transfixed, she stared at him. And saw him set his teeth.

"For Christ's sake, get moving!"

Shaken to her boots, furious to the point of incoherence, Kit wrenched Delia's reins from the bush and swung up to the saddle. She glared down at Jack, still standing before her, fists on hips, barring the way to the beach, then hauled on the reins and sent Delia up the cliff path.

On the western cliff top, Kit dismounted. She left Delia to graze the coarse grasses a few yards back from the edge. Seething, she threw herself down on a large flat boulder and, picking up a small rock, hurled it down onto the sands. She wished she could hit Jack with it. He was clearly visible, down by the beaching boats. A slingshot might just make it.

With a disgusted snort, Kit sank her elbows into her thighs and dumped her chin in her hands. God—could he shout. Spencer bellowed when in a rage, but the noise had never affected her. She'd always considered it a sure sign her grandfather had all but lost the thread of his argument and would soon succumb to hers. But when Jack had bellowed his orders, he'd expected to be obeyed. Instantly. Every vestige of defiant courage she possessed had curled up its toes and died. The idea of her doing anything to overcome such an invincible force had seemed patently ridiculous.

Thoroughly disgusted with her craven retreat, Kit glumly watched the gang unload the boats.

When the last barrel was clear of the surf and the pack ponies were all but fully laden, Kit stood and dusted down her breeches. Whatever happened, however much Jack bellowed, this was the last, the *very last time* she'd keep watch from the wrong position for the Hunstanton Gang.

"Well? What is it?" Jack dumped the keg he'd brought back from the run on the table and swung to face Kit. George had ridden straight home from the beach and, after one glance at Kit's rigid figure, Jack had sent Matthew directly on to the Castle. On the beach, he'd hoped that her knuckling under to his orders meant she'd forget her grievance over being a redundant lookout. He should have known better.

Kit ignored his abrupt demand and closed the door. With cool deliberation, she walked forward into the glow of the lamp Jack set alight. Pulling her hat from her curls, she dropped it on the table, then, in perfect silence, unwound her muffler.

Straightening from lighting the lamp, Jack pressed his hands to the table and remained standing. He felt much more capable of intimidating Kit when upright. Assuming, of course, that she, too, was upright. If she didn't hurry up and get to her point, he wouldn't give much for her chances of remaining so. Jack set his teeth and waited.

When her muffler had joined her hat, Kit turned to face Jack. "I suggest that in future you rethink your lookout policy. If you order me to a position in what is obviously the wrong direction, I'll move to a more sensible place."

Jack's jaw hardened. "You'll do as you're told."

Kit lifted a condescending brow.

Jack lost a little of his calm. "Dammit—if you're on lookout and the Revenue appear, how the hell can I be certain you won't do something stupid?"

Kit's eyes blazed. "I wouldn't just run away."

"I know that! If I thought you *would* run away, I'd have no qualms about putting you on the Hunstanton side."

"You admit you've been deliberately putting me on the wrong side?"

"Christ!" Jack raked a hand through his hair. "Look— you can't unload the boats, so you may as well be our lookout. As it happens—"

"At the moment you don't actually need a lookout." Kit's tone dripped with emphasis. "Because, as you well know, the Hunstanton Revenue men have been ordered to patrol the beaches south of Hunstanton."

Jack's eyes narrowed. "How did you know that?"

Kit lifted one shoulder. "Everyone knows that."

"Who told you?"

Kit eyed Jack warily. "Spencer. He had it from the owner of the Rose and Anchor in Lynn."

The muscles in Jack's shoulders eased. She didn't have any contact within the Revenue Office. He'd been away so long, he'd forgotten how things got about in the country. "I see."

"I take it that means I won't have to stay stuck on a cliff twiddling my thumbs next time?" Kit's look dared him to disagree.

He ignored it. "What the hell else can you do?"

"I can help unload the lace," Kit stated, chin high.

"Fine," said Jack. "And what happens the first time someone hands you a keg instead? Here, take this to the sideboard." Without warning, he lifted the keg he'd brought in and handed it to her.

Automatically, Kit put out her hands to take it. Jack let go.

Jack could carry the keg under one arm. He didn't have any idea how much Kit could carry, but he didn't expect her to sink under the weight.

Kit's knees buckled. Her arms slipped about the keg as she struggled to balance the weight against her own and failed. She went down, bottom first, and the keg rolled back to flatten her. The instant before it did serious damage, Jack lifted it from her.

In awful silence, Kit lay flat on the floor and glared at Jack. Then she got her breath back. Her bound breasts, swelling in righteous indignation, fought against the constraining bands; her eyes spat purple flame. "You bastard! What kind of a stupid thing was that to do?"

Carefully, Jack set the keg back on the table. He glanced once at Kit, sprawled at his feet, then rapidly away, biting his lips against the laughter that threatened. She looked fit to kill. "Here, let me . . ." Reaching down, he grasped both her hands. Gently, he hauled her to her feet. He didn't dare meet her gaze; it was sharp enough to slice strips off him. Doubtless, her tongue soon would.

Back on her feet, Kit was agonizingly aware that a certain portion of her anatomy was very bruised. "Dammit—that hurt!"

The accusation was softened by the way her lips trembled. She frowned, and Jack felt a patent fool. He'd been trying to protect her and instead, he'd nearly squashed her to death.

"Sorry." He was halfway into an apologetic smile, designed to charm her from her anger, when he remembered what would happen if he did. She'd smile back. He could just imagine it—a small, hurt little smile. He'd be felled. "But I'm afraid that's precisely what will happen if you play the lady smuggler with me." Realizing how close to danger he stood, Jack stalked back around the table.

Kit's spine stiffened. Her fingers curled in fury. Her wilder self came to life. *Remember your alternative to smuggling thrills?*

Kit smiled at Jack and noted his defensive blink. Her smile deepened. She put her hands behind her waist and turned slightly, grimacing artistically. "How right you are," she purred. "I don't suppose you have anything here for bruises?" She let her hands press down and over the ripe curves of her bottom.

Despite years of training in the art of dissembling, Jack couldn't tear his eyes from her hands. His body made the switch from semiarousal, his usual state in Kit's presence, to aching hardness before her hands reached the tops of her thighs. His brain registered the implication in her husky tone and scrambled what few wits he had remaining. Only his instinct for self-preservation kept him rooted to the floor with the table, a last bastion, between them.

It was the silence that finally penetrated Jack's daze. He glanced up and caught a gleam suspiciously like satisfaction in the violet eyes watching him.

"Er . . . no. Nothing for bruises." He had to get her out of here.

"But you must have something," Kit said, her lids veiling her eyes. Her glance fell on the keg. Her smile grew. "As I recall, there's a rub made with brandy." She looked up to see Jack's face drain of expression.

A brandy rub? Jack's mind went into a spin. The image her words conjured up, of him applying a brandy rub to her bruised flesh, his hand stroking the warm contours he'd just watched her trace, left him rigid with the effort to remain where he was. Only the thought that she was deliberately baiting him kept him still. Slowly, he shook his head. "Wouldn't help."

Kit pouted. "Are you sure?" Her hands gently kneaded her bottom. "I'm really rather sore."

Forcibly, Jack clamped an iron hold over every muscle in his body. His fists bunched; he felt as if he had lockjaw as he forced out the words: "In that case, you'd better get on your way before you stiffen up."

Kit's eyes narrowed, then she shrugged and half turned to pick up her muffler and hat. "So I can help with the boats from now on?" She started winding the muffler about her face.

Further argument was beyond Jack, but he'd be damned if he'd let her best him like this. "We'll talk about it tomorrow." His voice sounded strained.

Kit pulled on her hat and swung about to discuss the matter further, only to find Jack moving past her on his way to the door.

"We'll see what cargo Nolan has lined up for us. After all, you've only got a week more to go." Jack paused with his hand on the door latch and looked back, praying she'd leave.

Kit moved toward him, a considering light in her eyes, a knowing smile on her lips. "I thought you wanted two months?"

She was getting far too close. Jack drew a ragged breath and pulled open the door. "You agreed to one month, and that'll serve our purpose. No need for more." No need for further torture.

Kit paused beside him, tilting her head to look up at him from beneath the brim of her hat. "You're sure one month will be long enough?"

"Quite sure." Jack's voice had gained in strength. Encouraged, he grasped her elbow and helped her over the threshold, risking the contact in the interests of greater safety. "We'll meet here at eleven as usual. Good night."

Kit's eyes widened at his helping hand but she accepted her departure with good grace, pausing in the patch of light thrown through the open door to smile at him. "Until tomorrow, then," she purred.

Jack shut the door.

When the sound of the mare's hooves reached him, he heaved a huge sigh and slumped back against the door. He glanced at his hands, still fisted, and slowly straightened his long fingers.

A week to go. Christ—he'd be a nervous wreck by the end of it!

Pushing away from the door, he headed for the brandy keg. Before he reached it, the image of his torment, riding alone through the night, surfaced. Jack dropped his head back to stare at the ceiling and vented his displeasure in a frustrated groan. Then he went out to saddle Champion.

Chapter 13

"**W**ell, Kathryn dear, you're our local expert. If it's to be a real masquerade, with no one knowing who anyone is, how shall we manage it?"

Lady Marchmont sipped her tea and looked inquiringly at Kit.

Acquainted with her ladyship of old, Kit hadn't imagined she'd forget her notion of a ball. It was patently clear to all in Lady Marchmont's drawing room—Lady Dersingham as well as Lady Gresham with Amy in tow—that the ball was to serve a dual purpose, winkling the elusive Lord Hendon from his castle, and introducing Kit to him. Having expected as much, Kit had given the matter due thought. A masquerade provided a number of advantages.

"For a start, we'll have to make it plain the ball is a real masquerade—not just dominos over ball gowns." Kit frowned over her teacup. "Do you think there's enough time for people to get costumes together?"

"Time aplenty." Lady Dersingham waved one white hand dismissively. "There aren't that many of us, when all's said and done. Shouldn't be any problem. What do you think, Aurelia?"

Lady Gresham nodded. "If the invitations go out this afternoon, everyone will have a week to arrange their disguises." She smiled. "I must say, I'm looking forward to seeing what our friends come as. So revealing, to see what people fancy themselves as."

116

Sitting quietly on the *chaise* beside Kit, Amy shot her a glance.

Lady Marchmont reached for another scone. "We haven't had such promising entertainment in years. Such a good idea, Kathryn."

Kit smiled and sipped her tea.

"If you can't recognize anyone, how are you going to be sure none but the guests you've invited attend?" asked Lady Dersingham. "Remember the trouble the Colvilles had, when Bertrand's university chums came along uninvited? Dulcie was in tears, poor dear. They quite ruined the whole evening with their rowdiness and, of course, it took ages to discover who they were and evict them."

Neither Lady Marchmont nor Lady Gresham had any idea. The company looked to Kit.

She had her answer ready. "The invitations should have instructions about some sign the guests must present, so you can be certain only those you invited come but no guest identifies themselves beyond giving the right sign."

"What sort of sign?" asked Lady Marchmont.

"What about a sprig of laurel, in a buttonhole or in a lady's corsage?"

Lady Marchmont nodded. "Simple enough but not something anyone would guess. That should do it."

All agreed. Kit smiled. Amy raised a suspicious brow. Kit ignored it.

The ladies spent the next hour compiling the guest list and dictating the invitations to Kit and Amy, who dutifully acted as scribes. With the bundle of sealed missives handed into the butler's hands, the ladies took their leave.

Lady Dersingham had taken Kit up in her carriage; Amy and her mother had come in theirs. While they waited on the steps for the carriages to be brought around, Amy glanced again at Kit. "What are you up to?"

Her mother and Lady Marchmont were gossiping; Lady Dersingham had moved down the steps to examine a rosebush in an urn. Kit turned to Amy. "Why do you suppose I'm up to anything?"

Her wide violet eyes failed to convince Amy of her innocence. "You're planning some devilment," Amy declared. "What?"

Kit grinned mischievously. "I've a fancy to look Lord Hendon over, without giving him the same opportunity. Be damned if I let them present me to him, like a pigeon on a platter, a succulent morsel for his delectation."

Amy considered defending their ladyships, then decided to save her breath. "What do you plan to do?"

Kit's grin turned devilish. "Let's just say that my costume will be one no one will anticipate." She eyed Amy affectionately. "I wonder if you'll recognize me?"

"I'd recognize you anywhere, regardless of what you were wearing."

Kit chuckled. "We'll find out how good your powers of observation are next Wednesday."

Amy got no chance to press Kit for details of her disguise. The carriages rounded the corner of Marchmont Hall, and she was forced to bid Kit farewell. "Come and visit tomorrow. I want to hear more of this plan of yours."

Kit nodded and waved, but her laughing eyes left Amy with the distinct impression that she did not intend to reveal more of her plans.

Jack stood, feet planted well apart, resisting the tug of the surf surging about his knees. He glanced at Kit, slender beside him, and prayed she didn't overbalance. Even in the shadowy night, soaked to the skin, her anatomy was sure to show its deficiencies.

The yacht they'd been waiting to board came over the next wave and slewed as the helmsman threw the rudder over. Matthew, some way to their right, steadied the prow. Kit grasped the side of the boat with both gauntleted hands and hauled herself aboard. Or tried to.

Anticipating her helplessness, Jack planted a large palm beneath her bottom and hefted her over the side. He heard her gasp as she landed on the deck in a sprawl of arms and legs. Then he remembered her bruised posterior. He grimaced and followed her. Serve her right if she felt a twitch or two. He was in constant agony with a pain she delighted in compounding.

Kit scurried to get out of Jack's way as he clambered into the yacht, glaring through the night at him once he'd arrived on her level. She'd love to give him a piece of her mind, but didn't dare open her mouth. Just being where she was had stretched the tension between them to the breaking point; she was too wise to add fuel to the fire just at present.

As far as she was concerned, tonight was a once-in-a-lifetime chance, and she'd no intention of letting Jack spoil it. She'd gone with them to the Blackbird as usual on Wednesday, two nights ago. An agent had approached them with an unusual cargo—bales of Flemish cloth too unwieldy to be loaded into rowboats. To her surprise, Jack had accepted. The money on offer was certainly an incentive, but she couldn't imagine where he'd get large enough boats to do the job.

But he had—she knew better than to ask how.

She'd come to the beach tonight prepared to do battle if he dared suggest she be lookout. Although he'd eyed her with misgiving, Jack had included her in the group to go in the boats. The relief she'd felt when she'd learned she was to accompany Jack and the taciturn Matthew on board the yacht, rather than going on one of the other boats with the other men, was something she'd never admit. Its dampening effect was counteracted by her excitement over the yacht being the fastest boat in the small fleet. She'd always dreamed about sailing, but Spencer had never allowed her to indulge that particular whim.

Kit stood by the railings as the yacht cleaved through the swell. The ship they were to meet was a pinprick of light, gleaming occasionally well out in the Roads.

Jack kept his distance. He'd brought Kit along, unwilling to risk leaving her beyond his reach. Forcing his gaze from the slim figure with the old tricorne jammed over her curls, he focused on their destination, a black shape on the horizon, growing larger with every crest they passed. Via Matthew, he'd already started rumors of Young Kit's difficulties in continuing as part of the Gang. The stories revolved about Kit's grandfather, unidentified, kicking up a fuss at his grandson's frequent nocturnal absences.

Young Kit's retirement could not come soon enough.

Jack gritted his teeth as memories of their last evening at the Blackbird replayed in his mind. Kit had sat beside him in her usual place. But instead of keeping her distance as she'd done in the past, she'd shuffled closer, far closer than had been detectable from the other side of the table. The insistent pressure of her thigh against his had been bad enough. He'd nearly choked when he'd felt her hand on his thigh, tapered fingers stroking down the long muscle.

Luckily, she'd stopped when the agent appeared, else he'd never have had the wits to negotiate. In fact, he doubted he'd have had the strength to resist paying her back in her own coin which, given the predilection of females for forgetting where they were and what they were doing at such times, would probably have landed them in an unholy and potentially fatal mess.

After that, he'd kept Matthew with him, a fact that had his henchman puzzled. But he'd rather face a puzzled Matthew than a female determined to bring him low in typical female fashion. She might call him a coward—as she had last night when Matthew had dutifully followed them into the cottage after the meeting at the barn—but she didn't know what type of explosive she was playing with. She'd find out soon enough. Salacious imaginings of exactly how he'd exact his retribution filled his sleepless nights.

The yacht overtook three slower, square-rigged luggers, the rest of the Hunstanton Gang's fleet, then slewed sharply to come alongside the hull of the Dutch brigantine. Matthew stood in the prow, a coiled rope in his hands. The other two crewmen brought down the sails. As the waves drifted the hulls closer, Matthew threw the rope to waiting hands. Within minutes, they were secured against the Dutchman's side.

Jack turned to the helmsman. "Lash the wheel and let the boy watch it." The man obeyed; Jack turned to see Kit already on her way midships. He grinned. Bales of cloth were not packets of lace.

They unloaded the cargo smoothly, lowering the bales on sets of ropes over the brig's side, directly into the hold of the yacht.

Her hands on the fixed wheel, Kit watched, her heart

leaping when one bale swung crazily toward her, threatening to slip free of its lashings. Jack jumped onto the cabin roof directly between the wheel and the hold and steadied the large roll, reaching high with both hands and leaning his entire weight into it to counter its swing. Relief swept Kit when the bale settled; it was lowered without further drama.

The Dutch ship had been carrying a full load; at the end, each of the four smugglers' boats was fully laden, even carrying bales on deck, lashed to the railings. The entire process was accomplished in total silence. Sound traveled too well on water.

The men worked steadily, stowing the bales. Kit's mind drifted to the comment Jack had made the night before, when she'd been late for the meeting in the barn. She'd slipped unobtrusively around the door, but Jack had seen her instantly. He'd smiled and asked if she'd had trouble with her grandfather. She'd had no idea what he'd meant but had scowled and nodded, and then been astounded by the laughing understanding that had colored many of the men's faces. Later, she'd learned enough to guess that Jack had started paving her way out of the Gang. Clearly, he'd meant what he'd said about one month being more than long enough.

She'd gone on being Young Kit under duress; now, she was reluctant to part with her alias, her passport to excitement.

And you haven't had him at your feet yet, have you?

Kit eyed Jack's broad shoulders, presently directly in front of her, and fantasized about the muscles beneath his rough shirt. Before she broke with him, she was determined to convert at least some of her fantasies to reality. Thus far, the only response her tricks had brought was a general stiffening of his muscles, a clenching of his jaw. She was determined to get more than that.

A low whistle signaled that they were done. Ropes were released; the smaller boats poled off from the brig's hull, drifting until they were out of the larger ship's wind shadow before hoisting their sails.

Relieved of her watch by the wheel, which had been

every bit as useless as her lookout duty but infinitely more exciting, Kit strolled down the deck, heading for the bow. She'd cleared the cabin housing when the yacht passed the brig's prow and the wind caught its sails. The yacht leapt forward.

Kit screamed and just managed to stifle the sound. She was flung against the bale lashed to the railing. Her desperately groping fingers tangled in the lashings. Drawing a deep breath, she hauled herself upright.

Immediately she'd regained her feet, she heard an almighty crack, like a tree branch snapping.

"*Kit! Duck!*"

She reacted more to Jack's tone than his words, but duck she did. The boom went sailing past, level with where her head had been split seconds before. Kit stared at the long pole swinging outward over the waves, a rope dangling behind it. She grabbed the rope.

Instantly, she realized her mistake. The sudden tug on her arms was horrendous, and then she was being hauled in the wake of the boom, the wind filling the sail and causing the heavily laden yacht to list to starboard.

Kit's eyes widened in fright. She looked over the railings at the black waves and remembered she couldn't swim.

Her belly hit the bale. The next gust of wind would lift her from her feet, half over the rail. She was no expert seaman, but if she let go of the rope, the yacht looked set to capsize.

Hard hands locked about hers on the rope and hauled back. Kit added her weight to Jack's and the boom swung back. But the wind retaliated, filling the sail once more. The jerk on the rope pulled Kit hard against the bale, her arms outstretched over the railing. Jack slammed into her back.

Kit forgot the boom, the wind, the sail; forgot the waves and the fact that she couldn't swim; forgot everything but the awesome sensation of a very hard male body pressed forcibly against hers. She was jammed between the bale and Jack. She could feel the muscles in his chest shift against her as he struggled to haul in the boom. She could feel the muscles of his stomach brace into hard ridges as he used his weight to maintain their balance. She could feel the solid weight of his thighs pressed hard against her bruised bottom. On either side of her slender legs, she could feel the long columns of his legs like steel supports anchoring them to the deck, defying the wind's shrieking fury. She could also feel the hard shaft of desire that nudged into the small of her back. The discovery held her riveted.

Uninterested, was he? Found her unattractive, did he? What sort of game was he playing?

"For God's sake, woman! Lean back!"

Jack's furious whisper recalled Kit to the urgency of the situation. She dutifully added her weight to his as he drew in the boom.

Behind her, Jack was facing a conundrum unlike any he'd ever experienced. Having Kit trapped against him was pure hell. He'd give anything to be able to push her aside but didn't dare; he needed her additional weight to balance the wind in the sail. And he couldn't relax the tension on the rope long enough to wrap it about the rail.

The yacht raced before the wind, tearing through the waves. The helmsman tacked so they were driven by the wind-filled sail and were no longer in danger of capsizing.

Matthew appeared at Jack's shoulder, and shouted over the wind: "If you can hold it like that, we'll be all right."

Jack nodded and turned his head, intending to have Matthew replace Kit on the rope, but Matthew had already deserted him. He glared in disbelief at his henchman's retreating back.

Quite where the idea sprang from, Kit wasn't sure, but it suddenly occurred to her that Jack was every bit as trapped as she was. And, that being so, this was a perfect opportunity to further her aims in reasonable safety. She was screened from the other men by Jack's bulk. He had his hands full of rope, and he could hardly do much when the beach was only five minutes away. With a view to determining the possibilities, Kit pressed back against him.

A sharply indrawn breath just above her left ear was the result.

Her action had given her a little more room to maneuver. She wriggled her bottom, slowly, and felt a ripple of tension pass through the muscles in his thighs. The shaft rising between them was like iron, a solid but living force. Moving slowly, keeping her weight braced against the rope, Kit rubbed her body, from shoulders to hips and beyond, side to side against the man behind her.

Jack bit back an oath. He clamped his teeth over his lower lip to stifle a groan of frustration. Damn the woman! What devil possessed her wild senses to make her choose this precise moment to give him a demonstration of her potential? He could feel every undulation of her slender form, every purring stroke. She moved like a cat, sinuously against him.

The wind tugged again, and they were jammed together once more. Jack closed his eyes and forced his mind to concentrate on keeping his grip on the rope. His grip on his mind was dissolving.

Slamming into the bale knocked the breath out of Kit. She waited, but Jack made no move to pull back. His breath wafted the curls above her left ear.

Jack was content to remain where they were. He'd no intention of giving her the leeway to continue her little game. He considered whispering a few carefully worded threats but couldn't think of anything appropriate. He'd a nasty suspicion his voice would betray him if he tried to speak at all. He set his jaw and endured, cataloging every little move she made into his ledger of account against the time, almost a week distant, when payment would fall due. He'd every intention of making sure she paid. In full. With interest.

The sight of the beach was more welcome than the cliffs of Dover had ever been. Jack saw the helmsman wave. "Let go of the rope. Slowly."

Kit did as she was told, wary of the wind-whipped sail. Jack held on until he was sure her hands were free, then he let go as well. The boom swung away, but the wheel was also swung; the yacht slewed and slowed as the wind emptied from the sail. The boom swung inboard.

Jack was watching it. He ducked, taking Kit to the deck with him. She sprawled full-length beside him.

A quick glance showed Jack that the helmsman was concentrating on his yacht while the other men, including Matthew, were busy securing the boom. The moment was too tempting to pass up.

Kit had seen the boom returning but had not been expecting Jack's hands to close so abruptly on her shoulders. The deck was hard and uncomfortable, but it was doubtless better than a broken head. She saw the men struggling to tie the wretched boom back into position and placed her hands palm down on the deck. She braced herself to rise. Instead, she froze as a large hand splayed across her bottom.

Kit stopped breathing. The hand pressed gently, moving in a slow, circular motion, then its orientation shifted. Damp heat spread over her rear. Two long fingers slipped between her thighs.

With an audible gasp, Kit shot to her knees, but that only pressed her bottom more fully into that caressing hand, leaving her more open to those intimately probing fingers.

Too shocked to think, she leaned back on her haunches. The long fingers pressed deep. Kit leapt to her feet, her face flaming.

From behind came a mocking, very male laugh. "Later, sweetheart."

Two hard hands set her aside, and Jack moved past to check the boom.

Kit escaped Jack's dangerous presence as soon as she possibly could. Furious, nervous, and shaken, she bided her time until the difficult unloading operation began. Then she sought out Matthew. "I'll go up on the cliff and keep watch."

Matthew nodded. Unaided, Kit slipped over the side of the yacht, gently bobbing on the shallow swell, and waded to shore.

On board the yacht, Jack saw her in the surf. He swore and stepped to the rails, hands on hips. "Where the hell's he going?"

Matthew was passing. "Young Kit?" When Jack nodded, he replied: "Lookout."

Matthew moved on and so missed the devilish grin that broke across Jack's face.

Was he supposed to understand she'd rather do lookout duty than stay in his vicinity? Jack felt laughter bubble up. Like hell! He'd felt her heat, even in those few minutes on the deck. She was as hot for him as he was for her, his little kitten. And soon, very soon, he was going to have her purring and arching like she'd never done before.

With an effort, Jack forced his mind back to the mundane but difficult task of unloading bales.

Kit waited only until she saw the first men leave. Then she pressed her heels to Delia's sleek sides and headed home, her face still several shades too pink. She couldn't stop dwelling on those few minutes on the deck. And on the promise in Jack's final words.

Gone was any idea that he wasn't attracted to her. Instead, her most pressing concern should doubtless be whether it wouldn't be wise never to see him again.

To Kit's consternation, her mind flatly refused to consider such an option.

At least now you know a little of what Amy meant.

Oh, God, Kit thought, *that's all I need. I can't possibly be in love with Jack. He's a smuggler.*

Memories of how she'd felt on the deck crowded her mind. Even now, the skin on her bottom felt feverish as she recalled the play of his hand. Her bruises throbbed. Her memory rolled relentlessly on, to the delicious thrill she'd experienced when his fingers had probed the soft flesh between her thighs. Kit blushed. As her memory replayed his words, her heart accelerated. What if he really meant it?

She considered the implications and swallowed.

What did he actually mean? Was he really intending to . . . ?

Kit's thighs tightened, and Delia's stride lengthened alarmingly.

A mile behind Kit, Jack swung up into Champion's saddle. The last of the men had left, the cargo cleared. He turned to Matthew. "I'm going for a ride. I'll be in later."

With that, he set Champion up the cliff track, onto Delia's trail. Jack was very tired of his nocturnal rides, but he

couldn't have slept, even uneasily as he did, without knowing Kit was safely home. At least he only had less than a
week to go before Young Kit left the Hunstanton Gang.
When they met at night after that, if she left him at all, it
would be at a safer hour—one much closer to dawn.

Afternoon sunlight turned the streaks in Jack's hair to
brightest gold as he sat, lounging elegantly, in the carved
chair behind his desk. Huge and heavy, the desk was located before the library windows, its classic lines comple-
menting the uncluttered bookshelves lining the walls.

Bright blue fractured light fell from Jack's signet ring
onto the pristine blotter as his long fingers toyed idly with
an ivory letter opener. His attire proclaimed him the gentleman but as always held a hint of the military. No one,
seeing him, would find it difficult to credit that this was
Lord Hendon, of Castle Hendon, the High Commissioner
for North Norfolk.

A distant frown inhabited the High Commissioner's expressive eyes; his grey gaze was abstracted.

Before the desk, George wandered the room, glancing at
the numerous sporting and military publications left lying
on the side tables before stopping before the marble mantelpiece. A large gilt-framed mirror reflected the comforting
image of a country squire's son, soberly dressed, with
rather less of the striking elegance that characterized Jack,
a more easygoing nature discernable in George's frank
brown eyes and gentle smile.

George tweaked a gilt-edged note from the mirror frame.
"I see you've got an invitation to the Marchmonts' masquerade. Are you going?"

Jack lifted his head and took a moment to grasp the question. Then he grimaced. "Pretty damned difficult to refuse.
I suppose I'll have to put in an appearance." His tone accurately reflected his lack of enthusiasm. He wasn't the
least interested in doing the pretty socially—smiling and
chatting, careful not to overstep the mark with any of the
marriageable misses, partnering them in the dances. It was
all a dead bore. And, at present, his mind was engrossed
with far more important concerns.

He wasn't at all sure he hadn't overstepped the mark with Kit. She hadn't come to the meeting last night, the first meeting she had missed. He'd turned the event to good account by referring to her grandfather's influence. But, deep down, he suspected it was his influence that was to blame. Why she would take exception to his caresses, explicit though they'd been, he couldn't imagine.

She was a mature woman and, although she clearly liked to play games as many women did, her actions, her movements, the strength and wildness of her response, all testified to her knowledge of how such games inevitably ended. After her actions on the yacht, and at the Blackbird, it was difficult to doubt her willingness to pursue that inevitable ending with him. But he couldn't think of any other reason why she'd have stayed away last night.

The idea that she was a tease who didn't pay up he discounted; no woman who was as hot as Kit would draw back from the culminating scene. And even if she was that sort, he'd no intention of letting her shortchange him.

"What are you going to wear?"

George's question dragged Jack's mind from his preoccupation. "Wear?" He frowned. "I must have a domino lying about somewhere."

"You haven't read this, have you?" George dropped the invitation onto the desk. "It clearly states a proper costume is mandatory. No dominos allowed."

"Damn!" Jack read the invitation, his lip curling in disgust. "You know what this means? A string of shepherdesses and Dresden milkmaids, all either hitting you over the head with their crooks or knocking your shins with their pails."

George laughed and settled in a chair opposite the desk. "It won't be that bad."

Jack raised a cynical brow. "What are you going as?"

George flushed. "Harlequin." Jack laughed. George looked pained. "I'm told it's one of the sacrifices I must make in light of my soon-to-be-wedded state."

"Thank God I'm not engaged!" Jack stared at the invitation again. Then a slow smile, one George was well acquainted with, broke across his face.

"What are you going to do?" George asked, trepidation shading his tone.

"Well—it's perfectly obvious, isn't it?" Jack sat back, pleasurable anticipation gleaming in his eyes. "They're expecting me to turn up, disguised but still recognizable, prime fodder for their matrimonial cannons, right?"

George nodded.

"Did I tell you I've heard, from an unimpeachable source, that Lady Marchmont herself has me in her sights, for some nameless protégé?"

George shook his head.

"Well, she has. It occurs to me that if I'm to attend this event at all, it had best be in a disguise which will not be readily penetrated. If I can pull that off, I'll be able to reconnoiter the field without giving away my dispositions. I'll go as Captain Jack, pirate and smuggler, leader of the Hunstanton Gang."

George appeared skeptical. "What about your hair?"

"There's a wig of my grandfather's about somewhere. With that taken care of, I should be able to pass muster undetected, don't you think?"

At Jack's inquiring look, George nodded dully. With his hair covered, Jack's height was unusual but not distinctive. However . . . George eyed the figure behind the desk. There weren't many men in North Norfolk built like Jack, but he knew better than to quibble. Jack would do what Jack would do, regardless of such minor difficulties. The success of his disguise would depend on how observant the females of the district were. And most hadn't seen Jack in ten and more years.

"Who knows?" Jack mused. "One of these females might actually suit me."

George stared. "You mean you're seriously considering marrying?" His tone was several degrees past incredulous.

Jack waved one hand languidly, as if the subject was not of much importance. "I'll have to sometime, for an heir if nothing else. But don't get the idea I'm all that keen to follow your lead. A dashed risky business, marriage, by all accounts."

George relaxed, then took the opportunity provided by

this rare allusion to a topic that Jack more normally eschewed to ask: "What sort of wife are you imagining for yourself?"

"Me?" Jack's eyes flew wide. He considered. "She'd have to be able to support the position—be acceptable as Lady Hendon and the mother of my heir and all that."

"Naturally."

"Beyond that . . ." Jack shrugged, then grinned. "I suppose it'd make life easier if she was at least passably good-looking and could string a conversation along over the breakfast cups. Aside from that, all I'd ask is that she keep out of what are purely my concerns."

"Ah," said George, looking skeptical. "Which concerns are those?"

"If you imagine I'm going to settle to monogamous wedded bliss with a woman who's only passably good-looking, you're wrong." Jack's acerbity was marked. "I've never understood all the fuss about fidelity and marriage. As far as I can see, the two don't necessarily connect."

George's lips thinned, but he knew better than to lecture Jack on that subject. "But you don't have a mistress at present."

Jack's smile was blinding. "Not just at the moment, no. But I've a candidate in mind who'll fill the position admirably." His silver-grey gaze grew distant as his thoughts dwelled on Kit's delicate curves.

George humphed and fell silent.

"Anyway," Jack said, shaking free of his reverie, "any wife of mine would have to understand she'd have no influence in such areas of my life." With Kit as his mistress, he couldn't imagine even wanting a wife. He certainly wouldn't want one to warm his bed—Kit would do that very nicely.

Chapter 14

Noise, laughter, and the distant scrape of a violin greeted Kit as she strolled up the steps of Marchmont Hall. At the door, the butler stood, sharp eyes searching each guest for the required sprig of laurel. Drawing abreast of him, Kit smiled and raised her gloved fingers to the leaves thrust through the buttonhole in her lapel.

The butler bowed. Kit inclined her head, pleased that the retainer had not recognized her. He'd seen her frequently enough in her skirts to be a reasonable test case. Confidence brimming, she sauntered to the wide double doors that gave onto the ballroom, pausing at the last to check that her plain black mask was in place, shading her eyes as well as covering her telltale mouth and chin.

As soon as she crossed the threshold, she was conscious of being examined by a large number of eyes. Her confidence wavered, then surged when no one looked more than puzzled. They couldn't place the elegant stripling, of course. Calmly, as if considering the attention only her due, Kit strolled into the crowd milling about the dance floor. She'd had Elmina recut a cast-off evening coat belonging to her cousin Geoffrey, deepest midnight blue, and had bullied her elderly maid into creating a pair of buff inexpressibles that clung to her long limbs as if molded to them. Her blue-and-gold waistcoat had once been a brocaded underskirt; it was cut long to cover the anatomical inadequacies otherwise revealed by the tight breeches. Her snowy white cravat, borrowed from Spencer's collection, was tied

131

in a fair imitation of the Oriental style. The brown wig had been the biggest challenge; she'd found a whole trunk of them in the attic and had spent hours making her selection, then recutting the curls to a more modern style. All in all, she felt no little pride in her disguise.

Her principal objective was to locate Lord Hendon amid the guests. She'd imagined she'd find him being lionized by the local ladies, but a quick survey of the room brought no such interesting specimen to light. Lady Dersingham was by the musicians' dais, Lady Gresham was seated not far from the door, and Lady Marchmont was hovering as close as she could to the portal; all three were obviously keeping watch.

Kit grinned beneath her mask. She was one their ladyships would be keen to identify; their other prime target would be her quarry. Convinced Lord Hendon had not yet arrived, Kit circulated among the guests, keeping a weather eye on one or another of her three well-wishers at all times. She was sure they'd react when the new High Commissioner darkened the doorway.

To her mind, this opportunity to evaluate Lord Hendon was unparalleled and unlikely to be repeated. She intended to study the man behind the title, and, if the facade looked promising, to investigate further. Disguised as she was, there were any number of conversational gambits with which she could engage the new High Commissioner.

Kit glimpsed Amy in her Columbine costume at the other end of the room and headed in that direction. She passed Spencer, talking farming with Amy's father, and carefully avoided his attention. She'd convinced him to come alone in his carriage, on the grounds that she needed to arrive without his very identifying escort to remain incognito. Thinking she meant to hoodwink Amy and their ladyships, he'd agreed readily enough, assuming that she'd use the smaller carriage. Instead, she'd ridden here on Delia. She'd never brought Delia to Marchmont Hall before, so the grooms had not recognized the mare.

The Marchmont Hall ballroom was long and narrow. Kit sauntered through the crowd, nodding here and there at people she knew, delighting in their confusion. Throughout, she kept mum. Those who knew her might recognize the husky quality of her voice and be sufficiently shrewd to think the unthinkable. She was perfectly aware her enterprise was scandalous in the extreme, but she'd no intention of being within Marchmont Hall when the time came to unmask.

As she drew closer to the musicians' raised dais, she heard them tuning their instruments.

"You there, young man!"

Kit turned and beheld her hostess bearing down on her, a plain girl in tow. Holding her breath, Kit bowed, praying her mask hadn't slipped.

"I haven't the faintest notion who you are, dear boy, but you can dance, can't you?"

Kit nodded, too relieved that Lady Marchmont hadn't recognized her to realize the wisdom of denying that accomplishment.

"Good! You can partner this fair shepherdess then."

Lady Marchmont held out the young girl's gloved hand. Smoothly, Kit took it and bowed low. "Charmed," she murmured, wondering frantically whether she could remember how to reverse the steps she'd been accustomed to performing automatically for the past six years.

The shepherdess curtsied. Behind her mask, Kit frowned critically. The girl wobbled too much—she should practice in front of a mirror.

Lady Marchmont sighed with relief and, with a farewell pat on Kit's arm, left them in search of other suitable gentlemen to pair with single girls.

To Kit's relief, the music started immediately, rendering conversation unnecessary. She and the shepherdess took their places in the nearest set and the ordeal began. By the first turn, Kit realized the cotillion was more of an ordeal for the shepherdess than herself. Kit had taught her youngest two male cousins to dance, so was acquainted with the gentleman's movements. Knowing the lady's movements by heart made it easy enough to remember and match the appropriate position. Her confidence grew with every step. The shepherdess, in contrast, was a bundle of nerves, unraveling steadily.

When, through hesitation, the girl nearly slipped, Kit spoke as encouragingly as she could: "Relax. You're doing it quite well, but you'll improve if you don't tense so."

A strained smile that was more like a grimace was her reward.

With an inward sigh, Kit set herself to calm the girl and instill a bit of confidence. She succeeded sufficiently well for the shepherdess to smile normally by the end of the measure and thank her effusively.

From the other side of the room, Jack surveyed the dancers. He'd arrived fifteen minutes earlier, rigged out in his "poor country squire togs," a black half mask and a brown tie wig. For the first three minutes, all had gone well. After that, the evening had headed downhill. First, Lord Marchmont had recognized him, how he'd no idea. His host had immediately borne him off to present him to his wife. Unfortunately, she'd been standing with three other local ladies. He was now on nodding terms with the ladies Gresham, Dersingham, and Falworth.

Lady Marchmont had iced his cake with an arch pronouncement that she'd "someone" she most particularly wished him to meet. He'd suppressed a shudder, intensified by the gleam he saw in the other ladies' eyes. They were all in league to leg-shackle him to some damn drab. Sheer panic had come to his rescue. He'd charmed his way from their sides and gone immediately in search of refreshment, remembering just in time to redevelop his limp. At least it provided an excuse not to dance. Strong liquor was what he'd needed to regain his equilibrium. Matthew had gone alone to the Blackbird, to line up their next cargo. Jack wished he was with him, with a tankard of their abominable home brew in front of him.

In the alcove off the ballroom where the drinks were set forth, he'd come upon George, a decidedly glum Harlequin. At sight of him, he'd uttered a hoot of laughter, for which George repaid him with a scowl.

"I know it looks damn stupid, but what could I do?"

"Call off the engagement?"

George threw him a withering look, then added: "Not

that I'm not sure it constitutes sufficient cause.''

Jack thumped him on the shoulder. ''Never mind your troubles—mine are worse.''

George studied the grim set of his lips. ''They recognized you?''

Reaching for a brandy, Jack nodded. ''Virtually immediately. God only knows what gave me away.''

George opened his mouth to tell him but never got the chance.

''Christ Almighty!'' Jack choked on his brandy. Abruptly, he swung away from the ballroom. ''What the bloody hell's Kit doing here?''

Frowning, George looked over the guests. ''Where?''

''Dancing, would you believe! With a shepherdess in pale pink—third set from the door.''

George located the slender youth dipping through the last moves of the cotillion. ''You sure that's Kit?''

Jack swallowed his ''Of course I'm damned sure, I'd know her legs anywhere'' and substituted a curt, ''Positive.''

George studied the figure across the room. ''A wig?''

''And his Sunday best,'' said Jack, risking a quick glance at the ballroom. The last thing he wanted was for Kit to see him. If the Lord Lieutenant could recognize him immediately, it was certain Kit would. But she knew him as Captain Jack.

''Maybe Spencer brought him?''

''Like hell! More likely the young devil decided to come and see how the other half lives.''

George grinned. ''Well, it's safe enough. He'll just have to leave before the unmasking and no one will be any the wiser.''

''But *he'll* be a whole lot wiser if he sets eyes on either you or me.''

George's indulgent smile faded. ''Oh.''

''Indeed. So how do we remove Kit from this charming little gathering without creating a scene?''

They both sipped their brandies and considered the problem. Jack kept his back to the room; George, far less recognizable in his Harlequin suit, maintained a watchful eye on Kit.

"He's left his partner and is moving down the room."

"Is your fiancée here?" Jack asked. "Can you get her to take a note to Kit?"

George nodded. Jack pulled out a small tablet and pencil. After a moment's hesitation, he scribbled a few words, then carefully folded and refolded the note. "That should do it." He handed the square to George. "If I'm not back by the time for unmasking, make my excuses."

Jack put his empty glass back on the table and turned to leave.

Appalled, George barred the way. "What the hell should I say? This ball was all but organized for you."

Jack smiled grimly. "Tell them I was called away to deal with a case of mistaken identity."

Disentangling herself from the shepherdess's clinging adoration, Kit beat a hasty retreat, heading for the corner where she'd last seen Amy. When she got there, Amy was nowhere in sight. Drifting back along the room, Kit kept a wary eye out for the shepherdess and Lady Marchmont.

In the end, it was Amy who found her.

"Excuse me."

Kit swung about—Amy's Columbine mask met her eyes. Beneath her own far more concealing mask, Kit smiled in delight and bowed elegantly.

She straightened and saw a look of confusion in Amy's clear eyes.

"I've been asked to deliver this note to you—*Kit!*"

Kit grabbed Amy's arm and squeezed it warningly. "Keep your voice down, you goose! What gave me away?"

"Your eyes, mostly. But there was something else— something about your height and size and the way you hold your hands, I think." Amy's gaze wandered over Kit's sartorial perfection, then dropped to the slim legs perfectly revealed by the clinging knee breeches and clocked stockings. "Oh, Kit!"

Kit felt a twinge of guilt at Amy's shocked whisper.

"Yes, well, that's why no one must know who I am. And for goodness sake, don't color up so, or people will think I'm making improper suggestions!"

Amy giggled.

"And you can't take my arm, either, or come too close. Please think, Amy," Kit pleaded, "or you'll land me in the suds."

Amy dutifully tried to remember that Kit was a youth. "It's very hard when I've known you all my life and know you're not a boy."

"Where's this note?" Kit lifted the small white square from Amy's palm and unfolded it. She read the short message three times before she could believe her eyes.

Kit, Meet me on the terrace as soon as possible, Jack

"Who gave you this?" Kit looked at Amy.

Amy looked back. George had impressed on her she was not to tell the slim youth who had given her the note—but did George know the slim youth was Kit? She frowned. "Don't you know who it's from?"

"Yes. But I wondered who gave it to you—did you recognize him?"

Amy blinked. "It was passed on. I don't have any idea who wrote it." That, at least, was the truth.

Too caught up in the startling discovery that Jack was somewhere near, probably among the guests, Kit missed the less than direct nature of Amy's answer. Forgetting her own instructions, she put a hand on Amy's arm. "Amy, you must promise you'll tell no one of my disguise."

Amy promptly reassured her on that score.

"And I won't, of course, be here for the unmasking. Can you tell Lady Marchmont—and Spencer, too—that I was here, but that I felt unwell and returned home? Tell Spencer I didn't want to spoil his evening." Kit grinned wryly; if she stayed for the unmasking, she'd definitely ruin Spencer's night.

"But what about the note?" asked Amy.

"Oh, that." Kit stuffed the white paper into her pocket. "It's nothing. Just a joke—from someone else who recognized me."

"Oh." Amy eyed Kit and wondered. The male disguise

was almost perfect—if she'd had such difficulty recognizing Kit, who else would?

"And now, Amy dearest, we must part or people will start to wonder."

"You won't do anything scandalous, will you?"

Kit repressed the urge to give Amy a hug. "Of course, I won't. Why, I'm doing everything possible to avoid such an outcome." With a twinkle in her eye, Kit bowed.

With a look that stated she found the act of attending a ball in male attire inconsistent with avoiding scandal, Amy curtsied and reluctantly moved away.

Kit took refuge behind a large palm by the side of the ballroom. Caution dictated she avoid Jack whenever possible, but was it possible? Or wise? If she didn't appear on the terrace, he was perfectly capable of appearing in the ballroom, by her side, in a decidedly devilish mood. No—it was the lesser of two evils, but the terrace it would have to be. After all, what could he possibly do to her on the Lord Lieutenant's terrace?

She scanned the crowd, studying men of Jack's height. There were a few who fit that criterion, but none was Jack. She wondered what mad start had brought him to the ball. Unobtrusively, she made her way to where long windows opened onto the terrace that ran the length of the house.

The night air was crisp, refreshing after the stuffiness of the close-packed humanity within. Kit drew a deep breath, then looked about her. On the terrace, he'd said, but where on such a long terrace?

There were a few couples taking the air. None spared a glance for the slim youth in the midnight blue coat. Kit strolled the flags, looking at the sky, ostensibly taking a breather from the bustle inside. Then she saw Jack, a dim shadow sitting on the balustrade at the far end.

"What the hell are you doing here?" she hissed as she drew near. He was sitting with his back propped against the wall, one booted foot swinging.

Jack, who had watched her approach, was taken aback. "What am *I* doing here? What the devil are *you* doing here, you dim-witted whelp?"

Kit noted the dangerous glitter in the eyes watching her through the slits in his simple black mask. She put up her chin. "That's none of your affair. And I asked first."

Under his breath, Jack swore. He hadn't given his excuse for being at the ball a single thought, so fixated had he been on the necessity of removing Kit from this place of revelations. "I'm here for the same reason you are."

Kit bit back a laugh. The idea of Jack, in disguise, looking over a potential bride from among the local gentry was distinctly humorous. "How did you recognize me?"

Jack's lips twisted in a mocking smile. "Let's just say I'm particularly well acquainted with your manly physique."

Kit's chin rose along with her blush. "What did you want to see me about?"

Jack blinked. What the hell did she imagine he wanted to see her about? "I wanted to make sure that, having now seen how the other half comports itself, you'll realize the wisdom of making yourself scarce, before someone stumbles on your identity."

Behind her mask, Kit's frown was black. The man was insufferable. Who did he think he was, to hand her thinly veiled orders? "I'm perfectly capable of taking care of myself, thank you."

Her clipped tone convinced Jack she was not about to take his suggestion to heart. With an exasperated sigh, he got to his feet. "What sort of chaos do you think you'd cause if that wig slipped loose during one of the dances?" Jack took a step toward her but stopped when she backed away. A quick glance along the terrace revealed a single couple, physically entwined, at the opposite end.

Kit considered insisting Jack sit down again but doubted he'd oblige. He was very good at giving orders and highly resistant to taking any. And in the moonlight on the terrace, his height and bulk were intimidating. Particularly when she didn't want to do what he clearly wanted her to do. She took another step back.

"The ball's over for you, Kit. Time to go home."

Kit took a third step back, then judged the distance between them sufficient to allow her to say: "I've no intention of leaving yet. The person—"

Her words were cut off when Jack's hand clamped over her mouth. In the same instant, his other arm wrapped about her waist and lifted her from her feet. She hadn't even seen him move yet he was now behind her, carrying her to the balustrade. Kit struggled frantically to no effect.

Jack sat on the balustrade, Kit held on his lap, then rolled over the edge. He landed upright in the flower bed six feet below the terrace, Kit safe before him.

Seething with fury, Kit waited for him to release her. When he did, she spun on him. "You misbegotten oaf! How dare you—"

To her surprise, a large hand helped her spin until she was facing away from him again. Her words were cut off again, this time by her own mask, untied, folded then retied over her mouth. Kit's scream of rage was muffled by the black felt. She turned about again, her hands automatically reaching for the mask to drag it away, but Jack moved with her, remaining behind her. He caught her hands in his, his long fingers closing viselike about her wrists, pulling them down and behind her. In stunned disbelief, Kit felt material, Jack's neckerchief most probably, tighten about her wrists, securing them behind her back. Her temper exploded in a series of protests, none of which made it past the gag.

Jack appeared before her. Through the slits in his mask, his eyes gleamed. "You should be on your most ladylike behavior at a ball, you know."

Another volley of muffled protests greeted the sally. With a chuckle, Jack stooped; suddenly, Kit found herself looking down on Lady Marchmont's ruined petunias from a height of four feet. With Kit hoisted over his shoulder like a sack of potatoes, her legs secured under one muscular arm, Jack headed away from the house. Kit's muffled grumbles ceased abruptly when he ran his free hand over the ripe curves of her bottom, nicely positioned for his attentions. A fraught silence ensued. Giving the firm mounds a fond pat, Jack grinned and strode on.

He headed into the shrubbery at the end of the lawn. Taking a path enclosed by high hedges, he cast about for a niche to stow his booty. The walk ended in a fan-shaped bay just beyond the intersection with two other paths. A stone bench with a carved back stood in the bay. Behind it, between the curved hedge and the bench back, Jack found the perfect place to leave his unwilling companion.

Before he lowered Kit, he undid his belt, wrapped it about her knees, and cinched it tight. Then he shrugged her off his shoulder and into his arms.

Kit glared up into his face, silently fuming, her brain seething with the epithets she wished she could hurl at him.

Jack grinned and sat her on the bench. He pulled off his mask and tucked it into his pocket. "I'll have to leave you while I arrange our transportation. How did you get here? You may as well tell me—I'll find out soon enough."

Kit stared back at him.

Jack guessed. "Delia?"

Reluctantly, Kit nodded. A look in the stable would tell him as much.

"Right."

Jack picked her up, and Kit realized just where he was going to leave her. She struggled and shook her head violently, but Jack took no notice. Then she was laid out, full-length on her side, in the shadowy recess behind the bench.

Jack leaned over her. "If you keep quiet, no one will disturb you."

What about spiders? was Kit's agonized thought. She put every ounce of pleading she possessed into her eyes, but Jack didn't notice.

Unperturbed, he added: "I'll be back soon." Then he disappeared from sight.

Kit lay still and pondered her state. Disbelief was her predominant emotion. She was being kidnapped! Kidnapped from the Lord Lieutenant's ball by a man she wasn't at all sure she could trust. He thought she'd muff her lines and bring disaster on her head and, in typically high-handed fashion, had decided to remove her for her own good. There was no doubt in her mind that was how Jack saw it; his actions didn't really surprise her. What did worry her, what was looming as a potential source of panic in her brain, was what he intended doing with her.

Where was he taking her? And what would he do when they got there?

Such questions were not conducive to lying calmly in the dark while being kidnapped. That knowing hand on her bottom had sent a most peculiar thrill all the way to her toes.

In an effort to quell her rising hysteria, Kit forced herself to consider why Jack had been present at the ball. He'd said for the same reason as she. Presumably he'd meant he was here for a lark, just to see how the nobs lived. She could imagine he might do that, just for a laugh—the smugglers' leader at the Lord Lieutenant's ball.

In the shadows before the stable, Jack paused to take stock. Only two grooms sat in the puddle of light thrown by a lamp just inside the open door. The visiting coachmen, his own thankfully included, would be in the kitchen, enjoying themselves. All he had to do was pray that the groom who'd relieved Kit of Delia wasn't one of the two left to mind the stables.

"You two! My horse, quickly." Jack strode forward, habitual command coloring his words.

"Your horse, sir?" The men rose to their feet uncertainly.

"Yes, my horse, dammit! The black Arab."

"Yes sir. Right away, sir."

The alacrity with which the two scrambled up and made their way down the boxes told Jack his prayers had been answered. Delia, however, did not approve of the fumbling attempts of the grooms to saddle her. Jack pushed past them. "Here. Let me."

He'd handled Delia often enough for her to accept his ministrations. As soon as she was saddled, Jack led her to the yard. With a last prayer that Delia would not balk at carrying his weight and the grooms would not notice the stirrups were too short for him, Jack swung into the saddle.

The gods were smiling. Delia sidled and snorted but responded to the rein. With a dismissive nod to the grooms, Jack cantered her out of the yard. As soon as he was out of sight of the stables, he turned the mare toward the shrub-bery.

The first intimation Kit had that she was not alone was a soft giggle, followed by a low, feminine moan. She froze. An instant later, silk skirts rustled as a woman sank onto the stone bench.

"Darling! You really are *too* impetuous." The unknown female was a shady figure, the moonlight fitfully glinting on blond curls and bare shoulders.

"Impetuous?" A man sat beside the woman. His tone suggested pique, rather than pride. "How would you de-scribe your own behavior, making sheep's eyes at that devil Hendon?"

Kit's brows rose. *Devil?*

"Really, Harold! How common. I was doing no such thing. You're just jealous."

"Jealous?" Harold's voice rose.

"Yes, jealous," came the reply. "Just because Lord Hendon's got the most *wonderful* shoulders."

"I don't think it was the man's *shoulders* that impressed you, my dear."

"Don't be crude, Harold." A pause ensued, broken by the woman. "Mind you, I daresay Lord Hendon's equally impressive in other departments."

A growl of frustration came from Harold, and the two silhouettes above Kit fused.

Kit lay in her nook and tried to ignore the snuffles and slurps and funny little moans that came from the couple on the bench. It was enough to put anyone off the business for life. She turned to a contemplation of the new vision of Lord Hendon that was forming in her mind. Perhaps she'd been hasty in thinking him a fusty old crock. Certainly, a devil with impressive shoulders and equally impressive other parts did not fit the image she'd constructed. And the woman on the bench sounded as if she had the experience to know of what she spoke.

Perhaps she should give Lord Hendon a closer look. That had, after all, been her aim in coming to the ball, even if she hadn't had much hope of him then. Now—who knew?

But Jack would soon be back, determined to take her away.

Recalling that she'd yet to satisfy herself as to where Jack was taking her, Kit tested the bonds at her wrists. They gave not at all. She could moan and attract the attention of the couple on the bench, assuming she could make them understand it was not them doing the moaning, but the idea of the explanations she'd face defeated that thought.

Really, if there was any justice in the world, Lord Hendon would stumble upon her and rescue her from Jack and his altogether frightening propensities. Resigned, Kit stared at the small section of sky she could see and wished the couple on the bench would go away.

"Who's that coming?" The woman's voice held a note of panic.

"Where?" The same panic echoed in Harold's tone.

"From the side. See—there."

A long pause ensued. All three figures in the alcove held their breath. Then, "Dammit! It's Hendon." Harold rose and drew the woman to her feet.

"Perhaps we ought to wait for him—he might be lost."

Harold snorted in disgust. "All you females are the same. You'd crawl all over him if he gave you half a chance. But we can't let him catch us together, and how would you explain being here alone? Come on!"

The two figures departed, and Kit was alone.

Lord Hendon was close, but she couldn't even get to her feet. The chances of anyone walking up and looking over the back of the bench to find her were negligible. Kit closed her eyes in exasperation and swore beneath her gag.

Two minutes later, the hedge rustled. Kit opened her eyes to see Jack leaning over her. He lifted her from her bed, then propped her against his hip and bent down to undo his belt. Her legs free, Kit sank onto the bench.

While Jack replaced his belt, Kit stared about her, looking down each of the three paths leading from the bench. Where had Lord Hendon gone?

"Who are you looking for?" Jack asked, puzzled by her obvious search.

Kit glared at him.

With a lopsided grin, Jack reached for the ties of her mask.

Freed of her gag, Kit moistened her lips and glanced around once more. "There was a couple here, sitting on the bench. They left a few minutes ago because they saw Lord Hendon coming. Did you see him?"

Jack's stomach muscles clenched. He shook his head slowly and answered truthfully, "No. I didn't see him." What was it that made him so easy to recognize? The wig covered his hair and he hadn't even been limping.

He watched as Kit glanced around again. What was her interest in Lord Hendon? Had she heard the descriptions and been tantalized? Jack hid a smirk. If that was so, it might make telling her the truth later much easier. Taking her arm, he drew her to her feet. "Come on. I've got Delia."

They walked through the extensive shrubbery, Jack's hand on Kit's elbow. He didn't release her hands—he didn't fancy finding out what retribution she might visit on him if she had the chance.

Kit walked beside him, her insides in a most peculiar knot. The hold on her arm was proprietory, a feeling intensified by the fact that her hands were still tied. She didn't bother asking to be untied. He'd do it if he wished, and she wasn't going to give him the joy of refusing her.

Delia was tethered to a branch just beyond the last hedge. Jack walked Kit to the mare's side, then, to her relief, stepped behind her and untied her hands.

Her relief was short-lived. He untied only one hand, then brought both in front of her and lashed them together again.

"What on earth . . . ?" Kit's incredulous protest hung in the dark.

"You can't ride with your hands tied behind you."

"I can't ride with my hands tied, period."

Jack's lips quirked. "You didn't think I was going to put you on Delia and let you loose, did you?"

Kit swallowed. She hadn't thought that, no. But she wasn't at all sure what he was going to do.

"If I did," Jack continued, untying Delia's reins, "you'd be back at the ball as fast as Delia can go."

Kit could hardly deny that; she kept silent.

Jack pulled off his wig and stuffed it in the saddle pocket. "Up you go." The mare's reins in his hand, he lifted Kit up.

Kit swung her leg over and settled, then realized the stirrups had been lengthened. She stared at Jack. "We can't both ride—she'll never handle the weight."

"She will. We won't get above a canter, if that. Shift forward."

For an instant, Kit stared mutinously at him, but when he planted his foot in the stirrup, she realized that if she didn't do as he said, she'd be squashed. Slammed from behind—again. Even so, although she moved forward until the pommel pressed into her belly, it was a tight fit. Delia sidled but accepted them both. Jack, with his far greater weight, sank into the saddle seat proper and settled his feet in the stirrups. He lifted her, then resettled her against him, a more comfortable position but one every bit as unnerving as she'd feared.

Jack touched the mare's sides and Delia set off. Kit was too fine a rider for him to risk letting her have her feet in the stirrups. Which meant he'd have to endure her curves, riding in front of him, moving against him with every stride the mare took.

Within minutes, his patience was under threat. His jaw ached, a dull echo of the far more potent ache throbbing in his loins. The rubbing rhythm of Kit's firm bottom transformed mere arousal to rock-hard rigidity and reduced his resolution to almost nothing. Jack gritted his teeth harder; there was nothing else he could do. She was an itch he couldn't yet scratch.

Which, for a confirmed rake, was an agonizingly painful predicament.

Chapter 15

In the dark, Kit blushed and wished her mask was still on. With every step Delia took, the rigid column of Jack's manhood pressed into her back. No thought of teasing him entered her head. Instead, she fervently prayed he wouldn't think of teasing *her*. In a fever of irritation at an opportunity lost—when would she get a chance to size up Lord Hendon again?—compounded by the inevitable effect of Jack so close and her consequent fear of what might transpire, Kit fidgeted, wriggled, and squirmed in a hopeless endeavor to move farther away from him.

"Damn it, woman, stay still!"

Jack's growl was every bit as intimidating as the pressure in her back. Kit froze, but within seconds she was uncomfortable again. She had to get her mind off the physical plane. "Where are we going?" They were skirting Marchmont Hall in a northwesterly direction; they could be headed anywhere.

"Cranmer."

"Oh."

Jack frowned. Was that disappointment he heard in her husky voice? Perhaps he should change his plans and take her to the cottage instead. Was she ready to give over her games and take him on? The last question dampened his ardor. Despite her relative calm, he didn't think she was particularly pleased at being removed from the ball. A few more nights would dim the memory sufficiently. Two nights, to be precise.

Kit tried to stay still, but her mind wouldn't let go of the fascinating subject of Jack's anatomy. She wondered if Lord Hendon was better equipped and wished the woman in the shrubbery had been more explicit. Her own experience in the matter was all but nonexistent. But the insistent pressure in the small of her back provoked the most intense speculation.

Luckily for her peace of mind, recollection of Lord Hendon, that unattained object of her daringly scandalous escapade, rekindled her ire. Her brilliantly conceived and faultlessly executed plan to gain firsthand knowledge of his elusive lordship was ending in ignominious retreat, before her quarry had even been sighted. The thought lowered Kit's spirits dramatically. For a full mile, she sat engulfed in a mood perilously close to a petulant sulk.

Jack was taking her home. Gratitude was not the predominant emotion coursing through her veins. What right had he to interfere?

Abruptly, Kit sat bolt upright. No matter what rationale he gave, Jack had no right to meddle in her affairs. Yet here she was, being taken home like a wayward child who'd been caught watching the adults at play. And she'd let him! What was the matter with her? She'd never let anyone, even Spencer, treat her with such high-handedness.

"You really are an arrogant swine!" she exclaimed.

Jerked from salacious dreams, Jack didn't trust his ears. "I beg your pardon?"

"You heard me. If you had any real concern for my welfare, you'd turn Delia around this instant and take me back to the ball. Only now it's too late," Kit ended lamely. "There won't be enough time before the unmasking."

"Time for what?" Jack was puzzled. If she hadn't gone to the ball for a lark, what possible reason could she have?

"I wanted to meet someone—to see what he's like—but you kidnapped me before I got the chance!"

The aggrieved note in Kit's voice was genuine enough to touch a chord of sympathy. And awaken Jack's curiosity.

"You were waiting for a man? Who?"

Beneath her breath, Kit swore. Damn! How had that slipped out?

Despite her surge of temper-assisted courage, Kit hadn't lost her wits. "Never mind—no one you'd know."

"Try me."

Kit's senses pricked. Jack's deep voice was rapidly developing that tone of command she found particularly difficult to resist. "I assure you he's someone with whom you're definitely *not* on a first-name basis."

Jack's attention had focused dramatically. What man had Kit been waiting for and, more importantly, why? What reason could a woman of her ilk have for looking over a man incognito? The answer was so glaringly obvious that Jack wondered why he hadn't thought of it the instant he'd laid eyes on her in the ballroom. Kit, more than twenty if experience was any guide, had recently returned from London, where doubtless her life had been rather fuller. Particularly with respect to male company. She had no lover at present—a fact he'd bet his entire estate on—and was on the lookout for a local candidate. Obviously, she had someone in mind. Someone other than himself.

Then her preoccupation in the shrubbery flooded his mind with a radiant light. "You were waiting for Lord Hendon."

At the bald statement, Kit pulled a horrendous face. "What if I was? It's no concern of yours."

Hysterical laughter bubbled behind Jack's lips; manfully, he swallowed it. Christ—this mission was descending into farce! Should he tell her? What if she didn't believe him? A strong possibility, he had to admit, and one he couldn't readily overcome. *Convincing* her might jeopardize his mission. *Telling* her might jeopardize his mission. Hell! He was going to have to convince her he was a better lover than his reputation made him out to be.

A sudden vision of what his fate might have been, if he hadn't been previously acquainted with Kit and had remained at the ball, threatened his composure. Reappearing in North Norfolk as himself looked set to be even more dangerous than assuming the guise of a smugglers' leader. The local ladies were stalking him with a vengeance—on both sides of the blanket. He could have ended with Kit as his mistress and Lady Marchmont's drab protégé as a wife!

Jack's eyes narrowed. There was every possibility that scenario would still come to pass, but it would be on his terms, not theirs.

A disgusted snort brought his attention back to the slight figure before him. He felt the warmth radiating from her body, separated from his by a handbreadth. Only by exercising the most severe discipline had he resisted the temptation to pull her back against him, curving her body into his.

"Thanks to you, I'll probably never get another chance!" Disgruntled, Kit shifted and immediately remembered what was pressing against her back. Her temper overcame her maidenly reticence. "Damn it! Can't you stop that? Make it go away or something?"

She twisted about to try and get a look at the offending article. Jack's hands clamped about her shoulders and forcibly restrained her.

There was a distinct edge to his words. "There is a way to make it go away. If you don't sit still, you'll be providing it."

The raw desire in his voice petrified Kit into abject obedience. Inwardly, she railed. What was it about Jack that gave him this strange power over her? Not even the most ardent of London's rakes had made her feel like mesmerized prey about to be devoured, inch by slow inch. Her skin was alive, nerve endings flickering in fevered anticipation. He was her predator; every time he threatened, she froze. As if immobility could protect her from his strike! Her instinctive response was so illogical, she'd have laughed if she could have eased the knots in her stomach long enough to do so.

Jack stared at the back of Kit's wig, his frown only partly due to physical discomfort. He could hardly miss the effect his words had had—Kit sat as rigid as a poker, all her alluring warmth gone, an icily disapproving aura cloaking her slender frame. Inwardly, he swore. He wished she'd stop vacillating—first hot, then cold; steamy one minute, frigid the next. Every time he alluded to their inevitable intimacy, she pokered up. Maidenly virtue was certainly not the cause. Which left the irritating conclusion that her strange behavior was her idea of playing vixenish games.

Jack's eyes narrowed. "A word of advice—if you wish to secure Lord Hendon as your protector"—what a joke— she was going to have him as her protector regardless— "you'd be better served by curbing your hoity ways, dropping your manipulative playacting and relying on your *beaux yeux* to take the trick."

Kit's jaw dropped.

It wasn't the shock of why he thought she was interested in Lord Hendon that held her in raging silence—after her initial surprise that struck her as exquisitely funny. But that he had the nerve to suggest the effect he had on her was assumed, presumably to attract him, to suggest that she was *manipulative*, sent her temper into orbit. Her larynx seized; her fingers curled into claws. She'd seen manipulative fe- males aplenty in London—tizzy, dim-witted women with more hair than wit. And she'd laughed over their theatrical and frequently transparent antics with her cousins. To be classed with their kind was the lowest form of insult.

"My manipulative propensities?" she inquired silkily, as soon as she'd regained control of her voice. Her tone would have sent Spencer for the brandy, but Jack had yet to ex- perience her temper unleashed. "That, my good man, is certainly a case of the pot calling the kettle black."

My good man? Jack's scowl was as black as the night sky. "What the devil do you mean by that?" Had he said hoity? The damned woman ought to be on the stage. Now she was pulling rank on him like a bloody duchess!

To Kit's ears, Jack's growl was pure music. She was spoiling for an argument with him, infuriatingly arrogant oaf that he was. "I mean," she said, enunciating carefully, "it hasn't escaped my notice that anytime I'm in danger of winning a point, you wield that . . . that thing between your legs like a bloody sword of Damocles!"

Jack choked. "Winning points? Is that what you call your little exhibition on the yacht the other night?"

Kit shrugged. "That was just curiosity."

"*Curiosity*?" Jack hauled on the reins and brought Delia to a halt. "When you'd been waggling your tail at me for weeks?"

"*Oh!*" Kit shifted about to half face him. "*I* only did that because *you* were acting like a solid lump of cold stone. And *you* call *me* manipulative? Huh!''

Jack had had enough. How could he argue when all she had to do to demolish his arguments was wiggle her hips? He swung his leg over Delia's neck, taking Kit's along with it. Together, they slid to the ground.

Kit shook off his restraining hand and rounded on him. "When it comes to being manipulative, I'm a babe in the woods compared to you! You pretended to be totally indifferent to me, just so I'd feel piqued enough to try to capture your interest. *I'm* not manipulative—*you* are!''

Her accusation passed Jack by. One of her phrases had lodged in his brain, overwhelming it, obscuring all rational thought.

"Indifferent?" Jack stared at her. How the hell did she think he could possibly *pretend* to be indifferent to her? He hurt like hell, and she accused him of . . . He reached for her hands, still bound together with his neckerchief. "Does *that* feel indifferent?''

Kit's gasp at her first overt contact with an aroused male member never made it past her lips. Fascination smothered it. Between her hands, Jack's manhood pulsed, radiating heat through the corded stuff of his breeches. It felt hard, ridged, and curiously alive. Involuntarily, her slender fingers curled around it.

It was Jack who gasped. Unprepared for the outcome of his wild and undisciplined action, let alone her totally unexpected response, he closed his eyes and let his head fall back, hands fisting at his sides while he fought for control. In dawning wonder, Kit glanced up and saw the effect of her touch. Maidenly modesty did not rear its head as, her eyes straining to catch any change in his expression, she slowly slid her fingers up the long shaft until her questing fingertips found the smooth, rounded head.

She heard Jack's breath catch, saw the tension that already held him tighten its grip. His breathing faltered. Instinctively, she reversed direction, following the rigid rod down to its source amid flesh much softer. Her fingers discovered the round fruit within the soft pouches; she felt them tighten.

The groan Jack gave delighted her, thrilled her. Then he moved.

Jack gripped her shoulders between his hands. His mouth found hers unerringly, all manner of wildness unleashed by her bold touch. One arm slid around her back to gather her to him. The other hand slid into her curls, dislodging her wig. It fell to the ground, a pool of shadow in the moonlight, ignored by them both.

For the life of him, Jack couldn't regain control. Years of rakish plunder had hardened his heart; he was always in control of his senses, not the other way around. But her blatant yet oddly innocent touch had reached deep, to find something buried beneath layers of sophistication and stroke it to life, something buried so long ago he'd forgotten how it felt to be totally consumed by passion.

Urgency coursed through his veins. Experience told him the woman in his arms was far from the same state. He bent his considerable talents to rectifying the situation.

Kit was stunned. She couldn't move; her arms were trapped between their bodies, her hands still pressed intimately against him. But she'd forgotten all that. Her lips were on fire. And the heat came from him. She tried to appease the demand in the hard, hot lips pressed to hers; her lips softened but that wasn't enough. Then his tongue flicked along the swollen contours, and she shuddered and yielded the prize he sought.

She expected to be revolted, as she had been before. Instead, as his tongue stroked hers, flames flickered to life, warming her from within. His slow, sensuous plundering of her mouth shook her, draining the strength from her limbs. She wanted desperately to hang on to him but couldn't.

Totally engrossed in her responses, Jack sensed her need. He raised his head and thanked heaven for instinct. Distracted by their argument, he hadn't paid any attention to their direction, yet he'd stopped Delia beneath the spreading branches of a tree, shielded from any chance observer. Disengaging from Kit, he stepped back, lifting her tied hands around his neck. He straightened and pulled her hard against him.

Kit had no time for thought. No sooner had she been released than she was trapped again, this time breast to chest, pressed firmly against Jack from shoulder to thigh. His lips recaptured hers, and his tongue took up where it had left off, frazzling her defenses.

Defenses? What a joke! Her head was swimming, but her body seemed alive. Alive as it had never been before. Kit felt Jack's arms ease from about her and wondered at the warping of her senses. She couldn't see, she couldn't hear. She couldn't have strung two coherent words together. But she could certainly feel. His large hands came to rest just behind her shoulders. For one unnerving moment, she thought he intended to end the kiss. A shudder of relief ran through her as his palms swept her back, down over her waist, tracing her curves with authority. When his hands cradled her bottom, her fevered flesh burned.

With a low growl of satisfaction, Jack shifted his hold and lifted her, taking two steps to set her back against the trunk of the tree, bringing her head level with his. He let her slide slowly down until her feet just touched the ground, one of his thighs wedged firmly between hers.

Fire raged through Kit, leaving her scorched, parched, thirsty. Her lips clung to his, as if the passion in his kiss was her only salvation. Little rivers of flame ran through her veins, pooling in liquid fire between her thighs. She pressed her thighs hard against the muscular column between them but could find no relief. The flames flared briefly, then faded to a glow.

Then Jack's lips left hers. Too weak to complain, she let her head fall back, surprised at the soft moan that escaped her.

"Breathe out."

Without thought, Kit complied.

"More."

With a deft wiggle, Jack freed Kit's breasts from their bands. Her startled gasp was cut off as his lips returned to hers. Her mouth opened to his penetration, a honey-sweet cavern yielded like an offering. He might be in the grip of a raging lust unlike any other he'd ever experienced, but he still took time to savor her while his hands freed her shirt from the waistband, pushing the sides of her coat and waistcoat wide apart, baring her breasts for his ministrations. When his hand closed about one delectable globe, he felt a shudder of pure pleasure pass through her and knew she was his.

Kit was entirely beyond thought, her mind overwhelmed with feeling. Jack's confident possession of her breast brought a murmur of denial to her lips, but he ignored it. She ignored it, too, as his fingers sought her tightening nipple and caressed it to aching hardness. He seemed to know just what her flesh required, far more certainly than she did. When he turned his attention to her other breast, she pressed the soft mound into his palm, seeking relief from the driving need for satisfaction.

Jack drew back slightly, the better to view his conquests. The ivory skin of her breasts sheened like silk beneath his hands; it felt like satin. The rosy peaks were tight little nubs, dusky against the ivory. She had beautiful breasts, not overly large but firm and perfectly rounded. One strawberry-tipped peak beckoned; he dipped his head to taste it, drawing the succulent fruit into his mouth, swirling his tongue about the sensitive tip.

Kit lost the fight to stifle her gasps. Her fingers tangled in Jack's hair, pulling long strands free of the riband at his neck. He suckled, and her fingers tightened on his skull. God! She hadn't known she could *feel* so intensely. Her breathing was ragged, desperate yet disregarded. Feeling was all.

Desire drumming heavy in his veins, Jack released her breast. His lips returned to hers while his fingers sought her waistband.

Relief flooded Kit. Jack seemed content to nibble tantalizingly at her lips, allowing her mind to struggle free of the drugging effect of his kisses. She tried to ignore the peculiar hot ache deep within her, called to life by his passion, quietly building even though his own ardor seemed to have abated. Thank goodness he'd stopped! Her sense of right and wrong was hopelessly compromised.

What had Amy said? The kiss had come first—Jack had certainly cleared that hurdle. She'd willingly prop up the tree for the rest of the night if he'd only continue kissing her as before, deep, hot, and searing. What happened next? Her breasts—Amy had been right about that, too. Jack's hands on her breasts had been a purely sensual experience; she now understood that hitherto inexplicable female tendency to allow men to fondle their breasts. Kit shuddered at the memory of Jack's mouth on her nipple. Desperate to remember the next stage in Amy's scheme of loving, she pushed aside the recollection. What came next?

Whatever it was, Kit doubted she should wait to see if Jack would attempt it. Even her wilder self agreed it was time to take her newfound knowledge and run. In between savoring the heady taste of her teacher, warm, male, and aroused, she fought to regain some degree of control, some power to act. Jack had already gone too far, but at least he'd ceased his scandalously bold caresses. He'd drawn her into deep waters; it was time to retreat to safer shores.

With an effort, Kit gathered her wits and drew her lips from Jack's light, lingering kiss. He let her go without complaint, his head immediately dipping to her breast, tracing a path of fire to one burgeoning nipple.

Kit shook her head; words of firm denial formed on her lips.

They exploded in a long-drawn, half-sighed "*Ja-ack!*" of protest as she felt his palm flatten possessively over her naked stomach.

Kit's eyes flew wide. While she'd been gathering her wits, he'd been opening her breeches! Jack suckled on one nipple, and her fingers clenched in his hair, holding his head to her breast as her hips tilted into his shockingly intimate touch.

And then things got worse.

His long fingers slipped into the silky curls between her thighs.

Kit moaned and struggled to find the strength to break free of the conflagration of her senses. He was igniting it, and she couldn't stop the flames. She didn't even want to anymore.

But she had to make him stop.

His fingers parted her soft flesh and pressed gently.

Kit forgot about stopping. Pleasure streaked through her, sharp and tangible. His fingers set up a deliberate circular motion, first one way, then the other. His lips pulled hard on her nipple and a bolt of white-hot desire shot from her breast to the point where his fingers pulsed flame through her flesh.

His name was on her lips, a soft sigh he didn't mistake. Kit felt the low rumble of his satisfaction. Then his lips returned to hers. It never entered her head to deny him—she welcomed him, lips parting to receive him. She felt his weight as he pressed against her, the hard muscles of his chest comforting her aching breasts.

The material of her breeches strained across her hips as his hand pressed between her thighs. Mindlessly, she parted them further, wordlessly inviting the intimate contact. When one long finger slid slowly into her, she shuddered. Amy's words blossomed in her brain. Hot and wet. Kit knew then. She was hot and wet. Hot and wet for Jack.

Her every sense was centered on his finger, on his slow, inexorable invasion. Kit felt molten, her nerves liquefied. Heat beat in steady pulses through her. She tried to break free of his kiss, to draw breath, but he wouldn't allow it. Instead, his tongue set up a slow, repetitive dance of thrust and retreat. Inside her, his finger picked up the rhythm.

Beyond thought, beyond any sense of shame, Kit responded to the building beat, her body twisting and lifting in his intimate embrace, opening to his deepening caress.

Having made certain of his victory, Jack turned his mind to its accomplishment. And hit a snag. Several snags.

Three seconds of rational thought were sufficient to make clear the enormity of his problems. The ground about them was uneven and strewn with flints—an impossible proposition, even if they had a blanket, which they didn't. He didn't know what sort of tree they were under, but its bark was thick, rough, and sharp. If he took her against it, it would shred her soft skin. But the truly insurmountable difficulty he faced was her breeches. Tight-fitting inexpressibles, they clung to her skin as if she'd been poured into them. He was well accustomed to getting himself out of such attire—they peeled off his form readily enough. They didn't peel off Kit at all. He'd opened the flap to caress her. Now he needed far greater access, but try as he might, no amount of tugging seemed to shift them from her curvaceous hips.

Jack moaned deep in his throat and slanted his mouth over Kit's, deepening the kiss in an effort to deny the truth. Dammit! She was so hot—hot and ready for him. His finger slid effortlessly along her heated channel, slick with the evidence of her arousal. The urge to scorch himself in that slippery heat was overwhelming.

He was too well acquainted with the female body to miss her increasing tension. He didn't have time to stop and get her to assist; he couldn't afford to let her cool. He'd pushed her well along the route to fulfillment—impossible to draw back now.

Frustrated beyond measure, pulled by an urgency outside his control, Jack released his manhood. It sprang free, erect, engorged. He withdrew his hand from between Kit's thighs, ignoring her helpless moan. With a yank, he gained as much leeway as her tight breeches would allow. It wasn't enough.

With an anguished groan, Jack slipped his throbbing staff into the furnace between her silken thighs. If that was to be the only piece of heaven offered him that night, he was in too great a need to scorn it.

Kit groaned into his mouth. She had no doubt what the pressure that had replaced his hand was. But she didn't care. No—she did care—she wanted it there. Even more—she wanted him inside her. He drew back and thrust into the soft hollow between her thighs. In their curious, fully upright position, he could not penetrate her, yet she felt the swollen head of his staff nudge her soft center. Instinctively, she clamped tight about his hard smoothness, dragging her lips free to draw a shuddering breath.

Jack's head was bowed, his temple pressed to her curls, his breathing harsh in her ear. Kit felt him withdraw. She moaned her disapproval and tilted her hips, trying to draw him back. To her relief, he returned, his hips thrusting, the rigid column of his manhood parting her slick, swollen flesh and nudging deeper, the sudden friction sending shafts of pure delight coursing through her. With his next thrust, a furnace opened deep. Kit's hands clenched in Jack's hair; her body strained against his.

Then it happened.

Ripples of tension gripped her, surrounding and compressing her heat until it exploded, sending molten waves of sensation surging along every vein. Indescribable excitement gripped her, and her soul burned, consuming her overloaded senses. Caught on the crest of their passion, abandoned to feeling, she clung to Jack, his name soundless on her lips.

The flames fell and spread their heat through her flesh. Kit tilted her hips, instinctively seeking his fulfillment as part of hers.

Equally instinctively, Jack took the extra inch she offered him to penetrate more deeply into her slick heat. He gasped as the scalding softness of her swollen flesh engulfed him. Yet the ultimate caress of her body remained beyond his reach. His muscles quivered as frustration fleetingly impinged on rampant desire. His chest labored as he struggled for control. The hot honey of her passion poured over him; the faint, pulsing ripples of her release caressed him. Jack forgot about control. He withdrew and thrust again, over and over. The wave of his release hit him, crashing him into pleasured oblivion.

He'd missed seeing her eyes when she'd climaxed.

Jack's first thought on recovering from his exertions seemed perfectly rational. Next time, he'd make sure he satisfied his curiosity. Right now, he was too pleased with himself to allow any quibbles to dim his mood. Despite the limitations, the experience had been one to remember.

He glanced down at Kit. The aftershocks of her remarkable climax had died, but she was still dazed. Aware of the etiquette demanded of such intimate moments, even in such extraordinary circumstances, Jack carefully withdrew from the soft hollow between her thighs.

Kit's consciousness made contact with reality as Jack

settled her coat lapels in place. She stiffened, her eyes blinking wide. Had she dreamed it?

One glance at Jack's face dispelled that faint hope. His lips looked as if they couldn't stop smiling. Smugly. Kit felt faint. Her clothes were back in place, fastened, all except her bands, which he'd left about her waist.

She tried to ignore the dampness between her thighs.

Luckily, Jack took charge—without being asked, naturally. He settled her on Delia and then they were heading westward once more, at a walk.

The walls of Cranmer Hall were taking shape on the horizon before Kit came to grips with what had happened. She and Jack had been intimate. The thought sent her mind into a dizzying panic, only slightly ameliorated by the startling conclusion that, despite all, she was still a virgin. He hadn't breached her, of that she was certain. Years before, her grandmother had instructed her in the bald facts of wifely duty; Kit had felt no pain or discomfort—not the slightest. Neither had she felt any awkwardness or shyness in letting Jack caress her as he had, shockingly intimate though that had been, nor of letting him push that thing of his between her thighs—not at the time. Now, she was positively sunk in guilt, wallowing in the outraged modesty she hadn't felt while in his arms, kissed into complaisance. How could she have let it happen?

Easily, came the languid reply. *And you'd do it again, and more, if he wanted you.*

Kit smothered her groan and leaned her head back against Jack's shoulder, too exhausted to deny her wilder self's outrageous assertion. At least the comfort of her riding position had improved. Jack had untied her hands—afterward, damn him. There'd been moments under that tree when she'd have killed to have her hands free. Now they rested, crossed, on the pommel while Jack managed the reins. Her body fit snugly into his, the curve of her back settled into his midriff, his thighs on either side of hers, supporting her. The pressure in his loins had disappeared; she'd apparently been successful in taking care of that. There was nothing in their contact to cause alarm. She could fall asleep, if she wished.

Delia plodded on.

"Which way to the stables?"

Jack's quiet whisper brought Kit blinking awake. Familiar landmarks rose out of the dark. They were in a dip just behind the Hall. For a moment, she leaned against Jack's chest, savoring the hard warmth, wishing irrationally that his arms would come around and hold her. At the thought, panic pushed her upright. "I take Delia in through the paddock. I have to jump the fence."

The figure behind her was still, then said, "All right. I'll leave you here."

One hard hand closed on her waist. Kit stiffened, but Jack just needed her as balance as he swung down from the saddle. He handed her the reins. "Wait while I adjust the stirrups."

Shortening the straps so the stirrups sat once more in the groove they'd worn in the thick leather, Jack forced his mind to function—not an easy task in its present, slightly intoxicated state. If he was any judge of such experiences, what had happened beneath the tree should whet the appetite of a woman who was currently forced to a proscribed existence.

Yet there was something in Kit's response that warned him not to take her for granted. Her silence could simply be due to tiredness; her climax had been particularly strong. But there was more to it than that. Perhaps she was piqued he'd found her so easy to tame? Safely hidden by the dark, Jack grinned fleetingly. He had a premonition that she might be reluctant to yield more than she had already, not without a further concession from him. And at present he couldn't offer her anything, not even his name.

Whatever, two nights from now she would spend some time in his bed. And he'd stake his hard-won reputation that afterward, she wouldn't walk away from him with her pert nose in the air.

Jack straightened and pulled his wig from the saddle pocket. He stepped back. "I'll see you tomorrow at the Old Barn."

Excuses jostled on Kit's tongue, but she swallowed them. Four weeks she'd agreed to—four weeks he'd get. With a curt nod, she wheeled Delia and put her over the fence.

Cantering up the steep paddock to the stable, Kit resisted the temptation to look back. He'd be standing where she'd left him, hands on hips, watching her. She'd turn up tomorrow, and if they were doing a cargo, the night after that. But from then on, she'd give Captain Jack a wide berth. Distance was imperative. She knew the dangers now; there could be no excuse.

When the dark cavern of the stable had swallowed Kit, Jack turned and headed north. The moon sailed free of its fettering clouds and lit his way. Miles ahead, Castle Hendon awaited its master, his bed fitted with silk sheets, cool and unwarmed. Jack's lips quirked. He had an ambition to see Kit writhing in ecstasy on that bed, her curls a flaming aureole about her head, those other curls he'd touched but hadn't seen, burning him. He'd counted the nights ever since he'd first touched her and known his senses weren't playing him false. Now, she was damn near an obsession.

As his swinging stride ate the miles, his mind remained on the woman who'd captured his senses. She'd never be just another mistress—those who'd come before her had never intrigued him as she did. From her, he wanted much more than mere physical gratification, despite that every time he set eyes on her he was driven by a primal urge to bury himself in her heat. The need to possess her went much further than that.

He wanted to bring her to climax again and again. He wanted her cries of satisfaction to ring in his ears. He needed to know she was close and safe at all times.

Jack frowned. He'd never felt like that about a woman before.

Chapter 16

The slap of the waves against the fishing boat's hull was drowned by the roar of the surf. Thigh deep in the tide, Jack flexed his shoulders, then reached for the barrel Noah held out. With the keg balanced on his shoulder, he waded to the shore, to where the ponies were being loaded.

Jack waited for the men lashing the barrels to the ponies' saddles to take the heavy keg, then turned to survey his enterprise.

They had the routine down pat. Even as he looked, the men in the emptied boats bent to the oars and the six hulls slipped back out through the surf, off to find any fish they could before heading home. The last kegs were being lashed in place, then the parcels of lace, stacked against a rock nearby, would be balanced on top and secured.

As the lace was brought up, Jack let his gaze rise to the cliff overlooking the beach. He'd stationed Kit on the eastern point, but had no idea where she actually was. Doubtless the stubborn woman had made good her threat and moved farther west. She'd attended the meeting in the Old Barn the previous night, slipping in late to stand in the shadows at the back. Immediately after·he'd finished detailing tonight's run, she'd vanished.

He hadn't been surprised. But he'd be damned if he let her escape him tonight.

* * *

Two miles to the west, Kit halted Delia. She'd gone far enough. Time to turn back if she was to meet Jack at the cliff top as ordered. But still she sat, staring, unseeing, westward.

Her stomach was tied in knots. Her nerves wouldn't settle, fluttering like butterflies every time Jack's image hove on her mental horizon. His ideas for tonight, as far as she'd allow herself to imagine them, were pure madness, but what she could do to avoid them was more than she could fathom.

She would have to see him, that much was plain. Was there any chance she could talk her way free of his "later"? His words on the ride back from the ill-fated masquerade made it clear he'd read her teasing as encouragement. Kit grimaced. She simply hadn't realized how much she affected him. Whatever his reasons for reticence, she'd fallen into the trap.

With a tight little sigh, she plotted her course. She would have to explain. As a gently reared woman, she couldn't— simply could not—consider the alternative.

Light drizzle started to fall, misting Delia's breath. Kit's fingers were tightening on the reins to draw the mare about when she heard a jingle.

Followed by another.

Her senses pricked. The hairs on her nape rose. She'd heard that sound before. The heavier clink of a stirrup confirmed her deductions. An instant later she saw them, a whole troop, advancing at a steady canter.

Kit didn't wait to see more. She took the first path she found down to the sands and let Delia's reins fall. Her cheeks stung by the flying black mane, she clung to the mare's neck as the sand sped beneath the black hooves.

Automatically checking the ropes holding the precious cargo in place, Jack passed down the pony train. He'd made sure Kit wouldn't disappear like a wraith the instant the last pony gained the cliff top by the simple expedient of ordering her to meet him at the head of the path up from the beach—in the presence of half a dozen men. She wasn't a fool. She wouldn't risk the instant suspicion that failure to comply with such explicit orders would generate.

He was nearing the end of the pony train, and the men at its head were already mounting, when the reverberation of flying hooves on firm-packed sand brought him instantly alert.

Out of the night, a black horse materialized. Kit. Riding hard. From the west.

By the time she was slowing, so as not to spook the ponies, Jack was already running to the head of the train, where Matthew waited, mounted, Champion's reins in his hand. The big stallion was shifting, excited by the precipitous arrival of the mare, his huge hooves stamping the sand. Jack threw himself into the saddle as Kit pulled up before him, Delia pawing the air.

"Revenue. From Hunstanton," Kit gasped. "But they're still a mile or more away."

Jack stared at her. A mile or more? She'd been reinterpreting his orders with a vengence! He shook off the urge to shake her—he'd deal with her insubordination later and enjoy it all the more.

He turned to Shep. "Stow the stuff in the old crypt. Then clear everyone. You're in charge." The train had been intended for the Old Barn, but that was impossible now. Kit had given them one chance to get safely away; they had to take it. "The four of us"—his nod indicated Matthew and George as well as Kit—"will draw the Revenue off toward Holme. With luck, they won't even know you exist."

Shep nodded his understanding. A minute later, the train moved off, disappearing into the dunes cloaking the eastern headland. They'd go carefully, wending their way under maximum cover close by Brancaster before slipping south to the ruined church. Jack turned to Kit. "Where, exactly?"

"On the cliff, riding close to the edge."

Her voice, strained with excitement, showed an alarming tendency to rise through the register. Jack hoped George wouldn't hear it. "Stay by me," he growled, praying she'd have the sense to do so.

He touched his heels to Champion's sides and the stallion was off, heading for the path to the cliff top. Delia followed, with Matthew's and George's mounts close behind.

They swung inland to slip into the protection of the belt of trees running parallel to the cliff's edge, a hundred yards or more from it. They didn't have to go far to find the Revenue.

In the shadow of a fir, Jack stood by Champion's head, his hand clamped over the grey's nose to stifle any revealing whinny, and watched the Revenue men under his command thunder past like a herd of cattle without thought for stealth or strategy. He shook his head in disbelief and exchanged a pained look with George. As soon as the squad had passed, they remounted.

A sudden hoot from beside her startled Kit as she was settling her boot in the stirrup. She sat bolt upright, only to hear a long-drawn birdcall answer from a few feet away. Then Jack struck his knife blade to his belt buckle, muttering unintelligibly. George and Matthew responded similarly. Kit stared at them.

The retreating drum of the hooves of the Revenue's horses came to a sudden, somewhat confused halt. Matthew and George continued with their noises while Jack urged Champion to the edge of the trees. The muffled din continued until Jack turned and hissed: "Here they come."

George and Matthew held silent, watching Jack's upraised hand. Then his hand dropped. "Now!"

Amid cries of "The Revenue!" they spilled from the trees, heading west. Jack glanced about to find Delia's black head level with his knee, Kit crouched low over the mare's neck. His teeth gleamed in a smile. It felt good to be flying before the wind with her at his side.

They made as much noise as a fox hunt in full cry. Initially. When it was clear all the Revenue Officers were in dogged pursuit, floundering behind them, Jack pulled up in the lee of a small hill. Matthew and George brought their mounts to plunging halts beside him; Kit drew Delia to a slow halt some yards farther on. Her muffler had slipped slightly; she didn't want George or Matthew to see her face. The drizzle was intensifying into rain. A drip from the damp curls clinging to her forehead coursed down to the tip of her nose. Raising her head, she looked east. Low clouds, purple and black, scudded before the freshening wind.

Jack's voice reached her. "We'll split up. Kit and I have the faster horses. You two head south. When it's safe, you can separate and go home."

"Which way will you head?" George shook the water from his hat and crammed it back on.

Jack's smile was confident. "We'll head west on the beach. It won't take long to lose them."

With a nod, George turned and, followed by Matthew, slipped into the trees lining the road on the south. They couldn't head off until the Revenue were drawn away—the fields were too open and clearly visible from the road.

The squad of Revenue men were still out of sight on the other side of the hill. Jack nudged Champion close to Delia. "There's a path to the beach over there." He pointed. Kit squinted through the rain. "Where that bush hangs over the cliff. Take it. I'll follow in a moment."

Kit resisted the impulse to say she'd wait. His tone was not one to question. She kicked Delia to a canter, swiftly crossing the open area to the cliff's edge. At the head of the path, she paused to look behind her. The Revenue came around the hill and saw them—she at the cliff, Jack riding hard toward her. He'd dallied to make sure the troop didn't miss them. With a howl, the Revenue took the bait. Kit sent Delia to the sands, reaching the foot of the path as Champion landed with a slithering thump a few yards away. She'd forgotten that trick of his.

"West!"

At the bellowed order, Kit turned Delia's head in that direction and dropped the reins. Primed by the tension, the mare obediently went straight to a full gallop, leaving Champion in her wake. Kit grinned through the raindrops streaking her face. Soon enough, the thud of Champion's hooves settled to a steady beat just behind her, keeping pace between her and their pursuers.

Behind Kit, Jack watched her flying coattails, marveling at the effortless ease of her performance. He'd never seen anyone ride better—together, she and Delia were sheer magic in motion. She held the mare to a long-strided gallop, a touch of pace in reserve. Jack glanced behind him. The Revenue were dwindling shapes on the sand, outdistanced and outclassed.

Jack looked forward, opening his mouth to yell to Kit to turn for the cliff. A blur of movement at the top of the path, the last path before they passed onto the west arm of the anvil-shaped headland above Brancaster, caught his eye. He shook the water from his eyes and stared through the rain.

Hell and confound the man! Tonkin had not only disobeyed orders and come east, but he'd had the sense to split his men into two. He and Kit weren't leading the Revenue west—they were being herded west. Tonkin's plan was obvious—push them onto the narrow western headland, then trap them there, a solid cordon of Revenue Officers between them and the safety of the mainland.

Kit, too, had seen the men on the cliff; slowing, she glanced behind her. Champion did not pause; Jack took him forward to keep pace between Delia and the cliff. "Keep on!" he yelled in answer to the question in Kit's eyes.

"But—"

"I know! Just keep going west."

Kit glared but did as he said. The man was mad—all very well to keep on, but soon they'd run out of land. She could just make out the place ahead where the cliff abruptly ended. There was only sea beyond it.

Unconcerned by such matters, Jack kept Champion at a full gallop and pondered his new insight into Sergeant Tonkin. Obviously, he'd underestimated the man. He still found it hard to believe Tonkin had had wit enough to devise a trap, let alone put it into practice. It wasn't going to work, of course—but what could one expect? Tonkin's net had a very large hole which was one hole too many to trap Captain Jack.

A crack of thunder came out of the east. The heavens opened; rain hit their backs in a drenching downpour. Jack laughed, exhilaration coursing through him. The rain would hinder Tonkin; it would be morning before the sodden Revenue men could be sure the prey had flown their coop.

Kit heard his laughter and stared.

Jack caught her look and grinned. They were still riding

hard directly west. The tide was flowing in fast, eating away
the beach. On their left, the cliff swept up to a rocky outcrop, then fell to a rock-strewn point. The beach ran out.
Kit pulled up. Champion slowed, then was turned toward
the rocks.

"Come on." Jack led, setting Champion to pick his way
across the rocky point, waves washing over his heavy
hooves. Delia followed, hooves daintily clopping.

Around the point lay a small, sandy cove. Beyond,
sweeping southeastward, the beaches on the southern side
of the headland gleamed, a pale path leading back to the
mainland. But the Revenue would be skulking somewhere
in the murk, waiting.

In the lee of the cliffs, the rain fell less heavily. Jack
pulled up in the cove; Kit halted Delia alongside Champion.
She sat catching her breath, staring through the rain at the
headland on the opposite side of the small bay.

"Well? Are you ready?"

Kit blinked and turned to Jack. "Ready?" The sight of
his smile, a melding of excitement, laughter and pure devilry, set her nerves atingle. She followed his gaze to the
other side of the bay. "You're joking." She made the
words a statement.

"Why? You're already soaked to the skin—what's a little more water?"

He was right, of course; she couldn't get any wetter.
There was, however, one problem. "I can't swim."

It was Jack's turn to stare, memories of their night of
near disaster on the yacht vivid in his mind. In a few pithy
phrases, he disabused her mind of any claim to sanity, adding his opinion of witless women who went on boats when
they couldn't swim. Kit listened calmly, well acquainted
with the argument—it was Spencer's standard answer to
her desire to sail. "Yes, but what are we going to do now?"
she asked, when Jack ground to a halt.

Jack scowled, narrowed eyes fixed on the far shore. Then
he nudged Champion closer to Delia. Kit felt his hands
close about her waist.

"Come here."

She didn't have much choice. Jack lifted her across and

perched her on Champion's saddle in front of him. It was a tight fit; Kit felt the butt of Jack's saddle pistol press into one thigh. He took Delia's reins and tied them to a ring on the back of Champion's saddle, then his belt was in his hands. "Hold still." Peering at her waist, he threaded his belt through hers.

"What are you doing?" Kit twisted about, trying to see.

"Dammit, woman! Hold still. You can wriggle your hips all you like later but not now!"

The muttered words reduced Kit to frozen obedience. *Later.* With all the excitement, she'd forgotten his fixation about later. She swallowed. The moment hardly seemed ripe to start a discussion on that subject. He'd been half-aroused before she'd wriggled; now . . .

"I'm just making a loop so I can catch hold of you if you slip off."

The observation did nothing for Kit's confidence. "*If* I slip off?"

Jack straightened before she could think of any other route of escape. "Hold tight to the pommel. I'll swim alongside once we're in the water." With that, he set his heels to Champion's sides.

Both horses took to the water as if swimming across bays in the dead of night was a part of their daily routine. Kit envied them their dull brains. Hers was frantic. She clung to the pommel, both hands frozen and fused to the smooth outcrop. As the first wave lapped her legs, she felt Jack's comforting bulk, warm and solid behind her, evaporate. Swallowing her protest, she turned her head and found him bobbing in the water alongside her.

"Lean forward as if you were riding hard."

Kit obeyed, relieved to feel the weight of his hand in the small of her back.

A moment later, a wave crashed over her, drenching her with icy water. She shrieked and came up sputtering. Instantly, Jack was beside her, his face alongside hers, his arm over her back, one large hand spread over her ribs, and her breast. "Sssh. It's all right. I won't let you go."

The reassurance in his tone washed through her. Kit relaxed enough to register the position of his hand but was in no mood to protest. If she could have got any closer to him she would have, regardless of any retribution later.

The tide rushed through the narrow neck and into the bay. It carried them forward like flotsam and, in a short time, disgorged them on the sands of the mainland. As soon as Champion's hooves scraped the bottom, Jack swung up behind Kit. She heaved a sigh of relief and decided not to take exception to the muscular arm that wound about her waist, pulling her back tightly, tucking her into safety against him.

Jack countered the stallion's surge up the beach, holding him back until the mare's shorter legs reached the sand. As soon as they left the surf, he pushed Champion into a canter, heading for the closest path off the sand and the relative safety of the trees.

Kit held her peace and waited for Jack to come to a halt and set her down. But he didn't. Instead he steered Champion straight through the trees bordering the cliff and struck south through the teeming rain. Disoriented, Kit took a few minutes to work out where he was headed. Then her eyes flew wide. He was taking her straight to the cottage!

"Jack! Stop! Er . . ." Kit struggled to think of a pressing reason for a sudden departure, but her mind froze.

Champion's stride didn't falter. "You've got to get out of those clothes as soon as possible," Jack said.

Paralysis set in. Why as soon as possible? Wouldn't some other time do? For the life of her, Kit couldn't think of any words to counter his firm assertion. She decided to ignore it. "I can ride perfectly well. Just stop and let me get on Delia."

The only answer he gave was to turn Champion onto the road to Holme. A few minutes later, they reached the path that led south to the cottage. Fear loosened Kit's tongue. "Jack—"

"Dammit, woman! You're soaked. You can't ride all the way to Cranmer like that. And in case you hadn't noticed, the storm's about to break."

Kit hadn't noticed. A quick glance around his shoulder showed thunderheads lowering through the gloom. Even as she watched, a bolt of lightning streaked earthward. Kit stopped arguing and snuggled back into the warmth of Jack's chest. She hated thunderstorms; more importantly, so did Delia. Yet the mare seemed unperturbed, pacing steadily beside Champion. Perhaps she should ask Jack to ride home with her. No—they might have to stop under a tree.

There was no denying she could not afford a chill she couldn't explain. But what on earth was she to do when she got to the cottage? The thought focused her mind on what had hitherto proved the most reliable reflection of Jack's state of mind. To her surprise, she couldn't feel anything—there was none of the firm pressure she'd come to recognize, despite the fact that she was wedged more tightly against him than ever before. What was wrong?

Then the import of his words registered. He'd only meant she had to get out of her wet clothes, not that . . . Kit blushed. To her shame, she realized she felt no relief at her discovery, only the most intense disappointment. The truth hit her, impossible to deny. Her blush deepened.

Why not admit you wouldn't mind trying it with him? What have you got to lose? Only your virginity—and who are you saving that for? You know Jack would never hurt you—a bruise or two maybe, but nothing intentional. You'll be safe with him. Why not take the plunge? And what more perfect night for it—you know you hate trying to sleep during storms.

Kit remained silent, battling her demons.

Despite her beliefs, Jack's mind was well and truly occupied with her forthcoming seduction. But he was freezing, too. They both needed to get out of the rain-soaked wind whipping across the land. The double meaning in his first statement had been entirely intentional—he couldn't have planned this night better. He was looking forward to peeling Kit's wet clothes from her and, after that, he knew just how to warm them both. What he was planning would eradicate any residual chill.

There was no better way to while away a storm.

Chapter 17

The cottage loomed out of the dark, squat and solid, tucked into the protection of the bank behind it. Jack rode straight to the stable. He dismounted, then lifted Kit down. "Go in. The fire should be lit; there's wood beside it and towels in the wardrobe. I'll take care of Delia."

Kit stared through the darkness but couldn't make out his expression. Dully, she nodded and headed for the cottage door. His last comment was obviously intended to let her know she'd have time to get undressed and dried before he came in. Doubtless there'd be a robe or something in the wardrobe for her to wrap herself in. Presumably, getting into her breeches the other night had slaked Jack's lust, at least for the present. Either that, or the drenching had doused his ardor. Kit grimaced and reached for the latch.

The main room was lit by the red glow of a smoldering log. With a sigh, Kit fell to her knees on the mat in front of the fireplace. The wood was in a basket to one side. She laid logs on the flames, then sat back and watched them catch. The warmth slowly thawed her chilled muscles. With another sigh, she struggled to her feet.

There were towels on the top shelf of the wardrobe. Kit drew down an armful of blessedly dry linen and went to the fire. Leaving the pile on the end of the bed, she spread one towel on the mat, then pulled up a chair and proceeded to struggle out of her wet clothes. Hat, muffler, and coat she draped on the chair. She sat and pulled off her boots, then knelt on one end of the towel and, after one wary glance at the door, pulled her shirt over her head.

It was a battle to free her shoulders and arms, but eventually she managed it. Her bands were even more trouble, with the knot pulled tight and the sodden material clinging to her skin. She ran through her repertoire of curses before the knot finally gave way. It was a relief to unwind the yards of material and free her breasts.

Kit dropped the long band on the towel and sat back on her heels, letting the fire chase away her chills. Reaching back, she tugged a towel from the pile. Bending forward, she draped the towel over her neck, running the ends over her curls, scattering droplets into the fire. Once her hair had stopped dripping, she dried her arms and back, then started on her breasts.

The door opened.

Kit turned with a gasp, the towel clutched to her chest.

Jack stood in the doorway, looking for all the world as if he'd just forgotten what he'd come in to do. A deceptive expression. He'd come in to seduce Kit Cranmer, and there wasn't anything capable of making him forget that. His stunned look was due to the vision before him—Kit, bare to the waist, kneeling before his fire, her curls burnished by the flames. Kit, with wide eyes darkening from amethyst to violet, the towel clutched to her chest totally failing to conceal the twin peaks of her breasts jutting provocatively on either side, the long line of her legs revealed by her wet breeches.

Slowly, Jack shut the door, his eyes never leaving the woman silhouetted by the flames. Without turning, he slid the bolt home. He crossed to the table and laid his pistol down before shrugging out of his coat.

Held immobile by his silver gaze, Kit watched, helplessly transfixed. When he pulled his shirt over his head, she blinked free only to be mesmerized by the play of light over the muscles of his chest. She didn't notice him pause to release his hair, but it was swinging free, brown streaked with gold, brushing his shoulders, when he knelt on the towel beside her.

His hands closed on her bare shoulders. Gently, he drew her to face him.

Kit looked deep into eyes of brightest silver burnished with passion. Desire burned, a steady flame in their depths. Her mouth went dry. She shuddered, swept by a force beyond her experience.

Jack watched burgeoning passion turn Kit's eyes to glowing purple. When her tongue came out to moisten her lips, he judged it safe to reach for the towel. She relinquished it without protest. He glanced down at the treasure now completely revealed and watched as, caressed by his ardent gaze, her nipples crinkled tight.

With a slow smile of satisfaction, and anticipation, Jack returned his gaze to her face, noting her wide eyes and the lips already parted for his kiss.

Kit could barely breathe as Jack brought his hands up, skimming the contours of her neck, to cradle her face, his long fingers sliding into her curls. For a moment, he paused, his eyes holding hers, an unanswered question in their silvered depths.

She wanted this, she realized. Every bit as much as he did. In that instant, Kit made her decision. She put aside all the precepts of twenty-two years of training and reached for her heart's desire.

As Jack bent his head, she rose on her knees to meet him.

Jack took her mouth in a burning kiss, slanting his head as she opened to his penetration. Kit braced her hands against his upper chest and leaned into his caress. In seconds, her blood was alight, ignited by his fire.

Thank God her hands were free—free to roam the warm expanse of male skin, to caress the bands of hard muscle, to tangle in the springy brown hair. Kit's questing fingers found a hidden nipple. To her delight, she felt it harden to her touch. Hands spread, she explored the ridges of muscle above his waist before moving on to his broad back. Her hands found water. He was still wet.

Kit drew back from their duel of tongues. Jack's brow quirked. He reached for her, but she stayed him, one small hand braced against his chest as she reached for a towel.

A droplet of water fell from his hair and trickled, unheeded, down his chest. Kit saw it. She smiled, then leaned forward and licked it off. Jack shuddered and closed his eyes, his hands fisting by his sides.

Kit's seductive smile grew. She set to work drying his chest, working the towel in small circles, moving with a deliberate lack of haste. She stood and moved behind him to towel his back.

Jack sat on his heels and let her, held in thrall by her sensuous attentions. The tantalizing play of the towel would have melted a statue. Or at least sent it up in flames. His body was nearing that state.

When she reappeared before him, he caught her hands and drew her down to her knees again, taking the towel and tossing it aside. But he didn't pull her into his arms. He reached for her breasts, taking one luscious mound in each hand, squeezing gently, then circling the taut nipples with his thumbs.

Kit's eyes closed. She swayed toward Jack, her senses overloaded.

Jack kissed her, letting his hands drop to her waist. She was going too fast—he wanted to spin out her time as long as he possibly could. He didn't want her reaching her peak just yet—he had other plans.

The kiss slowed Kit down, easing her from a full boil to a bubbling simmer. Instinctively, she realized Jack wanted her in that state. She didn't know why, but conundrums were beyond her. His hands had moved to the fastenings of her breeches. The wet fabric trapped the buttons. It took the combined efforts of them both to win through. Once the flap was open, Jack eased the breeches down, running his hands over the cool skin of her buttocks.

Kit wriggled her hips free of the clinging folds, thanking all her angels that her riding breeches were not as tight as her inexpressibles. If she'd been wearing them tonight, she felt sure he'd have ripped them from her. At Jack's urging, she stood. He drew the breeches to her feet and helped her from them. But before she could sink to her knees again, his hands fastened about her hips, holding her where she was, totally naked before him.

For one long moment, Jack surveyed her beauty. Then he bent his head to pay homage.

Kit's gasp when his lips burned her navel echoed in the quiet room. Her fingers threaded into his hair; her hands clutched his head. She felt the thrust of his tongue, languid and rhythmic, and her flesh caught fire. When his lips finally moved on, her sigh filled the room.

She waited to be released, but Jack hadn't finished. His tongue explored the curve of her hip. Kit felt his hands shift down and around until each large palm cupped a firm buttock. His fingers gripped her, holding her prisoner. She smiled—she wasn't about to try to escape.

Then he shifted, settling lower on his knees. His lips dipped downward. And inward.

"*Jack!*" Kit's shocked protest ended in a whimper of pleasure. Her knees lost all ability to support her, but Jack held her steady as his lips closed over the bright curls at the apex of her thighs and his tongue probed the soft flesh they concealed.

Kit swayed, eyes closed. She'd wanted him at her feet, but this wasn't what she'd meant. *This* was beyond scandalous—it was a damned sight beyond anything Amy could even dream. Kit shuddered, and her head fell back. Her mind fragmented. Jack shifted his hold and lifted her left leg, hooking her knee over his shoulder, trailing hot kisses back up the satiny flesh of her inner thigh before settling to plunder her softness with the same unrelenting thoroughness he'd used earlier on her mouth.

Kit couldn't think. Her entire consciousness was centered on that point where Jack's hot mouth and even hotter tongue were drawing an answering heat from her. Her hands dropped to his shoulders, her nails sinking deep in convulsive reaction.

Concentrating on every spasm of her response, Jack knew when she approached the point beyond which her climax would become unavoidable. He changed tack, drawing her back from the brink, letting the flames he'd fanned die to a smolder before patiently stoking them to a blaze once more. From nibbling kisses about the curl-covered mound, he progressed to a slow exploration of the heated flesh that surrounded the entrance to her secret cave.

He had her balanced perfectly; her knee on his shoulder

let him steady her with that hand alone, leaving his left hand free to caress her bottom. Her skin was damp, but not from the rain. His hand skimmed one ripe hemisphere, then his fingers sought the cleft between, sliding down to find the spot where a little pressure went a long way. Kit's shuddering gasp told him he'd found it. He moved her knee, opening her fully, pausing to circle the swollen bud of her passion with his tongue before plundering the delights of her honey-filled cave.

He wondered how long she could take it. How long could he?

Sensation after sensation crashed through Kit. She felt battered by the volleys of passion rocketing along her veins. Hypersensitized, she was agonizingly aware of every erotic move Jack made. Wantonly, she abandoned herself to delight, reveling in the shocking intimacy. Again and again, he brought her to the point where she could sense those odd ripples of tension building within her. Then his attention would wander, slowing her down when she wanted to rush headlong to her fate. When he did it again, she moaned her displeasure. She struggled in his hold. "Damn you, Jack!" But she couldn't tell him to stop; she didn't know what she wanted.

But she was quite sure he did. She heard his deep chuckle, and felt its reverberations through her hands. He drew back to look up at her, his eyes alight with a searing silver flame. "Had enough?"

"Yes—no!" Kit glared as best she could, but it was a weak effort.

Jack laughed and let her knee down. He got to his feet and Kit swayed into him. His lips found hers and she tasted her nectar on his lips and tongue. The flames started to build again.

Then Jack drew away. Kit slumped against him, too weak to protest. He held her, his hands roaming her silken back, marveling at the texture of her skin. She was well and truly primed, ready to explode. And, thank Christ, he was still in control. God knew how long that would last.

Kit moaned her disapproval and lifted her face for his kiss. Jack obliged but kept the kiss light. He disengaged, and his lips brushed hers. "I take it that means you want me inside you?"

Kit blinked.

She couldn't believe her ears. After what he'd just done to her—after what she'd just let him do to her—he wanted her to say it. Aloud. She set her lips mutinously.

He raised his brows.

"Yes, damn you! I want you to put that bloody sword of yours inside me. All right?"

Jack crowed once in triumph, then swept her up into his arms. "Far be it from me to disappoint a lady." In two strides, he reached the bed. It wasn't his bed at the Castle, with its silken sheets, but it would do for now. The wind howled about the eaves as he laid Kit down, pulling the covers from under her. They wouldn't need them for an hour or two.

Deposited in the middle of the bed, Kit fought an automatic urge to cover her nakedness. But Jack's hungry gaze dispelled her inhibitions. She stretched, catlike, settling herself on the pillows, and watched him undress.

His boots came off first, then he stood and peeled off his wet breeches. Kit's heart leapt to her mouth when she saw what she'd previously only felt. Jack reached for a towel and dried his legs. When he turned his attention to what hung between them, Kit's mouth went dry. It had to be impossible, surely? But it was patently obvious that Jack had been accommodated by other women, although she couldn't imagine how.

A log settled in the hearth, sending sparks flying, recalling Jack to his duties as host. Dropping the towel, he crouched to tend the fire.

Kit drew a deep breath, then another. It would work— he knew what he was doing, even if she didn't. He wouldn't hurt her, she knew that. How was it going to feel, having that pushed inside her?

She forced her mind to other things—to the sheen of the flames on his skin, to the sculpted muscle covering his large frame. Her gaze was drawn to a number of scars scattered randomly over him. One in particular held her attention, a long gash on the inside of his left knee, highlighted by the flames as he stood and turned toward her.

His weight bowed the bed, rolling her into his arms. Kit lost all hope of retaining any degree of lucidity the instant his lips met hers.

Jack savored the taste of her, relishing the ardor he sensed beneath her calm. She'd cooled somewhat, but all that meant was that he'd have the pleasure of stoking her flames yet again. Regardless of her previous experience, he had every intention of making sure this was one night, one time, one man she'd never forget. He set his mind and his hands to the task.

His knowing fingers searched and found all her points of passion, those particular areas where she was most sensitive. The lower curve of her buttocks quickly became his favorite—she heated in an instant at the lightest caress. Anything more definite brought a moan to her lips. Satisfied she was safe from any chill, Jack gathered her to him, pressing her slim length to him, from shoulder to knee. But before he could roll her beneath him, he was seduced by the sensation of hot silken skin sliding sensuously over him.

Kit responded instinctively to the novel texture of Jack's body. She'd never felt anything like it before. Consumed by curiosity, she rubbed her soft thighs against his rough hardness, marveling at the friction of his hair against her skin, at the contrast between his lean muscle and her yielding flesh.

She sensed the hiatus in Jack's attention and assumed it was her turn to explore. She'd made her decision; there was no reason to shortchange herself. Whatever penance she'd pay would be the same. Opening her eyes, she spread her hands across his chest and wondered at the width of the muscles that spanned it. She glanced into Jack's face and found his eyes shut, his jaw set, his lips thin.

Smiling, she moved her hands lower and watched the tension in his face, his whole frame, grow. Tentatively, she reached for him, taking him between her hands as she had two nights before. Her fingers moved up the throbbing shaft and found the rounded head. A bead of moisture clung to her fingers.

Jack's control snapped. He forgot all thoughts of slow mutual torture, consumed by the need to douse the flames she'd set raging through him. His heat needed hers to come to fruition. In one smooth move, he pulled her beneath him, coming over her to settle on his elbows.

Kit's gasp was lost as Jack's mouth took hers in a relentless plunder of her senses. His fingers laced through her curls, holding her head steady while he ravished her mouth, sending heated longing down every nerve. His hips were heavy on hers, pressing her into the bed. She welcomed his weight and wanted more but he ignored her tugging. She felt him shift slightly, then his hand slipped between them to expertly caress the soft flesh between her thighs. Kit moaned and opened to his fingers, her breath catching as they slid slowly into her. She felt his thumb flick against her and sparks flew. The furnace deep within her ignited.

His hand withdrew and she frowned and shook her head, too breathless to find words to protest. She writhed, searching mindlessly for fulfillment. Then she felt his thighs press heavily between hers, nudging them farther apart. Smooth, hard pressure eased her aching flesh.

That was what she wanted. Kit moaned and tilted her hips in instinctive invitation.

Despite the mists of lust clouding his mind, Jack's faculties still functioned. They registered the unexpected tension in the ligaments of Kit's thighs and passed the information on.

With an effort, Jack drew his lips from Kit's. His head bowed, he drew a deep breath, then shook his head to clear it of the irritating niggle that was threatening to spoil his evening. But that only made the evidence more obvious. Dammit! It was as if she'd never spread her legs before. He frowned, and Kit moaned impatiently. Jack shook aside his ridiculous fancy. The woman writhing in urgent entreaty beneath him had most assuredly been this way before. He flexed his hips and entered her, slowly, letting her heat welcome him, the slickness of her arousal smoothing his way.

Three inches in, the truth hit him like a sledgehammer. Jack froze. In stunned disbelief, he stared at the woman lying naked in his arms, her creamy skin flushed with passion, her features rapt, her mind centered on the place where their bodies joined. He could feel her tightening about him, even though he was barely inside her.

"Christ!" Jack dropped his head, his jaw resting on her cheekbone.

Kit opened her eyes, bewildered and bemused.

Jack didn't look at her. He couldn't. "Kit, are you a virgin?"

Her silence was answer enough, but he needed to hear it, incontrovertible, from her lips. "Dammit, woman! *Are you?*"

Kit's soft "Yes," was drowned by Jack's groan. She felt him tense; his body went rigid. Then, slowly, he drew away.

The effort nearly killed him, but Jack forced his body to compliance. He pulled out of her clinging heat, then abruptly sat up and swung his feet to the floor. He dropped his head in his hands, shutting out the temptation to look at her. If he did, he'd lose the battle with his body, which was already in flaming rebellion.

He had to think. It wasn't just that she was a virgin and he'd long ago given up deflowering the little dears. There was something more significant about the fact. With a groan, he struggled to summon his wits from their preoccupation with attaining a goal he was no longer sure it was safe to gain.

Kit frowned at the broad back, which was all of Jack she could see. Something had given her away, but with passion beating steady in her veins, she was in no mood to pander to any peculiar rakish whim. She'd learned from her cousins that virgins were not the favored fare of rakes, the consensus being that experienced women gave better value besides being free of potential complications. It was too bad if Jack subscribed to such nonsense. He'd brought her this far; she'd be damned if she'd leave his bed untried.

When he gave no sign of coming to his senses and instantly returning to her arms, Kit sat up. Apparently, if she wished to get his mind back where she wanted it, and his body along with it, she was going to have to make her wishes plain.

She came up on her knees on the bed close behind him. Slowly, she placed her hands on his back, spreading the fingers wide, then sliding them around, pushing under his arms until she'd reached as far as she could. She clung to him, pressing her breasts, her hips, against his back, her fingers sinking into the deep muscles of his chest.

Jack stiffened. His head came up; his hands dropped, clenched, to his knees.

Kit nuzzled his neck, and whispered softly in his ear. "Jack? Please? Someone has to do it. I want it to be you."

The thought that this was the first time in his entire career he'd felt at a disadvantage in a bedroom floated through Jack's fevered brain. He couldn't think with her so close, in her present state. There was something important about her being a virgin that he should have grasped, but the elusive fact slipped further away as Kit laid her cheek against his shoulder.

"Jack? Please?"

What man of flesh and blood could resist such a plea? He certainly couldn't.

With a sigh of defeat, Jack pushed aside the disturbing conviction that he was about to commit an irrevocable act which would seal his fate forever, and turned. Kit was right behind him, waiting, her expression anxious.

Her heart in her mouth, Kit met Jack's gaze, smoldering silver fire. Would he? When his eyes held hers, as if trying to see beyond the passion of the moment, her confidence faltered. Her arms dropped to her sides. The silver gaze fell to her parted lips, then to her breasts, rising and falling rapidly, and finally, to the auburn curls between her wide-spread thighs.

Jack groaned and took her to the sheets, turning her into his arms. "Hell only knows, Kit Cranmer, but you're the most wanton virgin I've ever known."

It was the last lucid thought either of them had. Their lips met in a frenzy of need, too long denied to be gentle. The fire of their passion engulfed them, obliterating any lingering reservations. When Jack swung over her, Kit accepted his weight eagerly, her hands kneading his back in frantic entreaty.

Eyes closed, savoring the feel of her slim body arching against his, Jack grimaced. She was going to try his control as it had never been tried before. "Bend your knees up. It'll make it easier."

Kit complied with the rough command, too far gone in longing to be concerned over the intimate and vulnerable position. She felt his fingers part her, then hardness, smooth and solid, entered her. The pressure built as he pushed farther, inexorably inward, forcing her heated flesh to yield him passage. There was no pain, but she felt the tension when he abutted the barrier that marked her incontrovertibly virgin. To her dismay, he pulled back. Kit clamped her muscles tight to hold him within her.

Braced above her, he gave a chuckle that changed halfway through to a groan. "Relax."

Passion permitted her a spurt of resentment. Relax? He might have done this countless times before, but he knew she was a novice. Did he have any idea what it felt like, to have him invading her body in such an intimate way? At the thought, Kit pressed her head back into the pillow. She moaned, with relief, with anticipation, as she felt him return, surging up to the barrier, only to stop and retreat again.

Gradually, as he repeated the motion, Kit caught his rhythm. Instinctively, she matched it, tightening as he withdrew, relaxing as he entered. Even through her slickness, she could feel the friction in her flesh. A flame of a different sort grew steadily, ripples of tension concealed within it.

Jack's groan was encouraging. He dropped from his elbows, the pressure of his chest soothing her aching breasts. Kit hugged him to her. Her lips sought his, every bit as fervent as he. Her breath was suspended when his tongue delved deep. The sensation that streaked through her was quite different now that he was inside her. Her tension built. She felt her body arch hard against his, her hips lifting, searching. One large hand pushed under her until it cradled her buttocks. At the limit of his next outward movement, the long fingers slipped between her thighs, to the point of their union. And pressed.

Kit came off the bed, arching wildly in the grip of a passion she'd no hope of controlling. In desperate need of air, she dragged her lips from Jack's, pressing her head back into the pillows. She felt him thrust powerfully and a fiery pain flared inside. Her fingers dug into his back as he plunged deep into her body. Abruptly, the pain of his invasion disappeared in an explosion of delicious release, her tension peaking and overflowing in intense ripples through her straining muscles, the flames he'd stoked transforming pain to pleasure.

It took some minutes before Kit's mind registered anything beyond the warmth left behind by the flames. They continued to flicker, drawing her back to reality and the fact that Jack was holding still, his cheek pressed hard against her hair, his breathing a ragged, desperate sound by her ear. Her senses returned and she felt the steady throb of him, deep against her womb.

It was torture of the most exquisite sort, but Jack held still, every muscle clenched with the effort. He should have expected it. The damn woman had done everything she could to bring him low so of course she'd climax at just that moment. As their heartbeats mingled, the tension of her release dwindled. Her body's instinctive response to his invasion subsided as her muscles adapted to the novelty of having him buried inside her. When her hips tilted slightly, experimentally, as if to draw him deeper, he released the breath he'd been holding and started to move.

Kit responded immediately, caught by the discovery of how easily he rode her now that there was no barrier holding him back. His lips returned to hers and she accepted his kiss eagerly, her body straining against his as sensation washed through her. The tight buds of her nipples brushed his chest, over and over. With something very like awe, she felt that odd tension burgeoning once more, swelling and growing and expanding within her.

Jack released her lips, his breathing labored. His thrusts rocked her; she urged him on, her hips meeting his, her hands urgent on his back.

"Jack!" Kit's breath caught on a sob.

Her second climax overtook her, hurling her into the limbo of lovers. She was deaf to Jack's triumphant shout as he followed her.

Firelight filled the room with shifting shadows, gilding the heavy musculature of Jack's back as he stood at the end of the bed and stared, frowning, at the woman curled naked under the sheet.

The vision of how she'd looked, sprawled, sated and at peace beneath him, shook him. It took no effort to conjure up the rosy-tipped breasts, firm and proud, the tiny waist and those hips that had defeated him under the tree. And her legs—long and slender, thighs firm and strong from riding. She'd given him the ride of his life. He glanced down, and was relieved to see the memory hadn't stirred him beyond mild interest. She was exhausted—more from her own excesses than his. He'd no plans to mount her again that night.

Jack took a long sip of brandy from the glass in his hand. She'd fallen asleep virtually instantaneously the first time. He'd held her cradled in his arms, tired but not ready to sleep, prey to an emotion he couldn't define. He'd forgotten it when she'd stirred. Her lids had fluttered, then opened wide, the amethyst eyes large and shining. He'd been watching, interested to see her reaction. Having been in the same position often before, he'd been prepared for anything from shocked reproaches to smug self-satisfaction. He hadn't been prepared for the smile of dazzling beauty that had lit her face, or the warm tenderness in her eyes. And even less prepared for the kiss she'd bestowed on him.

His body had reacted with a vengeance. His control in abeyance, he'd been unable to rein in the passion that had flared. When her fingers had touched him, stroked him, he'd been rigid and ready for her. He'd heard her chuckle, delighted with his response as she continued to caress him.

"You fool! You'll be sore enough as it is."

She'd only laughed, a low, husky, mind-numbing sound that had frazzled his good intentions. "I'm not sore at all."

He'd lain on his back and tried to ignore her. She'd come

over him, her breasts brushing his chest, to kiss him long and lingeringly, exploring his mouth as he had hers. His control had been in tatters by the time she'd drawn back to whisper against his lips: "I want you Jack. Inside me. Now."

How he'd remained still in the face of such an invitation he'd never know. But she hadn't been defeated. "I'm hot and wet for you, Jack. See?" And the brazen woman had caught his hand and guided his fingers to where her warm honey was spilling onto her thighs.

With a groan, he'd delved deep and heard her breath catch. An instant later, he'd rolled her onto her back and, with one powerful thrust, had sheathed himself to the hilt in her welcoming warmth. And it hadn't stopped there.

He'd tried to remind himself she was new to the game, but her responses drove him far beyond rational thought. However hard he pushed her, she met him and urged him on, matching his passion with hers. Of her own volition, she'd wrapped her long legs about his waist, opening to him completely. As her tension had mounted a second time, he'd remembered what he'd promised himself.

"Open your eyes." Thankfully, she'd responded to his gravelly command, ground out through clenched teeth. His next thrust had sent her spiraling over the precipice. As her lids drooped, he'd closed his own eyes in satisfaction. Her eyes had gone black.

Sensing that her release had been total, he'd opened her even wider and thrust deeply, seeking his own ticket to heaven in her fire. He'd found it.

When next he'd been able to sense anything, he'd felt her soft breath on his cheek. She'd fallen asleep while he was still inside her, a small, satisfied smile on her lips. Feeling ridiculously pleased with himself, he'd held her close and turned to his side, careful not to disturb their union. He'd surrendered to sleep, feeling her heartbeat in his veins.

He'd woken ten minutes ago. After gathering his wits, he'd carefully unwound their tangled limbs and pulled the sheets over her. Then headed for the brandy.

The intensity of his satisfaction was one thing. What was

much more worrying was this other feeling, an irrational emotion which the events of the night had caused to grow alarmingly. Her whispered plea had been his undoing, in more ways than one.

Jack snorted and sipped his brandy, raising his head to listen to the storm as it swept past. The wind was still howling; the rain was still drumming against the shutters. There'd been a number of cracks of thunder; from them, he judged the worst was past. Outside. Inside, he was far from convinced Kit's seduction was the end of anything. It felt much more like a beginning.

His eyes traced the curves concealed beneath the sheet. If it'd just been lust, all would be well, but what he felt for the damn woman went far beyond that. Jack grimaced. No doubt George could define the emotion for him, but he, of his own volition, wasn't ready to do so yet. He didn't trust the feeling—he'd wait to see what came next. Who knew how she'd behave tomorrow—she'd been one surprise after another thus far.

With a sigh, Jack drained the glass and replaced it on the table. He stoked the fire, then joined Kit between the sheets. She stirred and, in her sleep, snuggled closer. Jack smiled and turned on his side, drawing her to him, curving her back into his chest. He heard her contented sigh as she settled under his arm. At least he wouldn't have to spend any more nights following her home through the dark.

Chapter 18

D awn was painting the sky when Kit rode up the paddock at the back of the Cranmer Hall stables. She dismounted and led Delia inside, then unsaddled the mare and rubbed her down. Delia had survived the storm, safe in her stall beside Champion. As for herself, Kit wasn't so sure.

She couldn't even remember any thunder, let alone the panic that usually attacked her at such times. What she could remember had kept her cheeks rosy all the way home from the cottage.

The weight of Jack's arm across her waist had penetrated her doze and brought her fully awake. She'd spent minutes in stunned recollection, as the events of the night had replayed in her brain. Jack had been sound asleep beside her. She'd edged from under his arm, conscious of a reluctance to leave his safe warmth yet quite sure she wouldn't want to be there when he awoke.

With a last pat for Delia, Kit left the stables. The morning-room windows which gave onto the terrace had long been her favored route for clandestine excursions. Minutes later, she was safe in her chamber. She discarded her clothes, a simple matter now that they were dry. She'd dressed in silent haste, petrified lest Jack should hear her and wake up. But he'd slumbered on, a smile she'd long remember on his lips.

She'd remember his lips for a long time, too. Kit blushed and clambered into her bed. Damn the man—she'd wanted to be initiated, but had he needed to go so far? She couldn't even think of the experience without blushing. She'd have to get over it, or Amy would become suspicious. The idea of confiding in Amy surfaced, only to be discarded. Amy would be horrified. Scandalized by her wildness. But then, Amy was marrying for love. She, Kit, was not marrying at all.

Kit pulled the covers to her chin and turned on her side, conscious of the empty bed behind her and annoyed at herself for it. She'd have to put the entire episode from her mind or even Spencer would notice. She wasn't up to analyzing how she felt and what her conclusions on the activity were—she'd do that some other time, when she could think straight again.

She closed her eyes, determined to find slumber. She'd learned what she'd wanted to know—Jack had been a thorough teacher. Her curiosity had been well and truly satisfied. She was free and unfettered. She was no longer in charge of smugglers; she no longer needed to appear at their runs to be a redundant lookout. All was well in the world.

Why couldn't she sleep?

Seven miles to the north, Jack came awake and instantly knew he was alone. He sat up and scanned the room, then, his privacy confirmed, fell back to the pillows, a puzzled frown on his face. Had he dreamed it?

A glance to the left revealed two bright strands of curling red hair, lying in an indentation in the pillow. Jack picked them up; the dim light filtering through the shutters struck red glints from their surface. Memories flooded him. One brow quirked upward. He lifted the sheet and looked down to where a few flecks of reddish brown stained the cream sheets.

No, he hadn't dreamed it. Once his mission was complete, he'd build on the start he'd made last night.

Jack groaned. Who was he fooling? His mission might take months. He couldn't possibly wait that long; after last night, he sincerely doubted she could. Not that she'd know that, but she'd find out soon enough. He might as well face it—for good or ill, Kit Cranmer and his mission looked set to stay entangled, certainly for the forseeable future.

His glance strayed to the bright strands wrapped around his fingers. He should, of course, feel irritated. But irritation was not what he felt.

Four days later, irritation was very close to his surface. He'd spent his Saturday and Sunday in a peculiar daze. On both nights, he'd gone to the cottage, but Kit hadn't shown up. He'd relieved his frustrations by visiting the Revenue Office at Hunstanton on Monday and making Sergeant Tonkin's life miserable. His questions had been phrased in an idle way, concealing the fact that he was intimately acquainted with Tonkin's unsuccessful attempt to trap his "big gang." He'd made Tonkin squirm, then later felt guilty. The man was a blot on the landscape, but in this instance he'd only been doing his job.

Jack had ridden to the Monday meeting at the Old Barn, silently rehearsing the words he intended to burn Kit's ears with, when they repaired to the cottage afterward. She hadn't shown her face.

What annoyed him most was that he actually felt hurt by her nonappearance. And the emotional hurt was much worse than the physical manifestation. At least, thanks to her earlier antics, he'd got used to that.

Now, he stood on the sands in the lee of the cliff and waited for his first "human cargo" to come ashore. He forced his mind back to the present, slamming a mental door against all thoughts of a redheaded houri in breeches. He glanced up at the cliff. Joe was on watch, but Jack doubted Sergeant Tonkin would try his luck quite so soon after his last dismal failure.

The first boat came in, swiftly followed by three more. A cargo of kegs and one man. He was in the first boat, a slight figure muffled to the eyes in an old greatcoat. Matthew, beside Jack, snorted at the sight.

Jack grimaced. "I know, you old warhorse—I'd like to get my hands around his throat, too. But he won't escape."

Matthew shifted, checking their surroundings. "D'ye think Major Smeaton'll have reached London by now?"

"George won't have dallied on the road. He should have

passed the news on by now. There will be a welcome awaiting this one when he gets to London. A welcome he wasn't counting on.''

"Why can't we just stop him here?''

"Because we need to know who he's meeting in London.'' Jack started down the beach. Reluctantly, Matthew followed.

Jack paid little attention to the spy, which gave the spy equally little chance of studying him. His disguise was good but not perfect; he'd no idea who the man was or what his station in life might be. A fellow officer, or the personal servant of a fellow officer, might well recognize him, or at least realize there was something a little odd about the Hunstanton Gang's leader. Jack busied himself with his material cargo and ignored the man.

The spy was put on a pony, and Shep and two of the older members of the gang set out to deliver him to the ruins of Creake Abbey. From there, he'd be spirited to London, the Admiralty's tracker on his tail.

Satisfied that all had gone smoothly, Jack followed the kegs to the Old Barn. They'd be taken to the abbey the following night. After the men had dispersed, he and Matthew rode to the cottage. From the first, he'd made a point of changing his clothes and his identity at the old fishing cottage; tonight, he had another reason for calling in. He didn't have much hope Kit would appear, but he wouldn't be able to sleep, alone between his silk sheets, if he didn't check.

The cottage was empty.

Lord Hendon rode home to his castle, cursing all red-headed houris.

There was no moon on Wednesday night. Astride Delia, Kit sat concealed in the deepest shadows under the trees in front of Jack's cottage and waited for him to return from the Blackbird. She'd determined not to come near him. Nothing could have got her to the cottage again—nothing except the news that the Hunstanton Gang had run a "human cargo" last night.

The past five days seemed an eon in time. She'd been

consumed by an odd restlessness that increased daily. Doubtless the effect of delayed guilt. It had even disturbed her sleep. She didn't need to convince herself of the threat Jack represented. He was a smuggler—not of her class, hardly an acceptable suitor. The events of Friday night were burned into her brain; the effects were burned into her flesh. She'd wanted to know—now she knew. But that didn't mean she could turn her back on Spencer and all he represented. She was a gentlewoman, no matter how much that sometimes irked. After the night of the storm, Jack was not just forbidden fruit—he was danger personified.

So she'd stayed away from the Monday night meeting but had dropped by the little fishing village this afternoon. Noah and the others had been there. Without hesitation, they'd filled her in on the previous night's activities.

Their lack of loyalty to their country didn't overly surprise her. She doubted that, living isolated as they did, they understood the implication of "human cargo." Jack hadn't spelled it out for them. But nothing could convince her Jack didn't have a military background. There was no possibility he didn't comprehend the significance of the men he was smuggling into the country.

Delia shifted. Kit sighed. She shouldn't have come—she didn't want to be here. But she couldn't let "human cargoes" be run and not do something about it. If she could make Jack stop, she would. If not . . . She'd think about that later.

A jingle of harness came to her ears, carried clearly over the silent fields. It was five minutes before they came into view, coming up the track from the northern coast, Matthew, George, and Jack. Kit held her breath.

They were walking their horses toward the small stable when Jack realized Kit was close. Or rather, Champion sensed Delia's presence and showed every sign of refusing to go into the stable without his lady love. Jack dismounted and took hold of the stallion's bridle above the bit. "Matthew, I'll be here for a while. You go on home."

With a mumbled "Aye," Matthew turned his horse and headed south for the Castle.

Jack turned to George, who was eyeing him suspiciously.

Captain Jack's devilish smile appeared. "I'd ask you in, but I suspect I've got company."

George looked down on him, his expression resigned. Jack knew he'd never ask who the company was. George didn't approve of his rakish ways.

"I take it you're sure you can handle this company alone?"

Jack's smile deepened. "Quite sure."

"That's what I thought." George pulled his chesnut about, then paused to add: "One day, Jack, you'll get bitten. I just hope I'm around when it happens, to say 'serves you right.' "

Jack laughed; George touched his heels to his horse and departed.

Jack noted the direction of Champion's fixed stare but didn't follow it. Instead, he spoke sternly to the horse. The stallion tossed his grey head at the rebuke but consented to be led to his stable. Jack unsaddled the great beast and rubbed him down in record time.

He'd expected Kit to appear as soon as the others left. When she didn't, Jack went back to stand in front of the cottage, wondering if Champion could have been mistaken.

From the shadows of the trees, Kit watched him. Up to the time he'd arrived, her course had been clear. But the sight of him had awoken memories of that stormy night in the cottage, reducing her to vacillating nervousness. Perhaps she'd do better to meet him in daylight?

Convinced by the pricking of his own senses that Champion hadn't been mistaken, Jack lost patience. He stood in the doorway of the cottage, hands on hips, and faced the trees across the clearing. "Come out, Kit. I've no intention of playing hide-and-seek in the dark."

The subtle threat in his tone made up Kit's mind for her. Reluctantly, she nudged Delia out of the trees. Suddenly remembering she'd no idea what Jack had made of her absence, she reined in. But she'd already gone too far. Jack stepped forward and caught Delia's bridle. The next instant, Kit felt his hands at her waist. She bit back a protest which wouldn't have been listened to anyway, too stunned by the force of her reaction to his touch to do anything more than summon up her defenses. Things were more serious than she'd thought; she'd have to ensure she didn't give herself away.

To her relief, Jack released her immediately. Without a word, he led Delia to the stable. Uncertain of her welcome and a host of related matters, Kit followed.

Jack hadn't noticed her reaction, for the simple reason he'd been too busy registering the violence of his own feelings. He'd never known a woman to affect him as Kit did. It was novel, unnerving and bloody annoying to boot. He hurt like hell in two entirely different places. He intended to see she eased at least one of the ills she'd inflicted on him—the more accessible one. The other he wasn't sure even she could cure.

Delia went readily into the stall next to Champion. Jack unsaddled her and rubbed her down. He was aware of Kit hovering at the stable door but ignored her as best he could. If he acknowledged her presence, she'd be on her back in the hay inside of a minute.

When she saw Jack unsaddling Delia, Kit sought for words to protest—she wasn't staying long. None came. In fact, she was seriously wondering if it was safe to talk to Jack at all. There was a certain tension in the large frame, a tension that was making her decidedly uneasy.

Before she'd time to think of anything to the point, Jack finished with Delia and strode out of the stable. "Come on."

To her annoyance, Kit found herself scurrying in his wake as he strode to the cottage door. He went through and held it open for her. Firelight cast a rosy glow through the room. Summoning what dignity she could, Kit sauntered to the table and dropped her hat on a chair. She was unwinding her muffler when the sound of the bolt on the door falling home set every nerve quivering. Her senses in turmoil, she forced herself to continue with her task, folding the muffler and placing it by her hat. Then she turned to face him.

Only to find he was right behind her. She turned into his arms and his lips came down on hers. Her moan of protest turned to a moan of desire, then faded to a whimper of pleasure as his tongue touched hers. Incapable of resisting, Kit placed her hands on Jack's shoulders and gave herself up to his embrace. She remembered her mission—to make him see sense, to promise not to run more spies—but she wouldn't be able to do anything until his passionate welcome came to an end. She might as well enjoy it until then. Besides which, thinking while Jack's lips were on hers, while his tongue played havoc with her senses, was well-nigh impossible.

Thinking was certainly not on Jack's agenda. What need was there for thought? He didn't even need to rein in his desire—she'd already given herself to him. His expertise as a lover would take care of her needs. His most urgent thought, the only one left in his brain, was to satisfy his needs. The primal lust he'd denied for too long, which she'd fed then let go hungry for five days and four nights, was on the rampage and had to be assuaged.

The softening of her body against his, her surrender implied, was all he waited for.

Kit felt his body envelop her, his hard heat both reassuring and exciting. His hands shifted and he backed her up until the table pressed against her thighs. Even in her semidrugged state, intoxicated with the taste of his passion, some small part of her brain was awake enough to register alarm. But before she could think, Jack's hands shifted. To her breasts, bound beneath her bands. Instantly, Kit felt discomfort which rapidly turned to pain. Her breasts swelled at Jack's touch; the bands cut into her soft flesh.

Luckily, Jack understood the source of her sudden gasp. He yanked her shirt free of her breeches and pushed it high to expose the linen bands. Kit lifted her arm so he could get at the knot. In a moment, it was undone; seconds later, the bands hit the floor and she breathed again.

Then Jack's lips found her nipple and her diaphragm seized. A sound halfway between a moan and a gasp was torn from her lips. As his tongue rasped her sensitive flesh, Kit arched into his hands. They fastened about her waist and he lifted her, setting her bottom on the table's edge, moving with her so that he stood between her wide-spread thighs.

The vulnerability of her position convinced Kit that Jack's welcome was not going to end with a kiss, or even with a caress, no matter how intimate. She wasn't entirely sure how he'd do it, but she knew what he intended.

A thrill of sheer delight coursed through her. She shuddered, and knew it drove him on. His lips returned to hers, his tongue instigating a duel of desire. She participated fully, all thought of her purpose drowned beneath the passion that flooded her. Wrapping her arms tight about his neck, she pressed her body to his. She could feel the evidence of his desire, pulsing hard and insistent against the softness of her belly.

When Jack's hands went to her knees, then skimmed the long muscles of her thighs back to her hips, Kit's stomach clenched in anticipation. One hand slid between her thighs to cup the mound between, long fingers stroking her through the stuff of her breeches. Kit moaned her displeasure, the sound trapped between them. A familiar heat was beating steady in her veins, a void had opened up deep inside. She needed him to fill her.

She felt Jack's knowing chuckle, then his hands moved to the buttons of her breeches. For the life of her, Kit couldn't imagine what he was about. Why not just take her to the bed? But she wasn't about to start an argument. With the flap open, his hands eased the garment over her hips. He lifted her, tipping her backward on the table, stepping back to draw the breeches to her boots. The boots pulled off easily; the breeches followed, leaving her naked from the waist down, her shirt pushed up to expose her breasts. Leaning back on her elbows, Kit blushed. But she forgot her inhibitions the instant her gaze collided with Jack's. Silver flames smoldered in his eyes. Sparks of pure passion lit their depths.

Kit watched him straighten, her breath caught in her throat, the sensation of being about to be devoured creeping over her. She shuddered in delicious anticipation and held out one arm to him. He smiled, supremely male, and closed the distance between them, his hands on the buttons of his corded breeches. As he stepped between her thighs, spreading them wide, his manhood sprang free, engorged and fully erect.

Kit's eyes flew wide, her mind seized, her heartbeat thundered in her ears. He was going to take her here and now— *on the table.*

She didn't have time for so much as a squawk. Jack's hands fastened about her hips and he drove into her. Kit's mind clenched in expectation of pain. There was none. Instead, her body welcomed him, arching, drawing him deeper. As Jack withdrew then thrust into her again, seating himself firmly within her, Kit felt the slipperiness that had eased his passage.

She'd been ready for him. She'd wanted him, and her body had known it. He'd known it.

Kit's eyes glazed as Jack's thrusts settled to a steady pounding. This was different from last time. The urgency coursing his veins communicated itself to her. She responded instinctively, lifting her hips, tilting them to draw him deeper still. She felt his fingers tighten about her hips. Her lids fell as she eased from her elbows to lie back on the table, her hands fastening on Jack's forearms, her fingers digging into muscles that flexed as he held her immobile against his repeated invasions.

The fever inside her burgeoned and grew, rapidly overtaking all other sensations. Her whole being was focused on his possession of her, complete and devastating as it was.

"Lift your legs."

Kit wrapped them about his waist.

Jack groaned and drove into her, wanting every fraction of an inch of penetration he could get. Her body welcomed him with heat and yet more heat, her muscles clenching about him in time with his thrusts.

A blinding explosion rocked Kit. Her body arched; her nails dug deep into Jack's arms. His response was to lean forward and take one nipple into his mouth. He suckled and she cried out. The waves of sensation abruptly intensified, breaking in a glorious climax to flow as molten passion through her veins. Her throbbing contractions continued long after. They were still with her when Jack reached his own release, spilling his seed deep within her.

Jack drew a shuddering breath and looked down at Kit, spread in wanton abandon before him. She was barely conscious, lying back on the table, struggling to breathe as he was, waiting for some measure of physical ability to return.

He couldn't resist a smug smile, but it turned to a half grimace as reality intruded. Five days had passed before she'd returned to his side. Once he touched her, she was his, but out of his reach, she was clearly one of those females with a very long fuse. There were ways to shorten that fuse, things he could do to ensure she burned with a passion to match his, not only in intensity, but in frequency, too. He didn't know where their lives were headed, only that they'd remain inextricably entwined, and, at least for him, the ties went deep. Strengthening the ties that held her to him seemed a good idea.

Kit lay still and waited for Jack to do something. She wasn't capable of doing anything herself. Her extended climax had drained her, physically and mentally. She remembered she'd come here to talk but couldn't recall any pressing urgency about the matter. While her flesh still throbbed and he remained inside her, she couldn't even recall what her point had been.

When he eased from her, Kit opened her eyes. From under weighted lids, she watched as he discarded his clothes. Naked, he came to her, a smile of male triumph on his lips, the expression echoed in his silver eyes. She suspected she should take exception but could only manage a weary smile.

"Come on. Up with you."

Jack caught her hands and drew her to sit on the edge of the table. While he divested her of her coat and pulled her shirt over her head, Kit wondered how she'd ever be able to face him across this particular table again. All he'd have to do was look at its surface and she'd curl up with embarrassment.

To her relief, he swung her up in his arms and headed for the bed, presumably understanding that her legs were as incapacitated as her brain. Kit sighed contentedly when Jack laid her between the sheets. She curled into his arms, entirely at peace.

Beds she could cope with. Tables were something else again.

Chapter 19

I t was a perfect summer night, the air soft and balmy. Kit stood beside Delia close by the cliff, waiting for Captain Jack. A sickle moon rode the purple skies, shedding just enough light to distinguish the huddled shapes a few yards away as men, rather than rocks. Their muffled conversation drifted past Kit's ears.

Facing the waves, Kit registered their regular ebb and flow, a parody of her confusion. Jack had unleashed all manner of wild longings; they sent her surging forward to some unknown fate. A deep-seated acknowledgment of what was due her position, her loyalty to Spencer, drew her back. Wednesday night had been a disaster. Kit's lips lifted in a self-deprecatory smile. A delicious disaster, but a disaster nonetheless. She'd intended to convince Jack of the folly of running "human cargoes." Instead, she'd been convinced of the folly of self-delusion.

No one, not even Amy, had warned her of the fever in her flesh. Of the aching void that, now the way was open, seemed to have grown within her. Her mind longed to recapture that moment of completeness. Her body yearned for the flame to transform her fever to consuming passion. She'd sensed it even after that first night at the cottage—a restlessness, a need she'd tried to ignore and had done her best to stifle. Wednesday night had left her with no alternative but to admit her addiction to Jack's loving.

Delia shifted, blowing low. Kit peered down the beach but could see nothing. She'd intended to bring up the subject of the spies once she'd recovered from Jack's amorous welcome. But he'd never let her recover. He'd stirred her awake far too soon; rational conversation had not been his aim. The night had dissolved into an orgy of mutual satisfaction. She couldn't deny she'd enjoyed it—her pleasure had been his command.

With a grimace, Kit shifted her stance. She might revel in Jack's attentions, but she wasn't about to let passion rule her life. Yet the niggling suspicion that Jack had *intended* Wednesday night, certainly the latter half of it, that he'd planned and executed their play like some campaign, had remained, a shadow in her mind. At dawn, he'd helped her dress, his touch deeply unsettling, then he'd saddled Delia. He'd told her of tonight's run, making it unnecessary for her to attend the meeting last night in the Old Barn.

Naturally, she hadn't gone, knowing that if she did show her face, she'd be admitting to him her addiction to his company. Instead, she'd gone early to bed. But not to sleep. Half the night had passed in tossing and turning, the fever burning slow and steady and unfulfilled.

Had he purposely drugged her with passion?

The broad shoulders of her nemesis hove into view. Kit watched as he rode up on Champion, George and Matthew, as ever, in attendance. Jack's silver-grey gaze swept her, the comprehensive glance followed by a fleeting smile. He dismounted, and the men milled about him.

Kit waited until the men moved to their positions, George and Matthew with them, before stepping forward. "Where do you want me tonight?"

Immediately, she bit her tongue. Jack had been glancing down the beach; at her words, his head swung about, an arrested expression on his face. For one fractured minute, she thought he'd answer with the words in his mind.

Jack was sorely tempted. The sound of her husky tones confidently voicing such a query sent a spasm of sheer desire through his veins. But he clamped a lid on that particular pot and set it aside to simmer. A slow, infinitely devilish smile twisted his lips. "I'll think about it for the next hour or two. I'll tell you my decision later—at the cottage."

Kit wished she could say something to wipe the smug expression from his face.

"But for now," Jack continued, suddenly brisk, "I need you on lookout. Wherever you like, since you won't obey my orders."

Kit tilted her chin. She turned and set her foot in her stirrup, pointedly getting on with her business.

The large hand that caressed her bottom shattered her complacency. After one leisurely circuit, it boosted her up to her saddle. Kit landed with a gasp. In daylight, her glare would have fried him. In moonlight, he stood, hands on hips, a patronizing expression on his face and gave her back arrogant stare for stare.

Sheer fury seared Kit's veins. She clamped her lips shut and hauled on Delia's reins. If she gave vent to her feelings here and now, her disguise would be blown past redemption.

Once on the cliff, she found a position overlooking Jack's operations and dismounted. Too furious to sit still, she paced back and forth, twitching her gloves between her hands, her gaze on the beach, her temper on the boil.

Exclamations crowded her brain. *How dare he?* seemed far too mild. Besides, she knew how he dared—he knew damn well she wasn't strong enough to withstand attack on that front, damn his silver eyes! If she didn't need to know about the spies, she'd never come near him again. But she'd been through all the arguments, assessed all the alternatives. Until she had some facts, a run date for instance, there was no point in revealing her masquerade. If Spencer heard of it, he'd forbid her to continue, and then they'd never stop the spies.

Anger was not the only emotion coursing through her. Kit shivered with reaction. Damn the man—if she'd needed any confirmation he'd planned Wednesday night's activities, that knowing caress had provided it. He'd purposely lit the fires of sensual pleasure in her flesh, so it would take just a caress to stir them to life. Kit ground her teeth and kicked a rock out of her way.

He was too damned sure of himself! He was too damned sure of her.

The run proceeded smoothly, as all Jack's enterprises did. Kit watched, mulling over that fact. Jack's cottage was on Lord Hendon's land. And Lord Hendon had conveniently sent Sergeant Osborne to patrol the Sheringham beaches and Sergeant Tonkin to watch the shores of the Wash. A cynic might imagine there was a connection.

Kit snorted. The only real connection would be that Lord Hendon, like all the surrounding gentry, tolerated the smugglers. But not the spies. On that point, Jack had stepped beyond the line.

As the ponies headed for the cliff, Kit rose and caught Delia's trailing reins. She mounted and urged the mare into the trees lining the first field. From there, she watched until the last of the pack train emerged from the cliff path. Then, before the grey stallion appeared, Kit turned Delia's head for Cranmer Hall and dropped her hands.

She kept the mare to a steady gallop, the black hooves eating the miles. When the shadow of the Hall loomed out of the dark, Kit uttered a small whoop and sent Delia flying over the stable paddock fence.

Safe home. She'd escaped Jack's trap, for one night at least. A fever might be the price she'd have to pay, but she'd pay gladly. Aside from anything else, it was safer this way.

Jack and his swaggering arrogance could spend the night alone.

On Sunday afternoon, after spending a virtuous morning at church, then presiding over the luncheon table, Kit sat Delia in the shadow of the trees facing Jack's cottage, her confidence at an all-time low. Distrustful of her reasons for being there, uncertain of her chances of success, she bit her lip and eyed the closed door. There was nothing to tell her if the cottage was inhabited or not.

If she sat still for long and Champion was in the stable, the stallion would sense Delia's presence and neigh, destroying any advantage surprise might otherwise give her. If she sat still for much longer, her courage would desert her and she'd turn tail for home. Kit directed Delia in an arc about the clearing. She approached the stable and dismounted, then led Delia inside.

Champion's huge grey rump loomed out of the dimness. Kit stopped, not sure if she felt relieved, excited, or dismayed. The stallion's head came around; Kit took Delia to the stall alongside. After tethering the mare, she debated whether to unsaddle or not. In the end, she did, refusing to acknowledge the action implied anything at all about her intentions, much less her hopes. She rubbed the mare down, ears pricked to detect any sound of approaching danger.

She knew why she was there—she needed to mend her fences with Jack; he was her only reliable source of information on the spies. Her wilder self jeered; Kit strangled it. There might be other reasons she'd ridden this way, but she wasn't ready to acknowledge them—not in daylight. Her innards were in a dreadful state; trepidation walked her nerves. She'd never felt like this before, not even when admitting to riding Spencer's favorite stallion at the age of ten. Spencer's rages had no power to make her quiver. The thought of how Jack would look when next she saw him, in a few minutes, did.

How would he welcome her this time?

The thought stopped her in her tracks as she headed for the stable door. She almost turned back to resaddle Delia. But her reason for being here resurfaced. She couldn't walk away from "human cargo." Kit set her jaw. With a determined stride, she made for the cottage door.

Kit paused with her hand on the latch, swept by the sense of being about to enter a potentially dangerous animal's lair. The cold iron of the latch sent a thrill through her fingers. Her whole being vibrated with anticipation. In truth, she wasn't sure where the danger lay—with him? Or with herself?

Inside the cottage, Jack lay sprawled on his back in the middle of the bed, his hands locked behind his head. He stared at the ceiling.

How long would it be before it got to her? How long before she came to find him?

He gave a disgruntled snort; his brows lowered. When

he'd embarked on his scheme to embed passionate longing firmly beneath Kit's satiny skin, he'd overlooked the inevitable effect such an undertaking would have on his own lustful appetites. Since Wednesday night, he'd been ravenous. And, thanks to Kit, he hadn't been able to sate his hunger. No other woman would do. He'd retired to the cottage, to brood on his desire.

He wanted *her*—Kit—the redheaded houri in breeches.

When he stroked her, she purred. When he mounted her, she arched wildly. And later, when their passion was spent, she curled into his side like a small cream-and-ginger cat. His very own kitten.

His very own pedigree kitten. When it came to making love, she was an aristocrat, no matter what her breeding. Her performances to date had been eye-opening, particularly to one of his experience. He'd thought he'd known all there was to know of women; she'd proved him wrong. The feigned responses of the gilded whores of the *ton* had always bored him. Kit's naturalness, her sincere enjoyment of their play despite the underlying prudery behind her occasional shocked protests, entranced him. He'd been able to turn her protests into moans with satisfying regularity.

With a stifled groan, Jack stretched his arms and legs, trying to ease the tension locked in the heavy muscles. His frown converted to a scowl. Twenty-four hours had been too long for him—seventy-two had been hell. The fact that she could deal with this particular disease better than he could was a severe blow to his male pride.

The latch on the door eased upward.

Instantly, Jack was alert, half-sitting before his mind took control and stilled his instinctive reaction. His impulse was to cross silently to stand behind the door. But if his visitor was Kit, he might scare her witless by appearing beside her so unexpectedly.

The door swung slowly inward. The shadow of a slender figure, topped by a tricorne, fell on the floor. Jack relaxed. He permitted himself a smug smile, then the memory of the past seventy-two hours intruded. He'd no guarantee she'd come to alleviate his discomfort. His expression bland, he settled back on the pillows.

Kit scanned the area revealed by the open door. Jack was not at the table. Swallowing her nervousness, she took a deep breath and stepped over the threshold. She paused by the door, one hand on the edge of the worn wooden panel, and forced herself to look at the bed.

There he lay, sprawled full-length on the covers, arrogant male inscribed on every line of his tautly muscled frame. Watching her. With a distinctly predatory gleam in his silver eyes.

Kit's breath suspended; her mouth went dry. She felt her eyes grow larger and larger.

Jack read her state in her eyes and knew precisely why she'd come. The news sent his senses soaring, but he clamped down on them before they addled his wits. His body had tensed with the instinctive urge to rise and go to her, to sweep her into his arms and crush her lips, her breasts, her hips, to his. But if he did, what would happen next?

The door was midway between the bed and the table, not particularly close to either. Judging by his last effort in welcoming her, they'd probably end up on the floor. While he had nothing against *al fresco* intercourse, he hadn't been particularly proud of his lack of control in taking her on the table. He didn't know what she'd made of the experience, but he'd seen the red patches on her buttocks later. And felt hideously guilty. Too often he'd ended giving her bruises, however unintentionally. Some, like the marks his fingers left in the soft curves of her hips, were unavoidable, given she bruised easily. But he didn't need to add to them through lack of thought.

"Bolt the door." He tried to keep the raw passion pulsing his veins from coloring his tone and only partially succeeded.

Kit's eyes grew rounder still. Her limbs felt heavy as, her gaze trapped in Jack's silver stare, she moved slowly to obey. Her fingers fumbled and she dragged her eyes from his. The bolt slid home with a metallic thud. Slowly, she turned back to face him, expecting to see him rising.

He hadn't moved. "Come here."

Kit considered that carefully. She might be mesmerized;

she wasn't witless. But she was caught, very firmly, in the sensual web he'd woven with such consumate skill, her pulse already increasing in anticipation of what was to come. Acknowledging the inevitable, she placed one foot before the other. Slowly, warily, she approached the bed.

"Stop." The gravelly command halted her a yard from the end of the bed. "Take off your hat and coat."

Kit's stomach contracted. She pulled off her hat and dropped it, then shrugged off her coat and let it slide to the floor. As the silver gaze dropped from her face to sweep her figure, Kit felt the embers of her passion glow.

"Take off those damned breeches."

Kit's embers burst into flame. She stared at Jack, shocked and tantalized by his suggestion.

Jack clenched every muscle in an effort to remain prone on the bed. Kit's eyes glowed violet, purple sparks of passion striking from their depths. He wasn't the least surprised to see her fingers move to the buttons which secured the drab breeches. He watched the slim digits work the buttons free. Then, slowly, she peeled back the flap, revealing an expanse of creamy stomach with a riot of red curls at its base.

Kit moved in a dream, sundered from reality. She saw the tension in Jack's frame increase and reveled in her power. Moving with deliberate slowness, she inched the garment off her hips, balancing on one foot to draw off her boot. When the second boot was off, she lifted first one leg then the other free of her breeches. She sent them to join her coat, then turned to pose, weight on one leg, the other knee bent inward, facing Jack.

He hadn't moved, but she could feel the effort it was costing him to remain where he was.

"Lift your shirt and free your breasts." Rigid with need, Jack forced the command from between clenched teeth. His eyes were glued to the rich bounty thus far revealed; his mouth was dry with anticipation of the revelations to come.

Wondering why he hadn't told her to take her shirt off, Kit obeyed the command literally, assuming there was some pertinent point she'd yet to comprehend behind it. She thought for a moment, then artfully rolled the front of her shirt up until she could hold the folds between her teeth. A sudden shift of the body in the bed told her the impulse was worth following. To her relief, the knot gave easily. She unwound the band. Slowly. The long strip went about her five times. She released her shirt just before the band dropped. Her breasts sprang free, proudly erect, semiobscured behind fine linen.

Jack swallowed a groan. His fingers, locked behind his head, clenched, biting into the backs of his hands. He couldn't imagine where she'd learned her tricks; the idea that they were instinctive started to unravel his much tried control. To gain a little time, and strength, he examined the figure before him critically. Light streamed through the window on the other side of the cottage. Kit stood directly between the bed and the window; he had an unimpeded view of her silhouette. Lingeringly, he examined every curve, knowing his gaze was heating her. The thought of what that meant forced him to speak. "Come and kneel on the bed beside me."

Without haste, Kit obeyed, climbing onto the horsehair mattress to sit on her knees by his side. In that position, her shirt covered her legs, giving her a modicum of relief from Jack's ardent gaze. He wasn't wearing a coat. His shirt was not of the same fine quality as hers; the muscles of his chest and arms showed as rounded ridges beneath its surface. Her gaze skimmed his chest, then dropped to where his shirt disappeared into the waistband of his breeches. She couldn't miss the bulge just below.

Jack saw the direction of her gaze. He kept his hands locked safely behind his head and fought to control his breathing. "Undress me."

Kit's eyes flew to his, startled conjecture in their purpled depths. Her lips parted but no protest came. Instead, she seemed to consider the idea; Jack wondered what form of slow torture she was planning.

Beneath her stunned surprise, Kit was aware of growing excitement. Never having attempted such an undertaking before, she took a minute to work out her approach.

Jack held his breath when she shifted, pressing her hands,

palms flat, against his chest. She swung over him, strad-dling him.

Boldly, Kit settled her bottom on his thighs. She heard his indrawn breath and felt the sudden leaping of the rigid rod half-trapped beneath her. She shuffled forward, pressing herself against him, protected from instant retribution by the material of his breeches. She glanced up; Jack's eyes were tight shut. A muscle flickered along his clenched jaw. With a smile of feminine triumph, Kit set to work, pulling his shirt from his breeches, tugging his arms from behind his head, eventually tugging him into a half-sit to drag the shirt off over his head.

Freed of his shirt, Jack fell back on the pillows, in pain, but eager to see how she'd manage the rest.

Flinging the shirt aside, Kit turned her attention to his waistband. It was the work of a moment to wriggle the buttons free. She laid the flap open and gazed down in awe at the prize revealed. Thick as her wrist, engorged and em-purpled, Jack's staff pulsed against the hair curling over the solid wall of his abdomen. Without thinking, Kit's fingers moved to touch it, to caress it.

Jack groaned, unable to keep the sound back. He shut his eyes, not wanting to see what she might do next. The soft caress of her lips sent him rigid; the wet sweep of her tongue, inexpert but guided by unerring instinct, broke his control. It was impossible to lie still in the face of such provocation. But he managed to keep his hands from tan-gling in her curls and guiding her lips to where his throb-bing flesh most wanted to feel them. Instead, he forced his hands to his hips, easing his breeches down. With his help, she managed the task efficiently, sliding down the bed to pull off his boots and free his legs.

Kit slipped from the bed, Jack's breeches in her fingers, and turned to survey her handiwork. Naked, displayed for her delectation, Jack was nothing short of magnificent. Not for the life of her could she keep the smile from her face.

"Come back here."

Kit's eyes flew to Jack's. What she saw in the silvered depths sent a thrill of sheer desire streaking through her. With unfeigned eagerness, she resumed her position at his side, gently simmering, intrigued to discover what next he had in mind.

Jack's mind wasn't functioning with its customary clarity. It was overheated. He watched Kit climb back on the bed, her bright eyes drifting down his torso. She knelt on her shirt and it drew taut, outlining the tight crescents of her nipples before she pulled it free. It would be easy enough to roll her beneath him and sheath himself in her heat, but in the past seventy-two hours, his imagination had been working overtime; he'd an ambition to turn some of his dreams to reality. But did he have sufficient willpower to do it?

"Ride me."

The command jerked Kit from her rapt contemplation. *Ride him?*

Jack read her question in her startled eyes, deep-hued violet and darkening rapidly. Despite the effort it cost him, he smiled. "When I mount you, I do all the hard work. This time, it's your turn."

Kit simply stared, trying to make sense of his words. Then she glanced down to where his member angled upward from its curly nest.

"Here. I'll show you." Jack caught her hands and drew her over him. "Straddle me like before."

Kit did, and nearly shot from the bed when she felt his staff leap under her. She froze, her weight steady against him, her thighs spread, her knees on either side of his hips. Breathless, she waited, stunned by the sense of vulnerability that washed over her.

Rigid with effort, Jack forced every muscle in his body to absolute obedience. A single upward thrust would sink his staff into her, hard against the source of the heat pouring over him from between her widespread thighs. But aside from the fact that he knew he might hurt her by such an aggressive entry in this position, she'd tensed and was probably dry.

He drew a ragged breath and avoided looking at the juncture of her thighs, where the head of his manhood nestled amidst her flaming curls. He eased his convulsive grip on her hands and raised them, placing them on the pillow, one above each of his shoulders. Another deep breath allowed him to run his hands back along her arms to curve about her shoulders. "Lean forward and kiss me."

Kit did as she was told, intrigued by this latest twist in his game. It started off as he'd said, with her kissing him, but he quickly took over, his fingers tangling in her curls, holding her head steady while his tongue plundered the soft cavern of her mouth. She made no protest at the change. Her furnace was alight; she needed to find the path to his flame.

Jack lowered his hands from Kit's head to her shoulders, then set them to mold her body as he wished, bringing her up on her hands and knees over him. He drew his lips from hers and urged her forward so he could take one shirt-veiled nipple into his mouth. Kit's gasp urged him on. He licked the material until it clung to the ripe peak, then drew the turgid flesh deep into his mouth. He suckled and Kit moaned, her body spasming in response. Her eyes were closed, her lips parted. Jack switched to her other breast and repeated the exercise.

Kit moaned with each successive onslaught on her senses. An urgent ache had developed between her thighs. She longed to ease it; she knew how. But Jack relentlessly stoked her fire, apparently unaware of her need.

"Jack!" Kit put all the longing she could into the syllable. Instantly, she felt his hands pushing aside her shirt to reach between her thighs. She sighed in relief when first one long finger, then two, slid into her. The fingers moved and she gasped, concentrating on their probing. They settled to a rhythm she recognized; she matched it. Jack's mouth continued on her breasts, his tongue laving the sensitized peaks, sending streams of fire coursing down her veins.

Jack waited until her gasps were quick and uneven, until her hips were pressing against his hand, her body seeking greater satisfaction. Her honey poured over his fingers as he drew them from her. "Now take me inside you."

The growled command was barely discernable but Kit heard and needed no further urging. She edged back, to where his member waited, throbbing with the desire to ease her need. She lowered herself onto it, tilting her hips to catch its head, drawing it into her. As soon as she felt him enter her, Kit sank back, taking him fully in one smooth movement.

Jack couldn't breathe. He grabbed her hips and raised her slightly. Immediately, Kit took the initiative, rising until he felt sure he'd lose her clinging heat, only to impale herself more deeply on the downward stroke. Once he was sure she was in control, Jack drew a ragged breath and refocused his attention on her breasts, warm and ripe beneath the tantalizing film of her shirt.

Kit savored the sensation of being in complete control, able to slide his strength into her at whatever pace she desired. She spread her thighs wide and took him deep; she experimented, clenching her muscles tight about him, closing her thighs to minimize penetration.

She felt Jack's hands close about her breasts, one hand covering each ripe mound, squeezing in rhythm with her ride. His fingers found her nipples. Then he started rocking his hips against hers, driving into her as she descended. Abruptly, Kit understood the purpose of her shirt. The edge floated on her thighs, rising and falling as she did, bringing home to her the view Jack would have if he was watching their bodies merge.

As she felt her fires coalescing, pooling into the conflagration that would ultimately consume her senses, Kit forced her eyes open. Jack was watching. Avidly.

With a groan she closed her eyes. Her head dropped back as the fires raged. She tightened her body, trying to hold back the inevitable, to prolong the sweet agony for just a little longer.

Jack wasn't up to prolonging anything. The sensual sight of their bodies fusing, of his staff driving into her, slickly penetrating her fevered body, was not designed to stave off consummation. He felt her body clench against release, tightening about him. He let go of her breasts and gripped her hips, holding her immobile. Drinking in the sight, he drove deeply into her.

That was all it took.

They climaxed together, gasping, their eyes open, gazes locked, their souls as fused as their bodies.

Kit's release swept her, draining her of all strength. She slumped forward and Jack gathered her to him, settling her legs so she lay on top of him, tucking her head under his chin.

She fell asleep with his arms about her.

When Kit awoke, they were lying entangled under the covers. She couldn't remember being moved, but Jack now lay sleeping beside her, one arm tucked protectively about her. Kit smiled sleepily, feeling the steady beat of his heart against her cheek. She was warm and secure, sated and content. Which was more than she'd been able to say since Wednesday night.

She squinted over the bedclothes at the window; the pink tinge of sunset was coloring the sky. It was nearly time to leave.

Memories of her recent activities drifted through her brain. She stifled a delighted giggle, then sobered. If she'd learned anything from today's episode, it was that she couldn't live without Jack. The fire in her veins was a drug she could no longer face the day without. Only he could stoke the blaze.

But Jack was smuggling spies.

Kit snuggled closer to his comforting warmth. She knew, beyond all doubt, that he was not personally involved with the spying. He was just misguided, believing it no different than smuggling brandy. She'd have to ensure, next time, that she explained it to him fully. It was up to her to make him see sense.

She had to succeed. There were three lives depending on it—Julian's, Jack's, and hers. Kit sighed. She'd speak to him about it next time she came. There was no point in spoiling the moment now.

Carefully, she eased from Jack's side, only to have him draw her back, his arm heavy in sleep. Kit glanced at the window. Perhaps it wasn't that late. She wriggled against Jack, rising up to find his lips with hers. And set about kissing him awake.

Chapter 20

The stars fell from Kit's eyes on Monday night. She'd decided to attend the meeting at the Old Barn. Although she no longer felt compelled to join the smugglers on their runs, she needed to see Jack, to try to learn more about his views on "human cargoes." When better to lead the conversation in that direction than on the slow ride back to the cottage after the meeting? She held few illusions as to how much rational discussion they'd engage in once they entered the cottage. But he'd only run one "human cargo" in the last two months; she had time, she felt, to pursue his conversion at a leisurely pace.

The meeting had already started when she got there. She slipped into the protective shadows at the back of the barn and found a dusty crate to perch on. Some noticed her furtive entrance; a few nodded an acknowledgment before returning their attention to Jack, standing in the cone of weak light shed by a single lamp.

Kit saw his grey eyes sweep her, but Jack's recitation of detail never faltered. He was midway through describing a cargo to be brought in the next night on the beaches east of Holme. Kit listened with half an ear, fascinated by the way the lamplight gilded the odd streaks in his hair.

Jack turned to address Shep. "You and Johnny collect the passenger from Creake at dusk. Bring him direct to the beach."

Kit froze.

Shep nodded; Jack turned to Noah. "Come in and pick

him up. Your boat should be the last to the ship. Transfer him and get the last of the goods.''

"Aye." Noah ducked his head.

"That's it, then.'' Jack scanned the faces, all weather-worn, most expressionless. "We'll meet again Thursday as usual.''

With grunts and nods, the band dispersed, unobtrusively slipping into the night in twos and threes. The lamp was hauled down and extinguished.

Still Kit sat her crate, head down, her face hidden by the brim of her tricorne. Jack eyed her silent figure. His misgivings grew. What the devil was wrong now? He'd expected her to arrive, but her pensiveness was unsettling. Eagerness was what he'd been expecting after her efforts of Sunday afternoon.

George and Matthew joined him by the now open door.

"I'm heading straight home." George spoke in a sub-dued tone, clearly aware Kit was behind in the gloom. He raised a questioning brow.

Jack's jaw set. He nodded decisively. George slipped into the night.

"You'd best be on your way, too.''

"Aye." Matthew went without question. Jack watched him mount and head south, through the shielding trees and into the fields beyond.

In the darkness behind Jack, Kit struggled to bring some order to her mind. Jack must have known about this latest "human cargo" since his visit to the Blackbird last Wednesday. Although she'd spent all Wednesday night and Sunday afternoon by his side, he'd not mentioned the fact. He'd not even alluded to it. So much for her ideas of learning of the spies ahead of time. Now, she'd less than twenty-four hours to make a decision and act.

When the silence of the barn remained unbroken, Jack turned and paced inside. He stopped where the moonlight ran out, and looked to where he knew Kit still sat. "What is it?''

At his impatient tone, Kit bristled, a fact Jack missed in the dark. Realizing her advantage, she took a long moment to weigh her strategy. She'd intended dissuading Jack from his treasonous enterprise; it was still worth a try. But the drafty barn, with its loose boards and warped doors, was no place to have a discussion on treason, particularly not with the person you suspected of committing it. "I need to talk with you."

Hands on hips, Jack glared into the dark. Talk? Was she up to her tricks again? He was getting damned tired of her changes in mood. He'd thought, after Sunday, that their relationship had got itself on an even keel—that she'd accepted her position as his mistress. Admittedly, she didn't know whose mistress she was, but he didn't think she'd jib at the change from smuggler to lord of the castle. He didn't think she'd jib, period.

Then he remembered she'd been watching him avidly when she'd first come in. Her attitude had changed later. An inkling of his problem blossomed in Jack's brain. "If you want to talk, it'd better be back at the cottage."

Kit stood and walked forward.

Jack heard her. He turned and strode to the door, not looking back to see if she was following. He went to where Champion stood tethered under a gnarled fir and vaulted into the saddle. He nudged the stallion into a canter, ignoring the horse's reluctance. Champion's gait didn't flow freely until halfway across the first field, when Delia drew alongside.

Jack rode in silence, his eyes probing the shadows ahead, his mind firmly fixed on the woman by his side. Why should she get her inexpressibles in a twist over him smuggling spies? Did she even know they were spies? The road appeared ahead, and he turned Champion onto the beaten surface.

Edging Delia up alongside Champion, Kit glanced at Jack's stern profile. It wasn't encouraging. Far from dampening her determination, the observation strengthened her resolution. Matthew was Jack's servant, George a too-close friend; neither had shown the slightest ability to influence Jack. Clearly, it was time someone forced him to consider his conscience. She didn't expect him to like the fact she intended to be that someone, but male arrogance was no excuse. She'd tell him what she thought regardless of what he felt.

They turned south and walked their mounts up the winding path to the top of the rise. Kit watched as Jack peered down, automatically ensuring that they hadn't been followed. The path below remained clear. She saw Jack grimace before he turned Champion's head for the cottage. Setting Delia in Champion's wake, she fell to organizing her arguments.

Jack dismounted before the stable and led Champion in. Kit did likewise, taking Delia to the neighboring stall. Having decided on her route of attack, she went straight to the point. "You do know the men you bring in and take out are spies, don't you?"

Jack's answer was to thump his saddle down on top of the partition between the stalls. Kit stared into the gloom. So he was going to be difficult. "You've been in the army, haven't you? You must know what sort of information's going out with your 'human cargoes.' "

When silence prevailed, Kit dropped her saddle on the partition and leaned on it to add: "You must have known men who died over there. How can you help the enemy kill more of our soldiers?"

In the dark, Jack closed his eyes against the memories her words unleashed. Known men who'd died? He'd had an entire troop die about him, blown to hell by cannon and grapeshot. He'd only escaped because a charger harnessed to one of the guns he'd been trying to reposition had fallen on him. And because Matthew, against all odds, had found him amidst the bloody carnage of the retreat.

Champion shifted, nudging him back to the present. Unclenching his fingers, he grabbed a handful of straw and fell to brushing the glossy grey coat. He had to keep moving, to keep doing, letting her words, however undeserved, wash over him. If he reacted, the truth would tumble out, and, God knew, the game they were playing was too dangerous for that.

When Kit realized she wasn't going to get any verbal reaction, she plowed on, determined to make Jack see the error of his ways. "Just because you survived with a whole skin doesn't mean you can forget about it."

Jack paused and considered telling her just how little he'd forgotten. Instead, he forced himself to continue mutely grooming Champion.

Kit glared in his direction, uncertain whether he could see her or not. She grasped some straw and started to brush Delia. "Smuggling's one thing. It might be against the law, but it's only dishonest. It's more than dishonest to make money from selling military information. From selling other men's lives. It's treason!"

Jack's brows rose. She should be in politics. He'd finished rubbing Champion down. He dropped the straw and headed for the door. As he crossed the front of the cottage, he heard a muffled oath from the stable. As he went through the doorway, he heard Kit's footsteps following. Jack headed straight for the keg on the sideboard.

Kit followed him into the room, slamming the door behind her. "Well, whatever . . ." Her voice died as she blinked into the black void left once the door had shut. She heard a muttered curse, then a boot hit a chair leg. An instant later, a match scraped, then soft light flared. Jack adjusted the wick, until the lamp threw just enough light to see by. Then he grabbed his glass, half-filled with brandy, and dropped into the chair on the other side of the table, his long legs stretched before him, his eyes broodingly watching her.

"Whatever," Kit reiterated firmly, trying to ignore all that lounging masculinity, "you can't continue to run your 'human cargoes.' They may pay well, but you're running too great a risk." She glared at the figure across the table, as inanimate as the chair he occupied. In the low light, she could barely make out his features, much less his expression. "What sort of leader knowingly exposes his men to such dangers?"

Jack shifted as her words pricked him. He prided himself on taking care of those in his command.

Kit sensed her advantage and pounced. "Smuggling's a transportable offense; treason's a hanging matter. You're deliberately leading these men, who don't know enough to understand the risks, to court death.'' When no response came, she lost her temper. ''Dammit! They've got families dependent on them! If they're taken and hanged, who's going to look after them?''

Jack's chair crashed to the floor, overturned as he surged to his feet. Kit's nerves jangled. She took an instinctive step back.

''What the hell would you know of taking care of anyone? Taking responsibility for anything? You're a *woman*, dammit!''

The outburst hauled Jack to his senses. Of course she was a woman. Of course she knew nothing of leading and the consequent worries. He should know better than to let a woman's words get under his skin. He frowned and took another sip of his brandy, holding her silent with a glower. What he couldn't fathom, what he should pay more attention to understanding, was why she was so opposed to him running spies. In his experience, women of her ilk cared little for such abstract matters. Whoever heard of a lowborn mistress lecturing her aristocratic lover on the morality of political intrigue?

With an effort, Kit shook free of Jack's intimidating stare and glared back. Setting her hands on her hips, she opened her mouth to put him right on the role of women.

Jack got in first, one long finger stabbing the air for emphasis. ''You're a woman. You're not the leader of a gang of smugglers—you played at being a lad in charge of a small group, but that's all.'' His empty glass hit the table. He placed both hands beside it and leaned forward. ''If I hadn't come along and relieved you of command, you'd have sunk without trace long since. You know nothing— *nothing*—of leading men.''

Kit's eyes sparked violet daggers; her lips parted on words of rebuttal.

Jack was in no mood to give her a chance. ''*And* if you've any notion on lecturing me on the matter, I suggest you keep your ill-advised opinions to yourself!''

Fury surged through Kit's veins, cindering her innate caution. Her eyes narrowed. ''I see.'' She studied the large form, bent intimidatingly over the table, the very table where she'd lain, sprawled in wanton abandon, five nights before, with him, erect, engorged, between her wide-spread thighs.

Kit blinked and shook aside the unhelpful memory. She rushed into speech. "In that case, I'll have to take..." Some sixth sense made her pause. She looked into the grey eyes watching her. Caution caught her tongue.

"Have to take...?"

Jack's soft prompt rang alarm bells in Kit's brain. Desperation came to her rescue. She put up her chin, cloaking her sudden uncertainty in truculence. "Take what steps I can to see that you don't get caught." Racked by nerves, she resettled her muffler. It was time for her to leave.

A cold calm descended on Jack, leaving little room for emotion. He saw straight through her obfuscation. "You mean to warn the authorities of our activities."

The statement brought Kit's head up so fast, she'd no time to wipe the truth from her eyes. The moment hung suspended between them, her silence confirming his conjecture more completely than any confession.

Realizing the trap she'd fallen into, Kit blushed. Denial was pointless, so she took the other tack. "If you continue to run spies, you leave me little choice."

"Whom do you plan to convince? Spencer?" Jack moved, smoothly, to come around the table.

Her mind on his words, Kit shrugged, raising her brows noncommittally. "Perhaps. Maybe I'll look up Lord Hendon—it's his responsibility, after all."

She swung to face Jack. And found him on the same side of the table and advancing slowly. Her heart leapt to her throat. She recalled the time on the Marchmont Hall terrace when she'd underestimated his speed. Cautiously, she backed away.

Her eyes rose to meet his. She read his intent in the darkened grey that had swallowed all trace of silver. "What do you think you're doing?" Irritation colored her tone. How like him to decide to play physical just now.

Despite his years of training, Jack couldn't stop himself from admiring the threat she posed. Satisfied he could reach the door before she could, he stopped with two yards between them and met her aggravated amethyst gaze. "I'm afraid, sweetheart, that you can't expect to leave just yet. Not after this little talk of ours." Jack couldn't keep a smile from twisting his lips as his mind assembled the rest of his plan. "You must see that I can't have you scurrying off to Lord Hendon." Heaven help him if she did!

Warily, Kit eyed the distance between them and decided it was enough. Despite his words, there was no overt threat in his tone or his stance. "And how were you planning to stop me? Wouldn't it be easier to just stop running spies?"

Jack's gilded head shook a decided negative. "As far as I can see,' he said, "the best thing I can do is keep you here."

"I won't stay, and you know you sleep soundly."

Jack raised a brow but didn't attempt to deny it. "You'll stay if I tie your hands to the headboard." When Kit's eyes widened, he added: "Remember the last time I had you with your hands tied? This time, I'll have you flat on your back in the middle of my bed."

Desire flickered hungrily in Kit's belly. She ignored it, blinking to dispel the images conjured up by his words, by his deepening tones. "There'll be a fuss if I disappear. They'll search the county."

"Perhaps. But I can assure you they won't search here."

His glib certainty struck Kit between the eyes. A conglomeration of disjointed facts fell into place. She stared at Jack. "You're in league with Lord Hendon."

Her tone of amazed discovery halted Jack; her words sent a thrill of expectation through him. She was so close to the truth. Would she guess the rest? If she did, what would she think?

It was his turn to be too slow with his denial to disguise the truth. Instead, he shrugged. "What if I am? There's no need for you to spend any of your time considering the subject. I've much more urgent matters for your attention." With that growled declaration of intent, Jack stepped forward.

Kit immediately backed away, her eyes wide. He was mad—she'd thought it often enough. "Jack!"

Jack took no notice of her imperious warning.

Kit drew a deep breath. And dashed for the door.

She'd taken no more than two steps before she felt the air at her back stir. With a shriek, she veered away from the door. Jack's body rushed past her, slamming against the wooden panels. Kit heard the bolt fall home.

Wild-eyed, Kit scanned the room and saw Jack's sword, propped against the wardrobe. Her heart thudding, she grabbed it up and whirled, wrenching the gleaming blade from the scabbard. She presented it, a lethal silver scythe transcribing a protective arc before her.

Jack froze, well out of her range. Inwardly, he cursed. Matthew had found the sword thrust to the back of the wardrobe. He'd taken it out and cleaned it before grinding the edge to exquisite sharpness. Apparently, he'd left it out in the belief his master should carry it.

Instead, his master, in full possession of his senses, now wished the sword he'd carried for ten years and more at the devil. If it'd been any other woman, he'd have walked calmly forward and taken it. But even though Kit had to use both hands to keep the blade balanced, Jack didn't make the mistake of thinking she couldn't use it. He didn't for a moment believe she'd run him through, but by the time she realized that, her stroke might be too advanced to stop, given her unfamiliarity with that particular blade, weighted for slashing swings, not thrust and parry. She might not kill him, but she could do serious damage. Even more frightening was the possibility she might get hurt herself.

That thought forced Jack to move cautiously. His gaze locked with Kit's, steadying, trying to will some of his calm into the frightened violet eyes. He wasn't sure how far she was from real panic, but he didn't think she'd hand over the sword, not after his threats. Slowly, he edged around the bed, away from her. Her eyes followed, intent on his movement, clearly puzzled by it.

Her breathing was too fast. Kit tried to contain her panic, but she was no longer sure of anything. She frowned when Jack stopped on the opposite side of the bed. What was he up to? She couldn't make for the door; he was far too fast for that. The corner of the room was just a step away; she'd already backed as far as she could into its protection.

Jack moved so fast Kit barely saw the blur. One moment he was standing still, feet apart, hands relaxed by his sides. The next, he'd grabbed the covers and whipped them over the sword, following them over the bed to wrench the blade from her hands. Over her shriek, Kit heard the muffled thud as the sword hit the ground, flung out of harm's way. Jack's arms closed about her, an oddly protective trap.

Struggling made no impression. Her legs were pressed against the bed, then she was toppled onto it. Kit's breath was knocked out of her when Jack landed on top of her. He used his body to subdue her struggles, his legs trapping hers, his hips weighting hers down, long fingers holding her head, gradually exerting pressure until she kept still. Half-smothered by his chest, Kit had to wait until he shifted to look down at her before opening her mouth to blister his ears. But no sound escaped her. Instead, his mouth found hers and his tongue filled the void with brandy-coated fire.

One by one, Kit felt her muscles give up the fight, relaxing as his intoxicating taste filled her senses, warming her from the inside out. The scandalous idea of being tied to his bedhead took on a rosy glow. As the insidious effect spread, her beleaguered mind summoned its last defenses. It couldn't happen. But she'd only have one chance to change her fate.

For one long moment, Kit flowed with the tide, then, abruptly, she threw every muscle against him, pushing hard to dislodge him and roll his weight from her.

Jack was taken aback by the force of her shove. But, instead of suppressing it by sheer weight, he decided to roll with her push and bring her up over him. Fully atop her, he couldn't reach that particular area of her buttocks that always proved so helpfully arousing. Reversing their positions was an excellent idea. He rolled, pulling her with him.

His head hit the bedend, concealed beneath the disarranged sheets.

Kit knew the instant he lost consciousness. His lips left hers; his fingers slid from her hair. She stared down into his face, oddly stripped of emotion, relaxed and at peace. In panic, she wriggled off him. She placed a hand on his chest and breathed a sigh of relief when she felt his heart beating steadily. Puzzled, she felt under his head and found the rounded wood of the bedend. The mystery solved, she sat up and tugged him farther onto the bed, then fetched a pillow to cradle his head.

Kit sat and frowned at her threat removed. How long would he remain unconscious? Reflecting that his skull had shown every indication of being thick, she decided a tactical withdrawal was her only option. She'd tried her best to make him see sense; his actions, his words, left her no alternative but to act.

Late-afternoon sunlight spilled through the cottage door, glimmering along the gilt edges of the playing cards Jack shuffled back and forth. His long fingers re-formed the pack, then briskly set them out.

Jack grimaced at the hand. All very well to play at Patience; he was desperately short of the commodity. But, despite the promptings of his wilder self, there was blessedly little he could do. When he'd woken in the dead of night to find himself alone, nursing a sore skull, he'd initially thought Kit had coshed him. Then the final moments of their tussle had cleared in his painful head and he'd worked it out. Small comfort that had been. She'd stated, categorically, that she was going to cause him heaps of trouble.

Irritation itched; he shook aside his thoughts and stared at the cards.

What would she do? He didn't feel qualified to guess, given he still couldn't fathom her peculiar intensity over the spies. She'd threatened to go to Lord Hendon. He'd considered that long and hard, eventually quitting home immediately after breakfast, leaving his butler, Lovis, with a most peculiar set of instructions. Luckily, Lovis knew him well enough not to feel the remotest surprise. Hopefully, no other redheaded woman would call unattended on Lord Hendon.

Driven by a growing sense of unease, he'd gone to Hunstanton and put Tonkin through his paces. His message ought to have been clear, but Tonkin's interest in his "big gang'' had grown to an obsession. Regardless of orders, Jack didn't trust the old bruiser an inch. He didn't think Tonkin trusted him, either. The man wasn't stupid, just an incompetent bully. He'd left Hunstanton even more disturbed than before.

The feeling that had taken root in his gut was all too familiar. Years of campaigning, both overtly and covertly, had instilled a watchfulness, a finely honed sixth sense, always on the alert for danger. With the steady drub of Champion's hooves filling his ears, he'd headed for the cottage, watching the storm gathering on his horizon swell and grow, knowing it would soon unleash its fury, wreaking havoc with his well-laid plans. And feeling totally impotent in the face of impending disaster.

But he was used to meeting that particular challenge and had long since perfected the mental and physical discipline needed to see any storm through.

However, the fact that Kit was enmeshed in the danger, up to her pretty neck, set a worried edge on his nervous energy. Theoretically, he should have already taken steps to nullify the threat she posed. In reality, there seemed little he could do without further jeopardizing his mission. Forced to spend the hours until the run in idle isolation, he'd had time to consider his options. The only one with any real merit was kidnapping. He'd have to be careful not to be seen by any on the Cranmer estate, but he could keep her here, in safety and comfort, for a week or so, until the worst was past. If the mission dragged on, as it quite possibly would, he'd move her up to the Castle once the first hue and cry had died. There, safety and comfort, both hers and his, would be assured. She'd be his prisoner, but after the first inevitable fury, he didn't think she'd mind. He'd ensure she was occupied.

The idea of having time to get to know Kit, of having the leisure to learn why she thought as she did, felt as she did, blossomed before him. Jack forgot his cards, mesmerized by a sudden glimpse into a future he'd never previously found attractive. Women, he'd always firmly believed, had but one real role in life—to pander to their man's wishes. An aristocratic wife—his, for instance—

would bear his children and manage his households, act as his hostess and support his position socially. Beyond that, she figured in his mind much as Matthew or Lovis did. His many mistresses had had but one sphere of responsibility— the bedroom—where they'd spent the majority of time flat on their backs, efficiently catering to his needs. The only communication he recalled having with them was by way of soft moans and groans and funny little gasps. He'd never been interested in what they'd thought. Not on any subject.

Absentmindedly gathering the cards, Jack refocused his abstracted gaze. The more he thought of it, the more benefits he saw in kidnapping Kit. After tonight, assuming they both survived the coming storm, he'd act.

Spencer, of course, would have to be told. He couldn't steal away the old man's granddaughter, whom he clearly cared for, and leave him to grieve unnecessarily. It would mean overturning one of his golden rules—he'd never, not even as a child, told people more than they'd needed to know, a habit that had stood him in good stead over the years. But he couldn't have Spencer on his conscience any more than he could tolerate Kit continuing her dangerous crusade.

At the thought of her, his redheaded houri, a stern frown settled over his face. He hadn't asked to feel about her as he did, but there was no point in denying it. She was more than the latest in a long line; he cared for her in ways he couldn't remember caring for anyone else in his life. Once he had her safe, he'd drum into her red head just what the upshot of that was. She would have to mend her ways— no more dangerous escapades.

Would she be silly enough to try to turn some of the men against him? Jack shuddered. There was no value in torturing himself. Shutting out his imaginary horrors, he purposefully reshuffled the cards.

Ten minutes later, the peace of sunset was interrupted by the steady clop of hooves, approaching from the east. Jack raised his head to listen. Both the confident pace and the direction suggested George had come to their rendezvous early. A glimpse of sleek chestnut hide crossing the clearing brought a half smile to Jack's face. He needed distraction.

George came through the door, his face set in disapproving lines.

Jack's smile of welcome faded. His brows rose.

George halted before the table, his gaze steady on Jack's grey eyes. Then he glanced at the keg on the sideboard. "Is there anything in that?"

With a grunt, Jack rose and fetched a glass. After a second's hesitation, he took a glass for himself and half filled both. Was this the start of his storm?

George drew up a chair to the table and dropped into it.

Placing one glass before George, Jack eyed his serious face. He resumed his seat. "Well? You'd better tell me before Matthew gets here."

George took a sip and glanced at the open door. He got up, shut it, then paced back to the table. He put his glass down, but remained standing. "I went to see Amy this afternoon."

When George fell into a pensive daze and yielded nothing further, Jack couldn't resist. "She wants to call off the wedding?"

George flushed and frowned. "Of course not! For God's sake, be sensible. This is serious."

Jack duly composed his features. George grimaced and continued: "When I was leaving, I got talking to Jeffries, Gresham's head groom. The man's a mine of information on horses."

Jack's stomach clenched, but his expression remained undisturbed.

George's gaze leveled. "We were talking of bloodlines in the district. He mentioned a black Arab mare, finicky and highbred. According to Jeffries, she belongs to one of Amy's friends."

"Amy's friend?" Jack blinked and the veils fell. He knew, then, what was coming. He should have guessed; there'd been enough inconsistencies in her performance. If he hadn't been so besotted with her, doubtless he'd have unmasked her long ago. The idea that some part of him had known, but he hadn't wanted to face the truth, he buried deep.

"Amy's bosom-bow," George confirmed, his voice heavy with disapproval. "Miss Kathryn Cranmer. Known as Kit to her intimates." George slumped into his chair. "She's Christopher Cranmer's daughter, Spencer's grandchild." George studied Jack's face. "His legitimate granddaughter."

Spencer's legitimate granddaughter. The thought reeled through Jack's brain in dizzying splendor. Stunned shock vied with disbelief, before both gave way to an overwhelming urge to lay hold of Kit and shake the damned woman as she deserved. How *dared* she take such scandalous risks? Clearly, Spencer had no control over her. Jack made a mental note to be sure the full magnitude of her sins was made clear to his redheaded houri in breeches— not that she'd get a chance to wear breeches again. She'd have to learn to take very good care—of herself, of her reputation. As Lord Hendon, he'd every right to ensure the future Lady Hendon played safe.

For that, of course, was the crowning glory of George's revelations. As Miss Kathryn Cranmer, Kit was more than eligible for the vacant post of Lady Hendon. And after their recent activities, there was no possibility he'd let her slip through his net. He had her right where he wanted her—in more ways than one. After tonight's run, he'd call on Spencer. Between them, they'd settle the future of one redheaded houri.

A smile of pleasant anticipation suffused Jack's face.

George saw it and sighed heavily. "From that besotted look, I take it affairs between you and Kit have gone a lot farther than I'd feel happy about?"

Jack grinned beatifically.

"Christ!" George ran one hand through his dark hair. "Stop grinning. What the hell do you plan to do about it?"

Jack blinked. His grin faded. "Don't be a fool. I'll marry the damned woman, of course."

George just stared, too astounded to say anything.

Jack swallowed his irritation that George should have entertained any other option. That George had thought *he'd* entertain any other option. It was all Kit's fault. Any woman running about in breeches was fair game. At least only George knew who she was. Then it hit him. "When did you guess she was a woman?"

George blinked, then shrugged. "A week or so ago."

Puzzled, Jack asked: "What gave her away?" He'd thought Kit's disguise particularly good.

"You, mostly," George absentmindedly replied.

"What do you mean—*me*?"

Jack's aggressive tone recaptured George's attention. Briefly, he grinned. "The way you behaved toward Kit led to only one conclusion. Which I'll be bound the rest of the Gang jumped to. Matthew and I know you rather better. Which made us wonder about Kit."

"Humph!" Jack took a swig of his brandy. Had any of the others guessed? Now she'd assumed the title of his future wife, he felt much more critical of Kit's wildness. He wasn't at all sure he approved of her having the nerve to do such outrageous things. It didn't auger well for a peaceful married life.

Jack glanced up to find the shadows deepening. The run was scheduled for immediately after nightfall. He hoped Kit would turn up. Now that he understood what a prize she was, he wanted her safe in his keeping. Quite how he'd handle her return to Cranmer and the inevitable interview with Spencer he hadn't yet decided. But he wanted her with him tonight.

He wanted to give her a piece of his mind, apologize, propose, and make love to her.

The order was beyond him; he'd leave that in the hands of the gods.

Chapter 21

A brisk northeasterly was whipping along the cliffs by the time Kit reached the coast. Dark clouds scudded before the moon. In the fitful light, she found the Hunstanton Gang already unloading their boats, the ponies lined up on the sands. The surf ran high; the crash of waves cloaked the scene in noise. As she watched, a light drizzle started to fall.

Squinting through the damp veil, Kit spotted Jack's lookout. The man was perched on a hillock commanding a fair view of the area. Her approach had been screened by wind-twisted trees, but he'd be unlikely to miss any larger mass of horsemen.

Staring at the boats, Kit picked out the figure of Captain Jack, tall and broad-shouldered, wading through the surf, a keg under each arm. The sight brought no comfort to her tortured brain.

What was she to do? Last night had passed in agonized self-argument as she sifted the possibilities, considered every avenue. In the end, everything had hinged on one point—did she really believe Jack was involved in spying himself? The answer was a definite, unshakable, albeit unsubstantiated, No. Given that, she'd concluded that speaking to Lord Hendon was the only safe way forward.

Jack had admitted a connection with the High Commissioner, one that presumably involved supplying brandy to the Castle cellars. Hopefully, his powerful benefactor would be able to succeed where she had failed and force sense through Jack's skull. She couldn't believe Lord Hendon would condone smuggling spies; she felt confident she could make him understand that Jack was not personally involved, just misguided.

But Lord Hendon had not been at home. She'd whipped up her courage and gone to the Castle on her afternoon ride. The head groom had been apologetic. Lord Hendon had left the house early; it was not known when he'd return.

She'd gone back to Cranmer even more worried than when she'd set out. She'd have to make sure she spoke to Lord Hendon soon, or her courage would desert her. Or Jack would catch her and tie her to his headboard.

His threat had forced her to face reality. Ever since their liaison had gone beyond the innocent, she'd been battling her conscience. Guilt now sat on her shoulders, a heavy and constant weight. She'd lost all chance of making a respectable match, a fact that caused her no regret, but she knew how saddened Spencer would be if he ever learned of it. Jack's hold over her, over her senses, was strong, but she was too wise to let it go on. Disaster skulked the hedges of that road—she knew it well enough.

So here she was, watching over Jack's operations in the hope of following the next spy he brought in. If she could find the next connection, she could give that to Lord Hendon as a place where official scrutiny could start, avoiding any mention of Jack and the Hunstanton Gang. It was one thing to hold to the high road and condemn men for running spies. It was another to betray men she knew to the hangman. She couldn't do it.

There were some among the Gang she wouldn't trust an inch, but they were not true villains. Misled, badly influenced, they might commit foul deeds, but ever since she'd known them they'd behaved as reasonable beings, if not honest ones. They'd done nothing to deserve death. Other than assist the spies.

The drizzle intensified. A raindrop slid under her tricorne and coursed sluggishly down her neck. Kit shifted and glanced west, toward Holme.

The sight that met her eyes tensed every muscle. Delia, alerted, lifted her head to stare at a small troop of Revenue

Officers picking their way along the cliffs. Another hundred yards and they'd see the activity on the beach.

Strangling her curses, Kit swung to stare at Jack's lookout. Surely he could see them? A small spurt of flame was her answer, followed by the noise of a shot, instantly drowned by the waves' roar. She heard the shot, but it was immediately apparent that neither Jack and his men, nor the Revenue troop, had. Both parties proceeded as before, unperturbed.

"Oh, God." Kit sat Delia in an agony of indecision. There was no way the lookout, scrambling from his perch, could get close enough to warn the men on the beach before the Revenue were upon them. Men on foot stood no chance against mounted troops armed with sabers and pistols. Her choice was clear. She could warn the Gang, or sit and watch their destruction.

Delia broke from the cover of the trees and went straight to the head of the nearest cliff path. In seconds, they were down, then flying over the sands toward the men by the boats.

Jack took another keg from Noah and waded slowly ashore. The tide was running high, the sands shifting underfoot. Spray and spume blotted out the cliffs; the roar of the waves drowned all other sounds. But the frown on Jack's face was not due to the conditions. He was worried about Kit.

Not even George knew of her threat to disrupt the Gang's activities; that information put her life in too much danger to be shared, even with his closest friend. But the sense that a storm was edging closer, that fate was closing in, on him and on her, was intensifying with each passing hour. And he didn't know where she was, much less what she was doing.

Matthew had arrived from the Castle with the disturbing news that she'd been there, but slipped through his net. The fact that she'd had the strength of purpose to try to see Lord Hendon was causing him grave concern. Unable to see the High Commissioner, would she take her information elsewhere? Jack hefted the keg to the back of a pony, wishing he could shrug off his worries as easily.

A black blur at the edge of his vision had him swinging around. He recognized Kit instantly. Equally instant came recognition of the reason for her speed. The storm was about to break.

His bellowed command saw all hands double pace, securing the last of the kegs, men scrambling aboard the lead ponies. The desperate struggle to clear the beach was already under way as he and George ran to the end of the line, to where Kit would pull up.

Kit saw them waiting, Jack's hands open at his sides, ready to catch Delia's bridle and quiet the excited mare. Abruptly, she pulled up ten yards away, out of their reach.

Jack swore and stepped forward.

Instantly, Kit pulled Delia back on her haunches, sharp black hooves flailing the air. When Jack stopped, she let Delia down but kept the reins tight. "Revenue. Only six. They'll be around the bluff any minute!" She had to scream over the sound of the waves.

Jack nodded curtly. "Go east!"

If there was any question as to the absolute nature of the bellowed command, his arm, pointing toward Brancaster, dispelled it. But Kit could see they'd never make it off the beach in time; the Revenue were too close.

A cry on the wind drew all eyes to the bluff. The troopers came tumbling over the ridge, their horses slithering through the sand dunes.

Kit looked back at the smugglers. The boats were pulling out; the ponies were almost ready to go. Matthew had left to get the horses. Five minutes would see them all safe. Her eyes locked with Jack's. He read her decision in that instant and lunged for her reins. Kit moved faster. She sprang Delia. West.

"Christ!" George joined Jack, staring aghast at Kit's dwindling figure. "She'll never make it!"

"She will," Jack ground out. "She has to," he added, under his breath.

The black streak that was Kit hugged the line of the waves, as far from the cliff as possible. The troopers saw her flying toward them and checked at the cliff foot. When it became clear she would pass them by, they milled uncertainly, then, with a bellow to stand, they set off to intercept her. But they'd misjudged Delia's speed and left it too late. Kit swept past and on toward Holme. With cries and curses, the Revenue charged in pursuit.

Biting back a curse, Jack swung and roared his orders, setting the men on their way. Soon, he and George were the only ones left standing. Matthew arrived with the horses; vaulting to the saddle, Jack yelled: "She'll have to go inland before Holme." Then Champion surged.

Jack leaned over Champion's neck, holding the grey to a wicked pace, trying, over the pounding of his heart, to take stock. Had Kit tipped off the Revenue, then changed her mind at the last minute?

The thought twisted through him, a sour serpent sowing seeds of doubt. Abruptly, he shook it aside. Kit had drawn the Revenue off at her own expense and was now in considerable danger. He'd concentrate on saving her satin hide first; learning the truth could come later.

Jack forced his mind to business. Kit was not well-versed in pursuit and evasion; on the other hand, Delia was the fastest thing on four legs this side of the Channel. But Holme, on its rocky promontory that blocked the beach, was close; Kit could not lose the Revenue before running out of beach. She'd have to go inland, taking to the fields or heading on to the west coast.

The drizzle intensified. Jack welcomed the sting of rain on his face. He swore, volubly, comprehensively, his gut clenched, the chill of doom in his veins. They'd started well behind the Revenue. When they sighted the promontory, the beach between them was deserted. Jack rode to where a well-worn cliff path led up from the beach. He drew rein where the path narrowed as it turned up the cliff. The sand was freshly and deeply churned. Jack drew his pistol and signaled to George and Matthew before sending Champion quietly up the path. There was no one at the top. Jack dismounted and studied the ground; George and Matthew rode in wide arcs.

"This way," George called softly. "Looks like the whole troop."

Jack remounted and walked Champion to view the barren stretch of track leading west. When he raised his head, his expression was grim. Kit had taken her pursuers as far from the Hunstanton Gang's field of operations as possible. She was making for the beach north of Hunstanton, to head south along the wide stretches of pale sand at a pace the Revenue could never match. Doubtless, she thought to come up to the cliffs somewhere near Heacham or Snettis-ham, to disappear into the fields and coppices of the Cran-mer estate.

It was a good plan, as far as it went. There was just one snag. With his sense of doom pressing blackly upon him, Jack prayed that, for the first time in his life, his premo-nition would be wrong.

Without a word, he set his heels to Champion's sides.

Far ahead, on the pale swathes of sand lapped by the waves of the Wash, Kit hugged Delia's neck and flew be-fore the wind. Once she was sure the Revenue had followed her, she'd watched her pace, holding back so they remained in sight, held firm to their purpose by her bobbing figure forever before them. She'd had to pull up on the cliff top near Holme, letting them get close enough to see her clearly. Like obedient puppies, they'd followed, noses glued to her trail as she'd led them onto the beach above Hunstanton. Now that they were too far from Brancaster to give Jack and his crew any trouble, she was intent on losing them and heading for the safety of home.

Delia's long stride ate the miles. Kit saw the indentation that marked the track up to Heacham just ahead. She checked Delia and looked behind her.

There was no sign of her pursuers.

Kit threw back her head and laughed, exhilaration pump-ing through her veins. Her laughter echoed back from the cliffs, startling her into silence. Here in the Wash, the waves were far gentler cousins of the surf pounding the north coast. All was relatively silent, relatively serene. Shaking off a shiver of apprehension, Kit sent Delia toward the track to Heacham.

She'd almost reached the foot of the track when a horde of horsemen broke cover, pouring over the cliff, another group of Revenue men, barking orders she barely heard. A spurt of flame glowed in the night.

A searing pain tore through her left shoulder.

Delia reared. Instinctively, Kit wrenched her south. The mare went straight to a gallop; the reins slack, Delia lengthened her stride, quickly travelling beyond pistol range. The Revenue Officers howled in pursuit.

Kit was deaf to their noise.

Grimly, she hung on, her fingers laced into Delia's mane, the stringy black hair whipping her cheek as she laid her head against the glossy neck. Delia's hooves pounded the sand, carrying her southward.

Jack, George, and Matthew caught up with the small Revenue troop on the beach south of Hunstanton. The Officers had given up the unequal chase. They milled about, disgruntled and disappointed, then re-formed and headed for the track up from the beach.

Concealed in the shadows of the cliff, Jack heaved a sigh of relief.

A shot rang out, echoing eerily over the water.

Jack's blood chilled. Under his breath, he swore. Kit had been hit—he was sure of it.

The Revenue troop also heard the shot. Instead of heading for home, they wheeled and cantered along the sands. Once they gained sufficient lead, Jack gave the signal to follow.

Battling faintness and a white haze of pain, Kit struggled to focus on what she should do. The hot agony in her shoulder was draining her strength. If she stayed on the sands, Delia would keep on until she fell from the saddle. As each stride the mare took pushed fiery needles into her shoulder, that wouldn't be long delayed. And then the Revenue would have her.

Spencer's image rose in her mind; Kit gritted her teeth. She had to get off the beach.

As if in answer to her prayer, the small track leading up the cliffs to Snettisham appeared before her. Gasping with the effort, Kit turned Delia into the narrow opening. The mare took the climb without further direction.

Waves of cold darkness welled about her; Kit fought them back. She rode with knees and hands, the reins dangling uselessly about Delia's neck. It was all Kit could do to discern the direction of the quarries and head Delia toward them.

In her wake, her pursuers came on, noisily clamoring for her blood, all but baying their enthusiasm.

A cold, shrouding mist closed in. Kit hugged Delia's glossy neck, her cheek against the warm wet hide. She tugged her muffler away from her dry lips and struggled to draw breath. Even that hurt.

The mouth of the quarries loomed out of the dark. Obedient to her weak tug, Delia slowed. Using her knees, Kit guided the mare into the quarries. If she could rest for a while and gather her strength, then Cranmer was not far away.

Delia walked among the jumbled rocks, hoofbeats muffled by the matted grass covering the disused tracks. Kit's cheek rose and fell with each stride. There was blackness all around, cold and deep, empty and painless. She could feel it enshrouding her. Kit focused on the black gloss of Delia's hide. Black rushed in and filled her senses. Black engulfed her. Black.

The scene Jack, George, and Matthew finally came upon was farcical. The Revenue troop had kept to the beach as far as the Heacham trail, then had gone up to the cliff top and continued south; they had followed quietly. The noise emanating from Snettisham drove them to pull away and enter the tiny village from the east, keeping within cover.

The place was in an uproar. The villagers had been woken and turned out of their houses; a large troop of Revenue men was searching the premises.

Jack, George and Matthew sat their mounts in stunned

disbelief. One glance was enough to convince them that Kit and Delia were not present. With a contemptuous snort, Jack pulled Champion about. They retreated to a shadowy coppice separated by a field from the activity around Snettisham.

George drew his chestnut up beside Champion. "She must have got away."

Jack sat still and tried to believe it, waiting for the explanation to unlock the vise that fear had clamped about his heart. Finally, he sighed. "Possibly. You two go home. I'll check if she's got back to Cranmer."

George shook his head. "No. We'll stick with you until all's clear. How will you know if she's already got in?"

"There's a way into the stables. If Delia's there, Kit's home." The memory of how the mare had stayed by Kit when he'd brought her down on the sands so many moons ago was reassuring. "Delia won't leave Kit."

George grunted, turning his horse toward Cranmer Hall.

Reaching the stables was no problem; ascertaining Delia's presence in the dark took much longer. Twenty minutes after he'd left them, Jack rejoined George and Matthew outside the stable paddock, his grim face telling them his news.

"Not there?" George asked.

Jack shook his head.

"You think she's been shot?" It was Matthew, lugubrious as ever, who put their thoughts into words.

Jack drew a tense breath, then let out a short sigh. "Yes. If not, she'd be here."

"She lost them at Snettisham, so presumably she's somewhere between there and here."

George jumped when Jack thumped his shoulder.

"That's it!" Jack hissed. "Snettisham quarries. That's where she'll have gone to earth."

As they swung up to their saddles, George grimaced. Snettisham quarries were enormous, new digs jostling with old. Neither he nor Jack knew them well; Snettisham was too far from Castle Hendon to have been one of their playgrounds. Not so for the Cranmers; Snettisham was on their doorstep. Finding an injured Cranmer in the quarries was going to take time, time Kit might not have.

George had reckoned without Champion. They returned to Snettisham to find the Revenue gone and the village quiet. At the mouth of the quarries, Jack let Champion have his head. The big grey ambled forward, stopping now and then to snuff the air. George wondered at Jack's patience, then caught a glimpse of his face. Jack was wound tight, more tense and grim than George had ever seen him.

Champion led them deep into a section of old diggings. Suddenly, the stallion surged. Jack drew rein, holding the grey back. Sliding to the ground, Jack quieted the great beast and signaled for George and Matthew to dismount. Puzzled, they did, then they heard the muttering coming from around the next bend in the track.

Matthew took the horses, nodding at Jack's silent direction to muzzle Champion. George followed Jack to the bend in the track.

His saddle pistol in one hand, Jack stood in the shadow of a rock and eased forward until he could see the next stretch. Moonlight silvered the hunched shoulders of Sergeant Tonkin, shuffling along, eyes on the ground, his mount ambling disinterestedly behind him.

"I swear we hit 'im. Can't be wrong. *Must've* at least winged 'im."

Still muttering, Tonkin followed the track on. A large opening to one side drew his attention. Abruptly he stopped muttering and disappeared through it.

Jack and George slid silently in his wake.

A clearing lay before them. At the far end, the entrance to an old tunnel loomed like the black mouth of hell. Before it, as black as the blackest shadow, stood Delia, head up, ears pricked. At Delia's feet lay a rumpled form, stretched out and silent.

"I knew it!" Tonkin crowed. He dropped his reins and raced forward. Delia shied; Tonkin waved his hands to ward off the skittish animal. Reaching the still figure, he grabbed the old tricorne and tugged it off.

Moonlight played on a pale face, haloed in red curls.

Tonkin stared. "Well, I'll be damned!"

With that, he slipped into peaceful oblivion, rendered

insensible by the impact of Jack's pistol butt on the back of his skull.

Swearing, Jack shoved Tonkin aside and fell on his knees beside Kit. With fingers that shook, he searched for the pulse at her throat. The beat was there, weak but steady. Jack drew a ragged breath. Briefly, he closed his eyes, opening them as George knelt on Kit's other side. She was lying on her stomach; with George's help, Jack turned her onto her back.

"Christ!" George blanched. The front of Kit's shirt was soaked in blood. The hole in her shoulder still bled sluggishly.

Jack gritted his teeth against the cold spreading through him; chill fingers clutched his heart. His face a stony mask, he lifted Kit's coat from the wound, fighting to conquer his shock and respond professionally. He had tended wounded soldiers often enough; the wound was serious but not necessarily fatal. However, the ball had lodged deep in Kit's soft flesh.

Turning, Jack called Matthew. "Go for Dr. Thrushborne. I don't care what you have to do but get him to Cranmer Hall as fast as possible."

Matthew grunted and went.

Jack and George packed the wound, padding it with the sleeves torn from their shirts and securing it with their neckerchiefs. Kit had already lost a dangerous amount of blood.

"What now?" George sat back on his heels.

"We take her to Cranmer. Thrushborne can be trusted." Jack rose and clicked his fingers at Delia. The mare hesitated, then slowly approached. "I'll have to tell Spencer the truth."

"All of the truth?" George clambered to his feet. "Is that wise?"

Jack rubbed a fist across his forehead and tried to think. "Probably not. I'll tell him as much as I have to. Enough to explain things." He tied Delia's reins to Champion's saddle.

"What about Tonkin? He saw too much."

Jack cast a malevolent glance at the Sergeant's inanimate

form. "Much as I'd like to remove him from this earth, his disappearance would cause too many ripples." His jaw set. "We'll have to convince him he was mistaken."

George said no more; stooping, he lifted Kit into his arms.

Jack swung up to Champion's saddle, then, leaning down, took Kit's limp form from George. Carefully, he cradled her against his chest, tucking her head into his shoulder. He looked at George, a worried frown on his face. "I'll need you to get into Cranmer. After that, you'd better go home." A weak, weary smile, a parody of Captain Jack's usual ebullience, showed through his concern, then faded. "I've enough to answer for without you added to the bill."

Chapter 22

The ride to Cranmer Hall was the longest two miles Jack had ever traveled. Kit remained unconscious, a minor mercy. To have her severely wounded was bad enough; to be forced to watch her bear the pain would have been torture. His guilt ran deep, increasing with every stride Champion took. His fear for Kit was far worse, dragging at his mind, threatening to cloak reason with black despair.

At least he now knew she hadn't betrayed them. If Tonkin had received word that his ''big gang'' was running a cargo that night, the whole Hunstanton Office would have been on the northern beaches. Instead, it seemed he'd set a small troop to patrol the area of his obsession. They'd just struck lucky.

Cranmer Hall rose out of the dark. Kit's home slumbered amid darkened gardens, peaceful and secure. Jack stopped before the front steps. With Kit in his arms, he slid from the saddle. George tied his chestnut to a bush by the drive, then hurried to catch Champion's reins.

''Once I'm inside, take him around to the stables before you go.''

George nodded and led the grey aside.

Jack climbed the steps and waited before the heavy oak doors for George to join him. When he did, Jack, his face impassive, nodded at the large brass knocker in the middle of the door. ''Wake them up.''

George grimaced and did. The pounding brought footsteps flying. Bolts were thrown back; the heavy doors swung inward. George melted into the shadows at the bottom of the steps. Jack strode boldly over the threshold.

"Your mistress has had an accident." Jack searched the four shocked male faces before him, settling on the oldest and most dignified as being the best candidate for Cranmer's butler. "I'm Lord Hendon. Wake Lord Cranmer immediately. Tell him his granddaughter has been wounded. I'll explain as soon as I've taken her upstairs. Which is her room?" During this exchange, he walked confidently toward the stairs. Turning back, brows lifting impatiently, he prayed the butler would hold true to his profession and not panic.

Jenkins rose to the challenge. "Yes, m'lord." He drew a deep breath. "Henry here will show you Miss Kathryn's room. I'll send up her maid immediately."

Jack nodded, relieved he wouldn't have to deal with dithering servants. "I've sent my man for Dr. Thrushborne. He should arrive soon." He started up the stairs, Henry hurrying ahead, holding a candelabrum aloft to light the way.

Jenkins followed. "Very good, m'lord. I'll have one of the men watch out for him. I'll inform Lord Cranmer of the matter directly."

Jack nodded and followed Henry down a dark corridor deep into one of the wings. The footman stopped by a door near its end and set it wide.

Worried by the chilled dampness of Kit's clothes, Jack's eyes went immediately to the fireplace. "Get the fire going. Fast as you can."

"Yes, m'lord." Henry bent to the task.

Jack crossed to the four-poster bed. Kneeling on the white coverlet, he gently placed Kit upon it, carefully easing his arms from under her then arranging the pillows beneath her head, pulling the bolster around to cushion her injured shoulder. Then he stood back.

And tried to hold his thoughts at bay. He'd experienced war firsthand; he'd nearly perished twice. But the mind-numbing fear that threatened to possess him now was beyond anything he'd previously felt. The idea that Kit might not live he blanked from his mind; that was a possibility he could not face. Drawing an unsteady breath, he fought to focus his mind on the here and now, on the tasks immediately before him. The next hours would be crucial. Kit had to live. And she had to be protected from the consequences of her actions. First things first. He had to get her out of her wet clothes.

Jack turned to survey Henry's handiwork. The fire blazed in the grate, throwing light and warmth into the room. "Good. Now go shake that maid awake."

Henry's eyes grew round. "Elmina?"

Jack frowned. "Miss Kathryn's maid." He nodded a curt dismissal, wondering what was wrong with Elmina.

Henry swallowed and looked doubtful, but went.

Jack paced before the fire, rubbing sensation and strength back into his arms. When Elmina failed to materialize, he swore and returned to Kit's side. Carefully, he untied their makeshift bandage. The wound had stopped bleeding. He started the difficult task of easing Kit from her wet clothes.

He'd removed her coat and was fumbling with the laces of her shirt when the door behind him opened and shut. Quick footsteps and stiffly swishing skirts approached.

"Mon Dieu! Ma pauvre petite! Qu'est-ce qui s'est passé?"

Jack blinked at the torrent of French that followed hard on the heels of that beginning. He stared at the small darkhaired woman who appeared on the other side of the bed to lean over Kit, laying a hand on her forehead. Then she noticed what he was doing and slapped furiously at his hands.

Jack recoiled from the ferocious attack and her equally ferocious words. Glancing toward the end of the bed, he saw two young maids hovering uncertainly. From their blank looks, Jack surmised they couldn't understand French. The virago, presumably Elmina, was dividing her time between verbally wringing her hands over Kit and hurling insults at him. What loosely translated as "blackguard" and "mountebank" were the least of them.

When Elmina bustled around and tried to shoo him from the room, Jack came to his senses. "*Silence!*" He spoke smoothly in French. "Cease your wailing, woman! We need to get her into something dry immediately." Jack leaned back over Kit and started on her laces again. His idiomatic French had set Elmina back on her heels. "We'll need bandages and hot water. Can you manage that?"

His sarcasm flicked Elmina to attention. She drew a fulminating breath; Jack looked at her and imperiously lifted one brow. Elmina's glance fell to the still figure on the bed, then she swung about and addressed the two maids. "Ella— get all the old sheets you can find. Ask Mrs. Fogg. Emily— run to the kitchen and fetch the kettle. And tell Cook to prepare some gruel."

Jack shook his head. "She won't be able to eat. Not until we get the bullet out of her."

"*Mon Dieu*! It's still there?"

The last lace unraveled. Jack looked up into Elmina's black eyes, pieces of coal in a face pale with anxiety. Despite her sprightly movements, she was a lot older than he'd expected. And, judging from her tirade, hellishly protective of Kit. How had his kitten escaped this mother cat? "Your mistress is lucky to be alive. She's going to need help to stay alive. Now help me get this off her." He pulled his sharp knife from its sheath in his boot and quickly slit the shirt. "Come around here. Bring that towel with you."

Picking up the small towel lying folded on Kit's washstand, Elmina hurried to obey. Jack freed the wound of torn fragments of shirt, then covered the angry flesh with the towel. "Help me ease off this sleeve."

With Elmina's help, the sleeve was removed without jarring the wound. Picking up his knife, Jack reached for Kit's wet bands.

"*Monsieur!*"

Jack all but snarled. "What now?"

Elmina's eyes were huge black orbs. Under Jack's glare, she clenched her hands tight. "*Monsieur*, it is not proper that you should be here. I will take care of her."

Proper? Jack closed his eyes in frustration. Neither he nor Kit possessed a proper bone in their bodies. He opened his eyes. "Damnation, woman! I've seen every square inch of skin your *pauvre petite* possesses. Right now, I'm trying to ensure that she lives. The proprieties be damned!"

He'd spoken in English. Elmina took a moment or two

to catch up. By then, Jack had expertly slid the knife between Kit's breasts and slit the bands.

Elmina's *"Sacre Dieu!"* was a weak effort as, grudgingly, she gave up her fight. Muttered references to the madness of the English, and the shocking want of delicacy displayed by unnamed peers, punctuated the next ten minutes.

The hot water and bandages arrived. Jack watched Elmina bathe the wound. The maid's hands were steady, her touch sure. When the ugly hole had been cleansed, he helped her tie a wad of torn sheeting over it. Kit's breathing had improved, but her complexion remained alarmingly pallid.

Jack left Elmina in charge with strict instructions to be called immediately should Kit regain consciousness or Dr. Thrushborne appear. In the corridor outside Kit's room, he slumped against the wall and shut his eyes. For one instant, despair overwhelmed him—Kit lay so very still, her skin so very cold. Her breathing was the only sign of life. Even if the wound didn't kill her, in her weakened state, an inflammation of the lungs might.

He tried to imagine his life without her—and couldn't. Abruptly, he opened his eyes and pushed away from the wall. Kit wasn't dead yet. If she could fight, he'd be by her side.

His face grave, Jack went to face Spencer.

Jenkins was waiting at the top of the stairs. "Lord Cranmer's in his chamber, m'lord. If you'll follow me?"

A weary grin twisted Jack's lips. The formal phrasing seemed out of place. He suspected he looked like a disreputable gypsy. And he was on his way to tell one of his father's closest friends that he'd seduced his granddaughter.

Spencer's rooms were in the opposite wing. Jenkins knocked, then held the door wide. Jack drew a deep breath and entered.

The dark was dispelled by a single lamp, turned low, set on a table in the center of the large room. In the uncertain light beyond, Jack saw the man he'd met in King's Lynn months before. Swathed in a dressing robe, Spencer sat in an armchair. The mane of white hair was the same; the shaggy brows overhanging his deep-set eyes had not changed. But the anxiety in the pale eyes was new, etching lines about the firm lips, deepening the shadows in the sunken cheeks.

Held by Spencer's gaze, Jack paused just inside the pool of lamplight, aware of Spencer stiffening as he took in his odd attire. Abruptly, Spencer raised a hand and dismissed the small man hovering at his side.

As the door closed, Spencer lifted his chin aggressively. "Well? What have Kathryn—and you—been up to?"

Feeling as if he was facing a court-martial, Jack clamped a lid on his natural arrogance and replied simply and straightforwardly. "I'm afraid Kit and I have become rather closer than is acceptable. In short, I seduced her. The only fact I can proffer in my defense is that I didn't know at the time she was your granddaughter."

Spencer snorted incredulously. "You didn't recognize the coloring?"

Jack inclined his head. "I knew she was a Cranmer but . . ." He shrugged. "There were other possibilities."

Spencer's gaze was sharp. "Led you to believe she was something she's not, did she?"

Jack hesitated.

"You may as well give me the whole of it," declared Spencer. "I'm not likely to faint from the shock. Told you she was illegitimate, did she?"

Jack grimaced, remembering that first night, so long ago. "Let's just say that when I made my supposition plain, she didn't correct me. I'd hardly expected your granddaughter to be riding the countryside alone at night in breeches."

Spencer sighed deeply. Slowly, his head sank. For a long moment, he stared into space, then in a gruff voice he muttered: "My fault—no denying it. I should never have let her grow so damned wild."

Minutes ticked by; Spencer seemed sunk in abstracted gloom. Jack waited, not sure what was going through the old man's mind. Then Spencer shook his head and looked him straight in the eye. "No sense in wailing over past history. You say you seduced her. What do you plan to do about it, heh?"

Jack's lips twisted wryly. "I'll marry her, of course."

"Damn right you will!" Spencer's shrewd eyes narrowed. "Think you'll enjoy it—being married to a wildcat?"

Briefly, Jack smiled. "I'm looking forward to it."

Spencer snorted and waved him to a chair. "You don't seem overly put out by the fall of the cards. But Jenkins said something about Kit's being hurt. What's happened?"

Jack drew an armchair to the table and sat, using the moments to assemble the essential elements of his tale. "Kit and I have been meeting by night at the old fishing cottage on the north boundary of my land."

Spencer nodded. "Aye. I know it. Used to go fishing with your father from there."

"I was on my way there tonight when I heard a commotion. Shots and horsemen. I went to investigate. From the cliffs I saw a chase on the sands—the Revenue following a horseman. Only the horseman was Kit."

"*They shot her?*" Spencer's incredulous question hung in the air. The sudden rigidity in his large frame was alarming.

"She's all right," Jack hastened to reassure him. "The bullet's lodged in her left shoulder but too high to be fatal. I've sent for Thrushborne. He'll dig it out, and she should be fine." Jack prayed that was true.

"I'll have their hides! I'll see them swing from their own gibbets! I'll . . ." Spencer ground to a halt, his face purpling with rage.

"I rather think we should tread warily, sir." Jack's quiet tone had the desired effect. Spencer turned on him.

"D'ye mean to say you'll let the bastards get away with putting a damned hole in your future wife?" Spencer's wild eyes dared him to confess to such weakness.

"Ah—but you see, that's just the point." Jack held Spencer's gaze. "They don't know they shot my future wife."

The silence that followed was broken by a creak as Spencer sank back in his chair.

Jack examined his hands. "All in all, I'd rather the authorities were not made aware that my future wife rides wild through the night dressed for all the world as a man.''

Eventually, Spencer sighed deeply. ''Very well. Handle it your way. God knows, I've never been much good at hauling on Kit's reins. Perchance you'll have more success.''

Recalling that he'd not succeeded in retiring Young Kit as he'd planned, Jack wasn't overly confident on that point. ''There's a complication.'' Spencer's head came up, reminding Jack forcibly of an old bull about to charge. ''Tonkin, the sergeant at Hunstanton, saw Kit without the hat and muffler she uses to conceal her face. He got a good look at her before I deprived him of his wits. When he comes to his senses, he'll be around here as fast as he can.''

The look on Spencer's face suggested he'd like to lock Tonkin in a dungeon and be done with it. Grudgingly, he asked: ''So what do we do?''

''He'll come asking questions, wanting to see Kit. The last person he'll expect to see will be me. He needs my permission to go any farther than questions. The story we'll tell is that I had dinner here this evening, with you and your granddaughter—a very private celebration of our betrothal. I remained until quite late, discussing the arrangements with Kit and you. Your health is uncertain, so the wedding will be a small affair, to be held as soon as possible.''

Spencer's expression turned grim, but he said nothing. Jack continued: ''Tomorrow morning, I'll call early to see you alone, to discuss the settlements. That's my reason for being here when Tonkin arrives.''

''What if he insists on seeing Kit?''

''I doubt he'll insist, not if I'm here. But if he does, Kit will have gone to visit the Greshams, to tell her friend Amy the news.''

Spencer nodded slowly, mulling over the plan.

The door opened and Jenkins entered. ''Dr. Thrushborne's arrived, m'lord. He's asking for Lord Hendon.''

Jack rose. Spencer started to rise with obvious difficulty; Jack waved him back. ''Kit's unconscious at the moment— there's nothing you can do.'' As Spencer sank back, softly wheezing, Jack added: "I'll come and tell you what Thrushborne says."

His face pale, his lips pinched, Spencer nodded. Jack returned the nod, then strode back to Kit's chamber.

God—let her live!

Telling Spencer had been bad enough; he shared some part of the blame for Kit's wildness. But Jack couldn't excuse his own behavior; he should have acted earlier, more decisively, more effectively. He should have taken better care of her. At least Thrushborne was here. He had been treating Hendons and Cranmers for decades. He could be relied on not to talk. So far, so good. But there was a long way to go before they were out of the woods.

Jack entered Kit's room without knocking. A small black whirlwind descended on him.

"Out! *Monsieur* we do not need you! You will be in the way. You'll—"

"Elmina, do stop that. I asked Lord Hendon to come." Dr. Thrushborne's mild tones halted Elmina in mid-stride. Jack sidestepped about her. Thrushborne was wiping his hands on a clean towel. Beyond him, his intruments were laid out on a table drawn up by the bed.

Thrushborne regarded Jack. He waved at Kit's still form and raised an inquiring brow. "I gather you know this lady rather well?"

Jack didn't bother answering. "Will she live?" It was the only question he was interested in.

Thrushborne's brows rose. "Oh, yes. I should think so. She's a healthy young woman, as you doubtless know. She'll do well enough, once we get that lump of metal out of her."

Jack suspected Thrushborne was enjoying himself. It wasn't often he had a Hendon at his mercy. But Jack couldn't drag his gaze from the still figure on the bed. He didn't care about anything—anyone—else.

Thrushborne cleared his throat. "I'll need you to hold her while I pull the bullet out. She's barely unconscious, but I don't want to give her a sedative yet."

Jack nodded, steeling his nerves for the coming ordeal. He obeyed Thrushborne's orders implicitly, trying not to bruise Kit as he held her right shoulder and leaned on her left arm to immobilize her. When the doctor's forceps probed deep, she gasped and struggled, furiously trying to pull away. Her whimpers shredded Jack's nerves. When tears welled beneath her closed lids and a choked sob escaped her, his stomach clenched. Gritting his teeth, Jack mentally ran through every curse he'd ever learned—and concentrated on obeying orders. Elmina hovered, murmuring soothingly, holding Kit's head through the worst, bathing her forehead with lavender water. As far as Jack could tell, Kit was oblivious to all but the pain.

Finally, Thrushborne straightened, flourishing his forceps. "Got it!" He beamed, then, dropping the forceps in a basin, gave his attention to staunching the blood, flowing freely again.

By the time Kit was bandaged and dosed with laudanum, Jack felt dizzy and weak.

About to leave, Thrushborne turned to him. "I take it I haven't seen anything at all of Miss Kathryn?"

Gathering his wits, Jack shook his head. "No. You were called to see Spencer."

The doctor frowned. "My housekeeper saw your servant come for me—why was that?"

"I was here when Spencer was taken badly and sent Matthew, rather than one of the Cranmer staff."

Thrushborne nodded briskly. "I'll call again in the morning—to see Spencer."

With a weary but grateful half smile, Jack shook hands. Thrushborne departed; Elmina followed, taking the bloody rags to be burned. Alone with Kit, Jack stretched, easing his aching back. He'd have to see Spencer and make sure the servants, both here and at Castle Hendon, understood their story sufficiently well to play their parts. He didn't doubt they'd do it. The Hendons and Cranmers were served by locals whose families lived and worked on the estates; all would rally to the cause. Tonkin was thoroughly disliked by all who knew him; the Revenue in general were favorites with no one. With care and forethought, all would be well. With a long-drawn sigh, Jack turned to the bed.

Kit lay stretched out primly, not wantonly asprawl as he

was used to seeing her. It would be some time before he saw her like that again. How long? Three weeks, maybe four? Jack contemplated the wait, by dint of sheer determination holding back the thought that he might never see her like that again. She would live—she had to. He couldn't live without her. The space beside her looked inviting, but Spencer was waiting, and Elmina would soon be back. With a wrenching sigh, Jack gazed down at the silent beauty. Her chest rose and fell beneath the sheet, her breathing shallow but steady. Jack put out a hand to brush a silky curl from her smooth brow, then bent to gently kiss her pale lips.

He dragged himself away. Elmina had said she'd watch Kit for what was left of the night, and Spencer was still waiting.

"Sergeant Tonkin, my lord." Jenkins held the library door wide, an expression of supercilious condescension on his face.

Stepping over the threshold, Sergeant Tonkin hesitated, his regulation hat clutched in his hands. Spying Spencer behind the desk, Tonkin headed in that direction, his stride firmly confident.

Spencer watched him approach, an expression of calm boredom on his aristocratic features. From an armchair halfway down the long room, Jack studied Tonkin's face. The sergeant hadn't seen him, so focused was he on his goal. An air of smug belligerence hung about Tonkin as he halted on the rug before the desk and saluted.

"My lord," Tonkin began. "I was a-wondering if I might have a word with Miss Cranmer, sir."

Spencer's shaggy brows lowered. "With my granddaughter? What for?"

The barked question, so direct, made Tonkin blink. He shifted his weight. "We have reason to believe, m'lord, that Miss Cranmer might be able to help us with our investigations."

"How the devil do you suppose Kathryn could know anything of your business?"

Tonkin stiffened. He shot Spencer a swift glance, then

puffed out his chest. In a portentious tone, he stated: "Some of my men were chasing a smugglers' leader last night. The man . . . that is, this leader . . . was shot. I found the fellow—the leader—in the quarries."

"So?" Spencer's gaze turned impatient. "If you've got the man, what's the problem?"

Tonkin colored. With one finger, he tugged at his collar. "But we haven't got him—that's to say, this leader."

"You *haven't*?" Spencer leaned forward. "The man was wounded and you let him get away?"

Watching, Jack sensed the moment when Tonkin's obsession came to his rescue. Instead of wilting under the heat of Spencer's glare, his backbone straightened like a poker, his beady eyes suddenly intent. "Before others of the gang knocked me out, I managed to get a good look at the fellow's—that is . . ." Gritting his teeth, Tonkin drew a deep breath then continued: "I got a good look at the leader's face. Red curls, my lord," Tonkin pronounced with relish. "And a pale, delicate-looking face with a small pointy chin." When Spencer merely looked blank, Tonkin added: "A *female* face, my lord."

Silence filled the library.

When Spencer frowned, Tonkin nodded decisively. "Exactly, m'lord. If I hadn't seen it with me own two eyes, I'd have laughed the idea aside, too."

Spencer's expression turned openly puzzled. "But I still don't see, Sergeant, what this has to do with my granddaughter. You can't seriously imagine she'll be able to help you?"

Tonkin's face fell; a second later, crafty suspicion gleamed in his small eyes. He opened his mouth.

Jack smoothly intervened. "I really think, Sergeant, that you'll have to explain why you imagine Miss Cranmer would be more help to you in identifying and locating a Cranmer . . . connection than Lord Cranmer himself. I must tell you such matters are not normally the province of the ladies."

Tonkin whirled, his expression, unguarded for an instant, a medley of fury and rampant suspicion. With the next breath, his unlovely mask fell back into place; he drew himself up and saluted. "Good morning, m'lord. Didn't see you there, sir." Then the implication of Jack's words registered. "*Connection*, m'lord?"

Jack raised a bored brow.

Visibly girding his loins, Tonkin shook his head. "No, sir." Chin up, at attention, he spoke to the air above Jack's head. "I know what I saw, sir. This woman rode a magnificent black horse. I saw with my own eyes the hole my men blew in her shoulder." Tonkin pressed his lips tightly together against the impulse to explain *whose* shoulder; meeting his eyes, Jack understood. Fanatical determination flared in those beady orbs as Tonkin, his chin pugnaciously square, glanced sideways at Spencer.

Jack smothered the urge to strangle the man. "Perhaps, Sergeant, if you'd tell us exactly what happened, his lordship might be able to clarify matters for you?"

Tonkin hesitated, eyes going from Jack to Spencer and back again before, very slowly, he nodded. And determinedly began his tale.

In her bed abovestairs, Kit lay flat on her back and tried to remember how she'd got there. Her shoulder was on fire; one minute she felt flushed, the next as cold as ice. Eyes closed against the light, she heard the door open and shut.

"Sergeant Tonkin's 'ere, miss." Kit identified the whisperer as Emily, one of the upstairs maids. "Jenkins just showed 'im into the library."

"This is the Revenue man, yes?" Elmina answered from the direction of the fireplace. Kit frowned. The Revenue? *Here*?

"He's a terrible bully, that one," Emily explained. "He's asking to see Miss Kathryn. Jenkins said as he'd seen her face."

Elmina's response was dismissive. "His lordship will take care of it. And Lord Hendon is there, too, is he not? Rest assured, all will be well."

"Elmina!" Kit struggled onto her good elbow, wincing at the pain in her left shoulder. Her weak call brought both Elmina and Emily rushing to the bed. "Get me my dove grey gown. Quickly."

Her face a mask of horror, Elmina remained rooted to the spot. "No, no, *petite*! You are much too weak to get up! You will reopen your wound."

"If I don't go down and let Tonkin see me, I might not live to heal anyway." Gritting her teeth, Kit managed to sit on the edge of the bed. Suddenly, she remembered all too well. Closing her eyes, she willed her dizziness away. "Dammit, Elmina! Don't argue—or I'll do it myself."

The threat worked, as it usually did; muttering, Elmina hurried to the wardrobe. Returning within minutes with the grey dress and Kit's underclothes, she ventured: "Lord Hendon is downstairs."

"So I heard." Kit looked at her clothes and wondered how she was going to cope. Lifting her left arm was to be avoided at all costs. She was wearing a fine linen night-gown with a high frilly neck. She'd chosen the grey gown because of its neckline, round and high enough to conceal her bandages. If she wore the dress on top of the night-gown, hopefully Tonkin wouldn't notice.

Battling dizziness, she stood; in a voice devoid of all unnecessary strength, she directed Elmina in helping her into the dress and easing the bodice up over her injured shoulder. She felt weak as a newborn kitten—just standing was an effort. While Elmina quickly laced the gown, Kit considered what might be transpiring downstairs. If Tonkin had seen her face, she doubted he'd go away without laying eyes on her. She hoped Spencer wouldn't lose his temper before she got down. The most puzzling aspect was why the elusive High Commisioner had chosen this particular day to pay a morning visit. Perhaps, if she could think straight enough, she might be able to enlist his aid in getting rid of Tonkin. Then, later, she could tell him about Jack and ask for his help in that matter, too.

How she was to manage that with Spencer looking on was beyond her at present. She'd worry about that once Tonkin was gone.

Elmina finished lacing the dress and hurried to get Kit's brushes. Kit looked down. The room swayed and she quickly raised her head. Fixing her gaze on her mirror across the room, she tried a step or two. It was going to be dicey, but she'd do it if it killed her. Her chin went up. She hadn't done anything she was ashamed of; she wasn't going to let a bully of a sergeant drag the Cranmer name through the mud.

Downstairs, Tonkin was struggling to keep his head above water. At Jack's artful prompting, he'd explained what had happened, in detail. When retold in such a way, his night's efforts lost much of their glory.

With that accomplished, Jack sat back and calmly engaged Spencer in a detailed discussion of all the Cranmer "connections" currently known. Throughout, he kept a careful eye on Tonkin, noting the sergeant's rising impatience—and his increasing irritation. Despite being subjected to considerable discouragement, Tonkin wasn't about to let go. When Spencer came to the end of the list of his sons' acknowledged bastards, Jack quietly put in: "But I believe the Sergeant said the face he saw was distinctly feminine. Is that right, Tonkin?"

Tonkin blinked, then nodded eagerly. "Yessir, your lordship. A woman's face, it was."

Spencer frowned, then shook his head. "Can't think of any male Cranmer with effeminate looks."

"I hesitate to suggest it," Jack said, "but could it possibly have been a female relative?" He could almost hear Tonkin's satisfied sigh.

"Aren't any," Spencer decisively replied. "Only girl in the family's Kathryn and stands to reason couldn't be her."

With a fleeting smile, Jack nodded in agreement.

Tonkin's face was a study in dismay. "Pardon me, your lordship, but why's that?"

Spencer frowned at him. "Why's what, Sergeant?"

Tonkin gritted his teeth. "Why *couldn't* it be Miss Cranmer, m'lord?"

As one, Jack and Spencer stared at him, then both erupted into laughter. Tonkin reddened; he looked from one to the other, ugly suspicion gathering in his eyes.

Spencer recovered first, waving his hand to and fro. "A rich jest, Sergeant, but I can assure you my granddaughter does not consort with smugglers."

Tonkin reacted as if slapped.

"I think, perhaps," put in Jack, sensing Tonkin's swelling belligerence, "that the Sergeant might as well know— just so he can accept Miss Cranmer's innocence as proven fact, my lord—that Miss Cranmer had dinner with both you and myself last night. We sat late, Miss Cranmer with us, discussing the details of our impending nuptials."

Jack smiled at Tonkin, the very picture of helpful assurrance.

"Nuptials?" Tonkin stared.

"Precisely." Jack adjusted the cuff of one sleeve. "Miss Cranmer and I will shortly be married. The announcement will be made in the next day or so." Jack smiled again, openly confident. "You can be one of the first to wish us happy, Tonkin."

"Er . . . yes, of course. That is . . . I hope you'll be very happy, sir . . ." Tonkin faltered to a halt.

The door behind him opened.

The three men turned. Three pairs of eyes fastened on the slim grey figure who appeared in the doorway; shock registered, in equal measure, on all three faces.

Kit saw it and glided forward, filling the telltale void. "Good morning, Grandfather." She crossed to Spencer's side. Placing her right hand on his shoulder, she planted a dutiful kiss on his cheek, grateful that impassivity had dropped like a veil over his features. Straightening, denying the wave of dizzying pain that threatened to engulf her, she looked directly at Tonkin. "I heard Sergeant Tonkin was asking after me. How can I help you, Sergeant?"

It was a bold move. Jack held his breath, wondering if Tonkin could see how pale she was. To him, her condition was obvious, but apparently Tonkin had never set eyes on Kit before last night. His heart in his mouth, Jack willed his muscles to relax. He'd shot to his feet the instant Kit had appeared; only by the most supreme effort had he stifled the overwhelming urge to go to her side. How on earth she'd got dressed and downstairs was a wonder; how long she'd remain on her feet was a major concern. She'd seen him as she'd entered. As her gaze had passed over him, he'd seen the shock of recognition flare beneath the haze of pain.

Sergeant Tonkin simply stared, speechless. His gaze flicked to Jack, then to Spencer, then, surreptitiously, he darted a glance at Kit, dwelling on her left shoulder.

Aware of his scrutiny, Kit held herself erect, her expression relaxed and open, waiting for Tonkin to state his business. Her grasp on Spencer's shoulder was nothing less than a death grip; luckily, Spencer had put up his hand to cover hers, the warmth of his large palm imparting strength and support enough to anchor her to consciousness. Kit drew on it unashamedly.

From where she stood, Kit could see Spencer's expression, arrogantly supercilious as he stared at Tonkin. A peculiar hiatus held them all.

Jack broke it, strolling casually forward to Kit's side.

The instant he moved, he drew Kit's gaze. Lips slightly parted to ease her increasingly painful breathing, Kit watched him approach. Her wits were slowing, becoming more sluggish. They'd said Lord Hendon was with Spencer. There was no one else in the room except Jack. And it *was* Jack, for all that he was far more elegantly dressed than she'd ever seen him, moving with a languid grace she recognized instantly. The man approaching her was a rake of the first order, one who'd learned his recreational habits in the hothouse of the *ton*. The man approaching her was Jack. Confusion welled; Kit resisted the urge to close her eyes against it.

Jack stopped by her side; she looked into his eyes and saw his concern and his strength. He reached for her right hand, lifting it from Spencer's shoulder. She let him, relief spreading through her at the comfort in his touch. His other arm slid about her waist, a very real support.

Aware of the picture he was creating for Tonkin, Jack raised Kit's fingers to his lips. "The sergeant thought he saw you last night, my dear. Your grandfather and I were just explaining that he must have been mistaken." Jack smiled reassuringly into wide amethyst eyes, hazed and dull with pain. "You'll be pleased to know I've given you an alibi. Even one so earnest as Sergeant Tonkin will have to accept that while you were having dinner with me, and later discussing our wedding, you couldn't possibly have been simultaneously riding the hills.''

"Oh?" It was no effort to infuse the syllable with bewilderment. Kit dragged her eyes from Jack's to gaze in confusion at Sergeant Tonkin. Dinner? *Wedding*? Her faintness intensified. The arm about her waist tightened possessively, protectively.

Kit's obvious confusion dispelled the last vestige of Tonkin's certainty. Jack could see it in his eyes, in the sudden slackness of his features. The pugnacity that had kept him going drained away, leaving him off-balance.

Swallowing, Tonkin half saluted. "I can see as you don't know nothing about it, miss." He glanced warily at Jack, then Spencer. "If it's all right with you, my lords, I'll be on my way."

Jack nodded; Spencer simply glared.

With a last salute, Tonkin turned and quickly left the room.

As soon as the door shut, Spencer turned in his chair, anxiety and relief flooding out in a fiercely whispered: "And what's the meaning of all this, miss?"

Kit didn't answer. As the door clicked shut, she'd leaned back against Jack's arm and shut her eyes. The willpower that had kept her going abruptly faded. She felt Jack's arms close about her. She was safe; they were all safe.

She heard Spencer's question as if from a distance, muffled by cold mists. With a little sigh, she surrendered to the oblivion that beckoned, beyond pain, beyond confusion.

Chapter 23

During the next week, the servants of Cranmer Hall and Castle Hendon struggled to preserve a facade of normality in the absence of their masters. Lord Cranmer was seriously ill and took to his bed. Miss Kathryn Cranmer stayed by his bedside, unable because of the exigencies of her nursing to see anyone. Lord Hendon was as mysteriously elusive as ever.

Behind the scenes, Spencer remained in his rooms, too worried to be of much practical use. Jack spent most of his time with Kit, helping to nurse her. Her shoulder wound healed well, but in her weakened state the cold she'd caught in the quarries rapidly developed into something worse. As the week progressed, Kit's fever mounted. Only Jack had the strength to hold her easily, to cajole and if necessary force her to drink the drafts the doctor prepared. Only his voice penetrated the fogs Kit wandered through, dazed, weak, and confused.

Dr. Thrushborne called every morning and afternoon, worried by Kit's state. "It's the combination of things," he explained to Jack. "The chill coming on top of a massive loss of blood. All we can do is keep her warm and quiet and let Nature work for us."

Two grim days later, he answered an exhausted Jack's unvoiced question: "The fact she's still with us is the brightest sign. She's a slip of a thing, but all the Cranmers are as stubborn as hell. I don't think she plans to leave us just yet."

Jack couldn't even summon a smile. His world centered on the room at the end of the wing. Other than an obligatory visit to Hunstanton to follow up Tonkin's suspicions, and an equally obligatory appearance at the church at Docking on Sunday, he'd not left the Hall. Matthew acted as his go-between, relaying his orders to Castle Hendon and supplying him with clothes, as well as taking messages to George, who'd temporarily assumed the leadership of the Gang. The bed in the room next to Kit's had been made up, so he could grab a few hours' sleep whenever exhaustion forced him to yield his place to Elmina.

It wasn't that he distrusted Elmina; he'd learned she'd been maid to Kit's mother and had been with her *petite* since her birth. However, like Spencer, she was incapable of exerting any control over her erstwhile charge. On the second night, he'd fallen into exhausted slumber, stretched, fully dressed, on the bed next door. He'd been awoken by a high-pitched altercation. In Kit's room, he'd come upon the staggering sight of Kit, out of bed, rummaging through her wardrobe, while Elmina remonstrated helplessly. He'd walked in and picked Kit up, ignoring her struggles and the curses she'd laid about his ears. He'd discovered she was fluent in two languages.

Even when he'd put her back in bed, she'd fought him, but eventually yielded to his greater strength. Delirious, she hadn't known who he was; her confusion that someone existed who could deny her had been obvious. The conviction that his kitten had gone her own way ever since she'd set foot from her cradle took firm root in Jack's mind.

And when her fever mounted, draining what little strength she still possessed, leaving him to watch, impotent, as death fought to claim her, he made a solemn vow that if she was spared, he'd keep her safe for the rest of her life. Without her, his life would be worthless—he knew that now. His vulnerability angered him, but he couldn't deny it. Nor could he walk away from his own part in her ill-fated masquerade. When all this was over, she'd be his responsibility—a responsibility he'd take more seriously than any other in his life.

For Kit, the week passed in a peculiar haze, lucid moments submerged in mists of confusion. Her body went from chilled shivering to heated dampness; her brain hurt dreadfully whenever she tried to think. Throughout it all, she was aware of a protective presence at her side, of a rock which remained steady within her whirling world. In the few scattered moments when she was fully conscious, she recognized that presence as Jack. Why he was in her bedroom was beyond her; she could only be grateful.

The end came abruptly.

She opened her eyes in the early dawn and the world had stopped spinning. She saw Jack, sleeping, slumped in an armchair facing the bed. Smiling, she wriggled to turn over, the better to appreciate the unexpected sight. A dull ache in her left shoulder stopped her. Frowning, she relived the night on the beach and her race from the Revenue. She'd been shot but had reached the quarries. After that came—nothing. Jack must have found her and brought her home.

Smiling at his evident concern, for it must have been that which had driven him to stay overnight, braving Spencer's wrath, Kit stumbled on her first difficulty. How had Jack convinced Spencer to allow him to stay, not just at the Hall, but in her room? She tried to concentrate, but her mind wasn't up to it. An elusive recollection niggled. Sergeant Tonkin was caught up in it somewhere; perhaps she'd been conscious for a time at the quarries and had overheard the sergeant and his men? Kit frowned, then mentally shrugged. No doubt it would come back to her.

Thoughts of Spencer reminded her she should go and reassure him as soon as possible; she knew how he fretted when she was hurt. Kit flexed her shoulder. She squinted down; all she could see was bandage. She felt nothing more than a mild ache.

Her gaze rested on Jack's sleeping figure, drinking in the familiar features like a soothing draft. His cheekbones and brow seemed more angular than she recalled. The normally smooth planes of his cheeks were roughened by stubble. He looked thoroughly rumpled, nothing like her last image of him. Kit frowned. Again, that elusive memory flitted past, tantalizingly insubstantial. She grimaced and shook her head. Her lids were heavy. It was too early to get up. Besides, Jack was still sleeping and looked like he needed the rest. Perhaps she should nap, just until he awoke?

Lips curved, she drifted back to sleep.

The sensation of being stared at penetrated Jack's slumber. Opening his eyes, he looked straight into shocked amethyst. Kit was awake and staring at him as if she'd seen a ghost. The look on her face told him he didn't need to worry about how to remind her of the scene in Spencer's library.

"Lord Hendon?" The weakness in her voice owed more to shock than illness. Suddenly, purple flares erupted in her violet eyes. *"You're Lord Hendon!"*

Jack winced at the accusation. He sat up and rubbed his hands over his face. It was just like her to return to the living with a rush. All his notions of gently explaining matters to a meek and confused woman went out the window. Kit was awake, alive and well, and in full command of her senses. And she hadn't changed one bit.

Kit jumped when Jack's hands dropped from his face to slap the arms of the chair. He surged to his feet, grinning inanely, his expression a mixture of joy, delight, and unadulterated relief. Before she could gather her wits, she'd been scooped from her bed and, in a tangle of sheets, deposited in his lap. Then he kissed her.

To Jack, Kit's lips, warm and sweet, tasted better than ambrosia. Stubbornly, she kept them locked against him. She struggled, but it was a weak effort—he felt perfectly justified in ignoring it.

Kit tried to protest, but her mumbles fell on deaf ears. She was confused and angry—and she intended telling him about it before he stole her wits. But it was already too late. A familiar warmth was spreading through her. She clamped her lips tight shut, only to feel her body respond shamefully to his nearness. Of their own volition, her lips parted, eager to yield him the prize he sought. Kit gave up. She wound her arms about his neck and returned his kiss with all the fervor of a woman too long denied.

It felt like heaven to be with him again.

Jack shifted his hold and Kit winced. He raised his head immediately. "Damn! I forgot about your shoulder."

"Forget my shoulder." Kit drew his head back to hers, but it was clear she'd unintentionally brought him to his senses. When he drew away again, she let him go.

Jack looked deep into Kit's eyes and wondered just how much she'd remembered. Whatever the answer, now was the time to tell her of their betrothal. Lifting her, he placed her back on the bed, plumping up the pillows at her back and tucking the coverlet about her. Kit accepted his ministrations, her expression turning suspicious.

Should he return to the formality of the chair? Jack temporized and sat on the bed, one of Kit's hands in his. He glanced into her eyes and squared his shoulders. Proposing would have been a damn sight easier. "As you've realized, I'm Lord Hendon."

"Not Captain Jack?"

"That, too," he admitted. "Lord Hendon is Captain Jack."

"When did you realize who I was?"

"The evening before you were shot." Memory stirred and Jack rose to pace the room. "I recognized you as a Cranmer at the outset, but I thought you one of the family's by-blows—as you well know." He shot an accusing glance at Kit. She met it with bland innocence. "That afternoon, George came to see me. He'd been visiting Amy—"

"Amy?" Kit stared.

Jack stopped and considered, but Kit's mind made the jump without further assistance.

"George is George Smeaton?"

Jack nodded. "We grew up together."

Kit tried to juggle the pieces of the jigsaw that were falling into her hands.

"The Greshams' groom told George who the black Arab mare belonged to. George came and told me."

Kit's mind was racing, filling in gaps, recalling snippets here and there. One particularly disturbing fragment was rapidly growing in importance. "My memory is still a little hazy," she began, "but I seem to recall some mention of a wedding?'' She tried to make the question as innocuous as such a question could be. When Jack's brows rose arrogantly, her heart stood still.

"Naturally, in the circumstances, we'll be married.'' Neither his tone nor the glint in his grey eyes suggested there was any alternative.

Kit blinked. "Married?'' Just like that? To a man like Jack? Worse—to a *lord* like Jack. Merciful heavens! She'd never be able to call her soul her own. "Just a minute.'' She tried to keep her voice even. "I'm not quite clear on what happened. When did we become betrothed?''

"As far as I'm concerned,'' Jack growled, his eyes gleaming, "we became betrothed when you begged me to take your maidenhead.''

"Ah.'' Kit's eyes glazed. Arguing that point was impossible. She tried a different tack. "When did this idea of marriage enter your head?''

Frowning, Jack tried to gauge her direction, wary of answering in the wrong way.

"After you'd found out who I was?''

Jack scowled.

Which was answer enough for Kit. "If you've determined on marriage purely to save my reputation, you can forget it.'' She sat up. "I'd already decided not to marry, so there's really no need for any charade.''

The idea that she was rejecting him held Jack speechless for all of ten seconds. "Charade?'' he growled. "Charade be damned! If you've a dislike of marriage—though what you can know of the matter defies me—you should have remembered that *before* you gave yourself to me. *You* offered—*I* accepted. It's too late for second thoughts.'' Hands on hips, he glowered at Kit. "And in case it hasn't sunk in yet, let me tell you that women of your station can't go about giving themselves to men like me and expect to get let off the hook!''

Kit's eyes blazed. "Dammit! There's no sense in marrying me if you don't want to!''

Jack nearly choked. "What's wanting got to do with it? Of course I want to marry you!''

The statement, uttered at half bellow, stopped them both in their tracks.

Turning it over in his mind, Jack decided there was nothing he wished to add. He had to marry. He wanted to marry Kit. In fact, as far as he was concerned, they were married already. He just had to get her to agree.

Kit watched him, a considering frown on her face. Lord Hendon was fast becoming a far greater threat to her future than Captain Jack had ever been. Jack was an arrogant rogue, who could send her senses spinning with a single caress and was quite prepared to tie her up and carry her off if she didn't obey his orders. But she'd been in no danger of having to marry Captain Jack. Lord Hendon had all Jack's attributes, if anything, in greater measure. While Jack might bellow to overcome any resistance, Lord Hendon, she suspected, would simply raise one of those supercilious eyebrows and people would fall over themselves to obey. Kit swallowed a snort. And he expected her to marry him?

She glanced up, into his silver-grey eyes, and saw something in their shimmering depths which made her throat contract. The implication of his watchful silence broke over her.

He wanted her to marry him. He wanted her.

Abruptly, Kit threw off the bedclothes and swung her legs over the side of the bed. She'd forgotten that curious sense of being stalked. Right now, she'd prefer to be a moving target.

"Stay in bed, Kit."

The undisguised command flicked Kit on the raw. She threw Jack a fulminating glance, but before she could take up her verbal cudgels, he was speaking again. "Dr. Thrushborne will be here soon, as he has been every morning for the past week."

"Week?" Kit stared. It couldn't have been that long. "What day is it?"

Jack had to think before answering: "Tuesday."

"God lord! I've lost a week!"

"You nearly lost your *life*."

The deliberate tones jerked Kit back to full awareness.

Jack had drawn closer. He stooped and scooped her legs in one arm and toppled her back on her pillows, tucking her legs under the covers.

"No more games, Kit. For God's sake, stay in bed and do whatever Thrushborne says. The story we've put about—"

While Jack sat beside her and filled her in on their tale, Kit struggled to regain some sense of reality, some semblance of normality. But nothing seemed the same anymore.

Jack came to the end of his tale. "Elmina will be here soon, and I should return to Castle Hendon. I'll be back this evening." He rose, wondering what more he could say. He wasn't sure if she'd accepted their marriage as inescapable fact; he hadn't yet told her how soon it would be. But it was high time someone took charge of Kit Cranmer; he was that someone.

Kit couldn't clear her brow of the frown, born of puzzlement and uncertainty, that had settled there. She glanced up at Jack, towering over her. To her surprise, his long slow smile transformed his face. Swiftly, he bent to run his lips along her forehead, easing the tension. Then, his fingers tipped up her face and his lips touched hers in a kiss of warmth and promise.

With a flick of her curls, he was gone.

Kit sank back onto her pillows with a groan. She needed to think.

But the time to think was hard to find.

Elmina entered the room before Jack could have reached the top of the stairs. Intrigued by her maid's apparent acceptance of a man in her life, Kit couldn't resist a few leading questions. What she learned left her even more adrift than before. It seemed that during her illness, Jack had taken over—taken *her* over—with Spencer's and everyone else's blessing.

Before she could decide what she felt about that, Spencer himself appeared. That interview was more painful than she'd anticipated. It very quickly became clear that Spencer blamed himself for her wildness, a fact which irritated Kit immensely. Her wildness was her cross to bear—it didn't owe its existence to anyone else; no one else was to blame. She'd always loved Spencer precisely because he'd never sought to draw rein on her. In her rush to reassure him, she found herself accepting her impending marriage with glib serenity. She convinced Spencer. When he left, much happier than when he'd entered, she was left wondering if she could convince herself.

Dr. Thrushborne was the next to cross her threshold. He was thrilled to find her awake and lucid. He examined her wound and declared it healing well. Pleased, he congratulated her on her forthcoming nuptials, teasing her on the anticipated date of her first confinement. As he was a favorite, Kit let him off with a glare.

In reply to her query, he agreed she could leave her bed, on condition she remained within the house and took care not to overtax herself.

Which was why, when Lady Gresham and Amy arrived that afternoon, she was lying on the *chaise* in the back parlor.

"Amy!" Kit sat up with a start, simultaneously remembering her wound and that she'd no idea how much Amy knew. Did George confide in Amy? Kit hesitated, just long enough for Lady Gresham to sweep in.

"Don't get up, Kit, dear." Her ladyship bent, offering a cheek for Kit to kiss. "The whole county knows how pressed you've been with Spencer so ill. I take it he's improved?"

Kit nodded, fervently hoping Spencer was still keeping to his rooms. "Greatly improved, I'm pleased to say." That, at least, was the truth.

While Lady Gresham settled her skirts in an armchair, Kit smiled at Amy, still wondering, but her friend only returned the smile gaily, apparently oblivious to any deeper currents. Perhaps George was as secretive as Jack.

"Well!" Lady Gresham smiled beatifically. "We called last week and again yesterday, as I hope they've told you. The first was simply to see how you were coping but, of course, we heard your news on Sunday and simply couldn't wait to congratulate you."

Kit tried to disguise her stare. What news? Sunday? The

suspicion she'd just set foot in one of Jack's webs grew.

"It was such a shock to hear the banns read out." Amy put a hand on Kit's arm. "Lord Hendon made your excuses quite beautifully, didn't he, Mama?"

"So accomplished," sighed Lady Gresham. "And so thrillingly handsome. Why—he's his father all over again."

Kit waited for the room to stop whirling. She could have told her ladyship just how accomplished Lord Hendon was—and how thrilling his handsomeness could be. "What was his father like?" She asked the question to gain time to gather her scattered wits and shackle her temper. If she screamed, she'd never be able to explain it.

But *banns?* Damn it, how had he managed that?

Her ladyship's reminiscences on the previous Lord Hendon were tame compared to what Kit knew of the present incumbent. But by the time Lady Gresham had recalled to whom she was speaking and curtailed her ramblings, Kit was in command of herself once more.

The rest of their visit was spent in joyous discussion of her wedding, on which subject Kit invented freely. What else could she do? She could hardly tell Lady Gresham that the banns had been read without her consent. Even if she did, they'd probably put the outburst down to exhaustion consequent on nursing Spencer. And no matter how angry Jack made her, she wasn't about to deny a betrothal. He'd made it perfectly plain how he saw that point. No—she was trapped. She might as well smile and enjoy it.

When she finally found solitude, in the peace of the gazebo with the red banners of sunset flying the sky, that attitude was close to the summation of her thoughts. She'd little choice but to marry Jack, Lord Hendon. Short of creating an almighty scandal, there was nothing she could do to avoid it. She'd made her decisions—her own mistakes; this was where they'd landed her.

Would marrying Jack be such a black fate? Settling on the seat, Kit couldn't suppress a smile. The prospect of being Lady Hendon was not entirely grim. Her physical satisfaction was guaranteed. Jack was a magnificent lover. Moreover, he seemed very interested in teaching her all she would ever wish to know. But she was not a dim-witted miss, entranced by a handsome face. She knew Jack too well. His autocratic tendencies, his habit of command, his determination to have things his own way—all these she'd recognized from the first. They'd been bad enough in Captain Jack but in Lord Hendon, her husband, they could well prove overwhelming.

That was what worried her.

Kit crossed her arms on the sill, sinking her chin into her sleeve. Her stomach knotted every time she tried to imagine how Jack would behave once they were married. In recent years, her freedom had become precious. As her husband, Jack would have more right to control her than anyone had ever had. And he'd served notice on her freedom—if not directly, then indirectly. Marriage to him would leave her with only as much freedom as he deigned to allow her. Could she tolerate such a situation?

Thoughts of Amy surfaced, bringing their childhood vow to mind. She'd marry for love or not at all. Did she love Jack?

Kit's brow creased. How to tell? She'd never been in love before—but she'd never felt for a man what she did for Jack. Was that love?

With a disgusted snort, she shrugged the question aside. It was irrelevant. She was marrying Jack.

Did he love her?

An even greater imponderable but far more to the point. He wanted her—not for a moment did she doubt that. But love? He wasn't the sort to make such an admission of weakness. That was how many men saw love, and who was she to deny it? Every time she thought of Jack, every time he kissed her, she felt weak. But the idea of Jack reduced by love to a weak-kneed state was simply too much to swallow.

Could she make him love her? He might be in love with her, but how would she ever know if he could never bring himself to admit it? Could she *make* him admit it?

A challenge, that.

Kit's brows rose. Maybe that was how she should approach this marriage—as a challenge. One to be grasped and made into what she wanted it to be. And before she'd finished, she'd make sure she heard him say he loved her.

The gentle breeze had turned cool, wafting the last of the perfume from the roses. Kit stared at the full blooms as they merged with the dusk. It was nearly time for dinner—time to go in and face her future.

A smile twisted Kit's lips. Undoubtedly, running in Jack's harness was going to try her temper to the limit. But there'd be compensations—she was determined to claim them.

"I might have guessed."

Startled, Kit swung about. Jack lounged in the doorway of the gazebo, his shoulders propped against the frame. With the last of the light behind him, she couldn't be sure of his expression.

"Elmina said Thrushborne told you to stay inside the house."

Kit's natural instinct was to ask who dared question her. But Jack's tone was not aggressive—was, in fact, close to tentative, as if he didn't know how she'd respond. Kit held her own features to impassivity as she rapidly considered her options. If she was to live with this man for the rest of her life, she'd do well to start practicing a little tact. According to Lady Gresham, a little of that commodity could go a long way in domestic affairs.

"I was miles away," she said, and watched his jaw harden in an effort to stifle his demand to be told what she'd been thinking of. Kit bowed her head to hide her smile. "It's getting rather chilly. I was about to go in."

She made to rise, and, instantly, he was there, by her side. Kit was glad to let him take her hand. She made no demur when his other arm slipped supportively about her waist. It was, she decided, quite pleasant to be treated like porcelain—at least, by Jack. As they walked through the darkened garden, whiffs of sandalwood mixed with the floral fragrance. That was something she should have picked up. An aroma of sandalwood had clung to Captain Jack, yet it was a rich man's scent. But the fragrance was so familiar, it hadn't registered as odd.

The warmth of the large body so close to hers was both comforting and distracting. Even in her weakened state, she could still feel the excitement his presence generated, setting her pulse beating in double time. She felt his gaze, still worried, scan her face. His arm tightened, almost imperceptibly. Kit knew that if she glanced up, he would pull her to him and kiss her.

She kept her gaze level. She wasn't ready for that yet. When he kissed her, she lost her wits. She became his, and he could do anything with her he wished. She needed time to adjust to the fact that in three weeks, that would be her permanent state.

As she went up the steps on Jack's arm, Kit wondered if she would be strong enough to be Lady Hendon—and still be herself.

Chapter 24

The wedding of Jonathon, Lord Hendon, and Miss Kathryn Cranmer was the highlight of the year in that part of Norfolk. Women from miles about crowded the yard of the tiny church in Docking that had served the Cranmers and Hendons for centuries. Maids from the surrounding houses jostled with farmers' wives, vying for vantage points from which to Ooh and Aah. All agreed that the bridegroom could not have been more handsome, in his bottle green coat and ivory inexpressibles, his brown hair, tied back in a black riband, glinting in the sunlight. He arrived commendably early and disappeared into the church, accompanied by his friend, Mr. George Smeaton of Smeaton Hall.

The subsequent interval was easily filled with satisfying gossip. The groom, with his military career as well as his natural heritage as a Hendon, provided much of the fare. The only stories known of Miss Kathryn dated from schoolroom days. While these were wild enough to satisfy the most avid gossip, all agreed the lady must have left such scandalous doings behind her. When she was handed down from the Cranmer coach, a slender figure in a cloud of ivory lace, beaded with pearls, the breath caught in every throat, only to be let out, a moment later, in the most satisfied of communal sighs.

The murmur which rose from the congregation behind him told Jack that Kit had arrived. He turned, slowly, and looked down the aisle. She'd paused just inside the church while a teary Elmina resettled her long train. As he watched, Kit started her walk toward him, her hand steady on Spencer's arm. Behind her veil, she was smiling serenely, her chin tilted at that particular angle he knew so well. As she neared the end of her walk to his side, Jack met her gaze. His lips curved in a slow smile, quite impossible to deny. She looked superb. There were pearls about her throat, others dangled from her ears. Pearl rosettes held the heavy train on her shoulders. Even the headdress that held her delicate veil in place was composed of pearls. None, in his eyes, could vie with the pearl the dress contained.

The service was short and simple. Neither of the chief participants had any difficulty with their vows, uttering them in firm accents perfectly audible to the many guests squeezed into the church.

And then they were running the gamut of well-wishers, lining their route to the Hendon barouche. Jack handed Kit in, then jumped in behind her. "To the Hall, Matthew."

To Kit's astonishment, the coachman's head turned to reveal Matthew's lugubrious features. "Aye," he chuckled. He nodded a welcome in her direction before giving the horses the office. A pair of high-stepping bays, they quickly drew the carriage free of the crowd.

Bowling along the country lanes, through shadows shot with sunlight, they had little chance to talk, too occupied with acknowledging the waves and wishes of tenants and other locals lining the way. Only when the carriage turned into the long Cranmer Hall drive did Jack get a chance to settle back and cast a knowledgeable eye over his bride's gown.

"How did you manage that?" It occurred to him that the gown was a feat bordering on a miracle, given the short notice she'd had.

"It was my mother's." Kit glanced down at a lace sleeve, closed with pearl buttons. "She was particularly fond of pearls."

Jack's lips twitched. He hadn't associated his Kit with anything so feminine as jewelry. He wondered how she'd look in the Hendon emeralds. They were somewhere in the

Castle. He'd hunt them out and take them to London to be cleaned and reset; their present heavily ornate settings would not suit Kit's delicate beauty.

They'd decided on a ceremony late in the day, to be followed by a banquet and ball. As the evening wore on, Jack sat at the high table and watched his wife enchant their acquaintances. There was, he reflected, nothing to complain of in Kit's social graces. Ever since that evening when he'd found her in the gazebo, she'd behaved perfectly. Her demeanor had supported the fiction of their arranged marriage; even the most sharp-eyed observer could find no inconsistency in her manner. So successful had she been in projecting the image of a woman well pleased that Spencer now behaved as if the arrangement had always been in the wind. She was confident and serene; while her attitude held no overt maidenly modesty, neither did it suggest she was aware of her husband in any intimate way.

All of which, of course, was the most complete humbug. But only he knew that the elegant Lady Hendon stiffened slightly whenever he was near, clamping a stubborn hold over her normal responses to him. Only he was aware that she avoided meeting his eyes, using every feminine wile under the sun to accomplish that feat.

He wondered whether she knew what she was doing.

Since that night in the gazebo, he'd not so much as kissed her. She hadn't given him a chance, and, wise enough to guess at her lack of enthusiasm for their union and the reasons behind it, he hadn't gone out of his way to create one. Time enough, he'd reasoned, to reel her in once they were married.

Now they were married, and he was rapidly losing patience.

He hadn't anticipated her degree of social confidence, either. He'd expected her to need help in taking up the role of Lady Hendon. Instead, the mantle had settled easily on her slim shoulders. He now understood why their story of an arranged marriage had been accepted so readily by their neighbors. Kit was the perfect candidate, one who, to all intents and purposes, could be said to have been bred for the position. Her six years in London were the icing on the cake. Aside from anything else, the fact she'd survived those years *virgo intacta* was the ultimate assurance she was not one of those women he mentally stigmatized as the gilded whores of the *ton*.

All in all, there was nothing in her manner or morals he wished to change. It was the distance she seemed intent on preserving between them that he could not abide.

Vignettes of memory, drawn from the hours they'd spent in the cottage, flashed through Jack's mind. With a smothered curse, he stifled them. He took another sip of brandy and watched his wife go down the dance with some local squire. She must know he liked her as she was—would she try to pretend that all the wildness had gone out of her, that by marrying her he'd tamed her?

Jack's lips twisted in a slow smile. If she thought that, she was in for a surprise. She might try to play the merely dutiful wife, but her fires ran deep. And he knew how to ignite them. Jack glanced at his watch. It was early, but not too early. And who was to gainsay him?

He raised his head and looked over the crowd to where Elmina sat by the door. She saw his nod and slipped away. Excusing himself to Amy, who was seated beside him in deep conversation with George, Jack rose and stepped from the dais.

Kit laughed at yet another weak joke elliptically alluding to her husband's sexual prowess and expertly turned the conversation into safer channels. There'd been more than one moment that evening when she'd been sorely tempted to let loose the reins of her temper and give her teasing companions the facts. In truth, the facts were far more torrid than anything they imagined.

The music ceased, and she thanked Major Satterthwaite before moving off down the room. Within minutes, she was surrounded by a party of the district's dames, the ladies Gresham, Marchmont, and Dersingham among them. Their talk was serious, revolving about the redecoration of Castle Hendon. Kit listened with half an ear, making the appropriate noises in the right places. She'd perfected the art of polite conversation during her stay in London. It was a prerequisite for retaining one's sanity in the ballrooms of the *ton*. At least the ladies' conversation was not peppered with allusions to the coming night's activities. Every teasing comment simply added to her nervousness, which in turn increased her irritation with her own irrationality.

Why on earth should she feel nervous over what was to come? What could Jack possibly do to her—with her—that he hadn't already done? Images of them, in various positions in the cottage, rose to torment her. Kit smiled and nodded at Lady Dersingham, and wondered whether her fever had truly addled her wits.

Then she saw him approaching through the crowd, stopping to chat here and there as people claimed his attention. But his silver-grey eyes were on her. Her breathing suspended. That familiar sensation of being stalked blossomed in Kit's midriff. No, it wasn't the fever that had addled her brain.

Kit wrenched her eyes from her approaching fate, fixing them on the mild features of Lady Gresham, and desperately tried to think of a reason why it was too early to leave for home. For Castle Hendon.

The instant Jack joined the group, she knew it was hopeless. All the ladies, *grandes dames* every one, positively melted at the first sound of his deep voice. She didn't bother trying evasion. Instead, she raised her chin and nodded polite acquiescence to his suggestion that they leave. "Yes, of course. I'll change my clothes."

With that, she escaped upstairs, not bothering to haul Amy from George's side.

In her bedroom, a surprise awaited her. Instead of the new carriage dress she'd ordered Elmina to lay out, her maid was smoothing the full skirts of a magnificent emerald velvet riding habit.

"Where did that come from?" Kit shut the door and went to the bed.

"Lord Hendon sent it for you, *ma petite*. He said you should wear it. Is it not enchanting?"

Kit examined the severe lines of the habit and could not disagree. Her mind raced, considering the implications. Her initial impulse was to refuse to wear clothes her husband had decreed she should wear. But impulse was tempered by caution. A habit meant horses. Kit slipped the heavy ivory wedding dress from her shoulders and Elmina eased it over her hips. Freed of her petticoats, Kit sat before her dressing table while Elmina pulled the pins from her headdress.

She hadn't discussed how they were to travel to Castle Hendon, leaving Jack to deal with that as his prerogative. She'd imagined they'd go in the barouche. The riding habit said otherwise.

Suddenly enthusiastic, Kit hurried Elmina. A wild ride through the night was just what she needed to dispel her silly trepidation. The knots in her stomach would disappear once they were flying over the fields.

Pirouetting in front of her long mirror, Kit was pleased to approve of her husband's taste. How had he known? A wry smile twisted her lips. Not only had Jack known she'd prefer to ride, he'd known she'd never refuse to wear the habit in such circumstances. As she'd once remarked, when it came to manipulation, he was a master.

When she appeared at the top of the stairs, it seemed that all of Norfolk had gathered in the front hall. Buoyed by the knowledge that she looked her best, Kit beamed upon them all. As she descended the stairs, an avenue opened from their foot, through the throng, to where Jack waited for her by the door. Even from that distance, Kit caught the glint in his eyes as they swept over her, appreciation glowing in their depths. Pride was etched in every line of his face.

She must have responded to the wishes of those lining her route for they seemed happy enough, but Kit was unaware of anything beyond Jack. He held out one hand as she approached and she slipped her fingers into his, dimly aware of the cheers that rose about them. Then Jack's fingers tightened about hers and he drew her out onto the porch.

Some had noticed her dress and started whispering. The whispers turned to exclamations when the crowd, pushing through the door behind them, saw the two horses Matthew held prancing in the moonlight. Delia was a shifting black shadow, highlighted by the white flowers someone had plaited into her mane; beside her, Champion's hide gleamed palely.

Kit turned to Jack.

He lifted one quizzical brow. "Are you game, my lady?"

Kit laughed, her nervousness drowned by excitement. Smiling, Jack led her down the steps and across to the horses. He lifted her to her sidesaddle before swinging up to Champion's broad back.

Only Spencer approached them, all others too wary of the sharp hooves striking sparks from the flinty drive. He came between them, reaching up to squeeze Kit's hand before placing it on her pommel with a valedictory pat. Then he turned to Jack. "Take care of her, m'boy."

Jack smiled. "I will." And that, he thought, as he wheeled Champion, was a vow every bit as binding as the ones he'd given earlier that day.

The horses needed no urging to leave the noisy crowd behind. Well matched for pace, they fell to the task of covering the five miles to Castle Hendon with highbred ease. Jack felt no urge to converse as the miles disappeared beneath the heavy hooves. One glance at Kit's face had told him his bright idea had been a master stroke.

His lips curved. In his present state, being forced to traverse the eight miles of road between Cranmer Hall and Castle Hendon in a closed carriage with Kit, knowing they'd have to appear before the Castle staff immediately upon their arrival, would have been nothing less than torture.

Riding was far safer.

Beside him, Kit gloried in the rush of wind on her face. The regular thud of Delia's hooves steadied her skittering pulse until it beat to the same racing rhythm. There was excitement in the air, and a sense of pleasure shared. She slanted a glance at Jack, then looked ahead, smiling.

They sped through the night, the moon's luminescence spilling softly over them, lighting their way. For Kit, the black mass of Castle Hendon appeared before them too soon, bringing her respite from jangling nerves to an end. Grooms came running. Jack lifted her down before the steps leading up to the huge oak doors of her new home.

Her feet touched the ground, then she was swung up into Jack's arms.

Kit bit back a squeal and glared at him.

Jack grinned and carried her up the steps and through the open door.

Kit blinked in the glare of lights that greeted them. As Jack set her on her feet, she adjusted her features and smoothly moved into the business of greeting her new staff.

She vaguely remembered Lovis from her single visit as a child. Jack hadn't been at home at the time. Many of the other staff had family at Cranmer, so her progress down the long line was punctuated by explanatory histories. When she reached the end and acknowledged the bob of the sleepy scullery maid, Kit heard Jack's deep voice just behind her.

"Lovis, perhaps you'd show Lady Hendon to her room?"

Lovis bowed deeply. "Very good, m'lord."

Kit hid a nervous grin, realizing there was a tradition to be upheld. Lovis led the way, positively steeped in ceremony. Kit followed him up the wide curving staircase. When she reached the bend, she was relieved to see her husband still at its foot, conversing with one of the male staff—the head groom, as far as she recalled. The thought that he would doubtless give her time to soothe her frazzled nerves before coming to her eased her skittish pulse.

Please, God, let it be slow and steady. Too often, their first encounters resembled a clash of the furies.

The chamber Lovis led her to was enormous. Castle Hendon had grown up about a medieval donjon. Looking about her, Kit surmised her room might well have been part of the donjon's main hall. The walls were of solid stone, papered and painted over, the doors and windows set into their thickness. Extensive reworking had enlarged the windows; Kit felt sure that when she drew the curtains the next morning, the views the Castle was famed for would greet her eyes. Her sleepy, sated eyes.

With a start, Kit fell to examining the furnishings. They were exquisite, every one. She stopped by the four-poster bed. It was huge, covered in pale green satin, the Hendon arms carved in the headboard.

Kit wondered what the pale satin would feel like against her skin.

Abruptly, she remembered she had no clothes with her. In a panic, she flew to the massive mahogany armoire, pulling open doors and drawers. She found a complete wardrobe—dresses, underwear, accessories—all put carefully away, as if she'd always lived here. But none of them were hers. Her luggage was somewhere between Cranmer and Castle Hendon, with Elmina.

Puzzled, she drew forth a fine voile nightdress. Shaking out its folds, she held up the almost transparent garment. That her husband had chosen this wardrobe—for her—was instantly apparent.

Muttering an imprecation against all rakes, Kit bundled the shocking nightgown into a ball and crammed it back in the drawer. Her fingers pulled at the next fold of material. They couldn't all be like that, surely?

"What are you doing?"

Kit jumped and whirled to face her husband. To her surprise, he was not where she expected—at the door from the corridor—but lounged against another door she'd yet to investigate. Presumably, it led to his apartments. Kit swallowed nervously. The smile on Jack's face sent the butterflies that had taken up residence in her stomach into a frenzy.

"Er . . ." *Think, dimwit!* "I was looking for a nightdress."

As she watched Jack's smile widen, Kit could have bitten her tongue.

"You won't need one." Jack pushed away from the door and started toward her, his smile growing more devilish with every stride. "I'll keep you warm."

"Er . . . yes. Jack, stop!" Kit held up her hand in panic. "Shouldn't you send for a maid?"

The witless question had the desired effect. It pulled him up short. It also brought a frown to his face and darkened his eyes.

Jack stopped in the middle of his wife's bedroom and

placed his hands on his hips, the better to intimidate her into dropping her silly pose. He'd had enough. "What the devil's the matter with you, woman? In case you've forgotten, I'm perfectly qualified to undress you. I hardly need a maid to show me how." With that statement of intent, he stepped purposefully forward but stopped when he saw sheer alarm flare in Kit's eyes.

What was the matter with her? Kit wished she knew. If he'd come to her as Captain Jack, she'd have been in his arms in a trice. Making love to Captain Jack had been easy. With Captain Jack there hadn't been a tomorrow.

But there was no way she could possibly confuse the man standing in the middle of her bedroom with Captain Jack. The physical manifestations were the same, but there the similarity ended. This was Lord Hendon, her husband. The superb cut of his coat, the fine linen of his shirt, the gleaming hair neatly confined, and especially the sapphire signet ring glinting on his right hand, all underlined the essential difference. This was the man she'd married, vowed to honor and obey. This was the man who as of this evening was all things to her. The man who now had legal rights over her far beyond those any other had ever had. Her mind was not capable of equating making love to this man with making love to Captain Jack.

It simply wasn't the same. *He* wasn't the same. Kit drew a shuddering breath. No matter what he thought, she'd never made love to him before.

Jack watched the expressions flit across her pale face and his confusion grew. She couldn't possibly be nervous, but he hadn't previously thought her such an accomplished actress. Her eyes were enormous pools of fright, skittering and restless. Her fingers were clenched so tightly on the door of the wardrobe her knuckles showed white. When a shiver of apprehension flickered over her skin, he gave up the fight against incredulity.

She *was* nervous.

"Hell!" Jack turned toward the bed, running one hand through his hair, disarranging it. Absentmindedly, he tugged at the black riband and freed the long locks, dropping the riband on the floor. He shot a glance at Kit, all but petrified by the wardrobe. If she was nervous, he hoped she'd keep her gaze level, and not let it drop to the bulge he was well aware was distorting the perfect cut of his inexpressibles. Hell and the devil! This looked set to be a long-drawn act, and he wasn't at all sure he was up to it.

"Come here." He struggled to soften the raw desire in his growl and only partly succeeded.

Kit's alarm flared again, but when he held out his hand, imperiously beckoning her forward, she hesitated, then came to his side, slipping a trembling hand into his. Smoothly, Jack drew her into his arms, turning to clasp her fully to him.

"Relax." He breathed the command into the soft curls by her ear. Now that he had his hands on her, he didn't need any further confirmation of her state. She was wound tight, quivering with tension. He wasn't fool enough to ask for explanations. Instead, his lips found the pulse point beneath her ear.

Kit shivered and wondered how she was to obey that order. His lips traveled her jaw, placing gentle kisses along the curve. Reassured she was not about to be devoured, she leaned into the warmth of his embrace, yielding her mouth to his expert attentions.

When her lips parted automatically to receive him, Jack clamped an iron hold on his reactions. What sort of hell on earth had he landed himself in this time? Not only did she need to be wooed gently, but her responses were ingrained, a natural part of her that he'd taken care, in their earlier engagements, to encourage. Now they looked set to drive him to the brink of madness. Every time he thought he had their relationship pegged, she invented a new twist to torment him. Mentally gritting his teeth, Jack set about the task of seducing his wife.

Unaware of the trouble she was causing, Kit felt the knots in her stomach ease as Jack's hands commenced a leisurely exploration of her fully clothed form, his tongue probing the soft contours of her mouth unhurriedly, as if he was willing to spend all night in such intoxicating play. She knew he wouldn't, but it was a comforting sensation. The kiss deepened by almost imperceptible degrees, his caresses becoming increasingly intimate until she was warmed through. She was glad to slip her arms free of her jacket. Snuggling closer, she pressed her tingling breasts to his chest. His hands roamed her back, molding her to him until her thighs were wedged firmly against his. The evidence of his desire pressed strongly against her stomach. Kit felt a familiar ache grow inside.

What followed was a carefully orchestrated journey into delight. Throughout, Jack held tight to the reins of his desire, not relinquishing his grip even when Kit lay naked beneath him, gasping with desire, her thighs spread, her hips tilting in unmistakable invitation. He sank into her welcoming heat, his jaw clenched with the effort to remain in control, determined that, whatever the cost, she'd have a night of loving she'd never forget.

He filled her and Kit sighed deeply. She closed her eyes, savoring the sensation of being so thoroughly possessed. Her skin was alive, her swollen breasts ached, her body yearned for completion. When Jack moved within her, she bit her lip and held still, sensing his strength, his hardness, his unrelenting need. Then she moved with him, letting her own need flower, feeding and assuaging his. She wrapped her arms about him, wound her legs about his hips, and let the dance consume them. Their bodies strove, intimately locked, heated and slick. As the glory drew nearer, Kit gasped and surrendered—to passion's flames, to mind-numbing delight, to incandescent sensation.

When, at last, they lay spent in each other's arms, and Jack felt the last of Kit's sweet spasms fade as her breathing slowed into blissfully sated slumber, triumphant possessiveness streaked through him.

She was his. He'd recaptured his wild woman. He'd never let go of her again.

With a sigh of contentment, deepened by the glow of achievement, of satisfaction in a job well-done, Jack turned on his side, taking Kit with him, carefully resettling her against him.

Halfway back from paradise, Kit felt his weight shift but was too deeply sated to protest. She'd forgotten what it was like—to lose her wits, to surrender her senses to the conflagration of their desire. Slow and steady she'd wanted; slow and steady she'd got. Jack's loving was a potent brew; she was addicted beyond recall. There was no hope of denying it, so she might as well accept it as her lot.

Who knew what lay in store—for her, for him? After tonight, whatever happened, she'd have to face it acknowledging that, for her, only one man held the power to open the doors of paradise.

Her husband. Jack—Lord Hendon.

Chapter 25

The next morning, Kit entered the breakfast parlor already flustered by the lateness of the hour. It was not her habit to keep servants waiting on her but she'd slept in, drained by Jack's method of waking her.

Instantly meeting her husband's all-too-knowing gaze, and his slow smile, did nothing for her composure. Drawing dignity about her as best she could, she busied herself at the sideboard, praying the blush she could feel warming her cheeks wasn't visible to the reprobate at the end of the table.

She'd thought he'd have left the house by now—doing whatever it was that gentlemen did—but she'd donned a new morning gown just in case. The delicate primrose shade was a favorite—she hoped he appreciated it. He was looking as hideously handsome as ever, lounging in his chair, long fingers crooked about the handle of a cup, yesterday's paper spread before him.

Her plate in her hands, Kit turned. The question of where to sit was answered by Lovis, who held the chair at the other end of the table. Ignoring her husband, Kit sat and picked up her fork. From the corner of her eye, she saw Lovis dismissed by a languid gesture.

Jack waited until the door closed behind his butler to remark: "I'm glad to see your appetite's returned."

Kit glanced down at her plate, seeing for the first time the mound of rice pie she'd piled on it, two kippers nestling on one side with a serving of kidney and bacon on the other. A slice of ham was laid atop, a dob of pickle in the middle. Head on one side, she considered the sight before replying: "Well, I'm hungry." It was his fault she was. How dare he tease her about it?

"Quite so."

Kit glanced up in time to catch his proprietary gloat before Jack substituted a more innocent expression. Her eyes narrowed. She wished she could say something, do something, to wash the smug glint from his eyes.

When she continued to stare, Jack's brows rose in deceptive candor. "You'll need to keep up your strength," he offered. "I suspect you'll find the role of Lady Hendon unexpectedly tiring."

Warning flames flickered at the back of Kit's glare. Jack laughed and, setting down his cup, rose, coming around the table to stand by her side. "I hadn't intended to leave you so soon, but I'm afraid I have to hie off to inspect some fields. I'll be back by midday."

Kit remembered her morning engagement and bit back her request to go with him. She looked up at him, her expression blank. "Mrs. Miles is to show me over the house this morning. No doubt I'll be so entralled I won't even notice your absence."

Jack tried to keep his lips straight and failed woefully. A rumbling chuckle escaped him. He put out one finger and wound it in the curls by Kit's ear. Then he bent his head and whispered: "Never mind. Why not use the time to consider the more interesting aspects of Lady Hendon's duties? Perhaps, when I get back, we could discuss those?"

Kit stiffened. He couldn't mean . . . ?

Jack's fingers drifted down the sensitive skin beneath her ear. His lips followed, leaving a tickling trail of nibbling kisses. Before she could gather her wits, he tipped her chin up, kissed her full on the lips, and was gone.

Stifling a most unladylike curse, Kit wriggled her shoulders to dispel the delicious shiver he'd sent rippling down her spine, drew a deep breath, and applied herself to her breakfast.

Her morning went in the inescapable task of being ceremonially inducted into the workings of Castle Hendon.

The staff was pleasant, clearly pleased to find a local filling Lady Hendon's shoes. The business of running a household was second nature to Kit—a legacy from her grandmother. She dealt with the staff with an innate confidence that had the inevitable result. By midday, the domestic reins were firmly in her hands.

Jack was not at the luncheon table; Lovis confirmed he'd not yet returned. Used to solitude, Kit walked the extensive gardens, then, tiring of such tame exercise, went upstairs to change into her new riding habit. The day was fine, the breeze beckoned—what better way to spend an afternoon than riding her husband's lands?

The stables were large, set around two interconnecting yards. Kit wandered along the rows of stalls, searching for Delia's black hide. The head groom came out of the second courtyard. Catching sight of her, he hurried over, doffing his cap as he came.

"Good afternoon, ma'am."

Kit waited for him to ask if he could help her. When he simply stood, plainly nervous, twisting his hat in his hands, she took pity on him. "I'd like my horse, please. The black mare."

To her surprise, the man subjected his hat to a further twist and looked even more uncomfortable. Kit frowned, a nasty suspicion displacing her good humor. "Where is Delia?"

"The master said to put her in the back paddock, my lady."

Kit put her hands on her hips. "Where is this back paddock?"

The groom waved in a southerly direction. "Over the hills a-way."

Too far to walk. Before Kit could ask her next question, the groom added: "The master said she was only to be brought up at his orders, ma'am."

Inwardly, Kit seethed. There was no point haranguing the groom; he was only obeying orders. The person she wanted to harangue, *needed* to harangue, was the giver of those orders. Abruptly, she turned on her heel. "Send word to me the moment Lord Hendon returns."

"Begging your pardon, ma'am but he came in not ten minutes ago."

Kit's eyes glittered. "Thank you—Martins, isn't it?"

The groom bowed.

Kit rewarded him with a stiff smile and marched back to the house.

She found Jack in the library. She sailed into the room and waited until she heard Lovis shut the door before advancing on her husband. He was standing behind his desk, a sheet of paper in his hand. Noting the arrested look in his eyes, she realized any attempt to hide her anger would be wasted. She drew breath, only to have him seize the initiative.

"I'm sorry I wasn't back for lunch. How did your tour with Mrs. Miles go?" Jack dropped his list on the blotter and came around the desk.

Thrown by the mild question, Kit blinked, then realized Jack was advancing on her. He was going to kiss her. Nimble-footed, she stepped around a chair. "Er . . . fine. What have you done with my horse?"

His flanking attack defeated, Jack halted and faced her guns. He contemplated her belligerent stance, muted in effect by her retreat behind the chair. "I've had her put in a paddock large enough for her to stretch her legs."

"She stretches her legs often enough. I ride her every day."

"Past tense."

Kit frowned. "I beg your pardon?"

"You *rode* her every day."

When no further explanation was forthcoming, Kit gritted her teeth and asked: "Just what are you trying to say?"

"As of now, you ride Delia only when I ride with you. Other than Champion, there's no beast in Norfolk that can keep up with that black streak you call a horse. I won't saddle my grooms with the responsibility of trying to keep you in sight. Hence, you ride with me, or accept a meeker mount and take a groom with you."

Kit had never known exactly what *flabbergasted* felt like. Now, she knew. She was so angry, she couldn't even decide which point to attack first.

The obvious riposte—that Delia was her horse—had an equally obvious answer. As his wife, all her property was his. But his dictates were outrageous. Kit's eyes glittered dangerously. "Jonathon," she said, using his given name for the first time since their wedding vows, "I've been riding since I could walk. In the country, I've ridden alone all my life. I will not—"

"Be continuing in such unacceptable style."

Kit bit her tongue to keep from screaming. The unemotional statement sounded far more ominous than Spencer's ranting ever had. She drew a deep breath and forced her tone to a reasonable pitch. "Everyone around about knows I ride alone. They think nothing of it. On Delia, I'm perfectly safe. As you've just pointed out, no one can catch me. None of our neighbors would feel the least bit scandalized to see me riding alone."

"None of our neighbors would imagine I'd allow you to do so."

It was an effort, but Kit swallowed the curse that rose to her lips. Her husband's calm gaze hadn't wavered. He was watching her, politely attentive but with the cool certainty that he'd be the victor in this little contretemps stamped all over his arrogant face. This was the side of Jack she didn't know but had surmised must exist; this was Jonathon.

Kit tried a different tack. "Why?"

Explaining was not his style, but in this case, Jack knew the ground to be firm beneath his feet. She was new to his bridle; it wouldn't hurt to give his reasons. "Firstly, as Lady Hendon, your behavior will be taken as a standard for others to follow, a status not accorded Miss Kathryn Cranmer but a point I'm sure Lady Marchmont and company would quickly make clear to you if I did not." He paused to let the implication of that sink in. Strolling toward the chair behind which Kit had taken refuge, he continued: "There's also the fact that your safety is of prime concern to me." Another pause enabled him to trap her gaze in his. "And I don't consider riding the countryside alone a suitably safe pastime for my wife."

Was he really just concerned for her welfare? Kit opened her mouth, but Jack held up a hand to stop her.

"Spare me your arguments, Kit. I won't change my mind. Spencer let you ride alone for far longer than was acceptable. He'd be the first to admit it." Kit stiffened as Jack's gaze slowly traveled the length of her slim frame. A subtle smile twisted his lips. "You're not a child anymore, my dear. You are, in fact, a most delectable plum. One I've no intention of letting any other man taste."

One arrogant brow lifted, inviting her comment. Kit bit her lip, then blurted out: "If I were in breeches, no man would look twice at me."

She shifted uneasily as she watched Jack's smile grow. It wasn't entirely encouraging, for it didn't reach his eyes.

"If I ever come upon Lady Hendon in breeches, do you know what I'll do?"

The soft, velvety tones transfixed Kit. She felt her eyes grow round, trapped in her husband's gaze. Little flames flickered deep. Slowly, all but mesmerized, Kit shook her head.

"Wherever we are, indoors or out, I'll take great delight in removing said breeches from her."

Kit swallowed.

"And then—"

"Jack!" Kit scowled. "Stop it! You're just trying to scare me."

Jack's brows flew. He reached out and, to Kit's surprise, pushed the chair from between them. She hadn't realized he was so close. Before she could react, he caught her elbows and pulled her to him. Trapped within the circle of his arms, Kit looked into his face, her pulse accelerating. A peculiarly devilish look had settled over his features. "Am I?"

For the life of her, Kit couldn't decide if he was teasing or not.

"Try me, by all means, if you doubt it."

The invitation was accompanied by a look which made Kit vow not to call his bluff. She became engrossed in smoothing his lapel. "But I need the exercise."

Even as the plaintive words escaped her lips, Kit realized her error. Her eyes flew wide; there was no way she would risk looking up.

A nerve-stretching pause ensued. "Really?" came the mild reply.

Kit wasn't about to answer.

"I'll bear that in mind, my dear. I'm sure I can devise any number of novel ways to exercise you."

Kit didn't doubt it. The tremor in the deep voice suggested he didn't either. A maxim of Lady Gresham's recurred in her mind. *When all else fails, try cajoling.* She looked up. "Jack—"

But he shook his head. "Give over, Kit. I won't change my mind."

Kit stared into his perfectly serious eyes and knew it was beyond her powers to sway him. With a sigh of exasperation, of deep frustration, she grimaced at him.

He kissed her pouting lips. And kept kissing them until she yielded. Feeling her wits slip their moorings, Kit summoned enough will for one mental curse against masterful men, before settling down to enjoy one.

For the rest of that day, she maintained an attitude that was the very essence of wifely complaisance. Her halo positively glowed. Her husband had insisted—she'd desisted. If she couldn't win the bout, she was detemined to make the most of her defeat. Unfortunately, Jack showed every sign of being overly understanding. When he used her newfound meekness to trap her into agreeing to retire early, Kit rapidly reverted to her usual argumentative self. Only by then it was too late.

She had her revenge two days later, when the question of her visiting the shops in Lynn arose. It quickly became clear that Jack was not enamored of the idea of her being simultaneously out of his sight and off Hendon lands. She simply shrugged. "If you want to come with me, I've no objection." She kept her eyes, wide and innocent, on the gloves she was buttoning up. "But I hadn't imagined you sitting in on all the visits I'll have to pay in a few weeks. Not but what the ladies would be only too pleased to see you."

She won her carriage by default. But when she descended the front steps on her husband's arm, it was to see, not one, but *two* footmen waiting in attendance. She hesitated only a moment, taken aback by the sight but, by now, too wise not to accept the better part of victory with good grace. The footmen dogged her steps throughout her expedition.

Despite such adjustments, the end of their first week of married life arrived without major drama. Settled in an armchair before the fire in the library, Kit yawned and gave in to one of her favorite fascinations, studying the way her husband's brown hair glinted gold in lamplight. He was seated at the huge desk placed across one corner of the room, going through a ledger. Their interactions had fallen into a routine, a fact for which she was grateful. After so many years essentially alone, she found it reassuring to know when Jack would be with her and when her mind would be free to deal with the more mundane of Lady Hendon's duties. To her surprise, she was fast coming to the conclusion that married life would suit her after all.

Her days tended to start at dawn, although she'd not yet managed to leave her bed before nine. Her previous habit of riding before breakfast had died a death, thanks to Jack's amorous inclinations. He still rode early, though how he managed it was beyond her. After the shortest of recuperative naps, he'd be up and about while she lay sprawled under her green satin coverlet, her limbs weighted with delicious languor, utterly incapable of moving, let alone thinking. After bathing, dressing, and breakfasting, usually alone, she would check with Mrs. Miles and issue her orders for the day. The time before luncheon was easily filled with trips to the stillroom, the laundry, the kitchen or the gardens. Jack usually joined her for luncheon, after which, on all but one day, he made himself available to escort her on a ride. She'd accepted his offers with alacrity, thankful not to have to forgo her daily round with Delia.

On the afternoon he'd been detained at Hunstanton, she'd swallowed her pride and asked for the mare he'd chosen as Delia's substitute to be saddled. Escorted by a senior groom, she'd set out for Gresham Manor.

As newlyweds, their first weeks would be theirs, to settle into married life without distraction. But after that, the bride visits would start. And the dinners. Kit knew what to expect; the prospect held no terrors for her, but she did wonder how her socially ept but reluctant husband would cope.

Her visit with Amy had been relaxing but had highlighted the truth of Jack's warning that her status as Lady Hendon was a far cry from the importance of one Miss Cranmer. The idea of taking precedence over Lady Gresham required some adjustment. Her ladyship commented favorably on the correctness of her escort. Kit bit her tongue. Amy was dying to hear her private news, but Lady Gresham, also curious, did not leave them alone. Kit departed the Manor with the definite impression that she'd disappointed her friends by remaining essentially herself, rather than being visibly transformed in some miraculous way by her husband's legendary skills.

She'd ridden back to Castle Hendon chuckling all the way, much to the confusion of her groom.

The fire crackled and hissed as a drop of rain found its way down the chimney. Kit stifled another yawn. Of all the times in their day, the evenings were the most peaceful. Until they went upstairs to her bedroom. But even there, the atmosphere had calmed. The tenor of their lovemaking had changed; knowing there was nothing to keep them from spending however many hours they wished on the road to paradise, Jack seemed content to keep progress as slow as she wished, spinning out their time in that bliss-filled world. His touch was exquisite, his timing faultless. Each night there were new doors to open, new avenues to explore. Each led to the same peak, beyond which lay a selfless void of indescribable sensation. Her delight in learning the pathways of pleasure was unfeigned; he was a patient teacher.

Kit sighed and smiled at his bent head.

She was eagerly awaiting her next lesson.

A boom of thunder shook Kit awake. She curled tight and clutched the covers over her ears, but still the reverberations echoed through her bones. Then she remembered she was a married woman and reached for her husband. Her groping hand met empty air. There was nobody in the bed beside her.

Kit sat up and stared, first at the rumpled sheets, then

about the empty room. Lightning lit the chamber, a bright beam shafting through a chink in the curtains. Kit flinched. Where was Jack when she needed him?

The following thunderclap propelled her to her feet. She snatched up the scandalous silk negligee Jack had insisted she wear so he could enjoy divesting her of it, and wrapped its gossamer folds about her, cinching the tie tight. With a determined frown, Kit made for a door beyond which she'd yet to explore—the one that led to Jack's rooms. Whatever his reasons for going to his own bed on this of all nights, she intended making it perfectly plain that during thunderstorms, his place was by her side.

As she'd suspected, the door led to the master bedroom. If her room was large, Jack's was enormous. And equally empty. Kit stared into the shadowy corners, then sank onto the bed as realization struck.

Lord Hendon is Captain Jack.

In the upheavals of the past weeks, she'd completely forgotten that fact. After recovering from her wound, she'd tacitly accepted that becoming Lady Hendon meant no more smuggling. She was convinced Lord Hendon would see it that way. She'd put all thought of the Hunstanton Gang from her. But, apparently, Captain Jack intended to go his own road, regardless.

Oblivious of the storm raging outside, Kit sat on Jack's bed and struggled to make sense of the facts in her hands. It was no use—they simply did not form a coherent whole. When the cold penetrated her thin gown, she crawled to the pillows and drew the coverlet about her. Lord Hendon had been appointed as High Commissioner specifically to stop the smuggling of spies. The same Lord Hendon, in his guise as Captain Jack, was actively engaged in smuggling spies. Despite his total disinterest in the subject, she'd gleaned sufficient snippets to confirm her vague notion that the same Lord Hendon had a war record—an exemplary war record. In fact, according to Matthew, he was a damned hero. So what the hell was he doing smuggling spies?

With a frustrated growl, Kit thumped the pillow and laid her head down. She was missing bits of this jigsaw. Jack, damn his hide, was playing some deep game.

Sleep tugged at her lids and she yawned. She could understand why he hadn't told her before. But she wasn't a smuggler anymore—she was his wife. Why shouldn't he tell her now? With a little nod, Kit settled her chin deeper into the pillow and closed her eyes. She'd stay here until he did.

The bed curtains stirred in the current of air as the door opened and shut. Kit came awake with a start. Her eyes adjusted to the dark, she instantly espied her husband's large form as he crossed the room to the washstand.

He hadn't seen her in the shadows of the bed.

Kit watched as he stripped off his shirt, then grabbed a towel and dried his hair. She tuned her senses to the night sounds; the storm had eased; it was raining. As Jack passed the towel over his shoulders and chest, Kit realized he must be soaked. He sat on a chair and, with an effort, pulled off his boots. When he stood, bending to place the boots aside, she asked: "What was the cargo tonight? Brandy or lace?"

She saw every muscle in his large frame tense, then relax. Slowly, Jack straightened and looked directly at her. Kit held her breath. The silence was so deep she could hear the rain spattering the window panes.

"Brandy."

Kit hugged her knees. "Nothing else?" she inquired innocently.

Jack didn't answer. Her presence in his room at this particular moment had not been part of his plan. Just as it formed no part of his plan to satisfy her curiosity about Captain Jack's nocturnal adventures. From Spencer, he had learned about her cousin Julian; he now understood her interest in stopping the spies. A praiseworthy ideal for the High Commissioner's lady. But telling her anything at all was out of the question.

This was the woman who'd blithely accepted a position as leader of a smuggling gang, the same woman who on more than one occasion had disobeyed his explicit orders. Even hinting at the truth was too dangerous.

Intent on getting warm as quickly as possible, Jack peeled off his sodden breeches, leaving them in a heap on the floor. He toweled his legs and cast a considering glance at the bed. Now she was here . . .

Kit tried to ignore the tingle of anticipation that flickered along her nerves. "Jack, what's—*Oh!*"

She bit back a squeal as Jack landed on the bed beside her. He wrestled the covers away from her. The thin film of her negligee was summarily dispensed with before he rolled her beneath him. His lips found hers as her hands, and the rest of her, made contact with his naked body. After a blood-stirring duel of tongues, Kit drew back to gasp: "You dolt! You're freezing! You'll catch your death of cold." His skin was iced, all except one part of him, which was already basking in the heat at the juncture of her thighs.

"Not if you warm me up."

Kit gasped as she felt one large hand slip beneath her bottom, tilting her hips, opening her to his invasion. She felt his spine slowly flex. Hard as steel, smooth as silk, he entered her. Kit gasped again, her body arching in instinctive welcome.

His lips sought hers. They moved together, Kit following his lead, rising to his thrusts, stoking the flames higher until they broke in a molten wave, sending heated pleasure coursing through them.

Later, he moved off her, drawing her about so she lay curled with her back to him. He settled his larger body around hers and immediately fell deeply asleep.

Snuggled beneath a heavy arm and halfway to sleep herself, Kit grimaced. Marriage to Lord Hendon had changed nothing. When it came to smuggling, he was Captain Jack. And Captain Jack kept his own counsel.

Chapter 26

Why wouldn't he tell her? Kit cantered up the Gresham's drive with that refrain ringing in her ears. She'd not seen her aggravating husband since dawn, when, after exhausting her thoroughly, he'd carried her back to her bed. She vaguely recalled him saying something about inspecting his coverts. She wasn't deceived. He'd purposely found some activity to keep him out all day so she couldn't pursue her questions. Doubtless, he thought time would blunt her curiosity.

With a snort, Kit slid from the saddle without waiting for the assistance of her groom. "Is the family in, Jeffries?"

"Lord Gresham's off to Lynn, miss—I mean, your ladyship." Jeffries smiled as he took her bridle. "Lady Gresham took the carriage out an hour ago. But Miss Amy's inside."

"Good!" Kit stalked to the house and entered by the morning room windows.

Amy was there, idly plying her needle. She jumped up as soon as she saw Kit. "Oh, good. Mama's gone to Lady Dersingham's. Now we can talk." Then Amy noticed Kit's high color and the brisk way she stripped off her gloves. Her eyes widened. "What's the matter?"

"That damned husband of mine's as close as an oyster!" Kit flung her gloves onto a table and fell to pacing the room, her long swinging strides more suited to Young Kit than Lady Hendon.

"What do you mean?" Frowning, Amy sank back onto the *chaise*.

Kit glanced her way. Amy knew nothing of her husband's alias but the need to unburden herself was strong. "What do you think of a gentleman who refuses to tell his wife," Kit paused, searching for words, "the details of a transaction he's involved in, when he knows she's interested and it would not be a . . . a breach of confidence or any such thing?"

Amy blinked. "Why do you want to know about Jonathon's business?"

The simple question sent Kit's temper into orbit. With a frustrated growl, she went about the room again, struggling for calm. Why did she want to know what Jack was up to? Because she did. While she'd been Young Kit and he Captain Jack, she'd felt a part of his adventures. She couldn't—wouldn't—accept that being his wife meant she had to remain distanced from what affected him most nearly. Besides which, if she knew what he was up to, she was sure she could help.

She stopped in front of Amy. "Let's just say that not knowing is driving me crazy. Besides which," she added, kicking her skirts out of the way to pace again, "there are reasons of . . . of honor which say he should tell me. If he had *any* gentlemanly instincts, he would."

Amy looked stunned—and thoroughly confused. "Do you mean that Jonathon's not truly the gentleman?"

It was Kit's turn to blink. "Of course not!" She frowned at Amy. "That wasn't what I meant."

Amy eyed Kit with affectionate understanding and patted the *chaise*. "Do sit down, Kit—you're making me dizzy. Now tell me—is it really as exciting as they say?"

The point of the question missed Kit entirely. She dropped into a chair opposite Amy and frowned. "Is what so exciting?"

"You know." Amy's slight blush jolted Kit's mind into the right rut.

"Oh, that." Kit waved dismissively, then abruptly changed her mind. She wagged a knowledgeable finger at Amy. "You know, you didn't have the half of it when you told me all that stuff about getting hot and wet.''

"Oh?" Amy sat straighter.

"No," Kit affirmed. "It's much worse than that.''

When Kit fell into a reverie and said nothing further, Amy glared. "Kit! You can't just stop there. I told you all I know—now it's your turn. I'm marrying George next month. It's your duty to tell me so I'll know what to expect.''

Kit considered; she decided her vocabulary wasn't up to it. "Do you mean to tell me your George hasn't gone beyond a kiss and a fondle?''

"Of course not." Amy's expression held more disgruntled disgust than shock. "Jonathon didn't go any farther with you before your marriage, did he?''

Kit's eyes glazed. "Our relationship didn't develop along quite the same lines as yours and George's.'' Her voice sounded strangled. Memories of how far Jack had gone threatened to overcome her. Even if she gave Amy an edited version, it would shock her to the core. "I'm sorry, Amy, but I can't explain. Why don't you press George for further details? Here he comes now.''

Through the morning room windows she could see George striding up from the stables. He reached the windows and checked at the sight of her. Then, smoothly, he entered and greeted Amy, bowing over her hand before raising it to his lips.

Watching closely, Kit noted the glow that infused Amy's face and the brightness in her eyes. When his eyes met Amy's, George's face softened; as his lips brushed Amy's fingers, his eyes remained on hers. The warm affection in his gaze was fully returned by Amy. Kit felt uncomfortably *de trop*.

Releasing Amy with understated reluctance, George turned to Kit and took her hand in greeting. "Kit.''

She returned his nod graciously. They'd met only twice since she'd dropped the guise of Young Kit—once at the wedding, once at their belated betrothal dinner. She'd always had the distinct impression that George disapproved of her wild ways far more strongly than Jack did. "Amy and I were discussing the merits of a husband being open with his wife.'' Kit kept her gaze innocent and unthreatening. ''Perhaps, in the interests of a well-rounded argument, you could give us your views on the matter.''

George raised his brows, his expression growing wary. ''I suspect it depends very much on the nature of the relationship, don't you think?'' With a smile for Amy, George sat on the *chaise* beside her.

''True,'' Kit acknowledged. ''But given the relationship was right, the husband's willingness to confide is the next hurdle, don't you think? What reasons could a man have for keeping secrets from his wife?''

Their next half hour was spent in a peculiar three-way conversation. George and Kit traded oblique references to Jack's reticence, none of which Amy understood. Amy, for her part, urged Kit to unburden herself and explain her problem more fully—an undertaking George endeavored to discourage. In between, all three traded local gossip, and George managed to discuss the details of their wedding, which he'd come to the Manor to clarify.

Sensing the currents between Amy and George, suppressed in her presence, Kit rose and picked up her gloves. ''I must be going. I feel sure my husband won't approve of my being out after dark.''

With that acerbic comment, she embraced Amy fondly, nodded to George, and sailed from the room.

Amy watched her go, sighed—then went straight into George's arms. They closed about her; she and George exchanged a warm and unrestrained kiss. Then Amy pulled back with a sigh. ''I'm worried about Kit. She's troubled by something—something serious.'' She met George's gaze. ''I don't like to think of her riding alone in such a mood.''

George grimaced. ''Kit's a big girl.''

Amy pressed closer. ''Yes, but . . .'' The eyes that met George's twinkled. ''And Mama will be home any minute.''

George sighed. ''Very well.'' He kissed Amy again, then set her from him. ''But I'll expect a reward next time I call.''

"You may claim it with my blessing," Amy declared. "Just as long as Mama is out."

George grinned, more than a touch wickedly. "I'll be back." With a wave, he headed for the stables.

He caught up with Kit as she left the stables, mounted on a chestnut mare. George stared. "Where's Delia?"

For one fractured moment, Kit thought she'd erupt in flames. Her glance seared George. "Don't ask!" She swung the chestnut toward the drive.

"Wait!" George called. "I'll ride part of the way with you."

When he rode out a minute later, Kit was schooling the mare in prancing circles, her groom watching from a distance. She fell in beside George; together they headed north and west.

George glanced at Kit. "I take it Jack hasn't explained about the smuggling?"

Kit narrowed her eyes. "Explanations do not seem to be his strong point."

George chuckled. When Kit glared, he explained: "You don't know how true that is. Neither explanations nor excuses are part of Jack's makeup. They weren't characteristics of his father's either."

Kit frowned. "Someone once said he was 'Hendonish.' Is that what that means?"

George grinned. "If it was a woman who said it, not entirely, but it's not unrelated to what I'm trying to say. Jack's a born leader—all Hendons have been for generations. He's used to being the one who makes the decisions. He knows what he wants, what needs to be done, and he gives orders to make it happen. He doesn't expect to have to explain his actions and doesn't relish being asked to do so."

"That much, I'd gathered."

George glanced at Kit's disgruntled expression. "If it's any consolation, despite the fact Matthew and I have known him for most of his life, and shared most of it, too, we received not the smallest word of explanation for your inclusion in the Gang. He didn't even tell us you were a woman."

They rode on in silence, Kit considering George's words. His confidence did, in fact, ease some of the frustration dragging at her heart. Clearly, her husband was an autocrat of long standing; if George was right, a hereditary one. Equally clearly, none of those close to him had made the slightest push to influence his high-handed ways. The determination to make him change his attitude, at least with respect to her, grew with every short stride her meek chestnut took.

The fork that led to Smeaton Hall appeared ahead. Kit drew rein. "You know the truth about the smuggling, don't you?"

Pulling up beside her, George sighed. "Yes, but I can't tell you. Jack's my superior in this. I can't speak without his approval."

Kit nodded and held out her hand. "Thank you."

George met her eyes, then squeezed her fingers encouragingly. "He'll tell you in the end."

Kit nodded. "I know. When it's over."

George could only grin. He bowed and they parted, understanding each other rather better than before.

Kit stared at the packages on the carriage seat opposite. Had she bought enough? She'd come to Lynn to get some cambric. After last night, she'd decided that cambric shirts would be much more sensible for Jack to wear around the estate. He'd spent all yesterday helping thin coppices. She hadn't known but should have guessed he'd be the sort of landowner who got off his horse, took off his coat, rolled up his sleeves, and helped his men. She'd come upon him entirely unintentionally, when, just before changing for dinner, she'd gone into his room in search of the sash that went with her silk negligee. It had been missing ever since the storm, three nights before. A groan emanating from the room beyond had drawn her to the open door.

The room had been fitted out as a bathing chamber, with a huge copper tub in the center. Jack had just sunk into the steaming water. He was facing away from her and as he bent forward to rest his head on his knees, she saw his back. It was covered with scratches.

"What on earth have you been doing?"

She'd strode forward, entirely forgetting her sash, oblivious of Matthew standing to one side.

Water had hit the floor as Jack swiveled, then he'd grimaced and leaned back in the tub, settling his head on the raised edge. "Falling through brambles." A wave of his hand had sent Matthew from the room, a fact of which she should have taken more notice.

She'd stood by the tub, hands on hips, and examined all of her husband that she could see. Jack opened his eyes and squinted up at her through the steam. "You'll be pleased to know it's only my back."

At his grin, she'd humphed. "Lean forward and let me see."

She'd had to nag but in the end, he'd let her examine his wounds. Some of the scratches were deep and had bled, but none qualified as serious.

"Seeing you're here, you may as well minister to my injuries." He'd held out the sponge.

She'd pulled a face and taken the bait.

She should, of course, have guessed which track his mind had taken. But it hadn't occurred to her that the tub was big enough for them both. And she'd certainly never imagined it was possible to perform the contortions they had within its slippery confines.

Yet another novel experience her husband had introduced her to.

Kit shook aside the distracting memory. She counted the ells of material again and wished she'd brought Elmina. Still, Lynn wasn't so far that she couldn't come again if they needed more. Kit turned to the window, to call to Josh the coachman that they could leave, when her gaze alighted on a natty trilby, entirely out of place in provincial Lynn.

Intrigued, she drew closer to the glass to view the body beneath the hat. "Good Lord!" Kit stared, seeing a ghost.

It was Belville—Lord George Belville.

Kit blinked, then stared again. The four years since he'd been a suitor for her hand had not treated him kindly. He still possessed a large, strong-boned frame, but his face was more fleshy and his girth had increased dramatically. His skin bore the pasty complexion of one who spent too much time in the gaming room. Features Kit remembered as finely chiseled had been coarsened by drink and general decadence, until he was but a bloated caricature of the man she'd nearly agreed to wed.

A cold shiver touched Kit's nape and spread over her shoulders. Keeping within the shadows of the carriage, she watched as her erstwhile suitor strolled across the square to the King's Arms, Lynn's most comfortable inn. Belville was addicted to town pursuits. What was he doing here?

At the door of the inn, Belville paused. He glanced about, studying all those his pale gaze could find. Then, slowly, he entered the inn and shut the door behind him.

Frowning, Kit sank back against the squabs. Then, shifting to the other side of the carriage, she called to Josh to take her home. For some reason, she was sure she didn't want Belville to see her. He represented part of her history that was no longer relevant; she didn't intend to let him cloud her present happiness.

As the carriage rumbled out onto the open road, Kit's frown deepened. Belville was nothing but a government official—he couldn't harm her. So why did she feel so threatened?

Kit was already in bed when Jack entered her room that night.

He paused in the doorway, studying her pensive face. What was she planning now? His gaze dwelled on the halo of curls, on the full lips and delicate features, before sweeping over the alluring figure outlined in ivory silk. She hadn't seen him yet; her nipples were soft rose circles at the peaks of her full breasts. Her arms were bare, as ivory as her nightgown and equally silky. The simple sheath clung to her curves, highlighting the indentation that marked her tiny waist before flaring over her luscious hips. The triangle of red curls at the apex of her thighs was just visible through the sheer material. The long sweep of her sleek thighs led to dimpled knees, peeking from the folds of the gown. Below her well-turned calves, her tiny feet were tinted a delicate pink. Slowly, Jack let his gaze travel upward once more. His lower chest contracted; a familiar tightening in his groin suggested full arousal was not far off. With a wry grin, he moved slowly into the room. It was comforting to know that these days, satisfaction was readily available. And guaranteed. It was, he felt, one of the less well publicized benefits of marriage.

As he circled the room snuffing candles and opening the curtains, he wondered again what devilry his wild woman was hatching. For once, her mind was definitely not on him.

"I went into Lynn today."

"Oh?" Jack paused in the act of snuffing the last candle in the candelabrum.

"Mmm." Kit looked around and located him, standing with the silver snuffer in one hand, the strong planes of his face lit by the single flame, his gilded hair winking wickedly in the golden light. "I saw Lord Belville."

"Who's Lord Belville?"

An impish grin twisted Kit's lips. "You could say he was an old flame."

Jack frowned and doused the candle, leaving the room lit by the wavering light of Kit's bedside candle and the moonlight streaming in. Laying the snuffer down, he walked to the bed. "What do you mean—an old flame?"

Inwardly, Kit was delighted with his raspy growl, but she needed no demonstration of Jack's possessiveness. She immediately dismissed the idea of making him jealous. But she was truly puzzled by Belville's presence and felt Jack should hear of her tenuous connection with that questionable peer from her, rather than from Belville. "When I was eighteen, I nearly accepted a proposal of marriage from him."

Jack tugged the sash of his midnight blue robe open and shrugged the silk from his shoulders. Kit's mouth went dry as her eyes disobeyed all injunctions and roamed his large and very aroused body, caressing each and every muscle, homing in on the promise of pleasure soon to be enjoyed. She fervently hoped her mention of Belville was not going to mar that pleasure.

But Jack's "Tell me," uttered as he stretched out on the bed beside her, was encouraging.

Kit moistened her lips and tried to drag her eyes up to his face and her wits back from whence they'd wandered. She fastened her gaze on Jack's silver eyes, gleaming under heavy lids. "Did I tell you my uncles and aunts kidnapped me and took me to London to be married for their convenience?"

Jack's lips twitched. He shook his head. "Lie back, close your eyes, and start at the beginning."

Kit drew an unsteady breath and did as she was told. His voice had dropped to a husky growl. She commenced her story with her grandmother's death and her removal from Cranmer Hall. She felt Jack shift and come up on one elbow beside her. As she reached London, she felt a tug loosen the first of the silk bows that held her nightgown closed.

Her narrative faltered. Her lids flickered.

"Keep your eyes shut. Go on."

Another unsteady breath was necessary before she could. Slowly, her story unfolded, kept moving by Jack's rumbling prompts. Equally slowly, her nightgown was opened all the way down to her feet. She'd got to refusing her first suitor when she felt the bow on each shoulder give way. A second later, the two halves of her nightgown were lifted from her.

Kit's voice suspended. She was lying naked beside her husband.

"What happened then?"

"Ah . . ." It was an effort to collect her wits but, falteringly, she took up her tale. Jack's fingertips touched her, tracing patterns over her skin. His lips followed the trails they'd laid, but his body, his limbs, never touched her. It was like being made love to by a ghost. Soon, her nipples were hard crests atop her swollen breasts. Her stomach was as tight as a drum. Her skin was a mass of sensitized nerves, flickering in anticipation of his next touch.

Kit had no idea how coherent she was, but Jack seemed to follow her tale. His voice, deep and vibrating with passion, urged her on whenever she failed. But when his lips touched her navel and his fingers grazed her thighs, she gave up.

Resisting the temptation to open her eyes, she replied to his "And?" with a simple, "Jack, I can't think, lying here like this."

"Turn over then."

She was halfway over before her mind focused. She hesitated, and would have turned back to ask why, but two large hands fastened about her hips and helped her onto her stomach. Resigned, Kit settled her cheek into her pillow, feeling the sensuous slide of silk and satin beneath her, the coolness soothing her aching breasts and that other ache buried in the soft fullness of her belly. Air played over the heated contours of her back. Jack still lay beside her, not touching her at all.

Assuming that after her protest he'd remain that way, Kit took up her story. She made it to Belville's offer before Jack's palm made contact with her bottom. Moving in slow, sensuous circles, barely touching, his hand stroked her body to instant life.

"Jack!" Kit's eyes flew open. She tried to turn, but Jack leaned over her, his chest angled across her back.

"What happened next?" His lips were at her nape.

In a garbled rush, Kit babbled the tale of her eavesdropping, barely aware of what she said. Jack's hand continued its gentle stroking, extending his area of attentions to the sensitive backs of her thighs. As she recounted her ultimate refusal of Belville's offer, she felt Jack's other hand slip beneath her to close possessively about one breast. Kit moaned softly. The hand on her bottom paused, poised on the fullest point in the curve. The fingers about her breast squeezed gently. Kit felt her body tense; her thighs parted slightly. Jack's hand slipped between, nudging them farther apart. Kit's tension wound tighter. A long finger slid effortlessly into her.

"*Oooh*!" A delicious shudder wracked her as the soft, long-drawn moan left her lips. The finger probed deeply. Kit bit her lip to stifle the moans of surrender that welled in her throat. A second finger joined the first and she gasped.

"Tell me again—what does Belville do?"

What was left of Kit's mind reeled. She told him, as

quickly as she could, as completely as she could, her mind centered on his fingers, sliding easily in and out of her body, delving deep one minute, twirling about the next. She got to the end an instant before her vocal cords seized. *"Jack!"* His name was all she could manage in her need, her voice low and weak.

He heard her. His fingers left her. To her surprise, Kit felt her hips being lifted and a pillow stuffed under her stomach. Jack's weight pressed against her, then she felt the pressure build between her thighs.

He came into her with a rush. Her mind disintegrated. She gasped, with shock. He held still for a few moments, allowing her to grow accustomed to this latest variation, to get used to the sensation of fullness and the deep penetration he'd achieved. Then he started to move.

Kit soon caught the rhythm, riding his downward thrusts before twisting her hips upward to capture and hold him, before he drew back again. He rode her long, he rode her hard, each deep, controlled stroke sending her closer to ecstasy; she writhed beneath him, wordlessly begging for more. When the final all-consuming wave of passion caught them and flung them clear, exhausted, wrung out, and deliriously sated, Jack collapsed on top of her. His lips caressed her earlobe, before, chuckling, he lifted away and dropped to the bed beside her once more.

"Kitten, if you were any wilder, I'd have to tie you up."

Moonlight patterned the floor of Kit's bedroom when Jack woke from his sated slumber. He lay still, savoring the deep contentment of the moment, the warmth of the silken limbs entwined with his. Kit's breath was a butterfly's kiss on his collarbone. He resisted the temptation to tighten his arms about her.

The long-case clock in the corridor struck eleven.

Jack stifled a sigh and carefully disengaged from Kit's embrace. He slipped from her warm bed and found his robe on the floor. Shrugging into it, he paused, looking down on his sleeping wife. Then, a smile on his lips, he turned toward his room.

The instant the door to Jack's room shut behind him, Kit

opened her eyes. She blinked rapidly, then sat up, shivering when the cold found her naked shoulders. She dragged the coverlet to her chin and listened.

The heavy tock of the clock was the only sound to reach her straining ears.

Quickly, she slipped from the bed and made for her wardrobe. She'd need to hurry if she was to have any hope of following her husband to his rendezvous.

Chapter 27

The soft shush of the waves on Brancaster beach filled Jack's ears. Leaning against a rock, he looked across the moonlit sands. In the lee of the cliff, Champion snorted, unhappy at being tied next to Matthew's gelding. The rest of the Gang had yet to arrive; the boats weren't due for another hour.

Crossing his arms over his chest, Jack settled down to wait. The memory of the silken limbs he'd left so reluctantly warmed him. She was a passionate woman, his kitten. She'd succeeded in dramatically altering his view of marriage. Before she'd burst into his life, the urge to settle down and manage his inheritance had been driven more by duty than desire. Now, there was nothing he wanted more than to devote his energies to being the lord of Castle Hendon, to watching his children grow, and to taking delight in his wife. He'd no doubt she'd keep him amused—in the bedroom and out of it. Once this mission was finished, he'd be free to follow his own road. Now, thanks to his wild woman, he knew where that road was headed.

His thoughts of Kit reminded him of Lord Belville. He wasn't sure why she'd mentioned him. He'd never met the man; the only piece of her information that had interested him had been Belville's connection with Whitehall. As for the rest, Kit was his now, and that was that.

A cloud of salt spray, whipped by the freshening wind, drifted past. Jack frowned. Could Belville be part of the network that he, George, and countless other careful hands had been slowly unraveling? It was possible.

After months of careful, cautious work, they were nearing the end of their trail. Originally, his mission had been merely to block the routes by which spies were smuggled out of Norfolk. But his success in becoming the leader of the Hunstanton Gang, and then monopolizing the trade in ''human cargo,'' had made Whitehall more ambitious.

Despite having closed the spy-smuggling routes operating out of Sussex and Kent, the government had failed to identify at least one of the principal sources. Which meant there were still traitors sending information out of London. But the plans for Wellington's summer maneuvers were too vital to risk their falling into French hands. So Jack, George, and a select group of others had been summoned from their military postings and asked to sell out of the services to take up civilian appointments under the control of Lord Whitley, the Home Office Undersecretary responsible for internal security.

When the first of the incoming spies the Hunstanton Gang had passed on had reached London and led them to the next connection, the government had moved cautiously. While one group of officers tracked the London courier back to his source, presumably buried somewhere in the British military establishment, the government had decided to turn the route Jack now controlled to their own ends. Sir Anthony Blake, alias Antoine Balzac, had been the spy they'd ''smuggled'' to France the night Kit had been shot. Instead of the real plans for Wellington's coming campaign, he'd carried information put together by a conglomerate of officers who'd seen active service only a short time before. The information had been accurate enough to pass the scrutiny of the French receivers. The government had already seen evidence that the false trails were being followed, translated into field movements that would help rather than hinder the duke's forces.

That sort of return was worth a great deal of risk. The number of lives saved would be enormous. So they'd decided to chance a final hand, a last throw of the dice.

Anthony was to carry another packet of information into France, but this time, he would bargain for information in return—information on who the London traitor was. On his last visit, he'd made contact with a French liaison officer who had a great liking for cognac. The man knew the details of the entire English operation. Anthony was sure he could extract at least a clue.

The government now needed that clue. The courier they'd been following in London had been killed in a tavern brawl. The unexpected setback had been disheartening, but all concerned were now even more determined to identify the traitors still remaining. Even if he learned no names, if Anthony could discover how many traitors were left within the military establishment, tonight's mission would be worth the risk.

Hoofbeats, muffled by the sand, approached. Jack recognized George's chestnut. At sight of the figure on the second horse, Jack grinned and straightened. When the horses pulled up beside him, he caught the newcomer's bridle. "Ho, Tony! Ready for another bout of *la vie française?*"

Sir Anthony Blake grinned and dismounted. Another of Lord Whitley's select crew, he was the scion of an ancient English house, but half-French. He'd learned French at his mother's knee and had absorbed the full range of French mannerisms and characteristic Gallic gestures. In addition, he was slim and elegant with black hair and black eyes. He looked French. His ability to pass as French had yielded considerable benefits to His Majesty's government over the many years of war with France. Anthony's black eyes gleamed. "Ready as I'll ever be. Any developments?"

Jack waited until George and Anthony tethered their mounts and rejoined him before answering Anthony's question. "Nothing's happened to change your direction. But I've just learned that a gentleman connected with Whitehall has been seen in these parts. Do you know anything of a Lord Belville?"

Anthony frowned. His estates were in Devon; London was no more his cup of tea than Jack's or George's. "If I'm thinking of the right man, he's a nasty bit of work. Got a position somewhere in the long corridors on the strength of his pater's influence. Unsavory reputation socially, but nothing in it that would interest us."

Jack grimaced. "That's much as I'd imagined. Still, if he's poking his nose about without good reason, I'll follow it up."

The three of them fell to discussing the details of Antoine's trip.

"I'll play it safe and take the usual route back unless there's good reason to do otherwise."

Jack nodded. "Here comes our little troop." The members of the Hunstanton Gang were gathering. "God only knows how they'll react when they learn they've been doing their bit for Mother England." With a wry grin, Jack moved forward to take command.

Above him, hidden by a spiky tussock close by the cliff's edge, Kit frowned. Who was the third man?

She'd had a time following her husband, the short strides of her obedient little mare no match for either Champion or Matthew's black. The need to wait until they were clear of the stables before entering to saddle her mount had meant she'd left the Castle well behind them. But, courtesy of the moon and the elevation of her husband's home, she'd seen enough to realize they were making for the cottage. She'd drawn into the trees surrounding it only minutes before Jack had reemerged in his Captain Jack costume. She'd thanked her stars she hadn't been riding Delia then. Champion had no interest in the chestnut mare; he'd obeyed Jack's instruction without hesitation. She'd dropped behind again on the ride to the coast, and had had to cast about to find their position on the sands. She'd been surprised to find no one else there.

Then George and his companion had arrived. There was something about the way the unknown man held himself, the way he conversed with Jack and George, that disallowed any idea he was a new recruit for the Gang.

Kit saw Joe split from the knot of men around Jack and head toward the cliffs. Jack's lookout. There was a small knoll a few feet from the cliff, about fifty yards from where she was crouching. Once on it, Joe would be able to see her clearly. As Joe started up the cliff path, Kit scrambled along the edge until she found a deeply shadowed crevice. There were tussocks growing from the walls every few feet. The area at the bottom looked sandy. With a last glance to where her mare was concealed in a stand of trees, Kit went over the edge.

She dropped to the sand and wiped her hands on her breeches, then slid to the end of the shadows. Glancing left, she saw the run in full swing. Immediately before her were the horses, Champion and three others, tethered under the overhang of the cliff. Beyond them lay a section of dunes, heavily covered with clumps of sea grass. Kit slipped out and around the horses, patting Champion's great nose on the way. She gained the dunes and worked her way cautiously forward, until she was mere yards from where Jack and George stood, their mysterious visitor between them.

The run was a small one, leaving Jack and George with nothing to do but watch.

Kit glanced back at the cliff. She couldn't see Joe, but if he came to the cliff's edge, he'd spot her immediately. Not that she was frightened of being discovered. Jack had drummed into his men's heads that on no account were they to shoot or knife anybody. The most she had to fear was being locked in her room in Castle Hendon. And learning what Jack would do on finding her in breeches. Kit shook aside the distracting thought and focused on her husband and his associates. Unfortunately, they said nothing.

When the last boat was being unloaded, Jack turned and nodded to Anthony. "Good luck."

Anthony ducked his head but gave no word in answer. He strode down the beach on the first stage of his journey into danger.

Jack watched him go, watched the boat disappear into the surf to make contact with the ship standing offshore. Then he gave the final orders to clear the beach, sending the cargo on to the old crypt. Both he and George lingered on the sands, strangely tied to the fate of their friend. Matthew ambled the beach before them, patiently waiting.

Behind them, Kit lay burrowed in the sand, thoroughly

perplexed. Why "Good luck"? And why was she so sure Jack would have shaken the man's hand, but had stopped himself from doing so? She'd sensed his intent quite clearly. Yet, from everything she'd been able to see, the man was French.

She bit her lip, then shook her head. She simply could not believe Jack was smuggling spies. Damn the man—why couldn't he relieve her of this miserable uncertainty? It was all his fault. Her peace of mind was in tatters purely because he had a constitutional objection to being understood!

Suppressing a snort, Kit glanced back over her shoulder. And froze.

A few feet away, so close his grey shadow almost touched her, stood the hulking figure of a man. A scream of fright stuck in her throat. Her wide eyes took in a heavy frame and fleshy jowls. The man was staring at Jack and George, still watching the waves some fifteen feet ahead, presenting her with a haughty profile. He was oblivious of her, prone almost at his feet. Moonlight glinted on the long barrels of the pistols he carried.

The man was Lord Belville.

Kit couldn't breathe.

"We may as well go."

Jack's voice cut through the frozen moment. It brought Belville to life. He stepped forward, passing Kit, still lying immobile, to drop the last few feet to the sand. Another step took him clear of the dunes to face Jack and George as they turned toward the horses, Matthew a few steps behind them.

"Not so fast, gentlemen."

Jack pulled up, startled by the appearance of an armed stranger from dunes he had every right to expect were safe. Where the hell was his lookout?

As if reading his mind, Belville's lips twisted in an unpleasant smile. "I'm afraid your lookout met with a fatal accident." He glanced at the fingers of his right hand, closed about a pistol butt. "Slitting a throat is silent, but such a messy business."

Kit felt her blood run cold. She saw the expression on

Jack's face harden. *Oh, God*! If she didn't do something, he would be shot! Pressing her fingers to her lips, she struggled to think.

Thankfully, Belville seemed inclined to conversation. "I must admit that when our courier died in that brawl, we originally believed it simply bad luck. However, when we had no further approaches from our French comrades, when, in fact, they suggested they no longer needed our services, we thought an investigation was in order." Belville rolled the syllables from his tongue, his genial manner counteracted by the menace of the pistols in his hands. "Perhaps," he suggested, "given the trouble you've put me to, you'd like to explain just who you are and who you're working for? Before I put a bullet into each of you."

Kit wished him luck. She couldn't believe Jack would tell him anything, even under such pressure, but she wasn't about to wait to find out. She'd remembered Jack's saddle pistol. Pray God he kept it loaded. As she wriggled back through the dunes, she heard her husband's voice.

"You're Lord George Belville, I take it?"

Kit wondered what her erstwhile suitor would make of that. She hurried toward the horses, protected from sight by the dunes.

His gaze steady on Lord Belville's malevolent eyes, Jack inwardly cursed himself for a fool. He should have taken the time to learn why Kit had wanted to tell him about Belville. She'd been uneasy enough to mention him in the first place. He should have trusted her instinct. Now Joe was dead. And God knew how he, and George and Matthew, were going to get out of this without ending in the same state.

"How do you know who I am?" Belville's honeyed tones had become a snarl.

"You've been identified by someone with a direct connection to the High Commissioner. You could say that person has his lordship's ear."

Jack heard George, beside him, choke. Carefully, he weighed up the odds. They weren't encouraging. Belville had only two pistols, but he could see the butt of a smaller gun glinting in the man's waistband. Presumably, he also had a knife somewhere about him. Even if he missed one shot—and why should he, he'd plenty of room and they'd no cover—he'd still have a weight advantage over either George or Matthew in a knife fight.

Keep talking and pray for a miracle seemed the best bet.

"Who is this person? This intimate of the High Commissioner's?"

Jack's brows flew. "Ah—now that would be telling secrets, wouldn't it?"

Belville leveled his pistols. "I don't believe there is such a person."

Jack shrugged. "But how did I know you? We haven't met before."

The barrels wavered. Belville stared, eyes narrowing. "Who are you?"

Out of sight and sound, Kit's fingers closed about the small pistol tucked into the pocket in Champion's saddle. She let out a sigh of relief. If only she could get back in time.

As she scurried into the dunes, she heard Belville's voice, angry and demanding. Clearly, he hadn't liked being known. Jack's voice answered, smooth and confident, which only seemed to wind Belville's spring tighter. Kit forced herself to take care twisting through the dunes, praying her husband's glib tongue wouldn't get him shot before she made it back.

"Let's just say I'm someone with an interest in the traffic." Jack kept his eyes on Belville's. "Perhaps, if we talk, we might discover our interests are complementary?"

Belville frowned, clearly debating the possibility. Then he slowly shook his head. "There's something damned odd about your 'traffic.' You sent a man out tonight—Henry and I would like to know what he was carrying. There's no other traitor in Whitehall bar us—Henry's quite sure of that. Which means you're running a double deal, one which may well rebound on Henry's and my necks." Belville smiled, a chilling sight. "I'm afraid, dear sir, that your days in the profession have come to an end."

So saying, he raised both pistols.

Ten feet behind him, Kit skidded to a soundless halt in

the sand, eyes wide and terrified. She jerked Jack's pistol up before her, clutching it in both hands. Screwing her eyes tight shut, she pulled the trigger.

An explosion of sound ricochetted from the cliffs. Both Jack and George rocked back on their heels, expecting to feel the searing pain of a bullet somewhere in their flesh. As the veil of powder smoke drifted past on the breeze, they looked at each other and realized neither had stopped a bullet. Matthew reached them, equally astonished to find both unharmed. In amazement, they all turned to stare at Belville.

His lordship's pasty complexion had paled, a look of incredulity stamped across his fleshy features. Both pistols were smoking but pockmarks in the sand at Jack's and George's feet bore evidence that he'd not raised his weapons far before discharging them.

Bewildered, Jack looked into the man's eyes, only to find them glazing. As he watched, Belville twisted to the right and collapsed in a heap on the sand.

Facing them stood Kit, now revealed, a smoking pistol in her hands, her eyes enormous pools of shock.

Jack forgot about Belville, about missions and spies. In a split second, he'd covered the space between them and wrapped Kit in his arms, crushing her to him, furious and thankful all at once. "Damn woman!" he said into her curls. "How the hell did you get here?"

He felt weak, shock and relief offsetting his anger that she was there at all. As he reached for the gun, hanging from her limp fingers, he swore softly. "What the hell am I to do with you?"

Kit blinked up at him, thoroughly disoriented. She'd just killed a man. She wriggled in Jack's arms, trying to peer around his shoulders to where George and Matthew were bent over Belville's body. But Jack held her firmly, using his body to shield her. "Be still."

With no alternative, Kit did. Almost immediately waves of nausea swept through her. She paled and swayed into Jack's embrace as faintness dragged at her senses.

"It's all right. Breathe deeply."

Kit heard the words of comfort and did as she was told. Gradually, the world stopped spinning.

Then George was beside them.

Jack held her tight, her face pressed to his chest. Beneath her cheek she could feel his heartbeat, strong and steady, very much alive. Tears started to her eyes. Annoyed at her weakness, Kit blinked them away.

One look at George's face was enough for Jack, but he had to know and Kit had to hear. "Dead?"

George nodded. "Clean through the heart."

Jack stifled a ridiculous urge to ask Kit whether, among her many odd talents, she included pistol shooting. Even at such close range, a clean shot under pressure took skill. And courage. But he had no doubt of her reserves of that quality.

The resigned overtones in each man's voice brought Kit's head up. She stared at Jack. "Didn't you want him dead?"

To his exasperation, Jack couldn't come up with a convincing affirmative fast enough to allay her suspicions. Instead, her shocked gaze compelled him to stick to something like the truth. "It would have been more help if we could have got him alive, but," he hurried on, "in the circumstances, Matthew, George, and I are perfectly happy to be alive. Don't think we're complaining."

Jack couldn't tell what she was feeling; her eyes reflected a turmoil far deeper than his own. To his relief, George came to his aid.

"Matthew says a body put in here will be taken out to sea."

Jack nodded. A disappearance would be easier all around. Bodies had to be explained, and explaining Belville's would not help their mission.

"Joe—we have to find Joe!"

Kit's voice jerked both her listeners to a sense of their duty.

"No!" came from both of them.

"I'll take you home," Jack continued. "George will deal with Joe."

But Kit drew back as far as he'd let her, shaking her

head vehemently. "But he might not . . . No. We have to look now!"

Both men registered the note of hysteria in her voice. They exchanged troubled glances over her head.

"Come on!" Kit was tugging at Jack's arm. "He might be dying while you argue!"

Neither Jack nor George held much hope for Joe but neither felt confident of convincing Kit of the fact he was almost certainly dead already. With a sigh, Jack released her but retained a firm hold on her hand. Together, the three of them mounted to the cliff and approached the hillock.

A pathetic bundle in worn clothes was all that remained of Joe. The sand about was stained with the blood that had poured from the gaping wound in his neck. Kit stared. Then, with a convulsive sob, she buried her face in Jack's shirt.

George checked but there was no vestige of life left in the huddled form.

Kit struggled to draw breath. For weeks, she'd been Jack's lookout, playing smuggler without a care in the world. It had all been a game. But Joe's death was no game. If she'd still been with Jack, she would have died. Instead, Joe had gone. Any possibility of feeling remorse for killing Belville disappeared, run to ground along with Joe's blood. She'd avenged Joe, and for that she was glad.

The sudden rush of emotions weakened her to the point where Jack's arms were the only thing holding her upright. He sensed her draining strength and swore.

To Jack, the sight of his murdered lookout was a scene from a nightmare. Of course, in his worst nightmare, the huddled figure was Kit. The fact that it was Joe who had died muted the shock, but it was still very real. Badly shaken, he swung Kit into his arms, drawing comfort from the warmth in her slim frame.

George looked up. "Matthew and I will sort this out. For the Lord's sake, get her home. And don't leave her alone."

Jack needed no further urging. He carried his silent wife down to the horses and set her on Champion. He swung up behind her and settled her against him. "Where's your horse?"

Kit told him as they negotiated the climb to the cliff. Jack rode to the trees and tied the mare to Champion's saddle before setting a direct course for the Castle. His one aim was to get a brandy into Kit and then get her to bed. She was already shivering. He'd no experience of deep shock in women, but he fully expected her to get worse.

As they traversed the moonlit fields, Kit struggled to find her mental feet. She'd killed a man. No matter how she viewed that fact, she was unable to feel anything like guilt. In the same position, she'd do it again. He'd been about to kill Jack, and that was all that had mattered. As Castle Hendon loomed on the horizon, she accepted reality. Jack was hers—like any female of any species, she'd kill in a loved one's defense.

"We'll have to do something for Joe's family."

The sudden comment brought Jack out of his daze. "Don't worry. I'll deal with it."

"Yes, but . . ." Kit went on, unaware she was babbling all but incoherently.

Jack soothed her with reassurances. Eventually, she quieted, as if her outburst had drained her remaining strength. She sagged against him, comfortingly alive. Jack concentrated on guiding Champion through the darkening fields. His mind was full of conflicting emotions. The moon was setting; it was full dark by the time he clattered into his stables.

He shouted for Martins. The man came at a run, tucking his nightshirt into his breeches. Jack dismounted, then lifted Kit down, ignoring Martins's shocked stare. His wife's breeches were the most minor of the concerns pressing for his attention. He left Martins to deal with the horses and carried Kit to the house. He let them in through a side door. A single candle waited on the table just inside. Jack ignored it. He carried Kit straight to her room.

Once there, he stripped her of her clothes, ignoring her protests, handling her gently, like a child. He grabbed a towel and rubbed her briskly, over every square inch, until she glowed. Kit grumbled and tried to stop him, then gave up and lay still, slowly relaxing under his hands. He left her for a moment, stretched naked on her bed, her coverlet thrown over her. When he returned from his room, he was also naked and carried two glasses of brandy.

Jack slipped under the coverlet, feeling Kit's satin skin warm against his. "Here. Drink this."

He held the glass to her lips and persevered until, under protest, she'd drained it. He drained his own in one gulp and put both glasses on the table. Then he slipped down into the bed beside her, gathering her into his arms.

To his surprise, Kit turned to look up at him. She put up one hand to draw his head down to hers. He kissed her. And went on kissing her as he felt her come alive.

It hadn't been his intention, but when later he lay sated and close to sleep, Kit a warm bundle beside him, he had to admit his wife's timing had not been at fault. Their union had been an affirmation of their need for each other, of the fact that they were both still alive. They'd needed the moment.

Jack yawned and tightened his hold about Kit. There were things he had to think of, before he could yield to sleep. Someone had to take news of Belville's death posthaste to London. It sounded as if "Henry" was Belville's superior in the spying trade, and presumably worked somewhere in Whitehall. Whoever Henry was, they needed to make sure of him before Belville's disappearance tipped him off. Could George go to London? No—whoever went would need to explain Belville's death. He could take responsibility for his wife's actions; no other man could.

He would have to go, and go early.

Jack glanced down at Kit's curly red head, a fuzz in the darkness. He grimaced. She wouldn't be pleased, but there was no help for it.

The vision of her, his smoking pistol in her hand, came back to haunt him. He hadn't known what he'd felt when he'd seen her standing there and realized what she'd done. He still didn't.

No husband should have to go through the traumas she'd put him through. When he returned from London, that was something he *was* going to explain.

Chapter 28

When Kit woke and saw the letter, addressed to her in her husband's scrawl, propped on the pillow beside her, she groaned and closed her eyes. When she opened them again, the letter was still there.

Damn him! What now? Muttering French curses, she sat up and broke the seal.

Her shriek of fury brought Elmina hurrying in. "*Ma petite*! You are ill?"

"*I'm* not ill—but he will be when I get my hands on the bloody high-and-mighty High Commissioner! How *dare* he leave me like this?"

Kit threw down the letter and flung the covers from her legs, barely noticing her nakedness in her anger. She accepted the gown Elmina, scandalized, threw about her shoulders, shrugging into the silk confection before she realized it was one of those he'd bought her. "What's the use of these things if he's not even here to see them?"

Her furious question was addressed to the ceiling. Elmina left it unanswered.

By the time Kit had bathed and breakfasted, very much alone, her temper had cooled to an icy rage. She read her husband's letter three more times, then ripped it to shreds.

Determined not to think about it, she tried to submerge herself in her daily routine with varied success. But when evening approached and she was still alone, her distractions became limited. In the end, after a lonely dinner, seated in splendid solitude at the dining table, she retired to the li-

325

brary, to the chair by the fire, to stare broodingly at the vacant chair behind his desk.

It wasn't fair.

She still had very few clues as to his purpose, but her suspicions were mounting. She'd helped him gain control over all the smugglers in the area—she didn't know why he'd needed that but was sure it had been his objective in joining his Gang with her small outfit. Despite her constant requests, he'd refused to divulge his plans. Even when she'd threatened him with exposure, he'd stood firm. Then she'd saved them from the Revenue, nearly dying in the process. Had he weakened? Not a bit!

Kit snorted and shifted in her chair, slipping her feet from her slippers and tucking her cold toes beneath her skirts.

His reaction to the latest developments was all of a piece. He'd hied off to London, to smooth things over regarding Belville's death, so he'd said. Kit's eyes narrowed, her lips twisted cynically. He'd slipped up there. Their story for public consumption was that Belville had disappeared, presumed a victim of the treacherous currents. She wished she knew who Jack was seeing in the capital. Doubtless, they were getting the explanation she'd been denied.

Kit sighed and stretched. The lamps were burning low. She might as well go up to her empty bed. There was no getting away from the fact that her husband simply didn't trust her, was apparently incapable of trusting her.

Full lips drew into a line; amethyst eyes gleamed. Kit put her feet back into her slippers and stood.

Somehow, she was going to have to make clear to her aggravating spouse that his attitude was simply not good enough.

With a determined tread, she headed for bed.

When Sunday dawned, Kit found herself both husbandless and filled with restless energy—the latter a natural consequence of the former. Flinging back the curtains, she looked out on a fairy-tale scene. The green of the fields was dew-drenched, each jeweled blade sparkling under a benevolent sun. There was not a cloud to be seen; the birds sang a serenade of joy to the bluest of skies. A glint appeared in Kit's eye. She hurried to the wardrobe. It would have to be her inexpressibles; Jack had been overly hasty in divesting her of her riding breeches and Elmina had yet to mend them.

Clad as a boy, she slipped from the still sleeping mansion. Saddling the chestnut with her convertible sidesaddle was easy enough. Then she was riding out, quickly, lest the grooms see her, heading south. She reached the paddock where Delia was held. The black mare came racing at her whistle. It was the work of a few minutes to transfer the saddle, then she turned the chestnut loose to graze in unwonted luxury, while she and Delia enjoyed themselves.

She rode straight for the north coast, passing close by the cottage, a black arrow speeding onward. When they pulled up on the cliffs, exhilaration pounded in her veins. She was breathing hard. Laughter bubbled in her throat. Kit held up her hands to the sun and stretched. It was wonderful to be alive.

It would be even more wonderful if her hideously handsome husband was here to enjoy it with her—only he wasn't. Kit pushed that thought, and the annoyance it brought, aside. She cast about for a cliff path.

She rode eastward along the sands, then came up to the cliffs to make her way onto the anvil-shaped headland above Brancaster. Kit let Delia have her head along the pale sands where the Hunstanton Gang had run so many cargoes.

She found the body in the last shallow bay before the eastern point.

Pulling Delia up a few yards away, Kit stared at the sprawled figure at the water's edge. Waves washed over his legs. He'd been thrown up on the beach by the retreating tide. Not a muscle moved; he was as still as death.

His black hair rang a bell.

Carefully, Kit dismounted and approached the body. When it was clear the man was incapable of proving a threat, she turned him on his back. Recognition was instant. The arrogant black brows and aristocratic features of Jack's French spy met her wondering gaze. He was deathly pale but still alive—she could see the pulse beating shallowly at the base of his throat.

What had happened? More importantly, what should she do?

With a strangled sigh, Kit bent over her burden and locked her hands about his arms. She tugged him higher up the beach, to where the waves could no longer reach him. Then she sat down to think.

If he was a French spy, she should hand him over to the Revenue. What would Jack think of that? Not much—he wouldn't be impressed. But surely, as a loyal English-woman, that was her duty? Which took precedence—duty to one's husband or duty to one's country? And were they really different, or was that merely an illusion Jack used for his own peculiar ends?

Kit groaned and drove her fingers through her curls. She wished her husband were here, not so he could take control but so she could vent her feelings and give him the piece of her mind he most certainly deserved.

But Jack wasn't here, and she was alone. And his French friend needed help. His body was chilled; from the look of him, he'd been in the water for some time. He looked strong and healthy enough, but was probably exhausted. She needed to get him warm and dry as soon as possible.

Kit considered her options. It was early yet. If she moved him soon, there'd be less chance of anyone seeing him. The cottage was the closest safe place where he could be tended. She stood and examined her patient. Luckily, he was slighter than Jack. She'd found it easy enough to move him up the beach; she could probably support half his weight if necessary.

It took a moment to work out the details. Kit thanked her stars she'd trained Delia to all sorts of tricks. The mare obediently dropped to her knees beside the Frenchman. Kit tugged and pulled and pushed and strained and eventually got him into her saddle, leaning forward over the pommel, his cheek on Delia's neck, his hands trailing the sands on either side of the horse. Satisfied, Kit scrambled on behind, drew a deep breath and gave Delia the signal to stand. She nearly lost him, but at the last moment, managed to haul his weight back onto the mare. Delia stood patiently until she'd settled him once more. Then they set off, as fast as she dared.

Dismounting was rather more rough-and-ready. Kit's arms ached from the strain of holding him on. She slid to the ground, then eased the leaden weight over until, with a swoosh, he left the saddle to end in a sprawled heap before the door. Exasperated with his helplessness, Kit spared a moment to glare at him. She paused to tug him into a more comfortable position before going into the cottage to prepare the bed.

She found an old sheet and spread it on the bed. His clothes would have to come off, but not until she'd used them as handholds to get him up onto the mattress. Returning to her patient, she dragged him inside. Getting him up on the bed was a frustrating struggle, but eventually, he was laid out upon the sheet, long and slim and, Kit had to admit, handsome enough to make her notice.

Jack didn't leave his knives lying about, but his sword still resided in the back of the wardrobe. Kit put it to good use, slicing the Frenchman's clothes from him. She tried not to look as she peeled the material away, turning him over on his stomach as she went and pulling the muddy sheet from under him. There were bruises on his shoulders and arms, as if he'd been in a fight, and one purpling blotch on one hip, as if he'd struck something. She flicked the covers over him and tucked them in.

Glowing with pride in a job well-done, she set about lighting the fire and heating some bricks. Later, when her patient was as warm and dry as she could make him, she made some tea and settled down to wait.

It wasn't long before, thawed by the warmth, he stirred and turned on his back. Kit approached the bed, confidently leaning across to lay a cool hand on his forehead.

Strong fingers encircled her wrist. Heavy lids rose to reveal black eyes, hazed with fever. The man stared wildly up at her, his eyes searching her face. *"Qui est-ce vous êtes?"* The black eyes raked the cottage, then returned to her face. *"Où sont-nous?"*

The questions demanded an answer. Kit gave it in

French. "You're quite safe. You must rest." She tried to ease her hand from his hold, but his fingers tightened instead. Irritated by this show of brute male strength when it was least helpful, Kit added with distinct asperity: "If you bruise the goods, Jack won't be pleased."

The mention of her husband's name saw her instantly released. The black eyes scanned her, more confused than ever. "You are . . . acquainted with . . . Captain Jack?"

Kit nodded. "You could say that. I'll get you something to drink."

To her relief, her patient behaved himself although he continued to study her. He drank the weak tea without complaint. Almost immediately, he sank back into sleep. But his rest was disturbed.

Kit bit her lip as she watched him twist in the bed. He was muttering in French. She drew closer, to the foot of the bed. In his present state, she wasn't certain how clear his mind was. Getting too close might not be wise.

Suddenly, he turned on his back and his breathing relaxed. To her surprise, he started speaking quite lucidly in perfect English. "There are *only two* of them—only two more of the bastards left. But Hardinges drank too fast— the cretin passed out before I could get anything more out of him, blast his ignorant hide." He paused, a frown dragging the elegant black brows down. "No. Wait. There was one more clue—though God knows it's not much to go on. Hardinges kept using the phrase 'the sons of dukes.' I think it means one of the two we're after is a duke's son, but I can't be sure. However, I wouldn't have thought Hardinges was given to poetic illusion." A brief smile flickered over the dark face. "Well, Jack m'lad, I'm afraid that's all I could learn. So you'd better get on that grey terror of yours and fly the news back to London. Whatever they do, they'll have to do it fast. The vultures are closing in—they know something's in the wind our side, and they're determined to extract the ore by whatever means possible. If there's a rat still left in our nest, they'll find him." The long speech seemed to have drained the man's strength. After a pause, he asked: "Jack?"

Startled, Kit shook off her daze. "Jack's on his way."

The man sighed and sank deeper into the pillows. His lips formed the word "Good." The next instant he was asleep.

With gentle snores punctuating the stillness, Kit sat and put the latest pieces of the jigsaw of her husband's activities into place. He was the High Commissioner for North Norfolk—he'd been specifically entrusted with stamping out the smuggling of spies. It now appeared as if, not content with chasing spies on this side of the Channel, Jack had been instrumental in sending some of their own to France.

All of which was very well, but why couldn't he have told her?

Kit paced before the fire, shooting glances every now and then at her patient. There was no reason why Jack couldn't have entrusted her with the details of his mission, particularly not after her sterling service to the cause, albeit given in ignorance. It was patently clear that her husband harbored some archaic idea of her place in his life. It was a place she had no intention of being satisfied with.

She wanted to share his life, not forever be a peripheral part of it, an adjunct held at arms' distance by the simple device of information control.

Kit's eyes glittered; her lips thinned. It was time she devoted more of her energies to her husband's education.

It was late morning before she felt comfortable in leaving the Frenchman—who was clearly no Frenchman at all. There was no possiblity of hiding her male garb, so she didn't try. She rode straight to the Castle stables and dismounted elegantly as Martins ran up, his eyes all but popping from his head.

"Take care of Delia, Martins. You can return her to the back paddock later and bring up the chestnut. I'll not be riding again today."

"Yes, ma'am."

Kit marched to the house, stripping off her gloves as she went. Lovis was in the hall when she entered. Kit sent one defiant glance his way. To his credit, not a muscle quivered as he came forward, his stately demeanor unimpaired by a sight which, Kit suspected, sorely tried his conservative soul.

"Lovis, I want to send a message immediately to Mr. Smeaton. I'll write a note; I want one of the men ready to carry it to Smeaton Hall as soon as I've finished."

"Very good, ma'am." Lovis moved to open the library door for her. "Martins's son will be waiting."

Pulling the chair up to her husband's desk, Kit drew a clean sheet of paper toward her. The note to George was easy, suggesting he go immediately to the aid of his "French" friend, whom she'd left in the cottage, somewhat *hors de combat*. She paused, then penned a final sentence.

"I feel sure that you, being so much more in Jack's confidence, will know better than I how best to proceed."

Kit signed the note with a flourish, a grim smile on her lips. Perhaps it was unfair to make George squirm, but she was beyond feeling amiable toward those who'd helped her husband attain his present state of arrogance. She addressed the missive, confident it would send George posthaste to his friend's help. He could take subsequent responsibility.

She rang the bell and gave the note to Lovis to speed on its way.

For the next twenty minutes, she barely stirred, her mind engrossed with forming and discarding various options for bringing Jack's shortcomings to his attention.

When it came to it, she could think of only one way to proceed. There was no point in any complex maneuvers—he was far more expert in manipulation than she. In truth, she had little idea of how to go about bringing him to her heels in true feminine fashion. If she went that route, she'd a shrewd suspicion she'd end on her back, beneath him, leaving him as arrogant as ever. And as unwilling as ever to make concessions. The best she could hope to do was to make a statement—something dramatic enough to make him sit up and take notice, something definite enough for him to be forced to at least acknowledge her point of view.

Determination beating steady in her veins, Kit set out another sheet of paper and settled to write a letter to her errant spouse.

*   *   *

Jack arrived home on Monday evening. He'd had to wait until that morning to speak to Lord Whitley. Various schemes were already afoot to flush out the man they believed was Belville's Henry. All that remained was to wait for Anthony's return, to see if there were any more traitors to track down. They were nearly there.

With a deep sigh, Jack climbed the steps to his front door. Lovis opened it to him.

"My lord. Mr. Smeaton asked you be given this the instant you crossed the threshold."

Jack tore open the single sheet. George's writing took a moment to decipher. Then Jack heaved a weary sigh. He hesitated, wondering whether to send a message up to Kit. He wouldn't be back in time for dinner. It was doubtful he'd be back before she was abed. With a slow grin, he went back out the door. Much better to take her by surprise. "I'll return later tonight, Lovis. No need to tell anyone I was here."

At the cottage, he was greeted by a much-improved Sir Anthony. George was not there to hear the recounting of Antoine's adventures; he'd been summoned to a Gresham dinner.

"One of the trials of an affianced man." Grinning, Jack pulled up a chair, straddling it. It transpired that the French had tracked Antoine down, not out of suspicion, but in order to interrogate him in case he knew more than he'd yet revealed. He'd escaped by stowing away aboard a lighter bound for Boston on the other side of the Wash. Unfortunately, it had also turned out to be a smugglers' vessel. Smugglers did not like stowaways; he'd had to fight his way off, throwing himself overboard before they'd skewered him.

Anthony's tale suggested that the French were desperate for information. The news that there were only two traitors left was music to Jack's ears. "We've got them." Quickly, he filled Anthony in on the happenings on the beach after he'd taken ship, referring to Kit only as another member of the Gang.

"George said something about that," Anthony said. "But he said he'd leave it to you to elaborate as you 'had a deeper interest in Belville's death.' What on earth did he mean?''

Jack had the grace to blush. "Don't ask."

Anthony threw him a look of mock surprise. "Keeping secrets from your friends, Jack m'lad, is most unwise.''

"You'll meet this secret eventually so I wouldn't repine.'' At the intrigued look on Anthony's face, Jack continued quickly: "Whitley thinks Belville's Henry, whom we believe is Sir Henry Colebourne, will be behind bars in a few days at most. Which, together with your information, means the end is nigh. We'll have got them all.''

Anthony lay back on his pillows with a deep sigh. "However will they get along without us, now we've all sold out?''

"I'm sure they'll manage. Personally, I've got fresh fields to plow, so to speak.'' Jack's smile of anticipation was transparent.

Anthony's gaze descended from the ceiling to examine the odd sight of Jack's eagerness for civilian life. "I don't suppose,'' he said, "your newfound liking for peaceful endeavors has anything to do with the redheaded lad who brought me here?'' At Jack's arrested expression, Anthony quietly added: "Taken to the other side, Jack?''

Jack bit back a distinctly rude reply. His eyes gleamed. "From which comment I take it my wife was wearing breeches when she brought you here?''

"*Your wife*?'' Anthony's exclamation brought on a fit of coughing. When he'd recovered, he lay back on his pillows and fixed Jack with an astonished stare. "Wife?''

Jack nodded, unable to contain his smile. "You've had the pleasure of meeting Kathryn, Lady Hendon, better known as Kit.'' He paused, then shrugged. "It was she who shot Belville.''

"Oh.'' Anthony struggled to match fact with memory. "How on earth did that slip of a thing get me from the beach to here?''

Jack stood. "Probably sheer determination. It's a quality she has in abundance. I'll leave you now, Tony.'' He walked forward to drop a hand on Anthony's shoulder. "I'll send Matthew in the morning with a horse to move you up to the Castle. Rest assured I'll get your news to Whitley as soon as possible. He'll be relieved to know we've got them all."

"Thanks, Jack." Anthony lay quiet on his pillows and watched Jack walk to the door. "But why the hurry to leave?"

Jack paused. "A little matter of propriety I have to discuss with my wife. Not something a rake like you would understand."

Closing the door on his friend's "Oh-ho!", Jack strode to the stable. He hadn't actually caught her in her breeches, but it was close enough, surely?

Anticipation was riding high by the time he reached the house. He entered through the side door, picking up the single candle to light his way. He went straight to his wife's room.

And stopped short when the light from his candle revealed an undisturbed expanse of green satin, with no deliciously curved form snuggling beneath.

For a moment, he simply stared, unable to think. Then, his heart thumping oddly, he went through to his own room. She was not in his bed, either. The sight of the simple white square propped against his pillow caused his hand to shake, spilling wax to the floor.

Drawing a deep breath, Jack put the candle down on the table by the bed and, sinking onto the mattress, picked up the letter. Kit's delicate script declared it was for Jonathon, Lord Hendon. The sight of his proper given name was warning enough.

His lips set in a grim line, Jack tore open the missive.

Her formality had apparently been reserved for the title. Inside, her message was direct and succinct.

Dear Jack,

I've had enough. I'm leaving. If you wish to explain anything, I'm sure you'll know where to find me.
Your devoted, loving, and dutiful wife,

Kit

His first thought was that she'd omitted the obedient, obviously realizing his imagination wouldn't stretch that far. Then he read it again, and decided he couldn't, in all honesty, take exception to the adjectives she had claimed.

He sat on his bed as the clock in the hall ticked on and struggled to make sense of what the letter actually meant. He couldn't believe Lovis had given him George's message but forgotten to tell him his wife had left him. Trying to ignore the empty void that was expanding inside his chest, threatening to crush his heart, he read the letter again. Then he lay back on his bed, hands locked behind his head, and started to think.

She was annoyed he hadn't told her the details of his mission. He tried to imagine George telling Amy and felt a glow of justification warm him. Abruptly, it dissipated, as Kit's image overlaid Amy's. All right—so she wasn't the same sort of wife, theirs wasn't the same sort of marriage.

He and his mission were deeply in her debt—he knew that well enough. That she yearned for excitement and would follow wherever it led was a characteristic he recognized. He could understand her pique that he wouldn't involve her in his schemes. But to leave him like this—to walk out on him—was the sort of emotional blackmail to which he'd never succumb. Christ, if he didn't know she was safe at Cranmer Hall, he'd be frantic! No doubt she expected him to come running, eager to win her back, willing to promise anything.

He wouldn't do it.

At least, not yet. He had to go back to London tomorrow, to convey Anthony's news to Lord Whitley. He'd leave Kit to stew, caught in a trap of her own devising. Then, when he came back, he'd go and see her and they could discuss their relationship calmly and rationally.

Jack tried to imagine having a calm and rational discussion with his wife. He fell asleep before he succeeded.

Chapter 29

Heaving a sigh of relief and anxiety combined, Kit plied the knocker on her cousin Geoffrey's door. The narrow house in Jermyn Street was home to her Uncle Frederick's three sons whenever they were in London. She hoped at least one of them was there now.

The door was opened by Hemmings, Geoffrey's gentleman's gentleman. He'd been with the family for years and knew her well. Even so, given her costume, a long moment passed before she saw his eyes widen in recognition.

"Good evening, Hemmings. Are my cousins in?" Kit pressed past the stunned man. Brought to a sense of his place, Hemmings rapidly shut the door. Then he turned to stare at her again.

Kit sighed. "I know. But it was safer this way. Is Geoffrey here?"

Hemmings swallowed. "Master Geoffrey's out to dinner, miss, along with Master Julian."

"Julian's home?"

When Hemmings nodded, Kit's spirits lurched upward for the first time that day. Julian must be home on furlough; seeing him would be an unlooked-for bonus in this thus-far-sorry affair.

She'd left Castle Hendon on Sunday afternoon, more than twenty-four hours ago, dressed as Lady Hendon with no incriminating luggage beyond a small black bag. She'd told Lovis she'd been called to visit a sick friend whose brother would meet her in Lynn. The note she'd left for her husband would, she'd assured him, explain all. She'd had Josh drive her into Lynn and leave her at the King's Arms. When the night stage had left for London at eight that evening, a slim, elegant youth muffled to the ears had been on it.

The stage had been impossibly slow, reaching the capital well after midday. From the coaching inn, she'd had to walk some distance before she'd been able to hail a sufficiently clean hackney. And the hackney had dawdled, caught in the London traffic. Now it was past six and she was exhausted.

"Master Bertrand's away in the country for the week, miss. Should I make up his bed for you?"

Kit smiled wearily. "That would be wonderful, Hemmings. And if you could put together the most simple meal, I would be doubly grateful."

"Naturally, miss. If you'll just seat yourself in the parlor?"

Shown into the parlor and left blissfully alone, Kit tidied the magazines littering every piece of furniture before selecting an armchair to collapse in. She'd no idea how long she lay there, one hand over her eyes, fighting down the uncharacteristic queasines that had overcome her the instant she'd woken that morning, brought on, no doubt, by the ponderous rocking of the stage. She hadn't eaten all day, but could barely summon sufficient appetite to do justice to the meal Hemmings eventually placed before her.

As soon as she'd finished, she went upstairs. She washed her face and stripped off her clothes, wryly wondering what it was Jack had intended to do if he found her in such attire. The thought brought a soft smile to her lips. It slowly faded.

Had she done the right thing in leaving him? Heaven only knew. Her uncomfortable trip had succeeded in dampening her temper but her determination was undimmed. Jack had to be made to take notice—her disappearance would accomplish that. And he would follow, of that she was sure. But what she wasn't at all sure of, what she couldn't even guess, was what he'd do then.

Somehow, in the heat of the moment, she'd not considered that vital point.

With a toss of her curls, Kit flung her clothes aside and climbed between the clean sheets. At least tonight she'd be able to sleep undisturbed by the snorts and snores of other passengers. Then, tomorrow, when she could think straight again, she'd worry about Jack and his reactions.

If the worst came to the worst, *she* could always explain.

She was at the breakfast table the next morning, neatly attired in Young Kit's best, when Geoffrey pushed open the door and idly wandered in. He cut a rakish figure in a multicolored silk robe, a cravat neatly folded about his neck. One look at his stunned face told Kit that Hemmings had left her to break her own news.

"Good morning, Geoffrey." Kit took a sip of her coffee and watched her cousin over the rim of the cup.

Geoffrey wasn't slow. As his gaze took in her attire, his expression settled into dazed incredulity. "What the bloody hell are you doing here?"

"I decided a week or so away from Castle Hendon was in order." Kit smiled. "Aren't you pleased to see me?"

"Dash it, Kit, you know I am. But . . ." Geoffrey ran a harassed hand through his dark locks. "Where the hell's your husband?"

Abruptly, Kit dropped her pose. "Coming after me, I hope."

Geoffrey stared. Abruptly, he reached for the coffeepot. "Cut line, my girl. Start from the beginning. What kind of dangerous game are you playing?"

"It's no game." Kit sighed and leaned both elbows on the table. Geoffrey drew up a chair. When he waved at her to continue, Kit related her story. In the cold light of morning, it didn't sound particularly sane. And trying to explain to Geoffrey why she felt as she did was even more futile. She wasn't surprised when he showed every indication of taking Jack's part.

"You've run mad," was Geoffrey's verdict. "What the hell do you suppose he's going to do when he finds you?"

Kit shrugged, dreaming of the moment.

Geoffrey stiffened. "Did you tell him you'd be here?"

Kit's shaking head let him breathe again. "But he'll figure it out."

Geoffrey stared at her. That wasn't the assurance he'd wanted. He studied Kit, then asked: "You're not breeding, are you?"

It was Kit's turn to stare. "Of course not!"

"All right, all right." Geoffrey held up both hands placatingly. "I just thought it might be a good excuse to have handy when Hendon makes his entrance. Everyone knows women do strange things at such times."

Incensed, Kit glared at him. "That's not the point! I want him to realize I won't be put aside, tucked safely away in some niche, every time he decides what he's doing is not . . . not suitable for me to be involved in."

Geoffrey clapped a hand to his forehead. "Oh, my God!"

The door opened to admit Julian, the youngest of the three brothers, the only one younger than Kit. Geoffrey sat, staring into his coffee while Julian and Kit exchanged joyful greetings over his head, and Kit filled Julian in on the reasons for her present excursion. When they finally turned their attention to their breakfasts, Geoffrey spoke. "Kit, you can't stay here."

Her face fell. "Oh."

"It's not that I mind, personally," Geoffrey assured her, ignoring the dark look his brother was throwing him. "But can you please try to understand how your husband is going to feel if he arrives here to find you cavorting about Jermyn Street in breeches?" Geoffrey paused, then added: "On second thought, rescind that 'personally.' I *do* mind, because it's *my* hide he'll be after."

"I've got a dress with me."

Geoffrey cast his eyes to the ceiling. "With all due respect, Kit, trotting about Jermyn Street in a dress is likely to prove even more dangerous to your reputation than the other."

Kit grimaced, knowing he was right. She'd lived in London long enough to know the rules. Jermyn Street was the haunt of the well-to-do bachelors of the *ton*. Women of her standing definitely did not live in Jermyn Street. "But where can I go? And for God's sake, don't suggest your parents.''

"I'm a coward, not daft,'' returned Geoffrey.

The three cousins sat considering their acquaintance. None of it was suitable. Then Julian bounced to life. "Jenny—Jenny MacKillop!''

Miss Jennifer MacKillop had been governess to Frederick Cranmer's sons and had filled in a few years more as governess-companion to Kit until the time of Kit's first Season. Subsequently, she'd retired to look after her aging brother in Southampton.

"I had a letter from her a few months back,'' said Kit. "Her brother died and left her the house. She thought she'd stay there for the rest of the year, before making up her mind what to do.''

"Then that's where you'll go.'' Geoffrey sat up. He studied Kit sternly. "How far behind you do you suppose Hendon is?''

Kit looked uneasy. "I don't know.''

Geoffrey sighed. "Very well. I'd better wait here in case he arrives, breathing fire. No!'' he said, as Julian opened his lips. "From everything I've heard about Jonathon Hendon, he'd eat you alive before he paused to ask questions. At least I'll have my wits to help me. You may escort our lovely cousin to Southampton.''

Julian beamed. "May I use your curricle?''

Geoffrey's sigh was heartfelt. "If I find a scratch on it, you'll be painting it with your eyelashes.''

Julian whooped.

Geoffrey raised his brows. "You wouldn't think he shaves yet, would you?''

Kit giggled.

Geoffrey smiled. "That's better. I'd started to wonder if you'd forgotten how.''

"Oh, Geoffrey.'' Kit put out a hand to clasp his.

Geoffrey gripped her fingers. "Yes, well, I suggest you leave as soon as possible. You should be able to make it by nightfall if Julian keeps a proper eye on the cattle. It sounds as if Jenny will be able to put you both up.''

Her immediate future decided, Kit poured herself another

cup of coffee. She didn't want to go to Southampton. It was too far away from Castle Hendon. But she had to agree with Geoffrey's reasoning. Jack wouldn't be pleased to find her frequenting a bachelors' residence. And she would enjoy seeing Jenny again. Perhaps catching up with her old mentor would distract her from the problems of her new role.

Jack woke on Friday morning feeling thoroughly disgruntled. He lay on his back and stared at the ceiling, his eyes devoid of expression. Life, full to brimming but short days before, had taken on a greyish hue.

He missed his wife.

Not only did he miss her, he couldn't seem to function, knowing she wasn't here, where she belonged. He couldn't sleep; he couldn't recall what he'd eaten for the last three days. His faculties were enmeshed in a constant retreading of their last encounters, of the opportunities he'd missed to read her mind and head off her startling, but characteristic action.

It had been a mistake to leave her at Cranmer Hall. He saw that now. But he hadn't known then how much the thought of her would prey on his mind.

With a half groan, he pushed back the covers and hauled himself upright. Without more ado, he'd rectify his error. He'd ridden in from London late the previous night, his hope that Kit might have reassessed her objectives and returned home dashed by the sight of her empty bed. His empty bed had proved even less inspiring.

He dressed with unusual care, choosing a morning coat of simple elegance, determined to impress his wife with every facet of his personality. He knew exactly what he'd do. After greeting her coolly, he'd insist on seeing her alone. Then, he'd *explain* to her why her action in leaving him was unacceptable behavior in Lady Hendon, why no circumstance on earth could excuse her absence from the saftey of his hearth. Then he'd kiss the damned woman witless and bring her home. Simple.

He grabbed a cup of coffee and ordered Champion brought around.

* * *

"If she's not here, where the devil *is* she?" Jack ran an agitated hand through his hair, dragging golden strands loose to fly in wisps about his haggard face. He paced the Gresham's morning room like a caged and wounded tiger.

Amy watched him, sheer amazement in her face.

"Perhaps, my dear, you should get us some refreshment." George smiled reassuringly into Amy's eyes. Drawing her to her feet, he steered her to the door and held it for her.

Once Amy had escaped, George shut the door and fixed Jack with a stern eye. "I told you not to leave Kit alone." His voice held a note of decided censure. "And if you left without explaining what was going on, I'm not surprised she's left you."

Jack paused to stare at him.

George grimaced and rummaged in his coat pocket. "Here," he said, holding out the note Kit had sent him. "I'd hoped I wouldn't need to show you this, but obviously your wife knows your stubbornness even better than I."

Puzzled, Jack took the note and smoothed it out.

"Read the last sentence," said George helpfully.

Jack did. *I feel sure that you, being so much more in Jack's confidence, will know better than I how to proceed.* Crushing the note in his hand, Jack swore. "How the hell was I supposed to know she felt that strongly over it?" He glared at George.

George was unimpressed. "You knew damn well she wanted to know. Dash it—she *deserved* to know, after what she did that night on the beach. And as for her recent efforts in the cause—all I can say is she's been damned understanding."

Jack was taken aback. "You don't even approve of her!"

"I know. She's wild beyond excuse. But that doesn't excuse you."

Hands on his hips, his eyes narrowed and smoky grey, Jack glared at George. "You're not going to tell me you've told Amy of our mission?"

Unaffected by Jack's belligerence, George sat on the

chaise. "No, of course not. But the point is, Kit's not Amy."

Jack's lips twisted in a pained grimace. He fell to pacing once more, his brow furrowed. "If I'd told her, God knows what she'd have got up to. Our dealings were too dangerous—I couldn't expose her to such risks."

George sighed. "Hell, Jack—you knew what she was like from the start. Why the devil did you marry her, if you weren't prepared to accept those risks?"

"I married her because I love her, dammit!"

"Well, if that's the case, then the rest should come easily."

Jack shot him a suspicious glance. "What exactly does that mean?"

"It means," said George, "that you wanted her for what she was—what she is. You can't start changing bits and pieces, expecting her to change in some ways but not in others. Would you be pleased if she turned into another Amy?"

Jack bit back his retort, his lips compressed with the effort to hold back the unflattering reply.

George grinned. "Precisely. Not your cup of tea. Thankfully, she is mine." The door opened at that moment; George looked up, smiling warmly as Amy entered, preceding her butler, who bore a tray burdened with a variety of strong liquors in addition to the teapot. Dismissing the butler, Amy poured tea for George and herself while George poured Jack a hefty glass of brandy. "Now that we've resolved your differences of opinion, what exactly has happened?"

With a warning frown, Jack took the glass. "I came back from London on Monday evening and got your message—as you'd instructed, as soon as I'd crossed the threshold. I went to see our friend, then returned to the Castle. Kit wasn't there." He took a swallow of his drink, then pulled a letter from his pocket. "As we seem to be passing my wife's epistles about, you may as well read that."

George took the letter. A quick perusal of its few lines had him pressing his lips firmly together to keep from grinning. "Well," he said, "you can't claim she's not clear-headed."

Jack humphed and took the letter back. "I assumed she'd gone to Cranmer Hall and reasoned she'd be safe enough there until I got back from reporting Anthony's news to Whitley."

George's gaze was exasperated. "Hardly a wise move."

"I wasn't exactly in a wise mood at the time," Jack growled, resuming his frustrated prowl. "I've just endured the most harrowing morning of my life. First, I went to Cranmer. I didn't even make it to the Hall. I met Spencer out riding. Before I could say a word, he asked how Kit was."

George raised his brows. "Could he have been protecting her—throwing you off the track?"

Jack shook his head. "No, he was as open as the sky. Besides, I can't see Spencer supporting Kit in this little game."

"True," George conceded. "What did you tell him?"

"What could I tell him? That I'd lost his granddaughter, whom I vowed not a month ago to protect till death us do part?"

George's lips twitched but he didn't dare smile.

"After enduring the most uncomfortable conversation of my entire life, I raced back to the Castle. I hadn't thought to ask my people about *how* she'd left, as she'd obviously made all seem normal, and I didn't see any point in raising a dust. As it transpired, she'd told Lovis she'd been called to a sick friend's side. She had my coachman drive her to the King's Arms in Lynn on Sunday afternoon, from where, according to her, this friend's brother would fetch her. I checked. She took a room for the night and paid in advance. She had dinner in her room. That's the last anyone's seen of her."

George frowned. "Could someone have recognized her as Young Kit?"

Jack threw him an anguished glance. "I don't know. I came here, hoping against hope she'd simply laid a trail and then gone to ground with Amy." He stopped and sighed, worry etched in his face. "Where the devil can she have gone?"

"Why the King's Arms?" mused Amy. Sipping her tea, she'd been calmly following the discussion. George turned to look at her, searching her face as she frowned, her gaze distant.

Then Amy raised her brows. "The London coaches leave from there."

"London?" Jack stood, stunned into stillness. "Who would she go to in London? Her aunts?"

"Heavens, no!" Amy smiled condescendingly. "She'd never go near them. She'd go to Geoffrey, I suppose."

George saw Jack's face and leapt in with, "Who's Geoffrey?"

Amy blinked. "Her cousin, of course. Geoffrey Cranmer."

The sudden easing of Jack's shoulders was dramatic enough to be visible. "Thank God for small mercies. Where does Geoffrey Cranmer live?"

Frowning, Amy took another sip of tea. "I think," she began, then stopped, her frown deepening. "Does Jermyn Street sound right?"

George dropped his head back and closed his eyes. "Oh, God."

"It sounds all *too* right." His jaw ominously set, Jack picked up his gloves. "My thanks, Amy."

George swung about as Jack made for the door. "For God's sake, Jack, don't do anything you'll regret."

Jack paused at the door, a look of long suffering on his face. "Never fear. Aside from giving her a good shaking, and one or two other physical treatments, I intend to spend a long, long time *explaining* things—a whole *host* of things—to my wife."

At five o'clock, Geoffrey studied the elegant timepiece on his mantel and wondered what he could do to fill the time until dinner. He'd yet to come to a conclusion when the knocker on his door was plied with the ruthless determination he'd been expecting for the last three days.

"Lord Hendon, sir."

Hemmings had barely got the words out before Jonathon Hendon was in the room. His sharp and distinctly irritated grey gaze swept the furniture before settling with unnerving calm on Geoffrey's face.

Geoffrey remained outwardly unmoved, rising to greet his wholly expected guest. Inwardly, he conceded several of the points Kit had attempted to explain to him. The man standing in the middle of his parlor, stripping riding gloves off a pair of large hands and returning his welcoming nod with brusque civility, didn't look the sort to be easily brought to the negotiating table. Now he could understand why Kit had felt it necessary to flee her home purely to gain her husband's attention.

His knowledge of Jonathon Hendon was primarily based on rumor—not, he was the first to admit, a thoroughly reliable source. Hendon was a number of years his senior; socially, their paths had crossed infrequently. But Jack Hendon's reputation as a soldier and a rake was close to legendary. Undoubtedly, had the country not been at war, he and Kit would have met much sooner. But how his slip of a cousin coped with the powerful male force currently making itself felt in all sorts of subtle ways in his parlor was beyond Geoffrey's ability to guess.

"I believe, Cranmer, you have something of mine."

The steel encased in the deep velvety tones brought Geoffrey's well-honed defense mechanisms into play. Angry husbands had never been his cup of tea. "She's not here." Best to get that out as soon as possible.

Arrested, the grey gaze trapped him. Some of the tension left the large frame. "Where is she?"

Despite Kit's instruction to tell her husband precisely where she was as soon as he appeared, Geoffrey found himself too intrigued to let the information go quite so easily. He waved his guest to a seat, an invitation that was reluctantly accepted. Smoothly, Geoffrey grasped a decanter and poured two glasses of wine, handing one to his guest before taking the other back to his armchair. "I've been expecting you for the past three days."

To his surprise, a slight flush rose under his guest's tanned skin.

"I thought the damned woman was at Cranmer. I went to fetch her this morning, only to find Spencer hadn't seen her. It took some hours to uncover her trail. If it hadn't been for Amy Gresham remembering you, I'd still be chasing my arse in Norfolk."

Hearing exasperation ring behind the clipped accents, Geoffrey kept his expression serious. "You know," he said, "I don't think Kit intended that."

"I know she didn't." Jack fastened his gaze on Geoffrey's face. "So where is she?"

The commanding tones were difficult to resist but still Geoffrey hesitated. "Er . . . I don't suppose you'd consider allaying my cousinly fears with an assurance or two?"

For a moment, Jack stared, incredulous, until the sincerity in Geoffrey's eyes struck him. Here was another who, while recognizing Kit's wildness, had learned to overlook the fact. With a grimace, Jack conceded: "I've no intention of harming a single red hair. However," he added, his voice regaining its sternness, "beyond that, I make no promises. I intend taking my wife back to Castle Hendon as soon as possible."

The strength in that reply should have reassured Geoffrey. Instead, the implication revealed a glaring gap in Kit's plan. "I'm sure she has no other intention than to return with you." Geoffrey frowned. Had Kit explained to her intimidating spouse why she'd taken to her heels as she had? "In fact, I was under the distinct impression she was waiting for you to arrive to take her home momentarily."

Jack frowned, not a little confused. If she didn't want to bargain with him, her return against his promises, what was this all about? Admitting she wished to return with him would leave her no leverage to wring promises from him.

His bewilderment must have shown, for Geoffrey was also frowning. "I don't know that I've got this entirely straight—with women one never knows. But Kit led me to understand that her . . . er, trip was solely designed to make you sit up and take notice."

Jack stared at Geoffrey, his gaze abstracted. Was she wild enough to do such a thing—simply to make him acknowledge her feelings? To force him to do nothing more than admit he understood? The answer was obvious. As the memory of the sheer worry he'd endured for the past four days washed through him, Jack groaned. He leaned his brow on one palm, then glanced up in time to catch the grin on Geoffrey's face. "Has anyone warned you, Cranmer, against marriage?"

Jack stretched his long legs to the comfort of the fire blazing in Geoffrey Cranmer's parlor. Kit's cousin had invited him to dine and then, when Jack had confessed he'd yet to seek lodgings, Hendon House being let for the Season, had offered him a bed. By now at ease with both Geoffrey and the younger Julian, who'd joined them over dinner, he'd accepted. Both he and Geoffrey had been entertained by the conversion of Julian from guarded civility to hero worship. Aside from the ease of an evening spent with kindred spirits, Jack doubted Kit would find support from these two the next time she made a dash for town.

Not, of course, that there'd be a next time.

Before leaving with Julian for a night about town, Geoffrey had filled Jack in on Jenny MacKillop and her relationship to the Cranmer family. Julian had painted a reassuring picture of a genteel household in one of the better streets of Southampton. Kit was safe. Jack knew where he could lay his hand on her red head whenever he wished. He wished right now. But experience was at last taking root. This time, he would take the time to think before he tangled with his loving, devoted, and dutiful wife.

His record in paying sufficient attention to her words was not particularly good. He'd ignored her requests to be told about the spies because it had suited him to do so. He'd not listened as carefully as he should have to her warning about Belville, oblique though it had been, too engrossed in delighting in her body to pay due interest to the fruits of her brain. And he'd put off fetching her from Cranmer, knowing it would involve him in a discussion of topics he had not wished to discuss.

Uneasily, Jack shifted in the chair. Admitting to such failures and vowing to do better was not going to come naturally.

It would have to come, of course. He knew he loved the damned woman. And that she loved him. She'd never said so, but she proclaimed it to his senses every time she took him into her body. Even when she'd offered herself to him that night in the cottage, he hadn't imagined she'd done so lightly; that was what had made the moment so special. For her, and now for him, although it hadn't been so in the past, love and desire were two halves of the same whole—fused, never to be split asunder.

So he would have to apologize. For not telling her what she'd had a right to know, for treating her as if she was outside his circle of trust, when in reality she stood at its center. He'd never imagined a wife would be close to him in that way—but Kit was. She was his friend and, if he would permit it, his helpmate, more attuned to his needs than any man had a right to expect.

Jack grinned at the flames and sipped his brandy. He was a lucky man, and he knew it. Doubtless she'd want some assurance that he'd improve in the future. No doubt she'd assist, prodding whenever necessary, reminding him of this time.

With a confident snort, Jack drained his glass and considered his next meeting with his wife. His part was now clear. What of hers?

There was one point he was determined to make plain, preferably in sufficiently dramatic fashion so that his red-headed houri would not forget it. Under no circumstances would he again endure the paralyzing uncertainty of not knowing where she was, of not knowing she was safe. She must promise not to engage willy-nilly in exploits that would turn his golden brown hair as grey as his eyes. She'd have to agree to tell him of any exploit beyond the mundane before she did her usual headlong dash into danger—doubtless he'd arrange to block quite a few; others he might join her in. Who knew? In some respects, they were all too alike.

Jack stared long and hard at the flames. Then, satisfied he'd established all the important points in their upcoming discussion, he settled down to plan how best to take his wife by storm.

Despite her interest in some of his affairs, she'd neglected to ask about the family business. Perhaps, as the Cranmers relied totally on the land, she hadn't realized there was a business to ask about? Whatever, one of his brigs was currently in the Pool of London, due, most conveniently, to set sail for its home port of Southampton on the morning tide. The *Albeca* was due to load at Southampton for a round trip to Lisbon and Bruges before returning to London. Like all his major vessels, the *Albeca* had a large cabin reserved for the use of its owner.

He'd commandeer the *Albeca*. It could still do its run, but, after Bruges, could lie in at one of the Norfolk ports to let them ashore. As a means of transporting his wife from Southampton to Norfolk, a boat had a number of pertinent advantages over land travel. Aside from anything else, it would give them countless hours alone.

It was definitely time to reel Kit back.

Back where she belonged.

Chapter 30

Kit stared at the forget-me-nots bobbing their blue heads in Jenny's small walled garden and wondered if Jack had forgotten her. It was Monday, more than a week since she'd left Castle Hendon. She'd been absolutely confident he'd be after her the instant he returned from London, which should have been on Tuesday at the latest. A minute should have sufficed to tell him where she'd gone. Cranmer was out of the question; likewise, her aunts could not be considered candidates. Her cousins should have stood out as the only possibility, and she'd mentioned Geoffrey was her favorite. Of course, her move to Southampton would have delayed him for a day, maybe two. But he'd yet to show his arrogant face in Jenny's neat little parlor.

Worry creased Kit's brow; she chewed her lower lip in something close to consternation. It had never occurred to her that he might not behave as she'd expected. Had she misread the situation? Men often had peculiar views and certainly, her flight was not the sort of action any husband would view with equanimity. But she hadn't expected Jack to be overly concerned with the proprieties, or with how her actions reflected on him. Had she miscalculated?

She knew he loved her; where that certainty sprang from she couldn't have said, but the fact was enshrined in her heart, along with her love for him. The whens and wheres and hows were beyond her. All she knew was those truths, immutable as stone.

But none of that answered her question—*where was he?*

Kit heaved a heavy sigh.

So deep in contemplation was she that she failed to hear the footsteps approaching over the grass. Nevertheless, despite her distraction, her senses prickled as Jack drew close. She whirled with a gasp to find him beside her.

Her eyes locked with his. Her heart lurched to a standstill, then started to race. Anticipation welled. Then she saw his expression—stern, distant; not a flicker of a muscle betrayed any softer emotion.

"Good morning, my dear." Jack managed to keep his tone devoid of all expression. The effort nearly killed him. He kept his arms rigid at his sides, to stop himself from hauling Kit into them. That, he promised himself, would come later. First, he was determined to demonstrate to his errant wife how seriously he viewed her actions. "I've come to take you home. Jenny's packing your things. I'll expect to leave directly she's finished."

Stunned, Kit stared at him and marveled that the words she'd so longed to hear could be delivered in such a way that all she felt was—nothing. No joy, no relief—not even any guilt. Jack's words had been totally emotionless. Searching his face, she waited, more than half-expecting his austere expression to melt into teasing lines. But his frozen mask did not ease.

For the first time in her life, Kit did not know what she felt. All the emotions she'd expected to experience upon seeing Jack again were there, but so tangled with a host of newborn feelings, disbelief and resurgent anger chief amongst them, that the result was total confusion.

Her mind literally reeled.

Her face was blank; her mind had yet to sort out what her expression should be. Her lips were parted, ready to speak words she could not yet formulate. It was as if she was in a play, and someone had switched the scripts.

Wordlessly, Jack offered her his arm. Speech was still beyond her; her mind was in turmoil. Kit felt her fingers shake as she placed them on his sleeve.

Jenny was waiting, smiling, in the hall, Kit's small bag at her feet. Still struggling to grasp what tack Jack was taking, and how she should react, Kit absentmindedly kissed her erstwhile governess, promising to write, all the while conscious of Jack's commanding figure, an impregnable rock beside her.

Surely he hadn't missed her point entirely?

Kit sank onto the cushions of the hired carriage, puzzled that it wasn't one of the Hendon coaches. She blinked when Jack shut the door on her. Then it dawned that he'd elected to ride rather than share the coach with her.

Suddenly, Kit was in no doubt of what she felt. Her temper soared. *What* was going on here?

Ten minutes later, the carriage jolted to a halt. Sitting bolt upright on the carriage seat, Kit waited. Jack called an order. The keening of gulls came clearly on a freshening breeze. She narrowed her eyes. Where were they? Before she could slide to the window and peer out, Jack opened the door. He held out his hand, but his eyes did not meet hers.

Her temper on the tightest of reins, Kit coolly placed her fingers in his. He handed her down from the carriage. One glance was enough to tell her that she would have to delay giving him her reaction to his stoic performance. They stood on a wharf beside a large ship, amid bales and crates, ropes and hooks. Sailors rushed about; bustle and noise surrounded them. At Jack's urging, she stepped over a coil of rope. His hand at her elbow, he guided her along the busy wharf to where a plank with a rope handrail led up to the ship's deck.

Kit eyed the gangplank, rising and falling as the ship rode the waves of the harbor. She drew a deep breath.

Her chillingly civil request to be carried aboard never made it past her lips.

As she turned, Jack ducked. The next instant, Kit found herself staring down at the choppy green waves as Jack swiftly climbed the gangplank. Fury cindered the reins of her temper. She closed her eyes and saw a red haze; her fingers curled into claws. She'd wanted to be carried, but carried in his *arms*, not over his shoulder like a sack of potatoes!

Luckily, the gangplank was short. The instant Jack gained the deck, he set her on her feet. Kit immediately swung his way, her eyes going to his. But Jack had already turned and was speaking.

"This is Captain Willard, my dear."

With an almighty effort, Kit shackled her fury—aside from not wanting to scare anyone else, she wanted to save it all for Jack. Her face set, expressionless, her lips a thin line, she turned and beheld a large man, potbellied and jovial, dressed in a braided uniform.

He bowed deeply. "Might I say what a pleasure it is to welcome you aboard, Lady Hendon?"

"Thank you." Stiffly, Kit inclined her head, her mind racing. The man's manner was too deferential for a captain greeting a passenger.

"I'll show Lady Hendon to our quarters, Willard. You may proceed on your own discretion."

"Thank you, m'lord."

The truth struck Kit. Jack owned the ship. Yet another not-so-minor detail her spouse had failed to mention.

Jack steered Kit aft, to where a stairway led down to the corridor to the stern apartments. With every step, he reminded himself to hold firm to his resolution. He had endured a full week of the most wretched worry—surely an hour of guilty misery was not unreasonable retribution? That Kit was shaken by his retreat, his withholding of the responses she would have expected from him, was obvious. The stunned, searching expression that had filled her eyes in Jenny's garden had wrenched his heart; the quiver in her fingers when she'd laid them on his sleeve had nearly overset his careful plans. He hadn't been game to meet her eyes after that.

Carrying her up the gangplank had nearly done him in. Even with her tossed over his shoulder, he hadn't been sure he'd be able to let her go, which would have shocked Willard out of his braid.

He couldn't take much more of his self-imposed reticence. He'd leave her in his cabin until her hour was up, then surrender as gracefully as possible.

As he followed Kit down the narrow stairs, Jack closed his eyes and gritted his teeth. His resolution was fraying with every step. The sight of her hips, swaying to and fro before him, was more than he could stand.

His quarters lay at the end of the short corridor, spread across the vessel's square stern. The door he held open for Kit led into the room he used as his study and dining room. A single door led into the bedroom, the two rooms spanning the stern. Both rooms had windows instead of portholes, set in under the overhanging poop deck.

The bright light reflected from the water hit Kit instantly as she entered the room. She blinked rapidly; it took a moment for her eyes to adjust. Then, drawing a very deep breath, she swung to face her husband.

Only to see him disappear through another door.

"The bedroom's through here." Jack reappeared immediately. Kit realized he'd left her bag in the room. His demeanor hadn't altered in the slightest. It was still politely blank, almost vacant, as if they were mere acquaintances embarking on a cruise. He still hadn't met her eyes.

"I'll leave you to refresh yourself. We'll be departing with the tide." With that, he turned to leave.

The rage that gripped Kit was so powerful that she swayed. She grabbed a chair back for support. *Just like that?* She was being deposited in the cabin like some piece of baggage, and he thought he could walk away?

She was beyond fury, even beyond rage. Kit's temper was now in orbit. "Will you be back?"

The words, uttered in precise and icy tones, halted Jack.

Slowly, he turned. He was nearly at the door; Kit stood with her back to the windows. The light streaming in left her face in shadow; he couldn't make out her expression.

Jack stared at his wife and felt a familar ache in his arms, in his loins. She was so damned beautiful. Despite her less-than-placatory tone, his righteous anger melted away, leaving a hollow ache. "Strange," he said. "That's a question I've been asking of you."

The sincere doubt, the vulnerability revealed, pierced Kit's rage; nothing else could have hauled her back to earth. She blinked—and suddenly felt cold. "You *couldn't* have thought I intended to leave you permanently?"

When Jack's face remained shuttered, Kit frowned. "I

didn't intend . . . that is, I . . .'' Abruptly, she shook her wits into order. This was ridiculous! What misguided notion had he taken into his head? Drawing in an exasperated breath, she laced her fingers together, fixed her gaze on her husband's grey eyes and clearly enunciated: "I only meant my absence to focus your attention on my wish to be informed as to what was going on. I never intended to be away from Castle Hendon for longer than a few days."

Slowly, Jack raised his brows. "I see." He paused, then, strolling forward, said: "I don't suppose it occurred to you that I might be . . . concerned for your safety?" Kit turned as he neared; he could now see her face. "That, given your propensity for landing yourself in dangerous situations, I might, with justification, feel worried over your well-being?" The arrested look in Kit's large eyes stated quite clearly that the idea had never occurred to her. Abruptly, Jack's mock anger crystallized into the real thing. "Damn it, woman! I was *worried sick!*"

His bellow shook Kit. She grasped the chair back with both hands and blinked. "I'm sorry. I didn't realize . . ." Her words trailed into fascinated silence as, wide-eyed, she watched her husband fight to shackle his temper, a temper she'd never seen unleashed. He vibrated with angry tension, muscles clenched as if to hold the violence in. His grey eyes burned with a dark flame.

Jack heard her words through a haze of conflicting emotions, the suppressed fears of the past week unexpectedly erupting. Anger overrode all else—the damned woman really *didn't* understand. "In that case," he said, his voice a steely growl, "I suggest you listen very carefully, my love. Because the next time you endanger yourself recklessly, without me by your side, I swear I'll tan your pretty hide."

Trapped in the grey fury of his gaze, Kit felt her eyes grow rounder, a species of delicious fright tickling her spine. He'd called her *his love*—that would do for a start. His confession sounded promising.

With an effort, Jack forced himself to remain where he was, a bare three feet from his wife. If he touched her now, they'd go up in flames. He fixed his eyes on hers and enunciated clearly: "I love you, as you damned well know.

Every time you head into danger, *I worry*!'' Her eyes
searched his; he saw her lips soften. Abruptly, he swung
away and started to pace. "*Not* a passive emotion, this
worry of mine. When in its throes, I can't think straight! I
know you've never run in anyone's harness before. But you
married me—you vowed to obey. Henceforth, you'll do
precisely that.'' Jack came to a halt and fixed Kit with an
intimidating stare. "Henceforth, you'll tell me *before* you
embark on any escapade beyond what your dear friend
Amy would countenance. And if I forbid it, so help me,
you'll forget it. If not, I swear by all that's holy, I'll lock
you in your room!''

His voice had risen. His final threat struck Kit while she
was still engrossed with his first revelation. He loved her.
He'd said so, in words, out loud. In silence, she stared at
him, her gaze softening, caressing the angry lines of his
cheek and jaw. Her mind belatedly scrambled to catch up.
Did worry over her truly affect him so? Is this what love
did to him?

With a frustrated groan, Jack turned and strode from the
room, slamming the door behind him. He swung up the
short stairway and headed for the foredeck, his only aim to
cool his heated brain before he returned to his cabin and
made passionate love to his wife. He was so wracked with
violent emotions he didn't trust himself to lay hands on her
delicate limbs. She bruised easily enough as it was.

Kit stared at the cabin door. Her face drained of emotion,
then she stiffened. Her eyes flared, purple flames erupting
from the violet depths.

How dare he? One moment, vowing love and demanding
obedience, the next, walking out on her, as if he'd said the
final word.

"*Hah!*'' Kit drew a deep breath and drew herself up, her
hands on her hips. Her eyes narrowed. If he thought he was
going to so easily escape the rest of their discussion, the
clear statement of what *she* wanted henceforth from *him*,
he was wrong! She'd wanted his attention—she'd got it.
But he hadn't left it with her long enough!

With a determined stride, Kit made for the door.

*   *   *

His arms on the foredeck railing, Jack watched the waves slide under the bow. They'd slipped their moorings and were heading for the mouth of the harbor. Soon, the heavy swell of the ocean would tilt the decks. He drew a deep breath and felt sanity return.

Looking back, he couldn't recall a single instance throughout their association when Kit had allowed his plans to proceed without remodeling. He'd had their recent discussion carefully organized. He'd intended explaining to her what he felt when she went into danger, that she'd have to learn to cope with the ramifications of his love. He'd managed that but her patent surprise that he should feel so strongly for her had slipped under his guard and distracted him. His statements of intent had been far more aggressive than he'd planned.

He grimaced. That wasn't the worst of it. He'd forgotten the rest of his orchestrated performance, arguably the most important part. He'd omitted to tell her that he understood her need to know what he was about and that, henceforth, he was prepared to share even that aspect of his life with her.

Jack was drawing a last deep breath of calming sea air when he sensed a disruption behind him. He swung about to see Kit making for the foredeck, oblivious of the sailors she swept from her path. One glance at the set of her chin told him she was about to upset the plans he'd just made.

For one instant, Jack paused to admire the magnificent figure she cut, her lithe body outlined by her elegant carriage dress, her halo of curls gleaming in the sunshine. But he couldn't afford more time to stand transfixed by admiration. His Kit was no angel. In another minute, when she reached the foredeck, she was going to irretrievably damage his reputation—if not worse.

Kit had to concentrate to manage the ladder to the foredeck with her skirts held before her. She'd seen Jack's tall figure at the rail and made straight for him. The foredeck looked a perfectly wonderful spot to tell him what she thought of his henceforths, limited, as they were, to her.

Gaining the foredeck, she dropped her skirts and smoothed them down, then glanced up to find her husband.

To her surprise, he was directly in front of her.

Angry violet eyes locked with laughing grey ones.

Laughing? Kit opened her mouth to wither him.

She'd forgotten how fast he could move. Before the first syllable of her tirade tripped from her tongue, his lips had closed over hers, stifling her angry words. Kit struggled and felt his arms lock about her, a tender trap. Her heart was already accelerating, leaping with anticipation. It was too late to close her mouth. He'd taken immediate advantage of her parted lips to lay claim to the softness within.

Damn him! She wanted to *talk*! This was precisely why she'd left Castle Hendon in the first place.

Disgruntled, Kit tried to hold firm against the tide of need rising within her. It was impossible. Little flames of desire greedily flickered and grew, swelling into the familiar warmth in her belly. With a stifled groan, Kit rearranged her plans and surrendered to the urge to press herself against the hard body that surrounded her, savoring the pressure that would bring her relief.

When Kit melted into his embrace, Jack knew he'd won the round. Despite the catcalls and whistles that rose about them, he kept kissing her, too hungry after the starvation of a week to call an early end to their exhibition. The need to repair to a place of greater privacy to embark on the next stage of their discussion finally brought his head up. He stared down into her wide eyes, already purpling with passion.

Jack smiled, his slow, wicked smile. Kit's heart lurched crazily.

"I'm going to carry you down to our cabin. Don't, for the love of God, say a word."

One arrogant brow rose, but Kit could only stare. Talk? That required being able to think. She was witless—how could she say anything?

Then, as Jack stooped and tossed her over his shoulder, reality returned to her with a thump. Heavens—everyone on the ship was staring at them! Kit felt her cheeks burn crimson as Jack went down the ladder. She could just imagine the grin on his face.

Her fears were confirmed when he shrugged her from his

shoulder into his arms. He strode the length of the deck smiling down into her anguished eyes. Cradled in his strong arms, Kit knew it was useless to struggle but she'd have given a great deal, at that moment, to wipe the triumph from his lips. Still, it was only a battle—she had set her sights on winning the war. He juggled her back to his shoulder to manage the narrow companionway and corridor, then strode through the door to their stateroom and kicked it shut on the world.

Her hands on his shoulders, Kit waited to be put down. Now was the time to make her stand, before he kissed her again. But Jack didn't stop in the stateroom. Kit blinked as she was carried into the bedroom beyond, ducking her head at his command to avoid the lintel.

She looked around wildly. Her stomach contracted as her gaze fell on the bed. Jack stopped at its foot, his intent clear. Any doubts she might have had on the point were banished as he let her slide down until her toes brushed the carpeted floor. Clasped against him, Kit could feel the evidence of his need pressed hard against her soft belly. Her eyes met his; her breath suspended as she saw desire etched in silver flame against the smoky grey.

With an effort, Kit pulled her mind free. She drew a deep breath. "Jack?"

"Mmm?"

He wasn't interested in talking. His large hands spread across her waist, moving down to mold her hips against his. One hand remained at the top of her thighs, trapping her in that intimate embrace, gently fondling her bottom. The other hand went to the laces of her gown. His lips grazed her ear, then lazily drifted to where the pulse beat strongly at the base of her throat.

Kit clenched her fingers on his shoulders, trying to hold on to her mind, but the heat trapped between their hips rose and cindered her resolution. She felt Jack tug at her neckline and the material ripped. As his lips moved down to taste the fruit revealed, Kit decided against protest.

He had stated that he loved her. Now he would show her, his loving a vibrant reiteration of what he'd found so hard to say. She'd be a fool indeed to interrupt him. Instead, she would enjoy him, enjoy his love and claim it as hers—then return to her point later, once their love had tamed him.

With a satisfied murmur, she dropped her arms to free them of her sleeves, then whimpered as Jack's tongue teased her sensitive nipples, aroused and covered only by the thin film of her chemise. She heard his knowing chuckle, then he moved closer to the bed, letting her down so she stood on unsteady feet, trapped between him and the end of the bed.

Her petticoats drifted to the carpet, freed by expert fingers. Gentle hands divested her of her stockings and shoes. Clad only in her fine silk chemise, she stood before her husband, half-expecting him to rip the garment from her. His eyes burned brighter than she'd ever seen them.

Jack feasted his eyes on her bounty, the ripe globes of her breasts tipped by ruched pink, duskier now that he'd claimed her. Below the swell of her hips, her sleek flanks beckoned, the heat between pulsing with her heartbeat. Every sweet inch of her was his—his to adore, his to devour.

Kit's heart was pounding, a slow steady beat, a march to take her to paradise. Her breathing was shallow. It dissolved into short little gasps as Jack's hands closed about her breasts. Long fingers slid beneath the lace edge of her chemise to draw her fruit to his lips. He suckled hard. Kit dropped her head back, her eyes closing, her senses burdened with sensation too exquisite to bear. Her fingers tangled in Jack's hair, frantically pulling the long locks from the riband that confined them. One strong arm slipped about her waist to support her as she arched her body, exposing her breasts fully to his mouth and tongue.

She was on fire. Kit drew a ragged breath as she felt one large hand drop to her silk-clad thigh.

"Oh, yes," she whispered, as she felt Jack shift her in his arms, so that her hips were now angled against his. Slowly, his fingers drifted beneath the silk chemise, tracing a long curve all the way up to her hip. She felt him tuck the end of her shift, which had risen with his hand, into the fingers at her back. The edge of the garment was now draped from hip to knee across her body, revealing the satin expanse of one thigh to her husband's ardent gaze, but hiding the red-gold curls of her mound from his view. Kit lifted her heavy lids. The silver eyes were indeed examining what they could see. Then she felt his fingers drift down and closed her eyes the better to savor the pleasure to come.

As his fingers reached her knee, Jack's head dipped to take one rosy nipple into his mouth, torturing it with his tongue. The effort to breathe became that much harder as he reversed the direction of his caress, languidly trailing his fingers up the back of her thigh. Delicate caresses, tantalizingly explicit, trailed fire over the fevered skin of her bottom. Kit moaned, delighted he'd chosen the long way to paradise.

Slowly, the tracery of flame laid down by his fingertips moved over the curve of her hip to encroach on the silken skin of her stomach. His mouth on her breasts played havoc with her senses. When he finally raised his head, his fingers hovered just above her curls, already damp from the fever surging through her. Kit kept her eyes shut, knowing he was watching her, watching the way her senses flickered in heated anticipation of his next move.

"Open your eyes, Kitten." The growled command was one she wished she could disobey. Her lids fluttered and she opened her eyes just enough to see the devilish smile that twisted her husband's lips.

"Wide."

Kit glared weakly, but obeyed, her breathing tortured and waiting.

His smile grew.

One long finger slid into her.

Her body arched slightly, invitingly, her thighs parting to give him greater access. He reached deep. Kit shuddered and closed her eyes.

His lips found hers in a long slow kiss as his fingers found her heat, stroking and teasing until she clung to him, fever raging in her veins, her body straining for release.

Then he laid her on the bed. He shed his clothes and joined her, his hands, his mouth, quickly, expertly, restoking the flames before, in a fire of need, he possessed her, riding her hard, her urgency driving him on. Kit raised her legs and wrapped them about his waist, tilting her hips to take all of him, drawing him in, reveling in the slickness that allowed him to drive so deeply into her.

The end was shattering, leaving them both gasping. As the fires about them died, they slipped into sleep, limbs entangled, sated and content.

Kit woke to the sensation of Jack kissing her, soft, nibbling kisses that stirred her body to life. Before she was fully awake, he possessed her, quickly, expertly, taking the edge from her need before she even realized it was there.

Lying wrapped in his arms in the warm afterglow, Kit smugly considered the benefits accrued through having a rake for a husband. Then she remembered their discussion, and the fact that she'd yet to have her say. She tried to sit up, but Jack's arms held her firmly.

"Jack!"

At her protest, he shifted onto his elbow and kissed the frown from her brow. "I know, I know. Just keep quiet for a moment, you redheaded houri, and let me explain."

Redheaded houri? *Explain?* Kit dutifully stayed silent.

"I apologize, all right?" He nuzzled one ear, then placed a trail of kisses along her jaw to the other ear.

Kit frowned. "Exactly what are you apologizing for?" Now she'd finally got him to the point, she wanted to be sure she got her due.

Jack drew back and considered her through narrowed silver eyes. "For not telling you about the damned spies."

Kit smiled beatifically.

Jack humphed and kissed her long and hard. "Furthermore," he said, when he was finished, "I promise on my honor as a Hendon to *try* to remember to tell you the details of any of my endeavors which might conceivably cause you concern."

Kit narrowed her eyes as she considered his wording.

Jack raised his brows, at first arrogantly, awaiting her acceptance, then more thoughtfully. "In fact," he mused, considering the delightful picture she made, lying naked in his arms, her skin aglow in the aftermath of their loving, "I'll make a bargain with you."

"A bargain?" Kit wondered at the wisdom of making a deal with such a reprobate.

Jack nodded, inspecting her nipples, shifting over her so he could weigh her breasts in his hands. Then he raised his head and smiled, directly into her large purple-shaded eyes. "We share—I'll tell you what I'm doing before you have to ask, and you'll tell me what you're doing before you do it."

Kit bit her lip on her acceptance. "That's not quite fair," she said, weighing his words every bit as carefully as he was weighing her breasts.

"It's the best you'll do, so I'd advise you to accept." The raspy reply jerked Kit's mind to attention. Too late. He was already lying between her thighs, her long limbs wide-spread. Even as her mind dealt with that discovery, he lifted her hips. The sensation of warm steel pressing into her overrode all other interests.

Kit arched her back, pressing her head deep into the pillows behind her, her lids drooping over her darkened eyes.

"Oh, yes!" she breathed.

Above her, Jack smiled and wondered just what she was agreeing to. As he flexed his hips and thrust deep into her welcoming heat, he decided he'd assume she wanted to share her life in the same abandoned way she shared her body. Then he stopped thinking.

"Lisbon?" Kit turned to look at Jack in surprise. "Why Lisbon?"

Jack chuckled and turned on his side to look at her. The ocean swell had finally registered and she'd got up, draping the counterpane over her nakedness, and gone to the window. "Because it's where the cargo is bound. This isn't a pleasure craft."

Kit's frown took in the sumptuous cabin. "I did think it was a bit big for a yacht." At Jack's laugh, she climbed back on the bed. "So where do we go after that?"

Tucking her curled warmth into one arm, Jack told her of their projected trip, six days in Lisbon followed by the long haul to Bruges, keeping well away from the French coast. After four days in Bruges, they'd head home to Norfolk.

She lay quiet in his arms, and Jack marveled at the peace that held them. They were both wide-awake, but content in their closeness.

Gradually, the perfume of her warm body reached out to flick his senses. He felt his body react and smiled at the ceiling. She'd been well loved, and it was a long way to Lisbon. He closed his eyes. He'd give her another hour or two.

He was woken by Kit scrambling over the bed. "My dress," she said, catching hold of the garment and kneeling on the bed to inspect it. "You've ripped it." She turned to throw an accusing stare his way. Then she glanced at the large armoire against one wall. "I don't suppose that contains any dresses?"

Jack grinned and shook his head. Then he frowned. "Haven't you got another in that bag of yours?" Her black bag had been left near the door.

Kit shook her head. "I didn't expect to be away from home for long, remember?"

"What's in there?"

Warily, Kit eyed the long muscled length stretched, relaxed, on the bed. "My breeches. Both pairs."

Jack's head came up; his eyes found hers. Then, to her relief, he chuckled and dropped his head back on the pillow. "Actually, I'd hoped you'd be reduced to wearing them when I found you at Jenny's. I spent the entire trip down from London fantasizing about your punishment."

Kit stared at him. Fantasizing? She licked her lips. "You never did say what my punishment would be."

"Didn't I?" Jack raised his head. One brow rose; his eyes glinted wickedly. "But that's half the delight. Your imagination running riot in anticipation."

"Jack!" Kit frowned and shifted on the bed, drawing the counterpane about her. Her imagination was stimulated enough already.

He dropped his head back again, then she felt the bed rock with his deep laughter. "I just had a thought."

She could see the smile on his face. It grew. He came

up on one elbow, the look on his face growing more wicked with every passing second.

"If your breeches are all you've got to wear, then perhaps you'd better put them on now. Then we can get your punishment over and done with and you can wear them in Lisbon, until we can buy you some new clothes."

Kit stared as one arrogant brow rose, sending delicious shivers skittering through her. His gaze held hers steadily, as if what he was suggesting was the most straightforward proposition in the world. Dazed, Kit reflected that if she had a single proper bone in her body, she would tell him that married women did not indulge in realizing fantasies. Particularly not his fantasies. She concluded she didn't have a proper bone to her name.

She ran the tip of her tongue over her dry lips. "What sort of punishment did you have in mind?"

Jack smiled. "Nothing too drastic. Nothing that would hurt. I'd intended it as a purely educational exercise." He sat up in bed and leaned back to study her, his arms crossed behind his head. "I thought I should widen your experience by showing you what could happen should you be caught by a man while wearing breeches. But you'd have to promise not to squeal."

Squeal? Kit blinked. This was madness. But she'd never be able to sleep without knowing what he'd planned. Now he'd told her that much, and no more, sometime, somewhere, she'd wear her breeches again just to learn the rest. Why not now?

Jack knew she'd never be able to refuse, to walk away without knowing. Curiosity was something his kitten possessed in abundance. He sat back, entirely confident, and waited for her agreement.

"Perhaps—"

A knock on the stateroom door interrupted Kit's tentative acceptance.

"Lord Hendon?"

Jack got up and reached for his breeches, a smile still on his lips. "I'll take care of whatever it is. Why don't you get dressed?"

Buttoning his breeches, he went out.

Kit stared at the door through which he'd disappeared. She could hear talk in the next room, the voices muffled by the panels. Her gaze dropped to her small black bag, resting where Jack had dropped it, just inside the door.

She was buttoning up the flap of her riding breeches, her back to the door, when she heard Jack enter.

He saw her and, with a half-suppressed whoop, swooped down on her, one arm slipping around her waist to drag her up hard against him, her back to his chest. Without effort, he lifted her feet clear of the floor.

"Jack!" Kit struggled, keeping her voice down, remembering that she mustn't squeal. She assumed his surprise attack was what he'd meant. He'd certainly startled her. Her hands fastened on the muscled arm about her waist. "Put me down."

A rumbling chuckle ruffled her curls. Then his lips nuzzled her ear. "Remember, this is your punishment, love. Not something you have any say in. Just something you *feel*."

Kit closed her eyes. She wished she hadn't heard that. Her nerves were in turmoil. What fiendishly arousing act had he planned? She hadn't a single doubt as to its nature. His shaft was already hard and throbbing, pressed between the firm hemispheres of her bottom.

She didn't have to wait long to learn her punishment.

"I really don't think," her husband continued conversationally, his fingers rapidly undoing the buttons she'd just done up, "that you appreciate just how fast a man can have at you when you're dressed in breeches."

With that, he pulled the offending garment down, letting it slip from her thighs to hang from the closures above her calves.

"And given that you're so easily aroused," he went on, moving closer to a chair which was facing away from them. He let Kit slide down until her toes touched the ground. With a gasp, she grabbed the back of the chair with both hands as she felt Jack's fingers slide effortlessly into her. They withdrew and returned, delving deep, then left her.

"It takes but a second before you've . . ."

She felt him, hard and hot, behind her.

"Been . . ."

He lifted her hips slightly, the head of his swollen shaft nudging into her.

"Had." Then he drove home.

The young cabin boy was leaving the Master's cabin when he heard a very feminine "*Oo-oh!*" emanate from behind the oak door at the end of the corridor. His eyes widened. He cast a glance at the stairs but there was no one about. Quickly, he put down his tray and hurried to press his ear against the door to the bedroom.

At first, he heard nothing. Then his sharp ears caught a low moan, followed by another. One particularly long-drawn moan made his toes curl. Then he heard, quite distinctly, a definitely feminine voice sigh, "*Oh, Jack!*"

The boy's brows flew to astronomical heights. He'd heard tales of Lord Hendon. Obviously, they really were true. With wide eyes, he hurried to pick up his tray.

Epilogue

November 1811
The Old Barn near Brancaster

The wind whistled in the eaves of the Old Barn. It sent cold fingers sneaking through the crevices between the boards to set the lamp hung from the rafters wobbling. Shadows dipped and swayed eerily, ignored by the men gathered under the derelict roof. They were waiting. Waiting for their leader to return.

Captain Jack had led them to success after success. Under him, they'd enjoyed stability and strong leadership; he'd welded them into an efficient force, one they all felt proud to be a part of. They'd steered clear of the Revenue and of any more heinous crimes. They'd suffered no losses, other than poor Joe. And, thanks to Captain Jack, his family had been well taken care of.

All in all, Captain Jack's reign had been one of prosperity. The news that he'd been forced to retire had hit them hard. George, Jack's friend, had brought the news, more than a month ago. Since then, they'd done little, too demoralized to reorganize.

Then, last week, the message had gone around. Captain Jack was back. They'd gathered this foggy Monday night in the expectation of seeing their leader return.

George and Matthew had arrived. As ever, they'd taken up positions on either side of the door. The men chatted quietly, anticipation riding high.

A sudden gust howled about the roof; fingers of fog wreathed about the rickety door. Then the doors opened and a man strode in, fog clinging like a cloak to his broad shoulders. He walked in as Jack had always walked, to stand directly under the lamp, swinging high above.

The smugglers stared.

It was Jack, yet a Jack they'd never seen. His clothes marked him clearly as one born to rule. From the high gloss of his Hessians, to the faultless crease of his cravat, he was Quality. The grey eyes they all remembered scanned their faces, impressing power just as they recalled, only this time the personal strength was backed by social standing.

"Jack?" The puzzled question was asked by Shep, his grizzled brows knitted in consternation.

The slow smile they all remembered twisted the man's lips. "Lord Hendon."

The name should have sent shivers down every spine, but they all knew this man, knew he'd smuggled alongside them, that he'd saved their hides a good few times. So they sat and waited to have the mystery explained.

Jack's grin grew. He took up his usual stance, feet apart, under the light. "It's like this."

He told them the story, simply, without detail or embellishment. The essential points were enough for them to grasp. He made no mention of Young Kit, a fact some noted but none made comment upon. When they grasped the fact they'd been helping His Majesty's government to apprehend spies, the atmosphere lightened considerably. When Jack showed them the pardon he'd brought for them all, and read the official decree, they simply stared.

"This will be posted in all the Revenue Offices in Norfolk. It means that as of today, you're absolved of any crime under the Customs Act committed up until last night." Jack rolled the parchment up and tucked it into his pocket. "What you do with your lives from now on is up to you. But you'll be starting with a clean slate, so I'd urge you all to think carefully before you re-form the Hunstanton Gang." He smiled, wryly, convinced that no matter what he said, after a spell, the Hunstanton Gang would live again. "You'll doubtless be pleased to know that I'm retiring as High Commissioner. In fact, it's doubtful there will be another appointment made to the post.''

His glance took them all in, every last unlovely face. Jack smiled. "And now, my friends, I'll bid you farewell.''

Without looking back, Jack walked to the door. Matthew opened it for him, then he and George followed him outside. There was a murmur of farewell from the men in the barn, but none made any attempt to follow.

Outside, Jack stood under the open skies, his hair glinting in the moonlight. He dropped his head back, his hands on his hips and stared at the pale orb, glowing amid the clouds.

George drew near. "And so ends the career of Captain Jack?''

Jack swiveled about. In the moonlight, George saw his devilish smile. "For the moment.''

"For the moment?'' Incredulous horror filled George's voice.

Jack threw back his head and laughed, then strode toward the trees.

Puzzled, George watched him go. Then he gasped and grabbed Matthew's arm as a rider burst from the band of firs directly in front of Jack. Jack's stride didn't falter; if anything, he moved faster. Then George recognized the horse, and noticed Champion behind.

"Dangerous fools!'' he said, but he was grinning.

"Aye,'' said Matthew. "Imagine what their young'll be like.''

"God preserve us.'' George watched as Jack swung up to Champion's saddle. Kit tossed some remark over her shoulder and set Delia for the road. Jack followed, bringing Champion up to ride by his wife's side.

George watched until their shadows mingled with the trees and disappeared. Smiling, he turned to fetch his horse, his ride home made light by anticipation of Amy, now his wife, waiting safe at home in their bed.

"Incidentally,'' Jack said to Kit, as Champion led the way up the narrow path onto Hendon lands. "You'll have to give up riding Delia.''

Kit frowned and leaned forward to pat the glossy neck as Delia followed the stallion at a slow walk. "Why?''

Jack grinned, knowing his wife couldn't see it. "Let's just say you and she have more in common than you might at first suppose."

It took Kit a moment to work that one out. On the ship, her bouts of queasiness had become more pronounced day by day, until, when they'd left Bruges, she'd had to admit to Jack that she suspected she was carrying his child. To her abiding irritation, he'd admitted he'd known she was since he'd first made love to her in the big bed in their stateroom. Ever since, he'd gone around positively glowing with a smug pride that never failed to get her goat. His protectiveness, of course, had reached new heights. She'd been surprised he hadn't yet taken exception to her riding; doubtless that would come. But what could Delia and she have in common?

The answer made her rein in with a gasp. "You mean . . . ? How . . . ?" Jack drew up and turned to look at her. The truth was easy to read in his smile. Kit's eyes narrowed. "Jack Hendon! Do you mean to tell me you've let that brute of a stallion get at Delia?"

Her husband's eyes widened with unlikely innocence. "But, my love, surely you wouldn't deny Delia a pleasure you take so much delight in?"

Kit opened her mouth, then abruptly shut it. She glared at her aggravating husband. Would he always have the last word?

With an irritated humph, she clicked her reins.

Jack laughed and fell in beside her. "Well, are you satisfied you've shared in Captain Jack's end?"

Wide eyes turned his way. "Has Captain Jack died?" Her voice was sultry. "Or has he simply changed his clothes for a while?"

Jack's eyes widened as he read her look. But before he could say anything, Kit urged Delia ahead. She led the way homeward, but pulled up in the clearing before the cottage.

Jack drew rein beside her. "Tired?"

Kit eyed the cottage. "Not exactly." She slanted a look at her husband.

Jack saw it. He groaned, mock resignation not entirely

concealing his anticipation, and dismounted. "I'll take care of the horses, you take care of the fire."

Kit laughed as he lifted her down. She reached up to draw his lips to hers, pressing her body against his in flagrant promise. Then, smugly satisfied with his immediate reaction, she released him and ran for the door.

Jack watched her go, a slow smile curving his lips. Despite all her adventures, Captain Jack's damned woman was every bit as wild as she'd ever been—outwardly conservative, in reality as untamed as he. She was headstrong but his, in his blood as he was in hers; there could be no tighter bond. Caring for her would fill the empty center of his life; she'd already filled his heart. He could count on her to exasperate, frustrate and infuriate—and love him with all her soul.

She would keep him on his toes. Jack glanced at the cottage. He hoped she was getting impatient.

With a conspiratorial wink for Champion, and a last smiling glance at the moon, he took the horses to the stable before swiftly returning to the cottage—and the warm, loving arms of his wife.

A Gentleman's Honor

The Bastion Club

"a last bastion against the matchmakers of the ton"

MEMBERS

Christian Allardyce,
Marquess of Dearne

Anthony Blake,
Viscount Torrington

Jocelyn Deverell,
Viscount Paignton

Charles St. Austell,
Earl of Lostwithiel

Gervase Tregarth,
Earl of Crowhurst

Jack Warnefleet,
Baron Warnefleet of Minchinbury

#1 ~~Tristan Wemyss,~~ Leonora
~~Earl of Trentham~~   Carling

Christian didn't bother keeping a straight face. "He didn't sound all that sincere. He wrote that he had more pressing engagements, but wished us joy in our endeavors. He expects to be back in town in a week, however, and looks forward to supporting the six of us through our upcoming travails."

"Kind of him," Gervase quipped, but they were all grinning.

Trentham—Tristan Wemyss—had been the first of their number to successfully achieve his goal, the same goal they all were intent on attaining. They all needed to marry; that common aim had spawned this, their club, their last bastion against the matchmakers of the ton.

Of the six of them as yet unwed, gathered this evening to share the latest news, Tony felt sure he was the most desperate, although why he felt so restless, so frustrated, as if poised for action yet with no enemy in sight, he couldn't fathom. He hadn't felt so moody in years. Then again, he hadn't been a civilian, an ordinary gentleman, for years, either.

"I vote we meet every fortnight," Jack Warnefleet said. "We need to keep abreast of events, so to speak."

"I agree." Gervase nodded across the table. "And if any of us has anything urgent to report, we call a meeting as needed. Given the pace at which matters move in the ton, two weeks is the limit—by then, the ground has shifted."

"I've heard the patronesses of Almack's are thinking of opening their season early, such is the interest."

"Is it true one still has to wear knee breeches?"

"On pain of being turned away." Christian raised his brows. "Although I've yet to ascertain just why that would be painful."

The others laughed. They continued trading information—on events, the latest fashions and tonnish distractions—eventually moving on to comment and caution on individual matrons, matchmaking mamas, dragons, gor-

ONE

The Bastion Club
Montrose Place, London
March 15, 1816

"WE'VE A MONTH BEFORE THE SEASON BEGINS, AND AL-ready the harpies are hunting in packs." Charles St. Austell sank into one of the eight straight-backed chairs around the mahogany table in the Bastion Club's meeting room.

"As we predicted." Anthony Blake, sixth Viscount Tor-rington, took the chair opposite. "The action in the mar-riage mart seems close to frenetic."

"Have you seen much of it, then?" Deverell sat beside Charles. "I have to admit I'm biding my time, lying low until the Season begins."

Tony grimaced. "My mother might be resident in Dev-on, but she has a worthy lieutenant in my godmother, Lady Amery. If I don't appear at her entertainments at least, I can be assured of receiving a sharp note the next morning, inquiring why."

There were laughs—resigned, cynical, and commiser-ating—from the others as they took their seats. Christian Allardyce, Gervase Tregarth, and Jack Warnefleet all sat, then, in concert, all eyes went to the empty chair beside Charles.

"Trentham sends his regrets." At the head of the table,

gons, and the like—all those who lay in wait for unsuspecting eligible gentlemen with a view to matrimonially ensnaring them.

"Lady Entwhistle's one to avoid—once she sinks her talons into you, it's the devil of a job to break free."

It was their way of coping with the challenge before them.

They'd all spent the last decade or more in the service of His Majesty's government as agents acting in an unofficial capacity scattered throughout France and neighboring states, collecting information on enemy troops, ships, provisions, and strategies. They'd all reported to Dalziel, a spymaster who lurked, a spider in the center of his web, buried in the depths of Whitehall; he oversaw all English military agents on foreign soil.

They'd been exceedingly good at their jobs, witness the fact they were all still alive. But now the war was over, and civilian life had caught up with them. Each had inherited wealth, title, and properties; all were wellborn, yet their natural social circle, the haut ton—the gilded circle to which their births gave entrée and in which their titles, properties, and the attendant responsibilities made participation obligatory—was an arena of operations largely unknown to them.

Yet in gathering information, evaluating it, exploiting it—in that they were experts, so they'd established the Bastion Club to facilitate mutual support for their individual campaigns. As Charles had described it with typical dramatic flair, the club was their secured base from which each would infiltrate the ton, identify the lady he wanted as his wife, and then storm the enemy's position and capture her.

Sipping his brandy, Tony recalled that he'd been first to point out the need for a safe refuge. With a French mother and French godmother intent on encouraging any and all comers to bat their lashes at him—both ladies were aware such a tactic was guaranteed to make him take the matter of finding a wife into his own hands without delay—it had been he who had sounded the warning. The ton was not safe for such as they.

Set on in the gentlemen's clubs, hounded by fond papas as well as gimlet-eyed matrons, all but buried beneath the avalanche of invitations that daily arrived at their doors, life in the ton as an unmarried, wealthy, titled, *eminently* eligible gentleman was these days fraught with danger.

Too many had fallen on the battlefields of the Peninsula, and more recently at Waterloo.

They, the survivors, were marked men.

They were outnumbered, but they'd be damned if they'd be outgunned.

They were experts in battle, in tactics, and strategy; they weren't about to be taken. If they had any say in it, *they* would do the taking.

That was, at the heart of it, the *raison d'être* of the Bastion Club.

"Anything more?" Christian glanced around the table.

All shook their heads; they drained their glasses.

"I have to make an appearance at Lady Holland's soirée." Charles pulled a face. "I gather she feels she lent Trentham a helping hand, and now wants to try her luck with me."

Gervase raised his brows. "And you're giving her the chance?"

On his feet, Charles met his gaze. "My mother, sisters, and sisters-in-law are in town."

"Oh, ho! I see. Thinking of taking up residence here for the nonce?"

"Not at present, but I won't deny the thought has crossed my mind."

"I'll come with you." Christian strolled around the table. "I want to have a word with Leigh Hunt about that book he's writing. He's sure to be at Holland House."

Tony stood.

Christian glanced his way. "Are you still glorying in solitary state?"

"Yes, thank heaven—the mater's fixed in Devon." Tony resettled his coat with a graceful shrug. "I have, however, been summoned by my godmother to a soirée at Amery House. I'll have to put in an appearance." He looked around the table. "Anyone going that way?"

Gervase, Jack, and Deverell shook their heads; they'd decided to retire to the club's library and spend the rest of the evening in companionable silence.

Tony bade them farewell; grinning, they wished him luck. Together with Christian and Charles, he went downstairs and into the street. They parted on the pavement; Christian and Charles made for Kensington and Holland House, while Tony headed for Mayfair

Reluctance dragged at him; he ignored it. Any experienced commander knew there were some forces it was wise never to waste energy opposing. Such as godmothers. French godmothers especially.

"Good evening, Mrs. Carrington. A pleasure to meet you again."

Alicia Carrington smiled easily and gave Lord Marshalsea her hand. "My lord. I daresay you recall my sister, Miss Pevensey?"

As his lordship's gaze was riveted on Adriana, standing a few steps away, Alicia's question was largely rhetorical. His lordship, however, had clearly decided that gaining Alicia's support was crucial to securing Adriana's hand; while acknowledging Adriana, he remained by Alicia's side and made conversation in a distant, distracted fashion.

That last, something Alicia viewed with amusement, was due to his lordship's absorption with Adriana, talking animatedly with a coterie of admirers all vying for her favor. Adriana was an English rose gowned in pink silk a shade darker than that generally worn by young ladies, the better to exploit her luxuriant dark curls. Those sheened in the chandeliers' glow, creating the perfect frame for her bewitching features, her large brown eyes set under finely arched black brows, her peaches-and-cream complexion and lush, rosebud lips.

As for Adriana's figure, deliberately understated in the demure gown that hinted at rather than defined, it enticed. Even gowned in sackcloth, Alicia's sister was a package guaranteed to capture gentlemen's eyes, which was the reason they were here in London, in the very heart of the ton.

Masquerading.

At least, Alicia was; Adriana was who she purported to be.

While making the appropriate responses to Lord Marshalsea, Alicia monitored all those who paid court to her younger sister. Everything to date had gone exactly as they, sitting in the tiny parlor of their small house in Little Compton, in rural Warwickshire, which along with the surrounding few acres were all they—she, Adriana, and their three brothers—jointly owned, had planned, yet not even in their admittedly unfettered imaginations had they envisioned that events, people, and opportunities would fall out so well.

Their plan, desperate and reckless though it was, might just succeed. Succeed in securing a future for their three brothers—David, Harry, and Matthew—and for Adriana. For herself, Alicia hadn't thought that far; time enough to turn her mind to her own life once she'd seen her siblings safe.

Lord Marshalsea grew increasingly restless; taking pity on him, Alicia eased him into Adriana's circle, then stepped back, effacing herself as a good chaperone should. She eavesdropped, listening as Adriana handled the gentlemen surrounding her with her customary confidence. Although neither she nor Adriana had had any previous experience of the ton, of the ways of society's elite, since their appearance in town and their introduction to those exalted circles some weeks ago, they'd managed without the slightest hiccup.

Eighteen months of intensive research and their own sound common sense had stood them in good stead. Having three much younger brothers whom they'd largely reared had eradicated any tendency to panic; both jointly and individually, they'd risen to every challenge and triumphed.

Alicia was proud of them both, and increasingly hopeful of an excellent outcome to their scheme.

"Mrs. Carrington—your servant, ma'am."

The drawled words jolted her from the rosy future. Concealing her dismay, calmly turning, lips curving, she gave her hand to the gentleman bowing before her. "Mr. Ruskin. How pleasant to meet you here."

"The pleasure, I assure you, dear lady, is all mine."

Straightening, Ruskin delivered the comment with an intent look and a smile that sent a warning slithering down her spine. He was a largish man, half a head taller than she and heavily built; he dressed well and had the manners of a gentleman, yet there was something about him that, even hampered by inexperience, she recognized as less than savory.

For some ungodly reason, Ruskin had from their first meeting fixed his eye on her. If she could understand why, she'd do something to deflect it; her ever-fertile imagination painted him a snake, with her as his mesmerized prey. She'd pretended ignorance of the tenor of his attentions, had tried to be discouraging. When he'd shocked her by obliquely suggesting a *carte blanche*, she'd pretended not to understand; when he'd later alluded to marriage, she'd feigned deafness and spoken of something else. To no avail; he still sought her out, increasingly pointedly.

Thus far she'd avoided any declaration, thereby avoiding having outright to refuse it. Given her masquerade, she didn't want to risk an overt dismissal, didn't want to draw any attention her way; the most she dared do was behave coolly.

Ruskin's pale gaze had been traveling her face; it rose to trap hers. "If you would grant me the favor of a few minutes in private, my dear, I would be grateful."

He still held her fingers; keeping her expression non-committal, she eased her hand free and used it to gesture to Adriana. "I'm afraid, sir, that with my sister in my care, I really cannot—"

"Ah." Ruskin sent a glance Adriana's way, a comprehensive survey taking in the besotted lordlings and gentlemen gathered around her, and Miss Tiverton, whom Adriana had taken under her wing, thereby earning Lady Hertford's undying gratitude. "What I have to say will, I daresay, have some impact on your sister."

Looking back at Alicia, Ruskin met her eyes; his smile remained easy, a gentleman confident of his ground. "However, your concern is . . . understandable."

His gaze lifted; he scanned the room, filled with the fashionable. Lady Amery's soirée had attracted the cream of the ton; they were present in force, talking, exchanging the latest *on-dits*, exclaiming over the latest juicy scandal.

"Perhaps we could repair to the side of the room?" Ruskin brought his gaze back to her face. "With this noise, no one will hear us; we'll be able to talk, and you'll be able to keep your ravishingly lovely young sister safe . . . and in view."

Steel rang beneath his words; Alicia dismissed any thought of refusing him. Inclining her head, feigning serene indifference, she laid her fingers on his sleeve and allowed him to steer her through the crowd.

What unwelcome challenge was she about to face?

Behind her calm facade, her heart beat faster; her lungs felt tight. Had she imagined the threat in his tone?

An alcove behind a chaise filled with dowagers provided a small oasis of relative privacy. As Ruskin had said, she could still see Adriana and her court clearly. If they kept their voices low, not even the dowagers, heads close swapping scandal, would overhear.

Ruskin stood beside her, calmly looking out over the crowd. "I would suggest, my dear, that you hear me out—hear *all* I have to say—before making any reply."

She glanced briefly at him, then stiffly inclined her head. Lifting her fingers from his sleeve, she gripped her fan.

"I think . . ." Ruskin paused, then continued, "I should mention that my home lies not far from Bledington—ah, yes! I see you understand."

Alicia struggled to mask her shock. Bledington lay southwest of the market town of Chipping Norton; Little Compton, their village, lay to the northwest—as the crow flew there could be no more than eight miles between Little Compton and Bledington.

But Ruskin and she had never met in the country. Her family had lived a circumscribed existence, until recently never venturing beyond Chipping Norton. In embarking on her masquerade, she'd been certain no one in London would know her.

Ruskin guessed her thoughts. "We never met in the country, but I saw you and your sister when I was home last Christmas. The pair of you were crossing the market square."

She glanced up.

He caught her eye, and smiled wolfishly. "I determined, then, to have you."

Involuntarily, her eyes widened.

His smile turned self-deprecatory. "Indeed—quite romantic." He looked back at the crowd. "I asked and was told your name—Miss Alicia Pevensey."

He paused, then shrugged. "If you hadn't appeared in London, no doubt nothing would have come of it. But you did appear, a few months later—as a widow of more than a year's standing. I wasn't fooled for a moment, but

I comprehended your need of the ruse, and appreciated your courage in implementing it. It was a bold move, but one with every chance of success. I saw no reason to do other than wish you well. As my admiration for your astuteness grew, my interest in you on a personal level firmed.

"However"—his voice hardened—"when I offered you my protection, you refused. On reflection, I decided to do the honorable thing and offer for your hand. Again, however, you turned up your nose—quite why I have no notion. You seem uninterested in attaching a husband, solely concerned with watching over your sister as she makes her choice. Presumably, given you transparently have no need of funds, you've determined to make your own decision in your own time."

His gaze returned to her face. "I would suggest, my dear *Mrs. Carrington*, that your time has run out."

Alicia fought down the faintness, the giddiness that threatened; the room seemed to be whirling. She drew a slow breath, then asked, her tone commendably even, "What, precisely, do you mean?"

His expression remained intent. "I mean that your performance as a hoity widow in dismissing my suit was so convincing I checked my information. Today, I received a letter from old Dr. Lange. He assures me that the Pevensey sisters—*both* Pevensey sisters—remain unwed."

The room gyrated, heaved, then abruptly stopped.

Disaster stared her in the face.

"Indeed." Ruskin's predatory smile dawned, yet his self-deprecation remained. "But fear not—having concluded that marrying you would be an excellent notion, nothing I've learned has changed my mind."

His gaze hardened. "So let us be clear, my dear. *Mrs. Carrington* cannot continue in the ton, but if you consent to become Mrs. William Ruskin, I see no reason the ton should ever learn that Mrs. Carrington did not exist. I'm renewing my offer for your hand. Should you accept, there's no reason your plan to establish the lovely Adriana will suffer so much as a hiccup." His smile faded; he held her gaze. "I trust I make myself plain?"

Triumph had turned to ashes; her mouth was dry. Moistening her lips, she fought to keep her tone even. "I believe I understand you perfectly, sir. However . . . I would ask for a little time to consider my reply."

His brows rose; his untrustworthy smile returned. "Of course. You may have twenty-four hours—there isn't much to consider, after all."

She sucked in a breath, frantically gathered her wits to protest.

His gaze, hard, trapped hers. "Tomorrow evening you can formally accept me—tomorrow night, I'll expect to share your bed."

Shock held her immobile, staring at his face; she searched his eyes but found no hint of any emotion worth appealing to.

When she made no reply, he bowed punctiliously. "I'll call on you tomorrow evening at nine."

Turning, he left her, strolling into the crowd.

Alicia stood frozen, her wits careening, her skin icy, her stomach hollow.

A burst of raucous laughter from the dowagers, ineffectually smothered, jerked her back to earth. She glanced across the room at Adriana. Her sister was holding her own, but had noticed her distraction; their gazes met, but when Adriana arched a brow, Alicia shook her head.

She had to regain control—of their plan, of her life. Marry Ruskin, or . . . she could barely take it in.

Faintness still gripped her; she felt hot one minute, cold the next. Seeing a footman passing, she requested a glass of water. He brought it promptly, eyeing her warily as if she might swoon; she forced a weak smile and thanked him.

A chair stood against the wall two yards away. She

walked to it and sat, sipping her water. After a few minutes, she flicked open her fan and waved it before her face.

She had to think. Adriana was safe for the moment . . .

Blocking out all thought of the threat Ruskin had made, she focused on him, on what he'd said—on what he knew and what he didn't. Why he was acting as he was, what insights that gave her, how she might press him to change his mind.

They—she, Adriana and the three boys—desperately needed Adriana to make a good match. Not with just any gentleman, but one with reasonable wealth and a sufficiently good heart not only to forgive them the deception they were practicing but to provide for the boys' schooling.

They were as near to penniless as made no difference. They were wellborn, but had no close connections; there were just the five of them—or more correctly Alicia and Adriana to look after them all. David was only twelve years old, Harry ten, and Matthew eight. Without an education, there would be no future for them.

Adriana had to be given the chance to make the match they felt certain she could. She was stunningly beautiful; the ton had already labeled her a "diamond of the first water" among other admiring epithets. She would be a hit, a wild success; once the Season proper commenced, she could take her pick from the wealthy eligibles, and she was wise enough, despite her years, to make the right choice, with Alicia's help.

One gentleman would be the right one for her, for them all, and then the family—Adriana and the three boys—would be safe.

Alicia had no other goal before her; she hadn't had for the past eighteen months, since their mother died. Their father had died years before, leaving the family with little money and few possessions.

They'd scrimped, saved, and survived. And now they'd

risked all on this one throw that fate, in creating Adriana's undoubted beauty, had given them. In order to do so, Alicia had behaved in ways she wouldn't otherwise countenance; she'd taken risks she otherwise never would have—and thus far won.

She'd become Mrs. Carrington, a wealthy and fashionable widow, the perfect chaperone to introduce Adriana to the ton. Hiring a professional chaperone had been out of the question—not only did they not have the funds, but to the ton, especially the upper echelons, a wealthy widow presenting her ravishing younger sister was a significantly different prospect to two provincial spinsters with a hired chaperone, one whose relative standing would have illuminated theirs.

With her masquerade in place, they'd cleared every hurdle and succeeded in insinuating themselves into the ton. The ultimate success beckoned; all was going so well . . .

There *had* to be a way around Ruskin and his threat.

She could marry him, but the recoil the thought evoked made her cast that as a last resort; she'd return to it if and only if there was no other way.

One thing Ruskin had said clanged in her mind. He thought they had money. He'd discovered she'd never married, but he hadn't learned she was first cousin to a pauper.

What if she told him?

Would that make him turn aside from his plan, or simply place another weapon in his hands? If he learned she came with no money but only costs and responsibilities, would he decide not to marry her after all, but instead force her to become his mistress?

The thought made her nauseous. She gulped the last of her water, then rose to set the glass down on a nearby sideboard. The movement had her facing down the side of the room just as Ruskin stepped out through a pair of glass doors.

Moving into the crowd, she looked more closely. The doors, left ajar, led outside, presumably to a terrace.

The very fact she'd seen him go out into a place that would afford greater privacy hardened her resolve; she would go and speak with him. Despite what seemed an unhealthy wish to "have her," there might be some other reward he would accept in return for his silence.

It was worth a try. She did have acquaintances with money she could—or at least thought she might be able to—call on. At the very least, she might be able to talk him into giving her more time.

Tacking through the crowd, she came up beside Adriana.

With a smile at her cavaliers, her sister turned to her. "What's wrong?"

Alicia wondered again at her sister's facility for seeing straight through her. "Nothing I can't manage—I'll tell you about it later. I'm just going out onto the terrace to talk to Mr. Ruskin. I'll be back shortly.

The look in Adriana's eyes said she had many more questions but accepted she couldn't ask them now. "All right, but be careful. He's a toad, if not worse."

"I say, Mrs. Carrington, will you and Miss Pevensey be attending the opening night at the Theatre Royal?"

Young Lord Middleton was as eager as a spaniel; Alicia returned a vague answer, exchanged a few more comments, then slid out of the group and headed for the glass doors.

As she'd surmised, they gave onto a terrace overlooking the gardens. The doors had been left ajar to let air into the crowded and overheated drawing room; slipping through, she drew them almost closed behind her, then, shrugging her shawl over her shoulders, looked about.

It was mid-March and chilly; she was glad of the shawl. Not surprisingly, there were no others strolling in the still and frosty night. She glanced around, expecting to see Ruskin, perhaps indulging in a cigarillo, but the terrace, overhung with shadows, was empty. Walking to the balustrade, she surveyed the gardens. No Ruskin. Had he chosen to leave the soirée by this route?

She glanced down along the path that, from its direction, she assumed led to a gate giving onto the street.

A flash of movement caught her eye.

She peered, and glimpsed a man-sized shadow in the gloom beneath a huge tree beside the path. The tree was massive, the shadows beneath it dense, but she thought the man had just sat down. Perhaps there was a seat there, and Ruskin had gone to sit and smoke, or to think.

Of tomorrow night.

The idea had her stiffening her spine. Pulling her shawl tight, she descended the steps and set off along the path.

With every step Tony took along Park Street, his resistance to attending his godmother's soirée and smiling and chatting and doing the pretty with a gaggle of young ladies with whom he had nothing in common—and who, if they knew the man he truly was, would probably faint—waxed stronger. Indeed, his reluctance over the whole damn business was veering toward the despondent.

Not by the wildest, most exaggerated flight of fancy could he imagine being married to any of the young beauties thus far paraded before him. They were . . . too young. Too innocent, too untouched by life. He felt no connection with them whatsoever.

The fact that they—each and every one—would happily accept his suit if he chose to favor them, and think themselves blessed, raised definite questions as to their intelligence. He was not, had never been, an easy man; one look should tell any sane woman that. He would not be an easy husband. The position of his wife was one that would demand a great deal of its holder, an aspect of which the sweet young things seemed to have no inkling.

His wife . . .

Not so many years ago, the thought of searching for

her would have had him laughing. He hadn't imagined finding a wife was something that would unduly exercise him—when he needed to marry, the right lady would be there, miraculously waiting.

He hadn't, then, appreciated just how important, how vital her role *vis à vis* himself would be.

Now he was faced with that anticipated need to marry—and an even greater need to find the right wife— but the right lady had thus far shown no inclination even to make an appearance. He had no idea what she might look like, or be like, what aspects of her character or personality would be the vital clue—the crucial elements in her that he needed.

He wanted a wife. The restlessness that seemed to enmesh his very soul left him in no doubt of that, but exactly *what* he wanted, let alone why . . . that was the point on which he'd run aground.

Identify the target. The first rule in planning any successful sortie.

Until he succeeded in satisfying that requirement, he couldn't even start his campaign; the frustration irked, fueling his habitual impatience. Hunting a wife was ten times worse than hunting spies had ever been.

His footsteps echoed. Another, distant footfall sounded; his agent's senses, still very much a part of him, flaring to full attention, he looked up.

Through the mist wreathing the street, he saw a man, well muffled in coat and hat and carrying a cane, step away from the garden gate of . . . Amery House. The man was too far away to recognize and walked quickly away in the opposite direction.

Tony's godmother's house stood at the corner of Park and Green Streets, facing Green Street. The garden gate opened to a path leading up to the drawing-room terrace.

By now the soirée would be in full swing. The thought of the feminine chatter, the high-pitched laughter, the giggles, the measuring glances of the matrons, the calculation in so many eyes, welled and pressed down on him.

On his left, the garden gate drew nearer. The temptation to take that route, to slip inside without any announcement, to mingle and quickly look over the field, then perhaps to retreat before even his godmother knew he was there, surfaced . . . and grew.

Closing his hand on the wrought-iron latch, he lifted it. The gate swung soundlessly open; passing through, he closed it quietly behind him. Through the silent garden, heavily shadowed by large and ancient trees, the sound of conversation and laughter drifted down to him.

Mentally girding his loins, he drew in a deep breath, then quickly climbed the steep flight of steps that led up to the level of the garden.

Through ingrained habit, he moved silently.

The woman crouching by the side of the man lying sprawled on his back, shoulders propped against the trunk of the largest tree in the garden, didn't hear him.

The tableau exploded into Tony's vision as he gained the top of the steps. Senses instantly alert, fully deployed, he paused.

Slim, svelte, gowned for the evening in silk, her dark hair piled high, with a silvery shawl wrapped about her shoulders and clutched tight with one hand, the lady slowly, very slowly, rose. In her other hand, she held a long, scalloped stilletto; streaks of blood beaded on the wicked blade.

She held the dagger by the hilt, loosely grasped between her fingers, pointing downward. She stared at the blade as if it were a snake.

A drop of dark liquid fell from the dagger's point.

The lady shuddered.

Tony stepped forward, driven by an urge to take her in his arms; catching himself, he halted. Sensing his presence, she looked up.

A delicate, heart-shaped face, complexion as pale as snow, dark eyes wide with shock, looked blankly at him.

Then, with a visible effort, she gathered herself. "I think he's dead."

Her tone was flat; her voice shook. She was battling hysterics; he was thankful she was winning.

Tamping down that impulsive urge to soothe her, shield her, a ridiculously primitive feeling but unexpectedly powerful, he walked closer. Forcing his gaze from her, he scanned the body, then reached for the dagger. She surrendered it with a shudder, not just of shock but of revulsion.

"Where was it?" He kept his tone impersonal, businesslike. He crouched down, waited.

After an instant, she responded, "In his left side. It had fallen almost out . . . I didn't realize . . ." Her voice started to rise, became thready, and died.

Stay calm. He willed the order at her; a cursory examination confirmed she was right on both counts. The man was dead; he'd been knifed very neatly, a single deadly thrust between the ribs from the back. "Who is he—do you know?"

"A Mr. Ruskin—William Ruskin."

He glanced at her sharply. "You knew him."

He hadn't thought it possible, but her eyes widened even more. "No!"

Alicia caught her breath, closed her eyes, fought to summon her wits. "That is"—she opened her eyes again—"only to speak to. Socially. At the soirée . . ."

Waving back at the house, she dragged in a breath and rushed on, "I came out for some air. A headache . . . there was no one out here. I thought to wander . . ." Her gaze slid to Ruskin's body. She gulped. "Then I found him."

Ruskin had threatened her, her plan, her family's future. He'd been blackmailing her—and now he was dead. His blood oozed in a black pool by his side, stained the dagger now in the stranger's hand. It was a struggle to take everything in, to know even what she felt, let alone how best to react.

The unknown gentleman rose. "Did you see anyone leaving?"

She stared at him. "No." She glanced around, suddenly aware of the deep silence of the gardens. Abruptly, she swung her gaze back to him.

Tony sensed her sudden thought, her rising panic. Was irritated by it. "No—*I* didn't kill him."

His tone reassured her; her sudden tenseness faded.

He glanced again at the corpse, then at her; he waved back up the path. "Come. We must go in and tell them."

She blinked, but didn't move.

He reached for her elbow. She permitted him to take it, let him turn her unresisting, and steer her back toward the terrace. She moved slowly, clearly still in shock. He glanced at her pale face, but the shadows revealed little. "Did Ruskin have a wife, do you know?"

She started; he felt the jerk through his hold on her arm. From beneath her lashes, she cast him a shocked glance. "No." Her voice was tight, strained; she looked ahead. "No wife."

If anything, she'd paled even more. He prayed she wouldn't swoon, at least not before he got her inside. Appearing at his godmother's soirée via the terrace doors with a lady senseless in his arms would create a stir even more intense than murder.

She started shaking as they went up the steps, but she clung to her composure with a grim determination he was experienced enough to admire.

The terrace doors were ajar; they walked into the drawing room without attracting any particular attention. Finally in good light, he looked down at her, studied her features, the straight, finely chiseled nose, lips a trifle too wide, yet full, lush and tempting. She was above average in height, her dark hair piled high in gleaming coils exposing the delicate curve of her nape and the fine bones of her shoulders.

Instinct quivered; deep within him, primitive emotion stirred. Sexual attraction was only part of it; again, the urge to draw her close, to keep her close, welled.

She looked up, met his gaze. Her eyes were more green than hazel, large and well set under arched brows; they were presently wide, their expression dazed, almost haunted.

Fortunately, she seemed in no danger of succumbing to the vapors. Spying a chair along the wall, he guided her to it; she sank down with relief. "I must speak with Lady Amery's butler. If you'll remain here, I'll send a footman with a glass of water."

Alicia lifted her eyes to his face. To his velvet black eyes, to the concern and the focus she sensed behind his expression, behind the masklike, chiseled, haughtily angular planes. His was the most strikingly attractive masculine face she'd ever seen; he was the most startlingly attractive man she'd ever met, elegant, graceful, and strong. It was his strength she was most aware of; when he'd taken her arm and walked beside her, her senses had drunk it in.

Looking up at him, into his eyes, she drew on that strength again, and felt the horror they'd left outside recede even further. The reality around them came into sharper focus; a glass of water, a moment to compose herself, and she'd manage. "If you would . . . thank you."

That "thank-you" was for far more than the glass of water.

He bowed, then turned and headed across the room.

Suppressing an inner wrench, not just reluctance but real resistance to leaving her, Tony found a footman and dispatched him to revive her, then, ignoring the many who tried to catch his eye, he found Clusters, the

Amerys' butler, and pulled him into the library to explain the situation and give the necessary orders.

He'd been visiting Amery House since he'd been six months old; the staff knew him well. They acted on his orders, summoning his lordship from the cardroom and her ladyship from the drawing room, and sending a footman running for the Watch.

He wasn't entirely surprised by the ensuing circus; his godmother was French, after all, and in this instance she was ably supported by the Watch captain, a supercilious sort who saw difficulties where none existed. Having taken the man's measure with one glance, Tony omitted mentioning the lady's presence. There was, in his view, no reason to expose her to further and unnecessary trauma; given the dead man's size and the way she'd held the dagger, it was difficult if not impossible to convincingly cast her as the killer.

The man he'd seen leaving the grounds via the garden gate was much more likely to have done the deed.

Besides, he didn't know the lady's name.

That thought was uppermost in his mind when, finally free of the responsibility of finding a murdered man, he returned to the drawing room and discovered her gone. She wasn't where he'd left her; he scouted the rooms, but she was no longer among the guests.

The crowd had thinned appreciably. No doubt she'd been with others, perhaps a husband, and they'd had to leave. . . .

The possibility put a rein on his thoughts, dampened his enthusiasm. Extricating himself from the coils of a particularly tenacious matron with two daughters to marry off, he stepped into the hall and headed for the front door.

On the front steps, he paused and drew in a deep breath. The night was crisp; a sharp frost hung in the air.

His mind remained full of the lady.

He was conscious of a certain disappointment. He hadn't expected her gratitude, yet he wouldn't have minded a chance to look into those wide green eyes again, to have them focus on him when they weren't glazed with shock.

To look deep and see if she, too, had felt that stirring, that quickening in the blood, the first flicker of heat.

In the distance a bell tolled the hour. Drawing in another breath, he went down the steps and headed home.

Home was a quiet, silent place, a huge old house with only him in it. Along with his staff, who were usually zealous in preserving him from all undue aggravation.

It was therefore a rude shock to be shaken awake by his father's valet, whom he'd inherited along with the title, and informed that there was a gentleman downstairs wishful of speaking with him even though it was only nine o'clock.

When asked to state his business, the gentleman had replied that his name was Dalziel, and their master would assuredly see him.

Accepting that no one in his right mind would claim to be Dalziel if they weren't, Tony grumbled mightily but consented to rise and get dressed.

Curiosity propelled him downstairs; in the past, he and his peers had always been summoned to wait on Dalziel in his office in Whitehall. Of course, he was no longer one of Dalziel's minions, yet he couldn't help feeling that alone would not account for Dalziel's courtesy in calling on him.

Even if it was just past nine o'clock.

Entering the library where Hungerford, his butler, had left Dalziel to kick his heels, the first thing he became aware of was the aroma of fresh coffee; Hungerford had served Dalziel a cup.

Nodding to Dalziel, elegantly disposed in an armchair, he went straight to the bellpull and tugged. Then he turned and, propping an arm along the mantelpiece, faced Dalziel, who had set down his cup and was waiting.

"I apologize for the early hour, but I understand from Whitley that you discovered a dead body last night."

Tony looked into Dalziel's dark brown eyes, half-hidden by heavy lids, and wondered if such occurrences ever slipped past his attention. "I did. Pure chance. What's your—or Whitley's—interest?"

Lord Whitley was Dalziel's opposite number in the Home Office; Tony had been one, possibly the only, member of Dalziel's group ever to have liaised with agents run by Whitley. Their mutual targets had been the spy networks operating out of London, attempting to undermine Wellington's campaigns.

"The victim, William Ruskin, was a senior administrative clerk in the Customs and Revenue Office." Dalziel's expression remained uninformative; his dark gaze never wavered. "I came to inquire whether there was any story I should know?"

A senior administrative clerk in the Customs and Revenue Office; recalling the stiletto, an assassin's blade, Tony was no longer truly sure. He refocused on Dalziel's face. "I don't believe so."

He knew that Dalziel would have noted his hesitation; equally, he knew that his erstwhile commander would accept his assessment.

Dalziel did, with an inclination of his head. He rose. Met Tony's eyes. "If there's any change in the situation, do let me know."

With a polite nod, he headed for the door.

Tony saw him into the hall and handed him into the care of a footman; retreating to the library, he wondered, as he often had, just who Dalziel really was. Like recognized like; he was certainly of the aristocracy, with his finely hewn Norman features, pale skin and sable hair, yet Tony had checked enough to know Dalziel wasn't his last name. Dalziel was slightly shorter and leaner than the men he had commanded, all ex-Guardsmen, yet he pro-jected an aura of lethal purpose that, in a roomful of larger men, would instantly mark him as the most dangerous.

The one man a wise man would never take his eye from.

The door to the street shut; a second later, Hungerford appeared with a tray bearing a steaming cup of coffee. Tony took it with a grateful murmur; like all excellent butlers, Hungerford always seemed to know what he re-quired without having to be told.

"Shall I ask Cook to send up your breakfast, my lord?"

He nodded. "Yes—I'll be going out shortly."

Hungerford asked no more, but silently left him.

Tony savored the coffee, along with the premonition Dalziel's appearance and his few words had sent tingling along his nerves.

He was too wise to ignore or dismiss the warning, yet, in this case, he wasn't personally involved.

But she might be.

Dalziel's query gave him the perfect excuse to learn more of her. Indeed, given Whitehall's interest, it seemed incumbent upon him to do so. To assure himself that there wasn't anything more nefarious than murder behind Ruskin's death.

He needed to find the lady. *Cherchez la femme.*

TWO

HE REGRETTED NOT ASKING HER NAME, BUT INTRODUC-
tions over a dead body simply hadn't occurred to him, so
all he had was her physical description. The notion of
asking his godmother occurred, only to be dismissed; alerting *Tante* Felicité to any interest on his part—especially
when he wasn't sure of his ground—didn't appeal, and
the lady might have arrived with others. Felicité might
not know her personally.

Over breakfast, he applied his mind to the question of
how to track the lady down. The idea that occurred
seemed a stroke of genius. Ham and sausages disposed
of, he strode into his hall, shrugged on the coat Hungerford held, and headed for Bruton Street.

The lady's gown had been a creation of considerable
elegance; although he hadn't consciously noted it at the
time, it had registered in his mind. The vision leapt
clearly to his inner eye. Pale green silk superbly cut to
compliment a lithe rather than buxom figure; the fall of
the silk, the drape of the neckline, all screamed of an expert modiste's touch.

According to Hungerford, Bruton Street was still home
to the ton's most fashionable modistes. Tony started at
the nearer end, calmly walking into Madame Francesca's
salon and demanding to see Madame.

Madame was delighted to receive him, but regretfully—and it truly was regretfully—could not help him.

That refrain was repeated all the way down the street. By the time he reached Madame Franchot's establishment at the other end, Tony had run out of patience. After enduring fifteen minutes of Madame's earnest inquiries regarding his mother's health, he escaped, no wiser.

Going slowly down the stairs, he wondered where the devil else one of his lady's ilk might obtain her gowns. Reaching the street door, he opened it.

And saw, large as life, walking along the opposite side of the street, the lady herself. So she did come to Bruton Street.

She was walking briskly, absorbed in conversation with a veritable stunner—a younger lady of what even to Tony's jaded eye registered as quite fabulous charms.

He waited inside the doorway until they walked farther on, then went out, closed the door, crossed the street, and fell in in their wake, some twenty yards behind. Not so close that the lady might sense his presence, or see him immediately behind her should she glance around, yet not so far that he risked losing them should they enter any of the shops lining the street.

Somewhat to his surprise, they didn't. They walked on, engrossed in their discussion; reaching Berkeley Square, they continued around it.

He followed.

"There was nothing you could have done—he was already dead and you saw nothing to the point." Adriana stated the facts decisively. "Nothing would have been gained and no point served by you becoming further involved."

"Indeed," Alicia agreed. She just wished she could rid herself of the niggling concern that she *should* have waited in Lady Amery's drawing room, at least for the gentleman to return. He'd been uncommonly sensible and supportive; she should have thanked him properly. There was also the worry that he might have become embroiled in difficulties over finding a dead body—she had no idea of the correct procedures, or even if there *were* correct procedures—yet he'd seemed so competent, doubtless she was worrying over nothing.

She was still jumpy, nervy, hardly surprising but she couldn't allow even a murder to distract her from their plan. Too much depended on it.

"I do hope Pennecuik can get that lilac silk for us—it's a perfect shade to stand out among the other pastels." Adriana glanced at her. "I rather think that design with the frogged jacket would suit—do you remember it?"

Alicia admitted she did. Adriana was trying to distract her, to deflect her thoughts into more practical and productive avenues. They'd just come from visiting Mr. Pennecuik's warehouse, located behind the modistes' salons at the far end of Bruton Street. Mr. Pennecuik supplied the trade with the very best materials; he now also supplied Mrs. Carrington of Waverton Street with the stuffs for the elegant gowns in which she and her beautiful sister, Miss Pevensey, graced the ton's entertainments.

A most amicable arrangement had been reached. Mr. Pennecuik supplied her with the most exclusive fabrics at a considerable discount in return for her telling all those who asked—as hordes of matrons did and would when they clapped eyes on Adriana—that insisting on the best fabric was the key to gaining the most from one's modiste, and the fabrics from Mr. Pennecuik's were unquestionably the best.

As she patronized no modiste, the presumption was that she employed a private seamstress. The truth was she and Adriana, aided by their old nurse, Fitchett, sewed all their gowns. No one, however, needed to know that, and so everyone was pleased with the arrangement.

"Dark purple frogging." Alicia narrowed her eyes, creating the gown in her mind. "With ribbons of an in-between shade to edge the hems."

"Oh, yes! I saw that on a gown last night—it looked quite stunning."

Adriana prattled on. Alicia nodded and hmmed at the right points; inwardly, she returned to the nagging possibility that continued to disturb her.

The gentleman had stated he wasn't the murderer. She'd believed him—still did—but didn't know why. It would have been so easy . . . he might have heard her on the path, propped Ruskin against the tree, hid in the shadows and waited for her to "discover" Ruskin, then walked up and "discovered" her. If anyone asked, she would be honor-bound to state he'd come up after she'd found Ruskin already dead.

Already stabbed.

The memory of the dagger sliding out . . . she shivered.

Adriana glanced at her, then tightened their linked arms, pressing closer. "Stop thinking about it!"

"I can't." It wasn't Ruskin she was thinking most about, but the man who had emerged from the shadows; despite all, it was he who lingered most strongly in her mind.

Determinedly she redirected her thoughts to the crux of her worries. "After all our luck to date, I can't help but worry that some whisper of my involvement with so scandalous a thing as murder will out, and will affect your chances." She met Adriana's gaze. "We all have so much riding on this."

Adriana's smile was truly charming; she was no giddy miss, but a sensible female not easily influenced by man or fate. "Just show me the field and leave the rest to me. I assure you I'm up to it, and while I'm swishing my skirts, you can retreat into the shadows if you wish. But truly, I think it unlikely any news of this murder, much less your part in it, will surface, beyond, of course, the customary 'How unfortunate.' "

Alicia grimaced.

"Now," Adriana continued, "I gather from Miss Tiverton that there'll be quite a different crowd at Lady Mott's tonight. Apparently, her ladyship has a wide acquaintance in the counties, and what with everyone coming up to town early, there's sure to be many at her ball tonight. I think the cerise-and-white stripes will be best for me tonight, and perhaps the dark plum for you."

Alicia let Adriana fill her ears with sartorial plans. Turning into Waverton Street, they headed for their door.

From the corner of the street, Tony watched them climb the steps and enter, waited until the door shut, then ambled past. No one watching him would have noticed his interest.

At the end of Waverton Street he paused, smiled to himself, then headed home.

Lady Mott's ball had been talked of as a small affair.

The ballroom was certainly small. The ball, however, was such a crush Alicia was grateful that the size of Adriana's court gave them some protection.

As was her habit, after delivering Adriana to her admirers, she stepped back to the wall. There were chairs for chaperones a little way along, but she'd quickly realized that, not truly being chaperone material, it behooved her to avoid those who were; they were too inquisitive.

Besides, standing just feet away, she was near if Adriana needed help in dealing with any difficult suitor or avoiding the more wolfish elements who had started to appear at the periphery of her court.

Such gentlemen Alicia showed no hesitation in putting to rout.

The strains of the violins heralded a waltz, one Adriana had granted to Lord Heathcote. Alicia was watching, relaxed yet eagle-eyed as her sister prettily took his lordship's arm, when hard fingers closed about her hand.

She jumped, swallowed a gasp. The fingers felt like iron.

Outraged, she swung around, and looked up—into the dark, hard-featured face of the gentleman from the shadows.

Her lips parted in shock.

One black brow arched. "That's a waltz starting—come and dance."

Her wits scattered. By the time she'd regathered them, she was whirling down the room, and it was suddenly seriously difficult to breathe.

His arms felt like steel, his hand hard and sure on her back. He moved gracefully, effortlessly, all harnessed power, hard muscle and bone. He was tall, lean, yet broad-shouldered; the notion that he'd captured her, seized her and swept her away, and now had her in his keeping, flooded her mind.

She shook it aside, yet the sensation of being swept up by a force beyond her control, engulfed by a strength entirely beyond her power to counter, shocked her, momentarily dazed her.

Tangled her tongue.

Left her mentally scrambling to catch up—and filch the reins of her will back from his grasp.

The look on his face—one of all-seeing, patronizing, not superiority but control—helped enormously.

She dragged in a breath, conscious of her bodice tightening alarmingly. "We haven't been introduced!" The first point that needed to be made.

"Anthony Blake, Viscount Torrington. And you are?"

Flabbergasted. Breathless again. The timbre of his voice, deep, low, vibrated through her. His eyes, deepest black under heavy lids, held hers. She had to moisten her lips. "Alicia . . . Carrington."

Where *were* her wits?

"*Mrs.* Carrington." She dragged in another breath, and felt the reel her wits had been whizzing through start to slow.

His eyes hadn't left hers. Then he slipped his shoulder from under her hand, and that hand, her left, was trapped in his. His fingers shifted, finding the gold band on her ring finger.

His lips twisted fleetingly; he replaced her hand on his shoulder and continued to whirl her smoothly down the room.

She stared at him, beyond astonished. Inwardly thanking the saints for Aunt Maude's ring.

Then she blinked, cleared her throat, and looked over his shoulder into safe oblivion. "I must thank you for your help last evening—I hope the matter was concluded without any undue difficulties. I do ask you to excuse my early retreat." She risked a glance at his face. "I fear I was quite overcome."

In her experience most men accepted that excuse without question.

He looked as if he didn't believe it for a moment.

"*Quite* overcome," she reiterated.

The cynical scepticism—she was sure it was that—in his narrowing eyes only deepened.

Theatrically, she sighed. "I was attending with my *unmarried* younger sister. She's in my care. I had to take her home—my responsibility to her came first, above all else, as I'm sure you'll understand."

For a full minute, not a muscle moved in his classically sculpted face, then his brows rose. "I take it Mr. Carrington was not present?"

A whisper of caution tickled her spine; she kept her eyes on his. "I'm a widow."

"Ah."

There seemed a wealth of meanings in the single syllable; she wasn't sure she approved of any of them. Her tone sharp, she inquired, "And what do you mean by that?"

He opened his eyes wider, the heavy lids lifting; his lips, thin, mobile, the lower somewhat fuller, seemed to ease. His black gaze held hers trapped; he made no move to answer her question.

Not with words.

She suddenly felt quite warm.

Flustered—she was actually flustered.

The music reached its conclusion; the dance ended. She'd never been so thankful of any event in her life. She stepped out of his arms, only to feel his hand close once more about hers.

His gaze on her face, he set her hand on his sleeve. "Allow me to escort you back to your sister."

She had little choice but to accept; she did so with a haughty inclination of her head, and permitted him to steer her up the room, tacking through the crowd to where Adriana had returned to the safety of her court.

Taking up her position a few steps away, close by the wall, she lifted her hand from Torrington's sleeve and turned to dismiss him.

His gaze had gone to Adriana; he glanced back at her. "Your sister is very lovely. I take it you're hoping to establish her creditably?"

She hesitated, then nodded. "There seems no reason she shouldn't make an excellent match." Especially now Ruskin was gone. The recollection had her meeting Torrington's black gaze; it seemed fathomless, but far from cold.

Oddly intriguing. His gaze seemed to hold her, yet she didn't, in fact, feel trapped. Just held. . . .

"Tell me." His expression eased a fraction more. "Have you seen the latest offering at the Opera House? Have you been in town long enough to do so?"

He glanced away; she blinked. "No. The opera is one experience we've yet to enjoy." Studying him, she couldn't see him enthralled by opera or a play. Couldn't resist asking, "Have you succumbed to its lure recently?"

His lips twitched. "Opera isn't my weakness."

Weakness—did he have one? Given all she could sense, it seemed unlikely. She realized she was gazing at him, trying hard not to stare, not to show any consciousness of him, of the potent masculine aura of which, as the confines of the crowded ballroom necessitated them standing mere inches apart, she was very much aware.

She'd been going to dismiss him. She drew in a breath.

"I thought you'd want to know that the proper authorities were informed of Mr. Ruskin's sad end." Those fascinating black eyes returned to hers; he'd lowered his voice so only she could hear. "In the circumstances, I saw no need to implicate you. You knew nothing of the situation leading to Ruskin's death—or so I understood."

She nodded. "That's correct." As if in support of his judgment, she added, "I have no idea why he was stabbed, or by whom. I had no connection with him beyond a few social exchanges."

Torrington's black gaze remained steady on her face, then he inclined his head and looked away. "So from which part of the country do you and your sister hail?"

Given he'd just informed her he'd been instrumental in protecting her from precisely the sort of imbroglio she'd been frantic to avoid, she felt compelled to answer. "Warwickshire. Not far from Banbury." She and Adriana had decided it would be wise henceforth to avoid all mention of Chipping Norton.

"Your and Miss Pevensey's parents?"

"Are no longer alive."

That earned her a glance, black and sharp. "She has no guardian other than yourself?"

"No." She lifted her chin. "Be that as it may, I believe we'll muddle through."

He registered her acerbic tone; he glanced again at Adriana. "So you're solely responsible for . . ." He looked back at her. "Do you have any idea what you've taken on?"

She raised her brows, no longer amused. "As I said, I believe we'll manage nicely. We have until now, and quite well, I would say."

His black gaze held hers with a disturbing intensity. "I

would have thought your husband would have had some hand in that."

She blushed. "Yes, of course, but he's been dead for some years."

"Indeed?" Torrington's black eyes gleamed. "Might one inquire from what he died?"

"An inflamation of the lung," she snapped, not at all sure to what in his question she was reacting. She looked away at the surrounding crowd, tried to realign her thoughts with the requirements of her charade. "It's unkind of you to remind me, sir."

After a moment came the dry comment, "My apologies, my dear, but you don't appear to be a grieving widow."

She made the mistake of glancing at him.

He caught her gaze, held it.

After a moment, she narrowed her eyes, then, deliberately, looked away.

Fought to ignore the soft, very masculine chuckle that fell, a distractingly warm caress over her senses.

"Tell me." He'd lowered his voice and shifted closer; the deep rumble teased her ear. "Why aren't you joining your sister in hunting for a husband?"

"I have other matters in hand, other responsibilities. I don't need to add a husband to the list."

She refused to look at him, but sensed she'd said something to make him pause.

Not for long. "Most ladies in your position would look to a husband to shoulder their responsibilities for them."

"Indeed?" Still surveying the crowd, she raised her brows as if considering, then shrugged. "Perhaps, but I have no ambitions for myself in that direction. If I can see my sister comfortably established, married to a gentleman worthy of her, then I'll retire from this Season well pleased."

Glancing at Adriana's court, she noted one particular gentleman who was making every attempt to monopolize her sister's attention. The surprising thing was he appeared to be succeeding.

"Well pleased from a guardian's point of view perhaps, but as a lady of some experience, a widow's lonely existence can hardly be fulfilling."

Distracted, she heard the deep, drawled words, but wasted no wit on divining their meaning. Frowning, she turned to him. "Instead of twitting me, you might attempt to be useful—who is the gentleman with my sister?"

Tony blinked. Thrown entirely off his stride, he looked. "Ah . . . there's at present seven gentlemen surrounding your sister."

She made a frustrated sound—the sort that intimated he was being willfully obtuse. "The one with wavy brown hair speaking with her now. Do you know him?"

He looked, and blinked again. It was several seconds before he replied, "Yes. That's Geoffrey Manningham, Lord Manningham."

An instant later, his prey prodded his arm. "Well? What can you tell me about him?"

He glanced at her. Far from observing the stiff formal distance she'd been working to preserve between them, she'd shifted closer; he could smell the perfume wafting from her throat. If he shifted his head just an inch, he'd be able to touch his cheek to her hair.

She'd been staring, frowning, at Geoffrey; now she glanced up at him, pointedly opened her green eyes wide.

"His estate is in Devon. It shares a partial boundary with mine. If I know anything of Geoffrey, and I've known him since childhood, then his estate, houses, and finances will all be in excellent condition."

Her green eyes narrowed. "You . . ." She glanced at Geoffrey.

"No." It was comforting to be with a woman he could read so easily; she made very little effort to hide her thoughts. "Geoffrey didn't send me to distract you so he could waltz your sister off from beneath your careful nose."

She looked up at him, still suspicious. "And why should I believe that?"

He held her gaze, then caught her hand, lifted it to his lips. Kissed. "Because I told you so." Her eyes flashed; he smiled, and added, "And because Geoffrey and I haven't met in over ten years."

Perfectly aware that with the simple caress he'd fractured her concentration, he gestured to the circle a few feet away. "Shall we join them?"

She gathered herself and managed a regal nod. Delighted, entranced, he tucked her hand in his arm and steered her to Geoffrey's side.

"Manningham?"

Geoffrey looked up from his pursuit of the lovely Adriana. The rivalry that in their youth had never been far beneath their surfaces instantly leapt to his eyes.

Tony smiled. "Allow me to present Mrs. Carrington—Miss Pevensey's sister and guardian."

Geoffrey's gaze deflected, then he threw Tony a speaking glance and made haste to bow and shake Alicia's hand. Others made hay of his distraction and reclaimed Adriana's attention. Tony noted that while she showed no partiality to those anxious to gain her approbation, she did sneak swift glances at Geoffrey, engaged by her sister in the customary social niceties.

Content to observe, he made no attempt to extricate Geoffrey. Instead, he listened to Alicia Carrington craftily confirm all he'd told her, and elicit a few details more. Her protectiveness toward her younger sister, her determination to ensure she was in no way taken advantage of, rang true and clear. Not one of the men gathered about Adriana could doubt it; her sister would always stand as her protector.

With her single-minded focus, she reminded him of a

lioness watching over her cubs; woe betide any who dared threaten them. She was calm, determined, sensible, and strong-willed, mature yet not old; she was as chalk to cheese to the young misses he'd been exposed to over the past weeks—the contrast was a blessed relief.

Via the groom he'd sent to chat in the mews near Waverton Street, he'd learned that Mrs. Carrington hired her carriage from the nearby stables, and also that, as was her habit, she'd sent her evening's instructions to the coachman at midday. Armed with the information, he'd arrived early, much to Lady Mott's delight; he'd been in the ballroom waiting when Alicia Carrington had walked in.

He'd watched her for an hour before he'd approached; in that time, he'd seen her dismiss without a blink three perfectly eligible gentlemen who, as he did, found her quieter beauty, with its suggestion of maturity and a more subtle allure, more attractive than her sister's undeniable charms.

As with all else she'd revealed in response to his probing, her dismissal of marriage rang true. She was truly disinterested, at least at present. She was focused on her task . . . the temptation to distract her, to see if he could . . .

He refocused on her; she was still interrogating Geoffrey who, to Tony's educated eye, was finding the going increasingly grim.

He'd done his duty. He'd convinced himself that his first impression of Mrs. Carrington had been accurate; she hadn't slid a stiletto between Ruskin's ribs, and he could see no reason to doubt her assertion that she had known Ruskin only socially. There was nothing there to interest Dalziel.

Mission accomplished, there was no reason he couldn't retire and leave Geoffrey to his fate. No reason at all to remain by Alicia Carrington's side.

The distant scrape of bow on string heralded the return

of the musicians and an impending waltz. Geoffrey straightened, stiffened, then threw him an unmistakable look of entreaty. Man-to-man. Ex-boyhood-rival-to-rival.

Tony reached for Alicia's hand. "If you would do me the honor, Mrs. Carrington?" He bowed.

Alicia blinked, startled by the sudden clasp of Torrington's hard fingers on hers. As he straightened, she glanced at Lord Manningham only to discover his lordship had grasped her single moment of distraction to turn to Adriana, who, from her smile, had been waiting, having already granted him this dance.

She opened her lips—on what words she didn't know—only to find herself whisked about. "Wait!"

"The dance floor's this way."

"I know, but I wasn't going to accept your offer."

He threw her a black glance, not irritated but curious. "Why?"

"Because I don't want to waltz."

"Why not? You're passably good at it."

"It's got nothing to do with . . . I'm a chaperone. Chaperones don't waltz. We're supposed to keep an eye on our charges even while they're waltzing."

He glanced over her head. "Your sister's with Manningham. Unless he's changed beyond belief in the last ten years, he's no cad—she's as safe as she can be, and you don't need to watch."

They'd reached the floor; the musicians had launched into their theme. He swung her into his arms, then they were whirling down the room.

As before, she found breathing difficult, but was determined not to let it show. "Are you always this dictatorial?"

He met her gaze, then smiled, an easy, warming, simple gesture. "I don't know. I've never been questioned on the subject before."

She threw him a look she hoped conveyed total disbelief.

"But educate me—I've been away from the ton for

more than ten years—should your sister be waltzing at all? Wasn't there some rule or other about permission from the hostesses?"

"She had to get permission from one of the patronesses of Almack's. I spoke to Lady Cowper, and she was kind enough to give her approval." Alicia frowned. "But why have you been away from the ton for ten years—and more? Where were you?"

He looked at her for a moment, as if the answer should be obvious, tattooed on his forehead or some such, then his smile deepened. "I was in the army—the Guards."

"Waterloo?"

The concern in her face was quite genuine. It warmed him. "And the Peninsula."

"Oh."

Tony watched her digest that. Despite the fact he waltzed well—always had—the waltz wasn't his favorite dance; with a woman in his arms, he'd much rather be involved in a romp that heated up the sheets on some bed, rather than a sedate revolution about some tonnish ballroom.

And in this case, the woman in his arms teased and challenged on a level he'd forgotten what it was like to be challenged on. For too many years, women, ladies and all, had come to him easily; generally speaking, he'd only had to crook his finger, and there'd always been more than one willing to slake his lust. He was an accomplished lover, too experienced to be anything other than easy and generous in his ways.

Too experienced not to recognize when his senses were engaged.

Taller than average, supple and svelte, she was less buxom than those ladies who normally caught his eye, yet she hadn't just caught his attention, she'd fixed it—quite why he couldn't say. There seemed a multitude of small attractions that made up the whole—the sheen of the candlelight on her perfect skin, a soft cream tinged with rose, a very English complexion, her eyes and their green gaze—direct, without guile, amazingly open—the lush, heavy locks of her dark mahogany hair, the way her lips set, then eased and lifted.

He wanted to taste them, to taste her. To tempt her to want him. And more. With her in his arms, his appetite, along with his imagination, was definitely inclined toward a bed.

Alicia was conscious of an escalating warmth, one that seemed to rise from within her. It was pleasant, even addictive—her senses responded with a wish to wallow and luxuriate. It was something to do with him, with the way he held her, whirled her so easily down the room, with the reined strength she sensed in him but which triggered her innate defenses not at all—that strength was no threat to her.

His effect on her, however, might be; she wasn't experienced enough to know. Yet it was just a dance—one waltz—and she'd never waltzed like this before, never felt quite like this. Surely it couldn't hurt. And he was a military veteran, an ex-Guardsman, and a viscount.

Quite what that said of him she wasn't sure, but it couldn't all be bad.

He swung her through the turns at the end of the room; her heart leapt as his thigh parted hers. Letting her lids fall, she concentrated on breathing—and on the warmth her senses seemingly craved.

The music slowed, stopped, and they halted. And she realized just how pleasant—how pleasurable—the dance had been. She glanced at him, met his black gaze, and thought she saw a fraction too much understanding in his dark eyes. How black could seem warm she had no idea, but his eyes were never cold . . .

She looked to where Adriana's court waited, and saw Adriana on the arm of Lord Manningham ahead of them, moving that way. Torrington took her arm and steered her in their wake.

As seemed normal for him, he didn't offer his sleeve or ask her permission . . .

And, as was starting to be normal for her, she'd let him.

She frowned. Not once during the waltz had she thought to check on Adriana and Manningham—her distraction had been that complete.

The man on whose arm she was strolling was dangerous.

Seriously dangerous; he'd managed to make her forget her plan for a full five minutes, in the middle of a ton ballroom, no less.

Tony saw the frown form on her face. "What's the matter?"

She glanced up. He looked into her green eyes, watched as she debated, then decided not to tell him the truth—that he was disturbing her, ruffling her senses, undermining her equanimity—as if he didn't know.

Frown deepening, she looked down. "I was just wondering whether my demon brothers had behaved themselves tonight."

He felt his brows rise. "*Demon* brothers?"

She nodded. "Three of them. I'm afraid they're quite a handful. David is a terror—he pretends to be a pirate and falls out of windows. I don't know how many times we've had the doctor to the house. And then Harry, well, he has a tendency to lie—one never knows if the house really is on fire or not. And as for Matthew, he is only eight, you understand, if we could just stop him from locking the doors after people, and slipping around the house at night—we've lost three parlor maids and two housekeepers, and we've only been in town for five weeks."

Tony looked into her face, into her green eyes so determinedly guileless, and struggled not to laugh. She was a terrible liar.

He managed to keep a straight face. "Have you tried beating them?"

"Oh, no! Well, only once. They ran away. We spent the most awful twenty-four hours before they came home again."

"Ah—I see. And do I take it these demons are your responsibility?"

Head rising, she nodded. "My *sole* responsibility."

At that, he grinned.

She saw. Frowned. "What?"

He lifted her hand from his sleeve, raised it to his lips. "If you want to scare gentlemen off, you shouldn't sound so proud of your three imps."

Her frown would have turned to a scowl, but her sister came up on Geoffrey's arm and effectively distracted her. Adriana's court trailed behind; within minutes they were once more part of a fashionable circle, within whose safety Alicia remained, shooting the occasional suspicious glance his way until, deeming his duty on all counts done, he bowed and took his leave.

THREE

He repaired to the Bastion Club.

With a sigh, he sank into a well-stuffed leather armchair in the library. "This place is a godsend."

He exchanged a glance with Jack Warnefleet, ensconced in another chair reading an issue of *The Sporting Life*, savored a sip of his brandy, then settled his head against the padded leather and let his thoughts roam.

To his life—what it used to be, what it now was, most importantly what he wanted it to be. The past was behind him, finished, brought to a close at Waterloo. The present was a bridge, a transition between past and future, nothing more. As for the future. . . .

What did he truly want?

His mind flashed on snippets of memory, a sense of warmth in company, of rare moments of closeness punctuating long years of being alone. Of camaraderie, a sense of shared purpose, a passion for life as well as justice.

Dalziel and his mention of Whitley had brought Jack Hendon to mind. The last he'd seen of Jack he'd been firmly caught in his lovely wife's coils, trooping, gesticulating and protesting, at her dainty heels. A vision of Kit with their elder son in her arms, Jack hovering protectively over them both, swam through his mind. And stuck.

Jack and Kit were coming down to London this Season; they'd be here within a few days. It would be good to see them again, not only to renew old friendships but to refresh his memory, to sense again how a successful marriage worked.

The restlessness that for a few hours had been in abeyance returned. Draining his glass, he set it aside and rose. With a nod to Jack, who returned a salute, he left the library and the club.

At that hour London's streets were quiet, the last stragglers from the balls already at home while the more hardened cases were ensconced in their clubs, hells, and private salons for what was left of the night. Tony walked steadily, his strides long, his cane swinging. Despite his self-absorption, his senses remained alert, yet none of those hanging back in the shadows made any move to accost him.

Reaching his house in Upper Brook Street, he climbed the steps, fishing for his latch key. To his surprise, the door swung open.

Hungerford stood waiting to relieve him of his coat and cane. The hall lights were blazing. A footman stood to the side, still on duty.

"The gentleman who called this morning has returned, my lord. He insisted on waiting for your return. I've put him the library."

"Dalziel?"

"Indeed, my lord."

From Hungerford's tone, it was clear that he, no more than Tony, was certain just who, or more correctly what, Dalziel was, other than someone it was unwise to disobey, let alone cross.

Tony headed for the library.

"The tantalus is well supplied. Do you require anything further, my lord?"

"No." Tony paused and glanced back. "You and the staff can retire. I'll see"—he'd been about to say his lordship; Dalziel was at the very least that—"the gentleman out."

"Very good, my lord."

Tony continued across the green-and-white tiles toward the library door. The hall was paneled in oak, an airy, high-ceilinged space . . . it was a night for memories. He could recall running here as a child, with a fire roaring in the hearth at the end, the dancing flames reflecting off the oak, a sense of warmth enveloping him.

Now the hall seemed . . . not cold, but it no longer held that encompassing warmth. It was empty, waiting for that time to come again, for that phase of life to return.

Hungerford and the footman had disappeared through the green baize door. Alone, Tony paused; with his hand on the knob of the library door, he looked around. Let his senses stretch farther than his eyes could see.

He was alone, and his house was empty. Like it, he was waiting. Waiting for the next phase of life to rush in and fill him, engage him.

Warm him.

For a moment he stood silent and still, then he shook off the mood and opened the door.

Dalziel was in an armchair facing the door, an almost empty brandy balloon in one long-fingered hand. His brows rose faintly; his lips curved, cynical and amused, in welcome.

Tony eyed the entire vision with a misgiving he made no attempt to hide; Dalziel's smile only deepened.

"Well?" Crossing to the tantalus, Tony poured a small measure of brandy, more to have something to do than anything else. He raised the decanter to Dalziel, who shook his head. Replacing the decanter, picking up the glass, he crossed to the other armchair. "To what do I owe this . . . unexpected visit?"

They both knew it wouldn't have anything to do with pleasure.

"We've worked together for a long time."

Tony sat. "Thirteen years. But I work for the government no longer, so what has that to say to anything?"

Dalziel's dark eyes held his. "Simply that there are matters I cannot use less experienced men for, and in this case your peculiar background makes you too ideal a candidate to overlook."

"Bonaparte's on St. Helena. The French are finished."

Dalziel smiled. "Not that peculiar background. I have other half-French agents. I meant that you have experience of Whitley's side of things, and you have a better-than-average grasp of the possibilities involved."

"Involved in what?"

"Ruskin's death." Dalziel studied the amber lights in the glass he turned between his fingers. "Some disturbing items came to light when they started clearing the man's desk. Jottings of shipping information derived from both Revenue and Admiralty documents. They appear to be scribbled notes for more formal communications."

"Nothing in any way associated with his work?"

"No. He organized Customs clearances for merchant-men, hence his access to the internal Revenue and Admiralty notices. His job involved the dates of expected entry to our ports. The information jotted down relates to movement of ships in the Channel, especially its outer-most reaches. There is no possible reason his job required such details."

Dalziel paused, then added, "The most disturbing aspect is that these jottings span the years from 1812 to 1815."

"Ah." As Dalziel had prophesied, Tony grasped the implication.

"Indeed. You now perceive why I'm here. Both I and Whitley are now extremely interested in learning who killed Ruskin, and most importantly why."

Tony pondered, then looked at Dalziel, directly met his eyes. "Why me?" He could guess, but he wanted it confirmed.

"Because there is, as you've realized, the possibility that someone in Customs and Revenue, or the Home Office, or any of a multitude of government agencies is involved, in one capacity or another. It's unlikely Ruskin could use the information himself, but someone knew he had access to it, and either made use of him themselves, or put someone else on to him. In either case, this nebulous someone might be in a position to know Whitley's operatives. He won't, however, know you."

Dalziel paused, considering Tony. "The only connection you've had with Whitley's crew was that operation you ran with Jonathon Hendon and George Smeaton. Both are now retired; both are sound. Despite Hendon's background in shipping, he's had no contact with Ruskin—and yes, I've checked. For the past several years, both Hendon and Smeaton have remained buried in Norfolk, and their only links in town are either purely social or purely commercial. Neither is a threat to you— and as I recall, no one else of Whitley's crew ever knew who Antoine Balzac really was."

Tony nodded. Antoine Balzac had been a large part of his past.

"On top of that, you found the body." Dalziel met his gaze. "You are the epitome of an obvious choice."

Tony grimaced and looked down, into his glass. It seemed as if the past was reaching out, trying to draw him back; he didn't want to go. Yet all Dalziel said was true; he *was* the obvious choice . . . and Alicia Carrington was, at least peripherally, involved.

She wasn't part of his past.

"All right." He looked up. "I'll nose around and see what connections I can turn up."

Dalziel nodded and set his glass aside. "Ruskin worked at the main office of Customs and Revenue in Whitehall." He gave details of the building, floor, and room. "I suggested that his papers, indeed, all his office be left as was. I gather that's been done. Naturally, I've asked for no clearances. Let me know if you require any."

Tony's lips curved; he inclined his head. Both he and

Dalziel knew he wouldn't ask for clearances. He'd been an "unofficial agent" for too long.

"Ruskin lived in lodgings in Bury Street—Number 23. His home, Crawton Hall, is near Bledington in Gloucestershire, just over the border of north Oxfordshire, southwest of Chipping Norton, the nearest market town."

Tony frowned, but his knowledge of England was nowhere near as detailed as his knowledge of France.

"Ruskin has a mother living, and an older spinster sister. They reside at Crawton Hall, and haven't left it in decades. Ruskin spent but little time there in recent years. That's what we know of him to date."

"Odd habits?"

"None known—we'll leave that to you. Obviously, we can't afford any overt activity."

"What about manner of death—any word from the surgeon?"

"I called Pringle in. According to him, Ruskin was knifed with the stiletto you found. Very professionally slipped between the ribs. Angle and point of entry suggest a right-handed assailant standing beside and a little behind his left side."

They both could see how it was done.

"So." Tony sipped. "A friend."

"Certainly someone he in no way suspected of murderous intent."

Such as a lady in a pale green silk gown.

Tony looked up. "Did Pringle give any guesses as to the murderer—size, strength, that sort of thing?"

Dalziel's eyes, scanning his face, narrowed. "He did. A man almost certainly as tall as Ruskin and, of course, of reasonable strength."

"How tall was Ruskin?"

"A trifle shorter than me. Half a head shorter than you."

Tony hid his relief behind a grimace. "Not much help there. Any other clues?"

"No." Dalziel stood, fluidly graceful.

Tony did the same, with even more innate flair.

Dalziel hid a grin and led the way to the door. "Let me know what you find. If I hear anything useful, I'll send word."

He paused as they reached the door and met Tony's gaze. "If I do have anything to send, where should I send it?"

Tony considered, then said, "Here. Back door. My butler's reliable, and the staff have been with me for years."

Dalziel nodded. They stepped into the hall.

Tony saw Dalziel out and locked the front door, then returned to the library.

He went straight to one of the bookcases and crouched, scanning the spines, then he pulled out a large tome. Rising, he crossed to where the lamp on the desk threw a circle of stronger light. Opening the book—a collection of maps of England's counties—he flicked through until he came to the pages showing Oxfordshire. He located Chipping Norton, and Banbury in the far north of the county.

It took a few minutes of flicking back and forth, comparing maps of Gloucestershire, Oxfordshire, and Warwickshire, before he had the geography straight. The only bit of Warwickshire "not far from Banbury" was also not far from Chipping Norton, and therefore, in turn, not far from Bledington.

Alicia Carrington's home lay within ten miles of Ruskin's.

Shutting the book, Tony stared across the room.

How likely was it, given the social round of county England that, living in such proximity, Alicia Carrington née Pevensey and Ruskin had never met?

The question suggested the answer. Ruskin hadn't spent much time in Bledington recently, and despite telling him she and her sister hailed from the area, Alicia Carrington could well have meant their home was there now. The home she'd made with her husband; most likely she was referring to his house, not necessarily the area in which she and her family, the Pevenseys, had lived most of their lives. Of course.

He returned the book to the shelf, then headed for the door.

Of course, he'd check.

That, however, would have to come later. The first thing he needed to do, and that as soon as humanly possible, before any whisper of an internal investigation into Ruskin's affairs could find its way to anyone, was search Ruskin's office.

The Customs and Revenue Office in Whitehall was well guarded and externally secure, but for someone who knew how to approach it from within, down the long, intersecting corridors, it was much less impenetrable. Even better, Ruskin's office was on the first floor at the back, and its small window faced a blank wall.

At four o'clock in the morning, the building was cold and silent. The porter was snoring in his office downstairs; lighting a lamp was safe enough.

Tony searched the desk, then the whole office methodically. He collected everything pertinent in the middle of the desk; when there was no more to discover, he transferred all he'd found to the deep pockets of his greatcoat.

Then he turned out the lamp, slipped out of the building, and went home, leaving not a trace of his presence, or anything to alert anyone that Ruskin's office had been searched.

Despite his late night, he was out again at noon, heading for Bury Street. It was a fashionable area for single gentlemen, close to clubs, Mayfair, and the seat of government; Number 23 was a well-kept, narrow, three-story house. He knocked on the door and explained to the land-lady that he worked alongside Mr. Ruskin and had been sent to check his rooms to make sure no Customs Office papers had been left there.

She led him up to a set of rooms on the first floor. He thanked her as she unlocked the door. "I'll return the key when I leave."

With a measuring glance that read the quality of his coat and boots in much the same way as a military pass, she nodded. "I'll leave you to it, then."

He waited until she was heading downstairs, then entered Ruskin's parlor and shut the door.

Again, his search was thorough, but in contrast to Ruskin's office, this time he found evidence someone had been before him. He found a pile of old IOUs lying in a concealed drawer in the escritoire atop more recent correspondence.

Dalziel and Whitley would never have permitted any other from either the official or unofficial sides of government to meddle in an affair they'd handed to him; who-ever had been through Ruskin's papers was from the "other side." Indeed, the fact the rooms had been searched—he found further telltale signs in the bedroom—meant there was, most definitely, an "other side."

Whatever dealings Ruskin had been involved in, some-one had believed there might be evidence they needed to remove from his rooms.

Presumably they'd removed it.

Tony wasn't unduly concerned. There were always threads left lying around in the aftermath of any scheme; he was an expert at finding and following such flimsy but real connections.

Such as those IOUs. He didn't stop to analyze them in detail, but a cursory glance revealed that they'd been paid off regularly. More, the sums involved made it clear

Ruskin had enjoyed an income considerably beyond his earnings as a government clerk.

Stowing the notes in his pockets, Tony concluded that discovering the source of that extra income was logically his next step.

After taking an impression of the key, he let himself out, returned the key to the landlady with typical civil service boredom, admitting to removing "a few papers but nothing major" when she asked.

Back on the street, he headed for Torrington House. He needed a few hours to study and collate all he'd found. However, the day was winging, and there was other information he needed to pursue that would, he suspected, be best pursued in daylight.

He'd been wondering how to approach Alicia Carrington and learn unequivocally all he needed to know. He'd left a corner of his brain wrestling with the problem; an hour ago, it had presented him with the perfect solution.

First, he needed to empty his pockets and let Hungerford feed him. Two o'clock would be the perfect time to essay forth to rattle Mrs. Carrington's defenses.

He found her precisely where his devious mind had predicted—in Green Park with her three brothers and an older man who appeared to be their tutor.

The two older boys were wrestling with a kite; the tutor was assisting. The younger boy had a bat and ball; Alicia was doing her best to entertain him.

He spent a few minutes observing, assessing, before making his move. Recalling Alicia's description of her demons, he grinned. The boys were sturdy, healthy-looking specimens with apples in their cheeks and shining brown hair. They were typical boys, rowdy and physical, yet they were quick to mind their elder sister's strictures.

Obedient demons.

Amused, he walked toward her. The bat in her hands, she had her back to him. The youngest—Matthew?— tossed the ball to her; she swung wildly and missed. The ball bounced past her, giving him the perfect opening.

He stopped the ball with his boot, with a quick flick, tossed it up, and caught it. Strolling forward, he hefted the ball; as he reached Alicia's side, he lobbed it to the boy.

And reached for the bat. "Here, let me."

He twitched the bat from her nerveless fingers.

Alicia stared at him. "What are you doing here?"

Torrington glanced at her. "Playing ball." He waved to the side. "You should stand over there so you can catch me out."

Matthew, blinking at the changes, shook his head. "She's not much good at catching."

Her tormentor smiled at him. "We'll have to give her a bit of practice, then. Ready?"

Alicia found herself stepping back in the direction Torrington had indicated. She was not sure about any of this, but . . .

Matthew pitched the ball to him, and he tapped it back between her and Matthew. Matthew squealed delightedly and pounced on it. A huge grin wreathing his face, he hustled to square up again.

After a few more shrewdly placed shots—one which came straight at her and surprised a shriek out of her— David and Harry left Jenkins with the kite and came hurrying to join in.

Normally, the older boys would have immediately taken over the game; she girded her loins to defend Matthew, but Torrington, bat still in his hand, elected himself director of play. He welcomed the older boys and waved them to fielding positions, leaving Matthew as bowler.

What followed was an education in how boys played, or could play if led by a competent hand. When Jenkins came up, the discarded kite in his hands, she waved him to take over her position. He might be more than twice her age, but he was better at catching.

The kite in her arms, she retreated to lean against a tree. Given the focus of the game, she naturally found herself gazing at Torrington.

Not a calming sight.

He literally made her pulse skitter and race. She was far enough away to appreciate his perfect male proportions, the wide shoulders and tapering chest, slim hips and long, lean legs. She'd yet to see him make an ungraceful move; she wasn't sure he'd know how. His reflexes were excellent.

She saw the laughing humor in his face as he skied a ball to Harry, who with a rowdy whoop caught it. Torrington's black locks, thick and lightly wavy, hugged his head; one fell forward across his broad brow as he good-naturedly surrendered the bat to Harry. He took the ball and bowled for a while, then tossed it to David.

And came strolling over the lawn to take up a fielding position near her. He grinned at her. "Coward."

She tipped up her nose. "As you've been informed, I'm hopeless at catching."

The look he gave her was enigmatic, but a ball hit his way recalled him to his duty.

She tried to watch the play and call encouragement as a good sister should, but having Torrington so close, watching him move and stretch and stand, hands on hips, then wave, directing her brothers, was distracting.

His occasional glances did nothing to slow her pulse.

What really worried her was why he was there.

As soon as David and Matthew had had a turn at batting, she called a halt. "Come along—we have to get back for tea."

Her brothers, flushed and glowing with happiness, ran up.

"I say." David tugged her hand. "Can Tony come home with us for tea?"

Alicia looked down into David's bright eyes. Tony—Torrington was *Tony* to them. That seemed dangerous. But David, even more than the other two, was lonely here in London, and what, after all, could Torrington do? She smiled. "If he wishes."

"Will you come? Will you come?" The chorus was instantaneous.

Joining them, Tony—Torrington—glanced at her. "If your sister doesn't mind."

She wasn't at all sure it was a good idea, and he knew it; she met his gaze, but kept her expression easy. "If you have no objection to sitting down to a nursery tea, then by all means do join us."

He smiled, not just with his lips but with those coal black eyes; if she'd had a fan, she would have deployed it. He bowed. "Thank you. I'd be delighted."

Thrilled, thoroughly pleased with their new acquaintance, the boys took his hands; surrounding him, they danced by his side all the way back to Waverton Street, peppering him with questions.

At first, following behind with Jenkins, she merely listened, learning that Tony was an only child and had grown up mostly in Devon, but also in part in London. He knew all the childhood haunts. But when Harry, military mad, asked if he'd served overseas, and he replied he had, her protective instincts flared.

Quickly lengthening her stride, she came up beside Matthew, tripping along, Tony's hand in his, gazing adoringly up at his new friend.

"So which were you in—the navy or the army?"

"The army—the Guards."

"And you were at Waterloo?"

"Yes."

"Did you lead a charge?"

She jumped in. "Boys, I really don't think we need to hear about charges and fighting over tea."

Torrington glanced at her briefly, a swift, penetrating look, then he turned back to her brothers. "Your sister's right—war is not fun. It's horrible, and frightening, and dreadful to be involved in."

David's eyes grew round. Harry's face fell.

Alicia only just managed to keep her own jaw from falling.

"But . . ." Harry blinked at Torrington. "I want to be a major in the Guards when I grow up. Or the cavalry."

"I was a major in both, and I'd suggest you rethink. Aside from all else, there are no more enemies to fight. Being in the cavalry in peacetime might not be the exciting life you imagine."

They'd reached the front steps of the house. Torrington waved the boys ahead of him, then waited for Alicia to precede him. She went quickly up the steps and opened the door, then stood back, and the three boys filed in.

Gracefully, Torrington waved her on, then followed.

"Upstairs and wash your hands, please." She shooed her brothers to the stairs. "Then you may join us in the parlor."

They flashed swift smiles at Torrington, then clattered up the stairs. Jenkins shut the door. She turned to him. "If you could order tea, Jenkins?"

"Indeed, ma'am." Jenkins bowed and left them.

She turned to Torrington. "Thank you." She met his black eyes. "That was just the right thing to say."

He studied her for a moment, then one black brow arched. "It's no more than the truth."

But one few ex-majors in the Guards would admit. Inclining her head, she led him to the parlor. Located at the back of the house, it was the room she and Adriana used most, when they were alone or with the boys, *en famille.* A comfortable room in which the boys could relax without worrying overmuch about the furniture, it was a trifle shabby, but she didn't care as she led Torrington in; she'd warned him it was to be a nursery tea.

Adriana was there, poring over the latest fashion plates. She glanced up, saw Torrington, and rose, smiling.

After Adriana and Torrington exchanged greetings, they all sat. Even though the room was decently sized, Alicia was aware of his physical presence, his strength. Adriana asked how he had come to join them; he related the story of the game in the park. Every now and then, his gaze would touch Alicia's, and a teasing smile would flirt about his lips. She was relieved when the boys rejoined them, bursting upon them in a noisy, albeit well-behaved wave, and the talk became more general.

Jenkins appeared with the tray; if Torrington noticed the oddity in that, he gave no sign.

She poured; on their best behavior, the boys offered Torrington the plate of crumpets first. He went up in their estimation—and hers—when he accepted one and smeared it with globs of jam, just as the boys did with theirs. All were soon munching happily.

Crumpet dealt with in three bites, Torrington wiped his fingers on his napkin, then reached for his teacup. He looked at her brothers. "Your sister told me you live in Warwickshire—is there much sport up that way? Shooting? Hunting?"

David wrinkled his nose. "Some fishing, some shooting, not much hunting just where we are. That's south Warwickshire."

Harry waved his remaining crumpet. "There's hunting around Banbury, but not down near us."

"Well," David temporized. "There's a small, really *tiny* pack runs out of Chipping Norton, but it's not what you'd call a real hunt."

From the corner of his eye, Tony saw Alicia and Adriana exchange a swift glance; the instant the boys had started mentioning towns, Alicia had tensed. He pressed harder. "Chipping Norton? Is that your nearest town? I've a friend who lives up that way."

Alicia leaned forward. "Harry! Be careful. You're about to drip jam."

Adriana grabbed his napkin and wiped Harry's fingers. Neither Tony nor Harry could see any physical reason for his sisters' sudden action.

"There." Adriana sat back. "Now why don't you tell Lord Torrington about that huge trout you caught last year?"

Instead, the boys fixed Tony with round eyes.

"Are you really a lord?" Matthew asked.

Tony grinned. "Yes."

"What sort of lord?" David asked.

"A viscount." Tony could see from their faces they were trying to recall the order of precedence. "It's a small lordship. The second smallest."

They weren't deterred. "Does that mean you get to wear a coronet at a coronation?"

"What sort of cloak do you get to wear?"

"Do you have a castle?"

He laughed, and answered as best he could, noting the relieved look Alicia threw Adriana; his presence in her parlor was making her skittish, and on more than one front.

Interrogating her brothers was not a gentlemanly act, yet he'd learned long ago that when it came to matters of treason, and that was what he and Dalziel and Whitley were dealing with in one guise or another, one couldn't adhere to gentlemanly scruples. In that particular theater, adhering to such scruples was a fast way to die, failing one's country in the process.

He felt no remorse for having used the three boys; they'd come to no harm, and he'd learned what he needed. Now he had to interrogate their elder sister. Again.

"Time for your afternoon lessons, boys. Come along, now." Alicia stood, waving her brothers to their feet.

They rose, casting glances at Tony; knowing on which side his bread was buttered, he gave them no encouragement to defy their sister, but rose, too, and gravely shook hands.

With resigned polite farewells, the boys trooped out; Alicia followed them into the hall, consigning them into Jenkins's care.

Seizing the moment, Tony turned to Adriana.

She'd risen, too, and now smiled. "I believe you're acquainted with Lord Manningham, my lord."

"Yes. He's an old friend."

Amusement flashed through her brown eyes, suggesting Geoffrey had painted their association with greater color.

He didn't have much time. "I wanted to speak with you. Your sister will have mentioned the matter of Mr. Ruskin." Adriana's face immediately clouded; like Alicia, she possessed little by way of a social mask. "I gather you hadn't met him in the country."

"No." Adriana met his gaze; her eyes were clear, but troubled. "He appeared a week or so after we arrived in town. We only met him a handful of times in the ballrooms, never anywhere else."

She hesitated, then added, "He was not a man either of us could like. He was . . . oh, what is the word . . . 'importuning'. That's it. He hovered about Alicia even though she discouraged him."

From her expression, it was clear that while Alicia was mother lion, Adriana would be fierce in her sister's defense. He inclined his head. "It's perhaps as well, then, that he's gone."

Adriana muttered a guiltily fervent assent.

Alicia reentered; he turned to her and smiled. "Thank you for an entertaining afternoon."

Her look said she wasn't sure how to interpret that. He

took his leave of Adriana, then, as he'd hoped, Alicia accompanied him to the door.

Following him into the hall, she shut the parlor door. He glanced about; fate had smiled—they were alone.

He gave her no time to regroup, but struck immediately. "Ruskin lived at Bledington, close to Chipping Norton. Are you *sure* you never met him in the country?"

She blinked at him. "Yes—I told you. We only met recently, socially in London." Her eyes, searching his, suddenly widened. "Oh, was he a friend of your friend? The one you mentioned?"

He held her gaze; he could detect not the slightest hint of prevarication in the clear green, only puzzlement, and a hint of concern. "No," he eventually said. "Ruskin's friends are no friends of mine."

The reply, especially his tone, further confused her.

"I understand he'd been bothering you—in what way?"

She frowned, clearly wishing he hadn't known to ask; when he simply waited, she lifted her head and stiffly stated, "He was . . . attracted."

He kept his eyes on hers. "And you?"

Irritation flashed in her eyes. "I was not."

He felt his lips ease. "I see."

They remained, gazes locked, for two heartbeats, then he reached out and took her hand. Still holding her gaze, he raised her fingers to his lips. Kissed, and felt the tremor that raced through her. Watched her eyes widen, darken.

She drew in a quick breath, tensed to step back.

He reacted. Tightening his grip on her fingers, he drew her nearer. Bent his head and touched his lips to hers in the lightest, most fleeting kiss.

Just a brushing of lips, more promise than caress.

He intended it to be that, not a real kiss but a tantalizing temptation.

Raising his head, he watched her lids rise, saw surprise, shock, and curiosity fill her eyes. Then she realized, stiffened, drew back.

Releasing her, he caught her gaze. "I meant what I said. I truly enjoyed the afternoon."

He wondered if she understood what he was saying.

Before she could question him—before he could be tempted to say or do anything more—he bowed and turned to the door.

She saw him out and shut the door.

Gaining the pavement, he paused, letting the last moments fade from his mind, turning instead to running through all he'd learned thus far.

His instincts were pricking. Something was afoot, but just what he'd yet to divine. Turning on his heel, he headed for home and his library. There was a great deal he had to digest.

FOUR

He spent the rest of that day and the entire evening analyzing all he'd retrieved from Ruskin's office and lodgings. Ruskin's scribbled notes and the receipts of his debts appeared to be the only clues, the only items warranting further investigation.

After assembling a schedule of the dates on which the debts, in groups, had been paid, along with the sums involved, Tony called it a night. At least working for Dalziel gave him an excuse not to attend the ton's balls.

The next day, just after noon, he girded his loins and dutifully presented himself at Amery House for one of his godmother's at-homes, to which he'd been summoned. He knew better than to ignore the dictate. Strolling into her drawing room, he bowed over her hand, resignedly noting he was one of only four gentlemen present.

Felicité beamed up at him. "*Bon!* You will please me *and* your *maman* by talking and paying attention to the *demoiselles* here, will you not?"

Despite the words, there was an ingenuous appeal in her eyes. He felt his lips quirk. Hand over heart, he declared, "I live to serve."

She only just managed to suppress a snort. She rapped his knuckles with her fan, then used it to gesture to the knots of young ladies gathered by the windows. "*Viens!*" She shooed. "Go—go!"

He went.

It was a cynical exercise; none of the young things to whom the matrons prayed he'd fall victim had any chance of fixing his interest. Why they thought he might be susceptible escaped him, but he behaved as required, pausing by first one group, then another, chatting easily before moving on. He did not remain by any lady's side for long; no one could accuse him of being the least encouraging.

He'd scanned the room on entering; Alicia Carrington had not been present. As he moved from group to group, he resurveyed the guests, but she didn't appear.

While moving to the fifth knot of conversationalists, he caught Felicité's eye, noted her puzzled expression. Realized he was giving the impression he was searching for someone, waiting for someone.

Mentally shrugging, he strolled on.

He was with the sixth group, inwardly debating whether he'd dallied long enough, when he heard two matrons standing a little apart exchanging the latest gossip—the items they considered too titillating for their charges' delicate ears.

His instincts flickered; he'd noticed there was some flutter—some piece of avid interest—doing the rounds among the older ladies.

The two biddies a yard behind him put their heads together and lowered their voices, but his hearing was acute.

"I had it this morning from Celia Chiswick. We met at Lady Montacute's morning tea. You've heard about that fellow Ruskin being murdered—stabbed—just along the path there?"

From the corner of his eye, Tony saw the lady point into the garden.

"*Well!* It seems he was blackmailing some lady—a widow."

"No! Who?"

"Well, of course no one knows, do they?"

"But someone must have some idea, surely."

"One hardly likes to speculate, but . . . you do know who he was speaking with just before he left this room and walked to his death, don't you?"

"No." The second woman's voice dropped to a strained whisper. "Who was it?"

Tony shifted and saw the first lady lean close to her companion and whisper the answer in her ear.

The second lady's eyes widened; her jaw dropped. Then she looked at the first. "*No!* Truly?"

Lips thinning, the first lady nodded.

The second flicked open her fan and waved it. "Great heavens! And she with that ravishing sister of hers in tow. *Well!*"

Tony fought to keep his expression from hardening, from revealing anything of the maelstrom of emotions that rose up and buffeted his mind—and him. Inwardly grim, he spent a few more minutes with the sweet young things, then excused himself and headed for the door.

Only to have Felicité step into his path. "You're not leaving so soon?" She put a hand on his arm; immediately concern flared in her eyes. She lowered her voice. "What is it?"

He hesitated, then said, "I'm engaged on some business. I have to go."

Her concern only deepened. "I thought you'd finished with such things."

His short laugh was harsh. "So did I. But not yet." He eased her hand from his sleeve and bowed over it. "I must go—there's someone I have to see."

Her gaze had flicked to where he'd been, then to the garden. He could see the connections forming in her mind. He stepped away.

She looked back at him. "If you must go, you must, but take care. And you must tell me later."

With a curt nod, he left. For once, he didn't stop to consider his plan.

* * *

Alicia strolled the clipped lawns of the park in the wake of Adriana and her swains. A morning promenade was becoming a regular event in their schedule. The gentlemen preferred the less-structured, less-cramped encounters such a stroll allowed; it gave them more time to worship at her sister's feet unfettered by any need to pay attention to any other young lady.

She'd countered that by inviting Miss Tiverton to walk with them. Adriana now strolled beside that young lady while five perfectly eligible gentlemen vied for their attention.

The most prominent, and most assiduous, was Lord Manningham. Alicia studied the undeniably attractive figure he cut in his morning coat, pale, tightly fitting breeches, and black Hessians. His address was polished without being oversmooth, his features were handsome rather than beautiful.

He was turning Adriana's head, and her sister knew it.

It was time, perhaps, to learn more of Geoffrey Manningham.

Especially as he was apparently a friend of Lord Torrington's. He who had almost-kissed her, who without provocation let alone permission had deliberately teased her in her own front hall.

The moment flared in her mind; her nerves tensed . . .

Ruthlessly, she bundled the memory aside—he probably did such things all the time. She refocused on Adriana and her court. Adjusting her parasol, she strolled on.

She had no warning, no premonition of danger, until she heard herself hailed in a voice that cut like a whip.

She whirled, but Torrington was already upon her. Hard fingers closing manacle-like about her elbow, he swung her around and marched her down the lawn, away from the carriageway.

"What—?" She tried to free her arm, but couldn't. She glared at him. "Unhand me, sir!"

He ignored her. He strode on, forcing her with him; she

either had to keep up, or stumble and fall. His face was set like stone, his expression unforgivingly grim. Thunderclouds would have looked more comforting.

She glanced back at the others, strolling on unaware. "Stop! I have to watch over my sister."

He glanced briefly at her—too briefly for her to read his eyes—then lifted his gaze and looked back at the others. "She's with Manningham. She's safe." Looking forward, he growled, "You aren't."

He'd lost his senses. She tugged against his hold, then dragged in a breath. "If you don't stop this instant and let me go—"

Abruptly, he did both. She'd been strolling along the periphery of the fashionable throng; they were now in an area where no others were walking. They were out of earshot of everyone, too far from the carriageway for any to discern even the tenor of their exchange.

On top of that, he stood squarely between her and the rest of the ton. Cutting her off from the world. Stunned, she raised her eyes to his face.

His black gaze impaled her. "What was Ruskin blackmailing you about?"

She blinked; her eyes grew wide. The world lurched and fell away. "Wh—what?"

He gritted his teeth. "Ruskin was blackmailing you. About *what?*" His eyes narrowed to obsidian shards. "What was the hold he had over you?"

When she didn't answer, couldn't get her wits to stop whirling quickly enough—dear God, how had he found out?—his jaw set even harder. From the corner of her eye, she saw his hands clench; locking eyes, she sensed he wanted to seize her, shake her, but was exercising quite amazing restraint.

"Was. He. Blackmailing you?"

The words were uttered with such force they dragged the answer from her. "Yes—*no!* That is . . ." She stopped.

"Which?" He took a half step nearer, towering over

her, menacing, intimidating. Aggression poured from him.

And ignited her temper. She straightened to her full height, tipped back her head, met his piercing black gaze. "Whichever, it is *no* concern of yours."

"Think again."

The low growl skittered over her nerves; she dug her heels in even deeper. "I beg your pardon?" Outraged, she held his gaze, absolutely determined not to quail. "You, my lord, are skating on thin ice. Don't *think* to browbeat me!"

For an instant, they stood, all but toe to toe, certainly will against will, then, to her surprise and immense relief, he eased back. Reined in the sheer male power that beat against her senses.

Yet he didn't shift back; his eyes didn't leave hers. When he spoke, his tone was dark, definite, but harnessed, fractionally more civilized.

"I've been asked to investigate Ruskin's death. I want to know what your connection with him was."

She stared. "Why? *Who*—?"

"Just answer the question. What was your connection with Ruskin?"

She felt the blood drain from her face. "We didn't have any—I told you!"

"Yet he was blackmailing you."

"No—at least, not in the way you mean."

He opened his eyes wide. "What other way is there?"

She had to reply; there was clearly no option. "It wasn't about money. He wanted me to marry him."

He blinked. His tone lost a little of it sureness. "He was blackmailing you to marry him?"

Lips tight, she nodded. "He . . . offered me a *carte blanche*. I refused, and he offered marriage. When I refused that . . . he thought to pressure me into agreeing."

"With what?"

She searched his eyes; his demand was precise, implacable. Who was he?—she didn't really know. "He'd learned something about us—about me—that if it became common knowledge, would make establishing Adriana . . . very difficult. It's nothing nefarious or terrible, but you know what the gossipmongers are like."

"Indeed." The word was clipped, imbued with meaning. "You spoke with him immediately before he left Lady Amery's drawing room. I want to know what was said, and exactly what happened to result in you going into the garden and finding his body."

Whoever he was, he knew far too much. The thought chilled her. He also knew how to interrogate; even restrained, there was a threat in his manner—avoiding his questions wasn't going to be possible. She had absolutely no doubt his claim of being asked to investigate was true.

"I . . ." Her mind slid back to that moment in the drawing room, when Ruskin had threatened to pull the rug from under their future. "As I said, I'd declined his offer of marriage. That evening, he came up and requested a private interview. I refused—I was watching Adriana. He insisted, so we retreated to the side of the room. He told me he lived near Bledington, and had seen us last Christmas, in the square at Chipping Norton."

She refocused on the black eyes fixed so intently on her face. "He'd seen us—we hadn't seen or met him. Not then. Only after we came to London."

"What was it he knew of you?"

Feeling compelled to keep her eyes on his, she considered, eventually moistened her lips. "It's not anything to do with his death. It can't be. It doesn't concern anyone but me."

Tony held her gaze for a full minute; she didn't waver, didn't offer anything more. She was no longer so defiant, but on that one point intractable; she wasn't going to tell him. He forced himself to look away, over her head, forced himself to take a deep breath and think. Eventually, he looked down at her. "Does anyone else in London know of this *thing* that Ruskin knew?"

She blinked, thought. "No." Her voice strengthened. "No one."

He digested that, accepted it. "So he propositioned you—threatened you with exposure." He forced himself to say the words, ignoring the violence the thought evoked. "What then?"

"I asked for time, and he agreed to twenty-four hours. He said he'd call on me the next evening." Remembered horror flitted through her eyes; he wondered what she wasn't telling him. "Then he walked away."

When she said nothing more, he prompted, "What then?"

"I was upset." She seemed not to notice the hand she raised to her throat. "I asked for a glass of water, sat, then I started to think again, and realized he . . . that it might be possible to buy him off. I stood and saw him slip out of the terrace doors. I decided to follow and speak with him—at least convince him to give me more time."

Remembered fear tinged her voice. Swallowing an oath, he suppressed the urge to haul her into his arms; she'd probably struggle. "So you followed him out?"

She nodded. "But first I crossed the room to Adriana. I told her where I was going."

"Then you went onto the terrace?"

"Yes, but he wasn't there. It was chilly—I looked around and saw movement beneath that huge tree. I assumed it was he, so I went down. Then I found him . . ." She paused. "You know the rest."

"Did you see anyone else go out on the terrace before you did—or before Ruskin did?"

"No. But I wasn't watching the doors."

Regardless, it was unlikely a gentleman wearing a coat and hat would leave Amery House via the drawing room and the terrace doors. Fitting her information with his, it seemed clear what had happened.

She'd taken advantage of his silence to regroup.

He met her gaze. "I take it Ruskin made no mention of going to meet anyone."

"No. Why? Oh . . . I suppose he must have met someone."

"He did. As I came up Park Street, I saw a gentleman in a coat and hat leave by the garden gate. He was too far away for me to identify, but he definitely came out of that gate. Allowing time for you to walk to the tree, and for me to walk to the gate, it must have been he—that man—you saw moving beneath the tree."

She paled. Looked at him, stared at him. After a long moment, she asked, "Who are you?"

He let two heartbeats pass, then replied, "You know my name."

"I know I have only your word that there was another man, that it wasn't you who stabbed Ruskin."

The accusation pricked; holding her gaze, he softly said, "You might want to consider that I'm all that stands between you and a charge of murder."

The instant he uttered the words, he wished them unsaid.

Her head snapped up. She stepped back. "I do not understand what right you have to question me—interrogate me—*or my family.*" Her eyes blazed; her tone was scathing. "In future, please leave us alone."

She turned.

He caught her hand. "Alicia—"

She swung on him; fury lit her eyes. "*Don't* presume to call me that! I have *not* given you leave—and I won't." She looked down at his fingers circling her wrist. "Please release me immediately."

He had to force his fingers to do it, to slide from her skin; she snatched her hand away, backed two steps, watching him—as if she suddenly saw him for what he truly was.

Her eyes had widened; for an instant, he glimpsed a vulnerability he couldn't place.

Alicia fought to subdue the emotions roiling inside her. Her stomach was knotted, her lungs tight. He'd played with her brothers, interrogated them and Adriana, flirted quite deliberately with her. All because . . . and she'd thought he was honest, that he was trustworthy, genuine . . . how foolish she'd been.

When he said nothing, she dragged in a breath. "I've told you all I know. Please"—for the first time, her voice quavered—"don't come near me again."

With that, she whirled and walked quickly away.

Tony watched her go. Then he swore comprehensively in French and strode off in the opposite direction.

He hailed a hackney and headed into the city. Resting his head against the squabs, he closed his eyes and concentrated on getting his temper under control and his thoughts straight; it had been years since they'd been so tangled.

He'd stalked into the park furious with her for concealing from him such a potentially dangerous connection. Not because that concealment interfered with his investigation, but purely because the damned woman hadn't availed herself of his abilities—his protection.

Because she deliberately hadn't trusted him.

Stalking out of the park, he'd been furious with himself. She'd questioned who he was, his integrity, and he'd reacted by taking a high hand, which any fool could have predicted would fail miserably—in his case, spectacularly.

He hadn't meant it to sound as it had, hadn't in the least meant to threaten her.

Eyes still closed, he sighed. In thirteen years of operations, he'd never let his personal life interfere with his duty. Now the two were inextricably entwined. She hadn't killed Ruskin, but courtesy of whoever had started the rumors, she was now involved. Worse, he had a nasty suspicion that the person who had started the rumors would prove to be Ruskin's killer. If threatened, he might kill again.

He spent the rest of the day in the city, using his erstwhile talents to gain access to Ruskin's banking records. A combination of suggestion and implied threat, together with his title and the supercilious arrogance he'd learned long ago worked so well with those whose status depended on patronage, got him what he wanted.

His first stop was Daviot & Sons, the bank Ruskin had favored, exclusively as far as the notes in his rooms went. Ten minutes, and he'd gained access to all documents relating to Ruskin's dealings. The records revealed no major sums credited to Ruskin's account, only a trickle of income the bank verified came from Gloucestershire, believed to be derived from Ruskin's estate. There were no large deposits, nor any large withdrawals. Wherever the wealth Ruskin had used to pay off his considerable debts hailed from, it had not passed through the hands of the Messrs Daviot.

He proceeded to check all the likely banks; they were located in close proximity, scattered about the Bank of England and the Corn Exchange. Using his success at Daviots to pave the way, he encountered no resistance; by afternoon's end, he'd established that the city's legitimate financiers had not facilitated the flow of pounds to Ruskin's gaming acquaintances.

Hailing a hackney, he headed back to Mayfair. On the evidence of Ruskin's IOUs, the man had been not only a poor gambler but an addicted one. He'd lost steadily for years, yet there was no indication of any panic in his dealings. He'd paid off every debt *regularly* . . .

Muttering a curse, Tony tapped on the roof; when the

jarvey inquired his pleasure, he replied, "Bury Street—Number 23."

There had to be—*had to be*—some record somewhere. Ruskin was a clerk by nature; the contents of his desks, both in his office and his rooms, testified to his compulsive neatness. He'd even kept those old IOUs in chronological order.

The hackney halted in Bury Street; Tony swung down to the pavement, tossed a coin to the jarvey, and strode quickly up the steps of Number 23. This time, an old man let him in.

"I'm from Customs and Revenue—I have to check Mr. Ruskin's rooms for something I might have missed when I checked yesterday."

"Oh, aye." The old man stood back. "You'll know the way, then."

"Indeed. I have his key. I'll be a few minutes—I can see myself out."

The old man merely nodded and shuffled back into the downstairs front room. Tony climbed the stairs.

Once in Ruskin's rooms with the door shut and re-locked, he stood in the center of the rug and looked around. He imagined himself in Ruskin's shoes; assuming he'd kept a record of his illicit dealings and had wanted to keep that record secret, where would he have hidden it?

The room was clean, neat, dusted; the furniture was polished and well cared for. Someone came in to clean. Whatever secret hole Ruskin had, it would be somewhere not likely to be found by a busy char woman.

Behind the solid skirting boards was unlikely; the cleared floor space, even under the rugs, would be too risky. Working as silently as he could, Tony shifted the heavy furniture and checked beneath and behind, but found only solid walls and solid floorboards, and dust.

Undeterred, he checked inside the small closet, shifting the items he'd searched before. He pressed, prodded, gently tapped, but there was no hint of any secret place. Next, he examined the door and window frames, searching for any crevice opening into a useful gap within the walls. There wasn't one.

Which left the fireplaces and their chimneys.

There were two—one in the parlor and a smaller one in the bedroom. The mantelpieces and hearths were easily examined; no luck there. With a resigned sigh, Tony stripped off his coat and rolled up his shirtsleeves before tackling the chimneys.

He saw the place as soon as he crouched down, ducked his head, and looked into the parlor chimney. Enough light seeped past his shoulders for him to discern the single brick, up on the side well above the flames' reach, that was considerably less grimed than its fellows. Its edges were free of soot and the detritus of years. Reaching in, he pressed one corner; the brick edged out of place. It was easy to grip it and drag it free.

Setting the brick down, he dusted his fingers, then reached into the gaping hole. His fingertips encountered the smooth surface of leather. He felt around, then drew out a small, black leather-bound book.

Grinning, he laid the book on the floor and replaced the brick. That done, he cleaned his hands on his handkerchief, then rolled down his sleeves and shrugged on his coat. Picking up the book, he hefted it—then gave in to temptation and quickly leafed through it.

It was exactly what he'd hoped to find—a miniledger that many gamesters kept, noting their wins and losses. The book was almost full; the entries stretched back to 1810. Each entry comprised a date, the initials of the opponent, and sometimes the name of the game—whist, piquet, hazard—and the sum involved; the latter was placed in one of two columns ruled at the right of the page—either a loss or a win.

In Ruskin's little black book, the losses greatly outnumbered the wins. However, the tally of wins and losses, scrupulously noted at the end of each page, was readjusted every few months, being brought back into balance by an entry, repeated again and again, of a substantial sum, noted as a win.

Tony checked back through the book. The regular "wins" started in early 1812. Although always substantial, the sums varied; the initials noted for each payment did not.

A. C.

Tony felt his face harden. He looked up. His mind in a whirl, he closed the book and slid it into his pocket. A moment later, he stirred, and headed for the door.

He was on his way down the stairs when the old man stuck his head out of the downstairs room. He squinted at Tony, then recognized him, nodded, and moved to retreat.

Tony reacted. "One moment, sir, if you would."

The old man turned back.

Tony assumed a faintly harrassed expression. "Have there been any other visitors to Mr. Ruskin's rooms since he died?"

The old man blinked, thought, then opined, "Well, not since you folk came by, but there was a gentl'man called here the night Mr. Ruskin met his end. It was late, so mayhap that was after he died."

"This gentleman, was he one of Mr. Ruskin's friends? A regular acquaintance?"

"Not that I ever saw. Never seen him before."

"What happened on that night?"

The old man leaned on his cane; he peered up at Tony with eyes that retained a deal of shrewdness. "It was late, as I said. The man rapped politely, and as it wasn't after midnight, I let him in. I was sure Ruskin was out, but the gentleman insisted he'd go up and check . . . didn't seem any harm in that, so I let him. He went up the stairs, and a minute later I heard the door open, so I thought, then, that Ruskin must have slipped in, and I hadn't noticed. I left them to it and went back to my fire."

Tony stirred. "Ruskin hadn't come home. He spent most of the evening at a soirée in Green Street. It was there, in the garden, that he was killed."

"Aye. So we heard the next day. Howsoever, that night, the gentleman that called and went into Ruskin's rooms stayed for more than an hour. I could hear him moving around; he wasn't thumping about, but it's quiet around here at night. One hears things."

"Did you see him when he left?"

"No—I'd put the door on the latch and gone to bed. They can still let themselves out, but the door locks as it closes."

"Can you describe this gentleman?"

Running his eye up Tony, the old man grimaced. "I can't recall much—no reason to, then. But he was decently tall, not so tall as you though, but more heavily built. Well built. He was nicely kitted out, that I do remember—his coat had one of those fancy fur collars, like rippling curls."

Astrakhan. A vision flashed into Tony's mind—the glimpse he'd caught at a distance as the unknown man leaving the Amery House gardens had passed beneath a streetlamp. His thought had been "well rugged up"—prompted by the astrakhan collar of the man's coat.

"And," the old man continued, "he was a toff like you. Spoke well, and had that way about him, the way he walked and carried his cane."

Tony nodded. "How old? What color hair? Was there anything notable about him—a squint, a big nose?"

"He'd be older than you—forties at least, but well kept. His hair was brownish, but as for his face, there was nothing you'd notice. Regular features"—the old man squinted again at Tony—"though not as regular as yours." He shrugged. "He was a well-dressed gentl'man such as you'd find on any street about here."

Tony thanked the man.

Once on the pavement, he paused, then set off for Upper Brook Street; the walk would do him good, perhaps clear his mind. An A. C. had paid Ruskin large sums for the last four years. Be that as it may, he was perfectly certain things were not as they seemed.

A few hours closeted in his library clarified matters, at least as far as identifying his immediate next steps.

Through Ruskin's blackmail and fateful coincidence, Alicia Carrington was being drawn further and further into his investigation. Given his personal interest, he needed to regain lost ground rapidly—needed to regain her trust. Doing so would require an apology, and worse, explanations. All of which necessitated a certain amount of planning, which in turn required a certain amount of reconnoitering. His groom returned from the mews near Waverton Street with the necessary details, by which time he'd formulated his plan.

He began its implementation with a note to his godmother, then sent a different note around to Manningham House.

When the clocks struck nine, he and Geoffrey were propping the wall of Lady Herrington's ballroom, keeping a careful eye on the arrivals.

"I would never have thought of sending around a groom." Eyes on the throng, Geoffrey seemed to be relishing his role.

"Stick with me, and you'll learn all sorts of useful tricks." Tony kept his gaze on the ballroom stairs.

Geoffrey softly snorted.

The strands of old companionship had regrown quickly, somewhat to the surprise of them both. Tony was four years Geoffrey's senior; much of their childhood had been colored by Geoffrey's need to cast himself as Tony's rival. Despite that, there'd been many occasions when they'd combined forces in various devilry; the friendship beneath the rivalry had been strong.

"There they are." Tony straightened. At the top of the

steps, he'd glimpsed a coronet of dark hair above a pale forehead.

Geoffrey craned his head. "Are you sure?"

"Positive." Which was of itself revealing. "Remember—the instant they reach the bottom of the steps. Ready?"

"Right behind you."

They swooped as planned, a perfectly executed attack that separated Alicia and Adriana the instant the sisters set foot on the ballroom floor. Geoffrey took Adriana's hand—offered with a delighted smile—and smoothly cut in, drawing Adriana forward while simultaneously insinuating himself between the sisters, cutting Alicia off from Adriana's immediate view.

Before Alicia could even gather her wits, she was captured, swept aside; Tony propelled her across the front of the ballroom steps and around into their lee, where a small and as yet uncrowded little foyer stood before a closed door.

They'd reached the foyer before she caught her breath.

Then she did. Her eyes swung to his face. They blazed.

He caught that scorching glance, held it. Her breasts swelled; her lips parted—on a scathing denunciation he had not a doubt. "*Don't* fight me." He spoke softly; there was steel in his voice. "Don't look daggers at me, and for God's sake don't rip up at me. I *have* to talk to you."

Her jaw set mulishly. She tugged her right arm, firmly gripped in his right hand; his left arm was around her waist, steering her on. She tried to stop, to dig in her heels, but she was wearing ballroom slippers. "If we must, we can talk here!"

He didn't pause, but looked down at her, leaned closer, drawing her into the shield of his body. "No, we can't. You wouldn't like it, and neither would I."

He released her arm to fling open the door, catching her in his left arm when she tried to step back. He swept her over the threshold and followed, shutting the door behind him, by sheer physical presence forcing her on along the corridor beyond.

She hissed in frustration, took two steps, then swung to face him and glared. "This is ridiculous! You can't simply—"

"Not here." He caught her arm again, propelled her on. "The door on the left at the end is our best bet."

He could sense her temper rising, seething like a volcano. "Our best bet for *what*?" she muttered beneath her breath.

He glanced at her, but held his tongue.

They reached the door in question; he sent it swinging wide. This time, she entered of her own volition, sweeping in like a galleon under full sail. He followed, shutting the door, taking note of her gown—a sleekly draped silk confection in bronzy, autumnal shades that became her extremely well.

She turned on him, faced him; the silk tightened over her breasts as she dragged in a deep breath—

He heard a click as the door at the head of the corridor opened. The noise of the ball washed in, abruptly cut off again as the door was shut. A woman giggled, the sound quickly smothered.

Reaching behind him, he snibbed the lock on the door.

Too far from the corridor to realize the danger, eyes blazing, Alicia opened her mouth to deliver the broadside he undoubtedly deserved.

He stepped forward, jerked her into his arms, and silenced her—saved them—in the only possible way.

FIVE

HE KISSED HER.

Her mouth had been open, her lips parted; he slid between, caressed, claimed—and felt her attention splinter. Her hands had gripped his upper arms; they tensed, but she didn't push him away. She clung, held on.

As a whirlpool of want rose up and engulfed them.

He hadn't intended it, had had no idea how much he wanted, how much hunger he possessed, or how readily it would rise to her lure. Hands framing her face, he angled his head and flagrantly feasted. Asking for no permission, giving no quarter, he plunged them both into the fire. She was a widow, not a skittish virgin; he didn't need to explain things to her.

Such as the nature of his want. His tongue tangling with hers, aggressively plundering, he released her face and gathered her to him. Into his arms, against his hard frame. Glorying in the supple softness that promised to ease his ache, he molded her to him, blatantly shifted his hips against hers. He felt her spine soften as she sank into him.

As her bones melted and her knees gave way.

Alicia struggled to cling to her wits, but time and again he ripped them away. Her breath was long gone; with their mouths melded she could only breathe through him—she'd given up the fight to do otherwise.

Her head spun—pleasurably. Warmth, burgeoning heat,

spread through her veins. Intoxicating. Shocking. She tried to cling to her anger, rekindle her fury, but could not.

She'd had only a second's warning, but she'd expected a kiss—a touching of lips, not this ravenous, flagrantly intimate exchange. Mild kisses she could cope with, but this? It was new territory, unknown and dangerous, yet she couldn't—*could not*—let her innocence, her inexperience show.

No matter how much her senses swam, how much her wits had seized in sheer shock.

She had nothing to guide her but him. In desperation, she mimicked the play of his tongue against hers, and sensed his immediate approval. In seconds, they were engaged in a duel, in a sensual game of thrust and parry.

Of lips and tongues, of heated softness and beguiling aggression, of shared breaths and, amazingly, shared hunger.

It caught her, dragged at her mind. Drew her in. Held her captive.

He urged her closer still, one hand sliding down her back to splay over her hips, her bottom, lifting her and pressing her to him.

Sensation streaked over her skin, prickling, heated; she clung tight, felt the world whirl.

And she was engulfed in his strength, enveloped by it, a potent masculine power that seemed to weaken every bone in her body, that promised heat and flames so dizzyingly pleasurable all she wanted was to wantonly wallow, to give herself up to them and be consumed.

On one level it was frightening, but she couldn't retreat—had wit enough left to know she couldn't panic, couldn't run.

She was supposed to be a widow. She had to stand there, accept all, and respond as if she understood.

Eventually his aggression eased, the tension riding him gradually, step by step, reined in. Gripping his arms, fingers sunk deep, she felt that drawing back; the kiss lightened, became a more gentle if still intimate caress, lips clinging, teasing, still wanting.

At last he raised his head, but not far.

Her lips felt swollen and hot; from beneath her lashes, she glanced at his eyes. His black gaze touched her eyes, held, then he sighed. Bent and touched his lips to the corner of hers.

"I didn't intend this. There were people in the corridor. A danger . . ."

Deep, gravelly, the words feathered her cheek; sensation, hot and immediate, flashed over her.

"I wanted to apologize . . ." He paused, raised his head. Again she met his eyes, again found them waiting to capture hers. Something predatory flashed in the rich blackness, then he continued, "Not for this. Not for anything I've done or even said, but for how what I said in the park sounded."

His tone was still low, slightly rough, teasing something—some response—from her.

Her gaze had drifted to his lips; his hands tightened on her back, and she looked up, eyes widening as she felt the heat between them flare again.

He caught her gaze, held it. "I'm not Ruskin. I will never hurt or harm you. I want to protect you, not threaten you." He hesitated, then went on, "Even this—I didn't plan it."

This. He was still holding her close, not as tight as before yet just as flagrantly. Only lovers, she was perfectly certain, should ever be this close. Yet she didn't dare pull back, fought instead to ignore the warm flush the embrace sent coursing through her. What had gone before no longer seemed terribly relevant.

"So—" She broke off, shocked by the sound of her voice, low, almost sultry. She moistened her lips, tried for a normal tone. Didn't quite manage it. "What had you planned?" She met his eyes, clung to her bold front.

He studied her face, then his lips twisted. "I spoke the truth—I do need to speak with you."

He made no move to release her. How would an experienced widow react? She forced herself to remain passive in his arms and raised a haughty brow. "About what? I wasn't aware we had anything to discuss."

One black brow arched—arrogantly; holding her gaze, he deliberately shifted her against him, settling her in his arms—sending her senses reeling again. "Obviously"— he gave the word blatant weight—"there's much we could, and later will, discuss. However . . ."

The room, a small parlor overlooking the gardens, was unlit, but her eyes had adjusted—she could see his face well enough. Although he didn't physically sigh, she sensed his mind lift from them and refocus on something beyond. A frown in his eyes, he looked down at her, studied her face.

"When did you marry Carrington?"

She stared at him. "Marry?"

His frown grew more definite. "Humor me. When was your wedding?"

"Ah." She struggled to remember when it must have been. "Eighteen months—no, more like two years ago, now."

She dragged in a breath, struggled to ignore the way her breasts pressed into his chest, how her nipples tightened, and dragooned her wits into order. He was investigating Ruskin's death; she couldn't afford to prod his suspicions. "It was a very short marriage. Poor Alfred—it was terribly sad."

His brow arched again. "So you've been Alicia Carrington for only two years?"

She checked her calculations. "Yes." She bit her tongue against adding anything more; better to keep her answers short.

He didn't seem to notice; he seemed, not exactly relieved, but pleased. "Good!"

When she looked her surprise, he smiled rather grimly. "So you can't be A. C."

"Who's A. C.?"

"The person who paid Ruskin for his treasonous services."

She stared at him. Her lips formed the word twice before she managed to utter it. *"What?"*

Tony grimaced. He looked around. "Here." Reluctantly releasing her, he steered her to a chaise. "Sit down, and I'll tell you."

It hadn't come easily, his acceptance that if he wanted her trust, he would have to tell her, if not all, then at least most of what was going on, how he was involved, how she was involved—how she was threatened. He needed her cooperation for reasons that struck much deeper than his mission; that mission—his investigation—was a whip he could use to command her, but only one thing would suffice to make her trust him. To lean on him as he wished her to.

Appeasement—a peace offering, some gift on his part—was the only way to nudge her onto the path he'd chosen. The most important element between them right now was the truth; as far as he was able, he would give her that.

He waited while, with a suspicious and wary glance, she sat and settled her skirts, then he sat beside her and took her hand in his. Looked down, played with her fingers as he assembled his words.

Then, keeping his voice low yet clear enough for her to easily hear, he told her simply, without embellishment, all he'd learned of Ruskin.

She listened, increasingly attentive, but made no comment.

But when he came to how and where he'd discovered the initials A. C., her fingers tensed, tightened on his. He glanced at her.

She studied his eyes, searched his face. Then she

breathed in tightly. "You know I didn't kill him—that I'm innocent of all this?"

Not so much a question as a request for a clear statement.

"Yes." He raised her hand to his lips, held her gaze as he kissed. "I know you didn't kill him. I know you're not involved in any treasonous use of shipping information." He lowered their locked hands, then added, "However, you—we—have to face the fact that *someone* started the rumor I heard."

"I can't understand it—*how* could anyone know?"

"Are you sure, absolutely sure, that your secret, whatever it is, was known only by Ruskin?"

Frowning, she met his gaze, then looked away. Her hand remained resting in his. After a moment, she replied, "It might be possible that, in the same way Ruskin had learned what he had, then someone else might have, too. But what I can't understand is how that someone could know Ruskin was using the information as he was."

She looked at him.

"Indeed. Blackmail doesn't work if others know." He paused, then added, "From what I've learned of Ruskin, he wasn't the sort to give away valuable information. He'd have charged for it, and—"

Releasing her hand, he stood; he thought better on his feet. "The dates of payments noted in his black book not only match the dates he paid his debts, but also follow by about a week the dates he noted for certain ships." He paced, caught her eye. "However, there's no other payment—any unaccounted payment—entered. So I think we're on firm ground in assuming he hadn't sold any information other than the shipping directives."

Halting by the fireplace, he considered her. "So the question remains. Who would he have told about you, and why?"

Her brow creased as she looked at him; her gaze grew distant.

"What?"

She flicked him an impatient glance. "I was just wondering . . ."

When he moved toward her, she quickly continued, "When he left me, Ruskin was sure—absolutely confident—that I'd agree to his proposal. He"—she paused, blushed, but lifted her head and went on—"was so certain he expected to call the next evening and . . . receive my acceptance."

After a moment, she met his eyes. "I didn't know him well, but given his nature, he probably couldn't help gloating. About me—I mean, about gaining a wealthy widow as his wife."

Tony could visualize such a scenario readily, but he doubted it was her wealth Ruskin would have gloated about. Nevertheless . . .

"That would fit." He paced again. "If Ruskin, quite unsuspectingly, mentioned his coup—and yes, I agree, he was the type of man to gloat, then . . ." Bits and pieces of the jigsaw slid into place.

"What?"

He glanced at her, and found her glaring at him; he felt his lips ease. "Consider this. If Ruskin was murdered by whoever he'd been selling his information to—"

"By this A. C., you mean?"

He nodded. "Then if he mentioned he was about to marry, quite aside from any risk from the blackmail going wrong—it's always a risky business—the knowledge that Ruskin would soon have a wife would have increased the threat Ruskin posed to A. C."

"In case he told his wife?"

"Or she found out. Ruskin even mentioning knowing A. C., even years from now, might have been dangerous."

Alicia pieced together the picture he was painting. At one level, she could barely believe all that had happened since they'd entered the room. That searing kiss—it was as if it had cindered, felled, and consumed all barriers between them. He was talking to her, treating her, as if she was an accomplice, a partner in his investigation. More, a friend.

Almost a lover.

And she was reacting as if she were.

She was amazed at herself. She didn't—never had—trusted so readily. Yet if she was honest, it was why she'd been so furious with him in the park, when, despite her totally unwarranted trust—one he'd somehow earned in a few short days—it had seemed his interest in her and her family had all been fabricated. False.

That kiss hadn't been false.

It had been a statement, unplanned maybe, but once made, it couldn't be retracted—and he hadn't tried. It had happened, and he'd accepted it.

She had no choice but to do the same.

Especially as she, innocent or not, was being drawn deeper and deeper into the web of intrigue surrounding Ruskin's murder.

"Is this what you think happened?" She didn't look up, but sensed his attention fasten on her. "Presumably the man—let's assume he's A. C.—had arrived in the Amery House gardens via the garden gate. Ruskin went out to meet him—it had to have been an arranged meeting."

Torrington—Tony—drew nearer. "Yes."

"So then Ruskin babbled about his soon-to-be conquest—me—but . . ." Frowning, she glanced up. "Had Ruskin some information to sell, or had A. C. come there with murder on his mind?"

Tony mentally reviewed all Ruskin's notes on shipping. None had been recent. Even more telling . . . "I don't think there could be anything worthwhile for Ruskin to sell. With the war over, the information he had access to wouldn't be all that useful. . . ."

He was aware of her watching him, trying to read his face, follow his thoughts. He glanced at her. "I haven't yet defined how the information Ruskin passed on was used, but it's telling his association with A. C. began in early '12. That was when naval activity once again became critical. From '12 up until Waterloo, shipping was constantly under threat. Now, however, there is no significant danger on the seas."

He was going to have to pursue that angle hard, and soon.

She took up the tale before he could. "If Ruskin no longer had anything of real use to A. C., then . . ." She looked up at him.

He met her gaze. "A. C., assuming he has a position and reputation to protect, would have been threatened by Ruskin's continued existence."

"If Ruskin was not above blackmailing me . . ."

"Indeed. He may not have called it by that name, but given his debts, he would have needed an injection of capital quite soon, and almost certainly would have looked to A. C."

"Who decided to end their association." She nodded. "Very well. So while Ruskin is gloating, A. C. stabs him and leaves him dead. I come down the path—" She paled. "Do you think A. C. saw me?"

He considered, then shook his head. "The timing—when I saw him on the street—makes that unlikely."

"But then how did he know it was me Ruskin was blackmailing? Would Ruskin have told him my name?"

"Unlikely, but A. C.—and I agree, it most likely was he—didn't need your name to start the rumors."

She frowned at him. "These rumors—what exactly do they say?"

"That Ruskin was blackmailing some lady—a widow."

Her frown deepened. "But there are many widows in the ton."

"Indeed, but only one was seen talking to Ruskin immediately before he died."

Her gaze remained locked with his, then, abruptly, all color drained from her face. "Oh, good heavens!"

She sprang to her feet; her eyes flashed fire at him as if he was in some way culpable. "If they've decided I'm the widow in question, then what . . . ? *Good lord!* Adriana!"

Whirling, she raced for the door. He got there before her, closing his hand about the knob. "It's all right—calm down!" He caught her gaze as she paused, impatient before the door. "Manningham's with her."

Her eyes flashed again. "You and he planned this."

He tried to frown her down. "I had to talk to you."

"That's all very well, but what's been happening out there"—she jabbed a finger toward the ballroom—"while we've been talking?"

"Nothing. Most will be waiting, wondering where you are, hoping to catch a glimpse but not surprised given the crush that they haven't yet succeeded." He took in her wide eyes, the tension now gripping her. "There's no need to panic. They don't know it's you, and they only will know if you behave as if it is. As if you're frightened, or watchful. Ready to take flight."

Alicia met his steady gaze. To her surprise, she drew comfort from it. She drew in a breath. "So I have to carry it off with a high head and a high hand?"

"Absolutely. You can't afford to let those hyenas sense fear."

Despite all, her lips twitched. Hyenas? The hard line of his lips eased; she realized he'd deliberately tried to make her smile.

Then his gaze flicked up to her eyes.

He lowered his head—slowly; she sucked in a breath.

Held it as her lids fell and his lips touched hers—not in a tantalizing teasing caress, yet neither with their earlier ravenous hunger.

A definite promise; that's what the kiss was—as simple as that.

Slowly, he raised his head; their lips clung for an instant, then parted.

Lifting her lids, she met his black gaze.

He searched her eyes, then turned the knob and opened the door. "Come. Let's face down the ton."

She returned to the ballroom on his arm, calm, her usual poise to the fore. It was all a sham, but she was now an expert in the art of pulling wool over the ton's collective eyes.

One thing he'd said stuck in her mind: watchful. She had to stop herself from looking around, from searching for signs that people suspected her. She had to appear oblivious; it was the most difficult charade she'd ever performed.

He helped. On his arm, she strolled; he was attentive, charming, chatting inconsequentially as two such as they might. He was a wealthy peer; she was a wealthy, well-born widow. They didn't need to hide a friendship.

They progressed down the room; she smiled, laughed lightly, and let her gaze rest on the dancers but no one else. He distracted her whenever the temptation to scrutinize those watching them burgeoned.

At one point, his lips curved rakishly; he bent his head to whisper, "They're totally confused."

She met his gaze as he straightened. "About what?"

"About which rumor they should spread."

When she looked her question, with a self-deprecatory quirk of his lips he explained, "The one about you and Ruskin, or the one about you and me."

She looked into his black eyes. Blinked. "Oh."

"Indeed. So all we need do is continue on our present tack, and their befuddlement will be complete."

Just which tack he meant she discovered a minute later.

She'd expected him to guide her to Adriana's side; her sister wasn't on the dance floor, which surprised and concerned her—she hadn't yet located her among the crowd. Instead, he led her to a chaise midway down the long ballroom. Lady Amery was seated on it, along with an older lady Alicia had previously met.

Nervousness struck; her fingers fluttered on Tony's sleeve. Instantly, his hand closed, warm and comforting, over hers. Steering her to the chaise, he bowed to the two dames. "*Tante* Felicité. Lady Osbaldestone."

Spine poker straight, Lady Osbaldestone nodded regally back.

"I believe you're both acquainted with Mrs. Carrington?"

Alicia curtsied.

"Indeed." Lady Amery reached for her hands; her eyes glowed with welcome. "My dear, I must apologize for this *dreadful* business. I am most distressed that it was your attendance at *my* soirée that has given rise to such unpleasantness. Why, there are any number of widows in the ton, and as we all know, many of those others are much more certain to have secrets to hide. So foolish of these *bourgeoisie*"—with a contemptuous flick of her hand she dismissed them—"to imagine you had any connection with Mr. Ruskin beyond the natural one of living nearby."

Her ladyship paused; bright eyes fixed on Alicia's face, she surreptitiously pressed her fingers. "Tony tells me you spoke with Mr. Ruskin, but it was purely an exchange about mutual acquaintances in the country."

In the corridor just before they'd reentered the ballroom, he'd primed her with that tale. Alicia longed to turn her head and glare at him; he hadn't mentioned this little encounter he'd arranged for her.

"Indeed." To her relief, the glamor she'd perfected over the last weeks didn't waver; she smiled with easy assurance tempered with just the right touch of innocent bewilderment. "We hail from the same area. Although we only met recently, here in town, we shared a number of mutual acquaintances. It was they we discussed in your drawing room that evening."

Lady Osbaldestone humphed, drawing Alicia's attention. The old black eyes assessing her were a great deal sharper and harder than Tony's ever were. "In that case, you'll have to excuse those with nothing better to do than wag their tongues and make mischief. For my money, they've hay for brains.

"I ask you," she continued, "even if Ruskin was blackmailing some widow, what has that to say to anything?" She gave a dismissive snort. "The idea of some lady in evening dress pulling a stiletto from her reticule and stabbing him to death is ludicrous. Aside from the fact he was no weakling, and would hardly have obligingly stood still while she poked him, where would she have carried the blade?" The black eyes flashed, at Tony as well as Alicia. "That's what I'd like to know. Have you ever seen one of those things? *Pshaw!* It's not possible."

Apparently entertained, Tony inclined his head. "As you say. I heard the authorities are looking for a man at least as tall as Ruskin."

"Indeed?" Lady Osbaldestone brightened at the news. "Not perhaps revealing, but interesting nevertheless." She rose; although she carried a cane, she rarely used it.

She was a tall woman, taller than Alicia; her face had never been pretty, but not even age could dim the strength of its aristocratic lines. Her piercing black eyes rested on Alicia, then her lips lifted, and she looked at Tony. "Send my regards to your mother when next you bestir yourself to write. Tell her Helena sends her fondest wishes, too." Lifting her cane, she jabbed it at him. "Don't forget!"

"Naturally not." Eyes on the cane, Tony bowed with a flourish. "I wouldn't dare."

With a glint in her eye, Lady Osbaldestone regally acknowledged Alicia's bobbed curtsy and Lady Amery's salute, then glided away.

"Well, there you are!" Lady Amery beamed at Tony and Alicia. "It is done, and Therese will do the rest, you may be sure." She lifted a hand, waved it at Tony; he took it and helped her to her feet.

"*Bien!* So now I am going to enjoy myself, too, and see

what a stir I can cause." She glanced at Alicia, and patted her arm. "And you must go and dance, and pretend not to notice, and it will all blow over, my dear. You'll see."

Alicia looked into Lady Amery's button-bright eyes, then impulsively squeezed her hand. "Thank you."

Her ladyship's eyes glowed brighter. "No, no, *chérie*. That is not necessary—indeed, it is I who must thank you." Her gaze shifted to Tony. "I am an old woman, and I have been waiting an age to be asked to help. At last it has happened, and you are the cause. It is good." She patted Alicia's hand and released it. "Now go and dance, and I will go and make mischief."

The first strains of a waltz were percolating through the room; Tony offered his arm. "I suspect your sister will be located most easily on the dance floor."

Alicia narrowed her eyes at him, but consented to place her hand on his arm. He steered her to the floor; seconds later they were whirling.

She took a few minutes to adjust, to regain her breath, realign her wits and subdue her clamorous senses. The physical power with which he so effortlessly swept her along, the shift and sway of their bodies, the subtle repetitive temptation of their limbs brushing, touching, then moving away—the waltz was a seduction in itself, at least the way he danced it.

Surreptitiously clearing her throat, she looked up; she studied his expression, arrogant, latent charm lurking, yet difficult to read. "Why did you ask Lady Amery to help?"

He glanced down at her. "She's my godmother. You heard her—she's been waiting for the bugle call for years." He looked ahead, then added, "It seemed appropriate."

"It's *you* she wanted to help, not me."

His lips quirked. "Actually, no—it's *you* she's been waiting all my life to aid."

She frowned and would have pursued the odd point, but a flash of dark curls caught her eye. Turning, she saw

Adriana whirling down the room in Geoffrey Manning-ham's arms. Her sister was . . . the only fitting word was scintillating. She drew eye after male eye, and a good many female ones, too. Her delight seemed to fill her and overflow.

Alicia looked at Tony, caught his eye. "Please tell me your friend is entirely trustworthy."

He grinned; after whirling her through the turns at the end of the room, he dutifully parroted, "Geoffrey is entirely trustworthy." He paused, then added, "At least where your sister's concerned."

"What does that mean?"

"It means he won't do anything you would disapprove of."

She blinked at him. "Why not?"

"Because if he makes you unhappy, then I'll be unhappy, and Geoffrey and I have been down that road before."

She studied his eyes. A vise slowly tightened about her lungs. Then she forced in a breath, lifted her head, fixed her gaze over his left shoulder, and stated, "If you imagine I'll be grateful . . ."

Her courage failed her; she couldn't go on. But he thought her a widow, and clearly had a certain interest, and just possibly imagined. . . .

He frowned at her; from the corner of her eye she watched . . . it took a moment for him to follow her reasoning, then his eyes flared. His lips set in a thin line. The fingers about her hand tightened; the hand at her back tensed . . . then, very slowly, eased.

Eyes narrow, Tony waited; when she didn't look at him, he looked away, unseeing. After a moment, he exhaled. "You are without doubt the most difficult female I've ever—" He bit the words off, abruptly stopped as his temper threatened to erupt. When he had his fury once more in hand, he drew breath and went on, his voice low, tight, very definitely just for her. "I'm not helping you in the expectation of gaining any specific . . ." He cast about in his mind, but could only come up with, *"Service."*

Her eyes flicked to his face, wide, curious, wanting to know.

He trapped her gaze. "I want you, but not as a result of any damned gratitude!"

Her eyes remained on his, then scanned his features. "Why, then"—her voice, too, was low, intensely private—"are you helping me?"

For an instant, he inwardly rocked, then he found the right words—words he could say. "Because you deserve it. Because you and your sister and your demon brothers *don't* deserve the censure of the ton, let alone being implicated in a murder."

For a long moment, she held his gaze, then her lips gently lifted. "Thank you." She looked away; he only just caught her last words. "You're a good man."

He wasn't quite so good as he would have her believe, but he definitely wasn't expecting her gratitude to stretch as far as an invitation to her bed. He *did* expect to be invited to her bed, but not because of his efforts on her behalf.

The next morning, he was still . . . not so much smarting as ruffled, a disordered sensation he appreciated not at all. A vague disgruntlement that she'd even *imagined* that he might *need* to resort to gratitude—

He cut off the thought and headed for the Bastion Club.

Sanity in a disconcerting world—a world with females in it.

He was looking for advice. In the club's drawing room, he found Christian Allardyce slouched in an armchair, his long legs stretched out, ankles crossed, a news sheet propped before his face. He lowered it as Tony entered.

"Ho! And here I've been wondering about these tales of you stumbling over a dead body."

Tony grimaced. "All true, I'm afraid, and there's a

deadly twist. The game's fallen into Dalziel's lap, and guess who he's tapped on the shoulder?"

Christian's brows rose. "And you agreed?"

Elegantly sitting in another chair, Tony shrugged. "Aside from the fact that refusing Dalziel is marginally more difficult than taking an enemy battery single-handed, there were other aspects that attracted me."

"Quite apart from tripping over the body."

"Indeed. From what we have, the man was a traitor of sorts." Crisply, he outlined what he knew of Ruskin, omitting all mention of one lovely widow. After describing the payments made by A. C., he went on, "I wondered if perhaps, if A. C. was truly wise, he might have channeled the payments through a moneylender."

Christian opened his eyes wide. "Used a moneylender to draw the large sums, then paid them back with numerous smaller amounts much easier to explain from his own accounts?"

"Exactly. Do you think that's possible?"

Christian nodded. "I would say so." He met Tony's gaze. "Certainly worth asking."

"Next question: who do I ask? I've never had any dealings with such gentlemen."

"Ah! You've come to the right source."

It was Tony's turn to open his eyes wide. "I would never have imagined you deep in debt and reduced to dealing with moneylenders."

Christian grinned and laid aside the news sheet. "No, I never was. But I once bailed out a friend, and along the way I made the acquaintance of a good handful of the gentlemen. Enough, certainly, to start you on your way."

Folding his hands across his waistcoat, Christian leaned his head back; eyes on the ceiling, he started recounting all he knew.

Tony drank it in. At the end of fifteen minutes, he knew exactly who to approach, and even more importantly, how.

Thanking Christian, he left the club and headed into the city.

His interview with Mr. King, the most famous—or infamous depending on one's point of view—usurer in London was an unqualified success. Mr. King's office was a stone's throw from the Bank of England; as Christian had prophesied, Mr. King was perfectly happy to assist the authorities given their investigation in no way threatened him or his trade.

A traitor lost all claim to confidentiality; Mr. King had ascertained that no gentleman with the initials A.C. had borrowed large sums of cash from him. He'd confirmed that the practice of disguising major debts in such a way was not uncommon, and had undertaken to inquire on the government's behalf among the other moneylenders capable of advancing such sums.

Tony parted from Mr. King on genial terms. Hailing a hackney, he headed back to Mayfair. With the money angle in hand, he had two other avenues of inquiry to pursue; as the carriage rocked along, he considered how best to tackle them.

Nearing the fashionable quarter, he glanced out at the pavement. It was a glorious day, ladies walking, children laughing and dancing.

Temptation whispered.

Reaching up, he thumped on the roof, then directed the jarvey to Green Park.

He arrived to an exuberant welcome, and had just enough time to have a quick turn flying the kite before Alicia, feigning primness, gathered them all and herded them back to Waverton Street.

Although he quizzed her with his eyes, she remained spuriously aloof, walking smartly along, the boys skipping about them.

He matched his stride to hers, inwardly amused, not only with her but with himself. It had been a long time—

thirteen years at least—since he'd felt so relaxed, experienced this kind of subtle content. He'd honestly enjoyed his time with her brothers; it was almost as if his military years, especially as he'd lived them, had been taken out of his life, excised, so the youth he'd been at nineteen had more in common with the man he had become.

Or perhaps all he'd seen, all he'd experienced in those thirteen years away, had left him with a deeper appreciation of life's little pleasures.

Reaching their house, she opened the door. The boys tumbled in.

"Blackberry jam today!" Matthew sang, and rushed for the stairs.

The older two raced after him, laughing and calling. Jenkins, the kite in his arms, smiled and trudged after them.

Alicia called after him, "Do make sure they're clean before they come down, Jenkins."

"Aye, ma'am." Jenkins looked back. "And I'll let Cook know about tea."

He nodded deferentially to the presence behind her; suddenly realizing, Alicia whirled. "Oh—yes." She met Tony's black eyes; uncertainty flared. "You . . . er, will stay for tea, won't you?"

They were suddenly alone in the hall. He smiled, slowly, into her eyes, then inclined his head. "Blackberry jam's my favorite."

His gaze dropped to her lips; the image that flashed into her mind was of him licking blackberry jam from them. Heat rising in her cheeks, she quickly turned away. "Adriana will be in the parlor."

She led the way, with some relief saw Adriana look up as they entered. Adriana and Tony exchanged easy greetings; as was her habit, Adriana was studying the latest fashion plates prior to designing their next round of gowns.

They all sat; a companionable, almost familial ease fell over them. From her corner of the chaise, Alicia watched as Adriana asked Tony's opinions on various styles depicted in the latest issue of *La Belle Assemblée*. He responded readily; it was quickly apparent he understood more about ladies' garments than one might suppose a gentleman would. . . .

She broke off the thought. His attention was on the plates Adriana had spread before him; she seized the opportunity to study him.

She wished she could see into his mind.

Since they'd parted the previous evening, she'd been plagued by one question: how did he think of her? How did he see her—what were his intentions, his expectations? What direction did he imagine they were headed in?

Given the circumstances, those were not only valid questions; learning the answers was vital to maintaining her charade and succeeding in their aim of having Adriana marry well.

Tony—*Viscount Torrington*—could easily scupper their plans. If he learned of them, and if he so chose. There was, at present, no reason he should stumble on their—her—crucial secret. That secret, however, was precisely the fact that most complicated her way forward.

Along with all the ton, he thought her a widow.

Last night had been a warning. If she was to maintain her charade long enough to establish Adriana, and then disappear, she was going to have to as far as possible restrict her interaction with Torrington.

And what she couldn't avoid, she was going to have to respond to as if she was indeed a widow; she couldn't risk all they'd done, all their success to date, by succumbing to any missish sentiment.

The thunder of feet on the stairs heralded her brothers' arrival. They burst in, full of chatter and exclamations. Jenkins followed with the tray. In seconds, the parlor was filled with rowdy, boisterous warmth and comfort; if anything was needed to remind her why she was playing the role she was, it was there before her in her brothers' smiling, laughing, happy faces.

Torrington—thinking of him by his title helped to keep a sensible distance between them, at least in her mind—gave his attention to the boys, answering questions, joining in their speculations and wonderings, occasionally teasing in a way the boys not only understood and accepted, but took great delight in.

As the guardian of three males, she'd long known they were incomprehensible beings; watching Tony—Torrington!—slouched on the floor, munching a muffin slathered with blackberry jam only compounded her wonder.

He caught her watching; their gazes touched, locked, then he smiled. A fleeting, wholly personal, even intimate gesture, then he looked again to David, who'd posed the question of when the animals in the zoo were most likely fed.

To the boys' disappointment, Tony admitted he didn't know; to their delight, he promised to find out.

It was time to step in. She leaned forward. "Enough, boys! Time for your lessons."

With artistic groans, they clambered to their feet; eyes alight, each shook hands with Tony. Armed with his promise to let them know what he learned with all speed, they left with remarkable alacrity for their books.

Inwardly frowning, Alicia watched them disappear. Jenkins entered and removed the tray.

As he was leaving, Adriana bounced to her feet. "I want to do some sketching. I'll be up in my room."

Before Alicia could think of a suitably worded protest, given he whose presence occasioned that protest was stretched at her feet looking thoroughly at home, Adriana had blithely taken her leave of him, then, without meeting her eyes, her sister whisked out of the room.

And closed the door behind her.

SIX

Alicia considered the closed door, then looked at Tony. *Torrington*! He remained on the floor, shoulders against the side of an armchair; his expression gently amused, he raised a brow at her.

She cleared her throat. "Have you learned anything more about Ruskin?" She needed to keep his mind away from her, from his interest in her; his investigation was assuredly her best bet.

His eyes opened a fraction wider. "Yes, and no. I haven't learned anything definite, but I have certain inquiries in train. Whether they bear fruit remains to be seen."

When she waited, pointedly, Tony grinned. "I spent a most illuminating morning learning about moneylenders."

"Moneylenders?" Alarm flared across her face; her hand instinctively rose to her breast.

"Not on my account." He frowned fleetingly at her. "It's not unknown for gentlemen like A. C. to move the large sums they use to pay their informants via moneylenders, thus concealing their part in the transaction. I visited Mr. King this morning, and asked if he knew of any gentleman with the initials A. C. who had borrowed large sums regularly over recent years."

She continued to stare at him; her stillness was

strange. "Any gentleman . . ." She drew breath. "I see. And did he?"

"No." Tony studied her, trying to fathom the cause of her reaction. "He had no such borrower on his books. However, he agreed to check with the other moneylenders. Given he's something of an institution in the field, if A. C. has been using moneylenders to cover his tracks, I believe we can rely on Mr. King to unearth him."

She blinked; some of her tension had faded. "Oh." She searched his face, then abruptly rose; with a swish of skirts, she went to stand before the window. "Ruskin's information must have some bearing on this. Presumably A. C. used it to his benefit, or why seek and pay for it?"

"Indeed." His gaze on her, Tony got to his feet, resettled his coat, then approached. "There are other avenues I'm exploring."

His voice warned her; she glanced over her shoulder as he halted behind her, so close she was to all intents and purposes—certainly his intents and purposes—trapped between him and the wide windowsill.

Her eyes widened; she sucked in a quick breath. "What avenues?"

Standing this close, with the perfume of her hair and skin rising, wreathing his senses, his mind wasn't on his investigation. "The shipping is one." He slid one palm across her waist, then splayed his fingers and urged her back against him.

She hesitated, then permitted it, letting him settle her, warm and alive, against him. "How are you going to investigate that?"

The words were thready, starved of breath. He inwardly grinned, and sent his other hand to join the first, anchoring her before him, savoring the supple strength of her beneath his palms, her warmth and the softness of the feminine curves riding against him. "I have a friend, Jonathon Hendon. He and his wife will be in London in a few days."

Bending his head, he set his lips to cruise the fine skin above her temple. "Jonathon owns one of the major shipping lines. If anyone can indentify the likely use of Ruskin's information, Jonathon will."

There was a nervous tension in her he couldn't place, didn't understand.

"So you'll learn what A.C. used the information for from Jonathon?"

Beneath his hands, she stirred. Her pulse had accelerated; her breathing was shallow.

"Not quite." He bent lower, let his breath caress her ear. "Jonathon will be able to say what the information might have been used for, but proving that someone did use it, then following the trail back to that someone won't be quite so simple."

"But . . . it would work."

"Yes. Regardless of how we identify A.C., we'll still need to piece his scheme together. Eventually." He breathed the last word as he set his lips to her ear, then lightly traced with his tongue.

A telltale shudder racked her spine, then she surrendered and sank back against him. Feeling ludicrously victorious, he changed position so he could minister to her other ear.

Her hands closed over his at her waist, gripped. "What other route . . . you said avenues . . . plural . . ."

Her voice faded as he artfully teased; when he lifted his head, she sighed. He grinned openly—wolfishly—knowing she couldn't see. "There'll be some other connection between Ruskin and A.C. They'll have met somewhere, have known each other, even if only distantly. Their lives will have touched somewhere, at some time."

Sliding his hands from under hers, he ran his palms slowly upward. Heard the swift intake of her breath as his thumbs brushed the undersides of her breasts. She stiffened, stilled. He caressed knowingly, reassuringly; gradually, almost skittishly, she eased back.

"How—" She cleared her throat. "How do you plan to investigate . . . that?"

She was having trouble finding breath enough to speak; he decided to make it harder still. "I have a friend, not exactly up that way, but close enough." Boldly turning his hands, he cupped her breasts.

Alicia thought she might faint. Her lungs seized; her head whirled. Desperate, she clung to her wits. Dragged in a tight breath. "Ah . . . what . . . ?"

"I'll ask him to check in Bledington. See if the initials A. C. mean anything to people there."

She jerked as his hands shifted, frantically fought down all further reaction. She hadn't imagined he would . . .

His voice had grown deeper, darker, more gravelly. Would a widow protest? On what grounds?

Giddiness threatened. She hauled in a breath, briefly closed her eyes, battered by conflicting impulses. Panic that his friend might stumble on more than she would wish. The urge to stiffen—not just in response to that, but to his boldness, to the liberties he was taking . . . her head was spinning. The countering instinct to sink against him, to arch her spine, press her breasts, now aching so strangely, into his hard hands only added to her dizziness.

Then he closed his hands and kneaded.

She lost the last of her breath. Her senses fractured. Her wits fled.

Beyond her control, her spine softened, gave; she had to lean fully against him, her hands dropping helplessly to brace against his muscled thighs.

His fingers shifted, then closed again. Tightened.

Fire lanced through her. She gasped, arched; eyes shut, she let her head fall back as he repeated the torture, then he bent his head to her throat, now exposed. His lips cruised, then settled.

Hot, wet, his mouth covered the spot where her pulse raced. He kissed, licked, laved, all the while massaging her breasts, sending wave after wave of pure sensation rushing through her.

Heat built beneath her skin; the rasp of his tongue over her pulse point shocked and teased her senses. His hands were strong, his grip confident, knowing, his body a wall of hard muscle and bone, holding her there, a captive to delight.

To the pleasure even in her innocence she knew he was orchestrating.

She felt totally at his mercy. And witlessly content to be so.

Madness—but an oh-so-pleasurable insanity.

This had to be lovemaking, a part of it, of the type a nobleman indulged in with his mistress.

Illicit. Exciting. Enthralling . . .

The moment for protest was long past. Her role was set; eyes closed, head back, she gave herself up to it—she couldn't draw back now.

Tony was intrigued by her response, with the ardor he sensed beneath her restrained veneer. As he ministered to her senses, learned the curves of her breasts, their weight, their wonder, he cataloged, analyzed, noted for future reference. She was amazingly responsive; her breasts, now sensitive and swollen, filled his hands. She shifted under them, pressing back against him, sirenlike, openly sensuous.

Despite her reserve, an understandable defense for an attractive well-born widow, she couldn't hide her reactions; she understood what lay between them as well as he. The flames that leapt into being at just a touch were more than strong—they were scorching. They could both feel them licking, beckoning, hungry yet held back.

They couldn't take things much further yet, but their time would come. On the physical plane, the path ahead was straightforward, but there was much about her he'd yet to learn.

"Your parents." Releasing her breasts, he nuzzled her ear, gently blew. "When did they die?"

Eyes still closed, Alicia dragged in a breath—it felt like her first in ten minutes. Then she felt a tug at her neckline; opening her eyes, she looked down—to see his long fingers easing the top button of her bodice free. "Ah . . . Mama died almost two years ago."

Good Lord! She had to stop this—had to call a halt. If he touched her . . .

"And your father? From your brothers, I gather he's been gone a long time."

Her mouth was dry; she nodded. "Years and years." Gaze fixed on his busy fingers, she licked her lips.

"And you have no other family? No one close?"

"Ah . . . no." She dragged in a breath. "I really think—"

"You're not supposed to think."

She blinked, lifted her gaze. "Why not?"

"Because"—his fingers were inexorably descending, leaving her bodice gaping—"at the moment, you're supposed to be enjoying, simply feeling. You don't need to think to do that."

He sounded eminently reasonable, even faintly amused; the idea of a missish protest and consequent retreat seemed unwise.

"Have you always lived near Banbury?"

"Ah . . . yes." Once he'd opened her bodice, what did he plan to do?

He shifted behind her, easing back; the realization that she wasn't the only one affected by his play burst across her mind, stealing what few wits she'd managed to reassemble.

"I assume Carrington hailed from that area, too?"

The words sounded distant, vague, but whether that was due to the drumming in her ears, the titillating panic locking her lungs, or because he was no more interested in the subject than she was, she wasn't sure.

A cool wash of air slipped beneath her gaping bodice;

she quelled a shiver. His hands drifted down, then fastened about her waist.

"Ah . . . y-yes. He came from there, too."

"How old are your brothers?"

She frowned. "Twelve, ten, and eight." His hands had settled; she gulped in a breath. "Why are you asking all this?"

His fingers gripped, then he stepped back, turned her and stepped forward once more, locking her against the windowsill, his hips to hers, his erection rigid against the softness of her stomach.

He trapped her gaze.

She couldn't think—not at all. Could only stare into his black eyes, and wonder if there really were embers glowing in them. The sheer maleness of him engulfed her; his gaze dropped to her lips—she felt them throb.

His lips quirked, wryly humorous. He released her waist; one hand rose to cup her jaw, angling her face upward as he bent his head. "Because I want to know *all* about you."

His lips closed on hers as his other hand slid boldly beneath her bodice, and closed about her breast.

She gasped, tensed; only a fine layer of silk lay between her sensitized skin and his burning palm. Her breasts instantly felt heavy, swelling, tightening, aching anew.

Then he entered her mouth, possessive and demanding, capturing her attention, insistent and commanding; she scrambled to meet him, to remember how, to play the experienced widow she was pretending to be. The hand on her breast shifted, knowingly cupping, then his fingers toyed with the silk, shifting it over the tightly ruched peak, heightening its excruciatingly sensitive state—then he closed his fingers around the pebbled tip, tugged gently, then tightened, tightened . . .

She tried to break from the kiss, but he wouldn't let her; his hand framing her face, he held her captive. Once again lavished delight and sheer sensual pleasure on her through the play of his lips and tongue, and the even more expert play of his fingers.

He captured her totally. Not just with the heat, with the sudden flare of hot desire, but with something simpler, more fundamental.

His hunger—and hers.

He didn't try to hide his want, his wish to have, to know, to take, to explore, to experience; it was there, laid before her, stated more clearly than in words. A hunger of her own rose in reply, not mere curiosity but something more definite—a need she hadn't known she had.

He angled his head, ravaged her mouth, and she consciously met him. Flagrantly urged him on. His fingers closed again and she shuddered, no longer trying to disguise her response. Her hands rose, of their own volition found his shoulders, then pushed on, around, back, then she speared her fingers into his black hair.

The silken touch of the heavy locks didn't distract, but only added to the tactile experience; her greedy senses, awakened and starved, welcomed and wallowed. His hand shifted on her breast, blatantly possessive; his fingers tightened again—hers clenched in response.

He moved closer, into her, deepening the kiss—and suddenly they were somewhere else, in some place they hadn't been before. Somewhere hotter, more fiery, where their needs escalated and their senses grew ravenous. Clamorous.

Urgent.

It was he who broke the kiss, lifted his head and hauled them free of the fire. Drew them back to earth, back to themselves, to their bodies locked close in the parlor.

To their breaths fast and shallow, to their pulses hammering in their veins. Lids lifting, their gazes locked; in his, the flames still smoldered. Her lips throbbed, appeased yet still hungry.

His gaze fell to them, then lower. To where his hand

lay over her breast. He closed that hand, slowly, deliberately. Desire welled and washed down her spine; something inside her clenched tight.

His eyes lifted to hers. "Not here, not now." He bent his head and kissed her, slowly, deeply, intimately, then drew back. "But soon."

His hand left her aching flesh, yet he didn't step back. Instead, his gaze returning to her eyes, trapping her, holding her, he deftly rebuttoned her bodice.

Her head was whirling, but some part of her no longer cared. That part of her that seemed new, different—changed. Or perhaps revealed, called forth. That part of her that thrilled to that decisive "But soon."

She might have thought she was mad, but knew she wasn't. This was a facet of life she'd yet to experience, yet to explore.

As a widow, she couldn't pretend not to understand. The look in his eyes convinced her she'd never succeed in denying what she'd felt, in pretending her hunger didn't exist. He'd seen it, felt it, understood it—almost certainly better than she did.

There was nothing she could say—that she could think of that was safe to say—so she merely held his gaze and, her pulse still thundering, waited to follow his lead.

That seemed an acceptable response. When, stepping back, he quizzed her with his eyes, she merely arched a brow, and saw his lips quirk.

He took her hand, raised it to his lips. "I'll leave you. I'm afraid I won't be attending the Waverleys' ball tonight." He turned to the door; she walked beside him. "I need to consult with some others about the investigation."

He opened the door; she led him into the front hall.

"The rumors concerning you and Ruskin should be fading."

She glanced at him, saw a frown in his eyes. "I'm sure we'll manage."

Her even reply didn't reassure him. "Lady Amery will

be attending, and Lady Osbaldestone, too, should you need any support."

Opening the front door, she held it, and looked at him. "I doubt that will be necessary, but I'll bear it in mind."

Pausing by her side, he looked into her eyes. She got the distinct impression he wanted to say something more, something other, but couldn't find the words.

Then he reached out, with the pad of his thumb caressed her lower lip.

It throbbed.

Swiftly, he bent his head, pressed a kiss, hard and definite, to the spot, then he straightened. "I'll call on you tomorrow."

With a nod, he went down the steps.

She stood at the door, watching him walk away, then shut it. She paused, waiting until her nerves steadied and untensed, then, lips firming, she headed for the stairs.

Alicia tapped on the door of Adriana's bedchamber, then entered.

Sprawled on her bed, her sketchbook before her, Adriana looked up, then smiled. Impishly. "Has he gone?"

"Yes." Alicia frowned as Adriana bounced into a sitting position. "But you shouldn't have left us alone."

"Why ever not?" Adriana grinned. "He was waiting to be alone with you, wasn't he?"

Sitting on the end of the bed, Alicia grimaced. "Probably. Nevertheless, it would be wiser if I didn't spend time alone with him."

"Nonsense! You're a widow—you're *allowed* to be alone with gentlemen." Adriana's eyes sparkled. "*Especially* gentlemen like him."

"But I'm *not* a widow—remember?" Alicia frowned. "And gentlemen like him are dangerous."

Adriana sobered. "Surely not—not him." She frowned. "Geoffrey told me Tony—Torrington—was totally trustworthy. An absolutely to-his-bones honorable gentleman."

Alicia raised her brows. "That may be so, but he thinks I'm a widow. His attitude to me is based on that."

"But . . ." Adriana's puzzlement grew; curling her legs, she shifted closer, studying Alicia's face. "Gentlemen do marry widows, you know."

"Perhaps." Alicia caught her eye. "But how many noblemen marry widows? I don't think that's at all common. And you know what the books said—unless of the nobility herself, a widow is often viewed by gentlemen of the haut ton as a perfect candidate for the position of mistress."

"Yes . . . but the books were warning of the general run of gentlemen, the bucks, the bloods, the—"

"Dangerous blades?" Alicia's lips twisted; reaching out, she squeezed Adriana's hand. "You're not, I hope, going to tell me Tony—Torrington—isn't dangerous."

Adriana pulled a face. "No. But—"

"No buts." Alicia spoke firmly, then stood. "In my estimation, it would be unwise for me to be alone with Torrington in future."

Adriana's eyes, fixed on her face, narrowed. "Did he kiss you?"

Her blush gave her away; she met Adriana's eyes fleetingly. "Yes."

"And?" When she said nothing, Adriana prompted, "How was it? How did it feel?"

The word brought back exactly how it had felt; warmth spread beneath her skin, her nipples tightened. One glance confirmed that Adriana was not going to be deterred. "It was . . . pleasant. But," she quickly added, "indulging in such pleasantness is far too risky."

She could see more questions forming in Adriana's inquisitive mind. "Now that's enough about me." She reverted to her firmest tone. "I intend to avoid Torrington in future. But what about you? You're the reason we're here, after all."

Adriana gazed up at her. After a moment, she said, "I like Geoffrey. He's kind, and funny, and . . ." She drew breath and continued in a rush, "I think he might be the one."

That last was said with an almost stricken look. Alicia sat again. "If you only *think* he might be, perhaps we should cast around a trifle more until you're certain. There are three weeks yet before the Season begins, so you've plenty of time—there's no reason to feel you must reach a decision quickly."

"Indeed." Adriana frowned. "I wouldn't want to make a mistake."

The sisters sat side by side, both staring into space, then Alicia stirred. "Perhaps"—she glanced at Adriana—"to help in deciding, it might be time to ask Mr. King to dine."

Adriana looked at her, then nodded. "Yes." Her chin firmed. "Perhaps we should."

Alicia held her head high, her parasol deployed at precisely the correct angle as the natty barouche she'd hired from the livery stables rolled smoothly onto the gravel of the avenue through the park.

The morning was fine; a light breeze drifted through the branches of the trees, just coming into bud. She and Adriana sat in elegant comfort; on the box before them and clinging behind, the coachman and footman were attired in severe black with bright red ribbons circling the crowns of their hats. That last was Adriana's suggestion, a simple touch to add a hint of exclusivity.

Such things mattered when going about in the ton.

"I still can't get over Lady Jersey being so attentive." Adriana lifted her face to the breeze; her dark curls danced about her heart-shaped face. "She has *such* a reputation, but I thought she was quite nice."

"Indeed." Alicia had her own ideas over what had prompted Lady Jersey's kind words, and those of the other senior hostesses who had found a moment during the Waverleys' ball to stop beside her to admire Adriana and wish them both well. She strongly suspected Lady Amery and her dear friend Lady Osbaldestone had been busy. And she knew at whose behest.

"Oh! There's Lady Cowper." Adriana returned her ladyship's wave.

Alicia leaned forward and directed their coachman to pull up alongside her ladyship's carriage, halted on the verge.

Emily, Lady Cowper, was sweet-tempered and good-natured; she had from the first approved of Mrs. Carrington and Miss Pevensey. "I'm so glad to see you both out and about. The sun is so fickle these days one daren't let an opportunity pass."

"Indeed." Alicia touched fingers; Adriana smiled and bowed. "One can only attend a few balls each night, and there's so many one simply cannot find in the crowds."

Lady Cowper's eyes gleamed. "Especially when so many need to have their notions set straight. But that small *contretemps* seems to be sinking quite as quickly as any of us might wish."

Alicia shared a satisfied, understanding smile with her ladyship. They chatted about upcoming events for five minutes, then took their leave; the carriage rolled on.

To Lady Huntingdon, then Lady Marchmont, and finally Lady Elphingstone.

"That color so becomes you, my dear." Lady Elphingstone examined Alicia's maroon twill through her lorgnette, then turned that instrument on Adriana's gown of palest lemon. "I declare you both are forever at the very pinnacle of modishness—always just so, never a step too far. I only wish my niece would take note."

Alicia recognized the hint. "Is your niece in town?"

Lady Elphingstone nodded. "She'll be at Lady Cranbourne's rout tonight. I take it you both will be attending?"

"Indeed." Adriana smiled warmly; she knew her role well. "I would be pleased to make your niece's acquaintance, if that might be possible?"

Lady Elphingstone beamed. "I'll be sure to make her known to you."

Alicia returned her ladyship's smile. "We'll look forward to it." By such little strategems were valuable alliances formed.

They parted from Lady Elphingstone. Alicia glanced ahead, then instructed the coachman to return to Waverton Street. Adriana cast her a questioning glance. Settling back, she murmured, "I've had enough for today."

Adriana accepted the decree with easygoing cheerfulness; Alicia shut her lips on her real reason—she didn't need to burden Adriana with that.

She had had enough—enough of deceiving others. But she'd accepted the role she had to play; any guilt associated with it was hers alone to bear.

As the carriage rolled under the trees, along the drive lined with the conveyances of the fashionable, she and Adriana continued to smile, wave, and exchange nods; the number of ladies with whom they were acquainted had grown dramatically over the past days. Or, more correctly, the number of ladies wishing to make their acquaintance had grown, courtesy of Tony—his lordship—and those he'd asked to look kindly upon them.

The gates of the park loomed; the carriage swept through, and they were free of the necessity of responding to those about them. Alicia couldn't help but wonder what their reception would be if the ton knew the truth.

The prospect increasingly impinged on her mind. Tony—Torrington—had allied himself with them; if her secret became known, he would be involved by implication. Guilt by association, something the ton was quick to indulge in.

That worry dragged at her; only when they turned into Waverton Street and her mind swung to her brothers and her small household did she realize her worry for Torrington was of the same type, that nagging insistent consideration that she felt for her dependents, all those in her care.

The carriage rocked to a halt. Inwardly frowning, she let the footman hand her down. She wasn't wrong in assessing how she felt, yet Tony wasn't a dependent, nor yet in her care. Why, then, was her feeling so strong—so definite? So *real*.

After handing Adriana down, the footman bowed, then left. The carriage rumbled off. Adriana started up the steps. Closing her parasol, Alicia followed more slowly.

Jenkins would be upstairs with the boys; Adriana opened the door and went in, then turned to take Alicia's parasol. "I'll put these in the parlor. I thought of a new design—a variation of that French jacket. I want to sketch it before I forget." With a swish of her skirts, she headed for the parlor.

Alicia paused in the hall, watching her sister . . . just for one instant pausing to give thanks, then she heard a footfall on the stairs.

She looked up—and her heart leapt.

There could be no doubt; as she watched Tony slowly, elegantly descend, his lips set in an easy line but his eyes watchful, intent, she understood what she was feeling, couldn't stop the welling tide of anticipation, the burgeoning of simple happiness.

She was in a very bad way.

With one hand, he indicated the upper floor. "I've been with your brothers." Reaching the bottom stair, he stepped down, walked closer.

With every step he took, she could feel her awareness

come to life, feel her consciousness expand, reaching for him.

He stopped directly in front of her. His eyes met hers, their expression quizzical, faintly amused. Then, before she could stop him, he bent his head and kissed her.

Gently, warmly.

He raised his head, met her gaze. "I need to speak with you privately." He glanced around, then gestured. "Shall we use the drawing room?"

She looked at the closed door. Her lips still tingled; it was an effort to bludgeon her wits into working order. "Yes. If . . ." Had her brothers said something they shouldn't?

That thought and the incipient panic it evoked helped get her mind functioning. Turning, she crossed the hall by Torrington's side, her protective instincts abruptly on full alert. No matter what she felt for him, she shouldn't forget that if he learned the truth, he could pose as big a threat to her and her family as Ruskin had.

Indeed, the threat he could pose was even greater.

Tony opened the door, waited for her to enter, then followed her into the elegantly appointed room. His gaze went first to the windows—two long panes looking onto the street. Shutting the door, he glanced around, but there was nothing of her or her family there, on the mantelpiece or the occasional tables set between the two chaises and the well-padded armchairs.

She stopped in the middle of the richly colored Turkish rug; head up, spine straight, hands clasped before her, she faced him.

"You don't have enough menservants." He had no idea what she'd expected him to say, but it assuredly wasn't that. She blinked, then frowned as her mind shifted to the domestic arena. If he told her he'd discovered a certain delight in throwing her off-balance, in confusing her, she most certainly wouldn't approve, yet such moments revealed an underlying vulnerability, one she didn't normally show, but which he treasured seeing and knew he responded to. As he presently was.

"Menservants?" Her frown was definite. "We have Jenkins, of course."

"One man for a house of this size, with a family of this size?"

Her chin rose as he closed the distance between them. "We've never seen the need for a large staff. We're quite comfortable as we are."

Halting before her, he caught her gaze. "I'm concerned."

She searched his eyes. "About what?"

"About the direction my investigation is taking, and the fact someone started rumors about you. Specifically *you*—the widow Ruskin was blackmailing."

She hesitated, then said, "Adriana and I are always careful."

"Be that as it may, this house is large . . . and you have three young brothers."

He didn't need to say more; he watched alarm flare in her eyes, only to be replaced by consideration, then consternation. He picked his moment to murmur, "I have a very large house with a very large staff, most of whom have very little to do given I'm the only member of the family in residence." Her gaze lifted to his; he held it. "I would feel much happier, less concerned, if you would allow me to lend you a footman, at least until my investigation is successfully concluded."

She returned his regard steadily. A minute ticked by, then she said, "This footman . . . ?"

"I have one in mind who would suit admirably—Maggs. He's been with me for years. He's well trained, and I can assure you he'll know how to deal with your brothers and the rest of the household, Jenkins especially."

Her eyes narrowed; her look stated that she understood his tactics, that she recognized he'd left her little room to maneuver, no real excuse to refuse. "Just for the duration of your investigation?"

"You may have him for as long as you wish, but I'd urge you to allow him to stay at least until we have Ruskin's murderer by the heels."

She pressed her lips together, then nodded. "Very well. I'll warn Jenkins."

They were standing close; he sensed her impulse to step back, away. Instead, she fixed him with a direct look. "It may interest you to know that at the Waverleys' ball last night and in the park this morning, Adriana and I met with, not just a gratifying degree of acceptance, but a quite astonishing level of support."

He raised his brows. "Indeed?"

"Indeed." She held his gaze. "You arranged it, didn't you?"

His face remained impassive, unreadable; his eyes, he knew, gave nothing away while he debated his answer. Eventually, he said, "Although she no longer resides in the capital, my mother has a large circle of friends among the *grandes dames* of the haut ton. I used to find their existence a trial. Now . . . I'm prepared to admit they do have their uses."

She drew a slow, deep breath; although he kept his eyes locked with hers, he was highly conscious of the swelling of her breasts. "Thank you." She hesitated, then added, "I don't know why you're doing this—"

Alicia broke off when something flashed in his eyes—an expression so vibrant, so powerful, even as fleeting as it was, the glimpse distracted her.

In the same moment, he reached for her; hands sliding around her waist, he drew her to him. Against him. Into his arms as he bent his head.

"The reason I'm doing this . . ."

The words washed over her lips, suddenly hungry; for a second, their gazes touched, locked, then his lids fell. She felt his gaze on her lips.

"Ought to be obvious."

Deep, low, the words sank into her brain as his lips covered hers, and he sank into her mouth. Claimed her attention, then sent it spinning, fractured, dispersed. Called her senses, drew them to him, then trapped them, held them enthralled.

She kissed him back, found herself mentally floating as the slow, drugging kisses took their toll. Sinking her fingers into his shoulders, she tried to hang onto her wits, to some degree of control, but steadily, inexorably, implacable and irresistible, he drew it from her grasp.

Then he drew her hard against him, locked her body to his, and the flames and the magic flared.

It had to be magic, that surge of sensation, the giddy delight, the anticipation streaking down her nerves, tingling, tightening so that the need to sate it was suddenly more important than breathing, far more important than any consideration of social strictures.

His hands spread over her back, stroked possessively down the long planes, curving over her hips to close proprietorially over her bottom, provocatively kneading, then boldly caressing. Hot as a flame, heat spread beneath her skin; a deep-seated yearning flowered in its wake.

Then he angled his head and ravaged her mouth, took more, demanded more. Unhesitatingly she followed him deeper into the exchange, encouraging and enjoying the ever more intimate melding of their mouths.

The first inkling she had that he'd opened her bodice was the slithering caress of her silk chemise as, loosened, it slipped down, helped by his long fingers. And then those fingers were on her skin, and she lost touch with the world.

And plunged into another.

Into a realm where sensation and emotions were the only reality, where touches and caresses formed the language, with needs, wants, and desires the only goals. Every slow, possessive caress heightened her need, made her want with an ever greater certainty fueled by escalating, burgeoning desire. Yet that desire seemed entwined with his, with him, with his obvious reason. With what she sensed, in her bones knew, he wanted.

Their lips parted; from under heavy lids, their gazes met, held as his fingers moved on her, upon her, drawing whorls of flame on her skin, tightening her nerves to an excruciating degree. Unable to bear it, she closed her eyes, with a soft gasp let her head fall back. Felt him bend near, felt his lips on her throat, sliding down to fasten over her thudding pulse.

His hands shifted; her gown slid over her shoulders, then cool air caressed her heated skin. The bared skin he set his lips to tracing, with flicking licks and long trailing laves teasing, the hot, wet promise of his mouth withheld . . . as the fever built, as some need within her grew, and grew . . . until she moaned.

The sound, soft, nearly suppressed, surprised her, but through the hands at her waist holding her, supporting her, she sensed his satisfaction. A wholly male triumph that he crowned by closing his mouth—every bit as hot and wet as she'd imagined—over the taut, aching peak of one breast.

She tensed, her nerves clenched, not with rejection but delight. Her hands slid through his hair, tightened on his skull as he swirled his tongue about the ruched peak, then sucked gently. Sensation, pure and elemental, streaked through her, racing through her body to pool deep and low, a warming glow within her.

Cracking open her lids, she looked down. Watched as he feasted on her bounty—and wondered at her reaction. Some part of her was shocked, yet she couldn't, even now, summon any will to refuse him, deny him—to push him away. She couldn't tense her muscles, couldn't break the spell. She didn't want to, couldn't pretend. Could only watch, feel, learn, and experience.

Something new, something novel, something she'd never felt before.

Tony sensed her fascination and was content. For now. He knew her acquiescence was not, yet, freely given; he could draw her into such sensual exchanges, but she did not, yet, seek them of her own accord.

That was what he wanted. Needed. For her to want him as he wanted her.

Overwhelming her natural resistance, taking over, controlling her—for one of his talents, that wasn't all that hard. For him, the challenge lay deeper, in making her come to him, making her desire him enough to set aside her reserve and actively seek to be intimate with him.

Only by that route would he gain the surrender he sought, the complete and conscious giving that, for one of his nature, was the ultimate prize.

He raised his head; their gazes briefly touched, then he covered her lips, and took her mouth again. In a slow, thorough, leisurely engagement that left them both starved of breath.

Gradually, he drew back. Her breasts were swollen, tight beneath his hands; her skin felt like hot satin beneath his fingertips. He kept his lips on hers as he searched for and found the top edge of her chemise, and drew it up, tugging the drawstring so it tightened and held.

She stirred in his arms. He ended the kiss and lifted his head. Their eyes met for an instant, then she looked down; drawing her hands from his shoulders, she resettled and retied the chemise, then, a blush tinting her cheeks, she rapidly did up the buttons of her bodice.

He couldn't keep his lips straight when she glanced at him; his satisfaction was too deep to hide.

She saw it, read it; a frown in her eyes, she waved him to the door.

Smiling, he turned, glancing at her as she fell in beside

him. Before the door, he halted, caught her eye as she looked up. "I'll send Maggs this afternoon."

She blinked at him. "Maggs?"

"The footman."

"Ah." She drew herself up, nodded. "Yes, of course. Thank you."

He grinned, ducked his head, and kissed her—stole one last kiss from her luscious lips—then straightened and met her eyes, green and slightly dazed. "I'll see myself out."

He managed to suppress a smirk; feeling positively virtuous, he opened the door, gracefully saluted her, then closed it.

Alicia stared at the panels. Beyond them, she heard his footsteps recede, then the front door opened, and shut.

He was gone.

Reason and logic returned in a flood; the last minutes—however many minutes it had been—replayed in her mind.

Her increasingly horrified mind.

Her lips still throbbed, her skin still tingled, her breasts . . . she could still feel the sensation of his mouth moving over them . . .

With a groan, she closed her eyes and slumped against the door.

What was she going to do?

SEVEN

"My dear Mrs. Carrington, may I present Sir Freddie Caudel?"

Lady Hertford beamed at Alicia, who divined that gaining Sir Freddie's notice was something of a coup. She extended her hand with a polite murmur.

Sir Freddie took her fingers and bowed gracefully. A gentleman in his middle years, he was handsome in a quiet, patrician way.

Alicia smiled. In a few short minutes, she established that Sir Freddie was a scion of an old and ancient house and consequently socially prominent, held a political post in the government, possessed a degree of polish and address to which younger men could only aspire, and was on the lookout for a wellborn, beautiful, and young bride.

Not surprisingly, Adriana had caught his eye.

Alicia hestitated, wondering if she should, in all compassion, nip Sir Freddie's aspirations in the bud; from all she could see, Adriana was fast losing her heart to Geoffrey Manningham.

Sir Freddie had followed her gaze to where Adriana stood by Lord Manningham's side. "I realize, of course, that youth and beauty go hand in hand, yet often you ladies have a remarkably discerning eye."

Alicia met Sir Freddie's blue eyes, guileless and amused. Geoffrey might be younger, yet Sir Freddie was undeniably distinguished, and his manners, while absolutely correct, had an ease about them, a comfortable confidence deriving from years of moving in the first circles.

Sir Freddie might give Geoffrey a run for his money.

More particularly for Adriana's heart, which her hand would follow.

Lips curving, Alicia inclined her head. "If you wish to join my sister's circle, I have no objection." She seriously doubted Sir Freddie would succeed, but there was no harm in him attempting to upset Manningham's applecart.

Sir Freddie offered his arm. "If you would introduce me?"

Placing her fingers on his sleeve, Alicia allowed him to lead her to Adriana's side.

Adriana was, as always, polite to anyone who sought her attention. Introduction completed, Alicia withdrew, rejoining Lady Hertford at the side of the room.

"He's very highly thought of," her ladyship whispered. "Marcus tells me he can be quite stiff-rumped on occasion, but always the true gentleman." Adriana drew Miss Tiverton into the conversation with Sir Freddie; Lady Hertford smiled delightedly. "Such a sweet girl, your sister. Who knows? If Sir Freddie doesn't fix her interest, perhaps he'll look at Helen. Of course, there's his age, but when men of his stamp look to take a wife, one can at least be sure they're in earnest. And his estates are quite respectable, I believe—they've been in the family for generations."

Alicia smiled easily; she let Lady Hertford's chatter wash over her, nodding here and there. Eventually, her ladyship departed, leaving Miss Tiverton along with Adriana under Alicia's watchful eye.

She did keep her gaze on her sister's circle, some yards away, but the instant Lady Hertford's distraction disappeared, Alicia's thoughts focused on her own distraction.

Anthony Blake, Viscount Torrington.

Her reaction to his practiced seduction surprised her;

she'd assumed she'd be uninterested, disinterested, that repulsing any gentleman's advances, especially those of a predatory nobleman, would be instinctive, a natural response she wouldn't have to pause to consider, let alone battle to achieve.

It was a battle she was losing; she'd already lost significant ground. Quite why, she didn't understand.

When she was with him, in his arms or even simply alone with him, the world seemed to shift, the frame of reference by which she'd lived her life thus far to alter. It swung to focus on him, to accommodate him, to center, not just on him, not just on his wishes, but on hers—those wishes she hadn't known she had.

When with him, her attention shifted to a different landscape, one encompassing all that was growing between them. That change was unprecedented, unsettling, yet fascinating. Even addictive.

Something in him called to something in her; from the coalescing of those somethings grew the power she sensed, the power that was strong enough to suborn her wits, shackle her senses . . . and seduce her.

She shivered, and refocused on Adriana's circle, and saw Sir Freddie successfully solicit her sister's hand for a waltz. Noting Geoffrey Manningham's studiously impassive countenance, she smiled.

Hard fingers, a hard palm, closed about her hand.

She turned as Tony—Torrington!—raised it; eyes capturing hers, he pressed a kiss to her fingers. Faintly smiled.

"Come and dance."

Within seconds, she was whirling down the floor. She didn't bother trying to resist; instead, she turned her mind to her most urgent need—trying to understand what was going on.

He seemed content simply to dance, to hold her in his arms and revolve about the ballroom, his gaze resting on her face, on her eyes.

Drinking her in.

She lowered her lids, screening her eyes, shifted her gaze to look over his shoulder. Smoothly, he drew her closer as they went through the turns, and didn't ease his hold; abruptly she was aware of their bodies, the subtle brushing of their hips, of his thigh parting hers as they turned . . . as if he'd reached for her and enveloped her in a flagrantly intimate embrace. The memory leapt to her mind, instantly impinged on her wanton senses.

Instantly stirred her hunger.

She looked up, met his gaze. "This is madness."

The words were low, breathy. He smiled, but his eyes remained on hers, his gaze intent. "If it is, we're both infected."

Beyond recall. She drew breath, read his eyes; their expression was openly predatory—his intent could not have been clearer. Realization, as inescapable as the dawn, burst upon her.

Deep within her, something quivered.

Tony looked up, over her head, wishing for once that she possessed a more definite mask, a countenance less easy to read. One long look into her eyes, and he was aching. If Cranbourne House had boasted any suitable room, he'd have whisked her off to it, there to pursue, however impulsively, the connection growing between them. Unfortunately, Cranbourne House was small, pokey, a totally unsuitable venue. Added to that, her sister was present, which meant she'd be distracted. When he finally had her beneath him, he didn't want her thinking of anything else.

He noticed Geoffrey standing by the side of the room, not exactly scowling, yet clearly not happy. A quick glance about the floor located Adriana waltzing in the arms of a somewhat older man.

"The gentleman waltzing with your sister—who is he?"

Alicia had been studying his face; she answered

evenly, "Sir Freddie Caudel." After a moment, she asked, "Do you know him?"

One distraction was as good as another. Resigning himself to yet another night of escalating frustration, he glanced down at her. "No, but I've heard of him. Very old family. Why? Is he interested in your sister?"

Alicia nodded. "How interested, I'm not sure, and I doubt his interest, at whatever level, will be reciprocated, nevertheless . . ."

His lips quirked; he glanced again at Geoffrey. "Another iron in the fire?"

Alicia narrowed her eyes. "Precisely." One with which she might prod things along.

"I take it the footman met with your approval?"

"Maggs?" Bearing a written introduction, the man had presented himself at the back door in Waverton Street. She met Torrington's gaze, let a moment pass; Maggs, as he had to be aware, was the most unprepossessing specimen. His features were irregular, his face appeared pushed in, yet he seemed possessed of an easy disposition and had already, in just a few hours, gained acceptance from Cook, Fitchett, and, most importantly, Jenkins. For which she was grateful. "I daresay he'll suit well enough. As I pointed out, we really have little use for a footman."

"Nevertheless." Torrington's black eyes quizzed her. "Just so that I can rest easy."

She suppressed a humph.

The waltz ended. Without instruction, Torrington led her back to her position not far from Adriana's court. He remained by her side, chatting inconsequentially on this and that, the customary exchanges of tonnish life. Others joined them, remained for a time, then moved on; she tried not to dwell on the fact that she preferred having him near, that his easy, in many ways undemanding presence made her evening distinctly more enjoyable.

More relaxing on one level, more unnerving on another.

It was the minor moments that tripped her up, that set her nerves jangling. That brought what was between them flooding back into her mind, blocking out all else, even Adriana.

Like the moment when having remained by her side, her cavalier through the rest of the evening, Torrington parted from them in the Cranbournes' front hall. They were among a small crowd of departing guests; to gain her attention, he touched her shoulder.

His fingertips brushed lightly. Despite being decently sheathed in ruby silk, her skin reacted. Goosebumps rose and spread in a wave; her nipples tightened.

Her eyes flew to his, wide, aware; he read them, his lips thinned, and she knew he knew, too.

Then he met her gaze fully. The expression in his eyes nearly slew her; the heat was so open, so intense, it was a wonder it didn't melt her bones.

His lashes swept down; he grasped her hand and very correctly took his leave of her.

She mumbled some response, then watched his back as he walked away through the crowd; only when he disappeared through the front door did she manage to breathe again. Manage to give her attention to the footman waiting to be told which carriage to summon. Thankfully, Adriana hadn't noticed; her sister seemed as distracted as she.

The journey back through the night-shrouded streets provided a welcome respite, a quiet moment all but alone when she could gather her wits, review what had happened, all she'd felt, how she'd reacted, without worrying about her betraying blush.

Finally to make some attempt at defining where she stood. And whither she was heading.

The first seemed all too clear; she stood teetering on the horns of a dilemma. As for the second, the possibilities were varied but uniformly unsettling.

Her dilemma was clear enough. She had to play the part of a tonnish widow, an experienced lady aware of, indeed personally acquainted with, all aspects of intimacy. The question now facing her was simple: how far should she go in preserving her charade?

To her perturbation, the answer was not at all simple.

Dedication to their cause argued the answer should be as far as she needed to go to see Adriana through her Season and secure their family's relief. But that immediately raised another highly pertinent question: how far *could* she go without Torrington realizing?

He was not just experienced; he was an expert. She'd been scrambling to keep up with him thus far; at some point she would falter, and he'd realize. . . .

The social strictures at least were clear. Regardless of her charade, she wasn't a widow, but a virtuous spinster—she shouldn't permit him even the liberties he'd already taken. Unfortunately, her inner voice was quick to argue, to speak in support of those wishes and needs she was only just realizing she possessed; where, that inner voice asked, was the harm?

She'd accepted over a year ago that she'd missed her chance at marriage; she was twenty-four—not unmarriageable by ton standards, yet in reality the likelihood had faded. Once Adriana was established, she, Alicia, would disappear from society; she'd imagined she'd retire to the country to watch over the boys, to keep home for them whether with Adriana and her husband or otherwise.

That plan still stood; nothing had happened to alter her path. Any liaison with Torrington would be, as such things generally were, temporary, fleeting. A liaison with him might, however, be her only chance to experience all she was presently pretending to know.

He was the only gentleman who had ever engaged her on that level; even now, she wasn't sure how he'd done it, how it had happened. Yet it had; the possibility now existed where it hadn't before. If she wanted to know more, wanted to experience all that could be between a man and a woman, all she had to do was let Torrington teach her.

The carriage rocked along, heading into Mayfair, pausing here and there as other carriages crowded the streets. She barely noticed the delays, indeed was grateful for the opportunity to let her mind range ahead, examining, imagining.

If she did indulge in a liaison with Torrington . . .

He would realize she was a virgin, would guess she'd never been married. However, she doubted he would expose her to the ton; there was no reason he should, not once she'd explained.

There was, however, another danger. One her instincts, uneducated though they were, had detected. Just how real that danger was she couldn't be certain, yet Tony—Torrington—was a nobleman to his toes. Arrogant, yes, with a definite streak of ruthlessness behind his charming facade, and . . . she searched for the word to describe what she sensed when he looked at her, held her, kissed her, caressed her.

Possessive.

If she gave herself to him, trusted him that far, would he agree to let her go?

She wasn't foolish enough to overlook the point; if she became his mistress, allowed him to become privy to her secret, he'd be in a position much as Ruskin had been, able to dictate her behavior. She recognized the possibility, viewed it clearly, yet she couldn't, despite all, see it happening. Adriana had mentioned Geoffrey's assessment of Torrington; it concurred with her own reading of the man. He was simply not the sort to hold a woman against her will. Regardless of all else, he was an honorable man.

If she did become his mistress, for whatever length of time, he would, in the end, let her go.

All of which left her precisely where she'd started, facing the question of what she should do and no nearer to finding an answer.

The only alternative to making a decision was to stave it off. Somehow to hold him off, to avoid the culmination he was clearly steering them toward. If she could hold to a line just short of surrender, then the instant Adriana was established, disappear . . .

With a creak, the carriage turned into Waverton Street. Adriana stirred, stretched. Alicia straightened, and gathered her shawl and reticule. The carriage halted; looking out, she saw the light burning above their door.

Thought of her brothers innocently asleep in their beds.

Resist Torrington. The problem with that strategy was that in order to implement it, she'd have to fight not only him, an experienced campaigner, but her own, largely unknown, desires.

She let the footman hand her down, then led the way up the steps. Their reckless but straightforward plan had developed serious complications.

The next morning, Tony headed for the Bastion Club. On foot. He needed the exercise.

Needed the physical activity to ease the building frustration of a type he'd rarely had to endure. Indeed, he couldn't remember ever wanting a woman so much, and not having her. Worse, in this instance, he recognized the need to go slowly, carefully; his relationship with Alicia was forever, not for a few weeks or a few months. It would be the most important relationship of his life; it demanded and deserved a degree of care, of respect, of attention.

He'd noticed her occasional hesitations, the sudden tensing, almost a skittishness that sometimes gripped her. He'd always succeeded in soothing it, in getting her to set it aside and relax, to trust him. To open her eyes, see and accept all that could be and would be between them.

Although he hadn't foreseen it, her reserve didn't surprise him; she might be a widow, but that wouldn't change the underlying truth of her nature—she was a virtuous lady, and as such would not easily be seduced. And in her case, there was yet more—a complicating factor. She was responsible for her family, and she took that responsibility seriously.

He hadn't imagined that in gaining his bride, he'd have to compete with her family for her attention. While the fact was a difficulty, and clearly would continue to raise hurdles, he didn't, as it happened, disapprove.

He enjoyed her family—enjoyed spending time with her brothers, even enjoyed watching Adriana make her choice, especially given Geoffrey was involved. But more, he found the circumstance of her family reassuring.

As an only child, he'd never experienced the relationships Alicia and her siblings took for granted. The warmth, the closeness that was simply there, the support it never occurred to them to question . . . all that was not only attractive, but spoke strongly of Alicia's ability to create for him, with him, the sort of home and family he wanted. And needed. How much he hadn't realized until he'd met her and her brood.

Regardless of his frustration, he wouldn't have her change, didn't wish she was otherwise. He valued her for what she was, as she was, and was fully prepared to accommodate that, to woo her as she needed to be wooed.

And pray he didn't do himself an injury in the meantime.

With a wrench, he hauled his mind away from that moment in the Cranbournes' front hall. Just thinking of that made him ache. Determinedly, he focused on the meeting he was heading for, with Gervase Tregarth and Jack Warnefleet.

They were waiting in the club's meeting room, comfortably slouched about the mahogany table. Christian Allardyce was also there; when he raised his brows, Tony waved him to stay. "You've already heard part of this affair—the more help the better."

Christian grinned. "And Dalziel is involved."

"Indeed." Tony sat and quickly, concisely, told them all he'd learned of Ruskin, his death, and his dealings with A.C. "This is a list of the ships mentioned in Ruskin's notes, and the associated dates, and these"—he handed over a second sheet—"are the dates on which Ruskin received large cash donations to his gambling fund."

Gervase studied the list of ships and dates, then compared them with the dates of the payments. Shifting to sit beside him, Jack perused the lists, too.

Christian, beside Tony, looked across the table at them. "I take it the payments in some way coincide with the shipping dates?"

Checking back and forth, Gervase nodded. "About a week in between, but not for every ship listed."

Tony sat back. "It appears Ruskin provided the information, it was used or in some way confirmed, and then he received payment."

"Whoever A.C. is, he ran a tight operation. No payment unless . . ." Jack stopped, looked up.

Grimly, Tony nodded. "Presumably no payment unless the information was useful."

"Which," Christian murmured, "suggests it was used for something."

"And if it was," Gervase was still studying the lists, "it wasn't for anything good."

"That," Tony agreed, "is the inescapable conclusion. What we need to determine is exactly how it was used."

Gervase nodded. "And trace it back to whoever that use benefited."

"Precisely." Tony paused, then asked, "Can you help?"

Gervase looked up, grinned. "I was intending to slip home for a few days. I can easily ask around in Plymouth, and along the coast there." He met Tony's gaze. "But you've more extensive contacts in the Isles and on the French side, and to the southeast on this side, I'd imagine."

"Yes, but my problem—our problem at present—is that that information"—Tony nodded at the lists in Gervase's hands—"is all we have. I compiled the list of ships from scattered jottings, more like reminders. Presumably the information Ruskin passed contained more detail."

"But what detail we don't know?" Jack asked.

"Exactly. Via the Revenue and Admiralty dispatches that passed through his hands, Ruskin had what amounted to each ship's sailing orders, at least for their approach to our shores." Tony looked at Gervase. "If you can find any hint of what was going on—how the information was used—I can put out feelers more widely. But given the nature of my contacts, if I ask general questions, rather than specific ones, I won't get any answers. Worse, I might alert whoever it is that's behind this."

They all understood how the informant system worked; he didn't need to explain further.

"Can I keep these?" Gervase held up the lists.

Tony nodded. "Those are copies."

Folding the lists, Gervase slipped them into his pocket. "I'll ask around and see if I can find any whisper of any action involving these ships on or about those dates. If I find anything, I'll bring it back immediately."

"Once we have a clue what we're dealing with, I'll follow up more widely."

Jack frowned. "Have you thought of inquiring via the shipping lines? If these ships are merchantmen . . ."

"I've a friend who'll be in town in a day or so—he has a similar background to ours. He's been out of the service for some years, but knows the game well. He also owns Hendon Shipping, one of the largest of the local lines. He has the contacts and will know how to make such inquiries without raising a dust."

Jack nodded. "So—what did you want me to pursue?"

"Ruskin himself, and how A. C. knew him. Ruskin lived at Bledington when he was in the country. Not often, admittedly, but it's an area we shouldn't overlook. Given you're the closest of us countywise, your inquisitive presence is least likely to attract attention. Our ultimate aim is to identify A. C. It's possible he's someone who lives out that way, and that's how he knew Ruskin, and most importantly where Ruskin worked."

"Right." Jack's gaze had grown distant. "I'll check into Ruskin's background and see if I can turn up anyone with the initials A. C. connected in however vague a fashion with our boy."

"While you're up there . . ." Tony hesitated, then went on, "You might check on a Mrs. Carrington and her family, the Pevenseys. Their connection with Ruskin appears to be via Chipping Norton. It seems Mrs. Carrington and the Pevenseys didn't know Ruskin, but he knew them."

"Carrington." Christian murmured. "That's a C."

"Indeed. More confusing, she's Alicia Carrington, so she is A. C., but she married Carrington about two years ago, so wasn't A. C. four years ago, when Ruskin first started receiving large sums from A. C. More to the point, her husband, deceased for two years, was Alfred Carrington. Although he can't be the A. C. involved either, given the way names run in families there may be a connection with Ruskin of which Mrs. Carrington is unaware."

"Oh, yes." Jack nodded; for one instant, the dangerous man behind his hail-fellow-well-met cheerily handsome facade showed through. "Second cousin, third cousin, whatever. I'll check."

They all exchanged glances, then, as one, pushed back their chairs. They stood, stretched, resettled their coats; as they turned to the door, Christian murmured, "That shipping business sounds decidedly nasty." He caught Tony's eye, then glanced at the others. They were all thinking the same thing—that someone had been using the war for their own ends.

"We definitely need to learn what the information was used for, and how," Gervase said.

"And, most importantly"—Tony followed Christian from the room—"by whom." That, indeed, was their primary interest.

Tony returned to Upper Brook Street and spent the next few hours attending to numerous matters of business. Under his father's hand, the Blake estates had grown considerably; he was determined that during his tenure, the family's fortunes would continue to expand.

The activity naturally brought to mind the family—the people—that fortune was intended to support. When the clock struck two, he set aside his papers and strolled around to Green Park.

David, Harry, and Matthew were delighted to see him. Alicia was rather more circumspect; she greeted him with a polite smile and suspicious eyes. The wind was brisk, perfect for kites; together with the boys, he spent a thoroughly satisfactory hour making theirs soar higher than anyone else's.

"It'll get trapped in the trees," Alicia grimly prophesied.

"Nonsense." Halting before her, he looked into her eyes. Fought down the urge to see how she would respond if he kissed her there, in the middle of the park with all the nursemaids and Maggs looking on. He forced himself to turn and look at the boys. All three were hanging on to the kite strings, shrieking and whooping as the kite, courtesy of his maneuvering now high above the treetops, swooped and tugged in the wind. "I assure you I manage the reins better than that."

An instant's pause ensued, then she replied, "You might. They won't."

She was right, but before the kite could come to grief in the leafless branches, he stepped in and took control again, and gradually brought the flapping creation with its long tail safely back to earth.

The boys were ecstatic, their eyes shining, cheeks rosy, glowing with happiness. Walking to join the group, Alicia studied the man about whom her brothers danced; no matter her suspicions, she could not doubt that he, too, had enjoyed the play. His black eyes gleamed as he shared the moment with her brothers; his lips were curved, the normally austere lines of his face relaxed.

As usual, he was dressed with consummate elegance in a perfectly cut dark blue coat over a white shirt, his long legs encased in tight buckskin breeches that disappeared into glossy black Hessians. The wind ruffled the black locks of his hair as he helped her brothers gather the long tail of the kite.

He was sophisticated, worldly, a gentleman of the ton, yet at moments like this she could almost believe she could see the boy he must have been, the boyishly open soul still lurking behind his adult glamor.

When she stopped beside the group, he looked up and grinned, still very much the boy. She smiled spontaneously in return. "Tea?"

The boys instantly raised a chorus of entreaty, but he didn't take his gaze from her; his grin eased into a smile of quite devastating charm. "Thank you. I'd like that."

With the boys about them and Maggs following with the kite in his arms, they headed back to Waverton Street.

Teatime was the usual relaxed and comfortable interlude. Maggs brought in the tray. The boys peppered Tony with questions on their latest interest—horses, curricles, and phaetons, and racing the same, while devouring their usual quota of crumpets and jam.

Alicia exchanged a smiling glance with Adriana and sat back, content to let Tony—Torrington!—manage as he would; although his knowledge of such male subjects was patently wide, she now trusted him to know what was appropriate to tell her brothers, and what was not.

It wasn't them he was intent on seducing; he was more than wise enough to know he'd have more chance with her—

She broke off that thought and looked at Adriana. Busy as usual with sketches of gowns, hats, and accessories, her sister seemed quieter than usual. She seemed to be thinking, mulling—over what Alicia could easily guess.

She leaned closer; under cover of a rowdy conversation about swan-necked phaetons and their propensity to overturn, she murmured, "Mr. King sent a reply. He'll gather his information and dine with us the day after tomorrow."

Adriana looked up, held her gaze for a moment, then, lips firming, nodded. "Good." After a moment, she added, "If there's any difficulty . . . I need to know now."

Alicia patted her hand, then drew back.

Although courtesy of her brothers' eager opinions Tony hadn't heard what was said, he noted the sisters' exchange and made a mental note to ascertain just how serious Geoffrey was. The last thing he wanted was for Alicia to become anxious over her sister's budding romance. He wanted her attention, as much of it as he could get, for himself.

Maggs reappeared to remove the tea tray, bending a glance on Tony that he read with ease: nothing to report. At Alicia's command, the boys stood and took their leave, resigned to returning to their lessons. As they trooped to the door, Tony looked at Adriana.

She met his gaze, then fleetingly, conspiratorially smiled. Gathering her papers and sketchbook, she stood; directing an airy, "I'll be in my room if you need me," to Alicia, she followed her brothers out of the door, shutting it behind her.

The instant the door closed, Tony rose and sank onto the chaise where Adriana had been. Alongside Alicia.

She directed a wide-eyed look his way. "Ah—have you learned anything more about Ruskin, about what he was up to?"

Habit prompted him to answer with a simple "No," and then distract her from the subject, but his decision not to conceal such matters from her weighed against such a tack. "Nothing specific—as I said, I've various inquiries under way."

Reaching into his coat pocket, he drew out the originals of the lists he'd made of ships' names, dates, and Ruskin's payments. "This"—stretching out his legs, crossing his ankles, he settled back. Straightening the lists, he held them up before him—"are all we have to work with at present."

She hesitated, but had to lean closer to look.

Her shoulder brushing his arm, Alicia read the entries; she was determined to keep their conversation focused on the safe and highly pertinent subject of his investigation. Relatively safe; clearly, he was not above using every opportunity that came his way to ruffle her senses, even this. His writing was neat, precise, but quite small; she had to press closer still to make out the dates—her senses flared with awareness, of him, of his strength, of the promise of sensual delight her wanton wits now associated with him.

She waved at the lists. "These dates. They seem to be related in some way—not exactly, but . . ."

He nodded. "We think—"

Without further prompting, he explained what the lists were, what he believed they meant. To her surprise, he even told her what his assumptions regarding the lists' significance were, what he hoped to learn from the shipping companies, the ports, and the mariners, and how that might indicate further avenues to explore . . . it was intriguing.

She found herself enthused with a zeal to in some way assist in working out the puzzle of what Ruskin's information was used for, and why. She'd intended to do something—pushing the investigation to a rapid conclusion would remove the most compelling excuse Torrington had to call on her, to be close to her.

About to ask how she could help, she stopped; why ask? Reaching for the lists, she drew them from his fingers. "May I make copies of these?"

His brows rose, but he nodded. "If you like."

Tony watched as she stood and crossed to the escritoire standing against the wall between the windows. She sat, drew out a sheet of paper, then settled to copy his lists. A slanting beam of sunlight struck coppery red glints from her dark hair. In the evenings, she wore it coiled high; during the day, the heavy loops were neatly constrained at her nape, the dark silk lustrous against her pale skin.

A fleeting notion of releasing that restrained abundance, of spreading it in a sheening mahogany veil over her bare shoulders, a distracting screen about her charms, filled him. Caught him. Momentarily held him.

She glanced at him, alerted, suspicious, but not knowing why.

He frowned, surreptitiously shifted. "What do you intend to do with those?"

Laying aside her pen, she blotted the lists, then rose and turned to him. "I don't know. If I have them, then when I think of something . . ." She shrugged. His originals in her hand, she walked back to the chaise.

His frown wasn't feigned. "If you do think of anything, or learn anything, promise me you'll tell me immediately."

Alicia halted before him, met his eyes. After a moment's consideration, she nodded. "I promise." What else was she to do with anything she learned?

She held out the lists. For one moment, his gaze didn't leave her face, then it slowly lowered, eventually fastening on the sheets in her hand.

He reached out—reached farther than the sheets and grasped her wrist. Long fingers locking, he tugged.

Before she could catch her breath, she was on his lap, in his arms. In a flurry of skirt and petticoats, she tried to right herself, tried to push back.

She heard a deep chuckle, felt it reverberate through her palms, braced on his chest. "We have a few moments . . ." His tone was pure temptation.

Resist, resist, resist.

She drew breath, looked up. And his lips came down on hers.

He captured them, captured her mouth, bewitched her senses. She was kissing him back, flagrantly participating in the exchange before her wits caught up with her actions. He shifted; she felt him pluck his lists from her nerveless fingers, fold them, and tuck them into his pocket.

Then his arms rose and closed about her, his head angled, and he parted her lips wider, his tongue evocatively thrusting deep, then settling to a typical, devastatingly intimate game. Of exploration, of enticement.

Soon her mind was whirling, senses locked with his as together they fed their mutual hunger, created and assuaged a mutual desire. Fingers tangled in his hair, she clung, savored, appeased, and demanded.

How long they indulged in the heated sensations she had no idea, but her wits returned with a jolt when she felt his hands between them, opening the buttons down the front of her walking dress.

It took a huge effort but she broke from the kiss; he was distracted, so let her go. On a gasp, she looked down, then glanced wildly around. "Ah . . ."

"Don't worry." From under his heavy lids, his black eyes caught hers. He searched, read, then his lips twisted wryly. "Your brothers are safe upstairs, so is your sister. Jenkins is with your brothers, and the rest are in the kitchens. No one is going to come through the door, not in the next half hour."

Half hour? What might he do in half an hour?

"That's—" She had to stop and moisten her lips, had to whip her wits into order. She was supposed to resist, or at least . . . she looked down, saw his fingers dark against the skin he was swiftly uncovering, couldn't quite suppress a tense, expectant shiver. "This is . . . really too . . . that is . . ."

Good Lord! Her words died along with her wits when he slipped a hand between the gaping halves of her bodice, with a flick of his fingers dispensed with her chemise, and boldly set his hand to her skin.

The touch was a sensual shock, not muted in the least by the fact she'd expected it, knew what his hand felt like there, cupping her breast, taking its weight, fingers gently kneading, then artfully teasing the already tightly ruched peak. Her lids drifted down, eyes closing as the sensations swept her—then she remembered and jerked her eyes open. Half-open. Enough to look into his face.

He was watching her. "Stop fighting it—just enjoy."

His hand moved on her, her wits started to slide . . .

"No! That is . . ." She drew a determined breath, only to discover she couldn't; her lungs had locked. Her nerves had tensed, not in rejection but in pleasured delight. The urge to press her breast into his warm hand was compelling, almost overwhelming. She held it at bay.

Fingers sinking into his shoulders, lids closing, she managed to shake her head. "I—you . . . this. We *can't*—"

She broke off with a sound very close to a moan.

His hand shifted, fingers closing more definitely about the aching peak he'd so effectively tortured, with expert ministrations soothed the pain, but that somehow only escalated the ache.

"I told you not to worry."

His words, deep and gravelly, reached through the fog of her whirling senses. "If you need to go slowly, we will. We have no need to rush."

On the words, his hand left her, fingers trailing upward, then she felt him ease her gown over the peak of her left shoulder. Baring her breast. His hand returned to its seductive play; she knew he was watching as he caressed her swollen flesh. As he knowingly tightened every nerve she possessed.

"We can take the long road." His voice had deepened, darkened, weaving a sorcerous spell. "And spend as much time as we wish enjoying every sight, every experience along the way."

Her breasts ached; her whole body seemed to throb.

He leaned nearer; his lips brushed hers. "Is that what you want?"

She nodded. "Yes." The word was a whisper between their lips.

"So be it," he whispered back. Then sealed the pact with a kiss.

A kiss that ripped her wits away and sent them spinning. That sent heat and flame pouring through her, down every nerve, down every vein. His hand left her and he gathered her closer; holding her in one arm, he sent his hand exploring again.

Caressing her through her clothes. Not just her breasts, but everywhere. His hand traced her shoulders, her back, her spine, delineated the muscles on either side, then spanned the back of her waist. His palm, hot and hard, passed over her hip, then boldly caressed her bottom. He traced the globes, over and around, all the while holding her to their kiss, to the slow, steady dizzying rhythm of thrust and retreat he'd established.

Her senses spun as he cupped the back of her thigh, then moved down, found her knee, then swept upward. Inward.

She gasped, would have stiffened in his arms, but he didn't allow it. His other hand shifted, gripping her bottom, holding her still. Then his questing hand splayed over her stomach; he pressed, kneaded, then held her tight, not just in his arms but sensually, too, as he reached lower, traced the tops of her thighs, then stroked, through the fine fabric of her walking dress gently probed the hollow between, caressed the soft curls beneath chemise and gown.

Teased her to life.

Until every nerve in her body was tingling, until heat pulsed just beneath her skin.

Eventually, gradually, he drew back. Eased her back.

Eventually he lifted his head, looked into her face, then brushed her lips once more with his. "If you want it slow, we'll go slowly. Very, *very* slowly."

From beneath her heavy lids, she caught the fire in his eyes.

The reassurance was what she'd wanted.

She wasn't sure she'd survive.

EIGHT

AFTERNOON TEA IN WAVERTON STREET WAS A SOCIAL engagement Tony felt he could easily grow fond of. In contrast, balls, routs, and soirées held far less appeal; there he had to share Alicia's attention with anyone else who thought to claim it.

However, she'd asked to go slowly, to rein in their progress, and if he was honest and viewed the whole dispassionately, there was much to be said in support of her request.

He was engaged in a serious and difficult investigation, one in which she was involved; it made sense to conclude the matter, to identify, locate, and nullify A.C. before addressing what lay between them. Before formally mentioning marriage and precipitating the associated hullabaloo.

She was right; they should take the long road. Entering Lady Cumberland's ballroom, he tried to tell himself he accepted the decree.

He found Alicia in her usual position by the wall near Adriana's circle. As more families returned to town, that circle grew; the quality of its members was also increasing. Adriana now had two earl's sons dancing attendance, along with six of lesser standing, including Sir Freddie Caudel and Geoffrey, who looked somewhat tense.

Recognizing in his childhood friend some of the impatience he himself was feeling, Tony inwardly raised his brows. Luckily in his case, Alicia seemed impervious to the frequent advances made by numerous gentlemen; she consistently dismissed them with an almost absent-minded air. He was the only one she'd allowed to draw close, to impinge on her personal world. Unlike Geoffrey, he didn't need to worry that some rake would appear and turn her head.

Reaching Alicia, all thoughts of Adriana and her swains disappeared; taking Alicia's hand—the hand she now freely offered—he bowed, then placed her fingers on his sleeve, covering them with his.

She looked up at him, faintly arched a brow.

He simply smiled at her.

With a haughty look, she returned to her watching brief.

He studied her. Her gown of apricot silk, a warm and subtle shade, deepened the rich mahogany of her hair and made her creamy complexion glow. The gown hugged her curves, the silk flowing over her hips and down the long line of her legs. For the moment, he was content simply to stand and let his senses drink her in.

Two days had passed since he'd last had her to himself. He'd spent those days and the intervening evening pursuing a whisper Dalziel had heard of a possible link between Ruskin and someone in the War Office. Nothing, however, had come of it; while there might be someone in the War Office interested in things that were no business of theirs, there was no hint of a connection between Ruskin and anyone bar the mysterious A. C.

He'd caught up with Alicia at a ball yesterday evening; he'd had to content himself with a waltz before leaving to spend the rest of the night trawling through gentlemen's clubs and exclusive hells.

Jack Warnefleet was busy, Gervase likewise in Devon, and Jack Hendon would arrive in town late tomorrow. Jack had conveyed his willingness to place his time and contacts at Tony's disposal, an offer he intended to take up with all speed.

Tonight, however, the single question nagging him was: how slow was slow?

Cumberland House was a massive old mansion, one with numerous useful little rooms; he'd explored it years ago with some amorous young matron who had known more of its amenities than he. Such knowledge, however, was never wasted.

The musicians were resting; he wondered at his chances of convincing Alicia that Adriana would be perfectly safe for a time.

He glanced at her; she straightened, coming alert. He followed her gaze and saw Adriana looking questioningly Alicia's way.

Alicia responded; he moved with her as she glided to Adriana's side.

Adriana looked uncertain. "Sir Freddie was wondering . . ."

Smoothly urbane, Sir Freddie stepped in. "I was wondering, Mrs. Carrington, if you would permit me to take Miss Pevensey for a stroll in the conservatory. It's been opened for the evening, and many others are enjoying the cooler air. I thought perhaps you and"—Sir Freddie's gaze flicked, man-to-man, to Tony—"Lord Torrington might accompany us?"

Alicia smiled regally. "A stroll in the conservatory sounds an excellent idea—it's quite stuffy in here." She nodded encouragingly to Adriana, who smiled and accepted Sir Freddie's arm. "You go ahead, we'll follow." Alicia glanced at Tony as Adriana and Sir Freddie turned away. "If you're willing . . . ?"

He looked down at her, then slowly arched a brow. She blushed lightly and glanced away.

Ignoring Geoffrey and his suppressed displeasure—an emotion Tony had no difficulty interpreting—he tucked

Alicia's hand more definitely in his arm and steered her in her sister's wake.

While crossing the crowded ballroom, they chatted of this and that, but once inside the long conservatory, with its glass doors latched open and a wide corridor down the center cleared for promenading, there was space enough to ask, "How lies the wind in that quarter?" With a nod, he indicated Adriana, conversing animatedly with Sir Freddie.

Alicia humphed. "Much as I feared. Your friend Manningham has stolen a march on all others. However, as the saying goes, true love never runs smoothly."

"Oh? How so?"

"Adriana believes she should be certain of her feelings before she bestows her hand on any gentleman. And how is she to be sure other than by testing the waters?"

"Ah. I take it Geoffrey isn't taking well to her testing program?"

"Indeed."

He glanced down; a distinctly satisfied expression was stamped on Alicia's fine features.

"It's only sensible that a lady should be sure of her choice before declaring it, and if a gentleman has problems with that, well . . ."

Her gaze was fixed on Adriana and Sir Freddie; Tony told himself she wasn't speaking of herself. Their conversation drifted to other things, yet as they returned to the ballroom, he couldn't quite rid himself of the suggestion.

If she needed assistance making up her mind, he was only too ready—and willing—to supply it. How slowly could slowly be, after all?

The musicians had resumed; Lord Montacute was waiting to claim Adriana's hand in a country dance. Sir Freddie nobly requested Alicia do him the honor; to Tony's irritation, she granted Sir Freddie's wish.

Deserted, he went searching for the refreshment room.

Geoffrey found him there. He eyed the glass in Tony's hand. "Don't tell me you've been given your congé, too?"

Tony humphed; through the arch, he was observing the dancers. "Just for this dance." He sipped, then said, "Incidentally, I was informed you're being tested."

It was Geoffrey's turn to humph. "So I'd supposed."

Shoulder to shoulder, they watched the couples swirl about the floor.

Geoffrey shifted, lifted his glass, and sipped. He glanced at Tony. "I don't suppose you'd consider staging a diversion?"

Tony's gaze was on Alicia, twirling down the set. "Divert the lioness while you whisk away her cub?"

Geoffrey swallowed a laugh, nodded. "Precisely."

Watching Alicia's body sway as, hand high, she turned beneath Sir Freddie's arm, Tony asked, "What's your interest there?"

Geoffrey's tone—insulted, a touch vulnerable—gave him his answer more than the words, "What do you think?"

Tony nodded. "Done." He set down his glass. "But I'll have to move first. If she gets any inkling of your intention, I'll never get her away."

"The field's yours." Setting down his glass, Geoffrey followed him into the ballroom. "Just make sure I get at least half an hour."

Tony glanced at him, then looked back at his prey. And smiled. "Half an hour won't be any problem."

Getting Alicia out of the ballroom and into the tiny withdrawing room at the end of the east corridor—a room Tony remembered from that long-ago exploration—was the principal difficulty. He managed it by the simple expedient of talking fast.

His topic was guaranteed to fix her interest—the contrast between sophisticated gentlemen such as Sir Fred-

die Caudel and backbone-of-the-country types epito-
mized by Geoffrey Manningham.

"I didn't know he'd been in the navy." Alicia looked
thoughtful. "I don't think Adriana knows that."

"Understandably he doesn't speak much of it, but he
served with distinction. And then, of course—"

He rattled on, borrowing from his knowledge of Geoffrey, inventing shamelessly with regard to Sir Freddie.
Her eyes on his face, her mind on his words, Alicia barely
registered entering the corridor running alongside the
ballroom; when she went to look around, he mentioned
Geoffrey's mother—her gaze immediately swung back to
his face. His fingers firmly over hers, resting on his
sleeve, he steered her on.

When he opened the door to the withdrawing room,
she swept over the threshold of her own volition, held by
the vision he'd painted of Geoffrey's manor house and
the surrounding countryside, the rolling fields leading
down to the river with the blue hills in the distance, the
lowering plateau of Exmoor stretching to the horizon.

Gesturing, she turned to face him. "It sounds an almost
idyllic place."

Much of what he'd described was his own land, his
boyhood memories of home; his smile was genuine. "It
is."

He closed the door; without taking his gaze from her
face, he snibbed the lock. The sound broke the spell.

She blinked, glanced around. A three-armed candelabrum threw a warm glow through the small room.
Aside from a chaise and a single armchair, the only furniture was a small table and a heavy sideboard. She looked
at him. Directly. "Why are we here?"

He raised his brows, approached. "Guess."

Suspicion burgeoned in her eyes; as usual, she made
no effort to hide it. He watched her cast about in her mind
for some deflecting comment, yet as he neared . . . her

eyes widened, darkened—he could almost see her senses awakening, stretching. Reaching for him. Could almost see her wits start to slow . . .

He reached for her, gently drew her to him.

She came without resistance, her hands rising to rest on his chest. Her gaze dropped to his lips. "I . . . ah . . . I thought we'd agreed to slow down."

"We did." He urged her closer, settled her against him, bent his head. "We are." He kissed her, made her lips cling. "Progressing step by small step."

He took her mouth again; she gave it freely, met him, parted her lips, welcomed him in. Her hands clenched, clutched as he captured her senses and drew her deeper into the exchange, into the sensual game they both so enjoyed.

Lips caressed, pressed, tongues tangled, stroked, probed, mouths melded. Both took, gave, delighted, then explored.

Sensation streaked through Alicia; warmth welled, pooled, and dragged her senses down to wallow, to luxuriate, to expand and experience a world of sensual delight, of wanton, illicit, addictive pleasure.

No matter how much a small part of her mind tried to warn her, tried to make her see how dangerous it could be, her body, her nerves, her skin and her senses, and the greater part of her whirling wits, were eager to go forward, to follow the path he opened before her, to seize the moment to learn and feel.

To learn of herself, of what could be, of all she could be. To feel the welling tide of compulsive emotions—the hunger, the need, the flagrant desire, and most especially the triumph.

A simple and pure triumph she hadn't known existed, the confidence, delight, and sheer pleasure of knowing he found her desirable, that he wanted her in the most blatantly sexual way, and the satisfaction that flowed from knowing not only that she could evoke his hunger, but also from the innate womanly knowledge that she could, indeed, sate it.

He'd drawn her close, fitting her body against his, but once they reached that plateau of more urgent, definite need—one she now recognized—his arms eased, then his hands, hard and demanding, slid over her silk-encased form. Over her back, over her sides, around over her already aching breasts.

Through the fog of desire flooding her mind, she inwardly smiled. She eased back from the kiss enough to murmur against his lips, "I'm afraid this gown has no buttons down the front." She'd worn her topaz silk for that very reason.

"I'd noticed," he murmured back.

His lips brushed hers, then settled, drawing her into a long, increasingly intimate exchange . . . as it ended her awareness slowly returned. And she realized the pressure about her breasts had eased.

Her bodice was loose.

She drew back from the kiss as he did. Looked down as he raised his hands to her shoulders. Slowly, very slowly, he pushed her now gaping gown off her shoulders, sliding the small puff sleeves down her arms.

He'd undone the laces.

Her mind seized; she stopped breathing. She hadn't thought . . .

The neckline caught across the peaks of her breasts. Leaving the sleeves at her elbows, he ran his fingers up, then slipped them beneath the neckline and eased it over and down.

She shuddered, told herself it was due to the cool caress of the air. Knew it wasn't. Desperate, she hauled in a breath. Ignored the sudden lifting of her breasts. "Wait—"

"Lift your arms." The words were half entreaty, half command. They were reinforced by his touch, fingertips running over her bared shoulders, down the sensitive skin of her arms to her elbows. He gripped lightly, urged.

She freed her arms from the clinging sleeves. "This—"

"Is the smallest step I could think of." His black gaze touched hers; the emberlike glow in the dark depths only heated her more.

She sucked in a tight breath. "But—"

"Going slowly isn't stopping." He held her gaze, his fingers lightly caressing—so lightly they barely touched the heavy, swelling curves of her breasts. "You don't want to stop."

Not a question, a statement, one verified by the shiver that streaked through her, a silvery sensation that brought every nerve alive.

His lips curved, openly predatory, entirely undisguised. He bent his head. His lips cruised over hers as his fingers drifted, as his hands followed, then firmed, taking possession as they had before. But before she hadn't been as aware, as blatantly near-naked. As heated.

Her breath caught.

One hand kneaded, the other slid away. His arm slipped about her waist; holding her, he backed her, step by slow, easy step until she felt the sideboard behind her.

Lifting his head, he fastened both hands about her waist and lifted her to the sideboard's top. He sat her there; hands clutching his shoulders, she glanced down. Her gown had slid to her hips. Before she could react, he bunched the skirts and raised them to her knees, allowing him to part them and step between.

Her mind was whirling, wits totally scattered.

He met her eyes; his lips curved, but it wasn't exactly in a smile. "For us . . . the only way to slow our inevitable progression is to indulge in more intensive play."

She searched his eyes, instinctively accepted that as truth. Yet . . .

He leaned closer, lips swooping, nearing as his hands rose, fingers reaching for the tiny ribbon bows securing her silk chemise. The last flimsy barrier screening her from his sight.

Dizzy desperation gripped her; she sank her fingers into his shoulders. "I—"

He hesitated, but when she couldn't find the words—any words that made sense—he closed the inch between their lips, kissed. Drew back enough to breathe, "You know where we're headed, don't you? You know what lies at the end of our road."

Her lips were dry, yearning, hungry. She forced herself to nod. "Yes."

"Then there's no reason I shouldn't see you, bare you, and look my fill. No reason I shouldn't take what pleasure I wish with you, in you—and you shouldn't take all you wish of me."

His lips closed on hers, warm and beguiling; he didn't rip her wits away, didn't send them spinning, but left her aware, attuned, every nerve tight and flickering.

So she knew when his fingers closed on the ribbon ties, so she felt the tugs as he unraveled the bows, then slowly, gently, inexorably eased the fine fabric down. Exposing her breasts.

And then his hands were on her, hot skin to hot skin. He caressed, fondled, kneaded, squeezed. Her senses filled, overflowed; sensation rushed through her, down her nerves, down her veins.

She couldn't think, no longer had space in her mind for that activity, swept away, consumed by the dizzying splendor, the bone-melting pleasure he pressed on her. His lips left hers; he nudged her head back, skated his lips down the taut tendon to settle over her pulse point, heating her blood still further. Her fingers, until then gripping his shoulders, eased; she sent her hands sliding over and back, found and caressed his nape.

His lips left her throat and slid lower. Splaying her fingers, she speared them through his thick locks, then clutched. Eyes closed, she held tight as his burning lips cruised the upper swells of her breasts. Then dipped lower still.

Her world stopped when his lips found one aching peak.

Splintered when he took it into his mouth.

Hot, wet, he caressed, laved, licked, than gently rasped.

Her breasts felt on fire, tight, taut; head tilting back, she gasped, spine tensing as he artfully teased, then openly feasted. Then he shifted, drew the aching, tormented peak deep, and suckled.

The jolt of sensation rocked her, shocked her, surprised a small cry from her. Her fingers spasmed on his skull. Eyes shut, she struggled to cope, to cling to sanity as with mouth, lips, and tongue, hard fingers and palms, he pressed sensation after sensation upon her.

Through her fingers, through the tension gripping her, Tony read her increasing desperation. Every sense he possessed was locked on her, watching, gauging . . . he eased back.

Heard in her tortured breathing a return from the brink of panic.

He didn't take his lips from her skin, but traced, kissed lightly, soothed with gentle caresses. When she'd calmed enough to be lucid, he cupped both breasts in his palms, straightened slightly, shifting between her spread thighs. Bent again to touch his lips to the hot satin skin of the now swollen mounds. "Didn't your husband caress you like this?"

Her lids cracked open. From behind the screen of her lashes, her eyes met his. A moment passed, then she licked her lips. Tried to speak, ended by shaking her head.

When he waited, she dragged in a breath. "No. He . . ."

Primitive joy streaked through him. He waited; when she remained silent, he prompted, "Wasn't inclined to see to your pleasure?" A common enough failing, after all.

She shuddered. Beneath his hand, he could feel her heart still pounding, but slower. Her skin was still heated; he kept it that way, idly kneading, caressing.

Again she drew breath, again met his eyes. "I . . . don't know all that much about . . . pleasure."

The word came out on a soft exhalation; she closed her eyes as he again bent and savored one tightly budded nipple. He released it, blew gently on it, then soothed it again.

Lifting his head to examine the effect, he murmured, "It'll be my pleasure to teach you." Shifting his hands, he set his thumbs to circle her nipples.

"I—that's why . . ." She broke off, drew in a hissed breath. "Why it must be slow . . ."

On his shoulders, her fingers tensed again, but not, this time, with any sense of desperation. He watched her face as he caressed. "Forget about your husband. Forget all you ever knew." Keeping one hand on her breast, he slid the other to the small of her back and eased her to the sideboard's edge. His hand still at her breast, he bent his head to take her mouth.

Before he did, he murmured, his voice low, gravelly, decided. "Start again. With me. I'll teach you all you should know, all you need to know."

Her fingers slid to his nape, cupped as he covered her lips, held tight as he plunged into her mouth and took possession. Plundered, ravished, devoured as he wished; she met him, went with him, followed him deeper. Until the exchange became a flagrant echo of that other intimacy, until hot and heated she clung to the rhythm, matching him, sating his hunger as it rose, learning of her own.

He'd pressed her thighs wide; her silk skirts lay in a spill covering her knees, but beneath . . . he knew precisely what he would find when he released her breast and slid his hand beneath the folds of silk.

The skin of her inner thighs was as fine as the silk, as delicate, but far warmer. She was too deep in the kiss to do more than vaguely register as he stroked, caressed. Deliberately, he let her surface, step by step until he sensed her sudden awareness, felt the gasp smothered between their lips as she realized.

She started to tense; he deepened the kiss, just enough to distract her, to fracture her attention long enough to let him explore further. To reach higher and find her, swollen and fever-damp, hot enough to scald.

Slow. Step by step.

He forced himself to do no more than touch her, to find the tiny nubbin within the folds and caress, but go no further.

Tiny shivers of sensation coursed through her as he stroked, gently pressed. He knew what he might do, knew the potential, but sensed she wasn't ready for that yet.

Alfred Carrington must have been an insensitive clod.

He continued to touch her gently, undemandingly exploring, letting her grow accustomed to him touching her there, to the intimacy, mild to his mind though it was.

Step by step.

He let her surface by degrees, let her awareness rise free from the drugging kisses, until at the last he could raise his head and watch her face. Watch her lips, parted and swollen as he circled, then pressed lightly. Catch her eyes as he stroked, and she shuddered.

Then softly sighed.

She dropped her forehead to his shoulder. After a moment, said, "This is all so—"

She broke off. He stroked again, felt her shiver. "More than you expected?"

Against his shoulder, she nodded. "Much, much more."

Satisfied with the way events were proceeding not just with Alicia but also with his investigation, Tony felt distinctly mellow, a prey to pleasurable anticipation as the next evening he went upstairs to change.

He'd reached the landing when a heavy knock fell on the front door.

He recognized the knock. Halting, he waited, one hand on the balustrade as Hungerford strode majestically to the door. He'd recognized the knock, too. He pulled open the door, revealing Maggs.

Hungerford looked down his nose. "I believe you know where the back entrance is?"

"'Course I do. Live here, don't I?" Maggs lumbered in, his hat in his hands. "But I'm supposed to be Mrs. Carrington's footman. If I came with a message, I wouldn't come to the back door, would I?"

Turning back down the stairs, Tony straightened his lips. "What is it, Maggs?"

Maggs looked up. "Oh, there you be." He hesitated, frown growing as Tony descended. As he gained the front hall, Maggs suggested, "You might want to hear this in private."

Brows rising, Tony looked at Hungerford. "Thank you, Hungerford. I'm sure Maggs can see himself out."

That last was said with a hint of understanding. Hungerford bowed stiffly. "Indeed, my lord. If you have need of anything, you have only to ring."

"Thank you." Tony turned to Maggs and waved to the study. Hungerford departed; Maggs opened the study door. Tony entered and went to sit behind his desk; closing the door, Maggs came to stand before it.

Maggs had been a stable lad at Torrington Chase when Tony had been a boy; he'd attached himself to the son of the house and followed him into the army. Whenever Tony had had need of a batman, Maggs had filled the position. He'd been a part of Tony's life for longer than he could remember, and continued as his most trusted servant. Despite Maggs's bruiser's countenance, the man was intelligent, capable, and effective.

"What is it?" Tony asked.

Maggs's frown hadn't eased. "I don't know as you'll

believe this, but the ladies, Mrs. Carrington and Miss Pevensey, are sitting down to dinner—well, they'd be near to finished by now—with a gentleman goes by the name of Mr. King. Wouldn't've thought much of it 'cept I've seen him before, and I'd swear on my mother's grave he's Mr. King, the moneylender."

Tony blinked. After a long moment of staring at Maggs, he nodded. "You're right—I find that very hard to believe."

Maggs sighed heavily. "Well, there you are. But Collier's on watch at the corner, so you needn't think I've deserted my post and left the lady unguarded."

"Good." Tony was finding it hard to focus his thoughts. Mr. King? As a *dinner guest*? He refocused on Maggs. "What's the relationship between Mr. King and the ladies? How did they react to him?"

"Friendly." Maggs shrugged. "Nothing heavy-handed, if that's what you're thinking. They treated him like he was an old friend of the family."

Tony inwardly goggled. He stood. "Come on. I'll know Mr. King if I see him." He shook his head as he rounded the desk. "I can't believe this."

"Aye, well." Maggs lumbered after him. "I did warn you."

Half an hour later, from the shadows of his town carriage pulled up by the curb close to the end of Waverton Street, Tony watched a large, burly gentleman take his leave of Alicia and Adriana. The sisters remained just inside the front hall, but the hall and porch lights were lit; it was easy to make out the genuineness of their smiles as the three shook hands.

Then Mr. King turned and descended to the unmarked black carriage that awaited him.

Maggs had returned to his duties. Collier, the man Tony had set to watch the street, was in his accustomed place. Tony sat back and waited until Mr. King's carriage rumbled past. He didn't bother to glance again at the occupant; it was definitely London's most famous moneylender.

He remembered Alicia's odd reaction when he'd mentioned he'd visited the man.

The door of the Carrington abode shut. Slumped against the cushions, Tony waited, totally unable to formulate any possible scenario to account for what he'd seen. Five minutes later, he tapped on the roof and directed his coachman to return to Upper Brook Street.

Courtesy of Maggs, these days he always knew where Alicia would be. That evening, she was attending Lady Magnuson's ball; as usual, he found her by the side of the room, watching over Adriana.

Who, he inwardly admitted, now needed to be watched. The Season was nearly upon them; the wolves of the ton were back in force, actively hunting in their favorite ground. As he approached, he saw Alicia step forward and engage one of the younger brethren who, until then, had remained unwisely oblivious of her presence.

It was instantly apparent from the young buck's face that a few words had sufficed for her to draw blood; his face hardened, lips thinning. After one last look at Adriana, he sloped off to find easier—less well guarded—prey.

A flicker of unease tickled Tony's shoulder blades. Adriana and her beauty posed a danger. She was too young to fix the interest of the truly dangerous blades, yet she nevertheless drew their eyes, which then passed on—to her sister. Who was much more the sort to attract a connoisseur's attention.

Reaching Alicia, gowned in a pale bronze creation edged with tiny pearls, he took the hand she offered, almost absentmindedly raised it to his lips, then met her eyes as he kissed.

He watched a light blush rise to her cheeks.

She tugged; placing her hand on his sleeve, he covered it with his.

"I need to speak with you." He glanced at Adriana's court. "And before you tell me you need to remain here and protect your sister, regardless of your recent intervention, you don't."

She frowned. "That doesn't make sense."

"It does if you consider." Casting a last glance at Adriana's circle, he turned her, steering her down the long room. "If you hadn't stepped in, either Sir Freddie or Geoffrey would have. Or even Montacute. They've been dancing at your sister's feet for weeks—none of them will take kindly to any rakish interloper thinking to poach their prize."

She still frowned, more in puzzlement than irritation, but continued strolling beside him. "You make it sound like a competition. A sport."

"It's a game no matter which side you're on." He spotted an opening between two groups of potted palms; deftly, he whisked them into it. "Now, quite aside from that . . ."

He stopped, unsure how to proceed. How to ask what he had to. He glanced at her; she was studying him, not suspiciously but directly. "I was passing along Waverton Street earlier this evening and saw Mr. King leaving your house."

Her gaze didn't waver; she continued to regard him attentively.

"I mentioned meeting Mr. King in the course of my investigations. Is he . . . an acquaintance?"

Without hesitation, she nodded, then looked out at the room. "Yes—he's just that, an acquaintance."

Alicia let a moment elapse, then, her gaze still on the crowd, asked, "Do you want to know why he called?"

She heard a hiss, an exhalation through his teeth.

"Yes."

She'd assumed he would hear of King's visit; she'd re-hearsed her explanation. "We made his acquaintance some months ago through matters arising from my late husband's estate. Mr. King knew of our wish to establish Adriana creditably." She glanced up, and found Tony watching her closely. "He offered to give us the benefit of his knowledge regarding the financial status of any gentleman Adriana was seriously considering."

The look in his eyes was priceless; he was astounded, could barely believe his ears . . . she sensed it the moment he did.

His gaze sharpened. "What did Mr. King say about Geoffrey?"

She grimaced, let her uncertainty show. "That he's perfectly sound. He's never had dealings with any money-lenders, but they would be happy to have him on their books. His credit is excellent, his estates are in exemplary order. Financially, he passed with flying colors."

"So why aren't you thrilled?" Two matrons took up position on the other side of one set of palms. Grasping Alicia's elbow, Tony guided her out of their nook. A waltz was just starting; the dance floor seemed the next safest place.

He drew her into his arms, looked down at her face as he started them revolving, noted the frown in her eyes. "It's obvious your sister favors Geoffrey, and he's intent on her. You've received reports from all and sundry that his character and situation are beyond reproach. Why, therefore, your hesitation?"

They revolved twice before she met his eyes. Her gaze was level and serious. "Money, title, and estate are all well and good, and character to date as well. But who can foresee the future?" She blew out a breath and looked away. "If I could be certain he's all Adriana *deserves*, I'd feel happier."

Tony steered her around the tight turn at the end of the

room; she remained relaxed in his arms, warm, at ease, yet as so often was the case, focused on her family, in this case, Adriana. He studied her face as they precessed up the room; he could read her abstraction clearly.

What a lady deserved.

He'd never heard that advanced as a criterion for marriage, yet for the sort of marriage Alicia wished for her sister it was perhaps more pertinent, more relevant. And she was right; such a stipulation was much harder to guarantee—that a gentleman could and would provide what a lady deserved.

The waltz ended, but her concept remained, inhabiting his mind, directing his thoughts as they strolled through the glittering throng. Lady Magnuson was old but wealthy and well connected; all those of the haut ton already in town were certain to attend, to look in for at least an hour and show their faces. Many stopped them, most trying their hand at divining just what their relationship was; neither he nor Alicia gave them any joy. Which only fed the whispers.

He glanced at her. She was frowning, trying to catch a glimpse of her sister's court. Lifting his head, he looked over the crowd. "Adriana appears hale and whole." He glanced at Alicia. "She's managing perfectly well."

She frowned at him. "I should return to her—"

"No, you shouldn't." He anchored her hand more firmly on his sleeve. "She's too sensible to go out of the ballroom without your permission, and with both Geoffrey and Sir Freddie standing guard, no bounder will have any chance of whisking her off undetected."

"Yes, but—" She broke off as he whisked her into a dimly lit corridor. "Where are we going?"

"I don't know." That was the worst of having spent the last decade elsewhere. Taking her hand in his, he strolled on. "I don't know this house."

His hearing was acute; he passed door after door, hearing muffled giggles or grunts from the rooms within.

She tried to slow, but he kept her with him. She tugged at his hand. "We can't just—"

"Of course we can." He stopped outside a door, listened, then hearing nothing opened it silently. Caught a glimpse of a white rump plunging, and swiftly closed it. "Just not there."

He heard the growing frustration in his voice; from the odd glance she threw him, she heard it, too.

They turned a corner; it was instantly apparent they'd reached a wing that was no longer in use. No lights glowed; there was dust on the sidetable farther along. He stepped to the side and opened a door, cautiously. Looking in, he breathed again. "Perfect."

He drew her over the threshold and closed the door, with one finger snibbed the lock. Busy looking around, she didn't hear.

"What a lovely room."

He released her and she headed for the windows; uncurtained, they looked out over a stone-flagged courtyard with a long pond in its center, a fountain, still and silent, rising from the black water. Lily pads were unfurling, spreading across the obsidian surface. Moonlight, stark and ghostly white, poured softly over all, casting black shadows in the lee of the creeper-covered walls, edging each new ivy leaf in silver.

She glanced at him as he joined her. "I wonder why the room's unused."

"The Magnusons were a large family, but there's only Lady Magnuson left now. Her daughters are married and gone." He hesitated, then added, "Both her sons died at Waterloo."

She looked around the room, at the furniture swathed in holland covers. "It seems . . . sad."

After a moment, she glanced up at him.

What a lady deserves.

How unpredictable, how ephemeral, how precious life was.

Slowly, he bent his head and kissed her, despite all gave her the chance to deny him if she chose. She didn't. She lifted her face, met his lips with hers. They touched, caressed, firmed. She raised a hand and gently, tentatively, laid her fingers along his cheek.

He slid an arm around her, smoothly yet more slowly than usual; it seemed important to savor each moment, to draw each instant, each movement, each acceptance, each commitment out. To fully know and appreciate every subtle nuance as they came together, as without words, he steered her to the next step.

Heat blossomed, spread beneath their skins, pooled low, then coalesced. Tightened. Throbbed.

Alicia opened her senses, tried for the first time to deliberately explore the effect of each touch, each caress. Whenever she tried to cling to control, she was swept away, so instead she went forward of her own accord, eyes open, senses aware, ready to learn, to see, to know. To, perhaps, understand what this was, what fed the power he could so easily conjure between them.

And learn to manage it herself.

As he did.

The kiss lengthened, deepened, yet not once did his control even quiver. He knew what he was doing, scripted and directed their play . . . this time she participated without hestitation, eagerly, determinedly following his lead. Waiting to see where it led.

She was trapped in his arms, locked against him, flagrantly molded to him when he finally raised his head. He looked down at her face. She could feel their mutual need, a well-stoked furnace seething between them.

He eased his hold on her, held her until she was steady on her feet. His eyes were dark as they held hers, yet she could feel the heat in his gaze.

"Open your bodice for me."

The words were gravelly, deep, and dark. She held his gaze for an instant, then calmly looked down. Lifting her hands, she slipped the tiny pearl buttons free.

She felt him exhale. His arms fell from her. He looked around, then stepped back and lifted the holland cover from a large shape, revealing a big, well-padded arm-chair. It was set facing the windows so any occupant could enjoy the view.

Dropping the dust sheet to the floor, he looked at her. Met her gaze as she slipped the last button free.

He reached for her, still moving with that measured grace that only heightened her expectations, that gave time for anticipation to well before she felt the next touch as he drew her to stand before him.

She watched him watching her as his hands rose and closed on her shoulders. He pushed the gown down, inch by inch steadily slipped the sleeves down. Without wait-ing for any instruction, she lifted her arms from the nar-row sleeves, then, emboldened, draped them about his shoulders and stepped closer.

Saw the dark flare in his eyes as she did. Felt his hands tense on the folds of silk at her waist, then, holding her gaze, he slowly slid his hands down, tracing the curve of her hips, sliding her gown over them until, with a soft swoosh, it fell to the floor.

She caught her breath, felt the air on her skin, felt panic rise—

He circled her waist, drew her against him, flush against his hard body, and kissed her. Not ravenously but forcefully, then he lifted his head. "Slowly. One step more." He lifted his lids, met her gaze. "Trust me. It'll be as you wish." His gaze dropped to her lips; he lowered his head. "And all you deserve."

The promise feathered over her lips. Then he kissed her.

She stood locked against him in a dark, deserted room clad only in her chemise and her even finer silk stockings.

If she wished, she could retreat—she knew it—yet as he kissed her she could feel the strength of his control, could feel the tight rein he kept on his passions.

Therein lay safety.

Nothing ventured, nothing learned. And she had to learn more. At least his next step, so she could predict the one after.

Tightening her arms about his neck, she kissed him back.

NINE

HER CHEMISE REACHED TO MIDTHIGH; IN THE POOR light, he wouldn't be able to see through it. Her stockings covered her legs, the garters hidden beneath the chemise's hem. She was clad, albeit thinly; wrapped in his arms, his lips on hers, his tongue tangling with hers, she certainly wasn't cold.

Committed to playing her part, she set aside all maidenly reserve and gave herself up to it—to his embrace, to the slow-burning embers that glowed between them. No flames yet; he kept them dampened, but she knew the potential was there. It was a measure of his control that he could so easily hold the conflagration at bay, at a safe distance so she could feel the warmth, experience the pleasure, but not be burned by it. Not be consumed.

He held to his slow, measured, almost languid pace. The intimacy deepened; the urgency did not.

His control—the trust she placed in him—was what allowed her to stand within his arms and with simple passion kiss him back. He took her invitation as offered, savored her mouth, her lips; she in turn savored his pleasure.

When he straightened, eased his hold on her, sat in the armchair and urged her onto his lap, her confidence, her need to know, and her trust in him held firm, allowing her to sit across his hard thighs, to let him lift her, arrange her as he would. Then he drew her to him, locking her again in the circle of his arms, and kissed her. She responded willingly, eagerly, waiting to learn.

They were taking the long road; there had to be more steps before they approached the ultimate intimacy. She'd done her homework as well as she could, yet although she'd found two texts purporting to describe the physical aspects of intimacy as indulged in by blue-blooded rakes, said texts were so riddled with euphemisms she'd ended more confused than instructed.

The manuals had, however, demonstrated that the spectrum of activity was wide, that if an experienced gentleman were so inclined, there were indeed a large number of steps between a first kiss and consummation.

From what she'd understood, his attentions to her breasts, even his stroking of her curls, were relatively early in the sequence. Tonight, he wished to take one step further; she wanted to know what that step was. With luck, it would allow her to gauge just how far along their long road they were and how fast they were progressing.

How much more time in his arms she had.

That knowledge—that her time with him was limited—dragged at her mind; he seemed to sense it. He lifted his head. Close, their breaths mingling in the darkness, from beneath his heavy lids, he caught her gaze. After a moment, he murmured, "You're not frightened, are you?"

She thought, then shook her head. "No." She hesitated, then boldly raised her hand, traced a fingertip down his lean cheek. "Just . . . unsure." As far as she could, she'd be honest with him.

His lips curved, but didn't soften. The lines of his face seemed harsher, harder. Swiftly turning his head, he trapped her fingertip between his teeth. Bit gently. Then he drew it into his mouth, sucked . . . she blinked, then shuddered lightly.

He released her finger. His grin was so fleeting she nearly missed it. His arms tightened; he drew her back down, bent over her, paused to whisper in his dark sorceror's voice, "Slow. As you wish. All you deserve."

Then he kissed her.

Tony pressed deep, let the kiss, not just a meeting of lips but a melding of mouths, sink into realms they'd not previously explored. Let the drugging, absorbing effect take full hold . . . until they were captive, both trapped, held but not tightly within the web of their mutual desire. A desire that glowed, warm, alive, real, not yet red hot but a thing of flame.

She was with him, as committed as he to their road; he read it in her lips, through the way she met each increasingly explicit exchange, in the way her body, lithe and supple, lay lightly tensed, poised and willing in his arms.

Regardless, he held back, held his own desires in a grip of iron and focused solely on hers. On awakening them, coaxing them, stirring them—step by step, as he'd promised—into full-blown life.

She hadn't been down this road before; to one of his experience that was clear. Her husband . . . was dead, of no importance now. He set himself to search out and eradicate any lingering difficulties, any unnecessary hesitations. Any instinctive drawing back. He was committed to teaching her what could be—what should be and would be between them. All the glory he was capable of summoning and laying at her feet.

Her chemise had no straps; a drawstring secured it above her breasts. He caressed, taunted, teased her breasts through the fine layer of silk, then tweaked the tie undone and slipped his hand beneath.

Closed it about one firm mound, and felt something in her, and in him, ease in sensual relief. He drew back from the kiss, lifted his head to look down as he played. As he filled his senses and hers with simple delight, with uncomplicated pleasure.

She—they—had been this far before; despite her harried breathing, despite her racing pulse, she didn't protest, didn't pull away. He could feel her gaze on his face, watching him savor her, watching him fall more deeply under her spell.

He glanced at her, caught the gleam of her eyes from under her weighted lids. His answering smile was tight, dangerous. Shifting his hold, he lifted her, raising her breasts, her spine bowing over his arm as he bent his head to do homage.

In that, he held nothing back. Deliberately sent fire racing through her veins, set desire chasing hard on its heels. Her fingers found his hair, tangled, clung, then clenched as he feasted. He took all he wished, all she wordlessly offered, gave her in return all the delight, all the tight, thrilling, illicitly intense pleasure his expertise could evoke.

Alicia gasped. Her body seemed no longer hers. He suckled more deeply. Taut in his arms, a soft moan escaped her, then the suction eased, and fire flared anew; hot and scalding, it raced through her to flow into the furnace building deep within her.

Her breasts were on fire, but it was the increasingly insistent, increasingly powerful demands of her body that gripped her, shook her. Unknown, as-yet-incomprehensible demands that threatened to overwhelm her, to sweep aside what wits she'd managed to cling to. She struggled against the tide; she wanted to know more, to learn what this and their next step would be. They'd gone no further than before—yet. He hadn't even touched her curls—yet.

This time, she knew, and waited—for that knowing touch, that oh-so-illicit caress. Her whole body was taut, quivering in anticipation. Of that, of what would follow the delight, the almost excruciating pleasure he, with clear intent, lavished upon her.

His mouth was scalding as he tasted her sensitized skin. Her nipples ached with a deep-seated pain that was intensely sweet. Then he placed his hand, large and heavy, over her waist; through the silk, she felt its heat and hardness, felt her muscles leap.

He raised his head. Looked down at her breasts. Even in the dimness, she could see the possessiveness limning his features.

His gaze rose. Black, hot, it searched her face, read her features, then his eyes returned to hers. He held her gaze, held her awareness.

His hand drifted lower.

The silk softly shushed, the last barrier between his hand and her flesh. Flesh that now pulsed hotly, nerves that slowly, slowly tightened with expectation.

Almost negligently, he caressed her stomach, then his hand drifted to the curve of her hip, then followed the line of one thigh.

Tony watched her, watched her senses follow his hand, his fingers. He did nothing to break the spell, held aside his own clamorous instincts and forced himself to keep to the same slow steady pace that had, from the moment they'd entered the room, contributed to the magic.

Orchestrated it, built it.

He needed that magic. He didn't just want to introduce her to passion, to take her and make her his. He wanted—needed—to expand her horizons, to bring her to know, to experience, and ultimately to want to explore the outer reaches of desire with him. To achieve that he needed to show her, to make her see and appreciate that there was a great deal more beyond the simple act.

So he held back his frustration, without compunction sacrificed it to their greater good, closed his mind against the drumming insistence of even deeper instincts, those that had reacted to the thought of other men—other rakes—coveting her as he did, those instincts that still, beneath all else, prowled, prodded to possessive life by the nebulous threat of her involvement with Ruskin.

He pushed them all aside, and concentrated on her. On the tale told by her rapid breathing, the way her nerves leapt as he stroked down her thigh. The armchair was commodious; her legs were a heated weight across his lap. Against one firm thigh, he was hard as rock, rigid and aching, but relief was not in the cards, not tonight. He'd survive, but he was determined in recompense to advance their one small step.

Still holding her gaze, he closed his fingers about one knee and lifted it, shifted it, parting her thighs. She permitted it, but tensed; her breathing tightened. Intent, he kept her with him and stroked his fingers, his palm, up the sensitive inner face of her thigh.

All the way to where her tight curls brushed his fingertips. He smoothed them aside, in the same movement boldly cupped her. Set his hand to her softness and covered it. Claimed it.

She caught her breath, stopped breathing entirely. His gaze locked with hers, he held still, then, adhering to that same slow steady beat, he eased his palm back, and with his thumb and one finger began to explore her.

Alicia quivered, and followed his every move. She couldn't do otherwise; he had her locked to him in some heightened state where she was shockingly aware of their flagrantly sexual play, where they were in some way connected so she both felt the sensations of his touch and simultaneously experienced something of his reaction.

Of what he felt as he learned her, caressed and boldly explored the soft, swollen folds between her thighs. She'd never known that part of her body to feel so hot, so wet, so achingly wanting. Pulsing, almost throbbing; her hips stirred, of their own volition lifted to his caress as if seeking more.

A glimmer of satisfaction flashed across his hard face. That he understood her body better than she did she didn't doubt; his caresses changed, became subtly more deliberate, more potent.

More satisfying to both of them.

He was showing her, teaching her. She remembered his

words as his thumb swirled knowingly about the tight pearl of sensation he'd found, that exquisitely sensitive spot that seemed pleasurably connected to every nerve she possessed. He swirled again and her whole body reacted; she arched lightly, heard herself gasp, let her lids fall.

"Stay with me."

The deep words were an outright command. She forced her lids up, met his gaze. Tried to read it and failed. "Why?"

To her surprise, the single word was all sultry temptation. Not like her at all, or so she had thought, yet it was. Emboldened, she shifted her hands, until then slack on his shoulders, let her fingers stroke his nape.

In response, his fingers stroked, but more slowly, as if savoring the wetness they'd drawn forth.

"Because I want you to know this, and I want to know you—all of you. All that you feel, all that you enjoy."

On the words, as if to demonstrate, his wicked fingers shifted, parting her folds, this time gently probing.

The action captured her attention. Completely. She moistened her lips; her gaze once again locked with his, she felt him ease one blunt fingertip between the slick folds.

Her body reacted, flushed, heated. She dragged in a tight breath. "One step."

He held her gaze, his eyes black, intent. "Just one step."

Slowly, he slid his finger into her.

Into the heated softness of her body, into the scalding furnace of her desire. Mentally gritting his teeth, Tony held tight to his reins and watched her outward attention splinter. Watched her focus inward, on the steady penetration of his finger into her tight sheath.

Her breathing was labored; she struggled to do as he'd asked and cling to the contact, to keep her eyes open, locked albeit unseeing on his.

Still keeping to their slow, steady rhythm, he reached as far as he could, gently pressed, then equally slowly reversed, until his fingertip reached the tight constriction that guarded her entrance. Then he reversed direction, deliberately pressing in, stroking the soft tissues, teasing the nerves and muscles beneath.

She lay in his arms, not passive but accepting, following, letting him learn her body even more intimately. Aware, as her widening eyes testified, of the building beat in her own body, of the heat, the burgeoning need.

Relentlessly, he built the rhythm until, with a small cry, she lifted against his hand. He pressed deeper, faster, clung to their visual contact as she climbed the peak, as her nails sank into his shoulders, her body bowing as the tension tightened. Heightened.

Then broke.

She came apart in his arms. The shocked awareness on her face, the stunned expression that was washed away as rapture took her, was a revelation—she'd never known the pleasure before.

As her lids drifted down, fierce satisfaction broke over him. His innate possessiveness roared, pleased beyond measure that it had been he who had brought her her first taste of sexual bliss.

He kept his hand between her thighs, one finger buried deep within her, savoring her contractions, the telltale ripples as her muscles relaxed into satiation. All her tension melted; as it did, he slid another finger in alongside the first, gently worked both deep. Stroked as she floated; she was so tight . . . Alfred Carrington had clearly been inadequate in more ways than one. When their time finally came, she'd need help stretching to accommodate him. Perhaps it was as well their time was not yet. Would likely be some while yet.

Eventually withdrawing his fingers from her softness, smoothing her chemise down, he settled back in the chair. And tried to ignore the musky scent that teased his senses, compounded by the warm weight of well-pleasured woman in his arms. Not an easy task.

Only one topic held the power to distract him; he turned his mind to scripting their next step.

Alicia reached home in the small hours, her wits in disarray. Her body . . . felt glorious. The former was a direct consequence of the latter.

She now understood something she never had before—why ladies allowed themselves to be seduced. If that evening's sample of what a noble lover could produce was in any way indicative, it was a wonder any lady remained a virgin by choice.

A gloating whisper in her brain suggested only those ignorant of the possibilities did.

Leaving her cloak in Jenkins's arms, leaving him and Maggs to lock up the house, she headed for the stairs.

Adriana joined her, glanced at her face. "What's wrong?"

Alicia looked briefly her way. Wondered that her experience hadn't left some tangible evidence in her face. She felt different from her head to her toes, yet no one in the ballroom, whence they'd eventually returned, had seemed to notice. Apparently not even her perceptive sister could see the change in her. "Nothing."

Looking forward, she remembered the two texts on lovemaking she'd consulted. Remembered their shortcomings. "I wonder if there are *advanced* manuals?"

She'd mumbled—grumbled—the comment aloud. Adriana, passing on her way to her bedchamber, cast her a puzzled look. "What was that?"

She tightened her lips. "Never mind."

Opening the door to her bedchamber, the one nearest the stairhead, she nodded a good night to Adriana and went in.

Closing the door, she stood for a moment staring into space, then she moved into the room, dropping her reticule on the dressing table, quickly unpinning her hair. She undressed and donned her nightgown—then couldn't remember doing it. Finding herself ready for bed, standing beside the bed, she climbed in and lay down. Drew the sheet and coverlet over her.

Lay flat on her back and stared at the canopy.

Every nerve she possessed was still humming; warm pleasure still coursed her veins. Yet there was an expectation, an underlying anticipation that the evening's small step had done nothing to assuage.

Instead, that nebulous but definite anticipation had grown.

She didn't truly know what it was, could only guess for she'd never felt it before. But then she'd never indulged as she had that evening, never let any man touch her intimately at all, let alone as he had.

And now . . . having learned what she'd wanted to know, she found herself facing an even bigger unknown. An even more frightening unknown.

Knowledge, it seemed, was a two-edged sword.

By the next morning, she'd talked herself around. Her analysis of her situation, her decision on her best way forward, had been right; there was nothing in the events of the past evening sufficient to deflect her from her path.

It would, however, clearly behoove her to make a serious effort to push Torrington's investigation along. The investigation provided his major excuse to spend time in her company, seducing her, being kind to her brothers, helping her with Adriana . . .

Pushing aside such thoughts, she rose from the breakfast table and went in search of the lists she'd made.

Tony sat comfortably slumped in a leather armchair in the library of Hendon House. Idly swirling a glass of brandy, he recited the story of Ruskin's death, the subsequent revelations, and the ongoing investigation to Jack—

otherwise Jonathon, Lord Hendon—who was similiarly comfortable in another chair, and his strikingly beautiful wife Kit, presently perched at Jack's elbow.

"So," he concluded, "Ruskin's been selling information on ships and dates to someone, who presumably used the information for their own gain—they certainly paid Ruskin well for it. However, we have no idea of the precise nature of the information Ruskin passed, so we don't know how it might have been used—"

"And therefore can't trace said user of same." Jack met his gaze, his expression hard.

"That"—Tony saluted him with his glass—"sums it up nicely."

Kit straightened. "Well, Jack will just have to help you learn what was important about those ships, but meanwhile, what about this widow? What was her name?"

Tony met Kit's violet gaze. The first time he'd met her, he'd thought she was a boy—understandable given he was half-dead courtesy of a brig full of smugglers, and she'd been traipsing about in breeches at the time. Now her glorious red hair was longer, elegantly cut to frame her piquant face. Her figure, previously slender and slim, had filled out a trifle, but that only made it all the more womanly. Two children had done little to curb her fire; she was one of the most disconcertingly active women Tony knew.

He was supremely thankful she was Jack's wife. "The widow isn't involved, other than by the unfortunate act of stumbling on Ruskin's body."

Kit frowned. "Why, then, are you being so careful not to use her name? You've mentioned her at least six times, but always as 'the widow.'"

Jack had turned to study his wife; now he turned, and studied Tony. "She's right. What going on with this widow?"

"Nothing." Tony sat forward, then froze. To Jack and Kit, who knew him well, both his tone and that movement had betrayed him. "Oh, all right." He slumped back. "The widow is Mrs. Alicia Carrington, and she is, as you've guessed, of more than passable charms, and . . ."

When he didn't go on, Jack pointedly prompted, "*And . . . ?*"

Kit was grinning.

Tony grimaced at them both. "And it's possible, perhaps, that . . ." He waved the question aside. "That's beside the point. The first thing"—he fixed Kit with a narrow-eyed look—"indeed, the *only* thing I need from you both is help with this shipping business. We need to make some headway on how the ships were involved."

Kit continued grinning. "And later?"

She wasn't going to give up. Tony closed his eyes. "And later you can dance at my wedding." Opening his eyes, he glared at her. "Good enough?"

She beamed. "Excellent." She looked at Jack. "Now what could be the crucial *thing* about those ships?"

Jack studied the list Tony had given him. "If I had information like this . . ." He looked up, met Tony's gaze. "These are all merchant ships. If the dates are convoy dates, the dates on which these ships were due to join convoys to come up the Channel, or alternatively the dates on which they left the protection of the convoy to turn aside to their respective home ports . . ."

"You think the information might have been used to take the ships?"

"As prizes?" Jack thought, then grimaced. "That's one possibility. Another is deliberate sinking to lay hands on the insurance—I won't tell you how frequent that is. Wrecking is another option."

Tony pointed at the list. "All those ships are still registered." That was the first thing he'd checked.

"That makes sinking or wrecking unlikely." Jack looked again at the list. "The next thing to determine is who owns these vessels and from where they were coming."

"Can you do that?"

"Easily." Jack looked at Tony. "It'll take a few days."

"Is there anything else we can pursue in the meantime?"

Jack pulled a face. "I can ask, quietly, as to whether there's anything noteworthy about one particular ship, and perhaps put out feelers about a few others, but until we know something more specific . . ." He grimaced. "We don't want to tip our quarry the wink."

"Indeed not. Anything I can do?"

Jack shook his head. "Lloyd's Coffee House is the obvious place to ask, but it's a closed group. I'm one of them, so I can ask nosy questions, but the instant you walk in . . ." He looked at Tony. "You'd have to make it official to get any word out of anyone there."

Tony grimaced, then drained his glass. "Very well, I'll leave it to you."

Kit rose in a rustle of skirts. "I'll tell Minchin you'll stay to luncheon."

"Ah—no." With a charming smile, Tony stood. "Much as I would love to grace any board presided over by your fair self, I've other engagements I must keep."

Taking Kit's hand, he bowed with consummate grace.

As he straightened, she arched a brow at him. "I must be sure to make Mrs. Carrington's acquaintance."

He grinned and tapped her nose. "I'll warn her to keep a weather eye out for you."

Coming up behind Kit, Jack wrapped his arms around her waist. "Well, you've one night's grace—we're staying in tonight."

Kit leaned back against her husband's broad chest. "It was a wrench to part from the boys. It's the first time we've left them."

Tony noted her misty-eyed expression as she thought of her two sons. Last time he'd seen them, they were robust and active—the sort to run their keepers ragged.

Jack snorted and glanced down at her face. "God knows, by the time we get home, they'll have exhausted everyone and be lording it over all and sundry."

Tony saw the pride in Jack's face, heard it in his voice. He smiled, kissed Kit's hand, saluted Jack, and left them.

TEN

"WE FOUND A CLUE! WE FOUND A CLUE!" MATTHEW rushed into the parlor and flung himself joyously into Alicia's arms.

"Well, we think it's a clue," David temporized, following Matthew in.

"We had a wonderful time!" Harry's eyes were shining as he plonked himself down on the chaise beside Alicia. "Are there any crumpets left?"

"Of course." Smiling, Alicia hugged Matthew, relieved as well as pleased. Five minutes of studying Tony's lists that morning had convinced her that she, personally, had no hope of making any sense of them. Adriana, too, had had no idea, but had suggested Alicia ask Jenkins and the boys, pointing out that their frequent excursions often took them to the docks.

She'd harbored reservations over the wisdom of such a course, but Jenkins had welcomed the challenge for himself and his charges. The boys, naturally, had been thrilled to assist Tony in any way. Soothing her sisterly concern by sending Maggs with them, she'd consented to an afternoon excursion.

Releasing Matthew, she signaled Adriana, who rose and tugged the bellpull. A moment later, Maggs and Jenkins both looked in. Alicia beckoned. "Come and tell us your news, but first we need to order tea to celebrate."

She wasn't sure how much credence to place in her brothers' "clue," but they undoubtedly deserved a reward for doing as she'd asked and looking.

Matthew and Harry told her which wharves they'd visited, glibly naming various seagoing vessels and their likely destinations. Then Maggs opened the door, Jenkins carried in the tea tray, and everyone settled to hear the news. Both Matthew and Harry were busy with their crumpets, today dripping with honey; by unspoken consensus, everyone looked at David.

He asked for the list; Jenkins handed it over. David smoothed the sheet. "There are thirty-five ships listed, and for many, there's nothing odd or unusual to report." He glanced at Alicia. "We asked lots of stevedores, and we found at least one who could tell us about each of these ships. So we know that for nineteen of them nothing odd has happened, nothing anyone knows to tell or talk about. *But*." He paused, making the most of the dramatic moment, checking to see that both his sisters had recognized its import. "We learned that the other sixteen ships were all lost—on or around those dates!"

David's eyes gleamed as he glanced from Alicia's face to Adriana's; hardly surprising, they were both agog.

"Sunk?" Alicia asked. "All sixteen were sunk?"

"No!" Harry's tone indicated she'd missed the whole point. "Taken as prizes during the war!"

"Prizes?" Puzzled, she looked to Jenkins.

He nodded. "During all wars, merchantmen are targeted by opposing navies. It's a customary tactic to deny the country one is at war with vital supplies. Even a shortage of, for instance, cabbages, could cause internal civil unrest and pressure an enemy's government. It's a very old tactic indeed."

Alicia tried to put the information into perspective. "So you're saying that sixteen ships"—she reached for the list David held; little 'P's had been written in the margin beside nearly half the names—"these sixteen ships were taken as prizes of war by . . ." She looked up. "By whom?"

"That we didn't learn," Maggs replied. "But those we asked thought it was most likely foreign privateers, or the French or Spanish navies." He nodded to the boys. "Your brothers hit the nail on the head over who to ask—it was their idea to approach the navvies. They unload the cargoes, so they remember the ships they've been hired to unload that don't come in, because then they don't get paid."

Alicia sat and absorbed all they'd told her while they consumed their tea and crumpets. When, finished, the boys eyed her hopefully, she smiled. "Very well. You've done an excellent job, and doubtless learned a great deal this afternoon, so you're excused from lessons for the rest of the day."

"Yayyyy!"

"Can we go and play in the park?"

She glanced out; it was still light, but night would soon start falling.

"I'll take 'em if you like, ma'am." Maggs rose. "Just for half an hour or so—let 'em run the fidgets out."

She smiled at him. "Thank you, Maggs." Then she looked at her brothers. "If you promise to attend Maggs, you may go."

With a chorus of assurances, they jumped up, jostling as they raced from the room. With an understanding grin, Maggs followed.

Alicia watched him go. She owed Torrington a debt for sending him. Maggs was as careful of her brothers as she could wish.

Jenkins cleared the tea things and removed the tray; Adriana returned to her sketching. Alicia sat with the list in her hand, and wished Tony—Torrington—was there.

* * *

That evening, Alicia had elected to attend Lady Carmichael's ball. Thus advised by Maggs, Tony saw no reason to arrive early; better to let the first rush ebb before making his way up the Carmichaels' stairs.

He'd spent the best part of his afternoon with Mr. King, learning more about Alicia, specifically about her finances. As he'd suspected, she had had a contract with King, but to his surprise, the man hadn't jumped at his offer to buy out said contract.

A degree of verbal fencing had ensued, until both he and King had agreed to show their hands. Once he'd made the nature of his interest clear, King had been much more accommodating; he'd agreed to burn Alicia's contract in Tony's presence in return for a bank draft for the appropriate amount. As King's goal was to ensure that no one, not even he, could hold the contract over Alicia's head, and as *his* only aim was to lift the financial burden from her shoulders, he'd been happy to agree.

The amount he'd paid had been another revelation. He knew how much it cost to run his various houses and to meet his mother's milliners' and dressmakers' bills; how Alicia was managing on the frugal sum she'd borrowed was beyond his comprehension. Her gowns alone would cost more.

Yet King had assured him Alicia was not in debt to anyone else. Understanding what had occasioned his query, he'd added that he, too, had thought the amount far too small, but when recently he'd dined with them, he'd detected not the slightest frugality or lack.

Tony now understood that the face the Carrington household presented to the world was a facade—a superbly crafted one with no cracks. Behind the facade, however . . . he'd recalled the lack of servants and the simple but hearty fare Maggs had described.

Like crumpets and jam for tea.

Alicia's payment to King, capital plus interest, would

fall due in July. Her life would have changed dramatically by then, but if she recalled the debt and inquired, as both he and King fully expected she would, King had agreed to simply say that an anonymous benefactor had paid the sum. She would guess it was he; he was looking forward to her attempts to make him admit it.

Lips curving as he entered Lady Carmichael's ballroom, Tony inwardly basked in a self-satisfied glow.

He made his bow to her ladyship, then joined the throng. The ball was in full swing, the ballroom a collage of silks and satins of every hue swirling about the black splashes of gentlemen's evening coats. He looked around, expecting to locate Adriana's court somewhere along the side of the room.

Instead, he saw Geoffrey Manningham, shoulders propped against the wall, his gaze, distinctly black, fixed on him.

Instincts pricking, he strolled the short distance to Geoffrey's side. Met his scowl with a questioning frown.

"Where are they?" Geoffrey growled. "Do you know?"

Tony blinked. Satisfaction fled. He turned to survey the room, but didn't see the crowd. "My information was that they'd be here."

"You can take it from me they aren't."

The tension in Geoffrey's voice, in his stance, had effectively communicated itself to him. Tony's mind raced; he tried to imagine what might have happened. Could Maggs have been wrong? He looked at Geoffrey. "How did you know they'd be here?"

Geoffrey looked at him as if that was a supremely silly question. "Adriana told me, of course."

That raised the stakes. The sisters had expected to be there, and were now seriously late.

A contained commotion by the door drew their attention. A footman was whispering urgently to the butler, proffering a note. The butler took it, straightened magisterially, then turned and surveyed the guests.

His gaze stopped on Tony.

The butler swept forward, not running, yet as fast as one such as he might go. He bowed before Tony. "My lord, this message was just delivered by one of your lordship's footmen. I understand the matter is urgent."

Tony lifted the folded note from the salver. "Thank you."

Flicking it open, he rapidly scanned the contents, then glanced at the butler. "Please summon my carriage immediately."

The butler bowed. "Of course, my lord." He withdrew.

Tony opened the note again, held it so Geoffrey, looking over his shoulder, could read it, too.

The writing was a feminine scrawl, the hand holding the pen clearly agitated. Adriana had been too overset even to bother with any salutation.

> *My lord, I don't know who else might help us and Maggs assures me this is the right thing to do. Just as we were about to set out for the Carmichaels', officers from the Watch arrived, along with a Bow Street Runner. They've taken Alicia away.*

The writing broke off; a blob of ink was smeared across the page. Then Adriana continued: *Please help! We don't know what to do.*

She'd signed it simply Adriana.

Geoffrey swore. "What the devil's going on?"

Tony stuffed the note into his pocket. "I've no idea." He glanced at Geoffrey. "Coming?"

Geoffrey sent him a grim look. "As if you need ask."

They went quickly down the stairs and reached the portico just as Tony's town carriage rattled up.

Tony reached for the door, opened it, and waved Geoffrey in. "Waverton Street! As fast as you can." With that, he followed Geoffrey, slamming the door behind him.

His coachman took him at his word. They rocketed along the streets, swinging about corners at a criminal pace. In five minutes, the coach was slowing; it lurched to a halt outside Alicia's front door.

Tony and Geoffrey were on the pavement before the carriage stopped rocking. Maggs opened the front door to Tony's peremptory knock.

"What's going on?" Tony shot at him.

"Buggered if I know," Maggs growled back. "Strangest bit of work I've ever seen. Nice thing it is when a lady getting ready to go to a ball is set on in her own front hall. What's the world coming to, I ask you?"

"Indeed. Where's Adriana—and do the boys know about this?"

"They're all in the parlor. Couldn't keep the boys from hearing—there was a right to-do. Mrs. Carrington gave the blighters what for, but they weren't about to go away, nor yet let her go out and wait until later. I'm thinking she went with them just to get them out of the house, what with the boys and Miss Adriana being so upset."

Tony's face hardened. He led the way to the parlor. The instant he opened the door, four pairs of eyes fixed on him.

A second later, Matthew flung himself at him, arms clutching limpetlike about his waist. "You'll get her back, won't you?"

The words, not entirely steady, were muffled by Tony's coat.

David and Harry were only steps behind. Harry caught Tony's arm and simply clung, the same question in his upturned face. David, older, tugged at Tony's sleeve. When Tony looked at him, he swallowed and met his gaze. "They've made some mistake. Alicia would never do anything wrong."

Tony smiled. "Of course not." Putting a hand on Matthew's head, he tousled his soft hair; laying an arm around Harry's shoulders, he hugged him, then urged the trio back into the room. "I'll go straightaway and bring her back. But first . . ."

One glance at Adriana's white face told him she was as upset as her brothers, but having to comfort the boys and contain their panic had forced her to master her own. Despite the shock, despite the way her fingers clutched and twisted, she was lucid, not hysterical.

Her eyes were wider than he'd ever seen them. "They said they were taking her to the local Watch House."

"South of Curzon Street, it is," Maggs put in.

Tony nodded. Urging the boys ahead of him, he made his way deeper into the room. Geoffrey followed on his heels. While Tony sat in the armchair, the boys scrambling to perch close on the padded arms, Geoffrey sat beside Adriana. He took her hand and squeezed it reassuringly. She smiled weakly, rather wanly, at him.

"Now," Tony commanded, "tell me exactly what happened."

Adriana and the boys all started talking at once; he held up his hand. "Adriana first—listen carefully so you can tell me anything she forgets."

The boys dutifully settled to listen; Adriana drew a deep breath, then, her voice only occasionally quavering, she described how, just as she and Alicia were about to leave for the ball, a heavy knock on the door had heralded the Watch, accompanied by a Bow Street Runner.

"There were two from the Watch, and the Runner. He was the one in charge. They insisted Alicia had—" She broke off, then dragged in a breath and continued, "That she had killed Ruskin. Stabbed him to death. It was ludicrous!"

"I presume she told them they were fools?"

"Not in those precise words, but of course she denied it."

"The men wouldn't believe her," Matthew said.

Tony smiled at him. "Fools, as I said."

Matthew nodded and settled back against Tony's shoulder.

Tony looked at Adriana. She continued, "We tried to reason with them—Alicia even used your name. She told them you were investigating the matter, but they wouldn't even wait while we sent for you. They were totally certain—absolutely—that Alicia was a . . . a *murderess!*"

Eyes huge, Adriana looked at him imploringly. "They were very rough men—they won't hurt her, will they?"

Tony bit back a curse, exchanged a swift glance with Geoffrey, and stood. "I'll go there now—I'll bring her back straightaway. Geoffrey will stay and keep you company. If I'm an hour or so, don't worry." Resettling his sleeves, he flashed the boys a reassuring smile. "I'll need to have a word with this Bow Street Runner, and make sure the gentlemen of the Watch don't make such a silly mistake again."

Five minutes later, he strode up the steps of the Watch House. Two stalwart members of the Watch were heading out on their rounds; they glanced at him—and rapidly got out of his way.

Tony's heels struck the tiles of the foyer; glancing swiftly around, he fixed his gaze on the supervisor behind the narrow desk, who was already eyeing him with increasing unease. This Watch House was situated on the edge of Mayfair; the hapless supervisor would know Trouble when he saw it. His expression as he hurriedly got to his feet suggested he recognized it bearing down on him now.

"Can I help you, sir—m'lord?"

I believe you have something of mine.

Tony bit back the words, reined in his temper, and quite softly said, "I believe there's been a mistake."

The sergeant paled. "A mistake, m'lord?"

"Indeed." Tony drew out his card case, withdrew a card and flipped it on the desk. "I'm Lord Torrington, and according to Whitehall I'm in charge of the investigation into the murder of William Ruskin, lately of the Office of

Customs and Revenue. I understand two of your men in company with a Bow Street Runner visited a private residence in Waverton Street an hour ago and removed, *by force*, a lady—Mrs. Alicia Carrington. The taradiddle I've been told—no doubt you and your men can explain it—is that Mrs. Carrington is accused of having stabbed Ruskin to death."

At no point did he raise his voice; he'd long ago learned the knack of making subordinates quake with a quiet and steely tone.

With his gaze, he pinned the supervisor, who was now holding on to his desk as if he needed its support. "I should perhaps mention that it was *I* who discovered Ruskin's body. In the circumstances, I would like an explanation and I would like it now, but first, before all else, you will release Mrs. Carrington into my care." He smiled, and the supervisor visibly quailed. "I do hope you've taken exceptionally good care of her."

The man could barely draw breath. He bowed, bobbed. "Indeed, m'lord—she did mention . . . we've put the lady in the magistrate's office." He hurried around the desk, almost stumbling in his haste to conduct Tony thither. "I'll just show you, then I'll get ahold of Smiggins—he's the Runner, m'lord. We was acting under his orders."

"Very well." Tony followed the bobbing supervisor. "What's your name?"

"Elcott, sir—m'lord, begging your pardon." Elcott stopped outside a door, and gestured. "The lady's in here, m'lord"

"Thank you. Please send Smiggins here immediately. I wish to attend to this business and remove Mrs. Carrington as soon as possible. This is no place for a lady."

Elcott kept bobbing. "Indeed, m'lord. Immediately, m'lord."

With a curt nod, Tony dismissed him. Opening the door, he walked in.

Alicia was standing by the window, dressed in all her finery for the ball. She swung around as he entered; the pinched look in her face dissolved as she recognized him. "Thank God!"

She didn't exactly fly to him, but she crossed the room quickly, her hands rising; shutting the door, he grasped them, and pulled her into his arms.

He held her tight, his cheek against her hair. "I came as soon as I could. You needn't worry about Adriana and the boys—they know I'm here, and Geoffrey's with them."

A large part of her tension dissipated; she looked up, pushing back to look into his face. "Thank you. I didn't know what to do—and I've no idea what's going on. For some reason they think I stabbed Ruskin."

"I know." Tony heard footsteps approaching. Reluctantly releasing her, he urged her to the chair behind the desk. "Sit down—try not to say anything. Just listen and watch."

A hesitant tap sounded on the door.

Resuming his previous, grim expression, he took up a stance beside Alicia's chair. "Come."

The door opened; a heavily built man in the distinctive red coat of a Bow Street Runner looked around the edge. He saw Tony; his eyes widened. He cleared his throat. "Smiggins, m'lord. You sent for me?"

"Indeed, Smiggins. Come in."

Smiggins looked like he'd rather do anything else, however, opening the door wider, he entered, then ponderously shut the door. He turned to face them; meeting Tony's eyes, he stiffened to attention. "Sir?"

"I understand you saw fit to apprehend Mrs. Carrington this evening. Why?"

Smiggins swallowed. "I had orders to bring the lady in to answer questions seeing as she was said to have stabbed some gentleman called Ruskin. To death, m'lord."

"I see. I take it Elcott informed you that I have been

placed in charge of the investigation into Ruskin's murder by Whitehall?"

Hesitantly, Smiggins nodded. "That were a surprise,
m'lord. We hadn't been told that."

"Indeed. Who gave you your orders?"

"Supervisor at Bow Street, m'lord. Mr. Bagget."

Tony frowned. "I assume a warrant has been issued—
who was the magistrate?"

Smiggins shifted; all color fled his cheeks. "Ah—I
don't know about any warrant, m'lord."

Gaze fixed on the hapless Runner, Tony let the silence
stretch, then quietly asked, "Are you telling me you
seized a lady from her own house *without* a warrant?"

Smiggins looked green. Spine poker stiff, he stared
straight ahead. "Information came in latish, about six,
m'lord. Sir Phineas Colby—the magistrate on duty—he'd
already left. It was thought . . . well, the information was
that the lady was looking to leave the country, so . . ."

"So someone had the bright idea to send you, along
with two ruffians, to take matters into your own hands
and forcibly remove the lady from her home?"

Smiggins trembled and said nothing.

Again, Tony let silence work for him, then softly
asked, "Who laid the information?"

It was abundantly clear that Smiggins wished himself
anywhere but there. He hesitated, but knew he had to answer. "From what I heard, m'lord, the information came
anonymous-like."

"Anonymous?" Tony let his incredulity show. "On the
basis of anonymous information, you acted to remove a
lady from her home?"

Smiggins shifted. "We didn't know—"

"You didn't think!"

The sudden roar made Alicia jump; she stared at Tony.
He glanced briefly at her, but immediately turned back to
the now quaking Runner. "What exactly did this anonymous information say?"

"That Mrs. Alicia Carrington presently residing in Waverton Street had stabbed Mr. Ruskin to death and was likely to do a flit any minute."

His gaze on the Runner, Tony shook his head. "We already know that whoever stabbed Ruskin was taller than he was and had to have possessed the strength of a man, not a woman. Ruskin was nearly as tall as me—taller than Mrs. Carrington. She could not have stabbed Ruskin."

The Runner glanced at Alicia, then quickly looked forward.

Tony continued unrelenting, his tone lethally quiet. "You, Smiggins, and your supervisor have acted completely outside the law—the law you are supposed to uphold."

"Yes, m'lord."

"In a moment, I will be taking Mrs. Carrington from here and returning her to her home. Henceforth as far as Bow Street are concerned, she is to be considered as being under my legal protection in this matter—is that clear?"

"Perfectly clear, m'lord."

"And in recompense to Mrs. Carrington for causing her distress, and to me for disrupting my evening, you will undertake, with your supervisor's full support, to track down the source of your 'anonymous information.' You will do nothing else, take part in no other duty, until you have accomplished that and made a full report to me. Do I make myself clear, Smiggins?"

"Yes, m'lord. Very clear."

"Good." Tony waited, then quietly said, "You may go. Report to me the instant you learn anything—Torrington House, Upper Brook Street."

Bowing, Smiggins backed to the door. "Yes, m'lord. At once."

The instant the door shut behind him, Tony reached for Alicia's hand. "Come. I'll take you home."

She rose with alacrity, more than ready to leave; as he led her to the door, she glanced at his face, at the hard, set planes, heard again his tone as he'd dealt with the Runner.

As she walked beside him out of the Watch House, her hand tucked possessively in his arm, she absorbed the other side of him she'd just seen.

It wasn't until the carriage moved off from the curb and she relaxed against the well-padded seat that the shock and panic hit her. Until then, she'd been thinking of her brothers, of Adriana, worrying about them; until then, she'd taken everything in, but hadn't spared any real thought for herself.

She shivered and twitched her cloak closer, huddled into its warmth. If he hadn't come . . . a chill washed through her veins.

He glanced at her, then his arm came around her; he hugged her to him, against his warmth.

"Are you truly all right?" He whispered the words against her temple.

Her teeth were threatening to chatter, so she nodded.

Even through their clothes, the solid warmth of him reached her; as the carriage rolled on, negotiating the swell of evening traffic along Piccadilly, her chill slowly faded. His strength, the decisive and effective way he'd dealt with the entire episode, the simple fact of his presence beside her, seeped into her mind, into her consciousness, and reassured.

Eventually, she drew breath, glanced at him. "Thank you. It was just . . ." She gestured.

"Shock." He looked out at the passing facades. "We'll be back in Waverton Street soon."

Silence descended. A minute passed, then she broke it. "I didn't stab Ruskin." She studied his face as he looked at her, but in the dimness couldn't read his expression. She drew a determined breath. "Do you believe me?"

"Yes."

Tony gave the word, simple, straightforward, unin-flected, and unadorned, its moment, let it sink into her mind. Then he looked down; taking her hand, he played with her fingers. "You heard me tell the Runner, and *Tante* Félicité and Lady Osbaldestone before that. Physi-cally, you couldn't have killed Ruskin. I—we—knew that from the day after his death."

Her fingers twined with his. He could almost hear her mind working, hear the questions forming, sense her searching for the words.

"I. We. You told me you'd been asked to investigate, but until this evening, in the Watch House, I didn't truly comprehend what that meant, that you were investigating at the behest of Whitehall."

He felt her gaze trace his features. Waited for the next question, wondered how she'd phrase it.

"Who are you?"

When he didn't immediately react, she drew breath, straightened within his arm. "You're not just a nobleman the authorities—even less the gentlemen in Whitehall—just happened to ask to look into a matter because you stumbled over a body." Turning her head, she studied him. "Are you?"

He let a moment pass, then met her gaze. "No. That isn't how Whitehall operates."

She didn't respond, but simply waited.

He looked away, rapidly sorted through his impulses. He shouldn't expect her to accept him as her husband without knowing who he was, all he truly was. Ingrained instincts urged continued and total secrecy, yet he re-called the trouble Jack Hendon had landed himself in when he'd failed to tell Kit the whole truth. He'd thought he was protecting her; instead, he'd hurt her, nearly driven her away . . .

He glanced at Alicia, then reached up and rapped on the roof. His coachman opened the trap. "Drive around the park." The gates would be locked, but the streets around the perimeter wouldn't be crowded at this time of night.

The trap fell shut; the carriage rolled on. The flare from a passing streetlamp briefly lit the carriage's interior. He glanced at Alicia; she met his eyes, and raised a brow. The light faded; the shadows closed in.

Fittingly, perhaps.

He leaned back, resetting his arm so she could rest more comfortably, curving his palm about her shoulder both to steady her and keep her close. He tightened his other hand about hers, locking their fingers; in the dimness he needed the contact to help gauge her reactions.

Telling her all was a risk, but a risk he had to take.

"I told your brothers I was a major in the Guards, in a cavalry regiment." Her fingers shifted; he squeezed them gently. "I was, but after the first few months, I didn't serve in either the Guards or the cavalry."

She'd turned her head and was watching his face, but he couldn't make out her expression. He drew breath and went on, "There was this gentleman named Dalziel who has an office in Whitehall—" He continued, telling her what he'd never told anyone, not Felcité, not even his mother; quietly, steadily, he told her the truth of the past thirteen years of his life.

His voice remained cool, steady, his tone dispassionate, almost as if his dark and murky past was at a great distance. The carriage rolled on; she didn't interrupt, didn't exclaim or ask questions. Didn't pass judgment, but he couldn't tell if that was because she was shocked speechless or hadn't yet taken in enough to believe and react.

He didn't know how she would react. A surprising number of those whose lives and privileges he and his colleagues had risked their lives repeatedly to protect held that such services as those he'd performed, predicated first to last on deceit, fell outside the bounds of all decency and branded him forever less than a gentleman.

The knowledge that some who welcomed him into their homes would respond to the truth of his life, if they ever learned of it, in such a way had never bothered him. But how she reacted . . .

It was tempting, oh-so-tempting, to gloss over the dark facts, to paint the details of his life in brighter colors, to lighten them. To hide and disguise their true nature. He forced himself to resist, to speak nothing more than the unvarnished truth.

To his surprise, his chest felt tight, his throat not as clear as he liked. At one point, when recounting in bleak black-and-white terms the cold facts of his existence among the seedier elements in the northern French ports, he realized he'd tensed, that he was gripping her hand too tightly; he paused and forced himself to ease his hold.

She tightened hers. Shifted on the seat, then her other hand touched the back of his, and settled, warmly clasping. "It must have been dreadful."

Quiet acceptance, quiet empathy.

Both flowed around him like liquid gold.

His fingers curled, gripping hers again; warmth blossomed in his chest. After a moment, he went on, "But that's all in the past. Along with most others, I got out last year." He glanced at her, sensed the contact when she met his gaze. "However . . ."

She tilted her head. "When Ruskin was stabbed, and *you* reported the body . . . ?"

"Indeed. Dalziel reappeared in my life." He grimaced. "If I'd been in his place, I'd have done the same. Whatever the business Ruskin was involved in, it's almost certainly treasonous."

They'd circled the park; ahead, the flickering streetlamps played over the stately mansions of Mayfair. He reached up, and instructed the coachman to head for Waverton Street. Once they were within the fashionable, well-lighted streets, he looked at her and found her watching him, not judgmentally, not even curiously, but as if she could finally see him clearly—and what she saw was something of a relief.

Her gaze shifted past him, then her lips eased and she sat back. "So that's why Whitehall—this Dalziel person—chose you for the investigation. Because you've proved beyond question to be true to the country's cause."

No one had ever described him like that, but . . . he inclined his head. "It's important that whoever is pursuing the investigation is beyond question true, because with Ruskin being within the bureacracy, it's likely whoever he was dealing with is in some way connected either with a relevant department, or the government."

Waverton Street was approaching; Alicia spoke quickly. Her mind was racing, thoughts tumbling. "So is your investigation supposed to be secret?"

His reply was wry. "It was."

She glanced at him. "But now you've had to step in and rescue me—I *am* sorry. I shouldn't have—"

"Yes, you should have." His hand tightened about hers. "Indeed, if you hadn't, I'd have been . . . displeased."

She frowned at him. "Are you sure?"

"Perfectly. Neither the Watch nor Bow Street will be falling over themselves to say anything about what occurred tonight. Unless whoever was behind this evening's events was actually watching the Watch House, they won't be any the wiser."

"Whoever was behind . . ." She stared at him. "You mean the person who laid the information . . . that was deliberate? I assumed it was just a mistake. . . ." Hearing the words brought home the unlikelihood of such a supposition. She faced forward. "Oh."

"Indeed." His tone had hardened.

She glanced at him as the carriage rocked to a stop; his face had hardened, too.

He shifted forward; reaching for the door latch, he met her gaze. "We need to consider how to react—how best to meet this new development."

"She's back!" Harry reached Alicia first, wrapping his arms around her waist and hugging her tightly.

"I'm all right." She hugged him back, then opened her arms to Matthew, who clutched and wriggled until, with an effort, she lifted him into her arms. David hung back, feeling his age, yet clearly wanting reassurance; she smiled, freed a hand, and drew him to her for a quick kiss. "Truly," she whispered, then let him go.

His somber expression eased; turning, he led the way to the chaise.

Having followed Alicia into the parlor, Tony pressed a hand to her back, worried about Matthew's weight. She flashed him a smile, then glanced down at Harry's head.

Transferring his hand to Harry's shoulder, he gripped lightly. "Come on—let's get her to sit down."

Harry glanced at him, then released Alicia; tucking his hand in Tony's, he went with him to the armchair and perched on the arm. Still carrying Matthew, Alicia walked more slowly to the chaise. Matthew slid down and she sat, then he crawled into her lap.

Beside her, Adriana laid a hand on her arm. "It must have been awful—you must have been so afraid."

Alicia smiled reassuringly. "I wasn't there long enough to get into a state." She glanced at Tony, then looked down at Matthew, snuggling close. She ruffled his hair. "Sweetheart, it's long past your bedtime."

He looked up at her, for a minute said nothing, then, smothering a yawn, mumbled, "Have you told Tony about the ships?"

She looked at Tony. Everyone looked at him.

He stared back. "What about the ships?"

Three pairs of eyes focused in brotherly admonition on Alicia. She waved in exculpation. "There's been so much happening"—she exchanged a glance with Tony, the memory of their drive around the park and all it had revealed high in her mind—"I haven't had a chance. But now you can tell him yourselves."

They did, in a chorus of statements and explanations that left him dazed. "Prizes? Sixteen of them? You're sure?"

Tony studied the list Alicia had fetched from her escritoire. The boys had gathered about him, David leaning over his shoulder, Matthew and Harry balancing one on each chair arm. Scanning the list and the inscribed "P"s, he listened as they explained how they'd gleaned their information.

All the ships were still registered, therefore presumably still afloat, as they would be if they'd been taken as prizes and subsequently ransomed by their owners.

Alicia sank back on the chaise. "Jenkins can tell you more if need be. And Maggs—he went, too."

He glanced at her, then looked around at the boys, meeting their eyes. "This is excellent." He didn't have to fabricate his enthusiasm, the sincerity of his thanks. "You've shown us which direction to pursue. Thank you." Solemnly, he shook each boy's hand.

They grinned, and continued pelting him with information about the ships. One part of his mind listened, cataloging useful details; most of his mind was racing, assessing, formulating.

When the boys' observations slowed, then stopped, Alicia rose, clearly intending to gather them and send them upstairs. He stayed her with an upraised hand. "One moment."

One glance at Geoffrey's face, and Adriana's, assured him neither would let him leave without a comprehensive explanation of what was going on; they were merely biding their time. His professional habits urged secrecy—information shared only with those who needed to know—yet this time other instincts, deeper instincts, were increasingly suggesting that sharing knowledge was a wiser, infinitely safer way to proceed.

His gaze came to rest on Alicia's brothers, on the three tousled, silky brown heads, currently bent close as they again examined the list of ships.

If he were on the "other side" in this affair . . .

They'd already targeted Alicia, not once, but twice. They knew where she lived. Anyone watching the house and her would quickly realize what her strongest instinct was—and therein lay her greatest weakness. It would be remarkably easy to engineer, and her reaction would be one hundred percent predictable . . .

Raising his gaze to her face, he waved her to sit. Puzzled, she sank down on the edge of the chaise. He glanced at Geoffrey and Adriana, then looked back at her. "This household—Adriana and Geoffrey, and the boys, too, and Jenkins, Maggs, and any other servants you have—all need to know the basic elements of what's going on."

Concern filled her eyes. She frowned. Before she could voice any protest, he glanced at her brothers; all three had come alert at his words and were now looking expectantly at him.

He smiled slightly, then raised his gaze and met Alicia's eyes. "It's the best way to protect everyone. They all need to know."

Geoffrey and Adriana were quick to voice their agreement.

Alicia glanced at them, then looked again at the boys. A moment passed, then she lifted her gaze to meet his, and nodded. "Yes. You're right. The basic facts so they understand why they need to take care."

He inclined his head. "If you'll summon the others?"

She rose. He watched her, inwardly acknowledging his

ulterior—ultimately his primary—motive: keeping her safe. Keeping her brothers safe was part of that, but it was she who stood in the line of fire. Conscripting her household in her defense was clearly in everyone's best interests; each of them needed her in their own way.

Within a few minutes, the entire household had assembled. He hadn't previously met the cook and their old nursemaid, Fitchett; both women bobbed deferentially, then retreated to sit on the straight-backed chairs Maggs and Jenkins fetched for them. Maggs had warned him of the small number of staff, so that came as no surprise; given what he now knew of the family's finances, the fact even made sense.

When everyone had settled, the boys seated in a semicircle before his chair, despite the hour alert and eager to hear of his investigation, he told them, simply and concisely, all they needed to know.

ELEVEN

HE STARTED BY TELLING THEM OF FINDING RUSKIN'S body, omitting to mention that Alicia had been there. Her gaze touched his face; he met it, held it, continued explaining who Ruskin had been, and what they now believed he'd been engaged in—selling information on ship movements that had led to at least sixteen ships being taken as prizes by the enemy.

The boys exchanged significant—excited—glances. Tony noted it; he bore their reaction in mind as he admitted to being an agent for the government, stressing that he was in charge of the investigation regardless of the Watch's and Bow Street's imaginings. The boys were, predictably, even more impressed, their approbation edging into awe.

From there, it was a small step to explaining that the investigation, while no longer strictly secret, would progress more surely if pursued with discretion to avoid alerting the mysterious A. C. He asked that they all continue as usual, but if anyone noticed anything out of place, no matter how small or mundane, they should tell Maggs or, if that wasn't possible, send word immediately to him or, failing that, to Geoffrey.

Able to read behind his careful words, Geoffrey, his expression impassive, nodded, accepting the unstated commission.

Finally, he came to his peroration, specifically intended to impress on his audience, especially the three boys, that the matter was serious—deadly serious. It required tact to walk the line between frightening the boys and fixing it in everyone's heads that in no circumstance were they to court any risk whatever. He alluded to Alicia's recent trauma—a trauma her siblings and the household had shared—as an example of how A. C. might play his game, but he also cautioned that whoever he was, A. C. would not balk at more violent deeds—it was assuredly he who had murdered Ruskin.

From the looks on the boys' faces, worry, concern, but also determination all present in their expressions, he succeeded in his aim.

He glanced at Alicia, faintly raised a brow; she met his gaze, read his question, nodded almost imperceptibly.

Glancing around, surveying the faces, he said, "So now you all know what the problem is, and that there's a need to keep alert at all times."

"Aye." Maggs pushed away from the wall. He looked to the other servants, getting to their feet. "We'll keep our eyes peeled, you can count on that."

"Thank you." With a nod, Tony dismissed them.

Alicia flashed them a grateful smile as they filed out of the room, then turned to her brothers. "Bed for you three, now. It's been a very long evening, and you have lessons tomorrow."

They looked at her, then, somewhat to her surprise, quickly rose. They came to hug her; she kissed their cheeks, then they hugged Adriana and, without any argument, headed for the door. Alicia turned. Maggs and Jenkins had dallied in the doorway; they took the boys under their wings and herded them upstairs.

She sat back on the chaise, hugely relieved, amazed, given the events of the evening, to feel so. Then Geoffrey was bowing before her. She gave him her hand, smiled in gratitude. "I can't thank you enough for coming to stay with Adriana and the boys."

He looked faintly irritated; he frowned at her, reminding her of Tony. "Nonsense. Any gentleman would have
done the same." He glanced at Adriana, who'd risen, too.

She beamed at him. "But you did." She squeezed his
arm. "Come—I'll see you out."

With a tired but genuine smile for Alicia, Adriana led
Geoffrey to the door; he closed it behind them.

Alicia turned to Tony. He'd been watching the door
close; now he looked at her.

His gaze rested on her face for a long moment, then he
said, "My apologies. I should have asked before I
spoke—do you expect any trouble with your staff?"

She blinked. "You mean because of . . ." She let her
words trail away, uncomfortable with their direction.

He refused to mince words. "Because despite the fact I
avoided using the term, a threat clearly exists toward this
household, and, consequently, there has to be a certain if
unspecified danger. Household staff aren't partial to getting caught in any cross fire."

She smiled at the military allusion. "In this case, you
needn't worry. Cook, Fitchett, and Jenkins have been
with us for longer than even I can remember—they won't
give notice. They're part of the family."

He looked at her—studied her—then inclined his head
and rose.

Quickly, she rose, too. In the distance, she heard the
front door shut; she paused, waiting, then the sound of
Adriana's light footsteps on the stairs came clearly to her
ears.

And Tony's. One glance at him—at the black eyes that
were watching her—was enough to assure her of that.
But he made no move, simply watched her.

There was a great deal she wanted, indeed felt compelled to say. Quite aside from her rescue, aside from his
revelations, his taking the lead in dealing with the matter,
here, within her household, had given her time to calm, to
reassess and catch her mental breath. She felt infinitely

more confident, more assured, than she had two hours earlier. Her latent panic had disappeared; she could face the immediate future sure in her ability to cope.

He didn't move, just watched, waited.

She drew breath, lifted her chin, and closed the distance between them. She stopped directly before him—or would have, but he reached out and smoothly drew her on, into his arms. Her heart leapt; her senses stirred, came alive. His arms settled about her, a loose cradle; her hands coming to rest on his chest, she looked into his face.

A face that gave little away; she couldn't guess what he was thinking.

"I wanted to thank you." Without his intervention, she couldn't imagine what might have happened, how matters might have developed.

He said nothing; instead, he slowly raised a brow. His black gaze touched hers, then swept down to her lips.

She knew exactly what he was thinking. She didn't stop to consider, to assess the wisdom of her response. Drawing in a quick breath, she gripped his arms, stretched up against him, and touched her lips to his.

It was an invitation rather than a kiss; when he didn't immediately respond, she eased back.

His arms tightened, locking her more definitely to him. Her lashes fluttered up; his dark gaze met hers for an instant, then he bent his head.

His lips touched her cheek, a light, insubstantial caress. He paused, then closed again; this time, his lips found the corner of hers, and slowly teased.

As he drew back, just an inch, she turned her head, fleetingly met his eyes. Then she raised one hand, laid her palm along his cheek, and guided his lips to hers.

He closed them over hers and took what she offered. Her mouth, herself. He drew her deeper into his arms, parted her lips, and sank deeper into the kiss. Into the explicit exchange she now knew well.

She responded, more than willing. It seemed very right that she should thank him this way, that she should give and appease the hunger she sensed in him, that elusive desire she exulted in evoking, equally exulted in sating.

As far as she dared.

The warning sounded in her mind—there could not be that many milestones left in the long road they'd agreed to travel. All but instantly, that small voice of caution was drowned out by the memory of his assurance that instead they would dally longer, more intensely, more intimately at every stage.

His mouth feasted on hers; his hands roamed, pleasuring her while feasting on her curves. He molded her to him, explicitly rocked the hard ridge of his erection against her.

Heat erupted inside her, spread through her veins, suffused beneath her skin. Raising her hands, she framed his face, then ran her fingers back, spearing them through his hair. She opened her mouth wider beneath his, with her tongue boldly taunted, deliberately incited him to take, and take more. Never had she felt so alive, so blatantly desirable.

So wanted.

They were standing locked together in her family's parlor; she was sure he wouldn't forget. Felt sure she could leave the decision on what was appropriate to him.

She knew, in her heart, in her soul, that he wouldn't let her down.

Tony had no intention of doing so, yet the demands of the moment were many. A wild and primitive emotion was burgeoning within him; he didn't recognize it, but he knew what it demanded.

Her. Not just her giving but his taking. A claiming, yet . . . this, he accepted, was neither the time nor place.

Not yet, not here. Soon, yes, but tonight . . .

He didn't question the instincts that told him what to do; he'd been their captive for too many years. Experience analyzed, instructed, informed; he fell in with its directives.

Breaking from the kiss, he murmured, unsurprised his tone was low, almost harsh, "Jenkins?"

Courtesy of their kisses, she was close to breathless. "Upstairs. He locks up the front of the house early, all except the front door."

Thank God. He kissed her again, ravenously, arms locking her against him, lifting her as he backed her toward the chaise. Stopping before it, he lifted his head and let her slide down until her feet touched the floor. "So we're alone?"

"Um-hmm." Her hand pressed under his collar and curled around his nape; she lifted her lips to his.

"Good." He took them, kissed her hungrily, in no way disguising his need. She met him, flagrantly urged him on—didn't so much as catch her breath when he eased her gown over her shoulders, then pushed it down to pool about her feet.

Still he held her to the kiss. Shifting to trap her between the chaise and him, he closed his hands about her breasts. Through the fine silk of her chemise, he teased the sensitive mounds, stroked and kneaded until they were full, until her breathing was tight, threatening to fracture.

Swiftly, he undid the ribbon ties and eased the fine fabric down; it fell in folds about her waist. Deciding his control didn't need further strain, he left the flimsy garment there. It was so fine, it was barely a sop to modesty, but having her completely naked on the chaise beneath him might be that one step too far.

At the first touch of his hands on her bare breasts, she murmured incoherently, the words trapped between their lips, and pressed closer.

He held her, for long moments simply savored the sensations—of her mouth freely offered, all his, of her tongue slowly tangling, caressing his, of the way she softened as he explored, claiming at will, then artfully stoking her fires. A deep pleasure coursed through him, part victory, part desire, at the tactile confirmation his hands reported; he had her in his arms all but naked, her breasts bare, pressed to his chest, her hips, the cradle in which he ached to lie, screened by nothing more than a thin barrier of silk.

Now she was his, it was time to feast.

His hands shifted over her body, then he lifted her, knelt on the chaise and laid her on the damask, following her down so their lips didn't part, settling beside her, his longer, harder frame trapping hers on the cushions. One hand rising to cradle her face, he plunged once more into her mouth.

Plunged them both back into the building flames.

Alicia went willingly, eager to know, to experience whatever and wherever he led. She knew it was dangerous, yet when he finally lifted his head and released her lips, and she struggled to breathe, to fill her starved lungs, there was no thought in her mind of drawing back.

Not when he looked at her with desire, hot and glowing, behind his black eyes. His gaze had dropped to her breasts; they were swollen and aching. Nerves tightening, she waited for his touch, waited for the burning delight of his mouth, for the sharp, addictive pleasure.

His gaze flicked up to meet hers, briefly locked, then his lips curved, knowing and sure. He looked down, bent his head, and gave her all she'd wanted, all her tight nerves craved, the intoxicating play of lips and tongue, the hot, wet suction of his mouth.

He orchestrated the whole until her gasps filled the room, until her fingers were clenched on his skull, her body bowing under the hand he'd splayed across her midriff.

A deep rumble of satisfaction reached her; he shifted lower, leaning over her. One hand still massaged her breasts, stroking, tweaking, caressing as his lips trailed down between, down over the centerline of her body. With one finger he drew the silk folds of her chemise aside, so he could continue his line of openmouthed kisses to her navel.

Raising his head slightly, he circled the indentation with one fingertip, then lowered his head and boldly probed with his tongue, an echo of their kisses, of the plunder, the claiming.

Dazed, her limp fingers retensing on his skull, she watched him minister to her body as if it was a thing worthy of his worship.

Finally lifting his head, his eyes met hers; they were dark and fathomless, hot yet unreadable. Watching her, he shifted, parted her legs and settled between, ran his hand up her thigh, sliding it under the layer of silk to lay it over her stomach, hard possessive palm to her hot, soft skin.

She couldn't take her eyes from his, from the intent, burning look burnished in the black, didn't dare shift her gaze even when she felt his hand move, felt his fingertips brush her curls, then slide further to caress her as he had before.

Her breath strangled, her lungs slowly seizing as he artfully, deliberately explored, then stroked, caressed, finally probed. One large finger slid a little way in, just enough to tantalize, to freeze her mind, and send her frenzied senses searching. Reaching.

He caressed and her body came to life, muscles tensing, flickering, her hips lifting in anticipation. Slowly, he slid one long finger into her, pressed steadily deeper, deeper.

Her lungs locked; her hips lifted, but he held her down, moving lower, his shoulders sliding from her weakened grasp.

He looked down, watched as he worked his hand between her spread thighs, as he worked his finger within her, then he glanced up at her face, with his thumb circled that critical spot he'd discovered before, simultaneously reaching deeper still.

On a moan, she closed her eyes, let her head fall back. This had to be wicked; it was too glorious to be right.

A wave of sheer sensual delight swept through her, caught her wits, trapped her mind in sensations. Wild, wanton, indescribable pleasure flooded her; this time, he seemed content to let the wave lap at her, lap at her, rather than build.

The deliberate, flagrantly intimate repetitive penetration encouraged her to wallow in the warmth, to let her body simply enjoy every moment.

She was hardly relaxed, yet with every minute the landscape grew more familiar, less threatening. The urgency hadn't infected her yet, but she knew it would. Before it did . . .

She managed to catch her breath and look down at him. Reach for him, with her fingers brush his shoulders. He looked up; his eyes were so black she could read nothing of his thoughts, but his face was a graven mask etched with a desire she comprehended instinctively.

"You . . ." She moistened her dry lips. "I'm the one who's grateful. I want to give to you, not . . ."

Her gesture encompassed her body, thrumming with warmth and pleasure, and him, now propped between her knees, one shoulder cushioned against one of her thighs.

His hot black gaze didn't flicker. He glanced briefly down to where his hand steadily pandered to her senses, then he looked up and met her eyes.

"Then lie back, close your eyes, and let me take this, at least." His thumb swirled about the tight nub nestled within the now slick and swollen folds.

She tensed, but he held her with his eyes.

His words reached her, gravelly, low, primitively dark. "If you can't be mine yet, give me this instead. Let me claim this much."

Caught in his eyes, captured by the sheer need she

could feel pouring from him, she tried to think, couldn't—didn't care. "Take—whatever you wish." Caution reared. "But . . ."

His gaze seemed almost blank. "Just one more step." He shifted further back. "Do as I asked—lie back and close your eyes."

He waited; she could feel her pulse hammering in the soft flesh his fingers were tracing. She had no real idea . . . couldn't imagine . . .

She closed her eyes, let her head fall back.

"Just like that—try not to move."

She didn't get a chance to reply. At the first touch of his lips, she lost all capacity even to think. Sensations buffeted her, rose and crashed through her. The intimacy all but slew her.

She heard her gasp, followed by a long moan as his fingers slipped from her sheath and blatantly, holding her thighs wide, he settled to feast.

His mouth worked, and she thought she might die. Of their own accord her hips lifted, twisted, but his hands had closed about them and he held her down, held her in position so he could, as he'd wished, claim her in this way.

A brutally explicit, intensely intimate claiming.

As she squirmed helplessly, struggled to breathe, the fact he knew of no reason to hold back, to withhold from her any degree of his transparently well-educated expertise, was forcefully borne in on her. He knew just what he was doing, to her, to her nerves, to her senses, to her mind.

To, in some way she didn't comprehend, her heart.

She might be giving, he might be taking, yet he gave selflessly, too. If she'd harbored any doubts that lovemaking was in essence a sharing, the long, heated moments she spent under his hands, under his mouth, with his tongue stroking, probing, lapping at her softness, burned every shred of doubt away.

The flames built, expertly stoked, until the conflagration simply became too much. Too much for her to resist, to hold back from the beckoning delight. She would have warned him if she'd been able, but he didn't look up, didn't pause in his increasingly potent ministrations even when she tugged his hair.

And then she was there, at the heart of the firestorm, and for one blinding moment nothing else mattered but the intense, golden glory. It held her tight, a vise of his making, then she fractured, and the glory shattered, sharp shards streaking down her veins to melt deep within her, beneath her fingertips, under her skin.

Exulting, Tony savored the powerful contractions, savored her release, then licked, lapped. Eventually, he eased back and lifted his head.

Ignoring the fiery pressure in his loins, he looked at her, spent, dazed, gloriously sated. Gloriously exposed. He let his gaze travel slowly down her body, seeing and claiming anew, then he bent and placed a kiss on her damp curls, pushed up her chemise, and dropped a gentle, lingering kiss on her belly.

Next time. He promised himself that.

Lifting away, he shifted higher and lay down once more beside her. Propping on one elbow, he laid a hand on her breast, and settled to watch her return to earth and welcome her back.

An hour later, lying in her bed with the house silent about her, Alicia tried to take in, to understand, all that had happened. Not physically; shocking though that had been, stunning beyond her wildest imaginings—or, apparently, those of the authors of both sexual texts she'd consulted—she knew, to her bones, exactly what had happened, what part of him had touched what part of her, and how.

That was a problem in its own right, but what consumed her, what mystified her, was the connection she sensed, the link that steadily, day by day, interlude by interlude, seemed to be growing, forged in the fires between them.

That was something else. Something beyond the facts she'd considered when she'd decided to adhere to her widow's role, to pretend to be as experienced as she was not.

He'd agreed to go slowly; by his standards, he probably had. Even though it was now patently clear that they'd all but arrived at their final destination, it wasn't panic over that that filled her mind.

From the first, she'd responded to his practiced caresses instinctively, had been forced to rely on instinct to guide her. It seemed instinct had, but in a way she hadn't foreseen, in a direction she hadn't intended to take.

She hadn't foreseen the danger. Not at all.

Rolling over on her side, she clutched a pillow to her and tried not to think about him, tried not to feel . . . tried not to be aware of the compulsion that had grown to give him more than she at any stage had contemplated.

Yet the more she fought it, the more she tried to turn her mind from the prospect, tried to deny it, the more it grew.

Fascination had turned into something more.

Something a great deal more powerful.

At an unusually early hour the next evening, Tony entered Lady Arbuthnot's ballroom. Without glancing at anyone else, he made his way to Alicia's side.

Truth be told, he didn't truly register anyone else's presence; his mind, all of his awareness, was centered on her.

Not by choice. He felt driven, whipped along at the mercy of emotions he'd never before had to conquer. Mild possessiveness was one thing, but this?

There was so much in her life he wanted to spare her— more, that some part of him felt driven to fix, almost as if his very self—his honor, his name, his self-respect—

depended on it. Taking care of her, protecting her, keeping her safe, ensuring her happiness, had become that important.

How, he wasn't sure, but to his mind reasons were by the by. He knew how he felt; he knew what he wanted. He knew how he needed to act.

Reaching her side, he took the hand she smilingly offered, raised it, and placed a kiss on her fingers, then without pause, pressed another to her palm.

Startled, she searched his eyes. "Are you all right?"

He hesitated, then nodded. "Perfectly."

A lie, but he didn't want her asking questions he couldn't answer.

Tucking her hand into his elbow, he pretended to survey the other guests. The dancing had not yet commenced. "Has anyone behaved oddly toward you or Adriana today—here, or in the park?"

She glanced at him. "No." After a moment, she went on, her voice lowered, "Are you expecting rumors about me being taken up by the Watch?"

"Possibly. I want to know if any surface."

He could feel her gaze on his face, studying; he glanced at her, arched a brow.

She held his gaze. "What have you done? Tell me."

He debated whether to inform her he wasn't one of her brothers, but couldn't see it stopping her interrogation. "I've asked *Tante* Felicité and her bosom-bows to keep their ears open. I told her the bare bones of what happened yesterday—she and the few other *grandes dames* who were present were shocked and suitably outraged." He squeezed her fingers before she could protest. "This is the sort of thing that in different circumstances might happen to them. They have a vested interest in ensuring the customs of the ton aren't manipulated for subversive purposes."

Alicia frowned, then nodded, conceding the point. "I'll tell you if Adriana or I encounter any difficulties."

She continued to study his face; he seemed more tense, more on edge than he usually was. "What else did you do today?"

He paused, to her now-informed eye deciding where to start rather than deciding whether to speak.

"I passed the information about the ships on to Jack Hendon."

"The friend who owns a shipping line?"

"Yes. Now he knows what to look for, we'll get along faster. I also sent word to another friend who's checking along the southwest coast. With luck, we'll have a clearer idea of what's been happening soon, then we can start following the trail back to the perpetrator."

"A. C." Remembering the fright of the day before, she shivered. Feeling Tony's gaze on her face, she met it. "He must be someone quite knowledgeable, mustn't he? He knew how to start those first rumors, knew how to trick Bow Street into seizing me."

Lips set, he nodded. "He's intelligent, and cold-blooded."

He hesitated, then went on, his fingers absentmindedly stroking the back of her hand. "I heard back from Smiggins. It seems his 'anonymous information' came via a flower seller who'd been paid by a well-to-do gentleman, one expensively dressed, to take the information to the Watch. She can't describe the man beyond that."

The vision of a gentleman wrapped in an expensive coat with an astrakhan collar, viewed through the mists of a chilly night, slid through Tony's mind. For him, A. C. was no phantom, but a dangerous adversary, one he'd yet to put a name to.

Which, of course, only made it harder to protect Alicia from the danger. He let his gaze drift to Adriana's circle; through her connection with Alicia, she, too, was in danger. There were six gentlemen gathered about her; Sir Freddie Caudel was, as usual, one of the crew. He was engaged in describing some play to Adriana; prettily, she hung on his words, her attention politely all his, at least for the moment. Tony was not at all surprised to see Geoffrey hovering even more determinedly, more definitely possessive.

From beside him came a small humph. "I daresay, if Lord Manningham is all you and Mr. King tell me he is, then I'll shortly be entertaining an offer from him."

He glanced at Alicia, caught her eye. "I should think that's a foregone conclusion." He paused, then asked, "Will she, and you, accept Geoffrey's suit?"

She looked at Geoffrey and Adriana, hesitated, then nodded. "If she's happy, and if he wishes to hold to his offer once he's fully informed of the family's circumstances."

He arched a brow. "Circumstances?" He knew precisely what she meant—the fact she and her brood were as poor as church mice. She, however, didn't know he knew; he wondered when she'd tell him.

She met his gaze, her expression open. "There's the boys, of course, and myself—not every gentleman wants to marry into such a close family."

More fool them. He raised his brows noncommittally, and let the matter slide. Time enough to see how she reacted to his proposal once he'd made it. With her and her family in A.C.'s sights, eliminating A.C. had to be his top priority; there would be time aplenty to speak of marriage once they were safe.

More guests were arriving; her ladyship's rooms were fast filling. He remained by Alicia's side; with only two weeks to go before the start of the Season, tonnish entertainments once more resembled the melee he recalled, one through which wolves of various hues prowled.

Félicité waved from across the room, then Lady Holland stopped by to compliment Alicia on her and Adriana's gowns. The comment drew his notice; as usual, the sisters were superbly turned out . . . again he wondered

how they managed it. Then he recalled Adriana's preoccupation with fashion; she was forever sketching the latest designs, or similar designs artfully modified.

He looked again at their stylish attire. Understanding
dawned; he saw Adriana in a new light.

"Good evening, Torrington—I trust you will introduce
me to your lovely companion. I do not believe I have yet
had the pleasure of making her acquaintance."

The perfectly modulated tones, still distinctly ac-
cented, jolted him from his thoughts. Lowering his gaze,
he smiled easily and bowed. "Your Grace." His gaze
passed on to the lady—yet another *grande dame* if ap-
pearances spoke true—by Her Grace of St. Ives's side.
The lady smiled with charm, and a hint of determination.

"Allow me to present my sister-in-law, Lady Horatia
Cynster." The Duchess of St. Ives smiled at him, pale
eyes alight. She waited while he bowed over Lady Horatia's hand, then continued, "*Bon!* And now you may introduce us both to this lady, if you please."

He nearly laughed; one of his mother's oldest and
dearest friends, Helena, Duchess of St. Ives, was both in-
corrigible and unstoppable. She was a petite force of nature, and woe betide any who thought to say her nay. He
turned to Alicia. She met his eyes; he smiled encouragingly. "Ladies—Mrs. Alicia Carrington, allow me to
present Helena, Duchess of St. Ives, and Lady Horatia
Cynster."

Alicia dipped into a curtsy of precisely the right degree.

Impulsively, Helena took her hand and waved her up.
"Your sister is *ravissante*, as all the ton now knows, but
you, too, will do very well I believe."

Alicia smiled, but demurred. "I seek only to establish
my sister."

Helena bent on her a look of patent incomprehension,
then glanced at her sister-in-law.

Whose lips were not straight. "My dear, a word of

advice—*you* may not seek, but the gentlemen assuredly will. Indeed"—her gaze slid teasingly to Tony—"I'm quite sure they already are."

The only way to deal with such females was to meet their jibes with polite impassivity; Tony did so. They stayed by Alicia's side, chatting about this and that, for nearly ten minutes, then moved on.

Before Alicia had time to draw breath, two other haughty matrons stopped to speak kindly. He stood by her side, suavely urbane, and thought cynical thoughts along the lines of: where Cynsters led, others followed.

He was grateful for Helena's support; he knew her well enough to know the gesture had been intentional. To be seen to be accepted by the elite of the haut ton provided a social cachet which was of itself a protection. Rumors were simply much less likely to be credited. Socially, Alicia and Adriana were gaining a status it would require a major public indiscretion to shake.

As more of the ladies on whose opinion the ton turned made a point of acknowledging Alicia, either by stopping for a few words or by exchanging nods across the room, he felt increasingly reassured on the social front.

Other fronts, however, were not so secure.

"Good evening, Mrs. Carrington."

The deep timbre of the voice sent Tony's hackles rising. He turned to see a dashingly handsome gentleman with unruly blond curls bowing over Alicia's hand; from the look on her face, she hadn't meant to surrender it. The gentleman had approached from the rear, escaping Tony's watchful eye, which endeared him to Tony even less.

The gentleman straightened and smiled at Tony. "Your servant, Torrington." Exchanging a brief nod, he looked back at Alicia. "My mama chatted with you earlier—she told me your name. I'm Harry Cynster."

His smile thawed Alicia; she returned it, relaxing. "It's a pleasure to make your acquaintance, sir."

It took Tony a few seconds to make the connections.

Harry Cynster, he of the guileless blue eyes and a distinctly predatory streak. Horses—he was a renowned whip, a legendary rider, in more than one sense, appropriately nicknamed Demon.

He was chatting with Alicia, his voice a deep, fashionable drawl, deploying the charm for which the Cynsters were notorious. "My mama dragged me along. Now we're all of us back from the wars, it seems our mothers and aunts are determined to marry us all off."

"Indeed?" Alicia returned his innocent look with one of polite scepticism. "And what of you? Doesn't marriage figure among your ambitions?"

His eyes met hers, their expression rather less innocent. "Not just yet."

The undercurrent beneath the words registered as a warning.

Harry raised a brow. "I believe that's a waltz starting up."

To her surprise, Tony reached across; his fingers closed about her hand. "Ah, yes. Thank you for reminding me, Cynster." He smiled urbanely, and drew her to him. "Mrs. Carrington has promised me this dance."

Over her head, blue eyes met black. There was something—some form of masculine challenge—behind Tony's polite mask. She glanced from one to the other, then Harry Cynster raised both brows, faint surprise in his face. "Well, well. I see." Then he grinned and saluted her. "A pity, but I wish you good riding, my dear."

Before she could reply to the strange comment, Tony whisked her away.

"Mrs. Carrington doesn't often dance at all," she informed him as he drew her into his arms.

He met her eyes. "Except with me."

With that, he whirled her into the revolving circle of dancers. The floor was crowded; he had to hold her close. So close his strength and that fascinating power he wielded, a potent blend of physical confidence and sexual prowess, wrapped about her, a seductive spell she wasn't even sure he knew he was weaving.

Then he guided her through the turns; his thigh parted hers, and all she could think of was . . .

She looked away, cleared her throat. Desperate to cool her thoughts, she struggled to find some distraction . . . "What did he mean?" Glancing up, she caught Tony's black gaze. "Harry Cynster—why wish me 'good riding'? He doesn't even know if I ride."

For an instant, Tony stared down at her; she couldn't interpret his expression. "He assumed," he eventually said. His tone seemed flat. "He's an exceptional rider himself . . ." He shrugged lightly. "Probably all he thinks of."

His lips tightened, as if he didn't want to say anything more. He looked up, steering her on; she wasn't sufficiently interested to pursue the point—whatever it was.

But that left her mind free, and her senses susceptible. Left her nerves leaping when they were jostled and he drew her protectively close, into the safe harbor of his arms. For a moment, their hips and thighs touched, brushed; when they moved on, she felt heated. She glanced up at him, praying the heat hadn't reached her cheeks, afraid it had, afraid that her eyes, too, would give her away, would hold some impression of her thoughts, reveal her sudden, unexpectedly flaring need.

His eyes met hers; darkly burning, they reflected thoughts that mirrored hers.

Abruptly, it seemed they were the only couple on the floor, the sole focus of their senses. They moved in a social vacuum charged with sensual heat, wracked with restrained passion. It flowed about them, caressed their skins. Teased, taunted, and left them yearning.

The music ended. It was a wrench to stop, to part, to step back even though both recognized they must. It was harder yet to pull back onto that other plane, to deny any expression to what was beating inside them, burgeoning between them, especially when each knew the other felt it, too. That the other wanted just as passionately, just as hungrily.

The need was there in his eyes; the answering tug was very real within her. But they had to play their parts, had to stroll easily, apparently nonchalantly back up the room, returning to take up her usual position near Adriana's circle, with him by her side.

Tony settled her hand on his sleeve, but didn't dare leave his hand over hers. He wanted her close, closer than she was; such unsatisfying skin-to-skin contact was almost painful.

Dragging in a breath, he glanced around, unseeing. How he would survive . . . one thing was certain—no more waltzes. Not until they'd danced to a different tune in a much more private setting.

Not until he'd felt her skin against his, naked body to naked body.

After . . . he assumed—fervently prayed—that the pressures that seemed to be building inside him, seething volcano-like from somewhere deep within, those emotions he accepted but didn't wish to examine, would ease. That he wouldn't feel like snarling when men like Harry Cynster hove near, that he'd be able to waltz with her without remembering . . . and imagining . . .

Without wanting to behave like some primitive caveman and toss her over his shoulder, seize her, and cart her away. And . . .

He had to stop thinking about it, or he'd go mad.

At the end of the ball, he and Geoffrey accompanied the sisters into the front hall. Adriana gave Geoffrey her hand; he bowed over it, whispered something Tony didn't catch, then took his leave of Alicia, who, distracted, had missed that little interaction entirely. With a nod to him, Geoffrey left.

Alicia turned to him, held out her hand. "Thank you for your company."

He looked at her, took her hand, and tucked it in his arm. "I'll escort you home."

She blinked, but allowed him to draw her close. "You don't need to do that."

He looked down at her, then softly stated, "I do." After a moment, his chest swelled; he looked ahead. "Aside from all else, you're in my custody."

She frowned. "I thought you just said that for the benefit of the Watch."

A footman came to tell them their carriage was waiting. Tony steered her onto the steps, then leaned close, and murmured, "I said it for my benefit, not theirs."

T WE LV E

AFTER THAT COMMENT . . . ALICIA SPENT THE ENTIRE journey home in a fever of speculation. The waltz had left her nerves, her senses, primed and flickering; rocking over the cobbles in the dark with Tony beside her, his hard thigh riding alongside hers, did nothing to calm them.

Last night—or had it been this morning? Whichever, there was no doubt in her mind that there were no further halts along their road. Yet she hadn't until now seriously considered, hadn't asked herself the fateful question.

If it came to that, would she?

If the moment arose and she had the chance, would she take it? Or try to the last to avoid it?

A small voice whispered . . . how did one avoid the inevitable?

By the time they reached Waverton Street, and he handed her down, she felt as tense as a bowstring. Adriana followed her up the steps. Tony brought up the rear. Maggs opened the door and held it wide; Alicia stepped back and let Adriana precede her. Tony, she noticed, cast comprehensive glances up and down the street as he climbed to the door.

She entered; he followed.

Adriana, no doubt thinking thoughts of Geoffrey Manningham, drifted upstairs without so much as a good night. Uncertain if she should be grateful or irritated, Alicia nodded to Maggs. "Thank you. You may retire. I'll see his lordship out."

Maggs bowed and lumbered away.

She watched the green baize door swing shut behind him.

Leaving her alone with the man who would be her lover.

Slowly, she turned . . . and found herself alone.

Tony had gone. The drawing-room door stood open.

Frowning, she went to the threshold; a dark shadow in the unlighted room, he was standing before the long windows. Puzzled, she went in. "What are you doing?"

"Checking these locks."

The windows gave onto the narrow area separating the house from the street. "Jenkins checks the locks every night, and I suspect Maggs does, too."

"Very likely."

Halting in the middle of the floor, she folded her arms beneath her breasts. "Do you approve?"

"No." Tony turned from the windows, through the dimness studied her. "But they'll do." For now.

Until he could think of some way to improve the defenses he felt compelled to erect about her. He needed to know she was safe. He wanted her his. In the circumstances, satisfaction would—indeed needed to—come in that order.

The reality had come crashing down on him as he'd sat beside her in the carriage and sensed the flickering and skittering of her nerves, her growing agitation. After all she'd been through in the last two days, what woman wouldn't be on edge?

This was not the time to press his suit, regardless of the strength of their passions. Aside from all else, he hadn't forgotten her earlier mistake over him expecting her to be grateful. Hadn't forgotten Ruskin's diabolical scheme— "gratitude" demanded as payment for protection.

Now *he* was her protector, in more ways, more arenas,

more effectively established than Ruskin had ever stood to be.

No. He wanted her safe, wanted her to know she was safe, and had no need to thank him further. No need to come to him out of gratitude.

He didn't want her in that way, didn't want her to come to him with any complicating emotions between them. He wanted much more from her.

When she came to him, it had to be because she wanted to, because she wanted him as he wanted her.

That simple—that powerful.

To gain all he wanted, to achieve all his goals, that point was critical. He didn't question why that was so, but knew absolutely that it was.

She was watching him, puzzled, increasingly tense.

He crossed the room to her. She watched him approach, but didn't move. Either toward him, or away.

Halting in front of her, through the shadows he looked down on her upturned face. Slowly raising both hands, he feathered his fingers along her delicate jaw, then cupped her face, framed it as he tipped it up, bent his head, and set his lips to hers.

She opened to him readily; she kissed him back, not urging him on, yet not denying their mutual hunger. Her hands rose, her soft palms lightly clasping the backs of his, a subtle, accepting, very feminine caress.

For long moments, they stood in the cool dark, their bodies inches apart and, mouths melding, giving and taking, drank each other in.

The distant chiming of a clock broke the silence, reminding him of time passing. Reluctantly, he drew back; equally reluctantly, or so it seemed, she let him.

Lifting his head, he looked into her face, into the soft pools of her eyes. He couldn't read their expression, but he didn't need visual cues to know that she was as aware as he, as achingly, tormentingly conscious of the sensual whirlpool that was swirling about them, of the sheer strength of the attraction that had grown into so much more between them.

He lowered his hands, had to clear his throat to find his voice. "I'll leave you then." Despite his determination, there was the tiniest hint of a question in the words.

She drew a deep breath, breasts rising, and nodded. "Yes. And . . . thank you for all you've done."

No words could have better convinced him he should go. He turned to the door. She followed. He stood back to let her step over the threshold; as she did, a heavy knock fell on the front door.

They both froze, then he reached forward and moved her to the side. "Let me see who it is."

She made no demur but stood quietly where he'd set her while he crossed the hall and opened the door.

One of his footmen looked up at him. The man smiled in relief. "My lord." He bowed and offered a letter. "This came from the Bastion Club with instructions it be delivered to your hand as soon as possible."

Tony took the missive. "Thank you, Cox." A quick glance at the seal informed him it was from Jack Warnefleet. "Good work. I'll take care of this. You may go."

Cox bowed and retreated. His footsteps faded along the street as Tony shut the door.

"What is it? News?" Alicia came to his side.

"Very likely." Breaking the seal, Tony spread the single sheet. Took in the single sentence with a glance.

"What? Who is it from?"

"Jack Warnefleet. He's been digging into Ruskin's county connections." Folding the note, Tony slipped it into his pocket. "He's returned with some news he thinks I should hear immediately."

Jack had written that he'd uncovered something significant and suggested Tony meet him at the Bastion Club "pdq." Pretty damn quick. Between such as they, that meant with all speed—urgent.

The possibility that they'd finally got some handle on

A.C. sent anticipation, a keen sense of the hunt, rising through him. "He's at the club—I'll go there now."

He glanced at Alicia. His welling excitement had communicated itself to her; eyes wide, she reached for the doorknob. "You will tell me if you learn anything major, won't you? Like who A.C. is?"

Already speculating on what avenues the new information might open up, he nodded as she opened the door. "Yes, of course."

The words were vague, the nod absentminded; Alicia stifled an oath. She caught his arm and tugged until he looked at her, actually focused on her. "Promise me you'll come and tell me the instant you learn anything significant."

She held his gaze, prepared to be belligerent if he turned evasive.

Instead, he looked into her eyes, then smiled. "I promise."

He ducked his head, kissed her swiftly, then slipped out of the door she was holding half-open. "Lock it—shoot the bolts. Now."

Grimacing at him, she shut the door, dutifully reached up, and shot the bolt above her head, then bent and slid home the other near the floor. Straightening, she listened. An instant later, she heard his footsteps descending the steps, then he strode away down the street.

Half an hour later, in the shrouded darkness of her bed, she sat up, pummeled her pillow, then flung herself down on it again.

She hadn't wanted to take the final step.

She reminded herself of that fact in inwardly strident tones—to no avail. They didn't impinge on her restless moodiness in the slightest, didn't alleviate the deflated feeling dragging at her—as if she'd been on the brink of receiving some wonderful gift, but it had been delayed at the last moment.

The feeling was nonsensical. Illogical. But very real.

She'd spent the entire evening on tenterhooks, increasingly sharp ones, worrying over what would unfold between them next, worrying that she knew all too well, that Tony would press ahead, engineer the moment, and . . .

That she felt so ungrateful for his forebearance was damning indeed.

He'd clearly decided to hold back; she should grasp the time he'd granted her to concentrate on those things that were most important—Adriana and their plan and the boys. Closing her eyes, settling her head on the down-filled pillow, she willed herself to keep her mind on such matters, on the things that had always dominated her life.

Determinedly, she relaxed.

Within seconds her mind had roamed, to a pair of hot black eyes, to the feel of his lips, firm and pliant on hers, to the sensations of his hands stroking, caressing, to the intimate probing of his tongue . . .

Sleep crept into her mind and swept her into her dreams.

She woke sometime later to a preemptory knock on her bedchamber door. She couldn't imagine . . . she stared through the shadows at the door.

It opened. Tony walked—stalked—in. He scanned the room and located her in the bed; even through the dark his gaze pinned her. Then he turned and quietly closed the door.

She struggled up onto her elbows, struggled to shake off the cobwebs of sleep and make her mind work. What? Why? Had something serious occurred?

Tony's calmly deliberate movements made that last seem unlikely. He'd crossed the room. Without meeting her eyes, he turned and sat on the end of her bed. It bowed beneath his weight.

She stared at his back, then wriggled and sat up, hugging the coverlet to her breasts. She'd caught only a glimpse of his face, but her eyes were adjusted to the darkness; it had seemed somewhat harder than usual, the harsh features sharply delineated, the angular planes set like granite.

He didn't turn around, but bent forward.

She frowned. "What's going on?"

Her whisper floated out through the room.

He didn't immediately answer; instead, she heard a thud.

Realized with a sudden clenching of nerves that he'd pulled off one shoe.

He shifted and reached for the other. "You made me promise to come and tell you the instant I learned anything significant."

Those had been her exact words. She shifted, wondering . . . "Yes? So what—" A sudden thought took precedence over everything else. She stared at the back of his head. "How did you get in?"

His second shoe hit the floor. "I slipped the lock on the drawing-room window. But you needn't worry." He stood and faced the bed. "I locked it again."

That wasn't what was worrying her.

Eyes widening, mouth drying, she watched as he shrugged out of his coat, glanced around, then flung it over her dressing table stool. Then his fingers rose to his cravat, smoothly tugging the ends free.

"Ah . . ." Good heavens! She had to . . . had to . . . she swallowed. "Did you learn something from your friend?"

She had to distract him.

"From Jack?" His tone was flat, his accents clipped. "Yes. As it happened, I learned quite a lot."

He had the cravat undone; dragging it free, he flung it on his coat, then his fingers went to the buttons of his shirt.

It was getting harder and harder to think, to swallow,

even to breathe. Had the moment really come? Just like that, without warning?

Panic inched higher and higher.

She clutched the edge of the coverlet. "So . . . what did you learn?" She tried to recall what had passed between them earlier—had she inadvertently issued some sexual invitation?

"Jack investigated Ruskin's background. In Bledington." Tony followed the line of buttons down, then glanced at her, yanked the tails from his waistband and stripped off the shirt. His eyes had adjusted; he could see how wide hers were. Wondered, cynically, intently, just how far she'd go before she broke.

He tossed the shirt aside, set his hands to his waistband, his fingers on the buttons of the flap. "Ruskin's estate amounts to little more than a few fields—he inherited his liking for gambling from his father. The income he enjoyed could not in any way derive from his ancestral acres." He slipped the buttons free. "If anything, the upkeep of the house in which his mother and sister live was a drain on his purse."

She didn't shift, made absolutely no sound as he removed his trousers and sent them to join the rest of his clothes. His determination hardened; it was an effort to keep his emotions—the mix of incredulity, anger, and hurt, and so much more he didn't want to examine—from his face.

Clothed only in shadows, he turned to the bed. Silent-footed, he prowled down its side; it was a large, canopied affair. He was aroused but, apparently stunned, she was following his face; she'd yet to look down.

She moistened her already parted lips. "Ah . . . so . . . what does that . . ." She made a valiant and quite visible attempt to focus her mind. "I mean, why is that important?"

"It's not." He heard the harshness in his tone. Watching her closely, primed to smother a shriek, he reached for the covers. "But there were other facts Jack discovered that were far more startling."

Her knuckles turned white as he grasped the covers, but when, jaw setting, he lifted them, her grip eased; the silky quilt slid through her fingers as he raised the sheets.

"Oh. I see . . ."

She was looking straight at him, but he would have sworn she wasn't seeing him. Her tone seemed distant, as if she was thinking of other things.

His temper, held in tight check until then, flared. He slid onto the bed, dropped the covers, and turned to her.

His plan—what plan he had—was to force her into admitting the truth, the truth Jack had uncovered. The truth she'd so artfully kept from him, her protector and would-be husband. He'd intended to shock her, to use that truth itself to chastise her, to embarrass her into admitting all; he'd imagined she'd succumb to virginal fluster long before now.

Still convinced she would, that at any second she'd panic, call a halt, and admit all, he reached for her. Closing his hands about her slender shoulders, feeling the fine silk of her nightgown slide over the soft skin beneath, he drew her to him.

Slowly, steadily, totally deliberately.

He looked into her face.

No hint of fear, of panic—of anything remotely resembling the frantic, embarrassed fluster he expected—showed in her features.

Quite the opposite. She was finally looking at him, studying his eyes, his face; her expression seemed almost serene, almost glowing.

Her eyes searched; her hands slid up to frame his face, then slid farther, her arms twining about his neck.

Abruptly losing patience, he pulled her to him.

Fully against him, body to body with only a fine layer of silk between.

He hadn't counted on the shock affecting him.

For one instant, the world about them rocked, quaked, then settled not quite as it had been before. His lungs seized; every muscle tensed; every nerve came alive.

Impulses—powerful, primitive, and sure—rose and rushed through him; his head spun.

He heard her breath catch. He looked into her eyes. Saw something like wonder in her expression.

Their gazes touched, held.

For three long heartbeats, time stood still.

Between them, heat welled. Flames ignited, greedily grew.

Her gaze dropped to his lips.

Beyond his control, his dropped to hers.

Who made the first move he didn't know. She lifted her head as he bent his. Their lips met.

And the fires leapt, then raged.

She pressed against him and he was lost. She opened her mouth to him, and he drowned in her bounty.

He sank against her, into her. In no way passive, she met him, her body firm and supple against his, her hands in his hair, her tongue dueling with his, inciting, inviting.

Wanting.

His control was gone before he even saw the threat. Vaporized by a need the like of which he'd never known. She was with him in want, in desire, in passion; her flagrant encouragement left no room for doubt.

Instinct claimed him, primal and unfettered. Unchained after being so long denied. He had to have her, all of her, had to have her beneath him, claimed and incontrovertibly his. It wasn't lust that drove him, but something deeper, more powerful, something that dwelled in his heart and his soul and paid scant attention to the dictates of his brain.

Within a minute, the kiss turned ravenous; his hands hardened, fingers kneading possessively.

Alicia sensed the change in him and exulted. Her own needs unleashed for the first time in her life, she wanted all he did, wanted to experience all he and she together could be.

She'd made her decision. Or had had it made for her; she wasn't sure, but either way she felt certain, confident beyond doubt, that this was meant to be.

The moment he'd turned to her, naked, aroused, yet somehow to her senses still unthreatening, she'd known. To her eyes, he was beautiful, incomparably male yet totally safe; never would she find another man she could trust as she trusted him—never with another would she feel the same certainty that she could go forward without fear, that she could surrender to him yet not lose herself.

That his victory would also be hers. That in his arms she would always be safe. Protected. Cared for.

Worshipped.

Despite the urgency that coursed through him, that hardened his body and shredded the veil of elegance that usually disguised his strength, that last was still apparent. His every touch was blatantly sexual, not rough but driven, forceful, demanding, even predatory, yet still each caress had only one aim, to awaken her senses and heighten their delight.

Pleasure was his currency, first and last.

She accepted it, and made it hers.

She sent her hands roaming, fingers flexing over his bare shoulders, glorying in the sculpted strength tensing beneath her fingertips, in the heavy resilence of his flesh, so unlike her own. He had her locked to him, lips devouring as his hands evocatively kneaded her bottom, his erection a hot heavy ridge impressed against her belly. She couldn't push back enough to press her hands between them; denied the chance of exploring his chest, she ran one hand down his back, reaching boldly for his waist, his hip, the subtle flare of his buttock. That was all she could reach, yet she sensed his pleasure in her touch; his lips clung to hers, distracted, then his attention returned to her in full measure, hotter, harder, more urgent.

Encouraged, determined, she pushed back, and he let her, shifting over her so his weight pinned her to the bed. His legs tangling with hers, he released her bottom; his hands rose to her breasts.

Their kiss continued unabated, mouths melding in a feast of mutual need, their hunger steadily growing, the heat between them swelling, escalating, this time out of control. Neither sought to rein it in; neither even considered it. By mutual accord, they let it rage, and rage it did.

He'd touched all of her before, had had her naked beneath his hands before, yet this was different. Her senses splintered, avidly trying to take in every new sensation. From the crisp, crinkly rasp of his hair-dusted legs against the fine skin of hers, to the unexpected weight of him above her, to the promise in the hard hot length now pressed to her hip, all was new, fascinating and enthralling.

As was the compulsion within her, building and swelling with every beat of her heart, with every knowing sweep of his hard hands. Without pause, he pushed her on and she went gladly, matching him, meeting him, even, when she sensed him struggling to regain control, goading him.

Her hands had been resting on his shoulders; she swept them down, pressing her palms to his hot flesh, fingers searching, exploring, as wantonly sensual as he in learning him, in tracing the muscle bands, letting her fingers tangle in the mat of hair across them, finding a flat nipple beneath the pelt and tweaking it to a tight bud.

His hips shifted against her. Emboldened, she sent her hands lower, caressing the taut, ribbed muscles of his abdomen, then reaching lower yet.

Until she found him, hot, heavy, velvet over steel.

He'd taken his weight on his arms, allowing her her way. She took full advantage and traced, caressed, then took him between her palms almost reverently, amazed, enthralled by the feel of him, the weight, the length and thickness, the baby-fine skin so obviously shatteringly sensitive. She could feel his reaction to her every touch, feel the flickering of his locked muscles, the heat that flowed through their kiss, welling and swelling with every sweep of her fingertips, every gentle squeeze.

Abruptly he broke from the kiss, and rolled onto his back, taking her with him. The sudden change in position momentarily distracted her; while she was reassessing, her attention deflected by the feel of his body now beneath hers, he reached down.

He caught her nightgown, gathered the skirts until he held them bunched at her thighs.

What he intended burst into her mind. She looked down, met his black eyes.

And suddenly they were themselves again, sane, rational—yet no longer who they had been. They'd moved on, traveled the very last stage of their road, and arrived at their destination.

It was different from what she'd imagined.

He said nothing, simply waited, his need in his eyes, in his body taut and tense beneath her.

Within her, she felt her own need swell, recognized it as similar yet subtly different from his. Knew in her soul that their needs were complementary—they would be assuaged by the one act, sated and fulfilled in the same moment.

Their gazes remained locked, their lips mere inches apart, their breaths, panting and ragged, softly filling the silence between them.

She found it was impossible to smile. Instead, she shifted; fingers tangling in the silk, she twitched it. Upward.

He didn't wait for more, but drew the gown up, past her hips, past her waist, tugging it up over her breasts, waiting while she disentangled her arms before dragging it free and flinging it away.

And she was naked in his arms.

He reached for her; giving her no time to think, to dwell on the intimacy, the vulnerability, he drew her lips down, took them, took her mouth, and dragged her back into the flames, into the furnace of their mutual need.

His hands were everywhere, claiming anew, drowning her in glorious sensation.

The flames roared; heat engulfed them.

She was suddenly sure her skin was on fire; as for him, he burned. His hands felt like brands, spreading liquid flame as he caressed, boldly possessed. Then he rolled again and pinned her beneath him.

He spread her thighs and settled between; braced on one arm, he hovered above her, his lips feeding from hers, his hips holding her down as with his other hand he reached between them, and found her.

She was swollen, wet and wanting, all but aching with the need to feel him within her. She knew it, didn't try to deny it, hide from it.

His fingers briefly played, then penetrated her. Once, twice, delved deep, then withdrew.

He shifted, his hips pressing between hers, then she felt the broad head of his erection part her swollen flesh, sliding easily between the folds to press in.

He stopped. Bracing both arms he lifted above her, simultaneously breaking their kiss.

With an effort, she managed to lift her lids; panting, barely sentient, she raised her eyes to his.

He trapped her gaze. Held it.

Desire wrapped them in a cocoon of flames; her body felt molten, yet achingly empty. The need to have him fill that emptiness thrummed, a steady, compulsive beat in her blood. Eyes locked with his, her every sense was focused on where they would join, on the soft swollen flesh between her thighs, on the hard heavy rod of his erection.

He pressed in. He kept his eyes on hers, holding her with him as slowly, steadily, he thrust in, and filled her. Not in a rush, but inch by slow inch. She felt her body give, stretch, felt every inch of his thickness as he pressed deeper, as her body struggled to adjust to the invasion.

The difficult moment came, as she'd known it would. She tried to cling to calm, tried to find some ease by breathing yet more rapidly, but the pressure and the pain steadily built, built . . . she would have shut her eyes, turned her head away, but his black gaze held her trapped.

Held her through it all, steady as a rock, a primitive promise beckoning as fraction by fraction he pressed her farther . . .

Her body tensed, arching under his, and still he held her with his eyes. And sank deeper.

The pressure gave.

In one sharp flash of pain it was gone, leaving her gasping, breasts rising and falling, yet still locked in his black gaze.

She sensed rather than saw his satisfaction. He halted, held still for some moments as she struggled to recover, to assimilate the change; he watched her, waiting. He seemed to know the exact moment the burning sensation faded, and the vise about her lungs eased and fear left her; he resumed his invasion, still slow, yet more assured.

Tony watched her, held her eyes, drank in every nuance of her response as he claimed her, filled her, and made her his. He'd surrendered to instinct long ago, in that first heated moment when his need had broadsided him. Subsequently, no thought had been required. He knew what he wanted, what he needed. Ruthlessly he took it—and her.

And part of that taking was this, this slow, excruciatingly complete first invasion. A branding, a declaration, an acceptance.

A sharing.

He'd needed to know, to be with her, to appreciate what she felt, know how she reacted. He'd always noted the responses of the women he bedded, yet this time he was not simply cataloging, gauging a reaction in order to capitalize on it. This time, he was immersed in the moment, experiencing both her pain and that glorious rush of release, of sexual interlocking, with her.

Experiencing, through it all, a deeper sense of connection, a deeper meaning beneath the sensations, beneath the physical pleasure.

He continued to press in; her body continued to give, to enclose him, until finally he was fully seated within her. Still holding her gaze, he withdrew halfway, then pressed in again, watching for any sign of discomfort.

Seeing none, feeling her body ease beneath him, her scalding sheath clasping tightly about him, he bent his head.

She raised hers, offered her lips.

He took them, claimed them. Without further direction, let his body do as it wished, as it had to do, and claim her.

The tiny fragment of his mind that remained lucid fully expected a fast and furious engagement. Instead, he rode her slowly; even now, even freed from all restraint, his body remained attuned to hers, gauging without conscious direction, responding to each quickening clasp of her sheath, to each restless shifting of her thighs, ultimately to the tentative rocking of her hips as she learned to match him and meet him.

Their progression was slow, measured, deliberate— and all-consuming. As she took him in, and his body followed hers, it occurred to him to wonder who had claimed whom. Who was leading, who was in charge . . .

Not him, and it couldn't be her.

Never had he been so totally absorbed, so totally submerged in the moment, so totally aware. Not just of the woman beneath him, but of his own body, his own pleasure. Hers heightened his; like a series of mirrors, reflecting back over and again, each tiny gasp, each soft moan, every sudden tensing of her fingers on his skin, washed over him and welled, swelled the exquisite tightness in his groin, fueled the tension driving him.

She'd tugged him down so his body met hers; her breasts were trapped beneath the heavy muscles of his chest, the rough hair abrading their sensitive skin, her nipples tight crests, their arousing pressure shifting with every deep thrust. Their skins were aflame, sheened, slick; her hands roamed his back, sweeping over the long planes, increasingly urgent. Their stomachs met, his hips locked in the cradle of hers, her thighs widespread, knees clasping his flanks, calves tangling with his.

Their mouths had fused, lips still greedily clinging, a connection that completed some circuit, that kept them immersed, locked in the compulsion that drove them, wholly given over to it.

Surrender came with a sudden quickening, first of her body, then of his. He was so deeply buried inside her, she took him with her; release swept them both in a long, glorious golden wave. Locked together, they rode it, let it take them and fling them high into the heavens, into the realms of pleasured bliss.

He emptied himself into her, felt her womb contract powerfully, holding him, accepting, taking.

The wave receded.

They drifted slowly to earth, their bodies eased, all tension gone, boneless in the aftermath. Their lips parted; breaths mingling, they clung, eyes still closed, savoring the closeness.

He felt her arms steal around him, then rest, lax. With the last of his strength, he slumped to the side, trying not to crush her as oblivion, deeper than he'd ever known it, caught him and drew him down.

THIRTEEN

REMARKABLE.

It had been that and more; an hour later, Tony still couldn't rationalize how very different the interlude had been, that she, a rank novice, had been the one woman in all his years to shatter his control, capture him utterly, forcing him to rely wholly on instinct, thus taking him to . . . wherever they had been.

A plane on which the pleasure defied all description, in which the physical had been a golden echo of something else.

An unworldly, unearthly, otherworldly place.

In all his years, through all his experience, he'd never even imagined such an exchange could be, or that such a place existed.

On rousing, he'd disengaged and lifted from her. Lying on his back, he'd gathered her to him; unresisting, she'd let him settle her against him, within the circle of his arms, her head on his shoulder.

The covers lay warm about them. Night lay like a blanket over the house; the moonlight had strengthened. He glanced at her face; she still seemed sunk in pleasured oblivion. Lifting his hand, he tentatively touched her hair. When she didn't stir, he set his palm to the silky tresses, smoothing them, drinking in the feel of their warm softness.

Lying back, he looked up at the canopy; slowly stroking, he tried to think.

The gentle, rhythmic comforting caress gradually drew Alicia back into the world. Warmth held her; pleasure still lay heavy in her veins. A sense of safety she'd never before known, so deep, so solid its existence was beyond question, wrapped her about, supporting, reassuring.

She sighed, and her wits returned.

And she remembered. Everything. All of it.

Every moment that had passed since he'd drawn her into his arms, every touch, every blissful second.

His arms remained around her, steel bands cradling her, gently enough, yet still overtly possessive.

The stroking slowed; his hand stilled. He knew she was awake.

Opening her eyes, she shifted her head and looked up. Met his gaze. Excruciatingly aware that she lay naked in his arms, that he was naked, too. Aware that their limbs were tangled, that they lay slumped together in a warm cocoon of rumpled sheets.

His black eyes held hers; it was impossible to read anything from them or his face. "When did you intend to tell me?" His tone was even, uninflected.

She searched his face, remembered . . . refocused on his eyes. "You knew."

He'd known she was—had been—a virgin; he'd watched for every second as he'd taken her virginity, as she'd willingly yielded it to him.

He looked down, at her hand spread on his bare chest. He took it in his; his long fingers toyed with hers. "There wasn't any trace of any Carrington anywhere near Chipping Norton. No entry in the parish records. No one of that name known at any of the stables or inns. Yet many knew the Misses Pevensey—*both* Misses Pevensey."

He glanced up; his eyes were sharp as they found hers. "I would have stopped if you'd wanted me to."

A statement, but there was a question buried in it. She held his gaze steadily. "I know."

She let the two words stand alone, a simple acknowledgment of the decision she'd made. She'd gone to him willingly; she wasn't about to pretend otherwise.

What was done was done; she was his mistress now.

She frowned. "How did you learn . . . ?" The truth struck her, left her horrified. "Your friend?"

Incipient panic flared in her eyes; Tony closed his hand over hers. "There's no need to worry." He hesitated, then explained, "Jack Warnefleet—Lord Warnefleet—investigated Ruskin for me. He also asked after your supposed husband, Alfred Carrington. Another A. C."

Understanding lit her eyes; he added, "We can rely on Jack's absolute discretion."

She studied his face, his eyes; a long moment passed, then she asked, "That was the urgent information he sent you the note about last night?"

He felt his jaw set. "He knew I'd want to know."

She blinked, then her lashes veiled her eyes. "I couldn't tell you." A heartbeat passed, then she added, "I couldn't risk it."

There was no hint of excuse in her tone; she was stating a fact, at least as she'd seen it.

He drew in a breath, lifted his gaze to look, unseeing, across the room. Given all he now knew of her, of the plan she and, he assumed, Adriana had concocted, of her commitment to her sister and even more to her brothers, he couldn't fault her; any hint that she wasn't the widow the ton thought her would, even now, result in complete and unmitigated disaster. Any chance of Adriana making a good match would disappear. They'd be social pariahs, expelled from society, forced to retreat to their cottage in the country to scrape a precarious existence for themselves and their brothers.

Trusting him with the truth . . .

He suddenly realized she had. She just hadn't told him in words.

His silence had bothered her; she tried to edge away. Even before he'd thought, his arms were tightening, holding her to him. "No—I know." She stilled; he drew in another breath, glanced down at her bent head. "I understand."

When she didn't look up, he bent close, placed a kiss on her crown, hesitated, then gently nudged her head.

Alicia looked up, into black eyes that promised far more than understanding. Safety, protection from both the finite and the nebulous dangers of the world, but more precious, at least to her, was the strange and novel relief of having someone with whom she could share her thoughts, her concerns, her schemes. Someone who did indeed understand.

His eyes searched hers; as if to confirm her reading, he asked, "Tell me how this all came about—you, your sister, your plan."

It wasn't a command, but a request, one she saw no reason to refuse; better he know all than half the story. She settled against him, felt his arms close tighter. "It started when Papa died."

She told him everything, even explaining her connection with Mr. King. Although he said not a word, she could tell he didn't approve, yet still he accepted, and made no protest. She was surprised when he questioned her about their gowns, and gave mute thanks not everyone was so acute.

When she in turn questioned why he'd investigated her supposed husband, he explained his thoughts of some other Carrington being involved. The comment led them deeper into the possibilities surrounding Ruskin; they discussed, tossed thoughts back and forth, argued likelihoods—the sort of exchange she'd never indulged in with anyone else.

Gradually, the silences lengthened. Blissfully warm, totally comfortable, she lay in his arms and listened to his heart beat steadily beneath her cheek. The covers lay over them; she still lay half-atop him, stretched alongside, her legs tangled with his, her hand spread over his chest. One muscled arm was wrapped around her, his hand heavy over her waist.

She should, she felt sure, feel some degree of fluster, of maidenly, feminine embarrassment over their naked state, let alone all that had led to it. Instead, the intimacy was addictive, a strange sense of closeness, of inexpressible comfort, of a simple rightness she was loath to shake.

He glanced down at her, then she felt his lips brush her hair.

"Go to sleep."

The whisper floated down to her. Turning her head, she looked up, met his eyes. Then she lifted her head, and touched her lips to his. He met them, returned her kiss, but gently. Briefly. Softly sighing, she drew back. Settling more definitely on his chest, spreading her hand over his side, she relaxed, and closed her eyes.

He merged with her dreams in the darkness before dawn. For long moments as he caressed her, sending sensation after sensation spiraling through her, each exquisite touch driving her higher into the clouds, she wasn't certain where her dreams ended and reality began.

Then he moved over her, spread her thighs wide, and slowly filled her.

She woke as he thrust deep and embedded himself within her, to the sensation of him hard and strong and rigid within her, of her body clamping tightly, joyously, about him, her arms reaching out to embrace him—and knew her life would never return to what it had been.

That was her first and last lucid thought; the instant he started to move within her, her wits deserted her, submerged beneath her clamorous senses, greedy for him, for what was to come.

He stayed close this time, his body moving over hers, murmuring gruff encouragement as she shifted beneath him, tilting her hips, adjusting to the rhythm and the depth of his penetration.

Her body seemed to know what to do; she let herself flow with the tide, gave herself up to the powerful surging rhythm, let it sweep her away into a whirlpool of shattering sensation. He kept them there, held them there, each rocking thrust swirling the vortex higher, tighter. Their lips found each other's without conscious direction, and then they were there again, in the heart of the flames, the center of the furnace.

The heat cindered all barriers, locked them together, desire flowing molten through them, between them. For one glorious instant, she lost touch with the world, couldn't tell where she ended and he began, knew only that they were together, one in thought, in mind, in deed.

Their lips clung, their hands grasped, slipped, gripped; their bodies strove to reach the elusive peak, just beyond their reach.

Then they broke through the clouds and the sunburst took them. The glory fractured, shattered, and poured through them. Rained down on them. Drove them at the last, gasping and shuddering, onto some far-distant shore.

They lay tangled, entwined, struggling for breath, the last shards of ecstasy still shivering through them. Heated, swollen, their lips touched, brushed, then parted. In the instant before she surrendered to beckoning oblivion, one simple truth floated through her mind.

Each time he came to her, each time they joined, left her one step further from the woman she had been.

Tony woke as dawn began to streak the sky. Satiation lay heavy upon him; he didn't want to move.

Eyes closed, he lay still, savoring the sensation of Alicia's soft curves pressed to his side; he consciously considered leaping a few steps and simply staying where he was.

Reluctantly, he accepted that might be going too far, too fast. Although where they were headed was perfectly clear, taking women for granted was never wise.

Stifling a sigh, he disengaged, trying not to disturb her. She murmured sleepily and clutched at his chest, but then slid back into slumber. Gently lifting her hand from him, he slid out of the bed. She snuggled down in the warm depression where he'd lain. The sight of her burrowed there made him smile.

Quickly, he dressed, dropped a light, fleeting kiss on her forehead, then slipped out of her room, and out of the house.

"Are you all right, Miss Alicia?"

Alicia woke with a start, realized it was Fitchett who had spoken. "Ah . . . yes." A lie, but she could hardly explain. "I, ah, overslept."

Struggling to sit up, her gaze fell on the rumpled disaster of her bed. Thank heavens Fitchett was outside the door.

"Aye, well, we was wondering, seeing as you hadn't rung. I'll bring up your water if you're ready for it."

Alicia glanced at the window. A shaft of bright sunlight lanced into the room. Dear God, what was the time? "Yes, thank you. I'm getting up now."

Fitchett lumbered off. Dragooning her wits and her still too-lax muscles into action, Alicia flung back the covers and got out of bed.

By the time Fitchett arrived with her water, she'd stripped the bed; there'd been no possibility of putting things right enough to pass muster. When Fitchett stared at the pile of bedclothes, she airily waved. "I decided to change the sheets. It's only a day or so early."

To her relief, Fitchett merely humphed.

She washed and dressed quickly, then hurried down-stairs to discover bedlam reigning at the breakfast table. Adriana had done her best, but she lacked Alicia's au-thority; called to order, the boys assumed their most an-gelic expressions and innocently resumed a more civilized rapport.

"I slept in," she replied to Adriana's questioning look. It wasn't a good excuse—she never slept in—but it was all she could think of. Reaching for the teapot, she poured herself a cup. She sipped, relaxed, then realized how hun-gry she was. Ravenous, in fact.

Jenkins came in, and they discussed the boys' lessons for the coming week while she polished off a mound of kedgeree.

When Jenkins departed, the boys in tow, Adriana frowned at her. "Well, you're obviously not ailing—there's nothing wrong with your appetite."

She waved the piece of toast she'd started nibbling and reached for her cup. "I just slept longer than usual."

Adriana pushed back her chair and rose. "You must have been dreaming."

Recollection flashed across Alicia's mind; she nearly choked on her tea.

"Are we still going to Mr. Pennecuik's warehouse to-day?"

She nodded. "Yes—we must if we're to make those new gowns." Setting down her cup, she picked up her toast. "In twenty minutes—I have to check with Cook be-fore we go."

The rest of the day passed in the usual busy fashion; she hadn't before noticed how little personal time she had, private time alone in which to think. If she and Adri-ana weren't out, attending some function or event, then some member of the household would want to speak with her, or her brothers needed supervising, or . . .

She needed to think—she knew she did, knew she

ought to stop and consider, and get her mind in order for when next she met Tony. She'd taken a major step, turned a hugely significant corner—one she definitely shouldn't have turned, perhaps, but she'd willingly taken that road; it was clearly imperative she stop and take stock.

All that seemed obvious, yet when she finally found herself alone in her room, bathing, then dressing for the evening, she discovered her mind had a will of its own.

When it came to all that had passed in the night, and in the small hours of the morning, while she could recall and relive every moment, every detail, her mind flatly refused to go any further. It was as if some dominant part of her brain had decided those events were in some way sacrosant, that they stood as they were and needed no further examination. No dissection, no analysis, no clarification. They simply were.

It was, indeed, as if she'd stood at a crossroads, and now she'd gone around the corner, she couldn't see where she'd been. Which left her facing forward along a road she'd never imagined traveling.

Putting the last touches to her coiffure, she paused and studied herself in the mirror. She still looked the same, yet . . . was it something in her eyes, or maybe in her posture, the way she stood, that assured her, at least, that she was no longer the same woman?

She had changed, and she didn't regret it. There was little in this world for which she'd trade so much as a minute of the time she'd spent in Tony's arms.

Indeed, there was no point looking back. She was his mistress now.

And if she didn't know what that new status would bring, or how to cope, she'd just have to learn.

She looked into her eyes for a moment longer, then let her gaze run down the sleek lines of the deep purple silk gown Adriana had designed and she and Fitchett had created. The heart-shaped neckline showcased her breasts without being obvious; the cut below the high waist made the most of her slim hips and long legs, while the small off-the-shoulder sleeves left the graceful curves of her shoulders quite bare.

Turning, she picked up her shawl and reticule, then headed for the door. Luckily, she learned quickly.

The cacophonous sound of the ton in full flight rose to greet Tony as he paused at the top of the steps leading down into Lady Hamilton's ballroom. Her ladyship's rout was one of the events traditionally held in the week before the Season began; society's elite were almost to a man foregathered in town—everyone who was anyone would be present.

Looking down on the sea of bright gowns, of sheening curls, of jewels winking in the light thrown by the chandeliers, he scanned the throng, relieved when he located Alicia standing by the side of the room, Adriana's court, some steps in front of her, partially screening her. Relief died, however, when closer inspection revealed that three of the gentlemen between Alicia and Adriana were not conversing with Adriana.

Jaw setting, he strolled with feigned nonchalance down the steps; cutting through the crowd, he made his way directly to Alicia's side.

She welcomed him with a smile that went some way toward easing his temper. "Good evening, my lord."

He took the hand she offered, raised it brazenly to his lips, simultaneously stepping close. "Good evening, my dear."

Her green-gold eyes widened a fraction. His easy, languid smile took on an edge as, setting her hand in the crook of his arm, he took up a stance—a clearly possessive stance—by her side.

With every evidence of well-bred boredom, he glanced at the gentlemen who had been speaking with her. "Morecombe. Everton." He exchanged the usual nods. The last man he didn't know.

"Allow me to present Lord Charteris."

The tall, fair-haired dandy bowed. "Torrington."

Tony returned the bow with an elegant nod.

Straightening, Charteris puffed out his narrow chest. "I was just describing to Mrs. Carrington the latest offering at the Theatre Royal."

Tony allowed Charteris, who appeared to fancy himself a peacock of sorts, to entertain them with his anecdote; he judged the man safe enough. Morecombe was another matter; although married, he was a gazetted womanizer, a rake and profligate gambler. As for Everton, he was the sort no gentleman would trust with his sister. Not even with his maiden aunt.

Both clearly had their eyes on Alicia.

Behind his polite mask, he took note of the undercurrents in the small group; focused on the men, it was some minutes before he noticed the swift glances Alicia surreptitiously cast him. Only then realized she was, if not precisely skittish, then at least uncertain.

It took a minute more before he realized her uncertainty was occasioned not by any of the three gentlemen before her, but by him.

He waited only until the notes of a waltz filled the room. Glancing at her, he covered her hand on his sleeve. "My dance, I believe?"

His tone made it clear there was no doubt about the fact; as he hadn't previously spoken, it should be patently clear that her hand being his to claim was an arrangement of some standing.

Fleetingly meeting his eyes, she acquiesced with a gracious inclination of her head.

The glances he noticed Morecombe and Everton exchange as, with a polite nod, he led her away gave him some satisfaction. With any luck, they would move on to likelier prey before the waltz ended.

Reaching the dance floor, he drew Alicia into his arms, started them revolving, then turned his full attention on her. He studied her eyes, then raised a brow. "What is it?"

Alicia looked into his eyes; she felt her lips firm, but managed not to glare. *I haven't been a nobleman's mistress before* hardly seemed worth stating. And now she was in his arms, sensing again the familiar reactions—the physical leap of her senses soothed by the feeling of comfort and safety—her earlier worries over how she should react—how he would behave and how he would expect her to respond to him—no longer seemed relevant. "Have you made any progress with your investigations?"

That, at least, was something she could ask.

"Yes." For a moment, he looked down at her as if waiting for her to say something else, then he looked up for the turn, and went on, "I heard from Jack Hendon this morning—he's confirmed all that your brothers learned." Glancing down, he met her gaze. "Incidentally, he was impressed—you might tell them."

"They don't need any encouragement."

His lips twitched. "Perhaps not." He looked up again, drawing her fractionally closer as they came out of the turn and headed up the long room. "Jack's pursuing the matter, trying to find a pattern to the ships that were taken versus those that were not. With luck, that might shine some light on who benefited from the losses."

He met her gaze. "I haven't yet heard back from the friend scouting down in Devon—he has contacts with smugglers and wreckers along that coast. As for myself, now I've got something specific to ask, I'll start putting out feelers among my own contacts."

He'd kept his voice low; she did the same. "Does that mean you'll be leaving London?"

The prospect filled her with a curious disquiet. An odd, novel, uncomfortable feeling; she'd never relied on others before—she'd always been self-sufficient. Yet the thought of coping with the unfolding events stemming from Ruskin's death by herself . . .

His arm around her tightened, drawing her attention and her gaze back to him.

"No—my contacts are primarily along the southeastern coast, from Southampton to Ramsgate, all within half a day from town. I can cover them in single-day journeys. Aside from all else, I need to be here to assess what the others discover, Jack Hendon from Lloyd's and the shipping lines, and Gervase Tregarth in Devon."

She nodded, aware of relief, but they were now *too* close, her bodice brushing his coat, her silk-sheathed thighs shushing against his . . . yet with the press of other couples about them, it was unlikely any would notice. And to the ton, she was still a widow after all.

Tony hesitated, debating, then murmured, "Incidentally, I've arranged for some men to keep a watch on your house. They'll be in the street—you won't know they're there, but . . . just in case you have need, there'll always be someone watching your front door."

She stared up at him; he could see her thoughts whirling behind the green-gold of her eyes. First Maggs, now . . . "Why?"

He had his argument ready. "First the rumor, then the Watch. I want to make sure whoever A. C. is, he gets no chance to do anything more to implicate you. Or your family."

He felt confident those last words would see her accept his arrangements without further question.

She frowned at him, but proved him right. "If you really think there's a need . . ."

Whether there was or not, he would feel much happier knowing that when he journeyed out of the capital, more of his trusted minions had her and her brood under their eye. The three men he'd set to keep a constant watch on the Waverton Street house were one hundred percent reliable; nothing suspicious would escape them.

The music slowed, then ended; they whirled to a halt. Reluctantly releasing her, he tucked her hand in his arm and turned her away from Adriana's court. "I'll go down to Southampton tomorrow."

Looking at him, she nodded, then cast a glance back up the room. "We should—"

"Behave as if we're lovers."

Her gaze snapped back to his face. "What?"

He resisted the urge .to narrow his eyes at her; he opened them wide instead. "No one will find anything odd in that—it's what they're expecting." Given he'd laid the appropriate groundwork over the past several weeks.

She frowned. "Yes, but—" Again she glanced back toward Adriana.

"Stop worrying about Adriana. Geoffrey's beside her, and even if he's distracted, there's always Sir Freddie." He paused. "Has he made an offer yet?"

"Sir Freddie? No, thank heavens." She turned and settled to stroll by his side.

"Why so relieved? I thought you wanted Adriana to be able to choose among many?"

She narrowed her eyes at him. "I did. But as you very well know, she's already made her choice, so Sir Freddie making an offer will simply be an unnecessary complication."

He grinned, making a mental note to prod Geoffrey when next he had a chance. "Actually, I'm surprised you haven't been inundated with offers."

"I daresay I would have been if Adriana hadn't hinted many of them away." She shot him a severe glance. "Strange to tell, she seems to feel that avoiding trying Geoffrey's temper unnecessarily is a sound idea."

He looked down at her—and hoped she read the message in his eyes; he concurred with her sister's judgment and sincerely hoped she herself would exercise similar restraint.

The way she looked away, the hoity angle to which she

elevated her nose, suggested she understood him well enough. Hiding an inward grimace at his own susceptibility, he steered her to where his godmother waited, surrounded by a number of her extremely interested friends.

Despite their interest and that shown by any number of the ton's matrons in the relationship between them, the rest of the evening passed well enough. Through a combination of exemplary scouting and good management, he kept Alicia to himself throughout, avoiding the other gentlemen who, prowling through the crowd and attracted by the faintly exotic, definitely sensual picture she presented in her deep purple gown—something he fully intended to enjoy removing later—continually hove on her horizon.

They indulged in another waltz, after which she insisted on returning to check on Adriana and her court. Instead of permitting her to hang back as she usually did, he led her to join the circle of gentlemen and two other enterprising young ladies gathered about Adriana.

Alicia shot him a suspicious glance, which he met with a bland, wholly deceptive smile, but she consented to do as he wished. Thus protected from further incursions— the gentlemen who looked her way were not the sort to dance attendance among the younger crew—they saw out the end of the evening.

As soon as guests started to leave, Alicia turned to him; he got the impression she was tired, then recalled . . . hiding a smug smile, he gathered Adriana and Geoffrey; together with Sir Freddie, they joined the exodus. In the foyer downstairs, they parted. Sir Freddie bowed easily over Adriana's hand, bowed courteously to Alicia, nodded to Tony, and lastly Geoffrey, then left. Geoffrey scowled after him, then turned to farewell Adriana and Alicia.

Tony exchanged a nod and a glance. Geoffrey returned both, an acknowledgment that Tony would see both ladies safe home.

When he accompanied them to their carriage, Alicia shot him a wary frown. He ignored it, handed first Adriana, then her up, and followed.

Adriana accepted his presence without the slightest question. Alicia glanced at him, then gave her attention to the facades they rolled past. He leaned back, content to feel her soft warmth beside him, perfectly aware of what was going through her mind.

When the carriage rocked to a halt in Waverton Street, he stepped down, and handed both sisters down. He shut the carriage door; the carriage lurched, then rumbled off. He turned to find Alicia standing on the pavement, eyeing him uncertainly. Suppressing a smile, he took her arm and guided her up the steps. Adriana had already knocked; Maggs opened the door, and she swept in. He steered Alicia in her wake.

"Good night." Adriana headed for the stairs with barely a backward glance.

Maggs shot the bolts on the front door, then bowed to them both and took himself off.

Alicia watched him go and wished she knew what would happen next. She shouldn't encourage any illicit interlude; she steeled herself to bid Tony good night. Determinedly ignoring the twitching of her senses, the skittering anticipation afflicting her nerves, she tensed to swing about—

His long fingers slid around her wrist. "Come into the drawing room."

She turned, tried to read his face, but he was already moving, drawing her with him. He opened the door; leaving it ajar, he led her into the dimness beyond the shaft of light shed by the candle left burning in the hall.

Halting, he faced her, smoothly drew her into his arms—and kissed her.

Stormed her senses.

She was kissing him back, fully participating in an increasingly heated exchange before she caught her mental breath. Even when she did, it was impossible to draw back, to pull away from the engagement and the spiraling escalation of hunger and need it fueled.

Whose hunger, whose need, she couldn't have said; they were both greedy, ravenous, both wanting.

Her hands were sunk in his hair, holding him to her as their tongues dueled, as their lips feasted. One of his hands had closed about her breast, kneading, leaving it swollen and aching; the other was wrapped about one globe of her bottom, crushing the silk as he held her to him.

He rocked against her, deliberately evocative; heat pulsed within her—she heard a soft moan.

Holding her tight, her body molded to his, he broke from the kiss, raised his head, but not far. With an effort she lifted her heavy lids, and found his black gaze on her eyes.

"There's no reason to step back."

She knew he didn't mean from their kiss.

His gaze fell to her lips, then returned to her eyes. "And don't think to deny this."

She couldn't; given what was so manifestly flaring between them . . . he was right—there was no point.

He bent his head again. She was lifting her lips to meet his when she heard his soft murmur, "Or me."

She set her hand to his cheek as he took her mouth again; he was all heat and fire, tempting and familiar. This, she accepted, was the way it would be; if he wanted her, she was willing.

A minute later, he broke from the kiss to murmur, his voice dark and gravelly, "Upstairs."

He turned her. His hand remained on her bottom as he guided her into the hall, then up the stairs to her bedchamber; her skin didn't cool in the least.

Then they were in her room, and he closed the door. She'd halted in the middle of the floor, the candle in her hand. The flame wavered, but was enough to shed a golden pool of light into the general gloom.

He glanced at her, then at her dressing table; he waved. "Put it down there."

She moved to do so. Leaning over the stool, she set the candlestick down on the polished top, straightened—and saw in the mirror that he'd followed her.

His hands slid around her waist. He shifted her slightly so that she stood directly in front of the three-paneled mirror with its wide central panel flanked by two narrower wings. The rectangular stool stood before her knees. She glanced down at it, then looked up as his hands slid farther and gripped, anchoring her as he stepped closer, trapping her before him.

She caught her breath as, in the shadowy mirror, she watched his dark head bend beside hers; releasing her waist, one hand rose, gliding upward over the purple silk, now deep as the midnight sky, to close possessively over one breast. His other hand splayed down, covering her stomach, pressing in, gently kneading, pressing her hips back against his hard thighs.

Turning her head, she glanced over her shoulder at his face; inches away, she saw his teeth gleam in a fleeting smile.

"Bear with me," he murmured, then his lips touched the corner of hers, then cruised back along her jaw to trace her ear. "I want to see you naked."

He whispered the words, dark and erotic, into her ear.

It took a moment before she realized what he meant—he wanted to see her naked in the mirror.

Her nerves seized; before she could think of any protest—even decide if she wished to protest—he nudged her head back. She complied without thought; his lips traced downward along the column of her throat, then fastened over the spot where her pulse leapt.

His lips moved on her skin; his hands moved over her

silk-clad body, roaming, caressing, then his fingers found her laces.

She closed her eyes, leaned back against him as he loosened her gown, then his hands rose to her shoulders and pressed the soft fabric down.

"Lift your arms."

Opening her eyes just enough to see beneath her lashes, she watched her reflection in the mirror as she obeyed, sliding her arms free of the tiny sleeves. His palms swept down, over her breasts; the gown slithered down to her waist. His hands followed, pressed the folds past her hips; with a soft swoosh, the dress pooled at her feet.

For an instant, he paused, surveying what he'd uncovered. She caught the gleam of his eyes from beneath his heavy lids, felt his gaze briefly roam. In the flickering candlelight her chemise was opaque, the shadowy valleys and contours it hid mysterious.

He looked down. His hands rose and gripped her waist. "Kneel on the stool." He lifted her, and she did; with his knees he nudged her ankles wide and stepped between, so his chest was again a warm wall at her back, his erection a promise against the swell of her bottom.

The candlelight reached her, but didn't light him well; he was a dark presence behind her, his tanned hands contrasting starkly against the whiteness of her skin, the ivory of her chemise. He was a phantom lover, come to claim her, to lavish pleasure on her and take his own.

Her breath caught. He looked up, in the mirror trapped her gaze—as his hands slipped beneath the front hem of her chemise. She steeled herself, anticipating his touch, the fiery delight of his hands on her flesh, skin to bare skin. Instead, he turned his hands, caught the fine fabric and lifted it. Without touching her at all, he raised the diaphanous garment; lungs seizing, she lifted her arms and he drew it off over her head.

She put out a hand to steady herself as the cool air caressed her skin—the only firm purchase she could reach was his thigh behind her. Sinking her fingers into the hard muscle, giddy, she stared at the vision in the mirror—that of a slim, slender woman, her dark hair elegantly high, totally naked but for her silk stockings and the ruched satin garters that held them in place, circling her thighs.

Lifting her gaze to his face, she sensed rather than saw his satisfaction; it was a tangible thing, filling the air, surrounding her. She realized she still had on her ballroom slippers; even as the thought occurred, she saw him glance down, then his fingers caressed each ankle, and he slipped the shoes from her feet and let them fall.

He moved close again, and reached around to her garters. But instead of easing them down, as she'd expected, he ran his fingertips around the upper edge of each. And smiled. "They can stay. For now."

The timbre of his voice sent a shiver down her spine. It took effort to remain upright, yet pride dictated she keep her spine erect; she could feel the fabric of his coat and trousers gently abrading her bare skin.

His gaze had returned, slowly, to her face. He studied it, then shifted back a fraction, just enough to shrug off his coat. Seconds later, his waistcoat joined it on the floor.

He had to step back to deal with his cravat and shirt; she had to let go of him. She watched as he flung the shirt aside, then looked down, his hands going to his waist. His trousers hit the floor, and he stepped out of them, returning to her, his hands sliding over her hips, over her waist, drawing her back against him, against the heat of his skin, the rock-hard wall of his chest and abdomen, the hard columns of his thighs.

"Lean back. Let me love you."

The words were an erotic whisper in the darkness.

"Let me see you. Watch you."

She did as he asked, leaning back against him, eyes almost closed, committed to following his lead, only later, as his hands made free with her body, with her senses, fully understanding what he meant.

At first, his hands simply roved her body, a basic pleasure, heating her skin, teasing her senses to even greater awareness, evoking a deeper, persistent hunger. Flaring need grew as he weighed and caressed her breasts, taunting the tight, aching peaks, then tracing the lines of her body, sculpting the curves with his palms before gliding his fingertips down her thighs, then nudging her knees farther apart.

She watched, immersed in the sensations as he stroked the quivering inner faces of her thighs, then laid his hand over her stomach, the other sliding across her waist, holding her, surrounding her with his strength, giving her a moment to assimilate the heated, raspy reality of his skin, his muscled body pressed to her, locked about her.

In the mirror, she could see his shoulders above hers; his chest was wider than her back, his arms a cage in which she willingly waited.

He murmured something in French—she didn't catch the words but let her head rest back against his shoulder, watching, watching as he shifted, then the hand at her stomach slid lower, long fingers gliding over, then through the dark curls at the apex of her thighs. He reached farther; the breath strangled in her throat, her lungs seized. The vise about her chest locked tight as he stroked, caressed, then deliberately probed.

Farther, then yet farther, until his hand was pressed between her thighs, until her body was awash with flame. Her hands fastened on the arm locked about her waist, fingers sinking into the hard muscle as she watched him watching her—watched his hand, so much darker than her skin, rhythmically lavish fiery delight upon her senses.

She gasped, felt her body tighten, arching, reaching for the beckoning peak. He didn't stop but steadily pushed her on, on, on—until she fractured.

Her soft cry hung in the air; he wrapped her in his arms, in his strength, held her safe as she slowly drifted back from the crest.

She turned her head, glanced at him. He met her gaze, but briefly. His lips curving in what wasn't quite a smile, he glanced down at her body, soft, pliant, still locked against the hard aroused length of his. Then he bent his head and pressed a kiss to the point where her neck met her shoulder.

"First course."

His tone made it clear he intended to feast.

Reaching out, he moved the single candle, still burning bright, across and back on the dressing table, positioning it near the central pane of the mirror, at the very center. Reaching farther, he tugged first one side panel, then the other forward, angling them so they reflected the candle-light back at them. At her—it was her smooth, white skin the light illuminated; in contrast, his darker, tanned, and haired limbs seemed to disperse the light. Yet she could now see him clearly. The new position of the side panels let her see beyond her shoulders.

His hands returned to her body; they circled her breasts, gently kneaded, then slid down, tracing her sides, then he gripped her hips. Bent his head and murmured, his breath a heated promise, "Lean forward—hold on to the edge of the dressing table."

She did, and felt his hand caress the globes of her bottom. He traced the backs of her thighs, then reached between. Touched, stroked.

On a shuddering sigh, she closed her eyes; she had only an instant's warning—an inkling of what he would do—before he shifted, pressed close, and entered her.

Instinctively she locked her thighs, braced her arms, held still as he sank in, gasped when, with a last thrust, he filled her completely. His hands gripped her hips, anchored her as he withdrew, returned, then settled to a slow, steady plundering.

Her senses shook; her wits had long gone. Her breathing sounded ragged in her ears. Beneath her skin, her pulse throbbed, her body aflame as she rode the increasingly powerful thrusts.

The tempo escalated, degree by degree, until she was barely clinging to sanity, wrapped in heat, driven by desire.

"Watch."

The command reached through the flames fogging her mind. She dragged in a breath, forced her lids up. Looked.

And saw.

Him, behind her, his face etched with passion, set, his whole being focused completely on her, on the pleasure he found in her heated body. A body aglow with desire, softly sheened, his hands curved over her hips, his fingers locked on her skin.

She moved with him, not by thought but in instinctive concert, taking, giving, wanting more. Glancing to the side, into the side mirror, she watched their hips move, locked together in their sensual dance.

Her lungs seized; she glanced back at his face, saw the gleam of his eyes beneath his lashes as he watched her.

Then he shifted, thrust deeper, harder, higher. She gasped, let her lids fall; he was impossibly high inside her.

Faster, faster—and the flames roared. Took them, consumed them in an orgy of feeling, of sensations too sharp, too bright, too excruciatingly powerful to survive. And they were whirling, trapped in a whirlpool of delight, passion still driving, ecstasy beckoning . . . until it broke over them, drenched them, washed through them.

Leaving them shuddering, locked tight together, his arms wrapped around her, hers wrapped over them.

The tide faded, and left them.

The bed was close. He lifted her, staggered the few steps, then they collapsed amid the covers. It was a long time before either could summon the will or the strength to move.

FOURTEEN

THE FOLLOWING DAYS WERE AMONG THE STRANGEST
Alicia had known. And quite the fullest.

With the Season about to commence, the social pace
approached the frenetic; not only were there three or
more major balls every night, but the days, too, were
crammed with activities—driving in the park, at-homes,
teas, luncheons, picnics, and all manner of diversions. So
established were they now among the ton that their absence at such events would have been remarked; people
expected to see them—they needed to be there.

She'd schemed, hoped, worked for, plotted so that at
the start of the Season she and Adriana would be accepted members, indeed fixtures on the social scene. Fate
had granted her wish, and they were dancing every night.

Those who had only recently come to town cast cov-
etous eyes at their now-combined circle, with Tony,
Geoffrey, Sir Freddie, and a bevy of others regularly
forming part of that select company. But most, certainly
the major hostesses and the matrons on whose opinion
tonnish acceptance hung, had grown used to them; they
merely smiled, nodded graciously, and moved on through
the crush.

Of course, given Adriana's clear preference for Geoffrey's company, and his for hers, such social prominence
was no longer necessary, yet Alicia would have managed
society's demands easily enough—if it hadn't been for

the distraction of all else in her suddenly and unexpectedly full life.

Tony left her bed every morning before dawn; through the day, he traveled—to the coast, to various towns and hamlets, over the Downs, to Southampton and Dover—speaking with his mysterious "contacts," constantly seeking information that might shed light on A. C.'s nefarious activities.

In the evening, he'd return, not to Waverton Street but his own house; later still, he'd join her at whichever ball or soirée, musicale or rout they had chosen to attend.

Each evening, she'd wait, chatting with those about her but with her thoughts elsewhere, wondering, circling . . . until he arrived. Every time he appeared to bow over her hand, then set it on his sleeve and take his place by her side, her heart leapt. Quelling it, she'd wait still further, impatient yet resigned, for the ballrooms were now too crowded to risk talking of his findings.

Only later when he'd escorted them home, then followed her to her bedchamber would they talk. He'd tell her all he'd done that day, all he'd learned. Snippets of information verified their suspicions that A. C. had somehow profiteered by ensuring certain ships had been taken by the enemy, yet nothing they'd discovered so far had shed enough light to show them how.

Later yet . . . they'd come together in her bed, and the day would fall away, and nothing else—nothing beyond the cocoon of the coverlets and the circle of each other's arms—seemed real, of any consequence.

Later still, she'd lie wrapped in his arms, surrounded by his strength, listening to his steady heartbeat, and wonder . . . at herself, at where she was, where she was heading . . . but those moments were fleeting, too brief to reach any conclusion.

And then the sun would rise, and there'd be another day of frantic activity, of ensuring her brothers' lives and their lessons stayed on track, that Adriana and Geoffrey's romance continued to prosper, and that all else—the facade of her making—continued as it needed to.

Beneath the social bustle, she was conscious of an undercurrent of action. Things *were* happening; Tony and his friends were steadily, quietly, chipping away at A. C.'s walls—at some point they'd break through. Twice, she glimpsed a watchful face in the street; the sight reminded her of the potential danger, kept her on her mental toes.

She tried, once, to find time alone to think, but Adriana burst in in a panic over a new gown that wouldn't drape straight, and she put aside her nebulous concerns. Time enough when the Season had run at least a few weeks, enough to take the edge from society's appetite, and A. C. had been exposed and her family was safe again, and Geoffrey had proposed . . . time enough, then, to think of herself.

That evening, she nearly suggested they stay home—perhaps send a note to Torrington House, and another to Geoffrey Manningham, inviting them to a quiet dinner . . . then she sighed and climbed into the fabulous apple green silk gown Adriana had fashioned. It was the Duchess of Richmond's ball tonight.

The traditional, recognized, start of the Season.

Even before they reached the duchess's door, it was clear the crowd would be horrendous; their carriage took forty minutes just to travel up the drive and deposit them beneath the awning erected to protect the ladies' delicate toilettes from the light showers sweeping past. Once inside, the noise of a thousand chattering tongues engulfed them; friends called greetings through the throng—it was impossible not to be infected with the gaiety.

Geoffrey was the first to find them. "Let me." He took Adriana's arm, offered Alicia the other, then steered them to where a trio of potted palms gave some respite from the packed and shifting bodies.

They stopped, caught their breaths. Alicia snapped open her fan and waved it. "Now I see why they refer to such events as 'crushes.' "

Geoffrey threw her a commiserating look. "Luckily, it doesn't get much worse than this."

"Thank heaven for that," Adriana murmured.

Gradually, the others with whom they'd become most friendly found them; it was a comfortable circle that formed by the side of the room, Miss Carmichael and Miss Pontefract, both sensible and well-bred young ladies, helping to balance the genders. They exchanged the latest stories they'd heard during the day; the gentlemen, most of whom kept to their clubs during the daytime, often had not heard what the ladies had, and vice versa.

Occasionally, a matron would stop by and engage Alicia; some brought their daughters to be introduced. Lady Horatia Cynster smiled and nodded; later, the Duchess of St. Ives stopped by Alicia's side and complimented her on her gown.

"You have become as *ravissante* as your sister." The duchess's pale green eyes quizzed her. "I confess I am surprised Torrington is not here. Do you expect him?"

She wasn't sure how to answer, in the end admitted, "I believe he'll arrive shortly."

"Indeed, and no doubt he will see you home." The duchess's smile deepened. She laid a hand on Alicia's wrist. "*Bien.* It is good. I am most pleased that he has had the sense to act, rather than prevaricate—it is pleasing to see that he takes such excellent care of you." Her pale gaze fell on Geoffrey. "And this one, if my eyes do not lie, will take good care of your sister, *hein*?"

Alicia raised her brows. "It appears he wishes to, certainly, although she has yet to tell him he may do so."

The duchess laughed. "*Bon!* It is wise to keep such as he wondering, at least for a little time."

With a nod to Adriana, and to Sir Freddie Caudel, who

had noticed her and bowed low, the duchess patted Alicia's hand, then moved on into the crowd.

The dance floor was in the next salon, separated by an archway. Alicia refused all offers to lead her thence, remaining by the palms chatting with whichever gentlemen were not engaged with the ladies on the floor.

Such was the crowd, she was almost surprised that Tony managed to find them. It was late when he did.

His fingers slid around her wrist; she looked up, smiling in welcome, aware as usual of faint but definite relief. A relief that turned to concern when she met his eyes and saw her weariness mirrored there.

He raised her hand to his lips, using the gesture to mask his grimace. "I'd forgotten how bad these affairs could be."

She smiled, and let him draw her close. "The dance floor is unnavigable, I've heard."

He raised a brow at her. "There's always the terrace."

"Is there a terrace?"

He nodded. "Through the drawing room."

She considered the question in his eyes, then faintly smiled. "I'd rather go home."

His black eyes held hers. After a moment, he murmured, "Are you sure?"

"Yes."

He held her gaze for an instant, then nodded. With a look and a quiet word, he gathered Adriana; not surprisingly, Geoffrey came, too. Sir Freddie bade them a suavely courteous good night, remaining to chat with Miss Pontefract and Sir Reginald Blaze. Leaving the group, they made their way through the still dense crowd to the foyer.

Tony sent a footman for their carriage. Richmond was a long way from Mayfair; in response to a pointed look from Adriana, Alicia invited Geoffrey to share their carriage. He accepted; minutes later, the carriage arrived, and they set off on the long rocking ride back to town.

Once they were free of the gate and bowling along the main road, Geoffrey looked at Tony. "Have you learned anything yet?"

Tony felt Alicia's glance, shook his head. "Nothing definite. Corroboration, yes, but nothing that defines the game A. C. was playing."

"Was playing? You're sure of that? That it's all in the past?"

He wasn't surprised to find Geoffrey interrogating him; if he'd been in his shoes, enamored of the lovely Adriana, he, too, would want to know. "That much seems certain. Indeed, that's why Ruskin was no longer valuable—why he became an expendable liability."

Geoffrey thought, then nodded.

Conversation lapsed, then Adriana asked Geoffrey something; he looked down at her, and replied. They continued talking, their voices low.

Tony wasn't in the mood to chat; he was in truth tired—he'd traveled down to Rye and spent much of the day chasing men who rarely ventured forth in sunshine. Nevertheless, he'd found them, and learned all he'd needed to know.

He looked at Alicia; shifting his hand, he found hers and wrapped his fingers about it. She glanced at him; in the weak light he saw her smile gently, then she looked forward, leaned her head against his shoulder, her other hand finding and covering their clasped hands. He sensed she was as tired as he; he was tempted to put his arm around her and gather her against him, but in light of the pair on the opposite seat, refrained.

It took nearly an hour to reach Waverton Street.

Geoffrey jumped down; Tony followed. They handed their ladies down, then Geoffrey took his leave of Adriana and Alicia, and walked off.

Tony followed Alicia up the steps of the house, glancing as always to left and right. He'd caught a glimpse of his man on the corner, recalled the report that had been on his desk when he'd returned home that evening.

In the front hall, he waited with Alicia while Adriana went upstairs, and Maggs retreated to the nether regions; he was perfectly sure their charade wasn't fooling Maggs, but he suspected it was important to Alicia, at least at that point, to preserve her facade as a virtuous widow.

Once Maggs's footsteps had faded and Adriana had disappeared down the corridor to her room, he turned back to the front door and slid both bolts home. Alicia had picked up the candle from the hall table; on the lowest tread of the stair, she glanced back at him. He joined her; together they climbed the stairs to her room.

Her bedchamber was the largest, closest to the stairs. Adriana's room lay along the corridor, two dressing rooms and a linen press separating the rooms. He had no idea whether Adriana knew he spent the nights in her elder sister's bed; given the distance between their rooms, there was no reason she would have guessed.

The boys' rooms were on the next floor, the servants' rooms in the attics above. Following Alicia into her bedchamber and shutting the door, he reflected that thus far, her reputation remained safe.

If there was any reason to imagine it threatened, he would make his intentions public, but as things stood, with the ton believing her a widow and thus according her the associated license, there was no compelling urgency to declare his hand.

Indeed, he prayed the necessity wouldn't arise, that once A. C. was unmasked and they were free of his threat, he would have time to woo her, to ask for her hand with all due ceremony. That was, to his mind, the least she deserved, regardless of their established intimacy.

He hadn't intended that, but having once spent the night in her bed, the notion of not continuing to do so

hadn't even entered his head. The fact he'd simply assumed her agreement occurred to him. He glanced at her.
She'd crossed the room to set the candlestick on the
dressing table; seated on the stool, she was calmly letting
down her long hair.

The simple, domestic sight never failed to soothe
him—to soothe that part of him that was not, even at the
best of times, all that civilized.

She had not at any time drawn back, either from him or
from their relationship; her quiet, calm acceptance was
both balm to his possessive soul and a wordless reassurance that they understood each other perfectly.

Indeed, words had never featured much between them.
Aside from all else, he'd always believed actions spoke
louder.

Sitting on the bed, he removed his shoes, then
shrugged out of his coat. He stripped off his waistcoat,
untied his cravat, all the while watching her brush the
long, mahogany tresses that spilled down her back, a
silken river reaching nearly to her waist.

When she laid down the brush and stood, he crossed to
her. Bending his head, murmuring an endearment, he set
his fingers to her laces, and his lips to the sensitive spot
where her white shoulder and throat met. When her gown
was loose, he forced himself to move away, allowing her
to remove the gown, shake it out, and hang it up.

Unbuttoning his shirt, he inwardly frowned, returning
to a thought that frequently nagged; it would be nice to
give her more servants, a maid at least to take care of her
clothes and see to her jewels . . . frowning, he pulled his
shirt from his waistband. As far as he'd seen, she didn't
have any jewelry.

"Oh." At her armoire, she turned, through the shadows
looked at him. "I meant to tell you—something rather
strange happened today."

Clad in her chemise, she headed for the bed. He started
unbuttoning his cuffs. "What?"

Picking up a silk robe, she slipped it over her shoulders. "A solicitor's clerk called this morning." Sinking onto the bed, she met his eyes. "Adriana and I were in the park. The man—"

"A weasely-looking fellow in black?" The description had been in Collier's report; he'd read it before setting out for Richmond.

She blinked, then nodded. "Yes—that sounds like him. He insisted on waiting to see me even though Jenkins told him I'd be a while. Maggs and Jenkins discussed it, then left him in the parlor, but when I arrived home with Adriana and Geoffrey, the man wasn't there." She shrugged. "He must have got tried of waiting and left by the front door, but it seems strange that he left no message."

He'd slowed, stopped undressing, giving her his undivided attention. He considered, then said, "The parlor?"

She nodded.

Biting back a curse, he swung on his heel and headed for the door.

"Tony?"

He heard her whisper, but didn't answer. Glancing back as he went down the stairs, he saw her following, belting the silk robe as she came, her bare feet almost as silent as his.

Reaching the parlor, he opened the door. The fire was still glowing; picking up a three-armed candelabrum, he lit each candle from the embers, then, rising, set the candelabrum on the table beside the chaise.

Alicia silently closed the door. Her eyes felt huge. "What is it?"

Slowly swiveling, he studied the room, the window seat beneath the bow window, the bookselves flanking the fireplace and one corner of the room, the escritoire against one wall, and a high table with two drawers. "How long was he here—do you have any idea?"

Drawing the robe close, she considered. "It could have been half an hour. Probably not more."

He waved to the armchair by the fire. "Sit down. This might take a while."

Sinking into the chair, she drew her legs up, covering her cold toes with the hem of her robe, and watched him search the room. He was thorough—very thorough. He looked in places she'd never have thought of—like the undersides of the drawers of the table against the wall. He found nothing there, and moved on to the escritoire.

"Does this have a secret drawer?"

"No."

He checked every possible nook and cranny, then shifted to the bookshelves. She quelled a shiver. Barefoot on the cold boards, he hunkered down; his shirt flapped loose about his chest, but he didn't seem to feel the chill. He ran his hand along the spines, then started pulling out individual books, reaching into the gaps to check behind.

Tony had no idea what he was looking for, but instinct told him there would be something to find. He pulled out a slim volume; the title caught his eye. *"A Young Lady's Guide to Etiquette in the Ton."* Briefly, he raised his brows. Setting it aside, he pulled out a few more. They, too, dealt with similar subjects; clearly Alicia and Adriana had done considerable research before embarking on their scheme.

Making sure he missed no section of the shelves, he worked his way along.

He found what he was searching for behind a set of books on the lowest shelf, close by the room's corner. A sheaf of papers had been jammed behind the books; drawing them out, he turned to Alicia. One look at her face, her eyes, assured him they weren't hers.

"What are they?"

Rising, he moved closer to the candelabrum, and flicked through the sheaf. "Old letters." He straightened them out, laying each on the table. "Five of them." Sinking down on the chaise, he picked one up.

In a rustle of silk, Alicia left the armchair and came to

join him. Sitting close beside him, she reached for one of the letters—he forestalled her, passing her the one he'd already scanned; she took it and he lifted the next.

When he laid down the fifth missive, she was still picking her way through the second. The letters were in French.

For a long moment, he sat, elbows on his thighs, and stared across the room, then he leaned back, reached for her, and drew her, letters and all, into his arms.

She shivered, and looked up at him. "I've only read one. Are they all similar?"

He nodded. "All to A. C. from French captains acknowledging ships taken on information supplied." Three of the letters were from French naval captains; he could personally verify two of the names. He could also identify from his own knowledge the other two correspondents, both captains of French privateers.

The letters were extremely incriminating. For A. C.

Alicia had never been A. C., and indeed, the letters all dated from before her fictitous marriage had supposedly taken place. The name wasn't what was worrying him.

She frowned at the letter she held, then shuffled the sheaf. "These are all addressed to A. C. at the Sign of the Barking Dog."

Her tone alerted him; he glanced at her. "Do you know it?"

She nodded. "It's not far from Chipping Norton."

He sat forward. "An inn?" Getting to his feet, he drew her with him.

She shook her head. "No, a hedge tavern. Barely even that. It caters to a very rough crowd—most of the locals avoid it."

He hid a grimace. The Barking Dog sounded like the perfect address for a villain. He doubted he would get any help from the innkeeper as to who had picked up the letters, but he'd send someone to inquire tomorrow.

Meanwhile . . . "Let's go upstairs. You're freezing."

He drew her out of the room; she went unresisting, frowning, refolding the letters. Closing the parlor door, he saw her tiptoeing awkwardly to the stairs. Shutting his lips on a query regarding the whereabouts of her slippers, he strode after her, bent, and hefted her into his arms.

She looked into his face, then settled back and let him carry her upstairs. She'd left the door to her bedchamber open; he entered and nudged it closed. The lock clicked shut. She shifted, expecting to be put down.

He strode to the bed and dropped her on it. Filched the letters from her grasp when she bounced. "I'll need those."

She struggled up, watched as he crossed to his coat and slipped the sheaf into a pocket. "That clerk put them there, didn't he? Why?"

"To confuse things."

She swung her legs off the bed, stood, shrugged out of her robe and laid it aside. "How?" Turning back to the bed, she frowned at him. "What do you think will happen?"

"I think"—he stripped off his shirt and dropped it on his coat—"that you can expect a visit from someone in authority within the next few days. They'll be looking for the letters, but"—he smiled evilly—"they won't find them."

Still clad in her chemise, she slipped under the covers. He looked down as he stripped off his trousers, hiding his smile, pretending not to notice as, once safely covered, she wriggled out of the fine chemise and tossed it to the floor. Once he joined her in the bed, it wouldn't stay on her; better she remove it than risk him tearing it, or so he had given her to understand.

She was still frowning. "What should we do?"

Naked, he crossed to the dressing table and doused the candle. "We'll talk about it in the morning. There's nothing to be done tonight."

He returned to the bed and slid under the covers beside her.

She was shivering, still frowning, but accepting his edict, turned into his arms as she always did, as ardent and as needy as he. Her openness was a blessing for which he would remain forever grateful; the instant their limbs met, and their lips found each other's, there was only one thought between them, only one goal, one aim, one desire.

Her chill, her concern over the letters—and his—faded as that simple reality took control, claimed them, heart, minds, and souls fused them. Slumped, exhausted, and thoroughly heated, in each other's arms, they surrendered, and slept. And left tomorrow's problems for tomorrow.

Again, Alicia slept in. Lecturing herself that she couldn't let the practice become habit, she climbed into a new morning gown of forest green, quickly coiled her hair, then hurried downstairs, expecting mayhem.

She came to a teetering halt on the threshold of the dining room. Alerted by the deep rumble of Tony's voice, she looked in—stared.

He was seated at the foot of the table, keeping order, clearly in charge. Her brothers, of course, were on their best behavior; expressions angelic, they hung on his every word. Adriana . . . one glance at her sister as she slowly entered was enough to inform her that Adriana was intrigued.

The boys noticed her, and smiled.

Picking up her pace, as nonchalantly as she could she went to her accustomed place at the head of the table. "Good morning." Sitting, she met Tony's gaze. Inclined her head briefly. "My lord. To what do we owe this pleasure?"

A smile flashed behind his eyes; she prayed Adriana didn't catch it, or if she had, wouldn't be able to interpret it.

"I came to enjoy your company"—he smiled briefly at the boys; he was clearly their hero—"and also to discuss the most recent developments and remind you all to take care." His gaze returned to her face. "It seems matters are progressing, just not as I'd thought, or hoped. You"—his gaze swept the table—"all of you, need to stay alert."

"Why?" Eyes wide, David waited.

Alicia felt Adriana's glance, then her sister leaned forward and looked down the table at Tony. "That odd man who called yesterday but didn't wait—is it something to do with him?"

Looking straight down the table, Alicia met Tony's eyes and read the question therein. Briefly, she nodded.

"Yes." Assembling their collective interest with a glance, he went on to explain about the letters.

She listened, on one level monitoring his words and her brothers' reactions, on another, thinking rather more personally.

At least he'd changed out of his evening clothes; he was wearing a morning coat of rich, dark brown over ivory inexpressibles reaching into gleaming black Hessians. His waistcoat was striped in ivory and browns, his cravat starched white, severely simple. On the little finger of his right hand the gold-and-onyx signet ring he always wore gleamed; his gold watch chain and the gold pin in his cravat completed the picture, one of simple yet formidable elegance.

He'd left her bed at dawn, as usual; he must have gone home, then returned. She hoped he'd rung the doorbell, and hadn't simply waltzed in . . . then again, would anyone have deemed it odd if he had?

Was this a taste of things to come—a guide to how their relationship would develop? That gradually he would become more than just a frequent visitor, over time gaining the status of accepted member of the household, moreover a member whose edicts carried weight.

As they clearly already did with her brothers. Yet he

was impressing on them the need to take care, more, to avoid taking any risks; she wasn't about to complain. They paid his warnings far greater heed than they would any from her.

Deep down, she was conscious of a small, very small, degree of irritation that he'd been able so easily to assume a role that for a decade had been hers, that her family—even Adriana—accepted his usurpation without question . . . yet as, with a glance, he extended his edicts to Adriana, too, who just as avidly as the boys had been drawn in by his glib, truthful but not unnecessarily revealing, or worrying, account of the planted letters and what he thought they would mean, she couldn't find it in her actively to oppose him.

Nevertheless, some part of her, the most private side of her, felt almost exposed. Most definitely uncertain, both of the rightness of the present and what next might come. Until this morning, what had grown between them had remained between them alone, yet now . . . perhaps this was how things were done in his world?

She honestly didn't know; she'd traveled far beyond the limits of the books in the parlor. Not one gave any description of the normal pattern of behavior, the day-to-day arrangements that might exist between a member of the nobility and his mistress.

Presumably he knew how things should be; she would have to, as she'd had to so often thus far, follow his lead.

"I don't know exactly what will happen, or when." Tony met the boys' eyes, then glanced briefly at Adriana. "It's possible nothing at all might occur—we might catch whoever it is before he takes the next step."

He didn't believe that for a moment; Alicia's slight frown suggested she didn't either.

Returning his attention to the boys, he reiterated, "But you can't be too careful—I want you all to be on guard, and not panic if there is some development. I, and others, won't be far away."

The boys, eyes wide, nodded solemnly.

Jenkins came in at that moment; Alicia forced a smile and spoke with him regarding the boys' lessons, then looked at her brothers. "Up you go."

Tony reinforced her command with a look. The boys finished their milk; he inclined his head as they bobbed bows before taking themselves off.

Letting his gaze drift past Adriana, he looked at Alicia. "If I could speak with you for a moment?"

She blinked, glanced at Adriana, and rose. "Yes, of course. If you'll come into the drawing room?"

Rising, he took his leave of Adriana, who seemed totally at ease over his unorthodox presence, then followed her across the front hall. She paused by the drawing room door; he waved her in and followed, closing the door behind them.

She stopped and faced him; halting before her, he met her gaze. "Regardless of what I just said, I fully expect something to happen." He grimaced, let her see his unease. "I just don't know what, or exactly when."

She studied his face, then said, "Thank you for speaking with them. We'll be on guard now."

"My men outside gave me a decent description of this clerk, but there must be thousands like him in London—I don't expect to be able to trace him, let alone his employer." He paused, wondered if she'd see his next maneuver for the revelation it was—decided he didn't care. "With your leave, I'll send another footman—he'll arrive within the hour. Maggs tells me there's room in the attics—I want him—Maggs—free to follow any other strange visitors who come to call."

She blinked. A frown grew in her eyes. "We have Jenkins. I'm sure he can cope—"

"Your brothers." Ruthlessly he fell back on the one argument he knew would overcome her resistance. "I'd rather Jenkins concentrated on keeping watch over them, and I don't want you and Adriana left without some degree of male support."

She held his gaze, evaluating, realizing he'd left her no option. Her lips tightened, but only fractionally. "Very well. If you truly think it necessary."

"I do." Absolutely, definitely necessary; if he thought he could get her to agree, he'd have half a dozen men about her. "I'll be staying in London—Gervase should be back from Devon, and with luck Jack Hendon might have something to report."

"If you learn anything, you will send word, won't you?"

He smiled, a flash of teeth and resolution. "I'll bring any news myself." He studied her eyes. "If anything happens, Scully, the new footman, or Maggs, will get word to those watching—they'll find me. I'll come as soon as I can."

For an instant, her expression remained serious, sober, the reality of the threat, the potential but unknown difficulty she and her family might have to face—that he and she both felt sure they would face—dulling the gold and green, then a smile softened her eyes. "Thank you." Putting a reassuring hand on his arm, she held his gaze. "We'll manage."

Her "we" included him; that was clear in her eyes, in her inclusive smile.

His expression eased. He hesitated, then bent his head. Cradling her face in one palm, he kissed her, briefly yet . . . the link between them was now so strong, even that brief caress communicated volumes.

Raising his head, he stepped back. Saluted her. *"Au revoir."*

Tony returned to Upper Brook Street to discover messages from Jack Hendon and Gervase Tregarth awaiting him. Both expected to have firm information by noon;

Gervase suggested they meet at the Bastion Club. Tony sat at his desk and dashed off a note to Jack, giving him directions and a brief explanation—enough to whet his appetite.

After that he sat and mentally reviewed all he knew thus far. Action was clearly imminent; why plant incriminating evidence if not to expose it? How, by whom, and precisely when he didn't know, but he could and did clear everything on his desk, all matters that might need his attention over the next few days.

Summoning Hungerford, he gave orders that would ensure, not only that his houses and estate would continue on an even keel were he to be otherwise engaged for a week or so, but also that the various members of his extended staff, some of whom did not fit any common description, were apprised of his intentions, and thus would hold themselves ready to act on whatever orders he flung their way.

At a quarter to twelve, he headed for the Bastion Club.

Climbing the stairs to the first floor, he heard Jack, already in the meeting room, questioning, clearly intrigued by the club and its genesis. He pricked up his ears as other voices answered—Christian, Charles, and Tristan were there, regaling Jack with the benefits of the club, especially as applied to unmarried gentlemen of their ilk.

"I'm already leg-shackled," Jack confessed, as Tony appeared in the doorway.

"To a spitfire, what's more." Tony entered, smiling.

Jack raised his wineglass. "I'll tell her you said that."

"Do." Unperturbed, Tony took a seat opposite and grinned at Jack. "She'll forgive me."

Jack mock-scowled. "I'm not so silly as to encourage her."

Quick footsteps on the stairs heralded Gervase. He strode in quickly, brown curls windblown, the light of the hunt in his eyes. Every man about the table recognized the signs.

Christian, Charles, and Tristan exchanged glances. Christian made as if to rise. "We'll leave you . . ."

Tony waved him back. "If you have the time, I'd value any insight you might have on these matters. For our sins, we're all sufficiently connected with Dalziel, and Jack worked for Whitley."

Gervase drew out a chair and sat. "Right, then." He looked at Tony. "Who do you want to hear from first?"

"Jack's been checking the specific ships." Tony looked across the table. "Let's start there."

Jack nodded. "I concentrated on the sixteen vessels listed in Ruskin's notes that we know were taken. Thus far, I've only been able to get a general picture of their cargoes—asking too many specific questions would attract too much interest."

"Were they carrying anything in common?" Christian asked.

"Yes, and no. I've got word on six of the sixteen, and each was carrying general cargo—furniture, foodstuffs, raw products. No evidence of any peculiar item common to all ships."

"Six," Tony mused. "If there's nothing in common between six, then chances are that's not the distinguishing factor."

Jack hesitated, then went on, "All the ships are still registered—there's no hint of any insurance fraud. On top of that, all the ships I've got information on were owned by various lines, their cargoes by a variety of merchants. There's no common link."

Tony frowned. "But if you think of what's lost when a ship is taken as a prize, rather than sunk . . ." He met Jack's eyes. "The lines buy back their ships—it's the cargo that's lost irretrievably."

"To this side of the Channel." Charles looked at Jack. "But aren't cargoes insured?"

His gaze locked with Tony's, Jack shook his head. "Not in such circumstances. Cargoes are insured against loss through the vessel being lost, but they aren't covered if the goods are seized during wartime."

"So it's considered a loss through an act of war?" Tristan asked.

Jack nodded. "The cargoes would be lost, but there'd be no claim to worry the denizens of Lloyd's Coffee House, no fuss perturbing any of the major guilds like the shipowners."

"And if the merchants were unconnected individuals, and the losses varied and apparently random . . ." Tony paused, frowning. "Who would that benefit?"

None of them could offer an answer.

"We need more information." Tony looked at Gervase.

Who smiled grimly. "It took a bit of persuasion, but I heard three separate tales from three unconnected individuals of 'special commissions' being offered in the Channel Isles. The contacts were all English, and all were miffed that these 'commissions' were being offered solely to, not specifically French, but only to non-English captains."

Gervase exchanged a glance with Tony. "You know what the sailors in and about the Isles are like—they consider themselves a law unto themselves, and largely that's true. It never was clear where they stood in recent times."

Tony humphed. "My reading is that they're for themselves, regardless."

"Indeed," Charles put in. "But I assume the links between our shores and the Isles, and the Isles and Brittany and Normandy continued to operate throughout the war?"

"Oh, yes." Both Tony and Gervase nodded; Jack, too.

"Located as they are . . ." Jack shrugged. "It would be wonderful were they not the haunt of 'independent captains.' "

Tony turned to Gervase. "Did you get any confirmation on those particular ships?"

Gervase shook his head. "None of my contacts had information on specific ships—they'd never been in the running for those 'special commissions' and it seems whoever was making the offer played his cards very close to his chest."

Tony grimaced. "I could go over and scout about, but . . ."

Jack shook his head. "Aside from all else, there'd be more than a few who might remember one Antoine Balzac, and that not fondly."

Tony raised his brows fleetingly. "There is that." He reached into his pocket. "Which brings us to my discovery, which makes me even less inclined to go fossicking on foreign shores."

He tossed the bundle of letters on the table; the others' eyes locked on them. "Yesterday, a greasy-looking clerk in dusty black called at Mrs. Alicia Carrington's house in Waverton Street while she and her sister were in the park, as might have been predicted, the hour being what it was. Said clerk insisted on waiting, and was shown into the parlor, but when Mrs. Carrington returned home, no sign of this clerk could be found.

"Later, when I searched the parlor, I found these, wedged behind books in a corner bookshelf."

The others all glanced at him, then reached for the letters. Their faces grew more and more impassive as they read each, passing them around the table. Finally, when all five letters had been tossed back on the table, Christian leaned forward and looked at Tony. "Tell me why Mrs. Alicia Carrington cannot be A. C."

Tony didn't bridle; Christian was playing devil's advocate. "She's been married just less than two years—before that, she was Alicia Pevensey, and that's been checked." He gestured at the letters. "All five of these were written while she would still have been A. P."

Christian nodded. "Her husband—what was his name?"

"Alfred." Tony didn't like pretending Alfred Carrington had ever existed, but life would be easier if he stuck to Alicia's fabrication. "But he died nearly two years ago, so he wasn't the A. C. who was continuing to seek and buy information from Ruskin. Further, the Carrington family have no connections through which they might have used such information, nor wealth enough to have played A. C.'s game. The payments, the system, are consistent throughout—we're looking for one man, A. C., who's very much alive."

"And up to no good, what's more." Charles flicked one of the letters. "I don't like this."

Tony let a moment elapse, then softly said, "No more do I."

After a moment, he went on, "However, the letters confirm that the track we're pursuing is correct. They show A. C. did engage French naval captains and French privateers to capture ships, presumably using information Ruskin supplied." He added his knowledge of the Frenchmen involved.

"Stop a minute." Tristan said. "What have we got so far? How could a scheme based on what we've surmised work?"

They tossed around scenarios, pooling their experience to approve some suggestions as possible, discounting others.

"All right," Tony eventually said. "This seems the most likely then: Ruskin supplied information on convoys, especially when and where certain ships would leave a convoy to turn aside to their home ports."

Charles nodded. "That, and also when frigates were called off convoy duty to serve with the fleets—in other words when merchantmen would be sailing essentially unprotected."

"The merchantmen would have made a good show"—Jack looked increasingly grim—"but against an enemy frigate, they'd stand little chance."

"So, armed with said knowledge, A.C. arranges for a foreign captain to pick off a specific merchantman. Once the deed was done, and Ruskin's information proved good, A.C. paid him, and both he and A.C. went home happy." Tony grimaced. "We need to work out why A.C. was so keen on removing specific merchantmen, thus preventing their cargoes from reaching London."

He looked at Jack, who nodded. "We need the specifics of the cargoes, not just the general description. The only way to access those details after all this time is via Lloyd's—they always keep records."

"Can you learn what we need without alerting anyone?" Tony held Jack's gaze. "We have no idea who A.C. might be, nor yet what contacts he might have."

Jack shrugged. "I wasn't planning on asking anyone— I know where the records are kept. No reason I can't drop by late one night and take a look."

Charles grinned. "A man after our collective heart— are you sure you don't want to join the club?"

Jack answered with a brief grin. "I have my hands full just at present."

"How long will it take you to gather what we need?" Tony asked.

Jack considered. "Two days. I'll need to scout things out before I go in. Wouldn't do to get caught."

"No, indeed." Christian looked at Tony. "This business of those letters planted in Mrs. Carrington's parlor more than worries me. Whoever A.C. is, he's blackguard enough to happily deflect blame onto an innocent lady, without regard for the damage to her—"

Heavy thuds fell on the front door, reverberating up to the meeting room.

They all froze, waited . . .

The door downstairs opened; voices were heard, then footsteps, not precisely running but hurrying, came up the stairs.

Gasthorpe, the club's majordomo, appeared in the doorway. "Your pardon, my lords." He looked at Tony. "My lord, a footman has arrived with an urgent summons."

Tony was already rising. "Waverton Street?"

"Indeed, my lord. The authorities have descended."

FIFTEEN

THEY'D ANTICIPATED SOMETHING OF THE SORT, BUT Tony was nonetheless surprised and made uneasy by how swiftly the expected had arrived.

Jack demanded the number of Alicia's house, then parted from him on the pavement outside the club, saying he'd meet him there. Together with Christian and Charles, Tony piled into a hackney; Tristan intended to join them, but just at that moment Leonora, his wife, emerged from the garden next door—her uncle's house where she'd been visiting. She saw them, and instantly wanted to know what was going on.

Tristan stopped to talk to her; behind his back, he waved to them to go on without him. They did.

In Waverton Street, Tony jumped down from the hackney. Collier, masquerading as a street sweeper, was lounging on the railings close by the Carrington residence.

The heavily built man tipped his cap as Tony paused beside him. "Five redbreasts, m'lord. Never seen the like in all my born days—they pushed in like it was a thieves' den. Pompous little sort leading from the rear."

Tony murmured his thanks. "Keep watching."

"Aye." Collier eased upright. "I will that."

Christian had paid off the hackney; he and Charles followed as, jaw set, Tony strode up the steps. He didn't knock, but flung the front door wide and stalked in.

A young Runner standing before the drawing room

door started, instinctively snapping to attention, then pausing, confusion in his face.

From the direction of the parlor, a stocky sergeant barreled forward, belligerence in every line. "Here, then! Who'd you think you are? You can't just barge in 'ere."

Tony reached into his coat pocket, and withdrew a card. "Viscount Torrington." Face impassive, he handed the card to the sergeant, gestured to Christian and Charles. "The Marquess of Dearne and the Earl of Lostwithiel. Where are Mrs. Carrington and her family?"

The sergeant fingered the expensive card, tracing the embossed printing. "Ah . . ." His belligerence fled. He glanced at his junior barring the drawing-room door. "The inspector placed the lady and her household under guard, m'lord. Took 'em all into custody, like."

"Your inspector seems to have overlooked the point that Mrs. Carrington is already in *my* custody, a fact of which the local office of the Watch is well aware." Tony let his fury ripple beneath his words, subtly scathing.

Yielding to instinct, the sergeant came to attention, eyes fixed forward. "We're not local, m'lord. We came directly from headquarters—Bow Street."

"That's no excuse. Who's in charge here? What's your inspector's name?"

"Sprigs, m'lord."

"Fetch him." Tony caught the hapless sergeant's eye. "I'm going to check on Mrs. Carrington, to make sure neither she nor any member of her household has suffered any ill effects from your inspector's reckless action. Your inspector better pray they haven't. When I return here, I expect to find him waiting, along with every member of your force currently within this house. Is that clear?"

The sergeant swallowed. Nodded. "Yessir."

Tony turned on his heel and made for the drawing-room door. The young Runner gave way, hurriedly stepping back. Tony opened the door; pausing, he scanned the room, then released the knob and walked in.

Relief flooded Alicia; she jumped up from the chaise and went quickly to meet Tony. Two other gentlemen followed him in; from their appearance and actions, they were friends. The one with black curling hair moved to intercept their guard, struggling out of the armchair he'd commandeered with a weak "Hey!"

Tony turned his head and looked at the man.

Suddenly the object of two unnerving gazes, he stopped, apparently paralyzed by caution.

She reached Tony; his gaze returned to her, searched her face. He took her hands, squeezed lightly. "Are you all right?"

His gaze had gone past her to the boys, Adriana, and all their staff gathered about the chaise.

"Yes." She glanced back to see them all on their feet. "Just a trifle shocked." In truth, she was furious, still seething; the inspector's insinuations had made her blood boil. Looking back at Tony, she lowered her voice. "Is this about the letters?"

He squeezed her fingers again; instead of answering— an answer in itself—he kept his attention on the others. "This is all a mistake—we're here to sort it out. I want all of you to stay here quietly. There's nothing to fear."

Adriana nodded; forcing her lips to curve, she sat down again. The boys glanced at her, uncertain, then looked again at Tony.

He nodded. "Stay here with Adriana. Alicia and I will be back in a few minutes." She was close enough to sense the tension that held him, yet he smiled with beguiling charm at her brothers. "I promise I'll explain all later."

The smile and that promise reassured them; with fleeting if brittle smiles, they went to cluster around Adriana.

Alicia noted the look Tony exchanged with Maggs, and more briefly with the new footman, Scully, both of whom had refused to be shifted from her and her family's sides, then he took her arm and turned her to the door.

The other two gentlemen flanked them. Beside her, the larger smiled, as charming in his way as Tony, and half bowed. "Dearne. A pleasure to meet you, Mrs. Carrington, even in such trying circumstances. Rest assured we'll have this settled in short order."

She bobbed a brief curtsy.

"Indeed," the second gentleman said. He saluted her. "Lostwithiel, for my sins." His grin was unrepentant. "We can deal with the introductions later."

Tony shot him a glance as he opened the door.

They emerged into the front hall just as the inspector, a short, red-haired man of uncertain temper with an aggressive attitude and an abrasive tongue, came charging up from the direction of the parlor. "What the *devil's* going on here?" The demand fell just short of a raging bellow.

Fixing on their company, his eyes momentarily widened, then he recovered. "Scrugs! Dammit, man—don't you know better than to allow visitors in?"

He rounded on the sergeant, who held his ground. Scrugs nodded at Tony. "This here's his lordship, what I told you about, sir. And the marquess and the earl." There was enough emphasis in Scrugs's tone to convey the fact that if his superior didn't know when to back off, Scrugs certainly did.

"Inspector . . . Sprigs, is it?" The words were mild, Tony's tone was not. It cut.

Sprigs swung to face him, glaring belligerently. "Aye. And I'll have you know—"

"I assume you checked with the local Watch supervisor before barging onto his patch? Elcott, that would be."

Sprigs blinked; faint wariness crept into his piggy eyes. "Aye, but—"

"I'm surprised Elcott didn't inform you that Mrs. Carrington is already in my custody."

Sprigs cleared his throat. "He did mention it—"

"Indeed?" Tony raised his brows. "And did he also happen to mention that my orders in this matter come from Whitehall?"

Sprigs drew himself up. "Be that as it may, my lord, the information we've received—'deed, the people we received it from—well, we couldn't hardly ignore such, Whitehall or no."

"What information?"

Sprigs pressed his lips together, glanced at Alicia, then ventured, "That Mrs. Carrington here had hired some villains to do away with this man Ruskin, on account of she was in league with the French. Word had it that if we searched this house thoroughly, we'd find evidence enough to prove it."

"From whom did this information come?"

Again Sprigs hesitated; again the stretching silence forced him to answer. "Brought to us indirect, it was." He saw Tony's welling contempt and rushed on, "From the gentlemen's clubs. Seems a number of the high-and-mighty heard the story—wanted to know what we were doing about it. Questions were asked. They even had the commissioner himself in to explain."

Sprigs glanced at Charles and Christian, then looked at Tony. "It's treason we're talking about here. Don't suppose toffs like you care all that much, but if you'd served in the recent wars—"

"I wouldn't suppose quite so readily, Inspector."

The voice, languid, even soft, chilled. Everyone looked toward the front door. They'd left it partially open. A gentleman stood just inside; he walked forward as they stared.

His dark eyes remained fixed on Sprigs. Alicia had grown used to Tony's elegance—this man was equally impressive, moving with innate grace, slim, dark-haired, dressed in dark clothes that exuded that same austere style, a reflection of bone-deep confidence, of their assurance in who they were.

There was one difference. While Tony's tones could cut, whiplike, this man's voice projected a patently lethal threat, quietly efficient, like a scimitar slicing, unhindered, into flesh.

Suppressing a shiver, she glanced at Tony, then at his friends, and realized the newcomer was both known to them and accepted by them. An ally, definitely, yet she sensed he was someone around whom even they trod carefully.

Sprigs swallowed. He glanced at Tony. Behind him, the sergeant and his other two men were rigidly at attention.

"Dalziel." The newcomer answered Sprigs's unvoiced question. "From Whitehall." He halted at Tony's side and looked the unfortunate Sprigs in the eye. "I've already spoken with your superiors. You are to report back to Bow Street immediately, taking all your men, leaving this house in precisely the same state as it was when you, so unwisely, entered. You will not remove so much as a pin."

He paused, then continued, "Your superiors have been somewhat forcefully reminded that, together with Lord Whitley, I am handling this matter, and that contrary to their suppositions, Bow Street's mandate does not extend to countermanding or interfering with Whitehall's actions."

Sprigs, now all but at attention himself, nodded. "Yes, sir." He sounded strangled.

Dalziel let a moment pass, then murmured, "You may go."

They went with alacrity. At a nod from Sprigs, the junior stuck his head into the drawing room and summoned his companion; in short order, the five men from Bow Street were clattering down the steps, routed by a superior force.

All four gentlemen—Tony, Dalziel, Dearne, and Lostwithiel—stood in and about the front door and saw them off, watched them go. Trapped behind, screened from the sight by their broad shoulders, Alicia waited, somewhat impatiently. She knew the instant they all let down their guards.

Tony and Dearne visibly relaxed.

"Importunate devils," Lostwithiel quipped.

"Indeed," Dalziel replied.

They all started to turn inside—

Then paused.

Along with the others, Tony watched two carriages come clattering up, one from each end of the street. Both carriages pulled up before the house. The carriage doors swung open. Tristan sprang down from one carriage; from the other, Jack Hendon stepped down to the pavement. Both turned back to their respective carriages; each handed a lady down.

Kit, Jack's wife, and Leonora, Tristan's wife.

Barely pausing to shake out their skirts, both ladies swept toward the house—and saw each other. At the bottom of the steps, they met, exchanged names, shook hands, then, as one, turned and, beautiful faces decidedly set, swept up the steps.

On the pavement, Jack and Tristan exchanged long-suffering glances, and followed in their wakes.

All four men at the door gave way.

With barely a glance at them the ladies swept in. They saw Alicia, and pounced.

"Kit Hendon, my dear." Taking Alicia's hand, Kit waved toward Jack. "Jack's wife. How terribly distressing for you."

"Leonora Wemyss—I'm Trentham's wife." Leonora waved vaguely at her husband, too, and pressed Alicia's hand. "Are your family quite all right?"

Alicia found a smile. "Yes—I believe so." She gestured to the drawing room.

"It's quite insupportable," Kit declared. "We've come to help."

"Indeed." Leonora turned to the drawing room. "This is going to need action to set right."

Together, the three entered the drawing room. The door shut behind them.

All six men in the front hall stared at the door, then glanced, briefly, at each other.

Dalziel sighed, pityingly or so they all took it, and turned to Tony. "I take it you have whatever Bow Street's minions were sent to find?"

"Yes." Succinctly, Tony described the letters, and how they fitted the scenario they now thought most likely, confirming that A.C. had used Ruskin's information to arrange for merchantmen to be captured by the enemy.

At the end of his explanation, Dalziel, still and silent, stared out, unseeing, through the open door. Then, quietly, he said, "I want him."

He glanced at Tony, then at the others. "I don't care what you have to do—I want to know who A.C. is. As soon as possible. You have my full authority, and as for Whitley, suffice to say he's ropeable. If you have need of his name, you have permission to use that, too."

Briefly, he glanced at them again, then nodded. "I'll leave you to it."

He walked to the door. On the threshold he paused, and looked back. At Tony. "Incidentally, the information against Mrs. Carrington—there's no way to trace it. I've tried. Whoever this man is, he's extremely well connected—he knew exactly in whose ears to plant his seeds. When asked, every concerned soul said they heard it from someone else. I'll continue to keep my ears open, but don't expect any breakthrough on that front."

Tony inclined his head.

Dalziel left, going lightly down the steps, then striding away along the street.

The five men in the front hall remained where they were until his footsteps had faded, then all dragged in a breath and glanced at each other.

"I'm suddenly very grateful I only had to deal with Whitley," Jack said.

"Indeed, you should be." Tony stepped forward and shut the door.

Charles met Tony's gaze as he rejoined them, then glanced at Christian and Tristan. "How did he know?"

Christian raised his brows, openly resigned. "I suspect he knows one of our staff at the club rather well, don't you?"

"Our club?" Charles looked pained. After a moment, he shook his head. "I don't even want to think about that."

Tristan clapped him on the shoulder.

They turned to the drawing room. The door opened; Maggs, Scully, Jenkins, Cook, and Fitchett all slipped out, bobbing before disappearing through the green baize door.

With a glance, Tony halted Maggs. "Check the parlor—I doubt the good inspector's men had time to put their mess right."

Maggs nodded and headed down the corridor.

Tristan opened the drawing-room door and led the gentlemen in.

Kit and Leonora were seated in armchairs facing Alicia and Adriana on the chaise. All four heads were together; they glanced up as the men entered, but the comments that clearly hovered on their tongues had to wait—the three boys had been crowding around the front window; seeing Tony, they flung themselves at him.

"Are they gone?"

"What did they want?"

"Who was that man? The one who just left."

Tony looked down into three pairs of hazel eyes, all very like Alicia's. When he didn't immediately reply, Matthew tugged at his sleeve.

"You promised to tell us."

He smiled and hunkered down to be more on their level. "Yes, they've gone, and they won't be coming back. They'd been given false information, and thought there were documents hidden here—those letters I found. That's what they were searching for. And that man who just left was from the government—he came to tell them they'd made a big mistake, and that they weren't to bother you or your sisters anymore."

Three pairs of eyes searched his, then all three boys smiled.

"Good!" Harry said. "It might be exciting, but they weren't nice."

"And they worry Alicia and Adriana," David whispered.

Both his younger brothers nodded solemnly.

Smiling, Tony rose, ruffling Matthew's hair. "You'll do." He exchanged a fleeting glance with Alicia; with her eyes, she indicated upstairs. He looked back at the boys. "Now you'd better go and see if they searched your rooms." He lowered his voice. "You could help Jenkins and Maggs make sure there's nothing around to upset your sisters."

The boys exchanged glances. Solemnly nodded again.

They looked at Alicia. "We're going upstairs," David said.

She smiled encouragingly. "You can come down for tea."

Everyone waited while the three boys filed out and closed the door behind them.

"Thank heavens," Kit said. She looked at the men, still standing in a loose gathering in the center of the room. "Now! We need to move quickly on this. The damage has to be contained—better yet, turned around."

Jack and Tristan strolled forward.

Tristan shrugged. "I don't know that it's all that serious." He glanced at the other men. "I can't see that A. C. is likely to gain much from this—"

"*Not* your investigation!" Leonora glared at him. "That isn't what we're concerned about."

Tristan blinked at her. "What, then?"

"Why the potential social disaster, of course!"

They were right—that was the most urgent threat arising from Sprigs's visit; this time, Bow Street had come calling in daylight, and there'd been considerable activity visible from the street. Luckily, their counterstrategy was easy to devise and quickly set in train. Aside from Alicia and Adriana, there were seven of them in the room; each had multiple contacts among the *grandes dames*, contacts they normally avoided, yet contacts who, in this instance, once they were apprised of the situation, were very ready to come to their collective aid.

By the time that evening's entertainments commenced, all was in place, the cannons primed.

Tony, accompanied by Geoffrey, made privy to the latest developments, escorted the ravishing Mrs. Carrington and her even more ravishing sister to a formal dinner, followed by three major balls.

They'd barely entered the first ballroom, Lady Selwyn's, when he overheard his godmother spreading the word.

"It is *quite* beyond the pale!" Lady Amery's tones were hushed yet outraged. "This secretive gentleman seeks to manipulate us, those of the haut ton, with rumors and sly tricks, to make us turn on Mrs. Carrington and drive her from town so that her fleeing our wrath will appear an admission of guilt, and so confuse the authorities and hide his infamous deeds."

Lady Amery twitched her shawl straight, both the action and her expression indicating absolute disgust. "It is beyond anything that a gentleman should seek to use us thus."

Wide-eyed, the Countess of Hereford had been drinking in her eloquence. "So none of the rumors is true?"

"*Pshaw!*" Lady Amery flicked her fingers. "Nothing

more than artful lies. The reason he has focused on Mrs. Carrington is purely because she had the ill fortune to be the last person poor Ruskin spoke with before going to his death—at this very man's hands, no less! She was attending a soirée—I ask you, what is one supposed to do at a soirée if not talk to other guests? But now the devil seeks to deceive and deflect the authorities, and to use us to accomplish his evil ends."

"How diabolical!" The countess looked shocked.

"Indeed." Lady Amery nodded significantly. "You can see why we—those of us who know the truth—must be vigilant in ensuring these lies are quashed."

"Unquestionably." Transparently horrified, Lady Hereford laid a hand on Lady Amery's arm. "Why, if the ton could be used so easily as an instrument of harm . . ."

Her thoughts were easy to follow: no one would be safe.

Lifting her head, the countess patted Lady Amery's arm. "You may rest assured, Felicité, that I'll correct any idle talk I hear." She gathered her skirts. "Poor Mrs. Carrington—she must be quite prostrate."

Lady Amery waved. "As to that, she is one of us and knows how to behave—she will be here this evening, I make no doubt, and with her head high."

"I sincerely wish her well." Lady Hereford stood. "And will do all I can to aid her and bring this dastardly plot to nought."

With a regal nod, which Lady Amery graciously returned, Lady Hereford stepped into the crowd.

From where he'd halted, two paces behind the chaise where his godmother sat, Tony moved quickly forward, drawing Alicia, another fascinated observer, with him. Courtesy of the dense crowd, neither recent occupant of the chaise had noticed them. Now he rounded the chaise and bowed to his godmother, then bent and kissed her cheek.

"You were superb," he murmured as he straightened.

Lady Amery humphed. "It's hardly difficult to act outraged when I am." She held out her hands to Alicia, and when she took them drew her down to the chaise. "But you, *chérie*—I vow it is unconscionable." She looked at Tony. "You will find him soon, yes? And then this nonsense will be over."

"There's a crew of us pursuing him—we'll unmask him, never fear."

"Bon!" Lady Amery turned to Alicia. "And now you must tell me how that lovely sister of yours is faring. Has Geoffrey Manningham truly turned her head?"

Standing beside the chaise, Tony scanned the company. A number of senior hostesses had nodded pointedly their way, their acknowledgment marked and openly so. Others less prominent had stopped by to assure Alicia of their support. The tide was already turning.

He saw Leonora and Tristan arrive, and promptly start circulating. Deeming Lady Selwyn's event well covered, he summoned Geoffrey and Adriana with a glance, and they moved on through the crowded streets to the next major event.

The Countess of Gosford's ball was in full swing by the time they arrived. There, they met more hostesses, more *grandes dames*, all supportive. Lady Osbaldestone summoned them with an imperious wave of her cane; she gave them to understand that she hadn't had so much fun in years, and fully intended to make "the blackguard's" attempt to use the ton against Alicia a *cause célèbre*.

"A judgment of sorts on our malicious ways—we'd be fools not to see it." Her black eyes locked on the golden green of Alicia's, she nodded curtly. "So you needn't think to thank us—any of us. Do us the world of good to realize we've created a system so amenable to such dastardly manipulation. Help keep us honest." She grimaced. "Well, more honest."

Switching to Tony, she fixed him with a basilisk gaze. "And how long do you expect to take to lay this villain by the heels?"

"We're doing all we can—some things take time."

She narrowed her eyes at him. "Just as long as you don't at the last seek to sweep this blackguard's name under any rug." Her expression was a warning. "Rest assured we—none of us—will stand for that."

Tony smiled urbanely. "Rest assured," he returned, "no matter who else might think otherwise, I won't be a party to protecting him."

His answer gave Lady Osbaldestone pause; she searched his face, then humphed, apparently appeased. "Very good. You may now take yourselves off. Indeed, I suggest a waltz—that ought to be one starting up now. Last thing you want to appear is too concerned to enjoy yourselves."

Tony bowed; Alicia curtsied, and he led her away. To the dance floor.

She went into his arms readily. After three revolutions, his hand tightened on her back. She dutifully shifted her attention to his face.

"What is it?" There was a frown behind his eyes.

She smiled—more easily than she'd ever imagined she would be able to in such circumstances. "I just . . . find it all a trifle unreal. I've been transported Cinderella-like to an unimagined place. I never expected so many would so readily give me their support." She blushed lightly. "For all that it's you, and Kit and Leonora and the others asking the favor, it's me they have to agree to back."

His smile was slow, genuine and warming. "You take too little credit to yourself." He looked up as they swept into the turn. "Consider this." He drew her closer, bent his head so his words fell by her ear. "You've made few, if any, enemies—you and Adriana have been openly friendly, you've made many real friends over the last weeks. You've been pleasant companions; you've not sought to cut others out, nor to blacken anyone else's name. You've not lent your standing to any less-than-admirable social thrust; you've avoided all scandal."

He caught her eye as they whirled out of the tight turn.

Lips curving, he raised a brow. "Indeed, you're the epitome of a lady of whom society is pleased to approve—one of those the *grandes dames* delight in holding up as an example to others less adept, living proof of the type of lady they are happy to acknowledge."

Except she wasn't. She returned his smile lightly and looked over his shoulder as if accepting his description. Inside, the small kernel of disquiet that had been with her for weeks—ever since he'd first singled her out in some long-ago ballroom—grew, but she didn't have time to dwell on it, not then.

After the waltz, she and Tony strolled the ballroom, eventually rejoining Geoffrey and Adriana; together, they left for their last port of call.

The Marchioness of Huntly was one of the ton's foremost hostesses. When they arrived, Huntly House was ablaze with lights. A theme of white and gilt was repeated throughout the imposing reception rooms; the ballroom was festooned with white silk sprinkled with gilt stars and looped back with gold cords. The light from three brilliant chandeliers winked and glinted in the jewels circling ladies' throats and encrusting the combs in their coiffures.

Born a Cynster, Lady Huntly had been watching for them; she swept forward to greet them, and strolled down the ballroom chatting amiably, then handed them into her sister-in-law's care.

The Duchess of St. Ives positively glowed with social zeal. She smiled brilliantly at Alicia. "He is defeated, you see." Irrepressibly French, she gestured about them. "Oh, it may take a day or so more to complete what we have begun, but there will be no repercussions. He will not succeed in using us in so cowardly a way to attack you, and thus hide his own infamy."

Here, the company were the *crème de la crème*; only those accepted into the most rarefied of tonnish circles were present. The duchess remained with them for some time, introducing them to numerous others. Her generosity and determination added to the weight bearing down on Alicia's conscience.

Then a waltz started up, and Tony swept her onto the floor and into an interlude of pleasant distraction. She knew better than to think of the nebulous worry dogging her, not while in his arms; he was guaranteed to notice, and question, then interrogate further, and that she was not ready for.

So she laughed and smiled at his witticisms, eventually insisting he return her to Adriana's side. They joined her sister's circle. Although in this venue the attractions of those who had gravitated into Adriana's orbit was exceptional, it was clear, at least to Alicia, that her sister's decision to lean on Geoffrey Manningham's arm was not affected in the remotest degree.

Inwardly sighing, she made a mental note to arrange to speak with Geoffrey soon, to explain their financial state. Oddly, the prospect did not fill her with the dread she'd once thought it would.

Brows faintly rising, she realized she now knew Geoffrey too well to imagine mere money, or even their scheme, would weigh overmuch with him. His devotion to Adriana had remained unwaveringly constant throughout the weeks; indeed, it had only strengthened and grown. Adriana, at least, would achieve the goal they'd aimed for.

Her thoughts turned to herself; feeling a stir beside her, she abruptly pushed them aside, away, and turned.

"My dear Mrs. Carrington." Sir Freddie Caudel bowed and shook the hand she offered. He glanced around, then met her gaze. He lowered his voice. "I can't tell you how distressed I am to have learned of the problem besetting you."

Alicia blinked; the phrasing sounded rather strange, but Sir Freddie was one of the old school, somewhat formal in his ways.

"However, it seems the ladies of the ton have rallied to your cause—you must be grateful to have gained the support of such champions."

She'd learned that many gentlemen disapproved of the social power the *grandes dames* wielded; the edge to Sir Freddie's words suggested he was one. "Indeed," she replied, calmly serene. "I can't tell you what a relief it's been. The ladies have been so kind."

He inclined his head, looking away over the crowd. "It's to be hoped this man will be identified soon. Is there any information as to who the blackguard is?"

She hesitated, then murmured, "There are a number of avenues of investigation in hand, I believe. Lord Torrington could tell you more."

Sir Freddie glanced at Tony, on her other side, presently engaged with Miss Pontefract. Sir Freddie's lips curved lightly. "I don't believe I'll disturb him—it was purely an idle question."

Alicia smiled and turned the conversation to the latest play, which she hoped to see during the next week. Sir Freddie remained for several minutes, urbanely chatting, then he excused himself and moved to Adriana's side.

Turning back to Tony, Alicia saw he'd been tracking Sir Freddie. She raised her brows quizzically.

"Has he spoken—or even hinted—yet?"

"No—and don't speak of it. I'm hoping not to tempt fate." On a spurt of decision, she made a silent vow to speak with Geoffrey as soon as possible. There was no need to put Sir Freddie to the trouble of asking for Adriana's hand—no need for her to have to face the ordeal of politely refusing him.

To her relief, the evening rolled on in pleasant vein. Nothing of any great note occurred, no difficult situation arose to challenge her, or them. The small hours of the morning saw them heading back to Waverton Street, tired but content with the way their plans had gone. Geoffrey parted from them at their door. Tony accompanied them in, ultimately accompanying her up the stairs to her bed-chamber, and her bed.

Tony shrugged off his coat, dropped it on the chair, felt very much as if he was shedding some physical restraint along with his social facade.

I don't like this. No more do I.

Charles's words, his answer. A statement that grew more accurate with each passing day. Despite his erst-while occupation, its shadowy nature and often nebulous threats, he and his colleagues had always, ultimately, dealt with foes face-to-face. Once the engagement had commenced, they'd always known the enemy.

Never had he had to cope with a situation like this. The action had commenced with Ruskin's murder; subse-quent acts, strikes at their side, had been mounted and ex-ecuted with impunity, causing damage and difficulty in their camp. A. C. had forced them to respond, to deploy to meet his threats and the actions he'd unleashed, yet even though they'd managed thus far to weather all he'd thrown at them, they'd yet to sight his face.

An unknown enemy, with unassessed capabilities, made the battle that much harder to win.

Yet it was a battle he could not lose.

Glancing across the darkened room, he watched Alicia, sitting at her dressing table, brush out her long hair.

He couldn't even contemplate conceding a minor skir-mish; there was too much here that was now too precious to him.

Yanking his shirt from his waistband, he looked down, started sliding buttons free. Beneath the loosening linen, he shifted his shoulders, aware of muscles subtly easing in one way, tensing in another. A primitive want welling as the civilized screen fell.

I want him.

Dalziel's tone had been lethal, yet no more than an echo of his own resolve. Whatever it took, he would find A. C. and ensure he was brought to justice. The villain had focused on Alicia, struck at her not once but multiple times; for him, there could be no rest until A.C. was caught.

Yet they did not, after weeks of searching, even know his name.

He shrugged off his shirt and felt the last shreds of social restraint fall from him. For a long moment, he stood, his shirt bunched in his hands, staring unseeing at the floor, inwardly watching the volcano of his emotions surge and swell.

The scraping of wood on wood snapped him out of his state. Alicia stood, pushing back her dressing stool.

He dropped his shirt on the chair; unbidden, he padded barefoot across the room to help with her laces.

She glanced at his face, then gave him her back. He could feel his need building; rapidly, with far less than his customary languid sophistication, he unpicked the knots, hooked the laces free.

He glanced up, met her gaze in the mirror.

Saw that she'd sensed the change in him.

She searched his face, then looked down.

Normally, he would have stepped back, given her space to remove her gown . . . he didn't move.

Nor did she. Instead, she looked up, again met his eyes.

Her gaze was direct, questioning, waiting.

He dragged in a slow, deep breath, and reached for her.

Stripped the gown from her, let it and her chemise pool about her feet. Murmured darkly as he stepped close and wrapped his arms about her, locking her silken back to his bare chest, spreading his hands and claiming her glorious bounty. He shifted evocatively against her. Bending his head, he whispered, half in French, half in English, asking her to put her foot on the stool and remove her ruched garters and silk stockings.

Her breath shuddered as she breathed in, and complied.

While she did . . . he let his hands roam. Let them take

and claim as his need willed, set his senses free to wallow and seize all she surrendered to him, would surrender to him, in that moment, and the moments to come.

One arm crossing her body, his palm covering one breast, fingers evocatively kneading, with his other hand, he lightly gripped her nape; as she bent forward to roll the first garter and stocking down, he traced her supple spine, possessively stroking down, over the back of her waist, through the indentation below it, smoothly stroking over the swell of her bottom, down and around to caress the soft, slickly swollen flesh between her thighs.

With one foot on the stool, she was open to him. He parted the soft folds and found her, flagrantly caressed, then worked two fingers deep.

By the time she'd paused, gathered herself, changed legs, when she finally dropped the second stocking to the floor, Alicia was hot, wet and quivering with need.

Her foot still on the stool, her body riding the repetitive probing of his fingers, she looked into the mirror, from under heavy lids met his gaze.

Breasts swollen and full, peaks tight and aching, her skin heated, her breathing already ragged, she waited.

Withdrawing his hand, he grasped her waist; the instant she straightened and her foot touched the floor, he turned her.

She'd expected something else. Instead, he stepped back, drawing her with him, with one hand unbuttoning the flap of his trousers, the only clothing he still wore.

The backs of his thighs hit the bed. He paused only to free his fully engorged staff from the folds of his trousers, then he lifted her. Ignoring her smothered gasp, he sat and brought her slowly down, setting her on her knees astride his hips.

With the broad head of his staff nudging into her body.

She could feel him there, throbbing, sense the promise

of all that was to come. The hot, aching emptiness within her swelled.

She looked into his face, into his black, fathomless eyes. Raising her hands, she framed his face as his hands closed hard about her hips. Under mutual direction, their lips met. Clung, held.

Beneath his control she sensed all he held back, sensed the power, the desperate need.

She shifted fractionally on him. He caught his breath, broke from the kiss. Screened by their lashes, their eyes met.

He whispered against her lips, his breath a hot flame. "Take me. Give yourself to me." His gaze dropped to her lips. "Be mine."

Gravelly, rough, another seduction, a dark temptation to a deeper level of giving.

She didn't hesitate. Drawing in a breath, tightening her hands about his face to anchor her, she angled her head, set her lips to his, and slowly eased down.

Inch by slow inch, she took him inside her, gloried in the feel of him filling her, stretching her. She'd never before been so aware of how her body closed about him, enclasped him. Took him in.

His hands were hard as iron about her hips as he ruthlessly guided her down; he let her set the pace only until he was fully seated within her, then he took the reins, took control, and the giving began.

Hard, hot, and complete.

Without restrictions, limits, or reservations.

Their bodies merged deeply, compulsively riding a wave of sensual desire higher than any before, a tide of need more desperately urgent, more powerful. More addictive.

Their tongues tangled, their mouths feeding in frenzy. He took her as he would, seizing and claiming every sense she possessed, demanding more even as she gave him all.

In the end, on a gasp, she surrendered completely, opened her body, her soul, her heart, and let him plunder.

Let him capture, take, and make her his.

Beyond all thought. Beyond all denial.

Beyond this world.

She was his. Forever. He would never allow anyone to take her from him.

When he slumped back on the bed, drained, replete, to the very depths of his soul sated, the darker side of his nature for the moment wholly satisfied, as he tumbled her down with him, then kicked off his trousers and wrapped them in the covers, those were the only thoughts to cross Tony's mind.

They were the only thoughts that mattered.

SIXTEEN

In the darkness before dawn, Alicia stirred.

Awareness slunk into her brain. Her body still thrummed; her hair was a wild tangle, a fine net ensaring them, wrapped about the muscled arm lying protectively about her. Eyes closed, she lay still, safe, secure, warm. Freed by the night, by the silence, her thoughts crept from the corners of her mind, dwelling on the strange twist her life had taken—the deception she'd never intended to practice, not on so many, not to this degree.

The role of her own making now haunted her.

Not in her wildest dreams had she expected to rise to such social prominence, never imagined calling so many of the powerful friend. Yet in her and her family's time of need, they'd come to her aid—how could she now draw back from them, from the protection they'd so generously offered?

Thanks to A. C. and his latest attempt to cast all suspicion on her, she couldn't even slip away, fade from the scene. She had to remain, head high, and face down his rumors, at least for the next weeks.

Had to continue to pretend she was the widow she was not, while parading through the haut ton, the subject of the latest *on-dit*, the central character in the most amazing, attention-getting story.

The idea that someone from her little part of the country might, like Ruskin, pop up and recognize her had assumed the status of a nightmare. No amount of reasoning, of reiterating that there truly were few families of standing near Little Compton, and none who had known her, did anything to lessen its effect; like a dark, louring cloud it hovered, threatening, not breaking but always there, swelling in the back of her mind.

What if the cloud burst and the truth came raining down?

Her heart contracted; she dragged in a breath, conscious of the vise closing about her chest.

Tony had so publicly nailed his flag to her mast, had so openly committed himself to her cause, and brought with him so many of his aristocratic connections . . . if the ton ever learned the truth of her widowhood, how would that reflect on him?

Badly. Very badly. She'd now gone about in society enough to know. Such a revelation would make her an outcast, but it would make him a laughingstock. Or worse, it would cast him as one who had knowingly deceived the entire ton.

They would never forgive him.

And no matter any protestations to the contrary, deep down, in his heart, he would never—could never—forgive her. By making him a party to her deception, she would have ripped from him and put forever beyond his reach the position to which he'd been born, the position she suspected he never even questioned, it was so much a part of him.

She wanted to twist and turn, but with him breathing softly, deeply, beside her, she forced herself to lie still beneath the heavy arm he'd slung across her waist. Dawn was sliding over the rooftops when she finally accepted that she could do nothing to change things—all she could do was move heaven and earth to ensure that no one ever learned her true state.

She glanced at his face on the pillow beside hers. His dark lashes lay, black crescents over his cheekbones; in sleep, his face retained the harsh lines, the austere angularity of nose and jaw. In her mind, she heard his voice dispassionately reciting, describing what the last ten years of his life had been, how they'd been spent, and where; he'd avoided stating in what danger, but she was not so innocent she couldn't read between his lines. When his mask was off, as now, the evidence of that decade still remained, etched in the lines of his face.

Last night—early this morning—he'd needed her. Wanted her. Taken all she'd given, and yet needed more, a more she'd found it possible to give.

His satisfaction was hers, deep, powerful, and complete. She had never imagined such a connection, that a man such as he would have a need like that, and that she would be able so completely to fulfill it.

Her joy in that discovery was profound.

Lifting a hand, she gently brushed back the heavy lock of black hair that lay rakishly across his brow. He didn't wake, but stirred. His hand flexed, lightly gripping her side before easing as, reassured, he sank once more into slumber.

For long moments, she looked, silently wondered.

Faced incontrovertible fact.

He now meant more to her, at a deeper, more intensely emotional level, than all else in her life.

Tony left Waverton Street before the sunshine hit the cobbles. The tide of satisfaction that had swept him last night had receded, revealing, to him all too forcefully, the vulnerability beneath.

He couldn't—wouldn't—lose her; he couldn't even readily stomach the fact she was at risk. Therefore . . .

Over breakfast that morning, as always efficiently served by Hungerford who, despite knowing full well Tony hadn't slept in his own bed for the past week and more, remained remarkably cheerful, he made his plans. Those included Hungerford, but his first act was to repair to his study and pen two summonses. The first, to Geoffrey Manningham, took no more than a few minutes; he dispatched it via a footman, then settled to write the second, a communication requiring far more thought.

He was still engaged in searching for the right approach, the right phrases, when Geoffrey arrived. Waving him to the pair of armchairs before the hearth, he joined him.

"News?" Geoffrey asked as he sat.

"No." Sinking into the other chair, Tony smiled, all teeth. "Plans."

Geoffrey grinned, equally ferally, back. "You perceive me all ears."

Tony outlined the basics of what he intended.

Geoffrey concurred. "If you can get everything into place, including your beloved, that would unquestionably be the wisest course." He met Tony's gaze. "So what do you want me to do? I presume there's something."

"I want you to remove Adriana for the afternoon—or the day, if you prefer."

Geoffrey widened his eyes. "That all?"

Tony nodded. "Do that, and I'll manage the rest."

Just how he would do that last . . . they sat for ten minutes debating various options, then Geoffrey took himself off to accomplish his assigned task.

Tony remained before the fire for a few minutes more, then, struck by inspiration, returned to his desk and completed his second summons, disguised as a letter to his cousin Miranda, inviting her and her two daughters, Margaret and Constance, to visit him in London, to act as chaperone while the lady he intended to make his viscountess spent a week or so under his roof.

If he knew anything of Miranda, that last would ensure her appearance as soon as he could wish—namely, tomorrow.

The letter dispatched in the care of a groom, he rang for Hungerford.

Dealing with his butler was bliss; Hungerford never questioned, never made difficulties, but could be counted on to ensure that, even if difficulties did arise and his orders no longer fitted the situation, that his intent would be accomplished.

Telling Hungerford that he proposed protecting his intended bride from social and even possibly physical attack by installing her under this roof, within the purlieu of Hungerford's overall care, was all it took to get everything in Upper Brook Street ready.

He had little notion of what arrangements would be required to prepare the house to receive not only the widowed Miranda and her daughters, ten and twelve years old, but his prospective bride, her family, and her household, but he was sure his staff under Hungerford's direction would meet the challenge.

Beaming, clearly delighted with his orders, Hungerford retreated. Tony considered the clock; it was not yet noon.

He debated the wisdom of his next act at some length; eventually, he rose, and headed for Hendon House.

At two o'clock, he paused beside Collier, leaning on his street sweeper's broom at the corner of Waverton Street.

The big man nodded in greeting. "Just missed her, you have. She returned from some luncheon, then immediately headed off with the three lads and their tutor to the park. Kites today, if you've a mind to join them."

"And Miss Pevensey?"

"Lord Manningham called 'bout eleven and took her up in his curricle. They haven't returned."

Tony nodded. "I'm going to talk to the staff, then perhaps I'll fly a kite." He paused, then added, "I plan to move Mrs. Carrington and her household to Upper Brook Street, but I'll want you and the others to keep up your watch here. I'll leave Scully and one other in residence, to keep all possibilities covered."

Collier nodded. "When will this move happen?"

Today if Tony had his way. Realistically . . . "At the earliest tomorrow, late in the day."

Leaving Collier, Tony strode on; reaching Alicia's house, he went quickly up the steps. Maggs answered the door.

Tony frowned; Maggs forestalled him. "Scully's with 'em. No need to fret."

His frown darkening at the thought that he was *that* transparent, he crossed the threshold. "I want to speak with the staff—all of you who are here. It might be best if I came down to the kitchens."

From beneath the wide branches of one of the trees in Green Park, Alicia watched, a smile on her lips, as Scully and Jenkins wrestled with the second of the two kites they'd brought out.

The first kite, under Harry's narrow-eyed guidance, was soaring over the treetops. David was watching Scully and Jenkins, a pitying look in his face; Matthew's eyes were glued to the blue-and-white kite swooping and swirling above the trees.

"There you are."

She turned at the words, knowing before she met Tony's eyes that it was he. "As always."

Smiling, she gave him her hand; his eyes locking on hers, he raised it to his lips and pressed kisses first to her fingers, then to her palm. Retaining possession, he lowered his hand, fingers sliding about hers, and looked out at the scene in the clearing before them.

"I wonder . . ." He glanced at her, raised a brow. "Should I rescue Jenkins and Scully from sinking without trace in your brothers' estimation?"

She grinned; leaning back against the tree trunk, she gestured. "By all means. I'll watch and judge your prowess."

Over numerous afternoons, he'd taught the boys the tricks of keeping their kites aloft. He'd transparently enjoyed the moments; something inside her had rejoiced to see him caught again in what must have been a boyhood pleasure.

"Hmm." Studying the kite flyers, he hesitated; she got the impression he was steeling himself to resist the lure of the kites and do something else, something he was reluctant to do.

A moment passed, then he looked at her. "Actually, I wanted to speak with you."

She widened her eyes, inviting him to continue.

Still he hesitated; his eyes searched hers—abruptly she realized he was metaphorically girding his loins.

"I want you to move house."

She frowned at him. "Move? But why? Waverton Street suits us—"

"For safety reasons. Precautions." He trapped her gaze. "I don't want you or your household subjected to any repeat of yesterday."

She had no wish to argue that; no one had enjoyed the experience. But . . . she let her frown grow. "How will a different house avoid . . ." The intentness in his black eyes registered. Her lips parted; she stared, then baldly asked, "To which house do you wish us to move?"

His lips thinned. "Mine."

"No."

"*Before* you say that, just consider—living under my roof you'll have the protection not just of my title, my status, but also of all those allied with me and my family." His eyes pinned her. "So will your sister and brothers."

Folding her arms, she narrowed her eyes back. "For the moment, let's leave Adriana and the boys out of this discussion—it hasn't escaped my notice that you're always quick to drag them into the fray."

He scowled at her. "They're part of it—they're part of you."

"Perhaps. Be that as it may, you can't seriously think—"

He cut her off with a raised hand. "Hear me out. If it's the proprieties that are exercising you, my cousin and her two young daughters—they're ten and twelve—will be arriving tomorrow. With Miranda in residence, there's no reason—social, logical, or otherwise—that you and your household cannot stay at Torrington House. It's a mansion—there's more than enough room."

"But . . ." She stared at him. The words: *I'm your mistress, for heaven's sake!* burned her tongue. Compressing her lips, she fixed him with a strait look, and primly asked, "What will your staff think?"

What she meant was: what will the entire ton think. To be his mistress was one thing; the ton turned a blind eye to affairs between gentlemen such as he and fashionable widows. However, to be his mistress and live openly under his roof was, she was fairly certain, going that one step too far.

His expression had turned bewildered. "My staff?"

"Your servants. Those who would have to adjust to and cope with the invasion."

"As it happens, they're delighted at the prospect." His frown returned. "I can't imagine why you'd think otherwise. My butler's going around with a smile threatening to crack his face, and the staff are buzzing about, getting rooms ready."

She blinked, suddenly uncertain. If his butler thought her living in the Upper Brook Street mansion was acceptable . . . she'd always understood tonnish butlers to be second only to the *grandes dames* in upholding the mores of the ton.

Tony sighed. "I know we haven't properly discussed it, but there isn't time. Just because we've trumped A. C.'s last three tricks doesn't mean he won't try again." His expression resolute, he met her eyes. "That he's tried three times to implicate you suggests he's fixated on the idea of using you to cover his tracks. I'm sure he'll try again."

An inkling of why he was so set on moving her into his

house, having her, at least for the present, under his roof, reached her. She hesitated.

He sensed it. Shifting closer, he pressed his point. "There's a huge schoolroom with bedrooms attached, and rooms for Jenkins and Fitchett nearby. There's a back garden the boys can play in when they're not having their lessons—and the staff truly are looking forward to having boys running up and down the stairs again."

Despite all, that last made her smile.

He squeezed her hand, raised it to his chest. "You and the boys and Adriana will be comfortable and safe at Torrington House. You'll be happy there."

And he'd be happy if she was there, too—that didn't need saying, it was there in his eyes.

"Please." The word was soft. "Come and live with me."

Her heart turned over; her resolution wavered.

"There's no reason at all you can't—no hurdle we can't overcome."

Lost in his eyes, she pressed her lips tight.

Felt a tug on her gown. She looked down.

Matthew stood beside them; neither of them had noticed his approach. Face alight, he stared first at one, then the other, then breathlessly asked, "Are we really going to live at Tony's house?"

By the time they got back to Waverton Street, Alicia had a headache. A frown had taken up permanent residence on her face; she couldn't seem to lose it.

She was seriously annoyed, not specifically but generally—she couldn't blame Tony for involving her brothers, but involved they now were, and determined to convince her of the huge benefits of removing with all speed to Torrington House.

If Tony was ruthless, they were relentless. She went up the steps, shooing them before her, feeling almost battered.

Despite their arguments, she felt very sure she needed

to think long and hard about this latest proposition. She needed to investigate, and make sure that her presence in his house wouldn't harm his standing.

Nor make her own any more perilous.

"Off to wash your hands. No tea until you do."

It was blackberry jam day again, so they rushed off without argument.

With a short sigh, she swung to face Tony.

He was watching her closely. "Come and sit down."

She let him steer her to the parlor. Scully and Jenkins disappeared. Sinking onto the chaise, she fixed Tony with a darkling glance. "I haven't agreed."

He inclined his head and, wisely, made no reply.

Tea should have soothed her temper. Unfortunately, her brothers were not so perspicacious as Tony; although clever enough not to directly argue their case, their artful comments, tossed entirely among themselves, on the possibilities they imagined might accrue should they go to live in Upper Brook Street—possibilities like having suitable banisters to slide down, possibilities they innocently requested advice on from Tony—filled the minutes.

She kept her lips shut and refused to be drawn.

Then she heard the front door open, and Adriana's and Geoffrey's voices. She turned as they came in.

Adriana's face glowed. "We had a lovely drive around Kew. The gardens were well worth the visit."

Alicia sat forward and reached for the spare teacups, wondering how to broach the subject of Tony's proposed move, preferably in a way that would ensure her sister's cooperation in holding back what had started to feel like an inexorable tide.

Adriana tossed her bonnet onto the window seat, took the cup of tea Alicia had poured to Geoffrey, sitting in the second armchair, then sat beside Alicia on the chaise. Taking the cup she handed her, Adriana's gaze went to Geoffrey; he was being served crumpets and jam by Harry and Matthew.

Following her gaze, Alicia watched, noted. Despite their love of crumpets, the boys had readily shared; they'd accepted Geoffrey, not perhaps in the same unquestioning way they'd accepted Tony, yet they clearly counted him one of their small circle and trusted him.

Smiling, Adriana turned to her. "Geoffrey told me about Tony's suggestion that we move to Upper Brook Street." She sipped, then met Alicia's eyes. "It sounds an excellent idea . . ." Her voice trailed away; seeing Alicia's reaction, she blinked. "Isn't it?"

Alicia looked at Tony. He returned her regard steadily, giving not an inch. She glanced at Geoffrey, but he was—quite deliberately she was sure—chatting with her brothers about the merits of blackberry jam.

Slowly, she drew breath, then met Adriana's gaze. "I don't know." The unvarnished truth.

"Well—"

Adriana tried to persuade her all over again; her arguments echoed Tony's, yet were sufficiently different to assure Alicia he hadn't been so foolish as to plot with her sister against her.

He knew the thought crossed her mind; when, recognizing her suspicion was misplaced, she glanced at him, he searched her eyes, then faintly raised a brow. Raising his cup, he calmly sipped. And left her fighting a rearguard action against everyone else in the room.

Her brothers didn't press her directly; instead, they supported and elaborated on Adriana's themes. And then Geoffrey, more quietly but also more seriously and with considerably more weight, threw his support behind Adriana and Tony.

Looking into Geoffrey's steady brown gaze, Alicia felt her resistance waver. She could see why Geoffrey wanted Adriana and the rest of them under Tony's roof. Glancing at Tony, she knew the same reason was a significant part of his motivation, too. Was she being irrational in refusing to agree?

She needed reassurance, but not the sort anyone present could give—

The doorbell pealed. She glanced at the clock; time had flown. Hearing feminine voices in the hall, she rose. She tugged the bellpull to summon Jenkins, and instructed her brothers they could finish the crumpets before returning to their lessons.

Turning, she headed for the door, Adriana behind her. Tony and Geoffrey followed.

"Ah—there you are, Alicia!" In the hall, Kit Hendon beamed at her.

Beside her, Leonora Wemyss smiled. "I hope we haven't called at an inopportune moment, but there's a gathering at Lady Mott's that it would be wise to attend, and we wanted to coordinate which events we'll go to tonight."

Alicia smiled, touched hands, waited while they greeted the others, then ushered both ladies into the drawing room. As they all sat, disposing themselves on the chaise and the chairs, she realized that neither Kit nor Leonora had evinced the slightest surprise at discovering Tony and Geoffrey present.

The middle of the afternoon was not a common time for gentlemen to call.

Leonora plunged immediately into a discussion of the most promising events planned for that evening. "I think Lady Humphries' rout, then the Canthorpes' ball and the Hemmingses', too. What do you think?"

They tossed around the possiblities, eventually replacing the Hemmingses' ball with the Athelstans'. "Much better connected," Tony said, his eyes capturing Alicia's, "and that helps at the end of a long night."

"Yes." Leonora nodded, gaze distant as if reviewing a mental list. "That should do it." She glanced at Alicia. "A very good night's work."

"Now," Kit said, sitting forward, "the reason we think visiting Lady Mott's in the next hour would be wise is that her gatherings invariably attract all the busiest bodies in town. They're of the older, more crotchety crew, and while our story will doubtless have reached some of them, there are others who are highly active but only during the day."

"If we concentrate our activities solely on the evening events, we'll miss them," Leonora put in. "Not only would that leave an avenue open for A. C. to exploit, but those old ladies themselves won't thank us—they hate to be behindhand with gossip."

The observation made them all grin.

Alicia glanced down at her lilac gown; she'd worn it to luncheon at Lady Candlewick's, but courtesy of her sojourn in the park, grass stains now adorned the hem. "I'll have to change my gown."

"So will I." Adriana waved at her carriage dress, quite unsuitable attire for an afternoon call on Lady Mott and company.

"No matter." Sitting back, Kit waved. "Leonora and I will wait."

Alicia looked at Tony and Geoffrey. The opportunity to talk privately to Kit and Leonora, to sound them out over Tony's suggestion, was a godsend—but she didn't want to leave Tony alone with them in case he wooed them to his cause before she'd a chance to assess their true reactions.

As if bowing to her wishes, he uncrossed his long legs and stood. With a glance, he roused Geoffrey, then turned to her. "We'll leave you. I'll call for you at eight, if that's suitable?"

She rose to see them out. "Yes, of course."

He and Geoffrey farewelled Kit and Leonora. Adriana also rose and accompanied them into the hall. Maggs stood ready to open the door.

Alicia gave Tony her hand. He held it, looked into her eyes; reading them, his lips tightened. "You will consider my suggestion, won't you?"

"Yes." She held his gaze. "But I don't know that I'll agree."

The urge to argue welled strong; she could see it in his eyes, feel it in the clasp of his fingers about hers. But he quelled it. Suavely inclined his head.

Releasing her hand, he nodded to Adriana. With Geoffrey following, he went out of the door and down the steps into the street.

Alicia let out the breath she'd been holding and turned.

Saw Adriana's lips open and held up a hand. "Not now. We need to get changed—we can't keep Kit and Leonora waiting."

Adriana, every bit as stubborn as she, pressed her lips tight, but acquiesced. They went quickly up the stairs side by side. Alicia turned into her room—and then hurried like a fiend, selecting a pale green gown of the finest twill and struggling into it, then expertly tweaking and resetting her coiled hair.

She was ready long before Adriana; quickly, shoes pattering, she hurried back down to the drawing room.

Regardless of the fact she'd only made their acquaintance yesterday, with Kit and Leonora she'd felt an instant rapport. Indeed, *they* had only met on her front step, yet the directness, the ready understanding on which friendship and trust were based, were already there between them. She could ask them about Tony's suggestion; they were two of the very few people whose opinion on such an issue she would trust.

Kit was describing one of her eldest son's antics; she smiled as Alicia rejoined them, and quickly brought the story to a close.

Sinking onto the chaise, Alicia clasped her hands in her lap. Both Kit and Leonora looked at her; she drew breath and stated, "In light of the difficulties A. C. seems intent on causing, Torrington has asked me to consider moving this household to Upper Brook Street. To his house."

Leonora opened her eyes wide.

Kit frowned, tapped her fingers on the chair arm. "Who else is resident there?"

"A widowed cousin and her two young daughters—ten and twelve—are expected tomorrow."

Leonora's face cleared; she glanced at Kit. "It would certainly be—" She looked at Alicia and grimaced. "I was going to say an improvement, but by that I mean that while this address is perfectly respectable, Upper Brook Street would place you in the heart of the ton. It would be a statement in itself."

"Indeed," Kit agreed. "And given we suspect A. C. knows the ropes quite well, it's a statement he'll understand." She shifted, her bluey violet eyes studying Alicia. "I know Torrington House—Jack and Tony are old friends. It's a *huge* mansion, and currently only Tony lives there—you can imagine him rattling around like a pea in a cauldron. And it's fully staffed—he's never been able to bring himself to let anyone go, even though there's really no call for three parlormaids when there's only a bachelor to cater for. From what I've seen of his butler, Hungerford, he'll be in alt at the prospect of having a houseful of people to organize for again."

"It sounds like an excellent suggestion." Leonora looked at Alicia. "And it certainly sounds as if your household—boys and all—will fit."

Alicia studied their faces. There was not the slightest hint that either saw anything in any way remotely socially unacceptable in the notion of her living at Torrington House. In the end, she put her question directly. "You don't think it will be seen as scandalous—my living there?"

Leonora opened her eyes wide, clearly surprised by the question. "With his cousin in residence, I really can't see why anyone would disapprove."

She glanced at Kit, who nodded in agreement.

They both looked at Alicia. She summoned a smile. "I see. Thank you."

Adriana came in, a stunning breath of fresh air in a frilled gown of white muslin sprigged with blue. "Ready?"

The three ladies seated smiled and rose. Linking arms, they headed for Lady Mott's.

How he managed to keep his tongue between his teeth Tony didn't know, but he held his peace on the subject of the move for the entire evening.

Kit helped. She swanned up to him in Lady Humphries' ballroom and claimed his arm for a waltz. Alicia laughed and waved them away, remaining chatting with a group of others, all sufficiently harmless. Reluctantly, he let Kit lead him to the floor.

"Mission accomplished," she informed him the instant they were safely revolving. "And I was superbly subtle, I'll have you know. I didn't even have to mention it—she asked, and Leonora and I reassured her. We told her it was an excellent idea."

She smiled at him. "So next time Jack's being difficult about something, remember—you owe me."

He humphed and whirled her about, and forbore to mention that if Jack was being difficult about something, he'd almost certainly agree with him. "How did she take it?" he asked when they were once more precessing sedately up the room.

Kit frowned. "I'm not sure, but the impression I got was that her resistance stemmed primarily from a concern that in accepting your invitation she'd be committing some sort of social solecism." She looked up at him. "She's more or less on her own, with no older lady to guide her. For what it's worth, I don't think her resistance is all that entrenched."

"Good."

They spoke no more of it; at the end of the dance, he returned Kit to Jack's side.

Jack sent a significant glance his way. "I'll be dropping

by that other venue later. I'll catch up with you tomorrow if I learn anything to the point."

He'd lowered his voice, directed his words specifically to Tony, yet Kit caught not only the words, but their subtext. "What point? What other venue?"

Jack looked into her narrowing eyes. "Just a little business matter."

"Oh? Whose business?" Kit sweetly inquired. "A. C.'s?"

"Sssh!" Jack glanced around, but there was no one close enough to hear.

Kit saw her advantage and pressed it, drilling one finger into Jack's chest. "If you imagine you're going out skulking tonight *alone*, then you'll need to promise to inform not just Tony but *all* of us of anything you discover."

Curling his hand around hers, Jack scowled at her. "You'll learn soon enough."

Kit opened her eyes wide. "When you deign to tell us? Thank you, but no—I much prefer to set a time and place for your revelations."

Tony nearly choked; he was privy to the story of what had happened in the early days of their marriage, when Jack had refused to tell Kit what he was involved in. Clearly, Kit had not forgotten. From the look on Jack's face, one of chagrin and uneasy uncertainty, he hadn't either.

When Jack glanced at him, Kit cut in, "And you needn't look to Tony for support." She fixed her violet eyes on him. "He already owes Leonora and me a favor. A very telltale favor."

In her eyes, he read a threat of doom should he fail to capitulate. He sighed and glanced at Jack. "I was going to suggest the club, but let's make it my library. What time?"

Jack humphed. "I'll send word first thing in the morning, once I know what I've managed to find."

Kit beamed at them both. "See? It doesn't hurt."

Jack snorted. Tony fought down a grin. He chatted for a while, then headed back up the ballroom to Alicia, still safe within Adriana's circle.

Which circle was growing less and less intent as more of those aspiring to Adriana's attention *vis à vis* claiming her hand took note of the glances she shared with Geoffrey, and sloped off to pay court to someone else. One gentleman who remained apparently oblivious of the clear firming of Adriana's intention was Sir Freddie Caudel.

As he drew near, Tony wondered if Sir Freddie was biding his time, perhaps thinking to give Adriana more experience of the ton before making his offer, or if he was instead merely using her as a convenient and unthreatening excuse to avoid all other possible candidates. If the man hadn't spoken yet . . . but then, he himself and Geoffrey were of a more direct generation.

Sir Freddie had been conversing with Alicia. He saw Tony approaching, smiled benignly, and excused himself as Tony joined her.

She turned to him, raised a brow. Wariness showed behind the green of her eyes; with an easy smile, he claimed her hand, set it on his sleeve, and inquired if she'd like to stroll.

She agreed, and they did. Because of the many eyes fixed on them courtesy of the story on so many lips, it was impossible to slip away. Resigned, he reminded himself of the true purpose behind their evening's endeavors and conducted her to chat with the next fashionable lady waiting to have her say.

They caught up with his godmother in the Athelstans' ballroom. Dispatched to fetch refreshments, he left Alicia seated on the chaise beside Lady Amery and shouldered his way into the crowd.

Alicia watched him go, then drew breath and turned to Lady Amery. "I hope you won't think me presumptuous, ma'am, but I need advice, and as the person most nearly concerned is Torrington . . ."

She and Lady Amery were alone on the small chaise; there was no one else close enough to hear—and she might never have another such opportunity to ask the one person in London who held Tony's welfare closest to her heart.

Lady Amery had turned to her; now she smiled radiantly. Reaching for Alicia's hands, she clasped them in hers. "My dear, I'd be delighted to help in any way I can."

Alicia steeled herself to see that sentiment change in the next minutes. Lifting her head, she confessed, "Torrington has asked that I and my household move into his house in Upper Brook Street—his widowed cousin and her daughters will be staying there, too."

Lady Amery's gaze grew distant as she considered, then she refocused on Alicia's face. "*Bon.* Yes, I can see that that would be much more comfortable, especially for him, what with this latest brouhaha." Her eyes twinkled, then, reading Alicia's troubled expression, she grew serious. "But you do not wish this? Would it be difficult to move to Upper Brook Street?"

Alicia stared into her ladyship's transparently sincere eyes. Blinked. "No . . . that is . . ." She dragged in a breath. "I just don't want to do anything to give the gossips food for slander—I don't want inadvertently to do anything to damage his name or his standing."

Lady Amery's concerned expression dissolved into smiles. She patted Alicia's hand. "It is very right that you think of such things—such sentiments do you credit—but I assure you in this case, there is nothing to concern you. The ton understands such matters—*oui, vraiment.*" She nodded encouragingly. "There will be no adverse repercussions to your moving to Upper Brook Street in such circumstances."

The assurance with which she made the statement put the matter beyond argument.

Her expression easing, the weight on her shoulders lightening, Alicia smiled and let herself accept it. Despite her worries, her reservations, everyone—absolutely everyone—insisted Tony's suggestion was not only sound, but an outcome to be desired.

Despite that . . . she said nothing when he returned bearing glasses of champagne. Lady Amery claimed his attention and chatted animatedly about shared acquaintances, to Alicia's relief making no allusion to their discussion or her advice.

Finally, the long evening drew to a close, and they headed home. Geoffrey held to his new habit and accompanied them to their door; Tony, as usual, stayed with them beyond it.

In her bedchamber, they undressed—in silence. She felt herself tensing, waiting for him to ask her again, to press his case . . . instead, he said nothing. She climbed into the big bed; he pinched out the candle, and joined her beneath the covers.

He reached for her, drew her to him, then hesitated. In the dimness, he looked at her face. "You're still considering?"

There was no hint of a frown, of irritation or impatience in his voice; he simply wanted to know.

"Yes." She held his gaze. "But I haven't yet made up my mind."

She felt him sigh, then he tightened his hold on her, lowered his head. "We can discuss it in the morning."

When she awoke the next morning, however, he'd already left her bed. She lay staring at the canopy as minutes, then half an hour ticked by, then she sighed and rose.

Washed, gowned, her hair severely coiled, she headed downstairs.

Pausing in the doorway of the dining parlor, she studied the back of Tony's broad shoulders; she wasn't surprised to find him there, in the chair at the end of the table.

Her brothers saw her and turned; Tony glanced around and rose as she entered. Going past him, she waved him back to his seat, exchanged greetings with her brothers and Adriana—then, to Adriana's amusement, remembered to bid their guest a good morning, too.

He returned it with aplomb, recommending the kedgeree. She poured herself a cup of tea, then rose and crossed to the sideboard. She made her selections, all the while conscious of her brothers' whispers, of the anticipation welling, notch by notch, around the table.

Calmly, she returned to her chair, set down her plate, then sat, thanking Maggs, who held the chair for her.

That done, she picked up her fork—and looked around the table.

At four pairs of expectant eyes. And one black gaze she couldn't read.

She drew in a deep breath, exhaled. "All right. We'll move to Torrington House."

Her brothers cheered; Adriana beamed.

She looked down at her plate, poked at the pile of kedgeree on it. "*But* only when Lord Torrington's cousin is ready to receive us."

The cheering didn't abate, instead it broke up into excited speculation, mixed with whispered plans. She glanced at her brothers, then looked at Tony.

Raised a brow.

Tony knew better than to allow his satisfaction, let alone its depth, to show; looking down the table, holding Alicia's gaze, he inclined his head. "I'll send word when Miranda is recovered from her journey and ready to meet you."

Knowing Miranda, he predicted that would be about ten minutes after she arrived.

SEVENTEEN

As he'd prophesied, so it proved. Miranda arrived agog to meet the lady who had finally, as she put it, snared him.

An openhearted lady of considerable charm, her husband's early death had left her sincerely bereft.

"Although I doubt that will last forever." Blond curls framing her heart-shaped face, she looked up at Tony as he stood before the fire in his drawing room. "Meanwhile, I'm on pins, positive pins, waiting to meet this widow of yours. Dare I guess she's ravishingly beautiful?"

Tony fixed her with a not entirely mock-severe glance. "You will behave. Furthermore, you will not regale Alicia with tales of my youth, nor yet of my childhood."

Miranda's grin deepened. "Spoilsport."

He snorted, and turned to the door. The clock on the mantelpiece chimed—twelve *tings*. "I'll go and inform her of your great willingness to make her acquaintance."

At the door, he paused, glanced back. "Just remember—she and I haven't yet formally discussed our marriage." By which he meant she hadn't yet, in so many words, agreed.

Miranda looked both intrigued and delighted. "Don't worry—I won't scuttle your punt."

Feigning disbelief, he left.

* * *

The atmosphere reigning in Waverton Street was as close to pandemonium as anything he'd experienced. He stood in the front hall transfixed by the activity. Crates lay open on the tiles; the green baize door stood propped wide, and a hum of noise pervaded the house. The boys were rushing up and down the stairs, calling to each other, ferrying books and toys, clothes and shoes, stuffing them joyously into the crates before, pausing only to flash him wide grins, racing up the stairs once more.

Through the open dining-room door, he saw Cook and Fitchett carefully wrapping glassware. A sound drew his attention to the gallery; he watched as Maggs, a heavy case on one shoulder, slowly descended the stairs.

"Madhouse, it is." Depositing the case beside two closed crates, Maggs grinned at him. "Almost as bad as one of your mama's journeys."

"Heaven forfend," Tony muttered. "Where's Mrs. Carrington?"

"In her room packing." Maggs stepped aside as the boys came whooping down once more. "Think she's nearly done, but she did say as she'd be out to organize these three devils betimes."

The boys looked up from where they were carefully squeezing slippers and dressing robes in around their toys. They grinned.

Tony fixed them with a direct look. "Do you three devils still need your eldest sister to organize you?"

"'Course not." David shrugged. "But she does anyway."

The other two nodded.

Tony raised his brows. "So if I take her away, you'll be able to manage on your own? My cousin is waiting to meet her, and I thought it might be easier if Alicia came first, on her own."

David and Harry exchanged glances, then nodded encouragingly.

"Good idea," Harry opined. "Then she won't be here to fuss over us."

Matthew looked less certain; Maggs lumbered forward and held out a hand. "Here then, I'll help. We can get you all packed, and meanwhile your sister can go and make Mrs. Althorpe's acquaintance, and make sure she's ready to meet you three, heh?"

Nodding, Matthew took Maggs's hand, but he kept his gaze on Tony's face. "So we'll come to your house later?"

Tony hunkered down, lightly squeezed Matthew's other hand. "I'll send my coach around for you as soon as I get home. It's large enough to take all of you at once, and the luggage can follow. That way, you'll be in Upper Brook Street, in my house, all the sooner."

"Hooray!" David and Harry turned and raced up the stairs. Grinning, reassured, Matthew dashed after them. Maggs brought up the rear.

Tony watched until they disappeared along the corridor, then he went up the stairs and along to Alicia's room.

She was bending over a box at the foot of her bed; straightening with a sigh, she shut the lid.

Smiling, he strolled in. "Finished?"

Alicia looked at him, returned his smile, then glanced distractedly around the room. "Yes—I think that's it for in here."

"Good." Halting before her, he reached for her.

Before she realized what he intended, he'd caught her, bent his head, and was kissing her . . . thoroughly. Her head spun pleasurably . . . then she remembered and struggled.

He ended the kiss; raising his head, he looked down at her. "What?"

She wriggled from his hands, firm about her waist. "The boys!" She peeked around him at the door, but there was no sign of them.

Tony met her warning look with a quizzical one, then he glanced around. "I came to take you to meet Miranda." His gaze returned to her. "She's waiting, so she assured me, on pins."

"Already? Oh." She scanned the room, but she had indeed packed everything. "But the boys aren't yet ready and—"

"The boys assured me they had their packing under control. Maggs has elected to watch over them, and you know Jenkins will as well, and Fitchett and Adriana." He fixed her with a direct look. "So there's no reason you can't come with me now. I'll send my carriage once we reach Upper Brook Street, so they'll all be only an hour or so behind."

She frowned. "But—"

"And don't forget the engagements we have tonight. You'll need to settle in, and then we have a meeting at two o'clock in the library—Jack sent word he's got what we wanted—I'm assuming you still wish to attend?" Innocently, he looked inquiringly at her.

She narrowed her eyes at him. "Of course."

He inclined his head. "And then we've dinner at Lady Martindale's followed by two balls, so we'll be out again within a few hours. I think you should look over the rooms before the others arrive, just in case there's any difficulty, anything you'd like changed."

Lips setting, she looked into his black eyes; she'd seen that expression of immovable purpose before—knew he wouldn't change tack, not easily . . . and perhaps he was right.

She grimaced. "Your cousin—she only has two daughters?"

Tony nodded; taking her elbow, he turned her to the door. "If you're worried she'll have the vapors over the boys' antics, you can rest easy—Miranda was a tomboy to the depths of her soul. We spent much of our childhood together—we were both only children. If anything, she'll be in her element with your brothers—and, incidentally, so will her daughters. If I'm any judge, they'll give your three a run for their money."

That distracted her, enough for him to steer her to the stairs. But—

"I must speak with Fitchett, and Cook, too, before I can leave."

At least she was going down the stairs. He went with her, resigned yet on guard. Stoically, he stuck to her side, determinedly herding her back to the front hall. Finally there, he picked up the pelisse she'd left lying on a chair and helped her into it.

Taking her hand, he drew her out of the front door, pulled it shut, then led her down the steps to where his curricle stood waiting. One of his grooms was holding his matched bays. He helped her in, waited while she'd settled her skirts, then climbed up beside her. Nodding to the groom, he set the horses pacing. Glancing at her, he saw her watching his hands on the reins, watching the horses, still skittish, coquettish.

He realized she was nervous; he kept the horses to a slow trot. "Don't worry—they won't bolt."

She glanced at him. "Oh—I just . . . have rarely had occasion to be behind such beasts. They're very powerful, aren't they?"

"Yes, but I have the reins."

The comment took a moment to sink in, then she relaxed. She looked at him. "You haven't driven me anywhere before."

He shrugged. "There hasn't until now been a need."

But today was different; he wanted her to himself, free of her family. When she first crossed the threshold of his house, he wanted to be with her, just her and him alone, without any distractions. He wanted to have that minute to himself; he refused to waste any time wondering why.

Luckily, she accepted his comment without question;

relaxing a trifle more, she looked around as he took her deeper into the heart of Mayfair.

The moment, when it came, was as simple and as private as he'd wished; only Hungerford was there, holding the door as, his hand at her elbow, Tony guided her into his front hall.

She glanced at Hungerford, nodded, and smiled, then looked up, ahead, and around, and paused, stopped.

Hungerford closed the door, but hung back in the shadows. There was no footman hovering in the hall, no one else to intrude.

Pivoting, she looked around; Tony wondered how she would see it, how she would react to his home.

After a moment, she met his gaze. She sensed his waiting, and smiled. "It's much less intimidating than I'd imagined." Her smile deepened, softened; she glanced around again. "More comfortable. I can see people here—children . . . it's a welcoming house."

Her relief was transparent. It warmed him, eased a small knot of trepidation he hadn't until then acknowledged he carried. Joining her, he took her hand. "This is Hungerford. He's the ultimate authority here."

Hungerford approached and bowed low. "At your service, ma'am. Should you need anything—anything at all—we are at your disposal."

"Thank you."

Hungerford stepped back.

Tony gestured to the drawing-room door. "I'll introduce you to Mrs. Swithins, the housekeeper, later—she can show you the rooms they've prepared. But first, come and meet Miranda."

Buoyed by her impression of the hall, Alicia went forward eagerly. Entering the drawing room, she glanced around—and was again struck by the house's warmth. Without consciously considering it, she'd been expecting a house like him, coolly, austerely elegant, but that wasn't the pervading atmosphere here. The furniture was not new, far from it; every piece looked antique, lovingly polished, the tapestry and brocade upholstery and hangings carrying the rich, jeweled tones of a bygone age.

An age that had valued comfort and convenience as well as luxury, that had expected pleasure and enjoyment to be part of daily life. Hedonistic, but rich, warm, and very much alive.

Like the bright-eyed lady rising from a chair by the hearth. She came forward, smiling widely, hands extended.

"My dear Mrs. Carrington—Alicia—I may call you Alicia, may I not? I'm Miranda, as Tony's doubtless told you. Welcome to Torrington House—may your stay be long and happy."

Miranda's smile was winning; effervescent laughter lurked in her blue eyes. Alicia gave her her hands, smiled back. "Thank you. I hope you won't be too inconvenienced by our descent."

"Oh, *I* certainly won't be, and I doubt anyone could inconvenience Hungerford—he's terrifyingly efficient— all the staff are." Miranda looked at Tony. "You may take yourself off—we want to talk, and we'll do so much more readily without you. I'll take Alicia to meet Mrs. Swithins, so you're relieved on that score, too."

Alicia barely smothered a laugh. She glanced at Tony, saw chagrin briefly flare in his eyes as he sent Miranda a sharp glance, then he turned to her. "I'll send the carriage around for your family."

She smiled. "Thank you."

He hesitated, then, reluctant to the last, nodded and left them.

"Now!" Miranda turned to her, curiosity and delight in her face. "You must tell me all about your family—you have three brothers and a sister, that's all Tony's told me." Waving her to a chair, Miranda resumed her seat.

Alicia sank into the velvet comfort of an armchair, felt a solid sense of safety and security reach for her and wrap her about. Meeting Miranda's expectant gaze, she smiled and assembled her thoughts.

By the time Hungerford brought in the tea tray and she and Miranda had shared a pot, they'd progressed from acquaintances to friends, to newly found bosom-bows. The fictitious nature of her widowhood notwithstanding, they shared many interests—family, country pursuits, household management, and social necessity.

Miranda sent for her daughters; the girls arrived and made their curtsies, then asked polite but curious questions about her brothers. Alicia answered, inwardly heaving a sigh of relief; the girls were well-brought-up, well-bred young ladies, but not in the least sweet, retiring, or weak. They would, indeed, give her brothers pause.

Then it was time to meet Mrs. Swithins and look around the rooms before the others arrived. After performing the introductions, Miranda hung back, letting the housekeeper, a woman of considerable age but imposing presence, softened by a twinkle in her eye, guide Alicia through the house.

"We thought your young brothers would be most comfortable up here, ma'am." Mrs. Swithins led the way into the schoolroom; she waved to rooms opening off the central room. "There's three beds in the long room, and two in the next, so they can sleep together or separate if they wish." She smiled at Alicia. "We weren't sure, so both rooms are prepared."

Alicia frowned. "They're used to being together, but David is twelve."

Mrs. Swithins nodded. "We can leave it to them to decide what's most comfortable."

With a grateful inclination of her head, Alicia allowed

herself to be led on to view the bedrooms for Fitchett and Jenkins.

"So they'll be close enough should the boys have need." With an airy wave, Mrs. Swithins sailed on.

The rooms on the first floor that had been prepared for her and Adriana filled Alicia, not with surprise, for she'd expected something of the sort, but with a sense of having stepped into a fairy tale, or, more specifically, into her own dreams.

Her room lay in the central wing of the mansion, above the long ballroom and overlooking the rear gardens. A wide, spacious chamber, it possessed a sitting area with two chairs before the fireplace, a delicate escritoire against one wall, a bank of large windows with a padded window seat beneath, a gigantic armoire, and a huge four-poster bed hung with pale green silks and covered with an ivory silk coverlet embroidered in green.

"The master mentioned your maid was not with you, so I've assigned Bertha." Mrs. Swithins beckoned to a young girl, who came forward and shyly curtsied. "She knows her way around a lady's wardrobe and is quick with her hands."

Alicia returned Bertha's smile, a trifle shy herself. She'd never had a maid, just Fitchett, not quite the same thing.

"I've hung your gowns in the armoire, ma'am." Bertha's voice was soft, carrying a country burr. Greatly daring, she glanced up and met Alicia's eye. "Absolutely stunning, they be."

"Thank you, Bertha." Alicia hesitated, then added, "I'll need you this evening to help me dress—we've a dinner and two balls to attend."

"Oh?" Miranda pricked up her ears; she came forward to link her arm in Alicia's. "What's this? Tony gadding about in society? Whatever next? You must tell."

Alicia laughed. She thanked Mrs. Swithins, then let Miranda sweep her back downstairs.

The others arrived just in time for luncheon. Emerging from a room Alicia took to be the library, Tony joined the melee in the front hall, then shepherded her family into the dining room, where Miranda waited with her daughters.

Introductions between children could sometimes be awkward; in this case, the arrival of the luncheon dishes cut short any difficult moment. Quickly wriggling onto the chairs to which Tony and Miranda directed them, both her brothers and Miranda's girls were at first on their best behavior, their responses stilted. That lasted only until the platter of sausages was uncovered. Thereafter, needing to ask each other to pass this or that, they quickly lost their shyness in the quest for sustenance.

Margaret and Constance were sturdy young ladies with long blond plaits; both ate heartily, showing no overt sign of consciousness of the boys. That piqued David's and Harry's interest enough for them to extend an invitation to go kite flying in the park.

The girls exchanged looks, then agreed.

When three faces turned up the table to Alicia, and two to Miranda, at the table's other end, the ladies exchanged pleased glances and nodded permission; with just one whoop—from Harry, valiantly smothered—they all pushed back from the table, bobbed curtsies or bowed, then, dismissed with nods, they headed in a bumbling crowd for the door, and Maggs, Jenkins, the park, and the sky.

"Well," Miranda said, turning back from watching them go, "they seem to have fallen on their feet."

Tony shrugged. "Why not?" His gaze went to Alicia, sitting beside him, lingered, then he looked down the table at Adriana, seated beside Miranda. "The others should be arriving any minute." To Miranda, he explained, "We're holding a council of war, so to speak, in the library this afternoon, to discuss the latest developments in our search for A. C."

Miranda's eyes opened wide; she glanced at Alicia. "Is this a private meeting, or can I listen in?"

Tony grimaced. "All in all, it might be as well if you did."

A knock sounded on the front door, and he rose. He didn't trust A.C., not on any level; given Miranda was here with her girls, sharing his roof with Alicia and her family, it was only fair she knew the whole score.

He ushered the three ladies, all determined to attend the gathering, into the front hall as Hungerford opened the door. Members of the Bastion Club streamed in. Tony nodded in greeting; beside him, Miranda murmured, "Well, well—you didn't mention them. And they are?"

The introductions took a few minutes, by which time Tristan and Leonora, Geoffrey, and, most importantly, Jack Hendon and Kit, had arrived. Once everyone was comfortably seated in the library, the large room looked unusually full.

A knock fell on the front door; it opened. A deep voice, not Hungerford's, was heard. An instant later, the library door opened, and Charles walked in. Seeing all eyes on him, he raised his brows. "Am I late?"

Tony waved him to a chair. "I thought you were away."

"No such luck." Charles drew up a chair and sat. "Merely a visit to Surrey with my sisters, sisters-in-law, and dear mama. I got back"—he glanced at the clock—"two hours ago, but matters are so fraught in Bedford Square, I dared not remain. I took refuge at the club, and Gasthorpe told me of the meeting."

His dark gaze, along with a piratical smile, swept the room. "So, what do we have?"

Alicia followed that sweeping glance around the faces, saw in each an impatience, an eagerness, a determination to get on with the business of unmasking A.C. They were quite a crowd, five ladies and eight gentlemen, an intelligent and talented company focused on their common goal.

"So what did you find?" Tony's gaze rested on Jack Hendon.

Jack had settled on a straight-backed chair. "I got the information from Lloyd's, unfortunately not as much as I'd have liked. There's a watchman who goes around every half hour. I could only chance three passes—I had to put out the light every time he came by. Without it, I couldn't see to make copies of the bills of lading." He drew a sheaf of papers from his inside coat pocket. "I got the full details of six ships before I called it a night. However—"

He distributed the papers, handing three to the men on his right, three to his left; the ladies, on the two chaises perpendicular to the hearth, had to contain their curiosity until the men had scanned the pages and passed them their way.

"As you can see," Jack resumed, as the men finished with the papers and looked up, "there's nothing obvious, no particular goods or commodities that were carried on all six ships." He paused, then added. "I'm not sure where that gets us. I was assuming there would be something in common."

The men frowned; they looked at the six sheets, now in the ladies' hands.

"How did you choose which ships to examine?" Christian asked.

"More or less randomly over the years '12 to '15." Jack grimaced. "I thought that would be most useful, but now I wonder whether whatever's the crucial element changes over time. One thing for so many months, another later."

Gervase Tregarth leaned forward, peering at the lists Kit and Alicia had spread on a low table before the chaise. "Is there definitely no item in common?"

Kit, Alicia, and Leonora shook their heads.

One of the men muttered something about the seasons.

Alicia tapped an item on one list. "Three hundred ell of finest muslin. Remember how expensive muslin was?

The price is much better now, but when this was brought in, it would have been worth a small fortune."

"Hmm." Leonora studied the entry. "I never thought of it before—one simply grumbles and pays the price—but it must have been due to the war."

"Supply and demand," Kit said. They were speaking quietly, their lighter voices a counterpoint against the men's rumblings. "Jack says it's the merchants who best supply the demand who get on in business."

"True," Miranda put in, "and during the war, the demand was always there, never satisfied. Anything imported was by definition expensive. Just think how the prices of silks—"

"Let alone tea and coffee." Alicia tapped another entry on one list.

Miranda nodded; so did the others. "All those things became hideously dear. . . ." Her words faded.

Their gazes met. They all exchanged one long wondering glance, then looked at the lists.

"You don't think . . . ?" Adriana leaned nearer.

All five ladies bent over the lists again.

The gentlemen continued to reassess and revisit their reasoning, trying to see a way forward.

Alicia straightened. "That's it." She pointed triumphantly to items listed on each of the six bills of lading. "Tea and coffee!"

"Yes—*of course*!" Kit snatched up one of the lists and checked the entry, then reached for another.

"Ah—I see!" Leonora, face lighting, picked up another list.

Tony, Tristan, and Jack exchanged glances. "What do you see?" Tristan asked.

"The item in common." Alicia picked up another list and pointed to a line. "Tea—one thousands pounds of finest leaves from Assam."

Handing that list to Tony, she picked up another. "On

this one, it's coffee—three hundred pounds of best beans from Colombia."

Kit sat back. "So sometimes it's coffee, and sometimes it's tea—one from the West Indies, the other on ships from the East."

"But they're often both handled by the same merchant," Leonora informed the men as the lists made their way around the circle again. "Not necessarily sold through the same shops, but it's usually the same supplier."

"Which supplier?" Christian asked.

The ladies exchanged glances. "There are many, I imagine," Miranda replied. "It's a profitable area, and fashionable in its way."

"But it's the price that's so important." Alicia looked around the male company. "It's always difficult to get good-quality coffee and tea—there never is enough brought into the country, even now. As Kit said, it's supply and demand, so the price always remains high."

"For good quality," Adriana stressed.

"Indeed." Kit nodded. "And that, perhaps, is where A.C. might have made his money. During the war, certainly over the years '12 to '15, the price of tea and coffee—the better-quality stuff—fluctuated wildly. It was always high, but sometimes it reached astronomical heights."

"Because," Leonora took up the tale, "you men always insist on your coffee at the breakfast table, and we ladies, of course, must have our tea for our tea parties, and the ton wouldn't go around if those things weren't there."

There was an instant's silence as the men all stared at them.

"Are you saying"—Charles leaned forward and fixed them with an intent look—"that during the war, the price of tea and coffee was often driven high—very high—because of sudden shortages?"

All five ladies nodded decisively.

Miranda added, "Only the best-quality merchandise, mind you."

"Indeed. But tea and coffee—the finest quality—appears on each of those lists? One or the other at least?"

Again, the ladies nodded.

"That," Alicia concluded, "seems the only link—the only thing in common, so to speak."

"Held to ransom over our breakfasts." Gervase gathered the lists and shuffled through them. "Doesn't bear thinking of, but it certainly looks—and sounds—right."

Tristan was looking over his shoulder. "Two ships from the West Indies with coffee, the other four, all East Indiamen, carried tea."

"These prices." Jack fixed his wife with a questioning glance. "How much of an increase are we looking at—prices twice as high, three times?"

"For the best coffee?" Kit glanced at Leonora and Alicia. "Anything from ten, to even fifty times the usual price, I would say."

"For tea," Miranda said, "it could easily be from ten to thirty times the price before the war—and even that price was always high."

"How high?" Tristan asked.

The ladies pursed their lips, then tossed around figures that made the men blanch. "Good God!" Charles stopped, calculating. "Why that's . . ."

"One hell of a lot of money!" Jack growled.

"One hell of a lot of profit," Gervase said.

"One very good reason to ensure that the supply failed at critical times." Tony fixed the ladies with an inquisitorial look. "From what you're saying, the person who would stand to gain—"

"Is the merchant who had brought in a cargo of tea and coffee safely just before any shortage occurred."

It was Jack who had spoken. Tony looked at him. "Before?"

Jack nodded. "The warehouses and docks know when a ship and its cargo doesn't arrive, and the merchants mark up the prices of the goods they have in stock accordingly—that I know for fact."

"So . . ." They all sat and thought it over, then Tony called them to order. "Assuming the answer is tea and coffee, how do we go on from here?"

"We first check the waybills of the other ten ships we know were lost courtesy of Ruskin's information." Jack glanced at Tony. "Two of us, now we know what we're looking for, could probably check all the waybills at once."

Tony nodded. "We'll do it tonight."

"Meanwhile," Christian said, "the rest of us can start investigating the merchants who specialize in tea and coffee. The connection to A. C. must be through them." He frowned, then glanced around. "What could the connection between A. C. and a merchant be, given we know, or at least can surmise, that A. C. is one of the ton?"

Charles grimaced. "Can we surmise that, do you think? That he is one of us?"

"I think that's beyond question," Tony answered. "Who else would have known how to manipulate the ton against Alicia? And Dalziel confirmed that the third round of information against her had been laid through the most exclusive gentlemen's clubs. There seems little doubt A. C. is a member not just of the ton, but the haut ton—our circle." A memory floated through his mind; he grimaced. "Indeed, I suspect I've seen him."

"You have?"

"When?"

He briefly explained, describing the man he'd seen through the mists in Park Street all those nights ago.

"Astrakhan—you know, that's not all that common," Jack Warnefleet said. "A point to remember, especially if he didn't know you'd seen him."

"That leaves us still facing the final question," Christan said. "What link could there be between a tea and coffee merchant and a member of the haut ton?"

The room fell silent; only the ticking of the mantelpiece clock could be heard, then Charles looked at Tony. "It couldn't be *that*, could it—the reason behind Ruskin's murder?"

"It's certainly feasible." Tristan leaned back in his chair. "There's many in the ton would move heaven and earth to hide any contact with trade."

"Add to that the illegality involved, let alone its treasonous nature . . ." Gervase glanced around. "That's a powerful motive for removing Ruskin."

"And then going to *any* lengths to cover his tracks." Tony's gaze was fixed on Alicia.

There were slow nods all around. Charles leaned forward, hands clasped. "That's it—we might not yet be able to see the player, but that assuredly is the game. A. C. is directly involved in trade via some tea and coffee merchant."

Suddenly needing to move, Tony rose. Crossing to the fireplace, closer to Alicia, he braced an arm on the mantelpiece and looked around the circle. "Let's recapitulate. A. C. is at the very least a sleeping partner with a merchant who imports the finest tea and coffee. In order to increase profits by driving up prices, he sets out to manipulate the supply of tea and coffee through having ships carrying competitors' supplies taken by the French."

He looked at Jack Hendon. "How did he know which ships to target?"

Jack shrugged. "Easy enough if you're inside the trade. The merchants know each other, and each merchant usually has contracts with only one or at most two shipping lines, and the ships run by each line are listed in a number of registers, none hard to access. It wouldn't have been difficult."

Tony nodded. "So he knows which ships to target to

make his plan work. With the information from Ruskin, he knows when each returning ship will not be under frigate escort, and thus an easy and vulnerable target for a foreign captain."

His voiced hardened. "So A. C. arranges for the target ships to be taken, then sits back in London and counts the inflated return from the cargo he's already landed."

A long silence followed, then Christian straightened. "That's how it worked. We need to identify all possible merchants, then investigate which one had safe cargoes to exploit."

"And from there," Jack Warnefleet murmured, "we dig until we uncover A. C.—there'll be some track leading back to him, one way or another."

The soft menace in his tone was balm to them all.

Christian looked at Tony. "I'll act as coordinator in the search for the merchant, if you like." He glanced at the other members of the club. "We can take that on. I'll let you know the instant we identify the most likely firm."

Tony nodded. "I'll go with Jack tonight and confirm that the link holds good—if there's any ship taken that wasn't carrying tea or coffee, it might give us a link to another aspect of A. C.'s trade interests."

"True." Christian stood. "The more links we can get to A. C.'s trading activities, the easier it'll be to identify him conclusively."

The men rose. The ladies did, too, exchanging plans for meeting that evening at the balls they'd attend.

As the group emerged into the front hall, Charles paused beside Tony, his gaze uncharacteristically bleak. "You know, I might have understood if A. C.'s motive was in some way . . . well, patriotic even if grossly misguided. If he was the sort of traitor who sincerely believed England should lose the war and follow some revolutionary course. But be damned if I can understand how any Englishman could so cold-bloodedly have sent so many English sailors to almost certain death at the hands of the French"—he met Tony's gaze—"all for money."

Tony nodded. "That's one point that sticks in my craw."

Along with the fact A. C. had cast Alicia as his scape-goat.

Expressions grimly determined, they made their farewells and parted, all convinced of one thing. Whoever A. C. was, the man had no soul.

EIGHTEEN

"TAKE CARE!"

In the crush of Lady Carmody's ballroom, Alicia watched Kit lecture her handsome husband, then she turned on Tony, standing beside Alicia.

"And you, too. I suppose I feel responsible after pulling you out of the water all those years ago, but regardless, I would prefer not to have to come to some dockside Watch House and explain to the interested who you both are."

Tony raised his brows. "If we're caught, it'll be your husband's fault—I haven't been retired as long as he."

From the look on Kit's face, she didn't know whether to take umbrage on Jack's behalf or be more worried still. When no eruption ensued, Jack, behind her, glanced around at her face. Sliding his arm around her, he hugged her. "Stop worrying. I'll—we'll—be perfectly safe."

Alicia turned to Tony. She fixed him with her most severe look, the one guaranteed instantly to wring the truth from her brothers. "Is he speaking the truth? *Will* you be all right?"

Tony smiled; lifting her hand, he pressed a warm kiss into her palm. "There's no danger to speak of. Lloyd's is just a coffeehouse—easy pickings."

She wasn't entirely convinced and let it show; his smile deepened.

Glancing around at the jostling throng, at the many

gentlemen moving through its ranks, looking over the available ladies, he murmured, "I'm more concerned about you. Geoffrey will stay close, and Tristan and Leonora will meet you at the Hammonds', then Geoffrey will see you home." He met her gaze. "You face more danger than I." He added, pointedly, "Take care."

It was her turn to smile. "If worse comes to worst, I can always claim Sir Freddie's arm." And perhaps divert him from Adriana's side; the baronet remained assiduously attentive despite Adriana's hints.

Tony grimaced. Jack tapped him on the shoulder; he looked around.

"We'd better go." With a nod, Jack took his leave of her.

Tony's eyes returned to hers, lingered, then he released her hand and turned. With Jack, he moved into the crowd. They were taller than most, yet in seconds, neither Kit nor she could see them.

"Humph!" Kit pulled a face, and linked her arm in Alicia's. "We've been deserted." Surveying Adriana's circle, she set her chin. "This is far too tame—come on." She set off into the crowd, drawing Alicia with her. "Let's find some useful distraction. I don't know about you, but without it, I'll go mad."

Alicia laughed, and let herself be towed into the melée.

Gaining access to the records they sought wasn't quite as easy as Tony had painted it, yet soon enough he and Jack were flicking through files in the offices above the coffee house, searching for, then poring over the bills of lading lodged for the other ten ships Ruskin had identified and which were subsequently taken.

While he worked, Tony's mind revisited their logic, their strategies. "The connection had better not be through Lloyd's itself."

"Unlikely," Jack answered from across the room. "As far as I know, they've never handled tea."

Half an hour later, Tony wondered aloud, "In all of

this"—he waved at the cabinets ringing the room—"do you think there's any chance of identifying ships that docked with cargoes of tea or coffee say in the week before one that was taken?"

Jack looked up, then shook his head. "Needle in a haystack. Virtually every ship that passes through the Port of London will have a waybill in here. That's often hundreds a day. We'd never be able to check enough to identify the ship we want."

He resumed his searching. "Mind you, we *will* be able to confirm the link once we know the merchant and his shipping line."

Tony nodded, and continued flipping through files.

It took them two hours to locate and examine the ten waybills. Then they quietly put the room to rights, eradicating any sign of their visit, and silently retreated from the room and the building.

By the time Tony reached Upper Brook Street, Mayfair was silent, the streets dark with shadows. Miranda, Adriana, and Alicia would have returned home long ago. They should all be asleep in their beds.

Closing the front door, he shot the well-oiled bolts, then crossed the hall. There was no lamp or candle left burning; Hungerford knew him better than that. Quite aside from his excellent night vision, he knew this house like the back of his hand, knew every creak in the stairs, every board that might groan.

At the top of the stairs, he turned away from the gallery leading to the east wing where Miranda, her daughters, and Adriana had their rooms, and headed for the room Alicia had been given, three doors from the master suite. Hand on the doorknob, he paused, struck by a sudden thought.

How had Mrs. Swithins known . . . ?

The answer was obvious. He really was *that* transparent.

Grimacing, he turned the knob.

Alicia was in bed, but not asleep. Cocooned beneath the luxurious embroidered silk coverlet, silk sheets sliding seductively over her skin, she'd been waiting for the past hour, waiting to at least hear Tony's footsteps, passing her door . . . or not, as the case might be.

Unable to sleep, made edgy by her own expectation—that he would come to her, that she wanted him to, even needed him to—an expectation she found somewhat damning—she was after all in his house, an old aristocratic mansion, yet while that fact might inhibit her, she doubted it would influence him—she had forcibly turned her mind to reviewing the day. A long day in which much had happened, and much had changed.

So easily.

That more than anything else, the ease with which the changes had been wrought, the ease with which she'd simply *flowed* into the position he'd created for her, niggled. In some odd way seemed to mock her. Everything had fallen into place so smoothly, she was still struggling to come to grips with the ramifications. As if he'd once more swept her off her feet, and her head had yet to stop whirling.

Not, for her, an uncommon feeling where he was concerned.

It wasn't that she wished things were otherwise; she couldn't convincingly argue against the move, not even to herself. But the uncertainty, the lack of clarity regarding her position here—the lack of sureness made it impossible to feel confident, at ease . . .

She never heard his footsteps; only a faint draft alerted her to the opening door. He was no more than a dark shadow slipping through; she recognized him instantly.

Her eyes had adjusted to the dimness; watching him cross the wide room toward her, she searched his face, all she could see of him, but could detect not even a limp.

Kit's worry had infected her, yet here he was unscathed, moving with his usual fluid grace toward the bed.

He stopped by a chair and sat, reaching down to pull off his boots. She sat up, wriggling in the sheets onto her side; he heard the shushing and glanced across, smiled a touch wearily.

"Did you find the lists? From the other ships?"

He nodded. Setting his boots aside, he stood, stretched. "We found all ten—your theory was right. It's tea and coffee that's the link."

He lowered his arms, weary tension falling from him.

She watched him undress—coat, cravat, waistcoat, and shirt hit the chair. Realizing her mouth was dry, she swallowed, forced her gaze to his face. "So now we have to look for the merchant."

He nodded, looking down, bending down as he stripped off his trousers. "With all of us involved, that won't take long." Straightening, he grimaced. "Maybe a week." He flung the trousers at the chair, then turned to the bed.

Her pulse leapt. "So we're one step away from identifying A. C?"

"One step." Lifting the covers, he slid in beside her. Dropping them, he turned to her. Framed her face with his hands and kissed her.

Deeply, thoroughly, druggingly . . . until she was swept away, her mind whirling on a sensual tide.

Leaving one hand cupping her jaw, with the other Tony reached down and tugged the sheet from between them, then settled his body against hers. Letting the sheets fall, he plundered her soft mouth while with his palm he traced the long, smooth curve from her shoulder, over the supple planes of her back to the swell of her bottom, molding her to him, easing her beneath him, spurred by the realization that her skin was already warm, by the immediate leap of her pulse to the caress, the dewed flush that spread over the silken skin of her bottom, the evidence of her arousal he discovered when he pressed his hand down between them, slid his fingers between her thighs, and found her.

Ready, waiting, urgent for him.

He pressed her back into the bed, parted her thighs with his and filled her, surged slowly into her, taking his time, glorying in the ease with which he could forge in, in the way she tilted her hips and took him deep, to the fluid harmony with which they then moved, sliding into the dance their bodies now knew so well.

A different dance to any he'd enjoyed with any other woman.

Mouths melded, tongues tangling, hot yet languid, their bodies moved, merged, flexed to a rhythm that held a deeper tune, a more powerful cadence.

A heady, dizzying delight, a pleasure that soared higher and reached deeper, that slid past their slick skins, through muscle and bone, past straining sinews and tightening nerves to their cores. To touch, sink into, and hold something there.

Something precious, fragile, yet strong enough to fuse their hearts.

He sensed it before they'd even started to scale the peak. Their bodies held, thrummed with, a driving urgency, yet they had the strength to dally—neither was in any rush, delighting instead in every small touch, each delicate caress.

Slowly, powerfully, he rode her, feeling her body surrender and take him in, feeling the heat of her draw him deeper, tempting him further into her fire. He went, but kept the reins firmly in his hands, as always orchestrating the moment; after all these years, pleasuring women was all but second nature.

Gradually, the tempo built. Beneath him, her body rose, meeting his, matching his, urging him on. Her fingers, on his back, tensed, nails lightly scoring. Without easing the steadily escalating rhythm, he drew back from the kiss, through the dimness studied her face; her eyes were closed, her lips swollen and parted, telltale concentration etched in every line.

He thrust deeper, harder, and she gasped, her body arching greedily under his.

Lifting his shoulders a fraction farther, enough to appreciate the way her body, all sumptuous curves and hot flushed skin, undulated with each thrust, absorbed each forceful penetration as he rode her, filled her, he watched as he pushed her step by slow step closer to sensual fulfillment.

He felt the tension inside her coil, felt her tighten beneath him, her thighs gripping his flanks as release flickered and beckoned. Her ragged breathing filled his ears, a softer sound overlaying his own raspy breaths.

She reached for him, tried to pull him down to her.

Without breaking their rhythm, he shifted his hips, pressing more intimately between hers, then thrust deeper still, harder still.

She gasped, tugged, but the sight of her held him. Eventually lifting his gaze to her face, he saw the glimmer of her eyes beneath her lashes.

Alicia studied his face, licked her lips, felt her world teeter. She was so close to that joyous edge, yet, as always since that first engagement, no matter how desperate the moment, he held to his control, waiting, watching, certain to follow her, yet still . . .

"Come with me." She struggled to find breath enough to add, "Now."

His black eyes, until then hooded, opened wide—enough for her to realize she'd asked something no other ever had.

Her nerves shivered, started to unravel. Dragging in a breath, she lifted a hand to his face, traced his cheek. "*Be* with me. Please."

She wasn't sure how, but she knew what she wanted. Needed.

He knew, too. He gave a shuddering sigh; the tension rippling through him increased, hardening his body as it rode against hers, thrust into hers.

Their gazes remained locked. He shifted his weight, freed a hand, held it open close by her head. "Give me your hand."

She did, shifting her hand from his face, watching as he interdigitated his fingers with hers, then closed them, locking their palms. Then he pressed their linked hands into the pillow.

"Wrap your legs about my waist."

She could barely make out the gravelly command. The silk sheets caressed her skin as she complied, then gasped as he shifted fully over her and drove deep. Her spine bowed, but his weight pinned her, held her down as his hips flexed in a faster, more urgent, more compulsive rhythm.

For an instant, gasping and breathless, she rode it, then she felt his eyes on her face, met his black gaze, once again screened. Felt the flames inside rise, coalesce, fuse to an inferno.

He lowered his head, drove into her harder, faster, more powerfully.

"Now." He breathed the word against her lips, then took them, took her mouth as the conflagration roared— and caught them. Overwhelmed them. Consumed them.

As one. Together, as she'd asked.

Tony felt the reins he'd released whip away, sensed them cinder, all control sundered and gone. For only the second time in his life, he plunged into the heart of that familiar fire *with* a woman, by her side. Her hand was his anchor; he clung to it as her body tightened beneath his, closed powerfully around his, hot, scalding, driving him on, taking him with her into the world beyond the flames, into the pleasure of sexual satiation.

If she wished, so he would; they whirled, joined more intimately than he'd ever been with any other, not just their bodies but their awarenesses fused, experiencing together, simultaneously soaring. Higher, then yet higher.

Until they were both gasping, bodies locked and straining. Until they were there, twined together at the peak.

Until they fell, hearts thundering, senses merged, glory pouring through them. Souls as one.

She was his. Totally, completely, beyond recall.

The words drifted of their own volition across Alicia's brain.

Her body, trapped beneath his, thighs vulnerably wide with him buried so deep inside her, was no longer hers.

Her lips curved in sleepy satisfaction. No matter her thoughts, her will, her determination, logic had no place here. Despite all uncertainty, despite the nebulous unease that even now she could sense, a fog hovering just beyond the bed, even now, despite all, her heart rejoiced.

Lifting the hand he hadn't claimed, she laid it on his hair, then gently stroked. Let her fingers play among the silky strands.

Let her emotions have their way.

Let them well, and fill her mind, fill her throat and her chest, fill her heart, and overflow. Let them slide through her veins and sink into her flesh, a part of her, forever.

He lay heavy upon her; she delighted in his weight. Within her, the warmth of his seed radiated a glow of deep and abiding pleasure. She'd given him all she was; tonight, he'd taken, claimed, but when she'd wanted and needed, he had surrendered and given, too.

No matter what else the days might bring, tonight, he'd been with her.

As totally hers as she'd been his.

The gentle tangling of Alicia's fingers in his hair drew Tony back to earth. To a world that was almost as wonderful as the one they'd visited; her body was a sensual cushion beneath him, her breasts beneath his chest, her hips and thighs cradling his, their bodies still intimately joined.

He was more comfortable than he'd ever thought to be, not just in body but on all other levels. Physically, mentally, emotionally, he was at peace, at home in her arms. Where he was meant to be.

His satisfaction was so profound it was frightening. It lay like a golden sea about him, deep, timeless, ageless, weighing on his limbs, soothing his mind, infinitely precious.

Eyes closed, he savored it, held it, let its waves lap about him—and tried not to think of ever losing it.

Eventually, he felt forced to stir, to draw back from that contented sea. Lifting from Alicia, he ignored her sleepy protest; she seemed as addicted to the moment as he. Settling beside her, he drew her to him, against him, brushing aside her long hair so he could see her face. He looked into her eyes, shadowed pools, mysterious in the night.

Marry me tomorrow.

The words burned his tongue; all the reasons he shouldn't say them—not yet—doused them. Instead, bending his head, he touched his lips to hers, and spoke from his heart.

"Je t'aime." He breathed the words across her lips; closing his eyes, he tasted them. *"Je t'adore."*

He wasn't even conscious of speaking in French; it had always been the language of love to him.

She touched his cheek, returned his kiss, soft, clinging.

Their lips parted; he drew breath, softly asked, "Is everything here as you wish? If there's anything you need—"

She stopped him, laying her fingers across his lips. "There's nothing—everything's perfect." She hesitated, then added, "I like your house."

They were speaking in whispers, as if not to disturb the

blanket of shared pleasure that still surrounded them. It was the deepest part of the night, the small hours of the morning, yet neither was sleepy. Sated, content, they lay in each other's arms, limbs tangled, hands occasionally touching, brushing, stroking.

Time drifted, and with it the tide of their loving. It slowly turned. Returned. Alicia didn't think, but simply flowed with it, knew he did the same.

Effortless. Their communication in that moment needed no words, no careful phrases. It was carried by their hands, their lips, mouths, tongues, every square inch of their bodies.

They moved over and around, worshipping, first one, then the other. Pleasure bloomed, ecstasy blossomed.

He opened her eyes to pleasures she hadn't imagined, sensual delights beyond her ken. In turn, she set aside her inhibitions and let instinct and his guttural murmurs of appreciation guide her.

When at last they joined and again crested the final peak, and found the now-familiar splendor waiting, they were again together, senses open yet wholly merged, deliberately and completely one.

Later, when they lay spent, exhausted, in each other's arms, Alicia heard his words echo in her mind. *I love you. I adore you.*

She wondered if he'd understood her reply.

Tony sank toward sleep, sated to his toes, his mind unfocused. Thoughts drifted, melted into the fogs as they closed in.

He'd told her he loved her, had said the words aloud. He'd surprised himself; he'd always imagined they would be so hard to say.

They'd slipped out, almost without conscious direction, a statement of fact with which he had no argument.

So easy. Now all that remained was to organize their wedding.

They were one step away from identifying A. C. One step away from being free to face their future, to give it their full and undivided attention.

If he had his way—and he was determined he would—the next time they indulged as they just had, they would be in his big bed at Torrington Chase, and Alicia would be his wife.

The following days passed in a frenzy of activity—social commitments on the one hand, covert investigation on the other.

To Alicia's relief, the staff at Torrington House truly were, as Tony had told her, delighted to have three boys rampaging through the house. Once she realized how safe, secure, and cared for the boys now were, with so many benevolently watchful eyes on them, she relaxed her vigilance—one item she didn't need to worry over.

She had plenty of others on her plate.

One was a lovers' spat between Adriana and Geoffrey. It blew over in twenty-four hours, but left Alicia, the recipient of both principals' outpourings, feeling battered. The event precipitated the long-desired meeting between Geoffrey, Adriana, and herself. She and Adriana made their financial situation crystal clear; Geoffrey looked at them as if they were mad, and then asked why they'd thought he would care. Without waiting for an answer, he formally offered for Adriana's hand. Adriana, somewhat stunned by his unwavering singlemindedness, accepted him.

Alicia retired, pleased, relieved, but wrung out. They all agreed that any announcement should wait until Geoffrey had written to his mother in Devon and taken Adriana to meet her. On all other counts, Alicia felt justified in leaving them to plan their own future.

When, later that night, she regaled Tony with a description of the meeting, he laughed, amused. Later still, when she was lying sated and warm in his arms, he murmured, "Did you tell him you weren't a widow?"

"No." He sounded serious; she glanced up. "Should I have?"

He was fiddling with a lock of her hair; he met her gaze, after a moment, replied, "There's no need to tell anyone, not anymore. It doesn't concern anyone but you and me."

She considered, then resettled her cheek on his chest. She listened to his heart beating strongly, steadily, and told herself all was well.

Only it wasn't.

It took her until her fourth day in Torrington House to realize what was wrong, what was increasingly troubling her, converting nebulous unease into a more tangible fear.

In addition to Hungerford's delight at her presence, the open acceptance by the *grandes dames* and hostesses of her sojourn in Upper Brook Street had allayed her concerns on one score. Contrary to her beliefs, it clearly was acceptable for a nobleman's mistress to reside openly under his roof, in certain circumstances. She assumed the ameliorating circumstances included that she was a fashionable widow of whom society approved, that Miranda was present, and that A. C. had attempted to use her as his scapegoat.

Regardless, her initial fears on that point had proved groundless; society took her relocation in its stride. So did everyone else—except her.

Only she was having difficulties, and that in a way she hadn't foreseen. At first, when Miranda had consulted her over this and that, deferring to her suggestions on the menus, the maids, the day-to-day decisions of managing the large household, she'd assumed Miranda was merely trying to ensure she felt at home.

But on the third morning, Miranda threw up her hands. "Oh, stuff and nonsense—this is all so silly. You're hardly an innocent miss with no experience. Here"—she thrust the menus at her—"it's only right and proper *you* should be handling this, and you don't need my help."

With a brilliant smile, Miranda rose, swung her skirts about, and left her to deal with Mrs. Swithins alone. Which, after swallowing her amazement, she did; it was transparent Mrs. Swithins fully expected her to.

From that point, the servants openly deferred to her. From that minute she became, in all reality bar the legal fact, the lady of Torrington House.

Tony's wife.

It was a position she'd never thought to fill; now, she found herself living it. Bad enough. The associated development that transformed the situation into a deeply disturbing, unsettling experience was something she not only hadn't foreseen, but hadn't even dreamed of.

On the fourth morning, the truth hit her like a slap.

Since she'd moved into his house, Tony left her bed only minutes before the maids started their rounds. That morning, she rose from her disarranged couch, only to feel the dragging effects of real tiredness. The first weeks of the Season were packed with entertainments, morning, noon, and night; she, Adriana, and Miranda had attended six events the day before.

When Bertha appeared, she retreated to the bed, and let the little maid tidy away her evening gown. "We've a luncheon at two o'clock—I'll dress for that, but now I'm going to rest. Please tell Mrs. Althorpe and my sister that I'm still sleeping." If they had any sense, they'd be doing the same.

Bertha murmured sympathetically, efficiently tidied, then with a last whispered inquiry if she wished for anything else, which Alicia denied, the maid whisked out.

Left in blissful peace, Alicia snuggled down, closed her eyes. She expected to fall asleep, there was after all no urgent matter awaiting her attention, nothing she need worry about . . .

Her mind emptied, cleared—and the truth was suddenly there, abruptly revealed, rock-solid and absolute. Inescapable and undeniable.

Being the lady of Torrington House was the future her heart truly craved.

The revelation rocked her.

Lying back in the bed, she stared up at the silk canopy and tried to understand. Herself. How, why . . . when had she changed?

The answers trickled into her mind. She hadn't changed, but never before had she allowed herself to think of what she wanted for her own life; she'd spent her life organizing the lives of others, and had deliberately spared no thought for her own. Intentional self-blindness; she knew why she'd done it—it had been easier that way. The wrench of sacrificing dreams . . . one never had to face that deadening choice if one never allowed oneself to dream at all.

Looking back at her younger self, to when she'd made that decision . . . she'd done it to protect her heart against the harsh reality she, even in her relative naïveté, had foreseen. But she was no longer that naive young girl trembling, trepidatious and alone, on the threshold of womanhood, weighed down by responsibilites and cares.

She hadn't changed so much as grown. She was now experienced, assured. Her own actions in formulating and successfully carrying out her plan, and all that had flowed through her association with Tony, had opened her eyes, not just to what might be, but even more powerfully to who she was and what lay within her. Her own strengths, her own will, her abilities.

Beneath all ran a belief, a conviction, in her right to her own life—and a determination, quiet, until now unrecognized and unstated but definitely there, to seize what she wanted.

With the position of Tony's wife hers in all but name . . . the role fitted her like a glove, soothed her by its rightness, fulfilled some deep-seated yearning, an un-realized but essential, fundamental part of her.

That was what she wanted.

Her breath caught; a vise tightened about her heart. Her determination didn't waver.

Yet she was his mistress, not his wife.

He'd said he loved her. Her French was not good—she'd never had time to do more than learn the rudiments; he often murmured phrases during their lovemaking that she couldn't make out, yet she felt confident she hadn't misheard or mistaken those particular words.

She even believed them, or at least believed that he believed them.

What he *meant* by them was another matter.

Marriage had never been part of their arrangement. Just because she now yearned for it, wanted it—and not just because he got along so well with her brothers and had the wherewithal and character to guide and support them precisely as she'd always wished—just because she now realized that marrying him would satisfy every dream she'd never allowed herself to have, she couldn't now turn back the clock.

Couldn't now expect him to think in those terms just because her eyes had been opened. Shouldn't be so naive as to read too much into a simple declaration of love. Pretending to herself would be the ultimate folly, the ultimate way to break her heart.

When Bertha returned at one o'clock, she rose, washed, and dressed. Calmly serene, she went downstairs and threw herself into the social round.

A note arrived from Christian Allardyce just as Tony was about to embark on another round of balls and parties at Alicia's side. Also gathered in his front hall waiting for the coach to be brought around were Adriana, Geoffrey, and Miranda. Lady Castlereagh's was to be their first port of call.

Tony scanned the note. Christian wrote to suggest they should meet at the Bastion Club to review progress. Tony surmised that the others—Christian, Charles, Tristan, Gervase, Jack Warnefleet, and even Jack Hendon—were keen to use the investigation as an excuse to avoid their social obligations.

Even with Alicia's presence as reward, he, too, felt the temptation. For men of their ilk, balls were boring, pointless, and severely drained their never very deep reserves of civility. They'd spent the last decade avoiding fools—why change their ways now? ·

Noting Alicia, beside him, watching him, he handed her the note. While she read it, he glanced at Geoffrey. If it hadn't been for the little chat they'd had that afternoon, he'd be irritated by Geoffrey's and Adriana's total absorption in the how and where of their nuptials; luckily, Geoffrey had had no argument with his assertion that he and Alicia should marry first, even if by no more than a week.

Given the way Geoffrey was watching over Adriana, as if determined now he'd won her no other would get close, it was clear he, at least, would resist the lure of the investigation.

Tony turned to Alicia as she looked up from the note.

"Are you going?"

He looked into her green eyes, hesitated. "If you would prefer I escort you to the balls tonight, I can put off the meeting until tomorrow."

She looked at him steadily; he couldn't tell what she was thinking. Then she glanced down at the note. "But that would mean actions that could be instigated tomorrow if you met tonight would be delayed, wouldn't it?"

She looked up again. He nodded. Put like that, it was almost incumbent upon him to leave her to Geoffrey's care and devote his attention to unmasking A. C. Still he hesitated, not liking the fact he couldn't follow her thoughts, or see her feelings in her eyes. He usually could. "Are you sure? Geoffrey will stay with you—"

She smiled, confident, and assured. "Yes, of course. Indeed, I'm sure we're starting to be the butt of comments about being forever in each other's pockets." Turning to Miranda, she caught her eye. "Tony's been called away—I'm assuring him we'll be perfectly happy with just Geoffrey as escort."

"Oh, indeed!" Miranda flicked her hand at him. "Go, go!" She grinned, a devilish light in her eye. "I assure you Alicia and I will be *excellently* well entertained."

She meant it in purely teasing vein, yet the barb slipped under Tony's guard and pricked. He glanced at Alicia; turning to him, she gave him her hand.

"I'll bid you a good night, then. I daresay we'll be home long before you get back." She raised her gaze to his face, but not as far as his eyes.

A sudden chill touched him.

Having heard his name and ascertained from Miranda what was going on, Geoffrey turned to him. "Don't worry, I'll bring them all safely back at the end of Lady Selkirk's affair." Meeting Tony's gaze, he quietly added, "Send word tomorrow morning if there's anything I can help with."

Tony nodded. He released Alicia's hand to shake Geoffrey's. When he looked back, he found she'd turned away and was embroiled in a discussion with Adriana.

There seemed no reason to dally. "I'll leave you, then." He made the comment general; with a single nod for everyone, he headed for the door.

What he learned at the club drove all other thoughts temporarily from his mind.

"We've narrowed the field to three possibilities." As he'd suggested, Christian had acted as a central contact, compiling and disseminating information as the others brought it in. They'd all been involved, but in order to keep things moving, they'd simply reported, then got on with the next task, and left Christian to make sense of the whole. This was the first time they'd all gathered since the meeting in Tony's library—the first time they'd heard the results to date.

"Between them, Jack"—Christian nodded at Jack Warnefleet—"and Tristan came up with a list of tea and coffee merchants they've since verified as exhaustive."

"Can one ask how?" Charles asked.

Jack Warnefleet grinned. "Not if you want details. But I'm sure those merchants would be amazed at how much their wives, especially their competitors' wives, know."

"Ah!" Charles turned a limpid glance on Tristan.

Who smiled. "I left that endeavor to Jack. My contribution was verifying the information via the appropriate guilds. By a sleight of argument, I convinced the guild secretaries that I needed to examine their registers for cases of accidental cross-listings, where coffee merchants had been listed as tea merchants, and vice versa."

"Which naturally left you with a list of those who were both. Very nice." Charles looked back up the table.

"The list comprised twenty-three companies," Christian continued. "We eliminated those we know lost cargoes, assuming no merchant is going to send a precious cargo to France just to cover his tracks. That took twelve names out—some of the sixteen ships carried cargoes for the same merchant."

"Poor beggars," Jack Hendon said. "Knowing how close some of them sail to the wind, I'd be surprised if none have gone bankrupt."

"Some have," Gervase answered. "Yet more damage to add to A. C.'s account."

Tony stirred. "So that left us with eleven companies."

Christian nodded. "Courtesy of you all and your chameleon like talents, passing yourselves off as potential coffee-shop proprietors and the like, not to mention your ability to tell barefaced lies, by focusing on who had stock after the last A. C.-induced shortage, we've ended with three names—three merchants. All had stock to sell when the price last soared, and even though that incident was nearly a year ago, we have enough corroboration to conclude that *only* those three had stock to sell at that time."

A general hubbub ensued, centering on whether there was any easy way to narrow the list further.

Tony didn't contribute; reaching out, he took the sheet lying in front of Christian and read the names. "So," his voice fell into the lull as the prospect of a simple next step faded, "A. C. is associated with one of these three."

"Yes, *but*," Christian stressed, "two of the three are not involved. Given what we'll need to do to ferret out a hidden partner, we need to be absolutely certain which of the three it is before we move in."

Tony nodded. "If we get it wrong, we'll alert A. C., and given his record in covering his tracks, all we'll find is another corpse."

Jack Warnefleet sat forward. "So how do we pinpoint the right merchant?"

"The right merchant landed cargoes before each prize was taken." Tony looked across the table at Jack Hendon. "You said once we had a merchant's shipping line, we could verify the safe landing of A. C.'s cargo via the records at Lloyd's. We have three merchants—if we learn which shipping lines they use, could we check all three lines for safe landings in the relevant weeks preceding each prize-taking, and check the cargoes landed?"

Jack held his gaze for a long moment, then asked, "How much time do we have?"

"By my calculation, not a lot. A. C.'s been quiet for nearly a week, but he must know we haven't given up. He'll try something else to deflect the investigation—he won't succeed, but the faster we can conclude it, the better." Tony paused, then added, "Who knows what he might do next?"

It was a point on which he tried not to speculate, yet it

hovered in his mind, a constant threat. To Alicia, to him, to their future.

Jack was thinking, calculating—glancing around the table, he nodded. "Given our number, it's possible. And it might be the best way. The first thing we need to learn is which shipping lines those three companies use, but to do that without alerting the companies, you'll need to ask the shipping lines."

"Can you do that?" Christian asked.

"Not me. As the owner of Hendon Shipping, the instant I start asking questions like that, there'll be hell to pay."

"No matter." Charles shrugged. "You tell us what answers we need, and what questions will best elicit them, and leave it to us."

"Right."

"Easy enough."

The others nodded. It was Tony who asked, "How many shipping lines are there?"

Jack met his gaze. "Seventy-three."

When the others stopped groaning, Jack continued, "I'll put a list together tonight—we can meet here first thing tomorrow. If we push, we should get the information by evening, and then"—he met Tony's gaze again—"we'll first need to get access to the shipping registers and get the ships' names, then we'll revisit Lloyd's. We'll be able to find the answer—which company A. C. is behind—there."

Tony returned Jack's gaze, then nodded. "Let's do it."

NINETEEN

THE NEXT DAY WAS CHAOTIC.

Six members of the Bastion Club attired as no gentleman would normally be met with Jack Hendon in the club's meeting room at eight o'clock. Over breakfast, they divided his list on the basis of the location of the shipping lines' offices, then each took a section and set out. They were masquerading as merchants, all appearing older and a great deal more conservative than they were.

Whoever discovered a link between any of the three merchants and a shipping line would send a messenger back to Jack at the club. They'd decided against calling a halt until all seventy-three shipping lines had been assessed; there was always the possibility that a merchant used more than one, especially if that merchant had something to hide.

Tony had taken a group of fourteen offices congregated around Wapping High Street. Charles, who had drawn the area next to that, shared a hackney down to the docks. They parted, and Tony began his search for a reliable shipping line to bring tea from his uncle's plantations in Ceylon. Once he had a shipping manager keen to secure his fictitious uncle's fictitious cargo, it was easy to ask for references in the form of other tea merchants the line had run cargoes for in the last few years.

By eleven o'clock, he'd visited six offices, and scored

one hit. One line which, so the manager believed, had an exclusive contract with one of their three merchants.

Tony stopped in a tavern to refresh himself with a pint. Sitting at a table by a window, he sipped and looked out. He appeared to be watching the handcarts and drays and the bustling human traffic thronging the street; in reality, he saw none of it, his mind turned inward to more personal vistas.

Things had started to move; the pace always escalated toward the end of a chase. They'd soon have A. C., or at least his name. Dalziel would have his man; Tony would take great delight in delivering him personally.

He needed to keep his eye on the game, yet the very fact it was nearing its apogee had him thinking of what came next. Of Alicia and him, and their future life.

The closer the prospect drew, the more it commanded his attention, the more sensitive to threats to it he became. Last night in the hall, he'd been touched by premonition, by an unfocused, unspecific belief that something was wrong, or at least not right. Something in the way Alicia had reacted had pricked his instincts.

Yet when he'd returned home just after midnight, it was to find the others already back, and Alicia waiting for him in her bed. Explaining that they'd all wished for an early night, she'd encouraged him to tell her all he'd learned; she'd listened, patently interested, to their plans.

Then he'd joined her under the covers and she'd turned to him, welcomed him into her arms, into her body with her usual open and generous ardor. No hesitation, no holding back. No retreat.

When he'd left this morning, she'd still been asleep. He'd brushed a kiss to her lips and left her dreaming.

Perhaps that was all it was—that the social round, now frenetic, combined with the stress of watching over Adriana, was simply wearying her. God knew, it would weary him. When he'd returned to her last night, there'd been no sign of whatever he'd detected earlier, that slight disjunction that had seemed to exist between them.

He spent another five minutes slowly sipping his ale, then downed the rest in two swallows. He had eight more shipping lines to investigate. The sooner they could bring A. C.'s game to a conclusion, the better for them all.

Tony got back to the Bastion Club just after three o'clock. He was one of the last to return; the others were lounging around the table in the meeting room with Jack Hendon waiting impatiently for his report.

"Please say you've found a line working for Martinsons," Jack demanded before Tony could even pull out a chair.

He sat and tossed his list on the table. "Croxtons in Wapping have, so the manager assures me, an exclusive contract."

"Thank God for that." Jack wrote the name down. "I was beginning to think our plan would go awry. We've identified two shipping lines for Drummond, one from the east, one from the west, reasonable in the circumstances, and four—two in each direction—for Ellicot. Croxton runs ships both east and west, so Martinsons can indeed use them exclusively. Now"—he looked down his list—"all we need is for Gervase to confirm none of the three—Martinsons, Ellicot, or Drummond—use any other line."

But when Gervase came striding in fifteen minutes later, it was with different news. "Tatleys and Hencken both carry goods for Ellicot."

They all looked at him; Gervase slowly raised his brows. "What?"

"You're sure?" Jack asked. When Gervase nodded, he opened his eyes wide. "That's six shippers who carry Ellicot's goods, and two of those lines run ships to both the East and West Indies."

Tony caught Jack's eye. "Is it wise to place any great emphasis on that?"

Jack grimaced. "No, but it's tempting. If you wanted to disguise any pattern in shipping around the dates the prizes were taken, then the use of multiple lines and therefore different ships for each safe cargo brought in would totally obscure any link."

"The most likely people to check any connection would be the Admiralty," Gervase said, "yet their records show only the ships and shipping lines. There's no way to detect a link that exists at the level of cargo."

Tony frowned. "Customs and Revenue have records of the cargoes, but even there, the records are sorted by ports, and different lines use different home ports."

"So," Charles said, "this was an extremely well-set-up scheme. It's only because we used Lloyd's that we've been able to put things together."

"Which leads one to conclude," Christian said, "that the scheme's perpetrator knows the administrative ropes well. He knows how the civil services work and which avenues to block."

"We'll still get him." Jack had been reexamining his list. "We have nine shipping lines—more than I'd like, but seven are small. We now need a list of all the vessels each has registered."

"Can we get that before tonight?" Tony asked.

Jack glanced at the clock on the sideboard, then pushed back his chair. "We can but try."

"I'll help." Gervase rose, too. "I know the business well enough to deal with the intricacies of the registers."

"You two concentrate on getting a list of the ships' names," Tony said. "We'll take care of the rest."

Jack and Gervase left, conferring as they went. The others turned to Tony.

"Once we have the list of ships," he said, "we're going to have to search Lloyd's records. We need to identify which merchant consistently brought in a cargo in, say, the week before a prize was taken. Searching in the weeks before three separate incidents should give us one name and one only. If not, we can look at a fourth incident, but chances are three incidents will give us only one merchant who fits our bill."

The others nodded.

"Once we know the particular merchant involved, we should confirm that in each case they did indeed bring in tea or coffee."

"Can we do all that via Lloyd's?" Charles asked.

"Yes. If Jack and Gervase get the ships' names by this evening, I'll revisit Lloyd's tonight."

"I'll come, too" Charles said. "There's this horrendous ball my sisters want to drag me to—I'd much rather hone my filing skills."

"You can count me in," Jack Warnefleet said. "I've never had to track anyone through such a maze before."

They made arrangements to meet later that night.

Only Tristan demurred. "I'll keep a watch on things in the ballrooms. Having had the good sense to get married, I, at least, am safe from the harpies."

Charles grimaced. "Half your luck. I don't know how you managed it so quickly—and now look at Tony. You're both safe. What I want to know is how long *I'm* going to remain dead center in the matchmakers' sights. It's deuced harrowing, I'll have you know."

Both Tony and Tristan made sympathetic noises. The mood of teasing camaraderie disguising their implacable resolve, the meeting broke up and they each headed home.

Tony found Alicia in the garden.

Admitted to the house by Hungerford, he'd slipped upstairs and changed into more normal attire before setting out to search for her.

She was walking alone; Hungerford had told him the

boys were in the park—it was a perfect day for kites. It seemed odd to find Alicia by herself; pensive, head down, deep in thought, she slowly, apparently aimlessly, wandered the lawn.

He watched from the terrace—Torrington House was centuries old, the gardens stretching behind it extensive—then went down the steps and set out to join her. She didn't hear him; not wanting to frighten her by suddenly appearing beside her, he called her name.

Halting, she swung around and smiled. She straightened as he neared. "Did you learn anything?"

He would have taken her in his arms and kissed her, but she held out a hand; the swift glance she cast at the house was a warning.

Reluctantly bowing to her wishes, he took her hand and raised it to his lips. Kissed it, then, noting that her smile had faded, an expression he couldn't read taking its place, he tucked her hand in his arm, anchored it with his. He let a frown show in his eyes. "What's wrong?"

She blinked her eyes wide. "Wrong? Why . . . nothing." She frowned lightly back. "Why did you think there was?"

Because . . .

He felt confused, not a normal feeling, not for him. The expression in her eyes assured him she honestly didn't think anything was wrong, yet . . .

She shook his arm and started to stroll again. "*Did* you learn anything? What has Jack been up to—I met Kit at Lady Hartington's luncheon, and she said he was out, too, looking for A. C.'s connections."

He nodded. "We've all been out for most of the day."

He explained. Alicia listened, put a question here and there, and continued to reiterate to herself: *You are his mistress, his lover, not his wife.*

That, she'd decided, was the only sane way forward, to keep their relationship on a fixed and even keel. If she let herself get seduced—emotionally seduced by her emerging dreams—she'd end hurt beyond measure. She'd accepted the position; if she adhered strictly to that role, she and he could continue as they were. That would have to be enough.

If she was forced to make the choice between being his mistress or not being with him at all, she knew which she'd choose. She never wanted to lose him, to forgo those golden moments when they were so close, when each breath, each thought, each desire was shared. If to hold on to that closeness she had to remain his mistress, so be it. It was, she'd decided, worth the price.

The news he had was exciting; they were clearly closing in on A.C. As they discussed their findings, she was conscious of Tony's gaze on her face, black as ever but not so much intent as keen, sharp. Observant.

Finally, she felt forced to meet his eyes and raise her brows in mute question.

He searched her eyes, then looked forward, steering her along a path leading to a fountain. "Given I need to visit Lloyd's tonight, I won't be able to escort you to whatever entertainments you're scheduled to attend."

She forced herself to smile easily; she patted his arm. "Don't worry—I'm perfectly capable of attending by myself." Even though, in his absence, there was nothing at such events to hold her interest. She didn't even need to watch over Adriana anymore.

She'd learned there were indeed couples, noblemen and their wellborn mistresses, of whose relationship the ton was patently aware, but to which it turned a blind eye. Her and Tony's situation wasn't unusual. However, one relevant and undoubtedly important aspect was that those involved in such accepted affairs never drew attention to their relationship in public.

Such couples did not spend time together in ballrooms or drawing rooms; she should undoubtedly grasp this opportunity to ease their interaction into a more socially acceptable vein.

"You find the balls a bore." She looked ahead at the circular fountain set in the lawn. "There's no reason you need dance attendance on me there. Not anymore."

She glanced at him. There was a frown gathering in his eyes. She needed to discourage him from acting so overtly possessively. She smiled, trying to soften the hint. "And tonight, you need to be elsewhere searching for A. C.—there's no need to feel it's necessary to escort me, or that your absence will bother me—that I'll be in any way discomposed."

Her words were gentle, clear, her expression as always open and honest; Tony heard what she said, but wasn't sure he understood. She was explaining something to him, but what?

His brain couldn't seem to function as incisively as usual. The odd feeling in his chest, a deadening, dulling sensation, didn't help. Halting, he drew in a breath, glanced, unseeing, at the fountain. "If you're sure?"

He looked at her face, into her eyes—and saw something very close to relief in the green.

Her smile was genuine, reassuring. "Yes. I'll be perfectly content."

The assurance he'd asked for, yet not what he'd wanted to hear.

A babel of youthful voices spilled down from the terrace; they both looked and saw the three boys and two girls come tumbling down to the lawns.

Turning, they headed toward the children. As they reached the main lawn, Tony felt Alicia's gaze, glanced down, and met her eyes.

Again, she smiled reassuringly, then patted his arm as she looked ahead. "I'll be here, waiting, when you get home."

He'd accepted the arrangement because he'd had little choice. Yet the suspicion—now hardening to conviction—that something was going awry between them grew, fueled by that part of him that had heard her words as something approaching a dismissal.

A dismissal he'd had neither justification nor opportunity to challenge.

The incident had jolted him in a way he wasn't accustomed to; faced with a raft of unexpected uncertainties, he'd concluded he needed to think before doing anything, before reacting. Yet by one o'clock the next morning, when he silently let himself into his house, his uncertainty had only grown, until he, his usual forceful personality, felt paralyzed.

One thing he'd realized: he didn't have any real idea of what she was thinking, of how she saw their relationship.

He'd told her he loved her; she hadn't reciprocated.

He'd never before said those words to any woman, but in the past he'd been the recipient of such declarations too often for his comfort.

Alicia hadn't said the words. Frowning, he climbed the stairs. Until now, he hadn't thought he needed to hear them; until now, her physical acceptance, all that had passed between them, had been assurrance enough, guarantee enough.

But no more. Now he was uncertain. Of her.

Even though she'd assured him she'd be waiting, he wasn't at all sure what he'd find when he entered her room. But she was indeed there, yet not quite as he'd expected. She wasn't in bed, but standing by the side of the bow window, wrapped in her robe, arms folded beneath her breasts. Shoulder and head resting against the window frame, she looked out on the moonlit gardens.

As usual, she hadn't heard him enter. He made no sound as he closed the door, then stood in the shadows and studied her.

She was deep in thought, her body completely still, her mind elsewhere.

He hesitated, then stepped forward more definitely; she heard him and turned. Through the shadows he saw her gentle smile. She settled back against the window frame. "Did you manage to identify A. C.'s company?"

He halted by the bed. "It's Ellicot."

"The one that used many different shipping lines?"

He nodded; the subject was not the one uppermost in his mind. He eased off his coat. "Tomorrow, we'll start closing in, but we'll need to be careful not to alert A. C. We want him still in England when we learn his name."

He tossed the coat onto a chair, then looked at her. She'd remained at the window, leaning back against the frame, the silk robe draped about her, her arms folded. He sensed she was comfortable, at ease, yet distant.

The bed was behind him; stepping back, he sat on its side. Through the shadows, continued to study her.

He'd manipulated the situation and gained his objective—her, here, under his roof. In his house where he could share her bed easily, where she was protected constantly by his servants. He'd achieved all he'd wanted, all he'd thought they needed, yet . . . something was askew. The situation had developed undercurrents, ones he couldn't read well enough to counter.

She seemed to be drawing back. Not turning away, but sliding from his grasp. Inch by inch, step by tiny step . . .

He needed to hear words, yet he couldn't—didn't know how to—ask for them. Dragging in a short breath, he looked down at his hands, loosely clasped between his thighs. "Perhaps"—keeping his tone ruthlessly even, he looked up—"we should discuss the wedding."

She shook her head—instantly, without the smallest hesitation. "No, not yet. There's no sense making any plans until Geoffrey tells his mother, and they set a date."

He opened his lips to correct her; there was no reason he and she had to wait on Geoffrey and Adriana's arrangements . . .

The realization she'd thought he'd meant Geoffrey and Adriana's wedding, not theirs, burst on him before he uttered a word. It was superseded almost instantly by a blinding insight—the idea of their wedding—that he might be alluding to that—hadn't even occurred to her.

She shifted to stare out of the window once more. "It'll be upon us soon enough, but you needn't worry about the details. I'm sure they'll want to marry in Devon, and that would be wisest . . ." She paused, then softly added, "Considering my deception. A small, private affair would be best . . ."

Alicia let her words trail away. She'd been thinking of the wedding, of Geoffrey and Adriana's growing happiness, and struggling to contain a reaction perilously close to jealousy.

She drew in a slow breath, felt a welling need to rail, not against Geoffrey and Adriana—heaven forbid, she'd worked so hard to bring about her sister's happiness—but against a fate that was so twisted as to make her live through, have to smile through Adriana and Geoffrey's joy while knowing she would never achieve the same. Worse, while knowing she'd willingly and intentionally sacrificed her own chance at such happiness to ensure her sister made the marriage she deserved.

When she'd made the decision to leave behind any thought of marriage and masquerade as a widow, the critical decision from which all else had flowed, she hadn't known what she'd been so ready to turn her back on. Hadn't appreciated her until recently suppressed dreams, hadn't felt their tug.

Now she knew, now she had. Fate was indeed cruel.

Yet among her regrets there was one she didn't have. She didn't regret, couldn't regret, her relationship with Tony. If she couldn't marry him, then she wouldn't marry anyone else, so there was, she'd finally, bitterly, ironically and rather sternly concluded, no point in dwelling on her dreams.

Aside from all else, given his possessiveness, given all she sensed in him, honor notwithstanding, she wasn't at all sure he'd let her go.

Her senses suddenly leapt; she looked up, eyes widening as she found him—as she'd suspected—by her side. Straightening, she faced him.

He met her gaze briefly, searched her face, then his eyes returned to lock on hers. "I'll never let you go."

The words were quiet, steely—infinitely dangerous.

Almost as if he'd been reading her thoughts.

She held his gaze steadily, returned his regard. As always, his black eyes held a measure of heat, yet tonight, she could almost feel the flames. Not simply caressing, languidly artful, but greedily reaching, engulfing, hungry and urgent. Passion fueled them, but tonight there was something else, too, something she couldn't identify— something hotter, more potent, more powerful.

Something that touched her, reached deep, and thrilled her, as nothing had before.

"I know." There was no point in denying the strength of what bound her to him. She held his gaze. "I haven't asked you to."

"Good." The word was guttural in its harshness. His hands closed hard about her waist; she was instantly and shockingly aware of his strength. He pulled her to him, the movement lacking his usual grace. "Don't bother."

That something she couldn't name flared in his eyes.

"You're mine." He bent his head. *"Forever."*

The word was uttered as a vow, with the full force of all he was. Then his lips closed on hers.

He took them, claimed them, then parted them. She offered her mouth, appeasing his demand, ruthless, intent and dominant. His tongue thrust deep, knowing, commanding, then settled to plunder.

Not, as usual, with heated but languid caresses that spun a seductive web, but with unveiled passion, with a driving, ravenous, ruthless desire that stormed her mind and sent her wits careening.

His need hit her, an elemental force that literally shook her to her toes. Before she could react, she felt his hands shift, felt the tug—almost violent—as he jerked the tie of her robe undone. Then his hands, hard and forceful, were at her shoulders, pushing the robe over and down, stripping it away.

He gave her no chance to catch her mental breath. In seconds, the ribbon ties of her chemise were loose, then he pushed the garment down, his hands rough on her skin as he thrust the folds past her hips until they slithered down her legs to the floor.

His hands spread over her naked back and he pulled her fully to him, locked her against him. Angled his head over hers and ravaged her mouth, seizing, taking, ravishing, presaging what was to come.

Hands on his shoulders, fingers sinking into the embroidered silk of his waistcoat, she clung desperately to sanity, held tight as about her the world whirled.

She was naked in his arms, locked against his hard and unquestionably aroused body, her bare skin pressed to his clothes, the steely muscles trapping her screened by fabric. Even in her close-to-witless state, she recognized his clothed state as a deliberate ploy, a sexual taunt expertly aimed. He never cared about his nakedness; him naked she could deal with. Being naked, exposed, disturbed her still, at least beyond the confines of a bed.

He knew it. The way his hands moved over her body, not just possessive but tauntingly so, made that clear. Every touch escalated the tension gripping her, made her even more aware, deepened her feeling of vulnerabilty.

Heightened every sense she possessed until all, every last shred of her awareness, was focused completely on her own body, on what he was doing, on what he made her feel.

His lips held hers trapped as his hard hands moved over her breasts, closing, weighing, kneading, then retreating to play with her tightly budded nipples, causing havoc with nerves already excruciatingly taut. When her breasts were swollen and aching, he moved on, his touch openly hard, demanding, commanding. Not rough, but ruthless, relentless in pushing her on, in demanding and taking from her a surrender beyond all she'd previously given.

She didn't hesitate, didn't draw back. She met his lips, met his ravaging tongue, and let him have his way.

Let him trace her curves as he wished, explore her body as he wanted.

Let him sit on the window seat and lift her over him, let him settle her on her knees straddling his thighs, her own spread wide.

Let him hold her there as he broke from the kiss and trailed hot, burning kisses down her throat. Clinging to his shoulders, she arched her head back, caught her breath as he laved the pulse point at the base of her throat, then moved lower. To the ripe swells of her swollen breasts. To the tight, painful peaks.

He feasted, laving, licking, nibbling, sucking. She slid her fingers into his hair and held tight. Just breathing was a battle, one that only grew worse.

Along with the hot, empty ache deep within her. It welled, swelled, until it seemed to fill her.

Usually, with his hot body pressed to hers, she wasn't so shockingly aware of it. Tonight, held as she was, naked, but with him clothed, her thighs widespread, her body open but unfilled, she felt her own need keenly, clearly, more physically hers, not clouded by his.

Her breasts felt tight, skin hot and burning. He licked one nipple, then rasped it with his tongue; she heard a soft cry, and realized it was hers.

His hands, until then locked about her waist, holding her steady before him, eased; his palms slid down, curved over and around her bottom, then closed, kneading powerfully, evocatively. He continued to tease and taunt her nipples, then releasing her bottom, he ran his cupped hands down the backs of her spread thighs.

Her muscles quivered, then locked; above her knees,

his hands swung around and he pushed both hands, lightly gripping, thumbs cruising the sensitive inner faces, up her thighs.

Slowly. Deliberately.

She stopped breathing when, reaching the tops of her thighs, he paused. Then his hands left her.

She sucked in a breath—lost it when he opened his mouth and drew one tortured nipple deep, and suckled. Her shattered cry echoed through the room.

Then she felt his left hand close about her hip, holding her steady once more. His other hand returned to her mons, with a strong, firm stroke brushed over her curls, then reached beyond.

He opened her, explored her, tracing the entrance to her body while he continued to suckle her breasts, first one, then the other, constantly racking the tension that held her tighter. The emptiness inside her expanded, waiting for him to slake it. Nerves flickering, she waited, breath bated, expecting the slow penetration of his fingers, needing his touch, wanting it.

It didn't come.

She was ready to beg when his hand left her. Desperate, she caught her breath on a sob, felt the fingers wrapped about her hip dig in, anchoring her. Releasing her breast, he lifted his head, found her lips—took them. Ravaged them.

Her world teetered, rocked, then she realized on a rush of quivering relief that his other hand was at his waist, flicking the buttons free. He laid the flap of his trousers open. She immediately went to press closer, to sink down and take him in.

His hands gripped her hips, held her still for an instant, poised as he adjusted himself to her. She felt the broad head of his erection touch her, press fractionally in.

Eyes tight shut, her whole body a mass of urgent, heated need, she tried to gasp through the kiss.

He pulled her down onto him. Impaled her.

Her senses shattered.

He was fully aroused, engorged, more rigid unforgiving iron than velvet.

A low moan escaped her; he lifted her and ruthlessly drew her down again. Further, this time, so she took more of him. He thrust deeper, shifted beneath her, then his hands were at her hips, sculpting her legs, lifting them, rearranging them. As he wished. As he wanted.

He didn't ask, didn't order. He lifted her knees and wound her legs about his waist, leaving her helpless with no purchase to move.

Totally in his control, totally at his mercy.

He showed none; for her part, she asked no quarter.

All she wanted was him deep inside her, and he gave her that, as much as she wished, as much as she wanted.

Arms twined about his neck, she clung as he moved her. He set a steady rhythm, hard and deep, the head of his staff nudging her womb. She felt so full of him, as if he was pressing against her heart—and he only drove deeper, sure and true.

He held her to their kiss, tongues tangling, mouths merged.

Held her on his lap, naked and exposed, more vulnerable in the moonlight than she'd ever been.

More his.

All his.

When he finally released her lips and returned his attentions to her breasts, she let her head fall back, eyes closed.

Tensing as he again teased her nipples until they ached, then suckled anew, hard enough to make her fight to swallow a scream.

The next time, she lost the fight.

He was lifting her, working her on him, around him; simultaneously he was feasting at her breasts. She couldn't take much more stimulation, more of the sensations he was ruthlessly pressing on her, heightened, made infinitely more powerful by their position.

She licked her lips, managed to gasp, "Take me to the bed."

He didn't miss a beat. "No. Here. Like this."

His voice, all she could hear in it, very nearly made her weep.

With joy, with a pleasure that was far beyond the physical.

Need—simple, abiding, far deeper than she'd expected.

Never before had he been like this, never before had he dropped all pretence, every last vestige of sophistication, and allowed her to see so far, so clearly, to see that naked need. To know by her own experience so no lingering doubt could remain what truly drove him.

I love you.

She wanted to say the words. They welled in her chest, pushed up through her throat, but she swallowed them. If she told him that . . .

She had no wits left with which to think; instinct was her only guide. So she left the words unsaid, sobbed instead as her body started to convulse.

And he slowed.

Thrust harder, deeper, but slower.

So she felt every tiny slither as her senses unraveled, felt every last fraction of her helplessness as she climaxed more powerfully than she ever had before.

Tony raised his head and watched her, her ivory limbs silvered by the moonlight as she came apart in his arms. He drank in the sight, one he'd needed, one the prowling beast inside him had simply had to have.

Sunk to the hilt in her body, bathed in its scalding heat, he set his jaw and relentlessly drove her through the longest, most extended climax he'd ever forced on any woman. The soft strangled cries that fell from her lips were balm to his raging soul; the ripples of her release, the contractions that beckoned, her body helplessly gripping and releasing his erection, soothed that most primitive side of him.

It would be an easy matter to finish with her there, but that wasn't what he wanted. Tonight he needed more.

He waited until her muscles relaxed, until she was limp, wholly pliant in his arms. Then he lifted her from him, simultaneously stood, and carried her to the bed. He laid her on the coverlet, then stepped back and stripped off his clothes.

Then he joined her.

Propped beside her, he ran a hand down over her back, over the smooth globes of her bottom. Slowly, surely, he roused her again, then positioned her curled over her knees before him. He entered her slowly, eyes closed, savoring every fraction of an inch as her soft, swollen sheath closed about him.

Then he rode her.

Slowly at first, then without restraint.

Until she was sobbing, hair threshing as she struggled for breath, incoherent in her need, totally wild, completely wanton.

She was usually neither; that last rein of restraint she'd not before released had snapped, broken.

He savored every second of her abandonment, of her complete and absolute surrender, listened to her cries as she fell from the peak—then found his own surrender beckoning.

This time he went willingly. He knew, in some dark corner of his mind, just what he'd been doing. Knew it wouldn't work.

Didn't care.

He'd had to do it—to show her all there was, to tempt that side of her he didn't think she realized she possessed. She was a deeply sensual woman, but exploring her sensuality, opening her eyes to its true nature, had only more clearly demonstrated his own weakness, his own vulnerability.

This was one battlefield on which he was helpless. This was one fight in which there was no enemy.

Only surrender.

On a groan, he did, gave her all he was, all he could ever be.

Spent, he collapsed, then gathered her to him. He'd given her far more than his body. He'd lost his soul. And his heart. And perhaps even more.

TWENTY

HE LEFT ALICIA'S SIDE JUST AFTER DAWN, EARLIER THAN recent habit but after last night, he wanted nothing more than to have done with A. C.

After last night . . . he had even less idea what was wrong between them. Something, yes, but he'd be damned if he had a clue. If he pushed, twelve hours might result in them unmasking A. C., then he would be free to devote himself to the most important endeavor of his life—wooing Alicia, even winning her anew, if that's what was required.

Frowning, he left his apartments. After last night, he could hardly have missed the fact that she was as he'd hoped, openly, generously, totally his. If that was so, then what else was there? From where did their problem, whatever it was, spring?

Confusion reigned. Reaching Alicia's door, he determinedly put it from him, turned the knob, and entered.

She was still asleep. He sat on the bed and looked down at her, then gently shook her shoulder.

"Hmm?" She opened her eyes; he notched up her lack of surprise when she focused on him as a minor victory.

"I'm off to hunt down A. C. We're breakfasting at the club to work out our best approach. We need to learn who owns Ellicot, then proceed from there, but whatever we do—"

"You have to make sure you don't alert A. C." She was

wide-awake now, studying his face, her gaze earnest but watchful.

He hesitated; he wanted to say something about last night, about them, but didn't know what, and couldn't find the words.

"Stay on guard." Squeezing her hand, he rose. "If we stumble and alert him, I'd expect him to run, but . . . he's kept his head until now."

"We'll be careful." She struggled up on her elbows.

"Good." Backing, he raised a hand in farewell. She was naked beneath the covers, now sliding slowly down; he didn't trust himself to kiss her, and stop at just a kiss. Last night had left them both with enough to think about. "I'll be back this evening, if not before."

She nodded. "Take care."

At the door, he glanced back and saw her watching him. He inclined his head, and left.

Closing the door, he turned. David, Harry, and Matthew stood shoulder to shoulder across the corridor staring unblinkingly up at him.

"I was just telling Alicia where I'd be today."

"Oh." David considered his reply to their unspoken question, then nodded and turned to the stairs. "Are you going down to breakfast?"

Harry and Matthew swung around and followed.

Drawing a relieved breath, Tony fell in in their wake. "No—I have to go out straightaway."

Reaching the stairs, David and Harry clattered down.

Matthew stopped and turned to him. "Are you going to marry Alicia?"

Tony looked down into the big eyes fixed innocently on his face. "Yes. Of course."

The other boys had stopped halfway down to listen; now they whooped joyously, and thundered on down.

Matthew simply smiled. "Good." He took Tony's hand and, with simple gravity, accompanied him down the stairs.

* * *

Two hours later, Alicia strolled the lawns in the park, alone but for Maggs, tactfully keeping watch from a distance.

All about her was quiet and serene. It was too early for the fashionable throng; a few latecomers were still exercising their horses on Rotten Row, but most riders had already clattered home while the matrons and their daughters had yet to arrive.

The solitude and fresh air were precisely what she craved.

After the door had closed behind Tony, she'd lain in bed for ten minutes before the insistent refrain playing in her brain had prodded her into action. Ringing for Bertha, she'd washed, dressed, and joined Miranda and Adriana in the breakfast parlor.

Miranda and Adriana had been busy organizing their morning's engagements; she'd excused herself on the grounds of a slight headache and her need for a quiet walk to refresh herself. Accepting her excuse, the other two had left to get ready to visit Lady Carlisle; she'd climbed to the schoolroom and checked on her brothers, then quit the house, Maggs at her heels as per his "master's orders."

She'd accepted his escort with equanimity; she'd grown quite fond of the unprepossessing man. Interpreting his orders to watch over her literally, he'd retreated to stand beneath a large tree, now some distance away, leaving her to her thoughts.

Which were what she'd come to the park to confront.

It—her present tack—wasn't going to work. She'd thought her best way forward was to adhere strictly to her position as Tony's mistress and not wish for more, to rein in her dreams and accept what she'd been given, what he'd freely offered. But that view was fatally flawed—last night had proved it, had illustrated the truth beyond doubt.

The connection between them, so much more, so much stronger than any mere physical link, was not compatible with, would not remain constrained within, the bounds of the relationship of a nobleman and his mistress. Their connection was a vital thing, a living force in and of itself; it was growing, burgeoning, already demanding more.

Last night, she'd nearly told him she loved him, had had to fight to swallow the words. Some night soon she'd lose that fight. One way or another, the truth would out— *in toto*, there was more to it, more depths, more aspects than even that powerful fact.

She might already be carrying his child; it was too early to know, yet the possibility existed. In the beginning, she'd assumed he'd know what to do, would take precautions, yet he hadn't, nor had he expected her to. If she'd been shocked by her wanton behavior last night, her reaction to the idea of bearing Tony's child had only confirmed how little attention she'd paid her to her latent hopes, aspirations, and dreams. Until now.

In her heart, and now very clearly in her mind, she knew what she wanted. The question facing her was how to get it; leaving matters as they were was, she now accepted, no longer an option.

Drawing in a breath, she lifted her head and looked unseeing at some distant trees. She'd taken serious risks to secure Adriana's and her brothers' futures, boldly gambled and won. It was time to act in pursuit of her own future—to realize the dreams she'd never allowed herself to dream but which Tony had brought alive.

She would speak with him. She felt her chin set. Just as soon as A. C. was in custody, she would talk to Tony, explain how she felt about them, about their future. How he would react was the risk, the unknown, yet . . . she had his declaration of love to lean on, and, indeed, more. Their connection itself; through it she sensed how he felt, his need, even if he didn't consciously acknowledge it. In time, he would recognize the truth as she had, and re-assess as she had, and adjust.

Grimacing, she looked down. She would be gambling that their love truly was as she saw it—a huge risk, yet one she felt compelled to take.

The thud of footsteps approaching over the grass reached her. Looking up, she saw a footman in plain black livery striding purposefully her way.

Glancing to the left, she saw Maggs, leaning against the tree trunk, come alert, but as the footman halted and bowed, Maggs relaxed and resumed his unobtrusive watch.

"For you, ma'am."

The footman proffered a note. She took it, opened it, read it, and inwardly cursed. Chickens were coming home to roost thick and fast. Sir Freddie Caudel most for-mally and politely requested an interview.

She looked across the lawn to the black carriage drawn up on the gravel drive. With a sigh, she tucked the note into her reticule. "Very well."

The footman bowed and escorted her to the carriage. Maggs, closer to the carriage than she, remained where he was, half-obscured by the tree.

Reaching the carriage, the footman opened the door and stood back, clearly expecting her to enter. Puzzled, she looked in, and saw Sir Freddie, dapper and urbanely elegant as usual, sitting inside.

Smiling easily, he half rose and bowed. "My dear, I hope you'll forgive this unusual approach, but for reasons that will become clear as we talk, I wished to speak with you in the strictest privacy. If you will do me the honor of sharing my carriage, I thought we might roll around the Avenue—it's quite peaceful at the moment—and conduct our discussion in relative comfort, out of sight of prying eyes." He smiled, his pale gaze somewhat rueful, gently humorous, and held out his hand. "If you would, my dear?"

Inwardly sighing, she gave him her hand; gathering her skirts, she climbed into the carriage. Sir Freddie released her and she sat opposite him, facing forward. Sir Freddie nodded to his footman. The man shut the door; an instant later, the carriage started slowly rolling.

"Now." Sir Freddie fixed her with a calmly superior smile. "You must let me apologize for this little charade. I'm sure you understand that, given the nature of my interest and thus the reason behind my request for an interview, there would be nothing more unappealing to me than in any way whatever giving the gossipmongers reason to wag their tongues."

Alicia inclined her head; from her experience, now extensive, of Sir Freddie's circumlocutory periods, she knew it was pointless to try to rush him. He would get to his peroration in his own good time. Nevertheless . . . "Now we are here, you perceive me all ears, sir."

"Indeed." Sir Freddie returned her nod. "I should also explain that I did not think it appropriate, in the circumstances, to call at Torrington House." He held up a hand as if to stem a protest she hadn't made. "I'm quite sure I would be treated with all due consideration, indeed graciousness, however, I am aware that Manningham is an old and valued friend of Torrington's." Sir Freddie paused, as if weighing that fact anew. Eventually, he said, "Suffice to say I deemed it impolitic to call on you there."

Again, she inclined her head and wondered how long he would take to come to the point. Given that point—his offer for Adriana's hand—she turned her mind to finding the words with which to refuse him.

Sir Freddie rambled on and on; his voice, polished, light, his accents refined, was easy on the ear. Smoothly, he described his current position, his reasons for looking for a wife, then moved on to Adriana's manifold charms.

The carriage suddenly rocked, the wheel dipping in a pothole; mildly surprised that such a thing existed on the fashionable carriageway, Alicia refocused on Sir Freddie's eloquence, and discovered he was still describing, in phrases both flowery and convoluted, just what it was about her sister that had attracted his notice.

Counseling patience, she folded her hands in her lap, and waited. Her mind slid away . . . she imagined Maggs, under his tree, watching the carriage go around and around the park . . .

Instinct flickered. The carriage blinds had been drawn from the first, she'd assumed to prevent the interested seeing Sir Freddie speaking with her. The carriage rocked again; the blinds swayed—and she caught a glimpse of what lay outside.

It wasn't the park.

She looked at Sir Freddie as the sounds outside registered. They were traveling down some major road, not one lined with trees, not even with shops, but with houses—a road that led not into the city, but out of it.

Her shock, her realization, showed in her face.

Something changed in Sir Freddie's expression, as if a thin, obscuring veil was drawn aside; abruptly she realized that he was watching her closely, a coldly calculating look in his eyes.

He smiled. Before the gesture had been urbanely charming; now it chilled.

"Ah—I did wonder how long it would take." His voice, too, had subtly changed, all pleasantness leaching from it. "However, before you think of making any heroic attempt to escape, I suggest you listen to what I have to say."

His eyes held hers, and they were colder than a snake's. Alicia sat transfixed, her thoughts tumbling, churning. "Escape" implied . . .

"The most important thing you need to bear in mind is that there's another carriage ahead of us on this road. It contains two rather rough men—I wouldn't distinguish them with the title of gentleman—in company with your youngest brother. Matthew, as I'm sure you know, has a habit of slipping outside when he grows bored with his lessons. He did so, with a little encouragement I admit, this morning, just after you'd left the house. He's an enterprising young chap, quite capable of evading all supervision when he chooses." Sir Freddie smiled. "But I'm sure you know that."

Alicia's heart lurched; the blood drained from her face. She did know of Matthew's occasional excursions—just to the area between the house and the street to watch the world rumble by—but since they'd moved to Torrington House, she'd thought they'd stopped. "What do you want with Matthew?"

Sir Freddie's brows rose. "Why nothing, my dear—nothing at all. He's merely a pawn to ensure *you* behave as I wish." His gaze hardened. "If you do as I say, no harm will come to him. Those two men I spoke of have strict orders, ones it's to their advantage to obey. They'll take your brother to a safe place, and wait with him there for word from me. Depending on how matters transpire, I will instruct them either to return him to Upper Brook Street unharmed"—his lips curved lightly, tauntingly, "or to kill him."

He held her gaze. "The instruction I send will depend on you."

Alicia fought to met his gaze levelly, to keep her expression impassive, to keep her fear, her panic, at bay. Icy chills ran up and down her spine. *Matthew* . . . a vise squeezed her heart even as, instinctive and immediate, she searched for the means to free him. Maggs—he would fetch Tony . . . she couldn't work out the how and when, not with Sir Freddie's cold and sharply observant eyes on her.

She licked her lips, forced her lungs to work. "What do you want me to do?" She frowned. "What *is* this all about?" Why kidnap her and Matthew if it was Adriana Sir Freddie wanted?

She allowed her confusion and total incomprehension to show in her face.

Sir Freddie laughed.

The sound chilled her to the marrow.

Then he smiled, and she wanted nothing more than to flee. "This, my dear, is about me covering my tracks, an unfortunate necessity brought on by Ruskin. He couldn't seem to understand that the war was over and the easy pickings with it."

She stared at him. "*You're* A. C?"

"A. C?" Sir Freddie blinked, then his face cleared. "Ah, yes, I'd almost forgotten."

He shifted. With a graceful sweep of his arm, he bowed, the gesture full of his customary elegant charm. Face, lips lightly curved, and manner were all one, but as he straightened, his cold, pale eyes met hers. "Sir Alfred Caudel, my dear, at your service."

Tony returned to Torrington House midmorning. After reviewing their information, the group had agreed that Jack Warnefleet and Christian, neither of whom had been visible thus far in the affair, should visit Ellicot's offices and extract by whatever means they could some idea of who was behind the company.

There was a limit to how unsubtle they could be; there was no guarantee of a quick and favorable outcome. Restless, impatient, sensing matters were nearing a head but with nothing he could reasonably do, Tony had returned home.

He'd only just settled behind his desk when the study door burst open and panic—carried by David, Harry, Matthew, and Jenkins—rushed in.

"*Alicia!*" Matthew shrieked. "You've got to go and save her."

Tony caught him as he charged around the desk and flung himself at him. "Yes, of course," he replied, his gaze locking on the others.

David and Harry had rushed to the desk, gripping the front edge, their expressions as horrified as Matthew's.

Jenkins, close on their heels, was not much better, and out of breath as well.

"My lord," Jenkins puffed, "Maggs sent us to tell you—Mrs. Carrington was inveigled into a carriage which then took off to the west."

Tony swore, started to rise. "Where's Maggs?"

Jenkins struggled for breath. "He's following the carriage. He said he'd send word as he can."

Tony nodded curtly. "Sit down." Lifting Matthew into his arms, he turned his attention to the older boys. "Now, David—tell me what you know, from the beginning."

David dragged in a huge breath, held it for a second, then complied. The story came out in reasonable order: Alicia visiting the schoolroom, mentioning she was going for a walk—Tony had imagined her out with Miranda and Adriana—the boys then prevailing on Jenkins to take their nature lesson in the park; they'd arrived to find Maggs running toward them, swearing and cursing, watching a black carriage that had passed the boys turn out of the park and roll away to the west. Maggs had pounced on them, given them the message, hailed a hackney, and set off after the carriage.

"All right." Tony felt none of their panic; he'd spent the last decade dealing with similarly fraught situations. He welcomed, even relished what he recognized as the call to arms; he couldn't yet see how it related, but he knew a bugle when he heard it. "Did Maggs say who was in the carriage?"

The boys shook their heads. So did Jenkins. "I don't think he saw who it was, my lord."

"It was Sir Freddie someone's carriage." The mumbled words, spoken around a thumb, came from Matthew.

Tony glanced at him, then sat him on the desk so he could see his face. He pulled up his chair and sat, too, so he wasn't towering over the boy. "How do you know that?"

Matthew took his thumb out of his mouth. "Horses.

This time, he had four, but the front two were the ones that always pull his carriage. I know them from when he came to call at the other house."

Tony wondered how much reliance to place on a small boy's observations. He felt a tug on his sleeve and looked into Harry's face.

"Matthew notices things—and he really does know horses."

Tony looked at David, who nodded, then at Jenkins, recovering in a chair. Jenkins nodded, too. "He's very good about details, my lord. Excellent memory."

Tony paused, then swallowed the curse that rose to his lips. Rising, he turned to the bookshelves behind the desk, scanned, then pulled out his copy of *Debrett's*.

A tap fell on the door, then it opened. Geoffrey Manningham strolled in. Across the room, Tony met his gaze.

Instantly, Geoffrey came alert. "What? What's happened?"

"Caudel has kidnapped Alicia." Tony opened the book, swiftly flicking pages. He found the entry for Caudel. He read it, and swore beneath his breath. "Sir *Alfred* Caudel."

He slammed the book shut. "A. C. Currently with the Home Office. From an old if not ancient family, his principal estate is in north Oxfordshire, near Chipping Norton, not far from the tavern where those letters from the French captains were sent."

Geoffrey's mouth had fallen open; he snapped it shut. "*Caudel?* Good God—no wonder he's so desperate to scotch the investigation."

"Indeed, and no wonder he knew so much about the investigation itself." Standing behind the desk, fingers lightly drumming, Tony rapidly assembled a plan, checking and re-checking, mentally listing all the necessary orders. He glanced at the three boys, spared them a reassuring smile. "I'll go after them."

Geoffrey frowned. "You know where they've gone?"

"Maggs has them in his sights—he'll send word as soon as he passes a hostelery." Tony spoke to the boys. "Maggs knows what to do—he won't stop following Alicia. I'll head out as soon as I know which road—Maggs and I have a system we've used before. It'll work, so don't worry that we'll lose the trail." He looked at Geoffrey. "I need you to get word to the others, and then wait here with Adriana, Miranda, and the rest—no need for vapors, I'll bring Alicia back."

Geoffrey nodded. "Right. Who do you want me to get hold of?"

Tony gave him a list. Dalziel first; Tony wrote a short note summarizing the evidence that Sir Freddie was A. C. He handed it to Geoffrey. "Give that to Dalziel—into his hand, don't show it to anyone else. Use my name, that'll get you through his pickets. Then go to Hendon House and tell Jack, then to the club, and tell the majordomo, Gasthorpe. Tell him the others—Deverell's out of town but the other five—all need to know."

While he'd talked, he'd risen and tugged the bellpull. Hungerford appeared; Tony ordered his curricle brought around with the bays put to. Without comment, Hungerford left.

Almost immediately he returned. "A message from Maggs, my lord, brought by an ostler from Hounslow. Maggs says it's the Basingstoke road."

Having assimilated the fact that Sir Freddie was A. C., which he verified beyond doubt by telling her the details of how his scheme had operated, and of how he'd worked since Ruskin's death to turn all blame on her, Alicia still didn't know the answer to her question. She fixed Sir Freddie with a steady gaze. "What do you plan to do now? What do you want me to do?"

"At the moment, nothing." Reaching out, he lifted a window flap, glanced out, then let the flap fall and looked back at her. "We'll be journeying through the night.

When we stop to change horses, you'll remain in the carriage, calm and composed. At no time will you do anything to attract attention. You won't forget that your brother's future lies in your hands, so you will do exactly as I say at all times."

She debated telling him that Tony and his friends knew about Ellicot, but decided to hold her fire, at least until she knew more. "Where are we going?" Through the night suggested deep into the country.

Sir Freddie studied her, then shrugged. "I don't suppose it will hurt to tell you." His tone was cold, unemotional. "Given how forthcoming I've been, I'm sure you've realized by now that this last and, I fancy, winning throw of the dice involves your demise."

She had, but refused to let it panic her. She raised a brow, faintly haughty. "You're going to kill me?"

He smiled his chilling smile. "Most regretfully, I assure you. But before you waste breath trying to tell me such an act won't get me anywhere, let me explain how things will appear once you're no longer about to state your case.

"First, I'm aware of the activities of Torrington and his friends. They really are quite tediously tenacious. Ellicot was an obvious liability—he, naturally, is no longer with us. His family, however, are most likely aware that he had a sleeping partner, so I took care to remove all evidence of my association with him . . . and replaced it with evidence of *your* association with him.

"When Torrington and his friends look, they'll find a circle of evidence that leads them back to you—where their attention should have stayed all along. I'm sure they won't be happy about it, but they won't have any choice in laying the blame at your door. I've become quite adept at bending society and the upper echelons to my bidding; there'll be such irritation that you've escaped, your guilt will be established by default.

"Naturally, you won't be there to answer the charges,

which will only reinforce them. Your disappearance will be seen as an admission of guilt, one your supporters will be at a loss to counter. When your body is eventually found, as I'll ensure it is, everyone will conclude that, weighed down with remorse, with the investigation closing in—something you would know with Torrington as your lover—with social disaster of ever-greater proportions looming over you and your precious family . . . well, you took the only honorable way out for a lady."

She let contempt infuse her voice. "You said you know of Torrington and his friends and how tenacious they are. My death won't convince them—it won't stop their investigation, it'll intensify it." She was perfectly certain of that.

Sir Freddie, however, smiled, coldly condescending. "The key is Torrington, and how he'll react to finding your dead body."

She couldn't stop her lashes from flickering.

Sir Freddie saw; his smile deepened. "He's in love with you, not just a passing fancy, I fear, but well and truly caught. What do you think it will do to him to be the one to discover you dead?"

She refused to react, to give him any indication of what she thought; the arrogant fool had just said the one thing above all others guaranteed to make her fight to the last.

"With you gone and nothing left to save, Torrington will retire to deepest Devon. The others won't be able to sustain the investigation without him." He paused, then added, "And that, my dear, will finally be the end of the story."

She drew breath, but didn't challenge him; there had to be some way to scuttle his plans. She kept her mind focused on that, refusing even to think of defeat. Defeat meant death, and she definitely wasn't ready to die.

Leaning her head against the squabs, she went over his plan. He was right in predicting she would do nothing to put Matthew at risk, but the risk came from Sir Freddie. He'd said his men would hold Matthew *until* they heard from him; if they didn't . . . there'd be time to find them and free Matthew unharmed.

She needed to escape and simultaneously take Sir Freddie captive, ensuring he could send no message. Once they'd turned the tables, Sir Freddie would tell them where Matthew was held . . . she needed Tony for that, but . . .

In her heart, she was sure he'd come for her. Maggs had been watching; he'd probably realized she'd been kidnapped before she had. Maggs would get word to Tony, and Tony would come. However, she couldn't rely on Tony catching up with her before Sir Freddie tried to kill her.

She looked across the carriage. Sir Freddie's eyes were closed, but she didn't think he was asleep. He was some years older than Tony, a few inches shorter, but of heavier build. Indeed, he'd be described as a fine figure of a man, still in his prime; he'd never looked out of place in Adriana's court.

Physically, she couldn't hope to win any tussle, yet if Sir Freddie had any weakness, it was his overweening conceit. He believed he'd get away with everything. If she played to that belief, there might be one moment, almost at the end of the game, when he might be vulnerable. . . .

It would likely be her only chance.

She saw a glint from beneath his lashes; he'd been watching her studying him. "You didn't say where we're going."

He was silent, clearly weighing the risk, then he said, "Exmoor. There's a tiny village I was once stranded in. The evidence will suggest you stopped there, then wandered out onto the moor, threw yourself down a disused mine shaft, and drowned."

Exmoor. Closing her eyes, leaning her head back

again, she focused on that. An isolated moor. They'd have to walk to any mine . . . the coachman would have to stay with the horses . . .

As the day rolled into evening, she behaved precisely as Sir Freddie wished. She considered pretending to fall apart, weeping and despairing, but she wasn't that good an actress, and if Sir Freddie suspected she wasn't resigned to her fate . . . instead, she behaved as she imagined a French duchess would have on her way to the guillotine. Head high, haughtily superior, yet with no hint of any struggle against an overwhelming fate.

He had to believe she'd accepted it, that she'd go haughtily but quietly to her death. Given his background, that was very likely the behavior he'd expect of her, a lady of his class.

The farther they traveled, stopping at inn after inn to change horses, the more evidence she detected of his natural conceit overcoming his caution. He even allowed her to use the convenience at an inn, although she had no chance to speak to anyone, and he remained within sight of the door at all times.

Night fell; four horses pulled the coach steadily on. Closing her eyes, feigning sleep, she felt her nerves tensing and tried to relax. Exmoor, he'd said, and Exeter was still some way ahead; it would be hours yet before she got her chance. Her one chance at the life she now knew beyond doubt she wanted. The life she was prepared to fight for, the life she was determined to have.

Not as Tony's mistress, but as his wife. As his viscountess, the mother of his heir, and other children, too. She had far too much to live for to die.

And she knew he loved her; not only had he said so, but he'd shown her. If she'd had any doubt over what his feelings truly were, the picture Sir Freddie had painted, the question he'd asked: how would Tony react to finding her dead? had blown all such doubts away.

Devastated was too small a word—she knew precisely how he would feel because it was the same way she'd feel in the converse circumstance.

They loved each other, equally completely, equally deeply; she no longer questioned that. Once they were past this, free of Sir Freddie and his deadly scheme, she would speak with Tony. He might not yet see things as she did, but she was perfectly marriageable, after all. He'd established her as his equal in the eyes of the ton; if his mother was anything like Lady Amery and the Duchess of St. Ives, she doubted she'd have any difficulties there.

She wanted to marry him, and if that meant she had to broach the subject herself, then she would. Brazenly. After last night, she could be brazen about anything, at least with him.

The prospect—her future as she would have it with Tony by her side—filled her mind. Joy welled; fear hovered that it would not come to be, but she shunned it, clung to the joy instead.

Held to the vision of a happy future. Let it strengthen her. Her determination to make it happen—that it would be—soared.

Unexpectedly, she slept.

The noisy rattle of the wheels hitting cobblestones jerked Alicia from her doze. It was deepest night, past midnight; she'd heard the sound of a bell tolling twelve as they'd passed through Exeter, now some way behind.

Sir Freddie had fastened back one of the window flaps. Through the window, she glimpsed a hedgerow; beyond it, the ground rose, desolate and empty. The coach slowed, then halted.

"Well, my dear, we're here." Through the gloom, Sir Freddie watched her. Holding to her resolve, she didn't react.

He hesitated, then leaned past her, opened the door,

and climbed down. He turned and gave her his hand; she allowed him to assist her to the cobbles, leaving her cloak on the seat. When the time came to run, she didn't want its folds flapping about her legs. Her skirts would be bad enough.

She'd slipped the cloak off sometime before; Sir Freddie didn't seem to notice—there was no reason he should care. He'd stepped forward to speak to the coachman; she strained her ears and caught the words she'd hoped to hear.

"Wait here until I return."

When she'd first emerged from the coach at an inn, there'd been no footman; she assumed he'd been set down in London. The coachman had avoided her eye; she knew better than to expect help from that quarter. All she needed was for the man to wait until his master returned. If things went her way, his master wouldn't return, not before she did and raised help from the cottages she could see just ahead, lining the road.

Sir Freddie turned to her. Again, he studied her; as she had all along, she met his gaze stonily.

He inclined his head. "Your composure does you credit, my dear. I really do regret putting an end to your life."

She didn't deign to answer. Sir Freddie's lips quirked; with a wave, he indicated a path leading from the narrow road. Within yards of the hedge, the path plunged into a dark wood; beyond, the moors rose, alternately illuminated, then shrouded in gloomy shadow as clouds passed over the moon.

"We have to walk through the wood to reach the moors and the mine."

Sir Freddie reached for her arm, but she forestalled him and turned, and calmly walked to the opening of the path.

* * *

Tony swore; hauling on the reins, he swung the latest pair he'd had harnessed in Exeter onto the road to Hatherleigh.

Why here, for heaven's sake? Was it the isolation?

He'd had hours to consider what Sir Freddie was about while following his path across the country. It had been decades since he'd driven at breakneck speed—he'd been pleased to discover he hadn't forgotten how—but even the exigencies of managing unfamiliar cattle hadn't stopped him from thinking first and foremost of Alicia, of the danger facing her.

Up behind him, Maggs was hanging on grimly, every now and then muttering imprecations under his breath. Tony ignored him. He'd caught up with Maggs at Yeovil; before then, whenever Maggs had stopped to change horses he'd sent a rider wearing a red kerchief back along the road. Tony had stopped each flagged rider, and thus known which road to follow.

As it happened, it was a road he knew well—the same road he'd traveled countless times between Torrington Chase and London. The familiarity had helped; he'd have missed their turning to Hatherleigh if he hadn't known to ask at Okehampton.

Sir Freddie taking Alicia so far from London had been a boon initially, giving him time to catch up. Even though Sir Freddie had been rocketing along, always using four fresh horses, Tony knew he was close on their heels.

While they were traveling, he had no fears for Alicia. Once they stopped . . .

His experience lay in pursuing someone he needed to catch, not save. Every time he thought of Alicia, his heart lurched, his mind stilled, paralyzed; shutting off such thoughts, he concentrated on Sir Freddie instead.

Why this route? Was Sir Freddie intending to drive through to the Bristol Channel and rendezvous with some lugger? Was Alicia a hostage? Or was she intended as the scapegoat Sir Freddie had from the first sought to make her?

That was Tony's blackest fear. The landscape, the desolate sweep of the moors rising up on either side of the road fed it. If Sir Freddie intended to stage Alicia's murder and make it appear a suicide, and thus quash the investigation . . .

Tony set his jaw. Once he got hold of her, he was taking her to Torrington Chase and keeping her there. Forever.

Sending the whip swinging to flick the leader's ear, he drove the horses on.

TWENTY-ONE

ALICIA EMERGED ONTO THE MOOR WITH A SENSE OF RE-
lief; the wood had been dark, the trees very old, the path
uneven and knotted with their roots. Here, at least, she
could breathe—dragging in a breath, she looked up, tracing the path they were following to where it skirted a pile
of rocks and earth, the workings of the disused mine in
which Sir Freddie planned to drown her.

Every nerve taut and alert, she kept walking, head
high, her pace neither too fast nor yet slow enough to
prompt Sir Freddie to hurry her. Scanning the area, she
searched—for a rock, a branch, anything she could use to
overpower him. Closer to the mine would be preferable,
yet the closer they got . . .

She was supremely conscious of him walking steadily
at her heels. He seemed relaxed, just a murderer out to
arrange another death. Quelling a shudder, she looked
again at the mine. The path rose steadily, steeper as it led
up the shoulder of the workings before leveling off as it
skirted the lip of the shaft itself.

The clouds were constantly shifting, drifting; there
was always enough light to see their way, but when the
moon shone clear, details leapt out.

Like the discarded spar she glimpsed, just fleetingly, to
the right of the steepest section of the path.

Her heart leapt; her muscles tensed, ready . . .

Quickly, she thought through what would need to happen. She had to distract Sir Freddie at just the right spot. She'd already decided how, but she needed to set the stage.

Reaching the spot where the steep upward slope commenced, she halted abruptly. Swinging to face Sir Freddie, she found the slope was sufficient for her to meet his gaze levelly. "Do I have your word as a gentleman that my brother won't be harmed? That he'll be released as soon as possible in Upper Brook Street?"

Sir Freddie met her eyes; his lips twisted as, nodding, he looked down. "Of course." After a fractional pause, he added, "You have my word."

She had lived with three males long enough to instantly detect prevarication. Lips thinning, she narrowed her eyes, then tersely asked, "You haven't really got him, have you? There is no second carriage."

She'd wondered, but hadn't dared call his bluff or even question him while trapped in the carriage.

He looked up, raised his brows. Faintly shrugged. "I saw no reason to bother with your brother. I knew the threat alone would be enough to get you to behave."

The relief that surged through her nearly brought her to her knees. The weight on her shoulders evaporated. She was *free*—free to deal with Sir Freddie as she wished, with only her own life at stake. A life she was willing to risk to secure her future—what choice did she have? She fought to keep any hint of her upwelling resolve from her face. She glared at Sir Freddie, then swung on her heel and walked on.

Trusting to his overweening confidence to keep him from wondering at her continued acquiescence for just a few steps more . . .

From behind, she heard a faint chuckle, then his footsteps as he followed. Up ahead to her right lay the wooden spar. Just a *little* farther; she needed the greater steepness, the change in their relative heights . . .

Again she stopped dead, swung to face him.

At the last second let her contempt show. "You *bastard*!"

She slapped him. With the full force of her arm as she delivered the blow, with him lower than she, his face at the right height to take the full brunt of her momentum.

He had no chance to duck; the blow landed perfectly. Her palm stung; he staggered.

She didn't pause but turned and raced, scrambling up the few steps to the spar. She heard him swear foully, heard his boots scrabble on the path. Bending, she locked both hands on the spar, hefted it, and swung around. Driven by resolution laced with very real fear, she put every ounce of strength she possessed behind her swing.

He didn't see it coming.

She wielded the spar like a rounders bat. He was still lower on the path than she; the spar hit him across the side of the head.

The spar cracked, broke, fell from her hands.

He slumped to his knees, groggy, dazed, but not unconscious. He weaved. Desperate, she glanced around.

There were no other spars.

She grabbed up her skirts, stepped around him, and ran. Fled like a fury down the path, leaping down from the workings and streaking across the moor to plunge into the dark wood.

Chest heaving, she forced herself to slow. The roots were treacherous; she couldn't afford to fall. If she could get to the cottages and raise the alarm, she'd be safe. She didn't even have to worry about Matthew anymore.

From behind her came a roar; the thud of heavy footsteps reached her, rapidly gaining.

Fighting down panic, she kept her eyes down, locked on the path, feet dancing over the tree roots—

She ran into a black wall.

She shrieked, then stilled as the familiar scent, the familiar feel of Tony's body against hers, of his arms wrapping about her sank into her senses. She nearly fainted with relief.

He was looking beyond her, over her head. "Where is he?"

His words were a lethal whisper.

"On the path leading up to a disused mine."

He nodded. "I know it. Stay here."

With that he was gone. He moved so swiftly, so silently, surefooted in the darkness, that by the time, dazed, she turned, she'd nearly lost him.

She followed, but carefully, as quiet as he. She'd expected him to wait in the shadows and let Sir Freddie blunder into him as she had, but instead, he paused, waited until Sir Freddie was nearly to the trees, then calmly, determinedly, walked out of the wood.

Sir Freddie saw him. Pure horror crossed his face. He skidded to a halt, turned, and fled.

Back up the path.

Tony was at his heels almost immediately. Following as fast as her skirts would allow, she could see that he could have overhauled Sir Freddie anywhere along the upward slope. Instead, he waited until Sir Freddie gained the level stretch beside the gaping mine shaft before he reached out, spun Sir Freddie around, and plowed his fist into his face.

She heard the sickening thud all the way down the path where she was laboring upward. The first thud was followed by more; she couldn't see either man but felt sure Sir Freddie was on the receiving end. She hoped every blow hurt as badly as they sounded. Gaining the level stretch, she looked, just in time to see Tony slam his fist into Sir Freddie's jaw.

Something cracked. Sir Freddie fell back, onto a pile of rubble. He slumped, winded, but quick as a flash he grabbed a rock and flung it at Tony's head.

She screamed, but Tony hadn't taken his eye from Sir Freddie. He ducked the missile, then, lips curling in a snarl, bent, grabbed Sir Freddie, hauled him to his feet, punched him once in the face, grabbed him again, shook him—and flung him backward into the mine shaft.

There was a huge splash; water sprayed out.

Tony stood where he was, chest heaving until he'd regained his breath, then he stepped forward and looked down just as Alicia joined him.

She cast one brief look at Sir Freddie, spluttering, desperately searching for handholds on the slippery shaft wall, then looked at him. Reached out with both hands and touched him. "Are you all right?"

He looked into her eyes, searched her face—saw she was far more concerned for his well-being than hers—and felt something inside him give. "Yes." He briefly closed his eyes. If she was all right, he was, too.

Opening his eyes, he reached for her, drew her to him. Wrapped her in his arms and gloried in the reality of her warmth against him. Cheek against the silk of her hair, he sent a heartfelt thank-you to fate and the gods, then, easing his hold on her, looked down at Sir Freddie, fighting to hold his head above the dank water. "What do you want to do with him?"

She looked down. Her eyes narrowed. "He told me he'd killed Ellicot, and he was going to kill me. I say we let him drown—poetic justice."

"No!" The protest dissolved into a gurgle as Sir Freddie's terror made his fingers slip. "No," came again as he scrabbled back to the surface. "Torrington," he gasped, "you can't leave me here. What will you tell your masters?"

Tony looked down at him. "That you'd sunk before I reached you?"

Folding her arms, Alicia scowled. "I say we leave him—a hemlocklike taste of his own medicine."

"Hmm." Tony glanced at her. "How about a trial for treason and murder?"

"Trials and executions cost money. Much better just to

leave him to drown. We know he's guilty, and just think—*who* forced him to come here from London? Did *I* make him spin me a tale about kidnapping Matthew?"

Tony stiffened. "He told you that?"

Lips tight, she nodded. "And just think of all the brave sailors he's sent to watery graves! He's a disgusting and debauched worm." She tugged Tony's arm. "Come on—let's go."

She didn't mean it, but she was more than furious with Sir Freddie, and saw no reason not to torture him.

"Wait! Please . . ." Sir Freddie coughed water. "I know someone else."

Tony stilled, then, releasing her, he stepped closer to the edge and crouched down to peer at Sir Freddie. "What did you say?"

"Someone else." Sir Freddie was breathing shallowly; the water in the shaft would be freezing. "Another traitor."

"Who?"

"Get me out of here, and we can talk."

Tony rose; stepping back, he drew Alicia to him, pressed a kiss to her temple, whispered, "Play along." More loudly, he said, "You're right, let's just leave him." His arm around her, he turned them away.

"No!" Spluttering curses floated out of the shaft. "Damm it—I'm not making this up. There *is* someone else."

"Don't listen," Alicia advised. "He's always making things up—just think of his tale about Matthew."

"That was for a reason!"

She glanced over the edge. "And saving your life isn't a reason? Huh!" She stepped back. "Come on, I'm getting cold."

They started walking, taking tiny steps so Sir Freddie could hear.

"*Wait*! All right, damm it—it's someone in the Foreign Office. I don't know who—I tried to find out, but he's wilier than I. He's very careful, and he's someone very senior."

Tony sighed; he moved back to crouch at the edge. "Keep talking. I'm listening, but she's not convinced."

In gasps and pants, Sir Freddie talked, answering Tony's questions, revealing how he'd stumbled on the other traitor's trail. Eventually, Tony rose. He nodded at Alicia. "Stand back—I'm going to haul him out."

Tony had to lie full length on the ground to do it, but eventually Sir Freddie lay like a beached whale, shivering, coughing, and convulsing. Neither Alicia nor Tony felt the least bit sympathetic. Yanking Sir Freddie's cravat free, Tony used it to bind his hands before hauling him to his feet and, with a push, starting him back along the path.

Alicia's hand in his, Tony followed his quarry back through the wood and out onto the road. Maggs was waiting beside Sir Freddie's coach.

Alicia looked up at the box. "He had a coachman—he told him to wait."

"Oh, aye. He's waiting right enough, inside the coach." Maggs held out Alicia's cloak and reticule. "Found these when I shoved him in."

"Thank you."

Maggs nodded at Tony. "I was thinking we'd best leave 'em in the cellars at the George. I've had a word to Jim—he's opening up the hatch."

"Excellent idea." Tony prodded Sir Freddie along the road toward the nearby inn. "Bring the coachman."

Maggs had to lug him, for the coachman was unconscious. After a brief discussion with the landlord of the George, they left their prisoners in the cellars under lock and key.

Jim came out and led Sir Freddie's carriage away. Alicia was on the seat of Tony's curricle and he was about to join her when they heard the unmistakable rumble of a carriage heading their way.

Tony exchanged a glance with Maggs, then reached for Alicia. "Just in case, get back down here."

He had her on the ground behind him when the carriage rocked around the corner. The driver saw them and slowed.

"Thank God!" Geoffrey pulled the horses to a halt beside them.

Tony caught the leader's head, quieted the team. "What the devil—?"

In answer the doors of the carriage burst open and Adriana, David, Harry, and Matthew came tumbling out.

They rushed to Alicia, hugged her wildly, a cacophony of questions raining down. They waited for no answers, but danced and jigged, cavorted around Tony, too, but then returned to hug and hang on to their elder sister.

Geoffrey climbed down from the box; he stretched, then came to stand beside Tony. "Don't say I should have stopped them—it was impossible. It's my belief once they take an idea into their heads, Pevenseys are unstoppable." He smiled. "At least Alicia's a Carrington—she's been tamed."

"Hmm," was all Tony said.

Both he and Geoffrey were only children. The performance enacted before them left them both bemused and a trifle envious. They exchanged a glance, for once had no doubt what each other was thinking . . . planning.

"Come on," Tony said. "We'd better get them moving, or we'll be here for the rest of the night."

They rounded up their charges. With joy in their faces, still asking questions, the triumphant Pevenseys eventually climbed back into the carriage. Climbing up to the box, Geoffrey looked at Tony. "The Chase?"

Tony turned from handing Alicia into his curricle. "Where else?" Taking the reins, he climbed up. "It's the only thing Sir Freddie got right."

The comment puzzled Alicia. She waited until they were rolling along, heading farther up the road not back toward town with the heavy carriage rumbling behind. "Where are we going?"

"Home," Tony replied, and whipped up his horses.

She was determined to speak with him, to address the subject of marriage, but no opportunity came her way that night. They traveled for nearly an hour, steadily northward along the country road, then Tony checked the horses and turned in through a pair of tall gateposts with huge wrought-iron gates propped wide.

He'd refused to tell her more about where he was taking her, but she guessed when she saw the house. A large Palladian mansion in pale brown and grey stone with both double-and single-story wings, it sat peacefully in the moonlight, perfectly proportioned, comfortable, and settled within its park.

Tony drew the horses to a halt in the wide gravel forecourt. He leapt down, scanned the house with fond satisfaction, then turned and held out his hand. "Welcome to Torrington Chase."

The next hour went in pleasurable chaos. Servants tumbled from their beds and came rushing, their eagerness a comment on how they viewed their master. Tony flung orders this way and that; in the midst of the flurry, a calm, feminine voice was heard inquiring what her son was up to now.

In the drawing room, Tony exchanged a glance with Geoffrey, then looked at Alicia. Briefly, he lifted her hand to his lips. "Don't panic."

Releasing her, he went out; a moment later, he reappeared with his mother on his arm.

There could never be any doubt of the relationship; the viscountess's dark, dramatic, rather bold beauty was the feminine version of Tony's. Before Alicia could do more than assimilate that, she was enveloped in a warm embrace, then the viscountess—"You will call me Marie, if you please"—was asking questions, meeting the boys, exclaiming over Adriana, all with an understanding that made it clear she was excellently well served by correspondents in London.

Hot milk arrived for the three flagging boys, then they were bundled upstairs to bed. Maggs said he'd stay with them; he lumbered off. The housekeeper—Alicia felt sure the woman must be Mrs. Swithins's sister—came to say that chambers had been prepared for Alicia, Adriana, and Mr. Geoffrey, and that, as usual, the master's apartments lay ready and waiting.

With a recommendation that they all get some sleep, saying she would speak with them all in the morning, the viscountess graciously retired.

Tony asked Mrs. Larkins, the housekeeper, to show Adriana and Geoffrey their rooms. Taking Alicia's hand, he led her up the stairs in their wake, but then turned down another corridor off the main gallery.

He opened a door at the end of the wing and drew her into a large room. It was a private sitting room overlooking the gardens; she got barely a glimpse as he led her through a doorway into a large bedchamber.

She glanced around, taking in the heavy dark blue hangings, the richly carved mahogany furniture, none of it delicate. Her gaze stopped on the huge four-poster bed.

Tony drew her into his arms; she met his gaze. "This is your room."

His eyes held hers for an instant, then he murmured, "I know." He bent his head. "Tonight, very definitely, this is where you belong."

The first brush of his lips, the first touch of his hands as they spread and held her, then moved over her back and pulled her against him, verified the statement, told her how true it was—how very much he needed her.

The raw hunger in his kiss, the undisguised passion, the raging desire that fueled it, spoke eloquently of all he—and she, too—had feared, all they'd known they'd had at risk. Now the threat was behind them, conquered, vanquished, and in the aftermath, in the clear light of their victory, nothing was more apparent than the wonder and rightness of their dreams.

Their strength, their vulnerability—both sprang from the same source. The same overwhelming emotion that laid waste to all barriers and left them burning with one urgent and compulsive need.

Neither questioned it.

They shed clothes in the moonlight, let their inhibitions fall with them to the floor. He lifted her and they came together in a frenzy of need, of lust, of greedy passion, of molten, exultant desire. His need was hers; hers was his. They fed and gave succor, took, yielded, and let the raging tide swell.

Wrapped together, incandescent with glory, they gave themselves up to it, surrendered anew. She gave him all and he returned the pleasure, again and again, over and over until ecstasy built, rose and engulfed them. Caught them, trapped them in its golden fire.

They burned, clung, gasping as they reached the peak and soared, and the flames fell away.

Leaving them somewhere beyond the stars, far beyond the physical world.

Locked together, merged, as one they breathed, and felt, and knew. The moment stretched; full and deep, awareness touched them. Their gazes locked. A moment of heartbreaking stillness held them.

Passion, desire, and love. The smallest word held the greatest power.

This—all of this—was theirs. If they wanted. If they wished.

They both breathed in. The shimmering net released and fell away; the physical world returned and claimed them. With soft murmurs, soothing kisses, and caresses, they sank onto his bed.

Tomorrow, Alicia promised herself as, wrapped in his arms, she drifted into sleep.

*   *   *

He woke her the next morning, fully dressed, to explain that he'd sent a messenger to London last night, and now had to take Sir Freddie back to the capital.

Watching her as she blinked, valiantly trying to re-assemble her wits, he grimaced. "I'll return as soon as I can. Stay here with the boys. I suspect Geoffrey will want to take Adriana to meet his mother."

He leaned close and kissed her, then rose and strode out.

Alicia stared at the doorway, then heard the door beyond close. *No—wait!* was her instinctive reaction. Instead, she sighed and rolled onto her back.

Foiled again, yet there was no point in ranting. Aside from all else, when she spoke to him of marriage, she wanted Sir Freddie and all his works finished with, no longer in any way hanging over them.

Which left her facing her current situation—in his room, in his bed—and how best to deal with it.

In the end, brazen and resolute, she decided to behave within his house precisely as she meant to go on; she had had enough of deceptions. She rang for water, washed while a round-eyed maid shook and brushed her gown, then, determined to be completely open and honest with Tony's mother, she found her way back to the hall and was deferentially conducted to the breakfast parlor.

There, she found her four siblings in high spirits. Geoffrey rose as she entered; she smiled and waved him back, then bobbed a curtsy to the viscountess, seated at the end of the table.

Marie smiled warmly. "Come and sit here beside me, my dear. We have, I think, much to talk about."

The light in her eyes was delighted, frank, and encouraging; Alicia took her words to heart, piled her plate high at the sideboard, then returned to sit at her side.

She'd barely taken the first bite when Geoffrey asked if

he could take Adriana to visit at his home. "I'd like her to see the house and meet Mama."

The viscountess, busy pouring Alicia a cup of tea, murmured, "Manningham Hall is but two miles away, and Geoffrey's mama, Anne, is waiting to welcome your sister."

Alicia glanced at Adriana, read the eager plea in her eyes. "Yes, of course." With a flicker of her own resolve, she added, "It's only sensible to seize the moment."

Geoffrey and Adriana glowed with happiness; with various assurances, they excused themselves and left.

They passed Maggs in the doorway. He lumbered in, saluting both ladies. "If you're agreeable, ma'am," he addressed Alicia, "I'll be taking these scamps down to the stream. I mentioned it this morning—seems they've been an age without holding a rod, and I'm happy to watch over them."

As Alicia glanced at her brothers, Marie again murmured, "Maggs is entirely trustworthy." She smiled at the large, homely man. "He's been watching over Tony since he was no older than your David."

Alicia regarded her brothers' shining eyes and eager expressions. "If you promise to behave and do exactly as Maggs says . . ." She glanced at Maggs and smiled, too. "You may go."

"H'ray!" Setting down napkins, pushing back their chairs, they rushed to Maggs, pausing only to make their bows to Alicia and the viscountess before happily heading off.

Alicia watched Matthew, his hand in Maggs's, walk confidently out, and felt a rush of emotion. Not just for Matthew, but for the children she would bear; here, like this, with this sort of continuity was how children should be raised.

"Now!' Marie settled back in her chair. At her signal, the young butler departed, leaving them alone. "You can eat, and I will talk, and we will learn all about each other, and you can tell me when your wedding is to be. With his customary flair for avoiding details, Tony hasn't told me."

Lifting her gaze from her plate, Alicia looked into Marie's bright black eyes. "Yes, well . . ." She dragged in a breath; she hadn't expected such a direct approach. "Indeed, that's a subject I wished to discuss with you."

She glanced around, confirming that they were indeed alone. She drew another breath, held it for a moment, then met Marie's gaze. "I'm Tony's mistress, *not* his intended bride."

Marie blinked. A succession of emotions played across her features, then her eyes flared; she pressed her lips tight and reached across to lay her hand on Alicia's arm. "My dear, I greatly fear I must, most contritely, apologize—not for my question, but for my oh-so-tardy son."

Marie shook her head; Alicia realized with some surprise that she was struggling to keep her lips straight. Then Marie met her eyes again. "It seems he hasn't told you either."

Over the next hour, she tried to correct Marie's assumption, but Tony's mother would have none of it.

"No, and no and *non, ma petite*. Believe me, you do not know him as I do. But now you have told me your background, I can well see how you, through his laggardliness, have come to think as you do. You have had no mentor, no guide to rely on—no one to . . . what is the word . . . 'interpret' his behavior for you. Rest assured, he would not have allowed anyone to know of you, much less established you as his consort in the eyes of the ton, or, indeed, brought you here, if he hadn't, from the first, seen you as his bride."

It was increasingly difficult to cling to her argument in the face of Marie's conviction, yet Alicia couldn't—simply could not—believe that all along . . . "From the first?"

"*Oui*—without doubt." Marie pushed back her chair. "Come—let me show you something, so you will see more clearly."

They left the breakfast parlor; while they walked through the large house, Marie quizzed her on her brothers' education. On the one hand, Alicia's heart soared; this—this house, this sense of family, of immediate and natural care—was the stuff of her dreams. Yet her wits were whirling—she couldn't accept it, couldn't take joy in it, stymied by her uncertainty over Tony's intentions.

Had he always seen her as his wife? Did he *truly* do so now?

Marie led her to a long gallery lined with paintings. "The *famille* Blake. Most we need not consider, but here—here are the ones that might make things clear."

She halted before the last three paintings. The first showed a gentleman in his twenties, dressed in the fashion of a generation before. "Tony's father, the last viscount." The middle picture was of a couple—Marie herself and the previous gentleman, a few years older. "Here is James again, now my husband." She turned to the last painting. "And this is Tony at twenty. Now look, and tell me what you see."

One aspect was obvious. "He looks very much like you."

"*Oui*—he looks like me. Only his height, his body, did he get from James, and that one does not notice. He looks French, and that is what one sees, but one sees only the surface." Marie caught Alicia's eye. "What a man is, how he behaves—that is not dictated by appearance."

Alicia looked again at the portrait. "You're saying he's more like his father inside?"

"*Very* much so." Marie linked her arm in hers; turning, they strolled back along the gallery. "In the superficial things, he is clearly French. How he moves, his gestures—he speaks French as well if not better than I. *But* it is always James in the words he speaks, always—without fail—his Englishness that rules him. So, in deciding the question of did he always mean to marry you or no, the answer is clear."

With a gesture encompassing all the Blakes, Marie said, "You are English yourself. You know of honor. A gentleman's honor—*a true English gentleman's honor*—that is something inviolate. Something one may set one's course by, that one may stake one's life and indeed one's heart on with absolute certainty."

"And that's what rules Tony?"

"That is what is at his core, an inner code that is so much a part of him he does not even stop to think." Marie sighed. "*Ma petite*, you must see that it is not so much a deliberate slight, but an *oversight* that he has not thought to tell you, to ask you to be his bride. To him, his direction is obvious, so, like most men, he expects you to see it as clearly as he."

They'd reached the top of the stairs. Alicia halted. After a moment, she said, "He could have said something— we've been lovers for weeks."

"Oh, he *should* have said something—on that you will get no argument from me." Marie looked at her, frowned. "*Ma petite*, in telling you this, I would not wish you to think that I would counsel you to . . . how do the English say it—let him off easily?"

"Lightly," Alicia absentmindedly returned. She told herself she didn't have a temper, that not being informed she was to marry him—that he intended to marry her, indeed, from the first had so intended—that he'd taken her agreement so completely for granted he hadn't even thought to mention it was neither here nor there . . . she drew a deep breath, felt her jaw firm. "No. I *won't*—"

The boys came clattering into the hall below them. Seeing her and Marie, they came rushing up the stairs; if any shyness toward the viscountess had ever afflicted them, it had already dissipated. A rowdy report of their excellent fishing expedition tumbled from their lips.

Both Alicia and Marie smiled and nodded. Eventually, the boys ran out of exciting news, and paused.

David fixed his bright eyes on Alicia. "When are you and Tony getting married?"

"What he means," Harry put in, jostling his older brother, "is if it's soon, can we stay here?"

Matthew lined up, too. "There's ponies in the stable—Maggs said he'd teach me to ride."

Alicia waited until she was sure she had her voice and expression under control. "How did you know we were going to get married?"

"Tony told us." Harry grinned hugely.

"When?"

"Oh, days ago!" David said. "But can we stay here, please? It's so much fun."

Alicia couldn't think.

Marie stepped in and assured the boys their request would be considered. They grinned, briefly hugged Alicia, then ran off to wash and get ready for lunch.

As their footsteps faded, Marie drew in a long breath. Again, she linked her arm in Alicia's. "*Ma petite*, I think—I really do feel"—she glanced at Alicia—"*not lightly.*"

"No." Jaw set, Alicia lifted her head as she and Marie descended the stairs. "And not easily, either."

The coach rocked and swayed. Beyond the flaps, the rain poured down; the wheels splashed through the spreading puddles. Evening had come early over Exmoor, dark clouds roiling up from the Bristol Channel to blanket the moors. Then the clouds had opened.

Alicia felt entirely at one with the weather, but she prayed they wouldn't get bogged. She'd hoped to get a lot farther before halting for the night; now her sights were set on the next town, South Molton, where Maggs had told her they could be sure of a decent inn.

Harry was curled up beside her, asleep with his head in

her lap. He shifted, snuffled, then settled again. Absent-mindedly, she stroked his curls.

Through the unnatural gloom, she looked across the coach at Maggs, burly and bearlike, with Matthew asleep in his arms and David slumped against his side. When he'd heard of her decision to quit Torrington Chase and go home to Little Compton, he'd volunteered to come with her and help with the boys. With no Jenkins or Fitchett, she'd accepted his help gladly.

Once the idea of going home had occurred to her, she'd seized on it and refused to be swayed. Not that Marie had tried; she'd considered, then nodded. "Yes, that will work. He'll have to speak then."

Indeed. Alicia's only question was what he would say, assuming, as both she and Marie had, that Tony would come after her.

Adriana, returning with Geoffrey and an invitation to visit for a few days with Lady Manningham, with whom Adriana had got on well, had been concerned, more about what was going on between Tony and Alicia than anything else. So Adriana was now at Manningham Hall; Marie had smiled and approved the arrangement.

The boys, of course, didn't understand. They'd argued vociferously when she'd informed them they were returning to Little Compton immediately, but Marie had broken in to state, in her most imperious tone, that if they wished to return to the Chase soon, they would go without complaint.

They'd considered Marie, exchanged glances, then consented to accompany Alicia without further grumbling.

Marie had lent her traveling coach and a knowledgeable coachman; she'd also insisted on a groom. "I have no intention of drawing Tony's fire by allowing you to set out insufficiently protected."

So the poor groom, as well as the coachman, was getting drenched up on the box. They would have to stop at South Molton.

She had no idea how long it would be before Tony returned from London. Three days? Four? She hoped to be home in two days.

Head back on the squabs, eyes closed, she tried yet again to calm her chaotic emotions, to bring order to her mind. The greater part was still seething, the rest confused, still innocently querying: he hadn't really intended to marry her, had he? But some part of her knew—he did, he had, from the first. She shouldn't have overlooked how dictatorial he was—how many times had he simply seized her hand and whirled her into a waltz, or into some room? She knew perfectly well how used he was to getting his own way.

In this instance, he still would—she wasn't so far gone in fury she'd deny herself her dreams—but not before, absolutely *not* before he got down on his knees and begged.

Jaw tight, she was imagining the scene when the rhythmic thunder of galloping hooves came out of the night behind them.

The coachman slowed his horses, easing to the side of the road to let the other carriage past. Disturbed by the change in rhythm, the boys stirred, stretched, and opened their eyes.

Listening to the oncoming hooves, Alicia wondered who else was out on such a night, chancing his horses at such a wicked pace.

That pace slowed as the carriage neared, then the sound of hooves lightened further, eventually disappearing beneath the steady drumming of the rain. She strained her ears but heard nothing more.

Then came a shout, indistinguishable from within the coach, but in response the coachman reined his plodding horses to a halt.

The coach rocked on its springs. The boys came alert, eyes wide.

Alicia looked at Maggs. Head on one side, he was listening intently.

No highwayman would use a carriage, surely, and it couldn't be—

The coach door was wrenched open. A tall dark figure was silhouetted in the opening.

Tony glanced once around the coach, then reached in and locked his fingers around Alicia's wrist. "Stay there!"

At his tone, one of rigid authority, the four males jerked upright. He didn't wait to check their expressions, but unceremoniously yanked Alicia—stunned speechless, he noted with uncompromising satisfaction—out of the coach.

He steadied her on her feet, then stalked down the road, towing her behind him. She gasped, but had no option but to go with him.

Courtesy of her totally witless flight, he was already soaked; she was, too, by the time he reached a point out of bellow range of the coach.

Releasing her, he swung around and faced her. He glared at her through the rain. *"What the devil do you think you're doing?"*

The question cracked like a whip. Over the miles, he'd lectured himself not to overreact, to find out why she'd run before reading her the riot act; just the sight of her in a coach leaving him had been enough to lay waste to all such wisdom.

"I'm going home!" Her hair clung to her cheeks, wisps dripping down her neck.

"Your home lies that way!" He jabbed a finger back down the road. "Where I left you—at the Chase."

She drew herself up, folded her arms, tipped up her chin. "I am not continuing as your mistress."

If Alicia had had any doubt that Marie had held to her promise to play the dumb innocent and not explain her complaint, it was put to rest by the expression on Tony's face. Expressions—they flowed in quick succession from totally dumfounded, to incredulous, to believing but unable to follow her reasoning . . . to not liking her reasoning at all . . . then back to absolutely incredulous dumbstruck fury.

"*You*—?" He choked. Black eyes blazing, he jabbed a finger at her. "You are not my bloody mistress!"

She nodded. "Precisely. Which is why I'm going home to Little Compton." Picking up her skirts, she went to swing haughtily about. Her skirts slapped wetly about her legs; catching her arm, he hauled her back to face him.

Held her there. He looked into her face; his, the austere planes wet, his hair plastered to his head, had never looked harsher. "I have no idea what"—he gestured wildly—"*idiot* notion you've taken into your head, but I have never considered you my mistress. I have always— since the first time I saw you—thought of you as my future *wife*!"

"Indeed?" She opened her eyes wide.

"*Yes*, indeed! I've shown you every courtesy, every consideration." He stepped close, actively intimidating; she quelled an instinctive urge to step back. "I've openly protected you, not just through the investigation, not only via your household and mine, but socially, too. As God is my witness I have never treated you other than as my future wife. I've never even *thought* of you as anything else!"

Male aggression radiated from him. Uncowed, she held his black gaze. "That's quite amazing news. A pity you didn't think to inform me earlier—"

"*Of course* I didn't say anything earlier!" The bellow was swallowed by the night. He locked his eyes on hers. "Just refresh my memory," he snarled. "What was the basis of Ruskin's attempt to blackmail you?"

She blinked, recalled, refocused on his face—read the truth blazoned there.

"I didn't want you agreeing to be my wife through any damned sense of gratitude." Tony growled the words; sensing her momentary weakness, he pounced. Lowering his head so they were eye to eye, he pointed a finger at her nose. "I waited—and waited—*forced* myself to wait to ask so you wouldn't feel pressured!"

Panic of a kind he'd never before known clawed at his gut; anger and a largely impotent rage swirled through him; an odd hurt lurked beneath all. He'd thought he'd done the right thing—*all* the right things—yet fate, untrustworthy jade, had still managed to trip him up. Yet the truth was slowly seeping into his brain—he wasn't going to lose her. He just had to find a way through the morass fickle fate had set at his feet.

He scowled at her. "Regardless of what I did or didn't say, or why, what the *devil* did you think the last weeks have been about?" He stepped closer, deliberately crowding her. "What sort of man do you think I am?"

"A nobleman." Alicia refused to budge an inch; elevating her chin, she met him eye to eye. "And men of your class often take mistresses, as all the world knows. Are you going to tell me you've never had one?"

A muscle leapt in his jaw. *"You are not my mistress!"*

The words resonated between them. Slowly, she raised her brows.

He dragged in a breath. Easing back, he released his tight grip on her arm, plowed his hand through his hair, pushing sodden strands from his eyes. "Damn it—the whole bloody ton knows how I see you—*as my wife!*"

"So I've been given to understand. The entire ton, all my acquaintances—even my brothers!—know you intend marrying me. The only person in the entire world who hasn't been informed is *me!*" She narrowed her eyes at him, then more quietly stated, "I haven't even been asked if I'm willing."

Precisely enunciated, the words gave him pause. He

held her gaze for a long moment, then, also more quietly, said, "I told you I loved you." His eyes suddenly widened. "You do understand French?"

"Enough for that, but I didn't catch much else. You speak very rapidly."

"But I said the words, and you understood." His voice gained in strength. "It was *you* who never returned the sentiment."

She lost her temper. "Yes, I *did*! Just not in words." She could feel the heat in her cheeks, refused to let it distract her. "Don't tell me you didn't understand." She gave him a second to do so; when his face only hardened, she jabbed a finger into his chest. "And as for saying the words, *believing* as I did that I was your *mistress*, such a confession would have been entirely unwise."

She realized the implicit admission, sensed by the flare of heat in his gaze that he hadn't missed it.

Lifting her chin, she continued, determined to have all clear between them, "It's all very well to say you love me, but many men doubtless think they love their mistresses, and tell them so—how could I tell what you *meant* by the words?"

For a long moment, he held her gaze, then he gestured, as if brushing the point aside. In the same movement, he reached for her; grasping her elbows, holding her steady, face to face, he locked his eyes with hers. "I need to know—do you love me?"

The question, the look in his eyes, went straight to her heart.

She closed her eyes, then opened them and searched his. The rain was cascading down, the night was wild and black about them, yet he was totally focused on her, as she was on him. She drew breath, shakily said, "In *my* world, love between a man and a woman usually means marriage. In *yours*, that isn't necessarily so. You said one word, but not the other. You knew my background—

knew I wasn't up to snuff. I couldn't tell what you meant, but . . . that didn't make any difference to how I felt about you."

He studied her for a long moment, then released her, stepped close, framed her face with his hands. He looked down into her eyes. *"Je t'aime."* The words resonated with a conviction impossible to doubt. "I love you." He held her gaze. "I want no other woman, not for a day, not for a night—only you. And I want you forever. I want to marry you. I want you in my house, in my bed—you already reside in my heart. You *are* my soul. Please . . ." He paused, still holding her gaze, then more softly continued, "Will you marry me?"

He didn't wait for her answer, but touched his lips to hers. "I never wanted you as my mistress. I only ever wanted you in one role—as my wife."

Another subtle kiss had her closing her eyes, swallowing to get her words out. "Do you think you could see me as the mother of your children?"

He drew back and met her eyes, his expression faintly quizzical. When she said nothing more, he replied, "That's understood."

"Good." She cleared her throat. "In that case . . ."

She paused, holding his black gaze; she still couldn't entirely take it in, that the future of her dreams was here, being offered to her, hers for the taking. He hadn't got down on his knees and begged, yet . . . smiling, she reached up and wrapped her arms about his neck. "*Yes*, I love you, and *yes*, I'll marry you."

"Thank God for that!" He pulled her to him, kissed her thoroughly—let her kiss him back in a wild moment of untrammeled joy with the rain drenching them and the moors a black void about them, then he sighed through the kiss, sank deeper into it, wrapped his arms about her and held her close. Until that moment, she hadn't appreciated just how tense—how keyed up, how uncertain—he'd been.

Through the kiss she sensed their emotions meet, touch, ease—the fraught worry of recent times, the uncertainties, the fears, all faded, submerged beneath a welling tide of unfettered happiness.

When he lifted his head, dragged in a huge breath, and eased his hold on her, all that fraught tension was gone, and he'd reverted to his usual dictatorial self.

"Come." He kissed her hand and turned her back to the coach. His curricle stood across the road, the pair with their heads hanging. "There's a good inn in Chittlehampton, just off the road a little way back. It's closest." Hard hand at her back, urging her along, he glanced at her—met her eyes. "We should get out of these wet clothes before we take a chill."

She seriously doubted, once they got out of their clothes, that they would be in any danger; she could feel the heat in his gaze even through the darkness.

He called orders to the coachman, then opened the coach door and looked in. "We're going back to the Chase."

A chorus of wild cheers and a "Good-oh" from Maggs greeted the pronouncement. She stuck her head past Tony to add, "But we have to stop at an inn for the night. I'm too wet to get back in. I'll follow with Tony."

Her brothers were thrilled, in alt at the prospect of returning to a house she suspected they saw as paradise, and not at all averse to spending the night at an inn along the way.

Tony helped the coachman turn his team, then he drew her protectively back while the coach lurched and started back down the road. In its wake, they walked to his curricle. Closing his hands about her waist, he lifted her to the seat. The rain was easing; she waited until they were rolling along before saying, "About my brothers."

He glanced at her. "What about them? They'll live with us, of course."

She hesitated, then asked, "You're sure?"

"Positive."

She tried to think of what else remained, what else needed to be settled between them . . .

"Good gracious!" She looked at him. "What happened with Sir Freddie?"

Later, kneeling before the fire roaring in the hearth of the best bedchamber of the Sword and Pike in Chittlehampton, one towel wrapped around her while with another she dried her wet hair, she remembered how Tony had laughed.

How delighted he'd been that he—the question of becoming his wife—had exercised her mind to the total exclusion of Sir Freddie.

She had Dalziel to thank for Tony's rapid return. Tony had sent a rider hotfoot to London as soon as they'd reached the Chase the previous night; by return, Dalziel had sent word to bring Sir Freddie to London, but then had changed his mind. He'd met Tony on the road, and taken Sir Freddie into custody; apparently Dalziel wanted to visit Sir Freddie's home in his company.

It seemed clear Dalziel's interest had been sparked by Sir Freddie's claims of another, still unidentified ex-traitor. For her part, she'd learned enough about ex-traitors to last her a lifetime.

Yet Tony's reaction out on the road buzzed in her head. Almost as if he hadn't been sure that her connection with him wasn't in some way dependent on the threat of Sir Freddie. That that threat somehow ranked more prominently in her mind than it did.

The latch lifted; Tony entered. He'd taken it upon himself to see her brothers settled; Maggs would sleep in their room, just to make sure.

A smile curved his lips as he paused, studying her, then, smile deepening, he came toward her.

"Stop!" She held up a hand. "You're still dripping. Take off your clothes."

His brows quirked, but he obediently halted. "As you wish."

The purr in his voice was distinctly predatory, the speculation in his eyes equally so. She inwardly grinned, turned back to the fire, and continued to dry her hair.

But the instant he was naked, she rose, crossed the few steps to him. Holding his gaze, with the towel she'd been using on her hair in one hand, with her other hand she whisked the towel she'd wrapped about her free.

One towel in each hand, she started to caress him, to dry him.

She tried to make him keep his hands to himself, but failed. Miserably.

Within minutes, their skins were hotter than the flames, their mouths and hands more greedy. Then she felt his hands close about her waist, his arms tense to lift her. She pulled back from their kiss. "No. On the bed."

She'd never given orders, never taken the lead before, but he acquiesced, releasing her and drawing her to the curtained bed.

He held back the drapes, caught her eye as she climbed through. "How on the bed?"

She smiled, and showed him.

Had him lie flat on his back, and let her straddle him, let her take him in and ride him to oblivion.

She'd taken an hour to ransack his library; as she'd suspected, he had an excellent collection of useful guides. She had every intention of studying them extensively and putting the knowledge to good use.

As she did that night, lavishing pleasure upon him, taking her own from his helpless surrender. Hours later, when the fire had burned low and she lay exhausted, deeply sated in his arms, she murmured, "I love you. Not because you'll protect me and our family, not because you're wealthy, or have a wonderful house. I love you because you're you—because of the man you are."

He was silent for a long moment, then his chest

swelled as he drew breath. "I don't know what love is, only that I feel it. All I know is I love you—and always will."

She lifted her head, found his lips and kissed him, then snuggled down in his arms, where she belonged.

He'd wanted a big wedding. At the Chase, with half the ton and all of the Bastion Club looking on. As he wished, so it was—the only person invited who sent his regrets was Dalziel.

Just over a week later, they all gathered to watch her walk down the aisle of the church in Great Torrington to take her place at Tony's side. Her gown was a confection of ivory silk and pearls that Adriana, her bridesmaid, assisted by Fitchett, Mr. Pennecuik, and numerous others in London, had slaved over to have ready in time. About her throat, three strands of pearls glowed; more pearls circled her wrists and depended from her lobes—a gift from Tony, along with his heart.

As, meeting his black eyes, she placed her hand in his, gave herself into his keeping, she had no doubt which gift was the most precious to her, and in that moment, what was most precious to him.

With him, side by side, she faced the minister, ready and very willing to claim their future.

The ceremony ran smoothly; the wedding breakfast was held on the lawns of the Chase. Everyone from the staff to the Duchess of St. Ives threw themselves into the celebration, resulting in a day filled to overflowing with happiness and simple, unadulterated joy. The boys were in fine fettle; along with Miranda's girls they dodged here and there among the guests, weaving laughter and exuberance through the throng, leaving benevolent smiles in their wake. The horrors of the wars still shadowed many minds; it was at moments like this that the future glowed most brightly.

Late in the afternoon, when the ladies had settled in

chairs on the lawn to chat and take stock, their husbands, released from attendance, gathered under the trees overlooking the lake or wandered down to stroll the shores.

Together with Jack Hendon, who along with Geoffrey had stood as his groomsman, and the other members of the Bastion Club—Christian, Deverell, Tristan, Jack Warnefleet, Gervase, and Charles—Tony retreated to a spot in the pinetum from where they could keep the ladies in view but also talk freely.

The topic that interested them most was Dalziel's absence.

"I've never seen him anywhere in the ton," Christian said. He nodded toward the assembled ladies. "I'm starting to think if he appeared, someone would recognize him."

"What I want to know is how he manages it," Charles said. "He must be in similar straits as we, don't you think?"

"It seems likely," Tristan agreed. "He's definitely 'one of us' in all other respects."

"Speaking of which," Jack Hendon put in, "what happened to Caudel once he was in Dalziel's clutches?"

"Oh, he sang loud and long," Charles replied. "And then sat in his library and put a gun to his head—only way left for a man of his name. Far less messy than a trial and the attendant flap."

"Did he have any immediate family?" Gervase asked.

"Dalziel said a distant cousin will inherit."

Tony looked at Charles. "When did you see him?"

"He called me in." Charles grinned. "Seems this other sod who's been using the war for his own ends has been active for the most part in Cornwall, from Penzance to Plymouth. My neck of the woods. He's in the ministries, most likely the Foreign Office, and he's apparently someone in the higher levels, someone trusted, which is what is most deeply exercising Dalziel. If Caudel was bad, this other has the potential to be even worse."

"Has he been actively spying, or was it something more like Caudel's racket?" Tristan asked.

"Don't know," Charles replied. "That's one of the things I'm supposed to find out. I'm to go in and ask questions, creating the sort of ripples no self-respecting spy wants to know about, and then watch what happens."

Christian grimaced. "A high-risk strategy."

"But oh-so-welcome." Charles glanced at the others, his dark blue eyes alight. "So now I must leave you and be on my way. I'm driving on to Lostwithiel tonight."

He grinned, a touch devilishly. "Courtesy of our erstwhile commander, I have a gold-plated reason to escape London and the ton, and my sisters, sisters-in-law, and dear mama, who are all up for the Season and now fixed in town for the duration. Of course, they expected to spend much of their time organizing me and my future. Instead, I'm on my way home. Alone. There to sit in my library, surrounded by my dogs, put up my feet, and savor a good brandy." He sighed contentedly. "Bliss."

With a rakish smile, he saluted them. "So I must leave you to fight your own battles, gentlemen."

They laughed. Charles turned away.

"Let us know if you need any help," Jack Warnefleet called.

Charles raised a hand. "I will. And if you need to hide, you all know your way to Lostwithiel."

The group under the trees shifted, broke up. Tony, Jack Hendon, and Tristan remained, watching Charles as he glibly made his excuses to Alicia and Tony's mother, then deftly extricated himself from the clutches of the other matrons present.

As Charles headed toward the stables, Tony took note of his jaunty, cocksure stride. He glanced at Jack and Tristan, briefly met their eyes, then all three grinned and looked at their ladies—Alicia, Kit, and Leonora—heads together as they chatted in the sunshine on the lawn.

"I fear," Tony murmured, "that Charles's view of bliss

is severely limited by his restricted experience of the state."

"He doesn't know what he's talking about," Tristan averred.

"True," Jack said.

Tony's grin widened into a smile. "He'll learn."

The three of them stirred and headed out onto the lawn.

New York Times bestselling author **STEPHANIE LAURENS** began writing as an escape from the dry world of professional science. Her hobby quickly became a career. Her novels set in Regency England have captivated readers around the globe, making her one of the romance world's most beloved and popular authors. Stephanie lives in Melbourne, Australia, with her husband and two daughters.

For information on Stephanie and her books, including details of upcoming novels, visit Stephanie's website at *www.stephanielaurens.com*.

Readers can write to Stephanie via email at *slaurens@vicnet.net.au*. Readers can also email that address to be included in the PRIVATE Heads-Up email book announcement list for notification whenever a new Stephanie Laurens title hits the shelves!